THREE PLAYER CO-OP

SERIES ANTHOLOGY

ALLYSON LINDT

ACELETTE PRESS

LOOKING FOR IT

ONE

Things I didn't know I didn't want to see until I saw them:

How hot dogs are made.

The Black Friday line at Walmart.

My brother's best friend, in my bedroom, with my vibrators and other assorted toys scattered at his feet.

Jax had been around almost as long as I could remember—hanging out with my brother since they were in kindergarten and I was a year too young to join them. There was a span of time when he wasn't welcome, but since we'd made things right, I didn't mind having Jax around. With his short brown hair, piercing hazel eyes, and a physique that didn't need a rubber suit to show off the definition, seeing him—the looking—was fantastic.

"Who knew little Dee Dee had a wicked side?" A smirk tugged up one corner of his mouth.

No one else had called me *Dee Dee* since high school, nearly a decade ago. It was *Sadie*, or *Mercedes* if the occasion was formal. But sometimes when Jax said it, I could pretend it was a pet name, and not just a long-time habit.

"Anyone who's watched the outtakes on her Patreon." Grayson's voice came from behind me.

He was referring to one arm of my business. I made costumes based on characters from video games, movies, and whatever else caught my eye. Usually anime. It was why my short hair was currently lavender. My last outfit had been Ayane from Dead or Alive. YouTube let me share how-to videos, print-on-demand gave me a way to sell books, and Patreon let the fans support my hobby. In exchange, they got access to some of the sillier, more sweary outtakes from my vids.

Jax tapped his chin. He perpetually had two days' worth of stubble on his face. I swore, even right after he shaved? Stubble. "Those are probably my favorites. Closest we get to seeing the real Sadie."

I crossed the short distance to Jax and took the broken cardboard box from his hands. "I've got this. Thanks." I tried to keep my tone even. To pretend I wasn't utterly embarrassed by the assortment of battery-operated latex toys on the carpet.

I was moving today, and my brother was supposed to help me. He had to take a last-minute weekend meeting with a client and asked Jax to step in. Since Jax was dating Grayson, and Grayson had the pickup truck to haul most of my stuff, that meant I got both guys for the price of one.

I liked Grayson's company too. His wit. How incredible he looked in the cosplay armor I designed. His mind, of course.

At least it wasn't my brother who picked up the less-than-secure box of toys. I shoved them back in their temporary home. I'd used more than one of these when I fantasized about being with Grayson. Or Jax. Or both. They liked to invite other people into their bed and share, and my imagination liked me being that person.

While I personally couldn't imagine loving sharing someone with another person, my mind could run a marathon with the idea of being with both men at the same time. My favorite accessory was probably the U-shaped toy, with the textured end that slid inside me, and the suction end that vibrated against my—

"I'll help." Jax's hand brushed over mine when he knelt next to me, and sparks danced along my skin. "These are a lot of fun with a partner."

I— What? He had to be teasing me. A glance showed his expression was playful.

"I have them for when there *isn't* another person." I could do this. I could talk about sex toys with a straight face. Without giggling like a kid. The heat flooding my face said I must be tomato red by this point, but I wasn't backing down.

"So you've never done it?" Jax asked.

Grayson cleared his throat. The sound was loud and exaggerated.

Good. He could shut his boyfriend down.

Jax glanced at him. "Sadie and I are having an adult conversation. If she doesn't like it, she can say so."

Do it. Tell him now to stop.

Or let him keep going, and see if he blinked first. Everything he said was going in the Fantasy Pile, and imagining the two of them helping me masturbate was a pretty good addition.

"*Done it?* As in *sex?* Are we twelve? No. I'm not a virgin." Wow. I actually said that without my voice cracking.

"Not that, gorgeous." Another nickname that always meant more to me than it probably should, coming from him. He had a way of making it sound sincere and light-hearted at the same time. Jax held up a bullet vibrator. "Played with one of these with someone else."

The fantasies existed because I didn't have many memories of good sex. Not that my love life was all bad; it just wasn't toe-curling, sheet-clutching, back-scratching amazing. That kind of thing was for the imagination and porn. "No."

"I'd be willing to give you a demonstration."

He was taking this a lot further than I expected. And what was I supposed to make of Grayson's silence?

I was going to see how far Jax ran with this idea. If the answer *all the way*, I still wasn't flinching first.

Who was I kidding? I loved every minute of it. Desire hummed through my veins, and the heat under my skin was as much need as it was embarrassment.

There was a big, gaping flaw in his proposal, besides the fact that I shouldn't even flirt with my brother's friends, let alone consider fucking one of them. "If it's all toys, even with a second person, is it really sex?" I asked.

"If it's not, you've got the wrong second person," Jax said.

Of course. "What about you?" I looked at Grayson. "Are you just going to stand there and watch?"

He shrugged. "Sometimes. In this case, I'm thinking *yes*."

Because their relationship was open. Adding the idea of Grayson, watching, to that of getting a taste of Jax drove my senses wild, and it was probably status quo for them.

It was a bad idea, for me to even pretend I could live in that part of their world, regardless of what the tingles racing through me wanted.

Apparently, I was going to blink first. "Lyn's waiting on us. We should finish packing up the cars."

I shoved the box of toys on my dresser, to grab last. This way, I could keep it in the front seat with me and make sure that tonight, when I fantasized about giving Jax a different answer, I had latex help on hand.

We resumed loading boxes—bigger and heavier ones in Grayson's truck, and smaller in my car.

I was moving into a spare bedroom, in my best friend's house. Lyn owned a corner lot shop she'd purchased for a steal at a foreclosure auction. She turned the main floor into a gaming café, complete with a bakery for her own sinfully amazing baked goods.

A few months ago, she did a massive remodel on the shop— fiber optics in the walls. High-end gaming chairs, top-of-the-line hardware, and her dream kitchen for producing mass quantities of sweets. Business slowed for her right after, and she was struggling to pay back the loan for the overhaul.

My lease was up and I needed a month-to-month deal until the jobs I was pursuing in L.A. panned out, but my living with Lyn would also help her make ends meet until things picked up again for her business.

I grabbed one of the last boxes from my bedroom and was heading outside, when I found Grayson in the living room. He'd taken my replica lightsaber from its cradle, a grin on his face.

"*Power.* Unlimited *power.*" He held the lightsaber above his head, and called out in his best Palpatine voice.

The replica had been a gift from him and Jax. I was on a Star Wars kick after *The Force Awakens* came out, and they gave it to me to accent my Rey costume. The only thing that made the gift more perfect was I had no idea they'd made the purchase when I'd gotten them each one too, as a *thank you* for Jax's being my Kylo Ren and Grayson's being my Poe.

I took the weapon from him. "So this is how liberty dies. With thunderous applause." The game was simple. Pick a quote from a series, and each person had to add onto it with another—not necessarily the right one.

"Count me outta dis one." Jax's high-pitched Jar Jar Binks impersonation came from behind. He rested a hand on the small of my back as he stepped around me, and warmth spread out from his touch.

It was a simple gesture, to let me know he was here, and one he'd made countless times in the past. Today, it sparked images that weren't ready to be shoved aside.

"Apparently, you left a lot of your toys out," Jax said.

"I wanted to make sure this one travelled safely. It's special and doesn't go in a box." It was tempting to say something more about the *toy* comment, but I needed to let that line of conversation die.

Even if my mind was taking Jax's hand on the small of my back and spinning it into a rom-com style hookup. Except, instead of an awkward kiss that ended in light laughs, the next step was Jax, lifting me onto the kitchen counter and fucking me until I screamed.

I mentally shook myself and got back to work. Now wasn't the time. I never had an issue separating fantasy from reality before. Then again, Jax never offered to help me play with my vibrator while Grayson watched before.

He'd only been teasing, to see how I'd react. My *no* ended the moment, as it should have, and it was time to let things go.

I climbed onto the bed of Grayson's truck, to settle a box in among the others. It was like Tetris, but sweatier. When I stepped back toward the edge, Grayson was waiting his turn. He reached up and grabbed my hips, to help me hop down.

Which was perfectly normal and nothing to get excited about.

"I think we're almost done," he said. "Want to do one last pass?"

"Yeah. Good call." I headed back into the house, and surveyed each room carefully. All of the boxes were gone. Every loose item I wanted to keep an eye on was secured in my car. Only furniture was left.

Last stop was my bedroom. I paused just inside the doorway, using the silence to collect my thoughts. I was about to make some huge changes in my life, and my mind spent its free time these days going over all the details again and again.

The lack of certainty in the rest of my life was the only reason Jax's playful offer wouldn't leave me alone. There was no other explanation for the excitement that thrummed under my skin at the thought of his hands, roaming over me. His lips. His everything.

No other explanation at all.

And the brief conversation about sex toys was no reason to let things become long-term awkward with my brother's friends. *My* friends.

I heard the front door close, and footsteps echoed through the apartment.

Jax stopped behind me, one hand on my back again. Even without the familiar gesture, I always knew it was him. His cologne was faint but distinct, and currently adding another level of reality to my fantasies.

"I wasn't joking." His voice was throaty. Intoxicating.

"About what?" I knew what, but I needed to hear him say it.

He moved his hands to my hips and pointed me toward the box on my dresser. The one I'd almost overlooked, and would have been super disappointed to find missing when I got to my new place.

"You're not the least bit curious?" he asked.

"Maybe." The answer slipped out without my permission. "But talk about making things awkward."

"It doesn't have to." Grayson had joined us.

The images surged in full force. Not just of Jax. Now Grayson watched us…

Desire sparked in my gut and spread through my limbs.

"We're all adults," Jax said. "This doesn't have to be a big deal." Did his voice catch?

No. That was my breath, hitching at the implication. Could I really do casual sex *with them*? Probably. I never had a problem looking either of them in the eye after fingering myself to visions of one of them going down on me while I sucked the other off. "Good point."

Jax turned me to face him and cupped my cheek. I could drown in those liquid-amber eyes. "I'll ask you directly, one more time. You tell me to drop it, and I'll never bring it up again. Are you interested in a hands-on demonstration of how much fun a toy can be with a partner?"

Yes. *God* yes. I should say *no*, but if I did, I'd regret passing up this chance for a long time.

"All right. Show me." My pulse hammered in my ears so loudly I barely heard myself speak. "Let's have some casual fun." Why did I add that last bit?

Jax's raised eyebrow echoed my question, but he rested his other hand on my cheek and brushed his mouth over mine.

The feather-light touch sent a million tiny jolts through me, and I gasped. How did he do that with just a kiss?

He glided his hand to the back of my neck, gripped my hair, and crushed his lips to mine. This kiss was hard. Demanding. He danced his tongue around mine in a hungry tango.

I planted my palms on his chest, to keep my balance, and fisted his T-shirt, gripping as though my life depended on it. A whimper escaped my throat.

Jax pulled away with a self-satisfied smirk.

I liked it. "That had *nothing* to do with a vibrator." My voice was breathy, and my head swam.

"I didn't see any lube." He grasped my fingers. "So it's either packed away, or you don't need it. Personally, I always imagined you with a sloppy wet pussy, but either way, I have to make sure you're nice and slick."

He'd imagined me...? I was definitely wet after a kiss and a line like that.

TWO

Jax trailed his finger down my neck so lightly, shivers raced down my spine.

I could remind him about the toys, but if his goal was to turn me on and make me slick, it was working.

He followed a different path back up, to brush my ear and then my jaw. My mouth parted in a silent sigh, and he drew his finger along my bottom lip. I pulled him in with my tongue. The twin groans that greeted me were intoxicating, and the reminder that Grayson was watching hammered in my ears to the beat of my pulse.

Jax moved his other hand to my breast, to tease through the heavy fabric of my sweatshirt. He brushed a thumb over my nipple, and the soft fleece tickled my sensitive skin. He kept up the attention until I was squirming and squeezing my thighs together.

"Let's see if you're ready." He undid my jeans and glided his hand over my panties. Dampness had to be seeping through. With a dangerously sexy grin, he shoved my pants and underwear to the floor, rested his hands on my hips, and guided me back to lie on my bed. "Don't move."

It was awkward being naked from the waist down, on a bare

mattress, with two men in my room. But he wasn't gone long enough for me to dwell on the thought. Jax held up a vibrator—my current favorite—and turned it on.

I reached for it.

"Hands off," he ordered, "unless you want me to bind them."

That was tempting. "I can't just lie here."

"You can, but if you need something to do, play with your breasts." Jax shoved my sweatshirt up to my neck.

I hesitated. Being on display? Not new. Doing so completely exposed, while one guy stroked himself through his jeans and the other teased me with a vibrator? The situation shouldn't be so tantalizing.

I did as he ordered, cupping my boobs and pinching my nipples the way I would if I were drawing out a personal-play session.

Jax paused, to free himself from his jeans and roll on a condom. "Don't want to forget in heat of the moment."

Why did using toys require him to wear a condom?

The question evaporated when he slid the vibrating head along my slit. I gasped at the rush of pleasure. He followed the same path a few times, brushing my clit but never lingering. My hips thrust on their own, needing more... everything.

When he finally slipped the toy inside me, I groaned at the penetration. He teased with both ends of the device, pushing me close to orgasm, then backing away each time my breath grew shorter.

He finally pressed the suction end to my clit, and I clenched around the device as I climaxed.

When Jax slid inside me, next to the vibrator instead of withdrawing it first, I cried out. *Oh God.*

The twin sets of pressure, him sliding back and forth, and it staying mostly in place, drew out my pleasure until bright lights sparked behind my eyelids.

I heard a duet of grunts, Jax and Grayson, but I was too lost in sensation to focus on either. I was pretty sure the vibrator slipped out, but I didn't care. Not with the way Jax slammed inside me, his pelvis rocking against mine and his cock hitting me at the perfect angle.

His groans grew tighter as his movements became more frantic, then a pause and a shudder. He gripped my hips tight, and released, I knew he came too.

Jax dropped to his elbows, barely holding himself above me. The heat of his chest mingled with mine. He dipped his head, mouth near my ear. "*God*, Dee Dee, you're incredible." His voice was so soft, I could have imagined the words. His breath on my skin said this was all real.

The desire to giggle like a little girl was back. I settled for a quiet, "You too."

"I think you're both pretty fucking amazing." Grayson's voice was strained. I rolled my head to the side, to see him with his dick in his slick, glistening hand. *Fuck.* He came to the sight of us.

This was better than any fantasy.

The opening strains of "Heathens" by Twenty One Pilots filtered through the room—usually one of my favorite sounds, because it meant one of my best friends was calling. "I should get that. It's probably Lyn." I couldn't keep the disappointment from my voice.

"Yeah." Jax slipped out of me and pushed to his feet. He grabbed my phone from my nightstand and handed it over.

I stared the way his jeans hung off his hips, his softening cock dangling loose. I mentally shook my head and answered the phone. "Hey."

"You all right?" Lyn asked. "You sound winded."

"Moving boxes does that." I'd probably spill the beans about this as soon as she and I were alone, but it felt awkward right now. In fact, a whole lot of uncomfortable was setting in. How was I supposed to act around Jax and Grayson?

"Good point," Lyn said. "Anyway, you were taking a while, so I called to make sure you were okay. See if you needed me to send the troops. Or a hot pizza guy."

I definitely didn't need the second one. The guys left my room, and the sound of running water came from the bathroom. "I'm good. Chase couldn't make it, so we made other arrangements. But I'm on my way soon, and I'll explain everything when I get there." The drive should give me a chance to figure out what *every-thing* was.

"A line like that, and I expect a story."

A story. "It's not a big deal." Understatement of the year. "See you soon."

The guys reappeared, both dressed again. Jax lingered in the doorway, watching me with an unreadable expression. Grayson sat next to me on the bed.

I tugged my sweatshirt down, suddenly intensely aware that I was still half-naked.

"Are we good?" Grayson's arm brushed mine.

Good? They were incredible. It didn't matter that he hadn't touched me. That he got off to the show made it that much hotter. But that wasn't what he meant. He wanted an assurance that nothing had changed between the three of us.

"We're good," I said.

He kissed me on the forehead—a gesture that had never seemed more than friendly until this moment. "We'll see you there."

"And we should keep this between us," Jax said from the doorway.

Grayson frowned.

My warm fuzzies vanished. Of course they'd want discretion. Why would Jax want anyone to know he'd done anything with me? "Of course." My tone was cool. "I'm not telling anyone."

Jax clenched his jaw.

"That's not how he meant it." Grayson's voice was hard.

How many ways were there to mean *don't tell anyone we had sex?*

"Forget it." Jax jerked his head toward the front door. "Let's go."

THREE

After a quick cleanup of my own, and a touch-up to my makeup and hair to get rid of that *freshly fucked* look, I was on my way to Lyn's.

I shouldn't be irritated about Jax's request. It wasn't like I thought that one moment would lead to more. Their future involved the two of them, and mine pointed toward a Hollywood career, a doting husband, an amazing wedding, and the most perfect dress anyone had ever seen.

But I didn't like the idea of being anyone's dirty little secret. That stung. It hurt worse that Grayson put up so little argument, than Jax's making the request in the first place.

I cracked the window in my ancient Subaru, to let the cold December air hit my hot face. I loved this time of year. Yeah, I was a Basic Girl. Uggs and Peppermint Mochas all the way. Most people expected me to love Halloween the most, but I dressed up year-round—bonus to being a cosplay queen. The only thing that made October different was everyone else did as well.

Some people said costumes were about pretending to be someone else for a night or two. In a way, I agreed. But it was more about embracing individuality. Not pretending I was someone else, but being me, in whatever package, job, and universe I chose. I loved to see people exploring that. Which was the reason I loved Christmas. For me, it was all about finding the perfect gift for each person.

The holiday lights were gorgeous too. I could wander for hours through a Christmas village, admiring the lights and losing myself in the cheery mood.

When I got settled in my new place, I had big plans for Christmas activities on my channel. Things like quick accessories and unique gifts for anime fans that anyone could make from supplies around the house. How to go from safe-for-work Christmas cheer to sexy-fun after with the same outfit. Grayson was even going to model the guys' stuff for me.

Would he still agree? How much had our friendship changed? Not at all?

I didn't believe that. Neither did they. *We should keep this between us.* Jax's voice was back in my head, taunting me.

Jax's mother was sick a lot while we were growing up, which made him a semi-permanent fixture in our house. By the time I reached junior high, I'd decided I was going to marry him when we grew up. Which was how I got into sewing, and then cosplay. The perfect wedding required the ultimate dress, and I didn't trust anyone else to make mine for me. Not that I ever told him any of that. Thank God.

Back then, I was certain our love was meant to be, and he'd figure it out sooner rather than later. I was such an idiot, but not in the *I should have approached him* sort of way. In high school, things changed. I hit my junior year, and Jax got friendly. He'd always been nice, but this was different. He started flirting. I ate it up.

There were rumors he was going to ask me to the New Year's dance, and I was figuring out what kind of dress I was going to make. Satin. Blue, to match my eyes. Gold ribbon and embroidery to match his.

Thinking about how naive I'd been clenched like a fist around my heart. Chase had stopped me before I spent an entire paycheck on fabric. He was so nice and sympathetic, and that didn't make his words any easier to hear. Jax had been bragging—locker room talk—about how awesome he was. He'd convinced the girl in the tacky outfits that he liked her.

Chase promised me he'd shut Jax down. Said no one could talk about his sister like that.

Jax hadn't stopped flirting, though. Nausea churned in my gut, at the reminder of his asking me to that dance. I'd told him—screamed in the middle of the school common area—that I wanted him to stop. I wouldn't be his joke.

He did stop. Stopped talking to both Chase and me. Stopped coming to the house. I still hurt over the entire thing. The day they graduated, he *apologized*.

I'm sorry. For whatever I did. I didn't mean it.

It took a few years, but I forgave him enough to be friendly with him. He and Chase made up sometime in college, and we all grew up and moved on. It had been a decade, and the way we got along now allowed me to separate that moment from him.

Today wasn't a mistake. I'd had fun. As far as I could tell, they did too. However, I needed to distance myself from what happened, the way I did with our past.

Which started now, since I was at Lyn's place, and she was helping Jax and Grayson carry in my boxes from Grayson's truck.

Fortunately, this part didn't require much interaction. Grab some stuff, take it up to my new room on the second floor, and go back for the next load. I swore the process took longer than loading the vehicles had.

As we moved the last few boxes, I worked on pasting a smile into place. The manual labor had pushed most of my muddled-brain-ness aside, as well as chasing away the winter chill.

I grabbed a couple of lighter tubs that stacked, and headed for the stairs, passing Lyn. She spun on her toe, fell into step beside me, and tugged the back of my hair.

"Ow." It didn't hurt so much, as caught me off-guard. "What was that for?"

She held up a piece of fuzzy lint, the same color as my mattress pad. "Love the new accessory. Are we calling this *Catch of the Day?*"

"I wasn't *catching* anything." I snagged the fluff from her hand and shoved it in my pocket. "That's what condoms are for." We were eternally teasing each other about our sex lives. I shouldn't have dropped the hint that she was right this time. Not while Jax and Grayson were here. Not after that exchange earlier.

"No shit. Is this why you took so long?"

At three-quarters excited and three-quarters confused, I was bursting to share. "Maybe."

"Since when are you seeing someone. Are you? Did you send Mr. Mysterio home before they showed up, or is he why Jax is scowling?" Lyn spoke quietly, but excitement hummed in her voice. She was about half a second from peppering me with questions so quickly I wouldn't be able to keep up. "Did they interrupt you?"

"No. That definitely wasn't an issue." There was no way I wasn't blushing. I set my load on top of an existing stack. This room was as big as my old bedroom and living room combined. The flat-white walls in here were going to be so much better for filming against when the occasion called for it.

I turned to see Lyn, staring at me with wide eyes, her mouth agape. "No shit," she said.

"We need your keys." Grayson's voice came from the doorway, both startling me and sending a pleasant shiver up my spine.

I whirled to face him, digging the ring out of my pocket. Did he overhear us? He was watching me with a strange expression, but it almost looked... sad. Or was that longing? Definitely not. "For what?" I asked.

"The rest of your stuff is in the hallway. We're going to grab a truck full of your furniture."

"Sounds good. I'll meet you there."

He held out his hand. "We'll do this run alone. It's really only a two-person job."

"Oh. Okay." I couldn't keep the hurt from my voice as I handed him the keys to my apartment. It was a reasonable request, but it felt like there was more attached to it.

Grayson dipped his head next to my ear, and a flash of memory overlapped Jax and that tender moment earlier. "It's okay. I promise," Grayson whispered. "We'll talk this afternoon."

I nodded and stepped back. "Text me when you leave there, and we'll order pizza."

I watched him until he disappeared around a corner and down the stairs. Normally, I'd be enjoying the view, but my mind was in other places.

"Oh. My. Lord." Lyn's exclamation dragged me out of my head. "Does Grayson know? Or was it with him? That's why Jax is upset—he walked in on you. No. You said you weren't interrupted. Was it both of them? *Holy shit*, what was that like? What were you thinking? Chase is going to flip. Not that it's any of his business. Was it amazing? I bet it was. *Tell me.*"

A tiny laugh escaped me, mingled with a sigh. Lyn was a literal genius, and her brain and mouth tended to lay out everything all at once, rather than pondering any of it first.

I was a master of acting without thinking everything through, but she thought it as she did it. When I met her I didn't know how to process her behavior. Now I adored it.

"It was amazing. And confusing. They were both there." I wasn't ready to share details. If I talked about it, the magic might vanish, and I was alrcady struggling with the fallout. "What was I thinking?"

"You were thinking you were tired of being trapped in a *shoujo*, where there's so much tension you think the room might explode, and you wanted to finally move past the final end credits and do more than gaze longingly at each other." Lyn grabbed my hand and tugged me toward the kitchen.

I rolled my eyes, but her enthusiasm was chasing away my dread. "We're not an anime. It was a one-time thing. There's no *happily ever after* here." For them, maybe. And for me separately, with my one and only guy.

"You say that now." She handed me a Mt. Dew and grabbed herself a Diet Coke from the fridge.

We took seats at the kitchen table. "Forever. I'm not supposed to tell anyone. They're embarrassed about it. I made a mistake, didn't I?"

"Does it *feel* like a mistake? Not the circles your brain is chasing you in, but the actual moment. Do you want to take it back?"

I wanted the awkwardness around it to go away, but not at the cost of… Yeah, I wasn't ready to give up the memory of Jax's touch. His kisses. Grayson's gaze on us. His groans. "No."

"So it wasn't a mistake. They're big boys; they can deal with it. They *are* big, aren't they?"

My laugh was back. "I'll never tell."

"Yes, you will." Lyn kicked me under the table. "And that's all the answer I need."

Thank God for friends who got me. If only what came next—talking through things with Grayson and Jax—was going to be even a fraction as simple.

FOUR

J ax and Grayson returned with my bed strapped to the bed of
Grayson's truck and the rest of my bedroom set underneath.
Most of my furniture was going into storage or to my other
best friend, Anne, since Lyn already had furniture here.

Seeing the guys bring my bed in summoned memories of the
last thing we'd done on it, and a knot formed in my gut. Fortunately,
the arrival of the pizza lady was the perfect distraction.

Lyn and I gathered sodas and stacks of plates from her upstairs
kitchen. She always had a massive variety of drinks on hand,
because she got a good deal buying them in bulk for the shop. I was
grateful when she suggested we set it all up on the coffee table in the
living room. I still needed to figure out simple things like, could I
make eye-contact with Grayson and Jax? The kitchen table would
make that a more pressing concern than I was prepared to deal
with.

When Lyn grabbed a small salad from the fridge, I frowned.
"It's moving day. Indulge." I kept my tone light.

Lyn was gorgeously curvy, and every other month she started
another diet to hide her amazing features. "Burning calories isn't an
excuse to consume more."

"That's exactly what it is." I wished I could make her see what I did—that her intelligence and beauty didn't need to bend to fit anyone else's perspective. She was perfect as-is. I wouldn't push the issue today, though.

Grayson joined us first, and then Jax, both of them grabbing a couple slices of pizza before settling on the couch next to each other.

I staked out one of the oversized beanbags, and Lyn perched on the edge of a chair. A heavy silence settled over the room as we gave our attention to our food.

"You ready for RinCon?" Lyn asked Grayson.

Thank God for her and small talk. RinCon was an international gaming competition, put on by Rinslet, one of the largest gaming companies in the world, started by a couple of local guys.

Grayson flexed his fingers and rolled his wrists. "As ready as I'll ever be. I'm up against a newcomer from Korea this year, but I've got a good luck charm."

Grayson was an exhibition gamer. He used to compete. It was how he'd met Jax, who worked in sales with Chase at Rinslet. Grayson had been thinking about stepping back from the competitions anyway, but dating Jax made the decision easier. *Retiring* kept Grayson from traveling so much and helped them both avoid any conflict of interest. Now Grayson did most of his gaming online, and appeared at shows like this as part of the hype, to play against other top-tier gamers.

I glanced up to see Grayson watching me with an unreadable expression, and heat flooded my cheeks. "You'll do great," I mumbled through a mouthful of pizza.

"Your interview is tomorrow, isn't it?" Jax looked at me. "You excited?"

Tomorrow's meeting was the first of several I'd lined up, to speak with Hollywood costume designers and get myself on someone's team. The next step in my plan. I was nervous as fuck. "Of course. Opportunity of a lifetime, and all that." My reply came out with less enthusiasm than I intended.

Lyn's phone rang. She glanced at the screen and sighed so heavily, her body deflated. "I need to take this." As she answered, she left the room at a quick pace. Her voice faded then vanished.

Jax met my gaze. "You have the worst poker face in history. You said you were okay with this morning. Second thoughts?"

"I'm pretending it never happened, just like you asked." My retort came out with a sharper edge than I intended. Where was the balance between discretion and embracing what we'd done? I'd had a total of two one-night stands in my life. Hookups with guys I met online, that ended with a walk of shame.

Grayson set aside his plate. "You're not pretending very well."

"And I could have sworn *you* called it *casual fun*. So what's with the silent treatment?" Jax said.

"I don't appreciate being treated like a dirty little secret." I winced at my immature retort. Neither of them was being aggressive. They seemed willing to talk through this, and I'd prefer to still be on speaking terms with them at the end of the day.

Jax scowled. "You think—"

"That's not what he meant." Grayson's tone was kinder than Jax's.

Calm down. Be a grown-up about this. "Explain it to me."

"Not if you're going to take it out of context." Jax sounded frustrated and… hurt?

"How else am I going to take you?"

"Tight and slick, just like earlier." He winked.

Heat flooded my cheeks. Effective way to shift the mood in the room. "One, that doesn't make any sense, and two, you said *we should keep this between us.* Not the sweetest thing to hear after sex."

"The *you're incredible* didn't stick?" Jax asked.

Grayson crossed the room to sit on the floor next to my beanbag. The nearness wasn't unusual between us, but today it made me question so much.

"We asked for discretion because of Chase," he said.

Bros before hos? "I don't talk about my sex life with my brother."

"But we run in the same circles… obviously." Grayson settled his hand on my arm, searing my skin. "It's going to get back to him. And in the past, he's asked us—"

"His exact words were, *Keep your grubby dicks off my sister*," Jax said.

Not the nicest way for Chase to address his best friends, but he'd always been protective of me.

Wait. This meant he felt like he had a reason to make that request. Was that good or bad? I couldn't find a reply.

"The point was… *is*"—Grayson sighed—"we're not looking at you any differently—"

"I am." Jax smirked.

Grayson rolled his eyes, but a hint of a smile shone through. *Comforting.* "We're not looking at you with any less respect or any more assumption."

Jax's grin grew. "The lust hasn't decreased any, either."

He was lusting after me before? A tiny nag in the back of my mind repainted that moment in high school. He'd apologized. We'd moved on, or I wouldn't be talking to him now. None of those reassurances extinguished that spark of doubt. And here I was, not responding, while they tried to soothe my mind.

I needed to say something.

Grayson placed a finger under my chin and raised my gaze to his. "If you're not okay with what happened, say so now, and we can figure it out." He sounded so genuine.

My racing thoughts were slowing, and the nagging in my gut was fading at their insistence we use now to make things right. "I'm okay with it. Great with it. It was amazing." Was it okay to say that out loud? It should be.

"Something we agree on." Jax winked.

"*…I said no.*" Lyn's shout echoed through the top floor of the building. "If you don't like my answer—even if you do—you can fuck all the way off." She stormed back into the room and threw her phone at her chair. It bounced once, and then settled. Red blotches marred her face, and she was shaking.

The conversation with Grayson and Jax took a backseat to Lyn's distress. It felt like we'd worked things out, anyway. I needed to adjust my perspective on how to act around them.

I extracted myself from my seat and approached Lyn, in case hugs were needed. "What happened?"

She pinched the bridge of her nose and took a few deep breaths. "It was that asshole, who wants to buy the building. I want to blast out a warning to any woman considering dating him that he doesn't know how to take *no* for an answer. Fucking troglodyte."

"I can pound his face in for you," Jax offered.

Lyn let out a tiny laugh. "I'm good, thanks. But I'll keep the offer in mind." She looked at Grayson. "You're still coming over for Cosplay Christmas, aren't you?"

In other words, she wanted to change the subject. I respected that.

Grayson nodded. "Absolutely. I'm Sadie's to use and abuse, while the entire internet watches."

Hello, new fantasies. I needed to redraw the lines between the vivid images my brain liked to provide me with, and reality.

FIVE

I'd never been more nervous about a job interview in my life. Not that I'd had to deal with them since my channel took off a couple years ago and I started earning enough to pay the bills.

But today wasn't just about a job. It was about *the* job. The career I dreamed about. I looked myself over in the mirror one more time. The violet in my hair was vibrant, no roots showing. My makeup was on point. My outfit was the perfect way to present myself. It was a business suit, with subtle hints of evening gown worked into the trim and blouse. Professional but creative, to show off what I could do when I was given freedom.

I took several calming breaths and sat in front of my laptop. The call wasn't for another ten minutes, but I didn't know what else to do besides pace until I wore a path in the carpet. I'd posted several pictures of the outfit online, with a teaser that I hoped to share good news soon.

I fiddled with my phone, which I'd set to silent. There were three text messages. The first two were from Anne and Chase, wishing me luck. I'd read the third a ridiculous number of times. It was a good-luck message as well, but Jax sent it and Grayson chimed in. For someone who insisted one-time sex wouldn't change anything, I couldn't stop thinking it had changed everything.

Did I mind? All I knew was I couldn't hook up with them again. But damn, I wanted to.

Falling into that merry-go-round of thought would wait. It was almost time. I sat myself in front of my camera. The lighting and angle in my new room were perfect—I tested both with a couple of livestreams since yesterday. Any still-packed boxes were tucked away, and just enough of my room was visible to imply my personality without saying too much.

My stomach dropped into my shoes when my video-chat software rang. One more deep breath, then I answered.

The woman who appeared on my screen wasn't the one I expected. She introduced herself as *Kayla*, Ms. G's Assistant. Perhaps this was a few minutes of screening, or she'd keep me company until my Ms. G was available. A designer with her skill and reputation had to have a packed schedule.

I gave Kayla my warmest smile and let everything fall away except the person I was on camera. "It's so great to talk to you. I've really been looking forward to this conversation. You and Ms. G and the entire staff do such amazing work. The outfits in the newest fantasy adaptation were one-of-a-kind incredible." I stopped myself before I dove into fangirl gushing. I wanted them to know I was familiar with their designs, without talking so much they couldn't.

Kayla's smile brightened. "We're glad you reached out to us as well. It's always wonderful to connect with fresh talent. Your work is amazing. Not quite up to the standard we require from our designers, but you do have potential."

Mentally, I wavered. Feedback was good, especially from someone of this caliber. And they'd agreed to talk to me, so it wasn't all lip service. "I'm always willing to learn. Teach me and mold me."

"I'm happy to hear that." Did her voice just become a little more artificial, or was the mask over my wounded ego projecting? "Ms. G is so sorry she couldn't speak with you herself, but she'd like me to introduce you to a course we offer. It's an intimate, online setting. Rarely more than thirty people."

I— What? Maybe this was how they trained new hires? "Tell me more. Is this like some sort of remote internship?"

"In a way, yes. Your final design, the one you create for your grade, will be considered by Ms. G. If she feels you've done exceptional work, we consider offering you an internship. That will be local to L.A., and we provide a small stipend once you arrive."

None of this sounded like what I expected, or even legit. "And then you hire those interns?"

"If they work out, absolutely."

"I see. And this course is free?" Of course it was. She was about to laugh at me for even asking.

Kayla chuckled. "Ms. G's time is valuable. The course is five thousand dollars, but we do offer installment plans. If you're hired, the remainder of your balance is waived."

Anger flooded in, to mingle with my hurt and disbelief. "So basically, these interviews are your way of taking advantage of potential designers looking for an in."

"They're an excellent opportunity for people serious about their craft." Kayla's sunny mask cracked. "This is a chance to work with the best and get a foot up in an industry that touches every genre of film. Open slots in this program are rare, and you're fortunate to be offered one."

"Wow. I bet the internet would love to hear about this." Fuck pretenses and false smiles. This was some serious bullshit.

Kayla glowered. "You signed a non-disclosure agreement as part of this interview. I assure you, our lawyers do not take slander lightly. If you pass up this chance, if you leave a bad taste in our mouths, you will *never* work in Hollywood."

The idea of losing access to my dream curdled in my gut. She had to be making an empty threat. "I'll take that chance. Thank you for your time." I disconnected before she could reply.

I made sure all connections were closed, and resisted the urge to slam my laptop shut as I lowered the lid. Tears pricked the inside of my eyelids, as I sank back in my chair. Were they sadness? Fury? A heavy dose of both?

Was Kayla right, that I wasn't as good as I thought? Was that why I couldn't get anyone else to talk to me? Or was this one designer taking advantage of people? How many costumers had they taken advantage of? And what was it about me that said, *I'm so desperate, you can scam me out of five grand?*

I sat there, as minutes ticked away, letting my rage simmer into a thick, gooey mess in my thoughts. Ms. G wasn't getting away with this. I'd write a scathing email. Would I be the first? Would it be used against me when it came to other career opportunities? Did I care?

I opened my laptop again. A barking laugh choked from my throat when I saw an email waiting for me from Kayla. She was definitely getting a piece of my mind.

The body of the message wasn't a nice, personalized little note. It looked more like a newsletter. It thanked me for my time and offered a link to more information about the course. And at the bottom of it all, it reminded me, *This email was sent from an unmonitored box. Do not reply.*

Fucking bitch. Curiosity and anger had me clicking the link. It took me to a pretty page with pictures of lots of smiling people near ornate costumes, and brief, content-less blurbs about how amazing this course was.

I was more interested in the *Terms and Conditions*. One lesson I was grateful I'd learned early on in my career—always know what people are doing with my intellectual property. This company was keeping it. Any designs submitted, proposed, or posted in the discussion room during the course were property of Ms. G.

Apparently, I could be more furious. I took screenshots of everything, and captured a PDF of the email as proof. I needed to call Anne and go downstairs to let Lyn know how things went. But I needed to type first, while the rage and thoughts were still fresh.

The world was going to know about this bullshit. I'd do a live feed. I'd link to evidence. As the list ticked off in my head, my fingers flew over the keyboard, composing a list of talking points for me to cover when I addressed my followers. In the next few hours, millions of people would know what was happening in one corner of Hollywood.

My anger didn't diminish as I re-read, revised, and relentlessly polished. A little voice I didn't care for joined the chorus, telling me this was a mistake. They'd threatened me.

It didn't matter. Ms. G was scamming people, and the world needed to know before they took advantage of anyone else.

A knock on my door made me jump. Shit, it was almost two. I'd been at this for hours. I was sufficiently collected to talk to Lyn. "Come in."

Jax poked his head into my room. Lust bounded in and muddled my fury at the softness around his eyes.

"Are you all right?" he asked.

"No, I'm not. What are you doing here?" I made sure to ask calmly. I wasn't angry at him.

He stepped inside and mostly closed the door behind him. Jax dressed for work was as delicious as Jax in jeans and a T-shirt. He embodied everything about the phrase *Suit Porn.* "We all got worried when you didn't message anyone back. I had a client lunch down the street, and it gave me an excuse to check on you. Did they tell you that you have to wait to start? Or are they making you pack up and leave us right away?"

My brain stalled. He was assuming I got the job. There was no doubt in his questions, only concern.

"I didn't get it," I said.

"What? But you're the best."

"Not according to them." I couldn't hold back any longer. I'd spent hours writing out my thoughts, and now I had an audience. I let the story spill out.

His expression shifted from sympathetic to one of an anger that matched my own. "Are you fucking kidding me? Who do I need to crucify?"

"I'm going to tell the entire internet." I was encouraged by his response. "You can give me a signal boost."

Jax frowned. "Don't do that."

There it was—the lack of support I'd feared. Any hope that had blossomed since he showed up wilted and withered and exploded in a cloud of disappointed dust.

SIX

I stared at Jax with disbelief. "Did you hear me?" He'd looked sympathetic. "They're ripping people off. Not just me. They didn't manufacture a several-thousand-dollar course specifically for me."

"And you signed an NDA."

Fucking logic. "If they come after me, at least I've warned others. I'll fight back." Could I? How badly would they ruin me? Damn him, for zeroing in on the one point that had me wavering.

"It's not that easy, and it's not going to be cheap. Even an initial push back, beyond yielding to their demands, will make their five thousand look like pocket change." He sounded kind.

I didn't want that. I wanted him to be sneering, all-but implying I was being stupid, so I could keep raging and suck him into the bubble of what irritated me. "Since when do you know so much about these things?"

He raised an eyebrow and pursed his lips.

Ah. Not a dumb question unless one knew who he worked for. Rinslet had built a large part of their reputation on not fitting in. They were strategic about who they pissed off, and they knew how to spin almost any bad press. As part of their sales department, Jax had to be familiar with all of their talking points. Chase had gone on about it at length and with great fascination when he was in training.

But— "I can't let this go. They're taking advantage of people. This isn't just about me."

"I'm not saying *walk away*. Be smart about how you retaliate."

"How?"

"Let me talk to a friend in Legal. Save your rant until I have answers, and once you're protected, we can tear them down."

"*We?*" I liked the warm glow that spread inside with his support and offer of help.

He flashed me one of those sexy smirks that sent my imagination running rampant. "You roped me in when you gave me deets. Now you're stuck with me until things are resolved."

"I won't complain about that." Damn him for making me almost smile in the midst of my rage.

Jax reached for the door. "Text Anne and Chase and tell them you're all right. Chase wants to take you out to celebrate. Tell him you're up for commiseration instead, and he's buying the drinks."

"Bossy much?"

"You know you love it." He winked and was gone.

My feelings about the not-interview hadn't changed, but I was doing better, thanks to Jax's surprise visit.

He was eye candy and taken by an amazing man. Fantasy material, not swoon-after and crush-on material. I had to remember that.

I also had to go online and tell my followers my big news had been postponed, and thank them for the good wishes. My heart sank again. Talk about a soul-crushing reality check.

LYN INVITED everyone to hold my commiseration party in her basement. The space had originally been built out as an over-sized den, complete with a pool table, bar, and kitchenette. I insisted she didn't need to cook for us. She countered she had new appetizer recipes and needed a test audience.

It was hard to argue against her cooking. Besides, if we drank here, no one had to be the designated driver. The basement had plenty of couches for everyone.

Chase brought Asahi beer, because he was a beer snob.

Anne brought Guinness because, *Chase brought that pale-ass lager, didn't he?* I'd known her most of my life. When we were kids, we'd tell people we were twins, both of us the same height and build, with dark-blond hair. Her hair was a shorter pixie cut now, and its natural color. We were about five-six and could share clothes, but she was more comfortable in jeans and baggy T-shirts, where I preferred things more form-fitting. And she was still as much my sister as anyone ever would be.

Jax and Grayson brought champagne and flowers. There was no explanation, but daises were my favorite, and I couldn't hide my grin when Grayson handed them to me.

Everyone offered hugs and sympathy. It killed me to keep my mouth shut. To not tell them, *Turns out it was a massive fucking scam.* I hated keeping secrets, and my job-interview news plus my *it's just casual fun* hook up with Jax and Grayson were bursting to get out.

I needed more of a distraction than rounds of pity and commiseration. "We should play something," I announced. It was almost a given that we'd split into teams of boys versus girls. We were evenly matched at all of our favorites, though some of us were better at each than the rest of us. Pool. Dance Dance Revolution.

"Darts," Grayson said.

Chase handed Grayson and me each a beer. "Neither of you is drunk enough for darts."

I turned wide, sad eyes toward Chase and batted my eyelashes. "But I'm so wounded and heartbroken." I managed the perfect balance of teasing and pathetic in my voice.

"Fine." Chase let out an exaggerated huff. "I suppose you've earned the right to throw sharp, pointy things at a target. But no one's going easy on you."

My grin was back. "Like that's a concern."

We didn't play with traditional rules. The team with the most points at the end of one round won. We did have an extra set of rules we tacked on to anything we played as a group. Trying to distract the other team was both allowed and encouraged, as long as there was no touching, no stepping in someone's line of sight, and no jump scares. The distractions were frequently more fun and competitive than the game itself.

When we were younger, it was Chase and Jax versus Anne and me. We stopped for a while after I met Lyn, because the teams were uneven. But once Grayson and Jax started dating, it was *game on*. It helped that Grayson was the only one of them who could match me at darts.

Anne was up first, with Lyn and me cheering her loudly.

Anne lined up her first throw.

"Shame we're not playing DDR." Chase's tone was deceptively casual. What was he up to? "You're always nice to watch on the dance pads."

Anne threw. She fell far right of center, but it was a steady toss. "You just hate that you suck at this as badly as I do." She readied her second dart.

"If we're having a sucking contest, I want different rules. The *no touching* has to go. A little privacy might be nice."

"I don't need to hear that." I exaggerated my protest. His teasing seemed to get to me more than Anne. Her next throw hit the board, and her third landed in the wall.

Pretty much what I expected. But she made me look like spastic rag doll in DDR, and I didn't have a problem admitting it.

Chase went next. With a glance from Anne, I knew what she was up to. We gave him silence for his first two throws, while the guys chanted his name.

He lined up his last shot.

Anne let out a sharp wolf whistle. "Wow. Did you see her?"

Chase whipped his head in her direction, and everyone laughed.

"No one here but us, bro." Jax slapped him on the back.

Chase fixed his gaze on Anne. "Thought maybe you saw your reflection."

"Right." She raised her eyebrows and pursed her lips.

Jax stepped up to the line next, all swagger and confidence.

"Cocky for a man who's about to lose," Anne teased.

He kept his attention focused on the dartboard.

Lyn had her phone out. She swiped the screen, and a cash register sound echoed from the speakers.

Jax didn't flinch. He also barely hit the board.

She cycled through several more sounds in rapid succession. Cheers. Boos. A rooster crowing.

Jax made his second shot.

A drawn-out gasp, like someone on the edge of ecstasy, echoed from Lyn's phone.

Oh God. That was me.

Jax's last dart landed flat side against the wall and tumbled to the ground.

She must have taken that from one of my videos when I was messing around. I shot Lyn a glare, and she shrugged.

"Fair's fair," she said, and grabbed three darts to take her turn.

Lyn and Grayson were impossible to ruffle. Neither of them flinched or faltered, regardless of what we said. And Grayson hit every shot beautifully, with two in the bullseye and one in the treble ring.

Which meant I had to be spot on my game. I should have made Grayson go last, to see if any pressure got to him. But as a competition gamer, he'd learned how to let most of that stress roll off him.

I took my place in front of the board, darts in hand. Grayson stepped up behind me. He didn't break the *no touching* rule, but he was so close I felt his heat.

"I want to watch how a real master works," he said. "See this from the same angle you do." He wasn't so near that his breath brushed my skin, but I swore I felt his words rolling over me.

Whatever he was doing, it wouldn't work. I grabbed my focus and landed my first throw in the treble ring.

"You ever have trouble with the tip not sticking in?" Grayson asked.

A laugh bubbled up inside at the innuendo. If I gave in to amusement, I wouldn't be able to recover. "No."

"Any problems with it going in too deep?" Everyone was silent except Grayson.

I threw again and hit the bullseye. "No."

"Hmm…" Grayson dragged out the sound. "So it never gets stuck because it's a tight fit?"

This was killing me. I was so close to done, though. If I could hit the treble ring again, we'd win. "Nope. Never been an issue."

"Never?"

"Not even once." I aimed.

"What about when the tip gets jerked up at the wrong angle, and you don't expect it, and you get jizz in your hair?" Jax asked.

Laughter and disbelief tore from me, and I completely missed my mark. It took me several seconds to collect myself and shoot a glare at him, but with his smug expression staring back, I couldn't hold onto my composure. "That was anything but subtle." I finally managed. "There was *zero* innuendo there."

"Innuendo isn't against the rules. And she started it." He nodded toward Lyn.

She smirked. "Don't know what you're talking about."

With the game over, we fell into other conversations. The night sped by quickly, the way it tended to when we were all together. A few hours later, I found myself in the upstairs kitchen, looking for juice or something else to drink that wasn't alcohol.

"So, what's up with you three?" Anne's soft question startled me.

I hadn't talked to her since *the event*—had it only been a day?—and it wasn't the kind of thing I wanted to share over text. I could imagine the message now. *Guess who I had sex with?*

I could also imagine what she'd say next. That was the other thing holding me back. She was there when Jax hurt me, so long ago. She helped me pick up the pieces. Anne was the one person most likely to remind me this was a mistake.

"What do you mean?" I winced even before I finished asking the question. I didn't want to lie to her.

She crossed the room, to steal a sip of my Coke. "I *mean* they're flirting with you. Okay, so Grayson always does—"

He did?

"—but I swear I heard Jax get an erection when Lyn played that sound clip of you."

"So... yeah, something happened. But it was a one-time thing, and we're all being discreet."

"*All?* As in—"

"All three of us." If my confession to Lyn was any indication, it was best to get some of the details out there up front.

Anne stared at me, mouth slightly agape. Here it came. "No shit. How was it?"

Not the first thing I expected her to say, but it was the perfect response. "Amazing. And I'm dying, not being able to tell anyone."

"Lyn knows."

"Lyn guessed. It happened yesterday. It made us late to her house, and she put some pieces together."

Anne leaned against the counter next to me, her arm pressed against mine. "But it was only a one-time thing, right?" The awe and surprise faded from her voice.

"I already said it was."

"Because if Jax hurts you again, I'll make him suffer," Anne said.

There it was. "He's not going to. It's not that kind of thing." Except the nagging part of my mind that agreed with her on the possibility was begging me to listen to it. To her.

"Okay." Anne let out a long breath. "Both of them. Really? Do I get details?"

"When we're not surrounded by prying ears, yes. Like I said, it was amazing." I really was dying to talk about it. But my nagging voice didn't shut up because Anne had moved past her concerns.

SEVEN

Between sitting on my plans to expose Ms. G, and trying not to overthink Grayson and Jax's behavior post move-in, I had a lot of excess energy to burn. I poured a bit of it into decorating my room for Christmas. Evergreen-colored garland decorated with strings of red and white lights hung along my wall, and I had holiday wall scrolls to break up the design. I loved the way it looked for me and on camera.

That was done now, and I could go back to focusing on acting normal around Grayson. That should be easy, since he and I did things together all the time similar to what I had planned for today.

I dropped into my computer chair, careful not to let my outfit ride too high or drop too low, and surveyed the filming corner of my bedroom. In a few minutes, I was taking the last clips I needed to create my *Furry Christmas Cosplay How-To* video.

The outfits themselves were easy to make, and I'd filmed myself doing so. The red fleece tops were trimmed with white and had hoods with puppy ears for the guys and kitty ears for the girls. My outfit had a skirt that barely covered my ass, and thigh-high stockings. There were two variations on each top. A long-sleeved, jacket style, and a sleeveless fitted vest.

Grayson was going to be my model for the puppy clothing, one piece at a time, to show them off, and then the entire outfit. He'd done this for me so often, I knew his measurements by heart, and the vest would give my subscribers the fan service they expected from him.

They'd get the same from me. I was wearing the skirt and the low-cut top that pushed my cleavage up. I was going to look incredible, helping him dress up.

There were two big upsides to these collaborations—they brought in both of our fan bases and pushed my viewer numbers through the roof, but more importantly, it gave me the perfect excuse to run my hands all over Grayson's body.

Which... How did I ever think that was innocent? Because he had a boyfriend? He'd watched—jerked off—while said boyfriend fucked me. A pulse throbbed between my thighs at the whispers of memory. Even if the touching *didn't* mean anything, I'd never believe it again.

A sharp whistle cut through my swelling desire, and I whirled to see Grayson in my doorway. It was instinct to strike a sexy pose— our joint videos frequently started with his appreciation for my outfit of the day—but today his reaction also cranked the heat racing through my veins. How long until my face matched my clothes?

The way he leaned against my doorframe accentuated the ripple of muscle along his torso and upper arms. "Where do you want me, bosslady?"

On the bed. On the floor. Pinning me against the wall... "It's a standard shoot." I jerked a thumb toward an empty space I'd set up for this part of recording. "A piece of clothing at a time, and pose."

"All right." He kicked away from the wall. His cheerful tone clashed with his frown.

"What's wrong?"

"When do we film me helping you into and out of your clothes?"

That was new, even for us. I'm pretty sure I wouldn't have brushed off something that direct as status quo, in the past. "I'm not taking it off the table."

His grin turned my insides gooey.

Act normal. That was all I had to do.

Had we ever really been *normal?*

"Shirt off." I had a remote for my camera tucked under my bra strap. It would make it easier to keep both of us in the right position without having to record *everything*.

"I love the way you say that." Grayson, stripping his T-shirt off was a gorgeous sight to behold.

I took advantage of the half second his eyes were covered, to stare, when I should have been using the time to compose myself. Something about this situation had to change, or we wouldn't get any work done.

"You ready for RinCon?" I asked as I handed him the tail belt and stepped out of the frame.

He raised his brows but fitted the belt into place without argument.

I should have picked a better question to change the subject with. Not because it was unusual for us to talk about it—exactly the opposite. Our circle of friends lived and breathed RinCon in the weeks leading up to it, and there wasn't much left to say at this point. He was going to use this video as a teaser, to draw in more interest to his livestreams during the event.

But the con was all business to me. It was kind of like thinking about baseball, to ignore horniness. It wasn't working.

"Specifically, do you have any details you can share that no one else has?" I grabbed his vest off its mannequin. This part needed to be hands on. It was always more effective this way. I set the camera to record again and slid the fleece up his arms. Made a generous show of smoothing everything out as I glided my palms over his chest. Kept his tattooed arm pointed toward the camera.

Failed to ignore the prickles of desire racing over my skin and tightening in my nipples. Good thing this was a padded bra.

I finished my part and stepped back, to let him pose for the camera alone. Hood down, and then up. I paused the recording.

"They tell me there's a surprise coming, but no details," he said.

Something none of us had heard yet? "You're not just holding out on me to be clever?" I teased.

He shrugged out of the vest and held it out for me. When I stepped in to take it, he tweaked one of my kitty ears. "You look so adorable in these, I'd tell you the secrets of the universe if I knew them."

My heated cheeks were back. I turned away to hang up the top and hoped it would give my face time to pale again.

He grabbed my wrist, startling me, and turned me to face him. "We need to talk about the other day." His tone was serious, but a spark of playfulness danced behind his eyes.

"What about it? We're good. We all agreed." I was being awkward, but that would pass with time.

"We did. But I can't move past the jealousy."

Oh. My heart sank. I never wanted to be a wedge in their relationship. "I thought you were okay with it. I'm sorry. I didn't—"

He pressed a finger to my lips. "Don't apologize. Let me finish. I thought I was okay with it too—and don't misunderstand, watching you with Jax was good—but there's this little slice of envy that he got to feel you and I didn't."

And now my heart was not only fine, but also skipping. "I wouldn't want to leave you out."

"Me neither. Go figure." Grayson tugged me closer, dipped his head, and trailed his nose up the side of my neck.

Want clashed with concern. When I was with Jax, Grayson was there to give his explicit *okay*. This was different. "I don't want to come between you."

"He's okay with wherever this goes. In fact, I'm planning to tell him *everything* about what happens between us."

"Like what?" My question came out timid and breathy. I had my own fantasies, but I'd never dare say them out loud.

"Hmm..." Grayson settled his hands on my hips, on the bare skin above my skirt. "I'll tell him if your nipples taste like sugar. If your pussy is peach-flavored. How incredible you feel when I'm buried inside you. So if you have issues with me kissing and telling, say so."

The only issue I had was that we weren't doing any of that yet. "Does that mean—" The question stuck in my throat.

"Does it mean what?"

"That he'll get off to the story of us together?" I barely heard myself ask the question, over the hammering of my pulse in my ears.

Grayson pressed his body into mine, heat searing through my thin outfit. "We both will." His voice was a low hum, licking temptation along my skin. "I'll be at his feet, sucking his cock, stroking my own during every delicious moment of the relived memory."

"Hot." I hadn't meant to say that aloud.

He scrapped his teeth along my neck and yanked down my hood. "My point exactly. Is that a *yes?*"

Was it? How many one-night stands did it take, before we passed some invisible line of *too many*? Everything had already changed. How much further was I willing to alter the relationship between the three of us?

EIGHT

I didn't need to think long about Grayson's offer. Longer than I did for most things, but he was too tempting to pass up. "That's a *yes*."

"Looks like I get to help you out of your costume, after all." Grayson grasped the hidden zipper on my top and tugged it down one agonizing tooth at a time, his gaze lingering on my breasts. "Every time you run your palms over my bare chest, I want to return the favor."

Seriously, how had I never noticed before that what we did was more than friendly? "Now's your chance."

"And what a chance it is." He glided his hands up my chest, to cup my breasts.

When he dragged his thumbs over my nipples, I felt the *zing* even though the padding of my bra. It was a sharp spark that raced along my every nerve ending.

Grayson pushed my top off my shoulders and tossed it aside. My bra came off next, leaving me exposed and topless. Every time he looked me over, a fresh wave of flames raced over me.

When his palms touched my bare skin, the heat intensified. He teased my pale pink swollen nubs. "Not just sugar. Bubblegum.

Yum." He dipped his head to flick his tongue over one nipple, before drawing it into his mouth. He sucked and nibbled one side, while kneading the other.

Pleasure sped over me, and I pressed into his mouth. He switched to the other breast when I started to squirm. The longer he sucked, the damper my panties got. I wanted to reach between my legs and relieve the building anticipation.

Grayson grasped my wrist and moved my hand to his erection. I'd gotten a hint of how big he was the other day, but stroking him drove the point home. I traced the outline through denim, and his groan hummed across my skin. We were hooked in a delicious loop of pleasure.

He drifted his kisses lower, moving down my stomach and pulling away from my touch as he knelt in front of me. He shoved my skirt up and over my hips—another reason to love fleece—and scraped his teeth over my panties. "You're already wet."

Massive understatement. My laugh was breathy and strained, and most of my brain power was focused on my arousal. *"Already? I'm surprised all that sucking and biting didn't make me come."*

"No?" The way he looked up at me with that dark, open gaze, I felt like I was being worshiped. "Time to try something else." He looped his fingers in my panties and slid them down my legs. When he licked once along my damp lower lips, I moaned.

Could they hear me downstairs? Did I care?

Grayson stood, to lift me onto a nearby stool. As he knelt again, he spread my legs. His soft kisses started at my knee and traveled up my inner thigh.

Each brush of his lips against my skin cranked my anticipation higher, and I gripped the edge of the stool tightly. When he reached my core, I shivered and gasped in delight. He wrapped his lips around my clit to, suck and tease. I swear to God he was writing the alphabet with his tongue.

He slipped two fingers inside me, and hooked up, hitting the right spot and stealing my thoughts.

My breath came in short gasps, and I lost track of my own

moans and whimpers. My head was light. He pushed me to the edge of climax and let me linger on that fine point.

I knotted my fingers in his hair. I didn't want to miss anything, and from the way his tongue was working frantically, neither did he.

Orgasm crashed over me in wave, tearing a scream from my throat. I ground into Grayson's face as I came, losing myself in the intense colors of pleasure that sparked in my thoughts and made my legs weak.

He pulled away as I loosened my grip, and sucked his fingers clean as he stood. "Definitely cherries and bubblegum. My new favorite flavors. Want a taste?" He pressed his mouth to mine, open and hungry.

Our first real kiss.

What an odd thought. I brushed it aside and dove into the feeling of him devouring my lips. The taste of myself. The way he kneaded my breast and swallowed my moans.

I wrapped my legs around his ass and pulled him in closer, until I could reach his belt.

He broke the kiss, to laugh against my lips. "Eager?"

"Aren't you?" I let desperation and need drive me as I undid his jeans. When I brushed his shaft, his throaty groan drilled into me. "Promises were made."

"They definitely were." Grayson reached into his back pocket while I worked him free. He rolled on a condom and pressed, to glide the head of his cock along the same path his tongue had followed.

I arched into the contact. He slid inside me, stretching me out and hitting deep. I needed to be a part of him. To feel as much as possible. I tightened my legs, to set a fast and frantic pace.

He gripped my hips tight, slowing me down. With each thrust, he withdrew almost to the tip before plunging back into me again. My opening clenched at the delicious repeated sensation of penetration.

Grayson slanted his mouth over mine, to kiss me hard, and increased the pace at the same time. As he slammed against me, he struck that perfect spot inside, nudging me toward another orgasm.

The build-up pushed me right to that point between pleasure and discomfort. He nipped my bottom lip and pinched a nipple, rolling the nub between his fingers. The extra sensations knocked me into climax. I clenched around him, milking him and keeping him buried inside me until it was too much and not enough at the same time.

His grunts told me he was close. His pounding hit frantic, before jarring to a shuddering pause, and then slowing again. He'd come too.

The desperation faded as he stopped, but the warm fuzzies flitting through me lingered.

Grayson rested his forehead on my shoulder while we both fought to catch our breath. My legs were too wobbly to stay wrapped around him, but I hooked my fingers in the waistband of his jeans, holding him close and feeling as much of his skin as possible.

"You paused the camera?" he asked softly.

"Yes."

"Shame. I'd have loved a souvenir of that. Then again, one with just you, legs spread and pussy exposed, giving us a private show…"

I liked every bit of that, except the *us*. That was what he and Jax were, though. An *us*. I wasn't a part of that, no matter how much I enjoyed these interludes. A stone settled in my heart. They had each other, and I was an intermission, like every other hookup they had. Was I okay with that?

NINE

Knowing people in the gaming industry had its perks. Today, it was backstage access to Grayson's opening day exhibition match. The audience would have a better view of his game, thanks to the giant screens that sat at the front of the room, but I had more fun watching him.

Being back here also gave me a much-needed respite from the crowds for a little bit and let me catch my breath. I could still hear them, but they weren't pressing in on me.

The last couple of days, I'd been too busy to put much thought into what happened with Grayson. I edited the video—which was a massive hit and led to dozens of extra pic requests today—and spent the rest of my time making sure my costumes and schedule were set for the con.

Everyone else had been as busy as me, but the couple of texts I got from Grayson lifted most of the lingering doubt I had about that incredible frozen moment. The texts were nothing overt, which was perfect; they let me know everything was all right. This morning's said, *See you at the match in a few hours x.*

Someone pressed into me from behind, and a faint but familiar whiff of cologne reached me. *Jax*. He was warm against my bare lower back, thanks to the exposed midriff on my costume de jour.

He brushed his lips along the outside of my ear, sending shivers over my skin. Though the assumption of his closeness wasn't new, I was enjoying it far more than I'd ever dared in the past.

"Grayson told me what you did." His whisper made his tone hard to decipher.

"He promised he would." And what a vivid, seductive promise it had been. Did Grayson use similar words telling Jax?

Jax nipped my earlobe, and a jolt raced through my veins. "The plan is to get you addicted to us, so you can't help but come back for more," he said.

The emcee started working the crowd, and cheers exploded around us. My focus was elsewhere. I leaned some of my weight against Jax. The magic in the air here added to the floating giddiness in my head. "I thought this was just casual fun," I teased.

"Your words. Though it *is* fun." He glided his hands down my exposed sides, to rest on my hips right above the waistband of my low-rise jeans. "If I feel you up right here, does it take us a step closer to being more than *casual?*"

Did he want that? He wasn't exactly being subtle.

What about his relationship? What about the past? The questions slammed into my thoughts with a quiet cruelty, bringing images with them of a decade ago—a piece of my life I'd forgiven him for. So of course the reminder chose now to gnaw at me.

That didn't mean I wanted to push him away. "It takes us a step closer to getting caught." I kept my tone light and playful.

"Tempting, isn't it?"

It was. Much more than it should be. A rush of desire pulsed under my skin, similar to what I felt when Grayson watched me with Jax, but this was peppered with a hotter blend of spice. I wasn't quite bold enough to fool around with nothing but a curtain between us and an audience of several hundred, but it could be fun… "We'll miss the match."

"He'll win. He always does."

Another reason Grayson was an exhibition player now instead of a competitor.

"But never if you're uncertain." Jax's hands fell away. He didn't step back, though. "I talked to a friend about your situation."

I didn't realize I hadn't expected him to follow through until he said he did. The way he changed the subject jarred me, and the topic dragged my stress back. "What did they say?"

"I have a letter for you to send Ms. G's office. It tells them you consider the NDA null and void because you signed on the promise of a job interview, and it's obvious they never had any intentions of interviewing you. Along with the letter, you reiterate that you're going to make their information public, and then you publish what you have."

It was too easy. I shouldn't complain. "Just like that."

"That's what I'm told."

"That won't stop them from coming after me."

Jax sighed. "No. They can—and probably will—still pursue. But other people will come forward when they see that you have. Especially if the reason you speak up is are part of your exposé."

"And if others have similar stories, it corroborates mine." I hated that my word about the situation wasn't sufficient, but one person claiming, *I was scammed by Hollywood*, would fade into the background. Numbers gave me credibility.

"I think, if you keep pushing any correspondence they send you while this moves forward…"

"The internet will bully them back." Large chunks of this situation were unfolding before my eyes.

"Basically."

Wow. "Normally I'm opposed to the dogpile mentality."

Jax rested his hands on my hips again. "What if it's more of a puppy pile? All three of us, collapsing in a tangled heap of exhaustion and limbs after some incredible sex?"

All of us… The longer he talked, the more I wanted to take him up on that *feel me up right here* offer. "You're horrible."

"You said I was good."

"You were incredible."

He rested his head against mine. "That does sound like me. When are you going live with this?"

Our not even thinly veiled conversation about me sleeping with him and his boyfriend? That was for us alone. But he was talking about Ms. G. "This afternoon, if I can. That gives me the extra viewership of everyone tuned in for RinCon." And plenty of time to stress, as I waited for the fallout.

"Do it. We'll take you out after, to keep you distracted."

I kind of loved how he was in my head. "I'm not going to be a lot of fun if I can't stop thinking about it." Not just the blowback from Ms. G, but the hate this would earn me because I dared speak up about *anything*.

"We can be *very* distracting."

I adored his confidence. The attention. How much he was doing on my behalf. "You've set my expectations high."

"Where they deserve to be," Jax said.

If only I could give all my attention to him and Grayson, and ignore the holes worry was trying to tear in my soul.

TEN

Mid-afternoon, I called it a day from RinCon and headed home. My *Expose Ms. G* post was written up, but I had to add my letter to her, then re-read it. Again. And then again. Before I recorded my video.

When that was done, I checked it over and over, the need for perfection warring with my desire to act now. It was time to hit *Post*.

My phone chimed with a new text from Grayson.

Where are you?

Home. Contemplating the fate of my career, I replied.

Knock knock. His text coincided with a knock on my bedroom door, making my heart leap into my throat.

Thank God for a distraction. "Why'd you ask if you knew?" I said as I swung the door open.

"Sorry, what?" Grayson's gaze drifted up my body, Jax's doing the same.

Maybe I should have gotten dressed after my shower. At least I was wearing a robe, and I didn't mind at all the way they were looking at me. "You wouldn't have made the trip if you weren't pretty sure I was here."

Grayson looked up first, an easy smile sliding into place. "It was more fun this way. Chase said Anne said you took off, so..."

"They didn't mention *what* you took off. Probably for the best." Jax was still staring at my chest.

I snapped my fingers in front of his face, finally drawing his attention. "Am I late?"

"We're early," Jax said. "Something told me you were sitting here, conflicted over whether or not your posts were perfect, so you're going to pull the trigger, hand him your phone to keep you from checking it, and get dressed so we can go mingle in the courtesy suites."

"Just like that?" I shouldn't protest—I desperately needed the distraction Jax had promised.

Grayson held out his hand. "Just like that."

I handed over my phone. Two seconds later, my post was live on the internet and my heart rate had doubled.

Wait. They said courtesy suites? "If you're talking to clients and vendors, I'm not going to be a great conversationalist."

"You'll be too stunningly gorgeous for anyone to notice." Jax assured me.

I raised my brows. "You only want me as an accessory?"

"I want you for so much more, but no. I'd never relegate you to something like *accessory*. That's what this pretty boy is for." Jax jerked his head toward Grayson.

Grayson chuckled. "Such an asshole. You're lucky I love you." He brushed his lips over Jax's.

It didn't matter that the kiss was quick and something I'd seen over and over. Tonight, the sight sent tingles prickling along my skin. It was sweet and hot at the same time. How had I never noticed before how sexy that was? Easy adoration flowed between them. What they had was so real. So tangible. So very much what I wanted to find with my perfect guy.

"Get dressed. We'll wait downstairs," Jax said.

Boldness rushed into my veins, buoyed by an excess of adrenaline that wanted me to run away from what I just put out into the world. "You're not going to help?" I looked up at Grayson through my eyelashes. "Pretty sure there was talk of you dressing me."

Jax sucked in a hard breath.

Grayson bit his bottom lip. "Pretty sure we already did that. Still, a repeat is tempting. But we'd be so late if we did to you now even a fraction of the things we want to."

"All right." I managed a pout despite the way his words made my nipples tighten and my thighs squeeze together.

As I dressed, I understood exactly what Grayson meant about certain activities making us late. The brief teasing alone tempted me to pull out my vibrator. Or even better, yank the guys back up here.

Instead, I smoothed my favorite little black dress into place—the one with the scoop neck, fitted body, and long skirt with the slits that ran most of the way up my thighs. It was a stretchy fabric that looked like satin that shimmered but allowed me to move freely. I'd done my hair and makeup for the video, so there was only a little touch-up there, and I was ready.

I twitched, to reach for my phone. To take *a quick glance* at my messages. Thank God for Grayson, confiscating the device.

When I descended the back stairs to where the guys and Lyn were chatting in the kitchen, I was greeted with a trio of whistles. I looked amazing, but the confirmation did great things for my ego.

Grayson grasped my fingers before I reached the bottom steps, and I felt like I was making a grand entrance at a ball.

Kind of like that New Year's dance would have been, so many years ago.

The thought slipped into my head without permission, carried on a cloud of doubt and history, and I shoved it aside.

We headed out to Grayson's truck. It was a snug fit, but since he had a bench seat, it would be far more comfortable than Jax's BMW Z4. Being pressed between them, with the weight of strong arms and thighs resting against mine, was a much better distraction from what I'd done than their random banter about who they met and what they talked about at the show today.

What should have been a five- or ten-minute drive turned into nearly thirty, thanks to holiday traffic downtown. Not that I minded. I was warm and safe.

We pulled into the line for valet parking at the hotel where the parties were taking place.

Grayson rested a hand on my upper thigh. "I changed my mind." His comment was casual. The way he teased the slit of my dress with his thumb was almost possessive.

My pulse hammered in my ears, as if my heart knew something my head hadn't figured out yet. "About what?"

"Helping you with your clothes. Take off your panties."

"Here?" I squeaked. We sat higher than most everyone else, and it was dark in the cab, but we were still crawling slower than foot traffic, and surrounded by people. So why did the command spread through me on a rush of desire?

Jax slipped his hand under my skirt, to brush my bare skin. He trailed his fingers up the inside of my leg. "Unless you want to wait until we're closer."

I could tell them *no*, but my heart slammed against my ribs with the need to see where this went. I tried to be discreet about lifting my butt off the seat, and both of their touches fell away. It took inching the slits of my dress up over my hips to grasp the elastic of my panties and slide them down my legs. Stretchy-sparkly dress for the win.

I slipped the underwear off my legs. The instant I straightened in my seat again, Grayson tugged the lacy clothing from my hands and shoved it in his pocket.

"For safe keeping." The gruffness in his voice was like desire gliding over me.

And then Jax's hand was back under my dress, as he teased his fingers along my bare mound. Could anyone see? Did I care? His touch was light and playful, slipping easily along my skin and between my folds.

I half-closed my eyes, falling into the sensation, as he glided closer to my opening.

When his touch fell away, my eyes flew open. We were at the valet station, and Jax was sucking on his fingers.

A groan bubbled inside, and I swallowed it. *Fuck me.* No, really. Here. Now. I didn't care who saw.

Jax helped me from the truck as though nothing out of the ordinary had happened.

Grayson joined us. "You didn't save any for me."

Jax stuck two fingers in Grayson's mouth. This time a whimper did escape my throat, earning me a pair of satisfied smirks. Would my magical dress hide any wet spots? Because it would need to if this kept up.

We headed inside. Limitless lights and trees and ornaments greeted us, brightening the hotel and the various conference rooms on the mail floor. RinCon during the day was for the fans and press —the big games rolled out, the demos happened. At night, in the multitude of vendor-sponsored rooms with open bars and buffets, the business deals were churned out.

People were just starting to trickle in, but Jax and everyone in sales would be here to mingle and eavesdrop and spread goodwill.

And I was wandering through these crowds of businesspeople with no panties on. It was insane, and I was so turned on, I wasn't sure I could talk without bursting into giggles if anyone addressed me.

"Hey, guys." Chase's voice cut through every layer of haze in my head.

Talk about an arousal killer. I turned to face him, and gave him a smile.

"You here for work?" he asked me.

"Exactly the opposite." I was going to give him as close to the truth as I could without saying, *Do you have any idea how fuckably hot your friends are?* "I'm stressed about my latest video, so they're distracting me."

He furrowed his brow, and I could almost hear the gears turning in his head. "Something's different between the two of you." He was talking about me and Jax.

"Help a woman move her mattress, and the dynamic changes. That's just the way things work." Jax's reply was smooth and without hesitation.

I was grateful we'd agreed to discretion. I'd have to apologize later for the fit I threw about their original request.

"Uh-huh," Chase said flatly.

Grayson tangled his fingers with Jax's. "Pretty sure you're imagining things."

"Hughes." Someone called Chase from across the room.

He glanced at us one more time, shook his head, and trotted off to catch up with the guy who summoned him.

"Just so you know, that wasn't because you're a dirty secret." Jax moved his free hand to the small of my back, his voice so low only we would hear. "All three of us need to be on the same page when we tell people."

Tell people. His statement added a reality filter to an erotically surreal situation, and my thoughts revolted. "What is there to tell?"

"Part of what we'll discuss when we're not in the middle of a crowd of software-company execs," Grayson said.

I didn't have an argument. What *were* we doing? I reached for Grayson's sleeve, to tug them aside and ask. Despite what he said, now was as good a time as any to talk.

"Grayson." A woman approached, putting a dent in my plan. "I was hoping you'd be here."

"Lee. Great to meet you face-to-face." Grayson shook her hand. "This is Sadie, and my boyfriend, Jax."

An ache pinged in my chest at the introduction. But it was a solid reminder, and one I needed—they were *them*, and I wasn't a part of that.

ELEVEN

I gave Lee a warm smile. "How do you and Grayson know each other?"

"Lee's my contact for the VR hardware I've been streaming with," Grayson said. He had early access to some top-of-the-line gear that was lighter weight and higher powered than anything on the market.

From what I'd seen and what he'd said, even with the bugs in the beta version, it blew everything else out of the water. "It's amazing tech," I said.

"I've got to know." Lee dropped her voice to a stage whisper. "Have you hacked it for porn yet?"

Her blunt question didn't surprise me. In the gaming industry, there was no flinching when it came to casual talk about sex. But the assumption caught me off-guard. "You have people doing that with beta hardware? And you're okay with it?"

"Absolutely. We're encouraging it."

Grayson shook his head. "Haven't gone there yet. It's no fun alone, but if you wanted to send me an extra set or two..." He brushed my hand before slipping his into Jax's.

Heat seared through me at the brief contact.

Lee chuckled. "I'll make a note and see what I can do."

Lee and Grayson chatted a few minutes longer about the hardware specs and upcoming fixes, before she gave us all another smile and headed after someone else.

"You're not really surprised by the porn thing, are you?" Jax asked as we resumed wandering through the crowds.

I shook my head. "Just that they're okay with it."

"They're encouraging indie games and mods from the start." Grayson rested a hand on the small of my back, branding a patch into my skin. "*Company sanctioned* means more control for us over what happens."

That made sense.

"The hardware has other applications too," Jax said.

"Besides jerking off to cartoon people? Are you sure?" I teased. "I know it's already being investigated for military- and medical-training purposes."

Jax led us to the bar and ordered two Cokes and a seltzer with lime.

"You're going to raise eyebrows if you're not drinking when there's an open bar. And thank you." I took my soda from him.

The seltzer was for Grayson. He dipped his head to rest his lips near my ear. "Let them talk. We want you sober tonight."

"Applications specifically for you." Jax talked over the questions that tried to bubble up in my head. The demand for answers. "Imagine being able to see a 3D mockup of your outfits before you start sewing, with no more work than what you do now, when you design them in Photoshop."

I liked the thought, and I loved that they were thinking about my work that way. "It's not that simple. Is it?"

Grayson sipped his drink. "Not yet. But it's getting there." He nodded across the room. "The guy over there, with the neon-purple hair? He's the head of digital output at that new studio. The one giving ILM and Weta Workshop a run for their money. He uses the hardware to storyboard."

"They did the effects for the hot new horror movie." I'd heard the guy was insanely brilliant. Like, talked above most people's heads, but came up with such groundbreaking ideas that no one minded. "The combination of digital and physical is supposed to be surreal."

Jax smiled. "That's him. *Supposed to be?* You haven't seen it yet?"

I gave him a look of disbelief smattered with *duh?* I loved horror movies, but Anne and Lyn weren't fans. I'd rather see the spectacular films with friends, so we could all *ooh* and *ah* at the same time, so I usually went with Grayson, but he'd been busy.

"Not yet," I said.

"We should go," Grayson said. "Christmas afternoon?"

"And you might be able to convince me to go." Jax didn't sound enthusiastic.

I was surprised he made the offer at all. "You can hide behind your popcorn during the scary scenes."

"I can squeal in terror and hide my face in your shoulder." Jax mimicked hiding behind me, brushing a light kiss on my shoulder in the process. "As long as you promise not to tell anyone I covered my eyes through half the movie.

A flash of need pulsed between my legs. How much longer did we have to be here? "Everyone already knows."

"Good point. I'm in anyway." Jax straightened again.

Aside from the questions their behavior was planting in my head, about what I was to them, this was nice. Normal. The way things usually were with us.

But those questions bounced against the reminder they were a couple, and regardless of anything else, that wasn't going to change. I certainly couldn't choose between them or push them apart.

It didn't matter how much teasing and flirting there was. I needed to be happy with being a horror-movie buddy. Nothing more.

When Jax and Grayson were pulled into separate conversations, my mind had room to wander. I could either focus on the impending inbox explosions waiting for me on all of my accounts, or direct my attention to what was going on with the guys. It seemed more likely I could act on the second one first, and it was a more pleasant thought.

Grayson said we'd talk about what we all were. How we introduced ourselves to people. That didn't make sense. This wasn't
exactly the kind of society where someone said *this is my boyfriend, and
this is our fuck buddy.*

Was he talking about me being more to them? I couldn't wrap
my brain around that. Sure, they hooked up with other people, but
it was never a long-term thing. And yeah, there was polyamory and
multiple-person relationships, but those weren't something I could
see myself doing.

Aside from the awkwardness of explaining it to Chase, which
they seemed a lot more concerned with than I was, I'd also always
seen myself as a one-guy girl. It came back to my dream future.
Find the perfect guy. Have the perfect wedding. Settle into a life that
wasn't perfect, because no life was, but we'd make it work, because
we loved each other.

Jax and Grayson had already found their perfect guy, in each
other. I was outside fun. I was enjoying it; this definitely wasn't a
one-sided arrangement. Did I want to be their booty-call long term,
though?

"Sadie?" An unfamiliar voice called my name, startling me, and
I turned toward the man. He wasn't anyone I recognized from
Rinslet.

"It is you. Wow," he said.

I pasted on a neutral smile. "It is. I'm sorry, I don't recall your
name." Was he a colleague of Chase's? Anne's?

"We've never met. I'm Chet." He extended his hand. "I'm a
huge fan of your work."

"Thank you." I let some warmth bleed into my expression and
returned the handshake. I was cautious about meeting fans in
person, especially male fans, but I also appreciated flattery. Grayson
and Jax were close enough that I had a back-up escape if needed.

"No. Thank *you.* The way you bring flat drawings to life in a
real-world setting is brilliant. That takes some serious talent. I'm not
just saying that; I speak from experience."

Possible connection? I never passed on one of those. "Are you in
costume design?"

"3D rendering. Our artists struggle to translate 2D into something with depth, and they don't have to do it with fabric." Chet's tone was friendly, and his enthusiasm felt genuine. His gaze never dropped below my neck.

I let the appreciation seep in. "3D rendering fascinates me. There's so much potential in the art form, and we're right on the cusp of crossing the uncanny valley."

"Maybe my team will be the first." He grinned. "I won't keep you long, but when I realized you were here, I wanted to tell you in person, I saw what you posted on your pages this afternoon."

My gut turned itself inside-out. "Oh?"

"It was brave and bold. I'm furious on your behalf that people are doing shit like that. To anyone, and especially to talented artists like you. You have my support."

My heart dislodged from where it was stuck in my throat. "Thank you." I poured my sincerity into my reply.

He gave me another smile. "I'll let you get back to mingling, but good luck. It was a pleasure meeting you."

"Same."

And he was gone, melting into the crowds, like everyone else we'd talked to tonight.

"Do you know who that was?" Jax asked, suddenly by my side again.

"Chet?"

He chuckled. "Charles Stanford. He's Senior Vice President of Art for KaleidoMation."

Dials and knobs clicked in my head, to draw an association. "The 3D-rendering company?" One of the biggest. Even Rinslet bought their assets—CGI models and objects to be used in video games. "Wow. He's a nice guy."

"That's what I hear."

Grayson joined us too. "Do you want to get out of here?"

Was it that late already? I looked at Jax. "Don't you have to stay until things wrap up?" I didn't mind the mingling.

Jax shook his head. "I've done what I need to."

"I'll rephrase the question." Grayson dropped his hand to his pocket and let a hint of black lace peek out. "I keep brushing against these." He dipped his head close to my ear. "Someone's going to notice soon that I'm a walking hard-on, and I'd rather we take you back to our place than hang out here."

Oh. "All right." Any witty reply I had evaporated, but intense, throbbing desire replaced it.

TWELVE

The drive back to the guys' place was painfully basic. Settled between them, warm and safe and very hands-off. It made the anticipation that lingered on the tip of my tongue that much sharper.

Then we were in their bedroom, and Grayson was kissing Jax, their mouths merging and their tongues dancing with such passion, I expected literal sparks. Love flowed and spilled from them in waves.

They broke apart, and Grayson turned to me. He kissed the tips of my fingers. "We talked about who gets to have you first."

"Seems like I should get a say in that decision." I still didn't know how to feel, besides turned on, that they talked about sex with me.

Jax grinned. "That's fair. What's your decision?"

I hadn't expected him to yield so quickly. "Both? Both is good."

"That's where we landed as well." Grayson slid a finger under the neckline of my dress and glided it along my collarbone.

I captured his hand, enjoying the feeling of his skin against mine. "Do I get to see the two of you naked?" These were the pressing questions that needed to be answered.

"Presumably." Amusement lined Grayson's voice.

"You say that, but I keep ending up missing more clothes than either of you." Two times weren't exactly a pattern, but now was the time to balance things out.

Jax pressed into my back. "Are you complaining?"

I liked being a Sadie Sandwich. "About the sex? Not even for a second. About missing out on what I imagine is an incredible view? A little."

"Wouldn't want to ruin the fantasy," Grayson said.

I worked the knot of his tie, to loosen it, then untied it and left the ends hanging loose. "I'm not worried about that."

My world went black when something slipped over my eyes. The texture of silk against my skin said it was Jax's tie, blindfolding me.

I laughed lightly. "Can't see any nakedness this way."

"You will," Jax whispered in my ear.

Shivers raced down my spine, chased by him tugging down my zipper and exposing my back. He pushed my dress to the ground, leaving me on display in the middle of their room, my body screaming in anticipation.

Jax's familiar stubble scraped along my skin when he kissed my shoulder, then nibbled playfully. He trailed a barely-there touch down my spine. Every new contact from him shuddered through my body on a wave of desire.

Where did Grayson go? More than a minute or two couldn't have passed, but the loss of one sense distorted time.

Lips brushed mine. Lightly. Sweetly. Grayson's kiss could have been innocent, if I were wearing more than a pair of heels. He tangled his fingers in my hair and tugged hard, making me gasp. He bit my bottom lip, and licked away the sting.

At the same time, Jax was teasing his fingers lower along my back then slipping between my legs. He caressed my slick skin but didn't part my folds.

Grayson pressed his body to mine. Every texture—fabric, skin, the smoothness and roughness of it all—lit up my senses.

Jax's touch fell away, but Grayson kept my mind and body busy. He glided his touch over my hips, lower, dipping toward my clit but not touching it. Nearly sliding inside me, before pulling away.

Jax was there again, bare skin against my back and his erection digging into me. He gripped my hips and nibbled my ear. "You're not the only one who's been fantasizing, but the reality is much better."

"It really is." My words came out on a gasp. My skin absorbed every sensation, but there was a tug in my chest as well. Jax's words and Grayson's attention warmed me in a way their kisses didn't. They made me want to swoon.

When Grayson's hands fell away, Jax's replaced them. He moved between my legs again, drawing a groan from me when he slipped two fingers inside me. He rested his palm on my stomach, holding me to him. This was more than physical intimacy. It was a feeling I didn't dare look at too closely.

He sought out my clit, dancing lightly at first, but increasing the pressure and speed as my hips bucked into his touch. Climax lingered just out of reach, then flooded through me. I leaned into him, needing the extra support when my legs wobbled. I wanted to memorize everything about this moment.

Jax guided me toward the bed slowly, making sure I didn't trip or run into anything, since I couldn't see. He turned me to lie back on the mattress, my legs hanging over the edge.

When he licked up the inside of my thigh, that scruff of barely-there beard scraped along my skin with a tantalizing burn. I arched into his touch. His open-mouth kisses. Every lick and nip made me squirm a little more. When he reached my core, I whimpered.

He dove in with enthusiasm. His tongue inside me was the only thing I could focus on.

Until Grayson wrapped his lips around my nipple and sucked.

My mind fuzzed, and I let myself fall into it. I lost track of where one touch ended and the next began, and this orgasm lingered just out of reach. When I came, my entire body shuddered.

The blindfold fell away, and Grayson was kissing me.

I blinked rapidly in the abrupt light. "It's bright."

"You wanted to see us," he murmured against my lips.

I had. I took them both in. Grayson, propped up next to me on one elbow, familiar ink trailing down his chest. His cock was large, erect, and wrapped. Jax stood at the foot of the bed, looking just as impressively aroused and sexy as fuck.

Grayson traced the edge of my ear. "How are your legs?"

"Non-functional." Not that I had any issue with that.

"On your side." He nudged me so my back was to him, crooked my leg, and teased my opening with the head of his cock. He glided inside me slowly, stretching me out an inch at a time.

This was a new angle of penetration, and it was an incredible one.

Jax knelt on the mattress in front of me. The way he leaned in, propped up on one knee and arm, was odd. He teased my clit with the head of his cock, then nudged my opening too. They couldn't both... Could they?

"It's like the vibrator. Tell me to stop if it's too much," Jax said.

When he wedged inside me, next to Grayson, the stretch drew a long groan from me.

"You okay?" Jax asked.

I nodded. It hurt, but in a good way. I was so slick and turned on, the pain was delicious. They built to a slow rhythm, rather than the frantic, hard pounding I usually associated with sex. I slipped into pleasure tinged with pain, riding the high of both. When Grayson sought out my clit again, it was too much but just right.

I melted into climax. Mine. Theirs. Ecstasy consumed me.

When they slowed to a stop, there was no subtle pulling out of me. My body contracted when each of them withdrew, but the phantom sensation remained.

Grayson held me tight, his heat spreading over me. Jax lay across from me, a silly smile on his lips as he brushed my hair away from my face.

This couldn't last. Not with the kisses I'd seen them share. Not with how much they loved each other. But for now... God, it was incredible.

THIRTEEN

Amazing sex and a solid night's sleep between two naked and gorgeous men didn't change the fact that I needed answers.

I was the only one in bed when I woke up, but a faint shuffling sound drew my attention to the closet, where Jax was straightening his tie. He looked good—of course. I could get used to mornings like this.

Another reason to have this conversation now. "Can we talk?"

He jumped, laughed lightly, then met my gaze in the full-length mirror on the back of the closet door. "Morning, gorgeous. I hope I didn't wake you."

"No. I don't think so, anyway."

"It's probably good you're up." He smoothed out his shirt and slacks, and turned to face me. "I have to run into work early. Emergency of some sort. Grayson went to get coffee, but he'll be back soon. He can take you home, or you can hang out here, or whatever you celebrity streamers do while the rest of us are chained to desks."

I couldn't hide my exasperation. "Jax."

"Hmm?"

"Are you ignoring my question on purpose?"

He sighed and knelt on the mattress next to me. "No. Sort of, but I heard you."

"Okay. Because I'm having a lot of fun with whatever this is, but I'm not sure how I feel about being your toy." I swore he looked pained when I said *toy*.

"You're not. I promise." He leaned in and brushed his lips over mine. "We'd talk now if I had time. Don't make any decisions until all of us can discuss this together."

Agreeing meant not diving into the conversation with Grayson until Jax was free. But they should both be there, and I didn't want to make Jax late for work. "All right."

Then he was gone, and so was my immediate chance at closure and answers.

Until I could get that, I should go home. Dig into the backlash that waited after my *big reveal* last night.

Slipping into my dress this morning didn't hold the same thrill as last night. Today, the fabric felt like a stretchy sleight-of-hand trick, rather than actual magic. I didn't know what to do with myself, so I took a seat at the kitchen table.

Grayson didn't keep me waiting long. He looked at me with surprise when he stepped into the room, coffees in hand. "You all right?" he asked.

"I should get home. Take care of the fallout from yesterday."

He gave me a cup and kept one for himself. "You could do a lot of that here, if you wanted."

"I can't." As much as I liked the idea of hanging out a little longer.

"Why not?"

A heavy sigh slipped out. "We *all* need to talk, and I'm not sure I can stay away from the topic until then."

"I see. I'll take you home, then."

The ride to my place was quiet. I was desperate to talk about what was happening between us, and since I'd promised to wait, I couldn't think of anything else Grayson and I had ever talked about before this point.

When we pulled up in front of Lyn's house, Grayson handed me my phone.

I reached for the truck door handle.

"Sadie—"

I paused at the catch in his voice and looked at him.

Grayson worked his jaw. "I want to—" He shook head. "You're right. We should all be here for this conversation."

Now I was extra curious, but I'd wait. "Yeah. Talk to you soon." I didn't dare look back as I headed inside.

When I reached my room, I turned on my phone and woke up my laptop. My notifications and unread emails were only in the hundreds. Not nearly as bad as the situation could have been.

I mentally rolled my eyes at myself.

"You back?" Lyn called.

"Yeah."

She poked her head into my room. "Some guy dropped this off for you this morning. Everything all right?"

I grabbed the stapled papers from her. *Cease and Desist* was in a neat typeface across the top, next to my name and address. "It will be." I gave her a tight smile.

"Okay. I have to get back to the shop, but holler down if you need anything."

I scanned the C&D and posted it online, along with a series of hashtags, including #wewontbesilenced

I couldn't avoid the messages anymore, so I dug in. They fell into three main categories.

I'm so sorry you got scammed.

They got me too. Thank you for speaking out.

And, *You're a fucking whore. Someone should rape you to death. You don't deserve how good they tried to be to you.*

Most days I loved the internet, but when the assholes came out…

I spent hours replying to the kind words and blocking everyone who sent the cruel ones. It was early afternoon when it weighed down my soul so much, I didn't know if I could breathe.

I couldn't face this onslaught this way. I recorded a quick video, thanking everyone for their support, and followed it up with a note that I would be off social media for the holidays. I'd planned on taking a break over Christmas anyway, and now seemed like a good time to put that plan into motion.

The air was too tight in here. The room too oppressive. I needed to get out and clear my head.

I got in my car and drove. West seemed like a good direction today. Out past the mountains, toward the lake. Maybe beyond it. Maybe I'd go to Wendover and drop fifty bucks in the slot machines. Have a late lunch and a free drink or two.

I'd rather not be inside my head. Talking to someone would help me sift through my thoughts. Anne was stuck in crunch time at work, Lyn was working the shop, and Grayson...

Well, that was the problem, wasn't it?

He'd listened to me talk through breakups before. About whatever asshole I'd let crawl under my skin. He understood. Had his own stories to share. Was I about to become one of them? The girl who couldn't accept a little fun when she had the chance?

I wasn't getting anywhere with this. I cranked the radio to sing along at the top of my lungs. Belting out classic hair metal always made me feel better. As long as I skipped every single song about love and broken hearts.

A loud *bang* sounded over the music, and the steering wheel jerked in my hands.

FOURTEEN

I gripped the wheel harder and turned into the skid, trying to regain control. The car came to a crooked stop at the side of the road.

The entire thing only took a few seconds, but it shaved years off my life. I turned down the radio, only to be inundated by the sound of my pulse hammering in my ears.

I took several deep breaths to calm myself, then climbed from the car, to see what happened. My back right tire was a shredded mess of rubber that barely covered the rim.

Blow out. Wonderful. But this was something I could act on, and that was more comforting than it should be.

Spare was in the trunk. I knew how to change the tire. I'd be back on the road in twenty minutes.

And eighteen minutes later, as I lowered the jack with frozen fingers, I was feeling pretty smug.

Until the spare tire hit the pavement, and then dropped another few inches. The bottom looked like a rubber pancake. My spare was flat.

"*Fuuuuuuuck.*" I let the day's frustration fill my scream into the air. I shouted again and again, until my voice was hoarse and my lungs begged me to stop.

Okay. I could do this. No big deal. I probably couldn't get an Uber out here in the middle of nowhere. Would the app even let me enter *mile marker 38 on I-80?*

I hated to call my friends while they were working, but I couldn't afford tow truck fees if I had to get my tires replaced.

I dialed Lyn first, then Anne, and wasn't surprised to not get answers.

Chase picked up. "I'm heading into a client meeting. Can I call you back?"

"Yeah." I'd find someone else.

"Sadie? What's wrong?"

If I told him *nothing*, he'd pry until he got an answer, and that would waste everyone's time. "I had a tire blowout, and my spare is wrecked too. But I've still got people to call. Don't worry about it."

"Where are you?" His hurried brushoff had vanished behind concern.

I gave him the closest location I knew of. "But don't miss your meeting for me."

His conflicted growl almost made me smile. "Fine. This won't take long. Text me if you find anyone in the next fifteen minutes. If I don't hear from you, assume I'm on my way."

"All right. And thank you."

Before I could make another call, my phone buzzed with a text from Chase. *Help is on the way.*

I hoped he didn't ditch his clients for me. I settled back in my seat and pulled my coat tight around me. I was at least forty-five minutes away from any help, and while I had a full tank of gas, I wasn't going to keep the engine running the whole time. I needed to strike a balance between not freezing and not burning through my gas. Why had I grabbed the fingerless gloves instead of the full-blown fuzzy mittens?

Out here, away from most of the city lights, it seemed to get dark faster. It was kind of eerie, watching everything vanish into the creeping night.

Headlights flashed in my rearview mirror, then pulled up behind me on the shoulder. *Please let that be Chase or a good Samaritan, and not some creepy creeper.*

They didn't turn their lights off, so I only saw a silhouette approaching. When Jax knocked on my window, I yelped. I was such a dork sometimes.

I grabbed my purse and keys and opened the door.

"You ordered one knight in shining armor?" He grasped my fingertips and helped me from the car.

"I definitely called for help. I didn't expect…" Should I be flirty or plain? It didn't matter now; I'd hesitated too long. "You."

Jax gave a deep bow. "At your service. Your fingers are frozen." He grabbed both of my hands and pressed them between his.

Heat seared through my icy skin, and I groaned in appreciation. I looked up to find Jax watching me with an unreadable look.

"I do love the sounds you make when you're content or happy," he said.

Thank God he couldn't see the blush that raced over my skin. A sliver of fear attached to a memory crowded its way into my thoughts and took me a moment to decipher. This wasn't the Jax who I had a friendly relationship with over the last few years. This was the guy who led me on and broke my heart in high school.

But he wasn't. He'd changed, and I'd seen that.

The knowledge didn't stop a whisper of doubt from burrowing under my skin. "We should get going before we both freeze."

"Yeah. Sure." He shook his head. "We'll get someone back out here in the morning to take care of your car. Grayson knows a guy." Jax held his passenger door open for me until I was secure in my seat, then hurried around to slide into the driver's side.

"Right. I'll make arrangements in the morning."

Jax pulled onto the freeway, and we headed toward Salt Lake. "May I bring you home again? Our place?" he asked. "For that conversation we all need to have?"

Right. *The Conversation.* That thing I'd been itching for since this morning, that suddenly loomed more terrifying than any monster. If we did this, how much of our relationship would I destroy?

Not as much as if I let things drag out. I'd hate myself and resent them, if this went on and I got attached before they cut me loose. "Yes."

"That's it? Just *yes*?" He glanced sideways at me.

"It's not. I want to say a lot more. But if I start now, I won't stop, and you were right that we should all be there." We all needed to be on the same page, and saying what I had to was going to be hard enough once. I didn't want to repeat myself.

"Yeah. Of course."

Silence settled between us, except for the faint music coming from his stereo. Almost like a movie, except at this point in a film, we'd probably be hearing some heartbroken ballad by Adele, and not the Blink182 whispering through his speakers.

Basket Case by Green Day popped up next, and I turned up the volume. It was as appropriate a song as any for my mood. Neither one of us moved to turn the music back down for the rest of the drive. Not the most awkward hour-plus ever of my life, but probably in the top ten.

When we got back to their place, Grayson was waiting. The quick kiss they shared was the same one I'd seen hundreds of times, but tonight it was another reminder that part of their life was for them alone, and that wouldn't change.

Grayson gave me a friendly smile. "I hope you didn't freeze out there. Do you want hot chocolate? A blanket?"

His sweet consideration tightened the already-clenching fist around my heart. "I warmed up in Jax's car." Did that sound dirty? "Heated seats and all. Nothing else."

"I didn't say anything." Grayson shrugged.

Jax gave a tight chuckle. "Sounds like us the entire way here."

That was as good an opening as any. "Speaking of... Thank you for comi—" My brain glitched on the unintentional innuendo. "For picking me up. I'm super grateful. I'm also wondering... Can we skip the small talk and get this over with?"

"That's a good idea." Grayson nodded at the couch.

I wasn't ready to sit, and it looked like neither of them was either. Because of us standing around was so much more comfortable. Not.

"It sounds like you have specific thoughts. You first," Grayson said.

How was that fair? Then again, would anything they said make a difference? This was where I cut us off, even if they wanted to keep up the fun. If I set the tone, I might save us a bit of saying things we might regret. "You're both wonderful—in bed and out of it—and this fling, whatever you'd like to call it, is amazing."

Jax opened his mouth, but Grayson rested a hand on his arm.

Not a subtle or unique gesture, but it added more weight to my decision. "But it's not going anywhere. I know that. The two of you are together, and I'm like the side dish. The longer we keep going with the sex, the more likely one of us will get hurt when it ends." The brief speech clawed at my throat.

Jax scowled. Did I steal his thunder by dumping myself?

I crossed my arms in front of my chest, feeling exposed in a decidedly non-delicious way.

"To us, it's not a fling. Or casual fun. Or whatever you're calling it today," Grayson said.

What else could it be?

Jax moved closer to me, lightly grasped my fingers, and pulled my arms down. He didn't let go of my hands as he met my gaze. "I've been attracted to you for a long time. Both of us have. We're not using you. You're not a side dish." He sounded sincere. But once, a long time ago, I'd fallen prey to his false adoration.

I pulled my hands away and shoved them in my pockets. "What about *being discreet?*"

"We didn't plan that morning any more than you did," Grayson said. "We'd talked about you before—we talk about you a lot—and what you are in our life is too important to toss away on *casual fun.*"

I was really starting to hate that phrase. "So we're on the same page." There was no relief in the realization.

"We're really not." Jax reached for me again, flexed his fingers, then dropped his hand. "We're not telling you it's over. We—

Grayson and I—want to see where things go with you. As in, dating. A relationship. The kind we don't keep a secret."

"But the two of you are already dating." I wasn't dim. I understood polyamory, loving more than one person, but it wasn't for me. I'd tumbled down that path mentally several times, trying out the weight, seeing if I could do what Jax and Grayson did by letting other people into their lives. I couldn't.

I didn't want to share my *happily ever after*. I wanted the one guy, the one dress, the one wedding… The one ring. That last one should have made me laugh at my own wit, but I was hung up on other things.

Grayson sank onto the edge of the couch. "We are. And we want to see where things go when you're part of that."

"Things don't *go* anywhere. You're together." I'd said that once. I didn't want to repeat myself. "It's not like I'm going to pick one of you and break you up. I couldn't if I wanted to, and that's the last thing I want. Don't get me wrong, I'm loving the sex and the attention, but I'm not… It's not a long-term relationship kind of thing."

"It's absolutely something people do long term." Grayson studied me with those dark eyes I normally wanted to fall into but today made me turn away with uncertainty.

This wasn't supposed to be so difficult. I expected pain, but not for them to argue with me. Why were they doing this? "Other people. Not me."

"What did you think we were doing?" Jax's scowl was back.

At least that was something I knew how to deal with. It was a hint to summon my emotional armor and close him off from anything I felt. But the wall I put up cracked. "Not every hookup ends in a relationship. I was having fun. I said exactly that. I got the impression both of you were as well."

"So we're back on that. *Casual fun*." Jax spat the words out with frustration.

Something we agreed on. "I feel like you're not hearing me."

"That makes three of us," Grayson said.

"It's not…" Frustration bubbled up in my chest and pricked the inside of my eyelids. "I'm trying to be clear and plain about this. I don't expect that every guy I date is someone I'm going to spend the rest of my life with. That doesn't make the time with them any less enjoyable."

"We're already spending most of our lives together." Jax took a seat, but not next to Grayson.

That should be better. It didn't give the impression of them standing against me. But now I was on trial, with them judging me because I wanted something different from my future than they saw. "Because we're friends. I'm not planning on pledging my love—not the way you're talking about—to Lyn or Anne either."

"But have you slept with them?" Jax asked.

I glared. What the fuck kind of question was that?

"You're not even willing to consider this." Grayson's tone had shifted to an irritation that I never heard from him. "In that case, doesn't that make us the fuck dolls? You had your fun, you got to be naughty, and now you're done and move on?"

Fuck dolls. Horrible phrase. "You're putting words in my mouth."

"We're trying to understand." Grayson spoke through clenched teeth.

"So am I. I don't see why you think this is going to work when I'm telling you it's not for me."

"What did you think was going to happen?" Jax's question bled accusation. "Or didn't you? Did you approach us like everything else in your life, diving in without thought, and enjoying what happens now, fuck the consequences?"

The bitterness in his words felt like a slap, and I fumbled for a response. He saw me that way?

FIFTEEN

"This conversation is over." Grayson crossed the room to the stand by the front door, and grabbed his keys. "I'll take you home."

"Everyone wanted to talk. Let's finish talking." Jax didn't move, and that included the glare he had fixed on me.

"I agree." I stared back with as much ice as I could muster. "I want to know what you meant."

Jax was on his feet now too. He stalked toward me, stopping when his nose was inches from mine, anger flashing on his face. "You're in your current place, staying with Lyn, because you let your lease run out. You're heading off to Hollywood on a whim, without any thoughts of what you're leaving behind—"

"*On a whim?*" I was only a few decibels from shouting. "I think you mean *pursuing my dream.* You know, that thing I've worked toward for years. Growing my skills, building a fan base, and making connections. That *whim?* I'm not leaving anything behind, because my friends, the ones who don't try to emotionally manipulate me into giving up something I love, will keep in touch."

Grayson sighed. "He didn't mean—"

"Oh. My. God." I turned my frustration on him. "How often are you going to say that? Maybe if Jax doesn't mean things, he should stop saying them." Like calling me a *girl in tacky outfits.* The memory surged back on a rush of bile and lodged in my throat. I swallowed it as best I could. "You're right. It's time for me to go." If I kept talking, none of this would be salvageable. Maybe it wasn't anyway.

"I think that's a good idea." Grayson reached for the door.

I brushed past him. "Stay here. I'll call someone." *Who tries to understand me.*

Was I as guilty of that as they were?

I didn't know. I did know it hurt when Grayson closed the door behind me, leaving me in the cold. Why couldn't I just give them what they wanted?

Because that wasn't who I was. And now it had thrown up a huge divider between us.

I could knock. Ask for a chance to make things right. But I said what I meant to. There might not be a *right* in this case. And it might have cost me good friends.

I grabbed my phone to call for a ride, and found a message waiting from Anne. *Did you make it home all right? Work's over. Let me know if you need anything.*

Actually, I'm at the guys' house. Can you come get me? It was a plain message that would raise a dozen questions. I'd answer them when she got here.

Her reply buzzed through seconds later. *Of course. On my way.*

I was sitting on the curb, using the cold concrete to numb my thoughts as effectively as it did my ass, when Anne pulled up.

"What happened?" she asked as soon as I slid into the car.

Where to start? "Jax..."

"I'm going to kick his ass." Anne reached for the door.

I grabbed her other arm. "Don't. It's not like that."

"Did he hurt you?"

Yes. "I think I hurt them first. I don't... I can't even make sense of it, to put it into words."

"That's not like you."

"I know, right?" I sank down in my seat. "I think I fucked up, but I'm not sure. It felt right at the time. Now it just hurts."

Anne pulled onto the road. "At the time?"

"All of fifteen minutes ago." I tried to laugh. "*Fuck.* Maybe he's right. Maybe. I am only capable of living in the moment."

"That's not true. What do you need?"

"I need… to not talk about it." It hurt too much to even think about, and my confusion muddied everything. "How did work go?"

Anne tugged on her hair. "We pushed back the deadline. We're not going to make it before the holidays."

She'd put way too many hours into their latest game, fighting to make it work amid setbacks and incompetence. Having the game pushed back had to be a slap in the face to Anne's hard work.

"I'm sorry." I'd rather focus on making her feel better. "Sounds like we both need an escape."

One corner of Anne's mouth tugged up. "Shopping?"

"The only place open this late is Walmart."

"Online." The *duh* in her voice was playful.

I liked that. "For board games?"

"Craft supplies."

Inspiration sparked in my head. Perfect distraction. "Craft supplies, to make board games."

"Who has to come up with the rules?" Anne's voice was lighter.

"Every game will be different. We'll make the rules up as we go." And Jax's words were back, both in high school and tonight. Taunting me for being awkward, impulsive, and not caring how my decisions impacted people.

Anne glanced at me. "Lord of the Rings marathon."

Thank God for intuitive friends. "Don't you have to work in the morning?"

"We get the weekend off."

First time in two months. It had to feel good and frustrating at the same time. "Extended edition it is."

Anne's place was a small house near downtown. A single floor with two bedrooms, a kitchen, and a living room. The brick exterior belied what was inside.

She'd converted one of the rooms into a theater-slash-gaming room. Chase, Anne, and I had spent a weekend soundproofing the place after she bought it, so she could turn up the bass without bothering the neighbors.

We settled into two recliners, a bowl of popcorn between us, and started *Fellowship*.

Anne was asleep before they reached Rivendell. It was good to see her getting some rest.

I wouldn't be anytime soon. I turned down the volume, but left the movie playing while I made myself some coffee. We'd both seen it so many times, it didn't matter what we missed.

Hot drink in hand, I settled back into my seat and tried to focus on the costumes. They were my favorite part of these films. So much incredible detail and hard work went into every piece. I loved studying them and working out the techniques that had been used.

I couldn't focus on them tonight, though. My fight with Grayson and Jax kept charging back into my thoughts.

I wanted to see their perspective. Tried picturing myself with both of them. Tonight was devouring me; it hurt to for them to take a position against me. How much worse would that be if we tried to be together romantically?

What happened if I got closer to Grayson than Jax?

My mind revolted on that thought too.

I didn't see any solutions. Only an endless loop of questions.

SIXTEEN

"You want coffee?"

Three of the sexiest words ever dragged me from sleep. I opened one eye to find Anne perched in the chair next to mine. She held out a mug with Ms. PAC-MAN on it.

I forced myself the rest of the way to consciousness and took the offering. Near-scalding liquid slid down my throat. "You really do love me."

"Always."

"What time is it?" Sunlight streamed through the cracks in the heavy curtains.

"Almost noon," Anne said. "You looked too cute, sleeping. I didn't want to wake you up, but Lyn texted. Someone called in sick, and she needs help with the Christmas rush."

Great excuse to immerse myself in socializing and ignore a problem I didn't have an answer for. "I'm in. Wait. Why are you in?"

Anne wasn't as fond of people as I was. She stood with a shrug. "I'm not going to turn down a plea for help. And she said I can mostly stick to kitchen and barista duty."

"That's fair."

I took a few more minutes to wake up, and we were on our way. A brief glance at my phone fractured my creeping good mood. A few missed calls and an ass-ton of emails, none of them from Grayson or Jax. What did I expect, though?

I apologized to Anne for tuning her out while I dialed into my voicemail.

"Ms. Hughes, this is Gregory London, Esquire." An unfamiliar man's voice greeted me. "I represent Ms. G and her associates. You've failed to respond to our cease and desist and have posted further inflammatory slander since. If you don't comply with our request, there will be dire consequences."

Fuck. Could he do that? It had only been a day. They were calling me already? That didn't seem right.

I itched to delete the message and pretend I hadn't heard it. Instead, I saved it in case I needed it later.

"Hi, Mercedes." The next message started off more chipper. "I represent Mr. Watanabe's office. Due to recent events, we're no longer able to meet with you, to discuss employment."

Bile rose in my throat, and that message got an instant delete. It was regarding one of the interviews I had lined up for Costume Designer. I had half a dozen others, though. One down wasn't a big deal.

Email was next. Make that three down, thanks to another two cancellations waiting for me. Why were all these people working on a Saturday? Couldn't they wait until Monday, or maybe after Christmas, to band together to crush my dreams?

Lyn's café was packed, which was nice to see. Not a lot of people were gaming, but dozens were buying snacks and trinkets. If she could keep up even half this pace after the holidays, she'd be on track to recover more quickly, financially.

I threw myself into working the register and chatting up customers, but my smile was painted on and I couldn't keep my thoughts from straying toward Jax, Grayson, and my deteriorating future.

When Grayson called, a spark of hope flashed inside. I was in the middle of helping a woman decide between the Minecraft and Pokémon bento boxes for her son, so I couldn't answer.

The instant I was free, I pulled up his message.

"Hey." His voice was flat. "Grabbed your car this morning. Tire's fixed. Let me know when I can drop it off." He had a spare key, the same way Anne did, for when I locked my keys in the car.

Guilt churned inside. My flat was so far down on my list of concerns today, I'd almost forgotten about it. And he'd gone out of his way to make sure I was set, despite last night's disagreement.

Calling him back would have to wait, but I did send him a quick *thank you* text.

The rest of the day passed without a response. I was painfully grateful when Lyn ushered out the last customer and locked the door behind them.

She grabbed my arm and pulled me back into the café kitchen. "Where were you today?" Her voice was kind as she nudged me into a chair.

"Nowhere. Everywhere." Still uncertain where to start.

Anne joined us. "Something happened with Jax and Grayson last night."

I wasn't upset with her for saying so. It was as good an opener as any.

"I'm guessing this wasn't the sexy kind of *something*." Lyn moved around the kitchen as she spoke, pulling plates from one spot and pastries from another. "You know, if you don't talk through it, you're going to drive yourself nuts." She knew me well.

I picked at the cheese Danish she put in front of me, and at a loose thread of last night's conversation. The story tumbled out in a rapid-fire mess of emotion. As I reached the end, the relief I wanted wasn't there. "Was this my fault?" It seemed like it, from an outside perspective.

"You can't change how you feel about the situation, just because they feel differently," Anne said.

Lyn tapped a nail on the edge of her plate. "I'm with her. If loving two people that way isn't for you, then it isn't for you."

Confirmation. Agreement. Why wasn't I reassured?

"This is making you miserable, though." Anne was sympathetic.

"It's like one of you being mad at me. It sucks." At least that was an easy emotion for me to zero in on. "Jax and I… That's always been weird. But Grayson? I fucked things up because I fucked them. I want to go back to the way things were, but I'll always be thinking about… them."

"You fantasize about them, anyway." Anne's food sat untouched in front of her.

In fact, except for the tiny flakes I'd picked from mine, none of us were eating. I took a big bite of the pastry. As the sugar hit my tongue, my stomach grumbled. Maybe I should have consumed something besides coffee between popcorn and now. In a few bites, my dessert was gone. My problems… not so much. "But now I have reality to compare it to."

"Unless the reality was bad, that makes the fantasies that much more vivid. Do you want to make things right with them, as friends?" Lyn slid me her Danish.

I should have insisted she eat it. But it wasn't as though it was the last one in the kitchen. I consumed it more slowly. "Yes."

"There's your answer." Lyn made things sound simple.

Anne shook her head. "It's not that easy."

"I need to call them. Or head over there." I didn't want to try to mend our friendship over the phone, and I could pick up my car. I looked at Anne. "Drop me off?"

"All right." She pushed her plate to Lyn. "Eat this. No arguments. It will taste better than salad."

"What about you?" Lyn asked.

Anne grinned. "I may have helped myself to a couple while I was back here today. I'm Danished out."

Despite my mood, that drew a laugh. I promised Lyn I'd let her know if I was going to be delayed for whatever reason, texted Grayson to say I wanted to talk if they were there, and was on my way with Anne.

She pulled up in front of their house and squeezed my hand. "We're here if you need anything."

"Thank you." I knew it—I'd do the same for her or Lyn—but hearing it was reassuring.

I strode up the front walk with my back straight and my thoughts racing. My apology and request hovered on the tip of my tongue, rewriting themselves an infinite number of times with each step I took.

The door opened before I knocked. Grayson stepped aside to let me in, and closed the door behind me.

Jax stood a few feet away, in the living room, and joined him.

The atmosphere was so heavy, I could choke on it. Instead, I lingered in the entryway, back and palms pressed to the door. The cool steel pressed into my skin, giving me a place to focus.

"I'm sorry for overreacting," I said. That wasn't so hard. Then again, it was the easiest thing I had to say. "I let the heat of the moment get to me."

Jax cleared his throat, staring at his feet. "I'm sorry too." He looked up. "I was hurt, and I didn't mean the things I said."

I dragged in a deep breath, to steady my thoughts more than anything. "I did. For the most part I meant all of it. I adore you both, but I'm not a two-guy girl. I can't see myself sharing my love like that." It hurt to say. I loved them the way I loved any of my friends, but romantically? I couldn't do that.

Grayson worked his jaw a few times, and I braced myself for Round Two of last night. "So now what?" he asked.

Now I said the rest of what I came to, and hoped it didn't cost me too much. "I want... Can we still be friends?"

"Yes." Jax's answer was instant.

So far so good.

"Maybe, eventually." Grayson's reply was a knife through my heart. "I need time, and I don't know if we can ever go back to what we were."

Anger rose inside, fueled by hurt. "So you were only ever friends with me for the hope of more?" The instant the words passed my lips and his face twisted to match what I felt inside, I wanted to rethink my approach.

"No." Grayson's voice was stone. "But we both made assumptions, and some of those can't be taken back. I can't pretend I'm okay, any more than you can step into a relationship that doesn't feel right to you."

"Fine." I reached for the doorknob.

"Sadie." Grayson's voice sent a shred of hope through me. I looked at him, not daring to say anything. He handed me my spare car key. "Probably give this to someone else, to hold onto."

And that was that. I closed my fingers around the cold metal, the teeth biting into my skin. That was that.

SEVENTEEN

Staying off social media for the couple of days leading up to Christmas was easier than I expected.

Not picking up the phone and calling Grayson when I wanted to head out to breakfast Christmas Eve was excruciating.

Every single interview I had lined up with Hollywood costume designers fell through. One even told me if I wormed my way into the industry under a different name, I needed to remember what a close-knit community they were, and that they wouldn't tolerate someone bullying them.

I was the bully. Right.

I hadn't lost everything. Not even close. I still had friends. My family. My channel. And it was Christmas—my favorite holiday of the year. My parents had gone on a cruise this year, but Chase and I would still have lunch at their house. He was cooking, and he liked their kitchen better than his own.

And Anne would be there, the way she had been for almost as long as I could remember. Her home life had been dark and painful when she was a kid. Mom and Dad made sure she had an escape, and that included spending Christmas with us.

Jax and Grayson would be there too. I was ambivalent about

seeing them again. Which was why I was lying on my bed, memorizing the patterns in my wallpaper and the way my holiday lights cast shadows, rather than getting ready for lunch.

"You still here?" Lyn knocked.

I sat up. "Yeah. Come in."

She stepped into my room. We'd exchanged gifts last night, and she was wearing the empire waist blouse I'd made her and a drug-store Santa hat. She was heading to her family's house for the rest of the day. "I'm out of here. Do you need anything?"

Answers. Direction. A way to make things right with Grayson and Jax. "I'm good."

"Okay." She didn't sound convinced. "I left a tray of treats on the kitchen table, for you to bring. Tell everyone I said *Merry Christmas.*"

I forced a smile. "Thank you. Tell Hollie and Alex the same." I hadn't made cookies to send her parents, but I did make sure she had a bottle of their favorite whiskey.

"I will." Lyn hesitated. "Are you sure…"

I climbed from my bed. "I appreciate everything. Go. Have fun. I'll see you tonight."

She left, and I needed to be on my way too. I should have gone half an hour ago.

My parent's house was only fifteen minutes away. Ten minutes, when the roads were this empty. The other cars were in the driveway when I arrived. I steeled myself. Things had been awkward with Jax at these things a few years ago, when he and Chase started talking again. This wouldn't be much different, and I could spend most of my time with Anne.

I didn't want it to work that way, but if the situation was too tense, that was the plan.

"Hey." Anne saw me the instant I stepped inside, and she joined me. "Chase was about to send out the search parties."

"Sorry about that. I was… Stuff." Wow. Brilliant, me.

She took the bag of gifts that hung from my right arm. "I'll put these under the tree."

I gave her a grateful smile, and retreated to the kitchen to stash the treats from Lyn.

Chase gave me a quick hug and pointed me toward the dining room. I was late enough that it was time to eat.

I sat next to Anne, disappointment swelling inside when Grayson refused to make eye contact with me. Jax spared me a glance, but nothing more.

The food was incredible. Not that I was surprised. Chase managed to outdo himself every year. The conversation—or lack thereof—was excruciating. It was limited to Anne and Chase, talking about the game Rinslet was pushing back, and everyone else occasionally asking someone to pass the salt or butter.

Grayson had barely finished eating, when he pushed back from the table. "We need to get going. Thanks for a great dinner."

"Whoa." Chase's exclamation was painfully loud, compared to the silence it shattered. "What's going on?"

Jax shrugged. "Nothing."

Chase looked at me.

"Nothing." Apparently. The guys hadn't wanted Chase to know before. They sure as fuck wouldn't be interested in filling him in now. Not that I wanted to, either.

He looked at Anne. "Don't suppose you know."

"Nope." I wouldn't have him drag her into an argument that had nothing to do with her beyond her being my confidant. "Nothing means nothing."

"Except it's not *nothing*," Chase said. "Someone's got an issue with someone, and I want to know why."

"Why? Why is it any of your fucking business? Why has it ever been?" Jax's retort was harsh.

The surprise on Chase's face matched what I felt. "Because we're all family. Aren't we?" he said.

"I wouldn't assume anything of the sort." Grayson gripped the back of his chair, a visible tremor running through his hands.

His words scraped across my already raw nerves. True, I'd turned down their offer to see where things went, but he hadn't exactly been up front about his intentions when this entire hookup thing started. "I don't know why you expect anyone else not to make assumptions. Seems a bit hypocritical to me," I said.

"People seeing the world differently than you do isn't hypocrisy; it's reality," Grayson fired back.

The way he twisted my words cranked my anger a notch higher. "And it's also not my fault. Are you going to guilt me into changing my mind? Pull some sort of *I was just being a nice guy* bullshit?"

Grayson's face shifted to that stony cold expression I was learning to dread, and he clenched his jaw.

"Nice guy…" Chase trailed off. "Did you… With one of them?"

"Both." I bit off the word. "And Jax is right. Since when is it your business who I hook up with?"

"Don't drag me into this after pushing us away." Jax's voice held a hash edge. "You're not even fucking interested. After all that."

"How does it feel?" My retort slipped out before my brain caught up.

Jax stared at me. Then again, everyone was staring at everyone. Poor Anne looked like she wanted to crawl under the table and hide.

"What are you talking about?" Jax asked.

The past I'd tried to pretend for so long was behind me, came rushing back. That frozen instance of— "Being led on. Having to find out from someone else that you convinced the girl in the tacky outfits that you liked her." Repeating the words tasted foul. Reliving that moment when Chase told me … The scars were fresher than I expected.

"You sound like you're referencing a specific thing, but I have no idea what you're talking about." Confusion bled in Jax's anger.

My hurt grew. "Of course you don't remember. Chase overheard you, back in high school. It's why he stopped talking to you for so many years?"

"Umm…"

"*I* stopped talking to *him*"—Jax cut Chase off—"because he told me not to date you, and I told him it was none of his business who I went out with."

The pretty story now didn't change what happened then. "Because you were leading me on."

"About that…" Chase worked his jaw.

"Because I was falling in love with you," Jax shouted.

Wha… The bottom dropped out of my reality, and my insides pooled in my feet. "But Chase said—"

"He wouldn't back off." Chase sounded sheepish. "So I made something up. I didn't think you still remembered."

He didn't think— "Do you have any idea how much that hurt me?" Tears clogged my throat, but I wouldn't break down here.

"It was a decade ago. You're friends now, so I figured you were over it," Chase said.

Anne smacked him on the arm. "What the fuck is wrong with you?"

Jax was still staring at me. "I can't believe you thought I'd say that about you."

"Who was I supposed to believe? My brother, or the guy he overheard talking shit about me? Besides, you apologized."

"Because you were upset. I wanted you back, and I didn't know what I'd done."

Fuck. I didn't even know which way was up right now.

"We're gonna go." Grayson's knuckles were still curled and pale when he let go of the back of the chair.

Chase nodded. "I think that's a good idea."

"No one asked you what you thought. At all." Anne rarely sounded so angry. "You're the last person who should ever have anything to say about this. *Ever.*"

"Except maybe me." Because I had no clue what I thought or felt anymore. "You guys do whatever you want. I'm going home." My brother had lied to me. I'd been hiding for years from an attraction I didn't want to deny, and harboring a grudge in the process. And my heart felt like a gaping chasm was running through it.

EIGHTEEN

I expected to cry on the way home, but the tears weren't there. *I was falling in love with you.* At least the Jax voice in my head was saying something different than it had for years. My own brother said… I'd been mad at Chase for a lot of things, but this one had me seeing red. And Grayson was, apparently, a *friendzone* asshole.

Not true. Part of me recognized he was hurt and struggling, like I was.

What was I supposed to do? Life had gone from just the right dash of chaotic to completely fucked up in such a short amount of time. I hated it. I was tired of not knowing where my future was, what I wanted, who I wanted to be with, or where I was going.

Lyn wasn't back when I got home. She would probably be out for a few more hours. I hoped her day was the polar opposite of mine.

The empty house felt like an expansion for my rambling thoughts. I headed up to my room and closed the door, to see if confining everything would help.

It didn't.

I sank into the chair in front of my computer, and screamed

wordlessly until my breath ran out. Then I inhaled and started again.

My thoughts were still as much of a wreck as my life. I needed control. To do *something*, anything, that I had power over.

My phone buzzed. A text from Chase. I deleted it without reading it. I couldn't deal with him. With what he'd done. It didn't matter that it was so long ago. The discovery—the hurt—was fresh.

And I wouldn't let myself think about Jax or Grayson. That was the path toward a swirling pool of insanity, because I had no answers.

I also refused to wallow and do nothing. Next year's design schedule was open, in anticipation of my picking up and moving. Time to fix that. I'd create new, more unique than ever designs, and fuck being stonewalled by Hollywood—I'd find another avenue for my future. I'd redefine everything.

I grabbed my sketchpad and colored pencils, rolled my chair to the clear part of my desk, and started to sketch. This was a project I'd wanted to do for years, a custom piece of female armor, but it wasn't work and it wasn't pressing, so I'd been putting it off.

Today I poured everything into it. Notes about textures. Fabric. Shapes.

Anne texted me. *You all right?*

I sent her back a quick *Yes :)* and kept my focus on my work.

Chase sent me another message, and then called. I ignored it all. The horror-movie date with Grayson and Jax was presumably off. Assumptions let things go this far. What was one more?

I lost track of time as I spilled different angles and dozens of notes onto one page after another. Then I moved onto a male version. A rough sketch. I wanted to see them together. I turned to a fresh page and let my pencils fly over the paper.

Who was I going to have model this for me? The picture in front of me blurred. I scrubbed away the tears with the back of my hand, and turned the page. Time for a different outfit. Something white. Maybe with gold accents. The faintest pink. Lace.

The rough outline of a wedding dress stared back at me. Forget worrying about two grooms; I didn't even have one.

I ripped the page from my sketchpad, crumpled it up, and tossed it at the wall. It hit without a sound and dropped to the floor just as silently

"Sadie." Lyn's quiet voice yanked me from whatever I was stuck in.

I looked up, to find her standing next to my desk, studying me with concern. I tried to grin, but it came out more like a grimace. "Hey. How was your Christmas?"

"A lot better than yours, from what Anne tells me. What can I do?"

"Nothing. What's done is done." I flipped back to the armor I'd started on. "I need some opinions about this."

"Of course." Rather than looking at my sketchpad, Lyn crossed the room and picked up the crumpled page I'd tossed away. She smoothed it out against her leg, then looked at me. "This is gorgeous."

I clenched my jaw and tried to collect my thoughts. "That's not what I'm working on." My voice cracked.

Lyn returned to crouch next to me, to look me in the eye even as I stared at the carpet. "Tell me," she said.

Talking about that wouldn't accomplish anything. I showed her the armor. "What do you think of this?"

She took my sketchpad from me, set it on the desk, and tugged me to sit next to her on the edge of the bed. Without my distraction in front of me, the rest of the day was free to rush back in.

"What if I never get to wear one?" The worry tumbled out without my permission. "It's a stupid question. It's not like I won't date other guys." Except the thought made my stomach churn. "And yeah, I can make one any time, but what if I never get to wear one for the intended purpose?" It was only one piece of my plan for the future, but it had been the impetus for so much else, and with my plans crumbling around me...

"What are we assuming is the intended purpose?"

I looked at her skeptically.

Lyn gave me a tiny smile. "Humor me. Answer the question."

"Getting married. Obviously being someone's wife isn't going to define me, but a girl has her dreams."

"Getting married is a lot of things to a lot of different people. For instance, I don't see you as someone who will be happy purchasing a license and letting a justice of the peace process you in the next room over. Where the only thing that says *we're married* will be signing your name on a piece of paper."

That sounded horrible. So bad, it almost made me smile. "No. That's not me."

"You want an outdoor ceremony on the lawn, in the sunshine. You and your girls in gorgeous dresses. The guys in matching tuxes. Everyone's friends and family, watching you declare your love for each other. Celebrating a moment no one else will ever have, because your love is yours and unique."

It was a painfully beautiful description, and it refractured my heart. My brain wanted to put either Jax or Grayson across from me, and at the same time, the *either-or* of the thoughts ached. "What if that's not an option for me?"

"Why wouldn't it be?"

"Because three people can't get married." Saying it aloud released a cork on my fears. They had a shape now, which made them sound silly and more terrifying at the same time.

Lyn shook her head. "Not in the first scenario, they can't. The state's not super flexible about that. But in the second—your dream wedding—why not?"

What about jealousy? And feeling left out? And everything that came with being a third wheel? "Because… it doesn't work that way." A weak answer, but it was all I had.

"Maybe not. But maybe it does." Lyn hugged me. "Come downstairs. I'll eat brownies if you will."

Brownies weren't a solution, but my thoughts spun in a different direction now, looking at things from an angle I couldn't see before, and chocolate sounded like a good way to help that along.

NINETEEN

Talking to Lyn didn't help me sort my thoughts so much as it lodged ideas in my head that I'd dismissed before. Which meant my brain was more of a mess than ever.

I was going to adjust my plan for the future. The career part of it.

But none of the plan stood alone. Thinking about my career goals led back to thoughts of love, and I couldn't see anyone but Jax and Grayson in that picture. The same old argument was there—it couldn't work. I couldn't share and be happy. But now I couldn't imagine it working any other way, with any other guy, either.

It was jumping the gun, to even take the thought that far. They wanted to see where things went, and I was planning the rest of my life around the idea. Then again, that was the only way to look at it. Sure, I didn't plan on marrying every guy I dated, but the possibility was there for each one.

And with them…

I couldn't linger in that corner.

Telling myself to stop thinking about Jax and Grayson was like ordering someone not to think about an elephant. Completely counterproductive. "When did this all start?" I asked my empty room.

With the sex was the easy answer. But they'd been thinking about it—about me in that way—before then, or Jax wouldn't have made the proposal. I wouldn't have accepted if the fantasies didn't already exist.

With both of them, regardless of what I told myself.

"When did it all start to fall apart?" The walls weren't going to give me answers, but asking the questions aloud helped me feel better. It dragged me out of my own head.

With the sex. Maybe. At the RinCon courtesy suites? That was when I started to put pieces together. Amid talk of hacking VR for porn and turning costumes 3D with rendered assets. When I couldn't ignore what was right in front of me any longer.

"Wait. What?" I rewound, and landed on my conversation with Chet. *Our artists struggle to translate 2D into something with depth.* "No…"

But yes. It was brilliant. What if his artists didn't have to imagine it? What if someone gave them a real-life model to work from? Maybe they already did that. Was that a thing? Could it be my thing?

I'd make it mine. I found contact information for Charles Sanford on the KaleidoMation website, but it was a generic email. I wanted to get to him directly and crossed my fingers he was as big a fan as he'd said.

I sent Anne a quick message, asking if she knew anyone at work who could help me out, then dove into my proposal. I'd want to start with a simple email, to request a meeting. Then something brief—a high-level overview, including a few portfolio shots but mostly a discussion of the concept. And a third that dove into details.

A reply came in to my message to Anne, but it was from Jax. Seeing his name in my email twisted me into a pretzel. The message itself, a digital copy of Chet's business card, complete with a personalized email address, was as benign as could be.

I typed a dozen different replies, before settling on *thank you*.

My letter for Chet was ready. Send it now, the day after Christmas, and take a chance on it getting lost in all the messages he'd get over the holiday, or hold onto it?

Who was I kidding? I couldn't sit on this for a week. I gave the thing another proofread and hit *Send*. Now I'd wait.

What next?

Talking to Grayson and Jax. I needed things to be right between us, and chasing them around in my head wasn't getting us there. I could also return Chase's messages, but I wasn't ready to forgive him.

I sent Grayson and Jax a shared message, asking if we could talk.

Grayson's reply came through seconds later. *Can't. Busy this week.*

Oh. There was no room there to pick a date—set a time at some point in the future. Just a *nope*.

I couldn't leave it at that. *My schedule is flexible. When are you free?*

Can't say, Grayson replied.

Jax's silence was at least as bad as Grayson's stonewalling. What were my options? Showing up to their house unannounced. But that was rude, and it also showed I didn't believe Grayson's *busy*. I wasn't sure if I did or not, but implying he was a liar wouldn't help the conversation.

I needed to give them a more concrete request. An invitation with a specific date and time, that didn't leave any room for guessing about when they were busy. They had plans for New Year's, but what if I could make things right and recreate that missed moment with Jax, way back when? Reset that first misunderstanding, when Chase tried to tear us apart? Except Grayson would be there, too, and I could show the both that I wanted the in my life.

I'd give it a day before I sent the request. Let them simmer on things, the way I'd been doing.

Another *ping* from my email derailed my thoughts. A reply from Chet. That had to be a good sign.

Sadie,

It's great to hear from you. I'm definitely interested in your proposal. If you have something you can email, send it over, and I'll get back to you.

I've been watching the public side of your legal situation. I hope things are all right on that front.

I need to talk to some people here before I can get you more of an answer.

Was this his polite way of brushing me off? He was being kinder about it than anyone in Hollywood. I sent my proposal over, as requested, but with his mentioning my legal issues, I didn't expect I'd ever hear back.

TWENTY

Grayson accepted my invitation for the night before New Year's Eve, on both of their behalves. It felt a little silly to make an appointment to visit them, but if this was what it took to make things right...

Was that an option?

God, I hoped so.

I wanted to dress up fancy. Relive that moment Jax and I never got in high school, but better since Grayson would be there, with the blue dress to match my eyes, and the jewelry to match theirs. Once things were better.

Instead, I went for casual but neat, in jeans and a flattering sweater, and now I stood on their porch, both relieved and terrified to finally be knocking.

Grayson answered. No smile. No expression I could interpret.

My heart cracked at seeing him again.

"Come on in." He stepped aside. One obstacle down. "It's just me. Do you want anything to drink?"

"I'd love to be drinking heavily right now." I laughed. He didn't join in. Noted. I wouldn't make any more drinking jokes. Jax was here—his car was in the driveway—but I'd say this twice or three times or a million if I had to. "I need you to know I'm sincere, though, so no thanks."

I did sit. Perched on the edge of a chair, trying not to look like I was ready to bolt. I'd never felt more uncomfortable here.

Grayson reclined on the couch, watching me warily. "What's up?"

"I thought we were going to be okay."

"No you didn't. Too many things were said. Too much hurt was passed around."

"I'm not done," I said. "When I asked if we could be friends, I'd convinced myself we could be okay. Before that, when we hooked up, I let myself believe it wasn't a big deal. I did know better, but it was easier to listen to the voice that wanted the world without offering anything in return."

Grayson raised his eyebrows.

A facial expression. I'd take it. "I'm sorry." Now that the words were flowing, they tasted better than any words had in ages. They didn't have the same foul bitterness of everything else I'd tried to pretend was real. "I'm sorry I couldn't understand what you were asking from me. I'm sorry I pushed you away because I couldn't see what could be—only what couldn't. I want to take it all back, and I know that's not an option. But I want to do things differently now."

"You thought you knew what you wanted before. Why should I listen? What makes this any different?"

Harsh questions, but fair. "I can't make you hear me out. One of the things I've always adored about you is that you're forgiving. That you allow people to learn and grow, and you understand changing an opinion based on new input."

"Tell me what you want to say." His voice wasn't as flat as before.

Skip all the drawn-out explanations and get to the point? Where was the fun in that? I kept the sarcastic thought to myself. I crossed the room, to kneel at his feet. I needed to look him in the eye for what came next, and this was the best way to ensure he would meet my gaze. "I want you back in my life. Both of you. I want to see where things go. I don't want to pretend this is just fun and games and *casual*."

I swore he was trying to peer into my soul. He was welcome to see it. I'd lay myself out bare, inside and out, to make them understand.

"Don't say any of this simply to make things right." Grayson leaned in, bringing his face closer to mine. "I need you to mean what you're saying."

That was fair. "I mean all of it. Yes, I miss you, and I thought a lot about how to bridge the divide between us. But I'm not going to make up something I don't feel—especially something like this—to put a fake bandage on the situation."

Something rustled behind me, possibly coming from the kitchen. Was Jax listening?

"I've been thinking about this—about us—for a long time. Fantasizing. Asking myself how two people who loved each other could share… It's been in my head for years, but I never looked too deeply into the why. When you told me you wanted me to be a part of that… I needed a new perspective, once everything started to come together. I'm sorry it hurt you, but I can't apologize for taking time to figure it out. That is what it is."

Grayson rested a finger under my chin, lifted my head, and brushed his lips over mine. It was a feather-light touch, but it still sent a shock crashing over me, like shoving icy skin under scalding water.

It ached all the way to my core, but I didn't want to pull away from the relief.

"I'm sorry." I didn't know what this apology was for. It didn't matter, if it earned me more tenderness and understanding.

"It's not your fault." Grayson's words were as soothing as the kiss. "I understand not getting it at first. I've had years to deal with the fact that Jax— I'm happy you see the situation from a new perspective. I'm happy it was you who made that decision. He may not come around so easily, but I fucking missed you, Sadie."

"I missed you too." I rose a little and stole another kiss. "I can't believe, all these years, I never thought what we did in front of the camera—"

"Was flirting? In a way, I'm glad, because it meant you never stopped."

I smiled. First real one in a few days. It felt incredible. "What about Jax?" Who I was almost certain now was listening.

"He's been waiting for you. And once he found out why you pushed him away…"

"He never told—" I clamped my jaw shut. He had told me how he felt. Several times. I ignored him, or threw it back at him for *teasing* me. I believed Chase had no idea back then what that one little lie would become, but it had shaped at least two lives for the next ten years. "I can't make things right if he won't talk to me."

Grayson grasped my fingers, tugged me to my feet, and wrapped an arm around my waist. He kissed me again, harder this time. It wasn't one of those ravenous, face-devouring kisses we'd shared before, but it was deep and intense, and I swore I felt his soul mingling with mine.

He pulled back and brushed a thumb over my bottom lip. "You already know he's in the other room, listening to everything."

"I guessed. How do I get him to talk to me?"

"He's still deciding if that's a good idea"—Jax's voice came from behind—"but watching you suck face with his boyfriend is forcing his hand."

What should have been playful words were carried on a stiff tone. If I couldn't make things right with Jax… I didn't know what I'd do.

TWENTY-ONE

I turned, to see Jax lounging against the wall that led to the kitchen, his arms crossed. He was as heartachingly sexy as he'd always been.

It was tempting to keep dwelling on *so much wasted time*, but this was a chance to move forward. "It doesn't matter if you heard it all. I'll repeat it over and over, if you want," I said.

"The day you moved, when I propositioned you, I was surprised as fuck you said *yes*. You'd pushed me away for so long. It's nice to finally understand why." Jax's voice was thick with the same emotion clogging my throat. "I only asked for discretion because being out—any kind of *out* that people don't think is *normal*—is hard. When you didn't react well, Chase was a convenient excuse, but not one I should have used. Maybe if I'd pushed harder, at any point between then and now—"

"I wouldn't have reacted any better." We could play the *what if* game for days, around that one little thing that kept us apart. It wouldn't change anything. "I'm not concerned about what other people think. My life is half on display anyway, and people can take their shitty judgments and go fuck themselves."

Jax smirked. I did adore that expression. "We've talked about you. A lot." He looked past me, to Grayson. "It was bad enough when one of us was smitten, but then he had to go and fall for you too."

"Smitten?" I loved it. Such a sweet, innocent word.

"Yes. And I understand your hesitation around being with both of us. When Grayson introduced me to the idea, way back when, I struggled with it too. Except it meant I could love him and not give up on you."

There was something in his words, the catch in his voice, that made my heart skip. I couldn't find a response.

Jax kicked away from the wall, walked up to me, and took my hand. "I tried to move on. Told myself it was pathetic that I couldn't get over a teenage crush. And I thought I had, until you were back in my life. Until Grayson, I never came close to feeling about anyone the way I did about you, and even now he lives in a separate place in my heart.

This wasn't *dating and seeing where things go*. He had a distinct destination in mind, and had for a while. I should be terrified or intimidated. Instead, I was settling into the relief that had been missing for weeks. "I'm sorry I believed the worst about you for so long. And that I don't have nearly as poetic a confession to make."

"That wasn't poetry, and all I need from you—ever—is the truth."

The truth. Should have been simple at any point along the way, but it always got muddled. Now it finally seemed so clear. "I'm glad you came back into my life. Chase's life, I guess. But he doesn't get any credit for this. Despite what I thought you'd done, I was happy to see you again. But I never dared think about you on that same level again. The hurt never left, and knowing now that it was misguided..." I wasn't going to tumble into hypotheticals. I had to remember that.

"You're committed to this idea now, of all of us?" Jax asked. "Because once you get past the hesitation, it feels really good, but you should know, it's hard falling for someone who already loves another person."

"I get that." I'd been getting that for years. "Believe me, I understand it implicitly."

Jax cradled my cheek against his palm. "Holding back all this time… Let's just say it's taught me infinite patience. But that day we hooked up, finally, the restraints snapped. I want you both, and I'm so happy you're good with that. I love you, Dee Dee."

I gazed back at amber eyes I used to think were cruel. Instead, he'd been as guarded as I was. "I hate that we wasted so much time." I had to say it. Voicing the regret made it easier to move past. "But we've got a lot of time ahead of us. And I love you too." Was I allowed to say that already? He said it first, and I meant it. Few things in my life felt more real or certain. Especially with Jax watching me in adoration, and Grayson wrapping his arms around my waist from behind.

Jax slid his hand to the back of my neck and crashed his mouth into mine. "I'm glad you wanted to do this here," he murmured between nibbles on my lips, "because we're not letting you leave for a few days."

I leaned into his kiss, letting the love and passion fill me. I turned to steal one from Grayson too. I'd almost walked away from this.

But I hadn't. That was what mattered.

Jax nudged my sweater up, and I stepped out of his grasp with a smile.

"It occurs to me"—or it was doing so as I spoke—"that having two boyfriends who are also dating each other means I get to watch you together." Which had recently become one of my favorite sights.

"What, specifically, do you want to watch?" Jax asked.

I hadn't gotten into many details yet. My fantasies tended to focus more on my pleasure. That would be changing. "Kissing and nakedness and stuff?"

"All right." Jax sounded far too casual.

Grayson kissed him in a way I recognized—his fingers gripping the short strands of Jax's hair, their mouths dancing hungrily together.

It wasn't just the watching that sang to my soul, it was also knowing how it felt when Grayson did that. Being able to place myself in the middle of that kiss. And seeing how much they both enjoyed it.

There was no hesitating, only frantic desperation, as they stripped off each other's shirts. Bare, well-defined chests molded to each other. They groped one another through their jeans.

Jax made quick work of Grayson's belt and zipper. He slid his hands under Grayson's waistband, to grab Grayson's ass and pull him closer. The kissing never paused for more than a second or two.

Until Jax broke away, to drop to his knees. When he worked Grayson's cock free, I whimpered. It earned me a pair of twin smirks that faded when Jax took Grayson into his mouth.

I'd never been this turned on by something like porn. Grayson, fucking Jax's mouth. The intensity. The enthusiasm. The low groans that reached deep inside me and stroked my every nerve ending.

Grayson's hips thrust in time with breaths that grew shorter and shallower. "Stop." He forced the word through gritted teeth and pulled back from Jax, who stood.

Grayson turned to me, shaft at full mast, lust splashed across his face. "Come here."

I couldn't disobey an order like that. The instant I was within his reach, he grabbed my hips and kissed me hard. I swore something ripped with the desperation he used undoing my jeans.

He shoved my clothes to the ground, the fabric scraping along my thighs on the way down. "Being away from you for so many days"—his voice was strained—"turns out absence makes the dick grow harder."

"I'm pretty sure that's not how the saying goes." I laughed.

"I get to decide how things go," Grayson said. "For instance, kneel on the couch."

Yes, sir. I was barely settled, when he grabbed my hips, pushed me forward, and thrust his cock inside me. No fanfare, just *slam*, and *God*, I'd missed the way he stretched me out. I gripped the cushions to keep my balance, my head level with the back of the sofa. He slipped in and out of me at an excruciatingly slow pace, but each push forward was hard, striking the perfect spot inside me.

Then Jax was in front of me, cock in his hand. I hungrily took him in my mouth.

My hands were occupied, keeping me from falling over, but the guys seemed to have the other mechanics figured out. Grayson teased my clit, keeping up the slow rhythm of fucking me.

Jax wasn't so patient, thrusting against my face.

The combination of the words shared, the things I'd witnessed, and the sensations now drew a long climax from me. My cries were muffled by Jax's erection when I came.

A salty spurt hit the back of my throat, then another, as he spilled inside my mouth. I devoured every drop.

As Jax slipped past my lips, Grayson picked up the pace. Grunting. Pounding. Hammering against and inside me. The sounds he made when he reached climax were deliciously intoxicating.

The world slowed to a stop, punctuated by the three of us struggling to catch our breath. This wasn't soft sweetness, but the spice was incredible, and it was love. More amazing than I ever could have imagined.

TWENTY-TWO

There was no going out for coffee or running off to work the next morning. We did force ourselves to get out of bed for the essentials, around midday on New Year's Eve. Spent way too much time figuring out if all three of us could fit in their small tub, for a shower at the same time. We didn't manage, but the trying was a lot of fun.

And I absolutely knew what the pizza girl was thinking when Grayson answered the door in nothing but a pair of gray sweats.

While we were eating, Chase texted me, as he had every day for the past week.

"When are you going to answer him?" Grayson asked.

I hadn't decided yet. The anger wasn't there anymore, thanks largely to the fact it was hard to be angry about anything when I was sitting with my back against Jax's shoulder and my legs across Grayson's lap. "I'm letting him simmer."

Jax tugged my hair playfully. "A decade seems fair."

"You haven't talked to him since Christmas?" Grayson managed to set his plate aside without disturbing my position. "You know he'd do anything for you."

"I haven't, and maybe next time he does something for me, he'll find out first if it's the thing I want."

"A person is allowed to learn and grow and change their mind." Grayson didn't even flinch at tossing my sentiment from yesterday back at me.

I stuck my tongue out at him. "Lying to and about people isn't the same as adjusting a perspective on how many people go in a relationship."

"Fair point." Grayson shrugged. "Then again, he didn't say it to or about me, so I'm not carrying the same kind of grudge."

Jax's barking laugh shook me. "Don't pull that bullshit. You were fuming after you heard what he'd done."

"It's true." Grayson lifted my legs and set my feet on the ground. "Speaking of Christmas— We never got to give you your gift. It wasn't in the stack at your parent's, because… we weren't sure anymore."

"We also haven't opened the ones from you yet. It didn't seem right," Jax said.

"What? You have to open them *now*." I'd forgotten about presents in middle of everything else, but now they could be a priority again.

Grayson kissed the palm of my hand. "Stay here."

He vanished into the other room and returned a moment later with a box that held two familiar wrapped packages. He handed Jax his, extracted his own, and set the box aside. "Who do you want to go first?"

Giddiness bubbled up. "It doesn't matter. Open them." It was a good thing neither of them were paper savers. I'd go nuts, watching them slowly cut around the tape.

I'd gotten Grayson a new set of headphones for streaming. He'd been eyeing them for months but kept putting off the purchase for one reason or another.

Jax's was a monogrammed leather portfolio, to hold documents for sales meetings. He gave me a curious look. "How did you…?"

"You said the one you carried was looking hammered." I was

pleased they both liked their presents. The pair of hungry kisses I got as *thank yous* didn't hurt, either.

"Your turn." Jax reached over, to grab something else from the box. He extracted a small package, barely bigger than a business card, and only maybe an inch high.

My heart jammed in my throat. It was a jewelry box—that much was obvious from the size and shape. I'd never had a guy buy me jewelry before.

He handed me the gift. "Merry late Christmas."

The gold foil paper glittered in the light. If I tore into it, the surprise would be over, but I was also dying to see what was inside. I slipped a fingernail under one flap, slicing the tape neatly.

"Are you kidding me with that?" Grayson asked.

I laughed and tore off the rest of the paper. Inside, nestled on a bed of cotton, was a gold bracelet. It looked like three delicate ropes braided together. I lifted it out gently, processing how gorgeous it was. Two charms dangled from it—a pair of scissors with sapphires in the handles, and a circle that read *weapon of choice.*

"It's gorgeous," I said.

"Here." Grayson held out his hand.

I handed the bracelet over. He unclasped it and gently secured it on my wrist.

"I may never take it off. Thank you."

We spent the rest of the day with movies playing in the background, while we groped each other as much as we paid attention to what was on the screen. We fucked to the ball dropping and ringing in the New Year, and collapsed in a tangled-but-happy heap for the second night in the row.

The next morning, we took our time getting up, and there was discussion of me maybe heading home for a few hours, for a change of clothes and to prove to Lyn that I was still alive. For now, I was happy in one of Grayson's shirts and a pair of Jax's shorts.

We hadn't managed to leave the bedroom, when someone rang the doorbell.

"Be right back." Grayson squeezed my fingers and gave Jax a quick kiss before leaving to answer.

"Is my sister here?" I heard Chase's voice distinctly as it drifted in from the other room.

Jax nuzzled my neck. "Make him suffer a little longer, or grant him a reprieve?"

"Not sure." I was going to forgive Chase. Maybe in about five or ten minutes.

"Are you here?" Grayson hollered through the house.

I laughed and rolled my eyes. "Depends on who's asking," I yelled back.

"I'm not going to do this in a shouting match." Chase was doing exactly that.

"Try."

"I'm sorry." Chase's voice carried better than mine. That deep tenor had a commanding quality to it.

Jax kissed the back of my neck and nudged me toward the door. As I stood, I grabbed his hand and tugged. "He owes you at least as much of an apology as he does me."

I recognized Chase's posture when we stepped into the living room. He had his back to the front door, and his arms were crossed. He looked me over, eyebrow raised. I stared back, unblinking.

"I'm sorry," he said again. "I didn't realize you'd held onto that, but I shouldn't have said it anyway. I was young. Stupid."

"*Was?* Past tense?" Jax said.

Chase snorted.

"Did you tell them to keep their grubby dicks off me?" I had to know. Because that wasn't nearly so long ago.

Chase nodded. "And they laughed at me for it."

Grayson moved to the side, so we could all see each other, and adopted a similar defensive posture to Chase's. "That's being kind."

"We told him to go fuck himself," Jax said.

Chase's shoulders drooped. He looked at all three of us again. There was no question *something* was going on, given my clothing. He didn't look upset. Not that his opinion would change my mind, but it would delay my forgiving him.

"They're good guys." Chase crammed his hands in his pockets. "I trust them implicitly, but you're more important. You're family.

My baby sister, even if it is only by a year. If they make you happy… I can accept that. If that changes, I'll start smashing skulls."

Grayson rolled his eyes. "How very caveman of you."

"Yup." Chase gave me all his attention. "I'm sorry. I really am. To both of you. I can't take it back, but I know it was stupid."

"I get it. I forgive you. But if you do something like that ever again…" I was happy letting the unspoken threat hang in the air.

"That's fair." Chase crossed the room to wrap me in a tight hug. He stepped back and looked at Jax, questioningly.

Jax's sigh was exaggerated, and I had to fight a smile. "I guess we're cool." Jax only held his stony expression for a few seconds before it shattered into a smile.

Telling Mom and Dad needed to be even a quarter this easy.

We sent Chase on his way, and I headed home to grab a change of clothes and take a quick shower where flipping a coin to see if anyone got to share wasn't required. Not that I minded the playful struggle between who got to spend more time with whom.

I was back at Jax and Grayson's place not long after. It wasn't as though I was moving in, but with Jax having the rest of the week off, and Grayson and me taking breaks from streaming, we were going to steal as much time together as we could.

Friday morning, I was surprised to see a phone call from an unknown number in California. "Hello?" I was prepared to hang up on a robodialer.

"Sadie? Hey, it's Chet Stanford."

My brain stumbled on the name, before catching up. "Yeah. Hi. I mean, how are you? How was your holiday?"

"Great. Look, I won't take a lot of your time, but I wanted talk to you sooner rather than later." He spoke more quickly than when we'd met in the courtesy suites, but he was just as friendly. "I'm sorry it took so long to get back to you. People have been in and out of the office all week, but I have the answers I hoped for."

I was missing something. "That's great?"

He laughed. "I missed a step. I do that when I'm excited. I loved your proposal, and so did the execs. We want to bring you on to do costume creation based on our specs, so our artists have something tangible to work from. But I needed a promise from Legal first that they could handle the fallout from the company pursuing you. They looked over your case, and they're going to take care of you."

I stared at Grayson and Jax, who were watching me with hopeful curiosity. Was this… It was the job I wanted. Creating for someone in public media. "Would I get artist credit?"

"Absolutely. And creative flexibility when it comes to making sure the designs are viable."

My name would be on video games. Asset sites. I'd get to make amazing new designs. I only saw one problem. "I'm not prepared to move to L.A. to do this." I had been a week ago, but my entire world had changed since then. Now Chet would tell me *never mind*, and I'd go back to that new life, missing the opportunity but knowing I couldn't leave my guys behind.

"That's okay. I didn't assume you'd want to," Chet said. "We will need you out here occasionally, to talk specs and look at what you come up with, but we're not equipped to have a seamstress in the building. This is a remote position."

"This sounds too good to be true." I meant to keep that to myself, but best to get it out now.

"I understand. I emailed you a contract. Look it over, take the weekend to think about it, and let me know."

"Yeah. Thank you." I couldn't think of anything else to say. I'd have questions once this sank in, but for now, I was basking in how amazing it sounded.

I disconnected, relayed the brief conversation to Jax and Grayson, and was promptly showered with hugs and kisses.

The contract came through as promised.

Grayson read it aloud.

"You even make legalese sound sexy," I teased him. The offer was exactly what Chet promised. Grayson handed me back my phone, and I set it aside.

"Would you really have given up a chance like this for us?" he asked.

"Yes." I didn't hesitate. "I love you too much to walk away from what we're discovering. Both of you." I hadn't said that specifically to Grayson yet, but the words felt incredible. "I love you so much."

He kissed me on the forehead. "I love you too. I'm glad you figured it out before it was too late."

"Arrogant asshole." I reached to smack him playfully, and he grabbed my wrist.

Heat rushed through me at the intensity in his gaze and the possession in his grip.

Jax pressed his lips to my neck, right below my ear. "What round will this be?"

"I'm not keeping count." I leaned back into him.

This was amazing. Whatever came next, we were ready for it. All three of us together, the way it should be.

EPILOGUE

August was the perfect time for a wedding. I was grateful to not be restricted to something like *saving myself for the wedding night,* but heading our separate ways had gotten harder and harder as the months passed by.

And for the last few weeks, I'd been too busy with wedding prep to spend much time with Jax and Grayson. Even with Anne and Lyn stepping in to help with the big things, my calendar had been full. Partly with finishing my wedding dress, which the guys hadn't seen yet.

I stood in what wouldn't be my bedroom after today, in Lyn's house, smoothing out the gown and studying my reflection.

"You look gorgeous." Anne tucked a loose strand of hair into the pins holding my updo in place. My hair wasn't quite long enough for a fancy style, but she'd given me ringlets and made my currently pale-pink tresses into a plaited design any woman would envy.

My hair color matched the embroidery and pearls I'd sewn into my gown. Lace hugged my torso, hips, and legs, and stretched into a short train behind me. It wasn't the princess dress that child-me imagined. It was stunning and elegant.

Lyn and Anne had similar style dresses, but in rich green and blue respectively, and minus the trains. I'd used the excess satin from my dress to make handkerchiefs for the guys' suits. Chase insisted I give him a blue one.

"Are you nervous?" Anne fidgeted with her skirt and shifted her weight from one foot to the other.

"Yeah. Not in a bad way. Like… I can't believe this is happening, you know?"

She grinned. "I do know. Me too."

Someone knocked, and she hurried to open the door.

My dad stood on the other side. "Are you ready?" He and Mom had barely flinched when I told them I was dating two men, especially when they found out who those men were. I'd taken the opportunity to point out to Chase that made him more uptight than our parents.

I nodded. "I'm ready." I wanted this to be over with, and at the same time, I wanted to savor every second of today.

Anne gave me a quick hug. "I'll see you downstairs." She hurried away, to take her place in the wedding procession.

Lyn was loaning us her house for the day, including her kitchen and back yard. She'd wanted to cater as well, but I made her promise if she cooked, she had to be done before the wedding, and someone else had to do the serving and the work. I wanted her and Anne by my side through this.

I descended the back stairs with Dad, and heard the electric organ kick up with the wedding march. The marriage wasn't state sanctioned or anything; we wouldn't have an official license for the three of us. But we'd have the ceremony and the promises we made here, and that meant everything to me.

When we stepped out the back door, I couldn't see anything but Jax and Grayson waiting for me at the altar. Their faces lit up. They were my entire universe. The best thing that ever happened to me.

I was on autopilot during the pastor's introduction. I managed my vows only because I'd practiced them a million times in front of the mirror. The rings Jax and Grayson gave me had been made to intertwine with each other, and I couldn't think of anything more appropriate as a symbol of our love.

The preacher said they could kiss the bride, and the both planted chaste kisses on my cheeks.

Then Grayson captured my face and pressed his mouth to mine, in a long, drawn-out vow that was the perfect seal to our recited words.

Jax cleared his throat, and stole me away for his own kiss. I was pretty sure people were cheering and clapping, but my new husbands were the only thing in my world right now.

Jax pressed his forehead to mine. "If you're leaving that mattress behind, we've got one last chance to abuse it before the reception starts," he whispered.

I grinned. "Let's do it."

This was nothing like what I'd dreamed of when I built my perfect-life plan. It was so much better, and I was looking forward to every single minute of it.

WAITING FOR IT

ONE

The one thing that made crunch time tolerable was my boss. It wasn't his fault we were working eighty-hour weeks to wrap up our company's most anticipated game ever; he took his directions from the people above him, like the rest of us.

Besides, even at eleven at night, when had both been staring at the same code problem for the last three hours and were punchy from lack of sleep, he was gorgeous. Dark hair that was cut close, piercing dark eyes, and tonight, a tantalizing hint of stubble.

Luke clucked. "Anne, Anne, Anne… Why the fuck isn't this working, Anne?"

"Gremlins?" I loved the way my name rolled off his tongue. And I was too tired to pretend I didn't want other bits of me on his tongue as well. I also didn't have any better answer to his question than any other time he'd asked it tonight.

We were in his office. As a director, he got one of the mid-range offices, with room for a small table in the corner and a great view of the mountains. I was sit-leaning against the edge of his polished-wood desk, watching him work. God, I loved the view. It almost made up for the fact that we were working on a Sunday.

Luke had returned to the flow chart we started an hour ago, and was drawing another series of lines. He jabbed the marker into the board several times, leaving a series of ink freckles. "The hobbits had a more direct, easy route walking to Mordor. Who wrote this shit?"

It didn't matter that his question wasn't funny. I still had to cut off my laugh before it became one of those drawn-out, sleep-deprived giggles. "We did."

I'd had more coffee in the last week than I used to drink in a year. Anything with high amounts of caffeine had been added to my *Best Friends* list since this project went sideways, shit itself, and landed face down, ass up in a ditch at the bottom of a deep ravine. Laughing was one of the only ways to stay sane in the midst of it all.

He sighed and dropped the marker. It clattered against the tray and bounced to the ground. "In hindsight, we should have just chartered a helicopter and flown into the mountain. The direct path is always the best."

And it was rarely the path a group of developers took. Partly because we all had different definitions of *direct*. "I'm at the point where I'd sell my soul to Sauron to fix this issue. I wouldn't hesitate."

"You'd make a horrible ring wraith. The hood and eternal damnation would obscure those gorgeous eyes." He turned back to the board and bent at the waist to pick up the marker, the muscles along his back and arms rippling under his T-shirt. He was a Marine-turned-developer and still had the physique.

"And you'd make a lousy hobbit." I smirked to hide my uncertainty. When he did things like compliment me in a way that sounded suspiciously like flirting, and then kept going as if nothing happened, it was almost impossible to take my eyes off him.

Too bad I was so lousy at seeing the signs of someone's intent. Misread it one too many times in an ex.

"Are you kidding? I'd make the best fucking hobbit. First of all, look at the size of these feet. Legit thirteens right here." He raised his foot.

I bit back my *you know what they say about guys with big feet* comment. That visual was for me alone. "And you'd forgo adventure, to stay home in the Shire and live a peaceful life?"

"I wouldn't forgo it, but I would make sure we were back in time for afternoon tea." He cupped his hand to the side of his head, like he was covering an earpiece. "Alpha Echo Sierra, this is Foxtrot One Half. We're ten clicks out from Mount Doom. Over."

My giggles threatened to return. I loved Luke's impersonations. I couldn't do the voices like he could, but that rarely stopped me from participating. "This is Sierra One Half, on your three. We've got orcs inbound. Spinning up the guns. Over."

"I'm going in. Give me cover." He mimed holding onto something, then made a tossing gesture. "Ring is in the fire. I repeat, ring is in the fire. Tea's getting cold. Let's head out, boys." He straightened again. "See how much easier that would have been?"

I laughed. "Tolkien fans everywhere would have your hide."

"They'd need to get in line, behind the X fans we're about to piss off with this plot twist." Luke winked.

And here were the giggles. I couldn't stop them this time. It was like being drunk without alcohol. The harder I tried to rein them in, the more my body shook.

"It's not that funny." But Luke was laughing too.

Several minutes—and my aching sides and cheeks later, we calmed down enough to stand upright again.

"Back to basics. The game is breaking on the call to the relationship AI." He spoke through gasps for breath, the occasional chuckle slipping through.

I composed myself and replied. "Are we passing too many variables? Not enough?" We'd asked the question before, in about fifty different ways. It wasn't the right direction to look in, but I was stuck on that point and couldn't move past it.

I could pretend there was no sexual tension between us better than he did. Even if he weren't my boss, I'd probably get stuck in the indecision of whether or not to say something to him.

My best friend, Sadie, would have made up her mind months ago and stuck to it. Either to pursue him or to ignore him. She was my exact opposite when it came to being outgoing and decisive.

She'd landed her dream job because of it, along with two gorgeous boyfriends.

Yup. Two. And I couldn't even hold onto one for more than a couple of dates, because I was busy drooling over men I couldn't have and didn't dare approach.

"This is why you don't let programmers write romance," Luke said. "They think falling in love should be as simple as ticking the right 1s and 0s."

"*They* includes you." And me. While I didn't believe romance was truly that straightforward, there were a lot of days I wished it was. I'd love a checklist, telling me exactly what to do, say, and look for, so I'd know if I was spending time with the right person. Then again, *Do you work for him?* would have a big fat 1 next to it, telling me to back off.

Luke shook his head. "I wasn't born a geek. I'm not one of them."

"One of us."

"Not you. You're different."

My breath caught from the way he looked at me, holding me with that deep, seductive gaze. I shook the lust aside... mostly. "Because I have tits?"

"Because you don't think the way they do. You know we've got people on the team who won't be able to process this new storyline. Linear is great for programming from specs, but sometimes sucks for troubleshooting, and it definitely doesn't work for falling in love."

The game had a twist. A bigger one than we ever included. Fewer than ten of us had been told how all the pieces fit together. "That would explain the blue screen of death when The X finally takes off his mask for the first time."

Luke put one hand over his heart, took my hand with the other, and held my gaze. "Art"—his voice dropped an octave and addressed me with the one of the game character's names—"I have to tell you something. I... I..." He stopped, eyes wide and expression frozen.

"I know. I've always—" I struggled to stay in character and not smile, as I waved my hand in front of his face. "Are you listening?"

Luke didn't move.

He didn't so much as blink.

I snapped my fingers. "Hello?"

He finally focused on me. "Give me a plasma rifle in the 40-watt range," he said in a near-perfect Schwarzenegger-as-The-Terminator voice.

And now I was giggling again. I wouldn't let it get out of control. I wouldn't.

I managed to stop laughing long enough to talk. "All right, Romeo. If the problem is *us geeks* don't know how to write romance, how are you going to woo your in-game love interest?"

"Not Romeo. *Gomez.* As in *Adams.*"

Seriously? I raised my eyebrows. "And that's going to work for you?"

"Oh, *cara mia.*" Luke brushed a thumb over my knuckles.

A gasp rose in my throat. It was just a touch. Nothing special. Nothing more significant than he'd been doing all night.

"How long has it been since we waltzed?" As always, his accent was dead on. He tugged me from my spot at the end of his desk, spun us in a fluid circle, and dipped me.

Fucking *dipped me*, without dropping me. My giggle died when I saw the intensity in his gaze.

"I would die for you. I would kill for you. Either way, what bliss." He pressed his lips to mine.

The rest of the world vanished. *Whimper.*

Did I do that out loud?

I kissed him back. His lips were soft, but his mouth was hard and demanding, and crushed into mine while he straightened us.

He tightened his arm around my waist, and my body molded to his like they were meant to fit together. Each nibble across my lips and hungry swipe of his tongue made my pulse pound harder in my ears. Had I ever been kissed like this?

It didn't matter. At this moment, nothing else existed. I dragged my nails up his back, wanting to feel *everything.* His groan when he pressed into me, his erection digging into my hip, was as intoxicating as fine whiskey.

He pulled away and put some distance between us. "I'm sorry."

My heart skipped, tripped, and landed flat on its face. "For what? Kissing me?" There was no way to keep from sounding hurt. I didn't just read a kiss wrong, did I?

"No. Definitely not." Luke reached for me but dropped his hand. "But I'm your boss. That's it. I quit."

I was typically pretty quick on the uptake, but my brain was struggling to keep track of this conversation. Maybe because that kiss had forced all the blood from my brain into every single extremity that could tingle with desire. "You can't get out of this project that easily." My laugh sounded as forced as it was.

"You were willing to sell your soul to Sauron to finish it."

"That's my soul. I'm not using it for much else, and these hours mean we're already the walking dead. But you're talking about—" his career. How did we go from fantasy kisses and dancing to this? I was taking things too seriously. Why did I always do that? I should have laughed off the *I quit* joke and gotten back to work like nothing happened.

Except Luke didn't look upset. Not with me. He was still watching me with those dark eyes that made my brain turn to mush. "Every time you laugh or sigh or say… anything—" He shook his head and let out a long breath. "This is so inappropriate."

"Yeah. Totally." I knew that. Or I might have, if it were happening with anyone besides Luke.

"I never want you to think you're in this job because of anything other than your skill, or that you have to do anything other than your work, to stay employed here."

Right. Because *sleep with me or I'll fire you* was a thing. I couldn't imagine Luke doing that, which was a good reason for me to be wary of it. I could imagine him doing a lot of other things to me, though I usually tried to keep those thoughts to a minimum. Getting work done would be infinitely harder if I actually let the fantasies run rampant—of him pinning me to the wall and kissing along my neck… my chest… lower…

"Anne?" He studied me with concern.

I didn't want to pretend the attraction didn't flow both ways. If work weren't an obstacle, would things go further?

What would Sadie do?

I didn't know.

Don't I?

Okay, I did, because Sadie and I might as well be twins, for as close as we'd been since we were kids.

"What if we pretended?" My voice cracked on the question.

"Pretended… I wasn't your boss?"

TWO

My heart was throwing itself against my ribs like it was in a one-man cage match, and I couldn't find my voice. I nodded.

"Strangers, then?" Luke stepped within arm's reach. "Random encounter? Undeniable chemistry? Two people who're definitely not us, even though we look and think exactly the same, who can't keep their hands off each other?" His voice rumbled over me with temptation.

Being picked up by him in a bar? Or anywhere? Yeah, that was hot. "Something like that." My response came out raspy.

He took my hand again and led me away from the desk. When we reached the small table at the other end of his office, he spun to face me. The toes of his shoes touched mine, and if I leaned in, our lips would meet.

"What's a nice place like you doing in a girl like this?" he asked.

I laughed at the Deadpool reference. If he was pretending to be a stranger, he had a pretty good knack for getting into my head. "I'd quote the movie back at you, but even if we're pretending we don't work here, Rinslet can't afford the copyright lawsuit."

Luke's throaty chuckle rolled over me. "Let's skip the pick-up lines," he said. "I'm not great at those anyway. How about we fast-forward to the part where I invite you back to my room?"

"Yes." *Fucking yes.* My voice had recovered.

He slid a hand to the back of my neck and kissed me again. There was no easing into this. He crushed against my mouth with an intensity I shared, and I parted my lips, to deepen the kiss.

Our tongues danced and thrashed against each other. He drew me closer, but I wanted to feel more than the pressure of his frame against mine; I wanted to be part of him.

I pushed his shirt up. One of us groaned—or was that both of us?—when my fingers met his bare skin.

His scent mingled with the faint musk of desire plus a full day's work. Everything about this, about us, was distinct and hyper-real. The way he tangled his fingers in my hair and tugged. The glide of his mouth along my jaw and to my collarbone. The barely-there fuzz of hair, when I slid my fingers up his torso and dug them into his chest, looking for something to hold onto.

"You're fucking incredible," Luke murmured against my shoulder, and the words vibrated through me. "I want to strip you down, and lick your pussy until you're grinding against my face and writhing in ecstasy. I bet you taste like peaches."

And he was a dirty talker. From the increased throb between my legs, apparently that was a turn-on.

The chime of his cell phone, unnaturally loud amid our panting and moaning, shattered the mood.

"I should get that," Luke said breathlessly.

"Right." I didn't know if I was hurt he didn't ignore it, or relieved he chose to answer.

As he crossed the room, cool air sank into my cheeks and pushed away the heat of fantasy.

I brushed my fingers over my tingling lips. The flesh was tender and swollen. My pulse wouldn't stop doing speed-trial laps. What the fuck was I doing? Was I really going to sleep with my boss?

Yeah, as far as bosses went, Luke was... *wow*, but I had to look him in the eye every day. Lust was one thing, but acting on it? Going further would be a mistake. I was a master of bad decisions, and that one would top the list.

"Sorry about that." He returned but kept his distance.

Good. It was. Really. I just needed *all* of me to be glad he wasn't close enough to touch. I wouldn't even ask what the apology was for —the interruption or what came before. "No worries. I think we should call it a night soon, anyway."

A shadow crossed his face, but it was gone before I could identify it. "You're right. It's late. Our brains are stuck in a debug loop."

"*That's it.*" I knew what the issue was with the code. Thank God, because it pushed the awkwardness out of my thoughts for a few seconds. "Check this out." I strode back to the white board, erased several of the lines in his flow chart, and drew in new ones. Not an easy trick while my brain was trying to remember if I knew any positions in the Kama Sutra. "This routine is stuck in a loop."

"You're right." He moved to stand behind me but kept a couple feet between us.

A couple feet of gaping chasm.

I ignored the thought and kept drawing. "We need to call this variable sooner and populate it at a higher level, so these modules can access it."

"Brilliant. If I'd know I had magic lips, I'd have done— *Brilliant.*"

My cheeks were burning again, but not from desire this time. *Done that sooner.* I knew what he wanted to say, because I was itching to joke that, *if your kisses come with programmer mojo, we need to do that more often.*

Not an option. I needed to relegate tonight's make-out session to storage, no matter how incredibly delicious and tempting his kisses were… How much I'd enjoyed his hands roaming my body—

"I'll get my team started on this in the morning. Which means we're done for the night." My words tumbled out in a rush.

"Smart thinking. We both need sleep." Was he looking at me funny? I couldn't bear to check. "Good work today." His tone was strained.

You too. You're an amazing kisser. "Thanks."

"Walk you to your car?"

"Sure." I had to accept. We always walked out to the parking lot together during late nights. He insisted it was to keep me safe, and I liked the idea of him looking out for me.

I grabbed my laptop—not that I would do any work between tonight and tomorrow morning, but just in case—and waited for Luke at the elevator.

The silence we rode downstairs in was deafening.

As we stepped into the parking garage, he coughed to clear his throat. "Anne…"

"Yeah?" I didn't pause in my stride or look at him. I couldn't.

He loosely grabbed my wrist, and a fresh shock of desire sped through me as he spun me to face him. "I don't regret what happened up there. I probably should, but I'm not sorry for kissing you."

"Okay." So not intelligent. "Me too." Only mildly better.

The corners of his mouth tugged up. His half-smile was as sexy as everything else he did. "But you're also one of the best employees I've ever had. And I'm not saying that because you've got incredible lips. You're one of my best hiring decisions."

"Thank you. I like working for you too. You're a good boss." The praise flushed me, but I could focus on the work parts of it and become a functionally vocal person again. I tugged free from his grip and kept walking. "Which is why I'm glad we stopped."

"Sure." He didn't sound convinced. "But it doesn't change anything else between us. I can't have this awkwardness. We need to be all right."

Easier said than done. "We're fine."

"Anne?" The *I call bullshit* was clear in his tone.

I should have assured him with more conviction.

We reached my car. I was both grateful and disappointed for the excuse to cut the conversation short. "We'll be fine. I just need some sleep."

"Okay. 'Night Anne."

I gave him one last glance. The lighting down here was harsh—

bright in some spots, dark in others to cast deep shadows, and a nasty shade of yellow—but he still looked amazing. Sympathetic, concerned, and fuckable, all at the same time.

"Night," I said.

As soon as I hit the main road, I cranked my radio and cracked my window to let the cold air hit my face.

None of it erased the repeat in my head. The memory of making out with Luke like we were horny teenagers alternated between ending the way it had in his office and continuing as though we hadn't been interrupted.

By the time I got home, my body was on fire with fantasy fed by memory.

I made it inside, and locked the door behind me. I'd purchased it when I started making good money, right as the market crashed, because I'd been convinced property was a good investment. Turned out my ex just wanted a bigger place I was paying for and he was crashing in.

. There were days when living in this big a house by myself felt lonely. Tonight I didn't mind the rambling house. The solitude meant I didn't have to worry about anyone walking in on me.

Sparks of desire danced under my skin, prompted by the images in my head of Luke gliding his palm up my chest, to tease me through my bra. My nipples, still rock hard, strained against cotton, begging for attention.

I dropped my laptop by the front door and stripped off my shirt, letting my hands roam where Luke's did in my head. To tug down the cups of my bra and free my breasts. To knead, and pinch and tug.

The pleasure that spilled through me was different than me just feeling myself up. It was fueled by whispers of *him*. What if he'd come home with me?

I backed myself to the wall at the fantasy of both of us being too eager to wait.

He'd press into my body again, him dressed, me half-stripped down. Would he be gentle? God, I hoped not.

I swore I could feel his hungry kisses, devouring me. Gliding down my neck. Alternating with playful nips and the occasional hard bite. Sucking on my nipples until I squirmed at the attention.

In my mind, we fumbled with each other's zipper, not wanting to break away from the kissing and exploration to give the task proper attention. In reality, I'd have to undo my own jeans.

When I wrapped my fingers around his shaft, his groan echoed in my ear. It was the kind of sound that said, *I'm tired of ignoring this.*

He'd shove my bottoms down as far as possible without breaking any other contact, and dip his fingers between my legs.

I mimicked the motion, and my body jerked at the new touch. I'd prefer his hand, but wrapped in fantasy, mine would do. I was already wet and slick, thanks to a night of better-than-should-be-allowed making out.

In my head, we were impatient. There was no more time for seduction. I stroked along my slit, dipping near my opening and then away, the way I wanted him to. My senses were screaming for relief, and my breath came in short gasps.

I honed in on my clit, sliding my fingers on either side and stroking. Orgasm built inside but didn't grant me relief.

Was I whimpering out loud?

I worked myself harder. Faster. The images in my head bled into the physical, until everything was a blur, except the sharp, disparate focus of my need.

Come for me, Anne. I swore I heard his voice in my ear and felt the playful sting of teeth biting the lobe.

Climax spilled through me, yanking a cry from my throat and shuddering over me.

I kept up the frantic self-attention until I was too sensitive and jerking away from my own touch.

Another gasp escaped when I rested fully against the wall. My legs were wobbly. I bet they'd be more so if Luke was here.

I sank to the ground, and the cold entryway tile bit into my ass.

I'd never dared entertain these thoughts before. Not consciously. Sure, my dreams betrayed me sometimes, and Luke visited me in them. But *letting* myself think about being with him gave the idea more shape and weight than it should have.

Heat still flooded me. I'd linger in the afterglow a little longer.

And hope post-coital bliss numbed the pit in my heart that reminded me this could only ever be a dream.

THREE

Hangovers had never been an issue for me. I could hold my liquor with the best of them, and had drunk my friends under the table more than once.

But as I got ready for work, my eyes burned in protest of being open, my skull throbbed, and my mouth felt like I'd slept with cotton stuffed in it. I could stand to sleep for another fifty years.

Which meant never seeing my friends again. And surrendering my dream of moving into a Director position similar to Luke's. That would suck. It also meant not working with Luke anymore. That would save me a lot of awkwardness... but it would also suck.

I shook aside the darkish gray thoughts and got ready for work. I wasn't running late according to office time, but I was for me. I liked to get there by seven thirty, because it gave me time to settle into the day before anyone else showed up.

Was last night a mistake? Obvious answer was *yes*, but every time I brushed something across my lips—my fingers, the toothbrush, lip gloss—I swore I still felt Luke. And now we could never do that again.

Was it really better to have made out and lost than never to have made out at all?

Depended on how the next few weeks of fumbling through, pretending nothing happened, went.

That should have been the last of those thoughts, but no, variations on the same repeated my entire drive to work, and when I settled into my desk, I was treated to the sequel.

No new email should have come in between last night and this morning, so I let my computer load while I went to fetch coffee from the break room. If I ventured to the cafeteria downstairs, I could get extra espresso and more sugar than should be possible in a single drink, but that meant facing other people. I wasn't quite ready for that yet.

When I got back to my desk, there was an email from Luke. Just his name made my heart do a funny dance, set to the Final Fantasy battle music. I needed to get that under control. How long could I hide in my office before anyone wanted face-to-face interaction?

According to Luke's email, another thirty-seven minutes. *Mandatory team meeting. Bullpen. 8:30.*

Hurrah.

There was another email from Mike, my counterpart in our Sacramento office. I didn't always care for him, but I respected his work ethic, considering it was an hour earlier there.

You didn't get those files delivered that you promised. Waiting since last week.

Yeah, I didn't care for him at all, especially since he'd copied Luke in a way that felt like *I'm telling the boss on you.*

I forwarded him the message in question, that I'd sent when I said I would, with my nauseatingly polite *Here you go. You must have missed this.*

His reply came in seconds later. *I didn't miss it. You didn't send it before.*

I bit the inside of my cheek. If I didn't have proof, I might believe him that I hadn't done it. That I remembered wrong. Thank God for *Sent Mail* history.

As people trickled in for the day, some of them waving as they passed my open office door, and others engrossed in their phones, I had zero focus.

Get it under control, me. I have work to do.

At 8:24, Chase knocked on my door. "Any idea what this is about?" he asked.

"Nope."

"Interesting. Let's go find out." He gestured toward the Bullpen.

Chase was Sadie's older brother, and by proxy as good as my stepbrother—the sexy kind of stepbrother, people wrote romance novels about. If I hadn't basically grown up in their house, I'd let myself pay more attention to how attractive he was. Dark hair, the same pale-blue eyes Sadie had, and the perfect amount of muscle in his arms to dip a girl and kiss her.

I might be fooling everyone else, but I couldn't lie to myself. I knew exactly how sexy Chase was, and unlike with Luke, I didn't pretend the fantasies didn't exist. I'd been daydreaming about Chase longer than I understood what the pulsing need between my thighs meant, when I thought about him kissing me.

And now last night with Luke was back in my head, overlapping my Chase repository like a scorching double exposure.

I gently tucked it all aside and fell into step beside Chase. He worked in Sales, not Development, but he was part of our team because he'd sold merchandising rights to several companies, for the game we were currently behind on. He had as much of a stake in the game hitting market as any of us did.

We took a spot near the *front* of the area we called *Bullpen*. It was an empty space amid the cubicles, near the windows, where we would set up gaming parties, pizza days, or whatever required a little extra space.

Including stand-up meetings.

"Where's the boss?" Chase whispered, when the clock ticked past 8:30.

I shrugged. Good question. Luke was never late.

When he finally stepped in front of the group a couple minutes later, his brow was pinched and his lips drawn in a thin line. A smile flickered across his face when he glanced at me.

My stomach did little a series of little flip flops.

"Someone looks like they've been force fed shit this morning," Chase muttered.

Luke's glare said Chase hadn't been as quiet as he'd intended.

"Sorry for being late. I was talking to Zach." Luke's voice carried across the room without a problem, and all the chatter stopped. Zach was one of the two company owners, and not the one who usually dealt with developers. If he was taking up Luke's time, odds were it included bad news.

"This won't take long," Luke said. "You know I'm always as direct with you as I can be. *Full transparency* and all that."

And now the flips in my stomach had turned into gnawing edges of tension. Something was wrong, and Luke hadn't been able to stop it. I rarely saw him like this, but when I did, he never had good news.

He always went to bat for us with management, but some things couldn't be diminished or erased. How badly this launch had gone, for instance.

Luke scrubbed his face. "I know crunch has been hard on everyone, but I have to ask you to hold on a little longer."

In the history of the company, this was the first time employees had been asked to do something like put in sixty- to eighty-hour weeks, for months on end, to meet a deadline. In the past, a couple of days at a time or an extra weekend here and there was the most anyone saw. The overtime was voluntary and paid, but our team was so invested in this game, we'd all agreed.

Rinslet was careful with their launch dates. They never made one public until they were ready to release, because they refused to miss a launch. This game was done six months ago. Everyone had signed off, alpha and beta tests were solid, and we were ready to go. And then everything fell apart. QA started failing. User acceptance testing. They were minor issues at first, but with each problem we fixed, more of the game broke.

Chase raised his hand. Which—okay? This wasn't that kind of an environment, and he'd never been a *wait for my turn to talk* kind of person.

I didn't think it was possible, but Luke's expression grew darker. "Hughes."

"Your people are the best"—Chase nudged me lightly—"but my programming skills aren't going to make anything better for anyone. What do you need me to do?"

Sell the big bosses on going easy on us?

Luke sighed. "That's where full transparency comes in. Management is watching us closely. If we don't get this right, other people may be brought in to help."

"And that's… bad?" I could spin up another dozen developers in a day, and more staff would be wonderful.

Chase tensed. I actually felt the slight tremor where his arm rested against mine. "*Help* to fill the gap left by anyone who won't be here."

A wave of murmurs rolled through the room. Rinslet was going to fire people if we didn't pull this off. Most likely starting with Luke and me, since we were overseeing development.

"Are you threatening us?" someone else asked.

Luke shook his head. "No. I'm telling you the way things are. I can't guarantee jobs—yours, mine, anyone's—if we miss this new deadline."

Here in Salt Lake City, there were only two big game developers —Rinslet and Digital Media—and working for DM meant full-time crunch and a lot less understanding from management.

I didn't want to find a new job. I liked working here. With good bosses and great benefits. With Luke. With Chase.

Losing my job was definitely more terrifying than whether or not I had someone fun and sexy to watch during meetings.

My lips tingled with a ghost of a memory of Luke's kisses and the intensity in his. It was going to take a while to pretend I didn't want that again.

"I have faith in you guys." The strength and confidence were back in Luke's voice. "You're going to rock this release. Back to work, and remember to clock all overtime."

The meeting broke up, and I headed back to my office, Chase walking next to me.

"I'm guessing this means you don't have time for lunch," he said.

I gave him a look I hoped properly conveyed *are you fucking kidding me?* I was considering tossing a cot in the corner, so I didn't have to waste time commuting. Going out to lunch was a luxury I couldn't afford.

He gave me a dry half-smile. "I'll bring you some General Tsao's?"

"That would be amazing." I'd made him grovel for what he did to Sadie, but she'd forgiven him and so did I. Which was good, because I hated being mad at him.

He squeezed my arm. "See you in a few hours. You've got this."

What would it be like, to have as much faith in our ability to deliver as Chase and Luke seemed to?

He left, and I dove back into work. I shut out the rest of the world and focused on code. We'd moved past the *fingers flying over keys* stage, and were in the *stare at the screen and see why things were breaki*ng point.

A knock on my door startled me. I looked up, to see Chase holding a bag from our favorite Chinese place.

"Sorry I'm late." He crossed the room to hand me the food.

I glanced at my clock. Almost one-thirty. Talk about losing track of time. My stomach grumbled at the scent of food. "I didn't notice, so no worries" I took the bag, resisting the urge to tear into it and eat like an animal. I shouldn't have skipped breakfast. "You're the best. Thank you."

"Anytime. Really. You want dinner, too?"

"We're having pizza brought in." Luke's comment made me jump for the second time in as many minutes. He stepped into my office. "I need to talk to you for a minute."

I swore I could smell his cologne from here. I couldn't really, but my brain was bent on convincing me otherwise. My thoughts ran rampant with memories, and my skin heated everywhere he'd touched last night.

I wasn't ready for one-on-one time in a closed space. Not yet. How were we supposed to pretend nothing had happened?

FOUR

I nodded at Chase, to imply I was in the middle of another conversation. "Can it wait just a few?"

"It won't take long, and it's not top secret or anything. He can stay if he wants."

Was it weird that Luke wouldn't look directly at Chase, or was I searching for a distraction, outside of the way my body was screaming to be closer to Luke?

Door was open. We had witnesses. I could rein in my imagination under these circumstances.

Unless Chase wants to join us.

What the fuck, brain? No. I was *not* going down that path. "What's up?" At least I could still speak normally, even if my thoughts were trying to sabotage my composure on every level.

"You and I are heading to Sacramento tomorrow, to meet face to face with Team Percival."

"Hey, me too," Chase said. "I have a vendor out there I need to play nice with."

This trip wasn't happening for me. And not only because I wasn't ready for that much alone time with Luke. "I can't go with you. I have too much work." We were behind, and I was going to fly off to the other offices for what? A friendly visit? Besides, Mike already thought I was trying to overshadow him. No reason to get in his face about it.

"I need you there." The undercurrent in Luke's tone sent pleasant shivers up my spine. "Give me specific concerns and let me address them."

I have too much work to do felt pretty specific to me. "It doesn't matter that it's a short flight. Once you factor in travel, boarding, security, any delays, we've wasted at least half a day each way. And only some of that time can be used for work. Why aren't we doing this via video? In fact, why am I involved at all, beyond the usual coordination?" Not that I minded the sound of Luke, saying *I need you.*

"Scott and I have some concerns about Mike, and I want you there as a second opinion, while we immerse ourselves in their culture."

Scott was the other owner, and the genius behind Rinslet's early tech.

I knew exactly what Luke was talking about. I had concerns about Mike's behavior too—though that didn't always mean anything in my case. And the more I thought about it, the less I wanted to turn down a trip with Luke, even if it was all business.

But I really did have too much work. "Mike's going to be on his best behavior if upper management is in the office."

"Some things can't be hidden, especially if they're a part of his everyday business," Chase said.

Luke raised his eyebrows. "Did you just back me up?"

Why was he surprised? Chase was outspoken but not argumentative.

"Don't get used to it." The sudden edge in Chase's voice caught me off guard.

Was there some sort of tension between the two of them I never noticed before? Who the hell knew? I hadn't even wanted to admit until last night that Luke's flirting meant anything.

And now that I knew, I couldn't use that information to my advantage.

Back to business. "I don't really have a choice, do I?" I asked.

"You always have a choice. I'd rather have you with me for this, but you get final say." Luke sounded sincere.

"I guess I'll go." I let out an exaggerated sigh. We had too much work, for this to be any sort of vacation, but I didn't want to let him down, and I was having a hard time remembering we should keep some distance between us.

Luke's smile was warm enough to make my pulse skip. "Thank you," he said. "I'll have Jamie make reservations. Expect to fly out tomorrow. I'll let you eat." He gave me one final glance and was gone.

"Is something weird between you two?" Chase stole the question I meant to ask him.

There was no way I was giving him an honest answer. "No. Why do you say that?"

"No reason. Just curious. Eat your food before it gets cold, Annie."

No one was allowed to call me that, except him. I had no idea why I let him get away with it, but the way he said *Annie* always made me smile. "I'm waiting until you leave, so I'm not rudely eating in front of you."

"And once I go, you'll forget for the next two hours. Eat." He knew me too well.

I set up my food on the corner of my desk and took a bite. The spicy-sweet of General Tsao's chicken washed over my tongue, and my stomach grumbled in appreciation. I shoved another forkful into my mouth quickly.

"How's development going?" Chase asked.

I stared at him, eyebrows raised and mouth full of food.

He laughed. "Sorry."

"No you're not," I said around my food. I chewed, swallowed, and washed it down with a swig of Coke. He'd even brought me the bottled kind with real sugar. He was too good to me. "Latest bug is that things are freezing right before… things." I wasn't supposed to share that detail.

"The big plot twist, right? If I beg and look pretty, will you tell me?"

I never had before, though it was silly to keep it from Chase. *Tell no one* meant *tell no one*. "Nope. But I'll give you a hint. It does have to do with the big confession of love."

"You sure you guys didn't write it that way? To freeze right before the good stuff, I mean," he teased.

I twisted my mouth in mock frustration. "You sound like Luke."

"You take that back." There was no power in his retort. "In fact, I bet when he said it, he did so in some sort of bad accent."

"It was a perfect accent." My reply came out more defensive than I intended, and I took another bite of food, letting the heat from the spice distract me so my mind didn't pick the situation apart.

"I accept that."

"If you want me to eat, you tell me about your day, so I can," I said.

Chase looked up for a moment. before focusing on me again. "Staff meeting this morning. Yoshi was in office."

My *oh?* came out muffled. Yoshi was VP of Sales and Marketing, which meant he was Chase and Jax's boss. Everyone had a story about him, in a good way. He was quirky, like so many of us, but he was as kind and genuine as anyone.

"Jax is supposed to be drilling down on a new merchandising contract, and none of us knows Yoshi is going to be there. He walks in five minutes into things, and everyone stops. He must have some sort of announcement or something important to share, right?"

I shrugged in agreement. Usually when a big boss crashed a meeting that was the case.

"He doesn't want a seat at the table," Chase said. "Instead he sits in one of the chairs against the wall, and sets a Taco Bell bag next to him. Everyone's staring and waiting for him to say something, and he's digging into a Chalupa. He looks up, mouth full, and says, *Don't let me interrupt.*"

"I bet Jax appreciated that," I said sarcastically. Jax had been negotiating this contract for months.

Chase grinned. "He cranked the cheer and enthusiasm to eleven."

"Extra irritated," I said in understanding.

"So Jax falls back into it. He's explaining how we're going to do a *Console Power Magazine* tie-in, and Yoshi asks, *What does this look like?* He's holding up a burrito."

There was a punchline in here, and knowing Yoshi, it would be a pun. I preferred the stories second hand, because Chase had better timing, and I loved watching him—well—do anything. "And Jax said *a burrito?*"

Chase nodded. "Yoshi can't stop smirking. He says, *A baby donkey.*"

A little burro? I groaned at the bad pun, but I was also laughing. "Worst one this week."

"Worst one I've told you about. I save you from the really bad ones."

"You're such a gentleman."

He tapped me playfully on the nose. "I absolutely am. I'm going to let you work, now that you've eaten. See you tomorrow?"

"See you tomorrow."

After Chase left, the amusement he'd brought faded quickly. I tried to concentrate on code. Exhaustion, food coma, and lust wanted me to daydream about either Luke or Chase instead. Or both together. Sleep-deprived me lacked a few filters. I had less than a day to get the potent desire out of my system and go back to the passive attraction.

I forced my gaze to my screen. The focus lasted about five minutes, before Luke knocked.

"Do you have a minute?" This time he stepped into my office and closed the door behind him.

No. The refusal froze in my throat. My insides twisted, and my brain grasped how intimately small my office was when the door was closed. How had I never noticed that before?

It only took him a couple of steps to move to the side of my desk. There was no furniture barrier now. "I want to make sure things are all right between us." His voice was low.

This wasn't exactly a private place to talk, even closed off from the office. "Fine." I needed to keep my answers vague. "I just had to—"

"Get home. Yeah. I meant everything I said."

That he was willing to quit his job to kiss me? That we couldn't continue what we'd been doing? That he imagined I tasted like peaches? "That's a lot of conflicting information."

"It's all true. I know what I'm saying. If you weren't under me —" His wince matched my mental one. Did he just get the same image I did? "Things are the way they are, and none of what happened has an impact on your job."

So he kept insisting, but it very much did. I'd never look at him the same way again. I wasn't saying that out loud, especially not here. If I was more like Sadie, would I stop thinking about this, and act?

I was me, though. "Good to know."

"Then we're all right? I don't have to worry about you hiding from me, or anything?" The lightheartedness in his question was strained.

I forced a smile. "Yup. Things are great."

He raised an eyebrow. "I'll take that for now."

As he left, I sank a few inches in my chair. Things would get back to normal between us. It would take time some time, though.

Did I want my relationship with Luke to go back to the way it was?

It didn't matter what I wanted. Returning to pretending it wasn't him was the only choice I had.

FIVE

After another night of working past ten, this time isolated in my office, and with an entire floor of developers between me and Luke, morning came too soon.

Taking a seven o'clock flight should get us into the Sacramento offices by about ten, which only meant a few hours of missed work. Still time I dreaded not having, almost as much as I missed the sleep I wouldn't be getting anytime soon.

At least I could dress in comfortable clothes, rather than business attire. Our company dress code was basically *clean, and make sure your genitals don't hang out.*

I sleepwalked my way through a quick shower, checking in online for my flight, and doing one last inventory of what I'd packed.

All set.

My phone buzzed with a new text.

I'm here. It was Lyn, my other best friend, who was dropping me off at the airport.

She'd been Sadie's friend first, and when the two of them met, I didn't know what to think of Lyn. She had that Sadie-confidence I envied, but something less self-assured hid underneath, and back then, I didn't know if I was jealous of her for covering up the insecurity, or hated her for not owning it like I did.

Lyn and I had moved past that, partly thanks to a little *experimenting*, that was physically incredible but emotionally didn't have the spark either of us wanted. Now, I was glad for her friendship.

Speaking of—if Lyn and I worked things out, Luke and I could still be friends too, right? Except my heart didn't want Lyn, and I was pretty sure it was interested in more from Luke.

I grabbed my suitcase, laptop, and purse, gave the house one last look—not that I'd spent enough time here in the last few months to miss the place—and headed out to her small SUV. After setting my luggage in the back, I joined her up front.

"I brought you a present," Lyn said in a sing-song tone as she held up a coffee cup.

I kissed her noisily on the cheek, and took the drink as I dropped into my seat. "My hero." The coffee scalded just a little going down, and left the burn of extra sweet in its wake. "Perfect."

"How's work?" Lyn pointed us toward the airport.

I made out with my boss two nights ago. You know—Luke, the hot one—and now I can't stop thinking about fucking him. I wanted to spill everything, but I needed to wrap my brain around it first. "It's work. How 'bout you?"

She drummed her fingers rapidly against the steering wheel and let out a subdued but happy squeal. "So, you know how I was talking to Roxie?"

I rolled the name in my brain until I made a match—names weren't my specialty. "The podcaster Sadie knows?"

"That's her. She came by the café yesterday, and she loves it. She's going to have me on her show, because—and I quote—*everyone needs to know about this place.*"

That was a happier wake-up call than the coffee. "*Yay.*" I clapped as best I could with a cup in my hand. "Tell me when, and I'll make the whole office listen."

Lyn twisted her mouth. "That won't be necessary, but you can listen and tell me how awesome I am."

"Duh." I was excited for the news.

Lyn owned a gaming and anime café called *Loading Java*. For a long time, she'd only spent what the business could afford, to keep it open. But almost a year ago, she took out a loan to expand. Business slumped off right after, and she struggled to stay in the black since. Christmas rush helped. A shout-out from a gaming podcaster with a huge platform could help even more.

We chatted about other random things while she drove. The airport was less than fifteen miles from my place, and this early in the morning, there was no traffic. Before I knew it, she was pulling up to the drop-off curb.

"Thank you for the ride," I said as I hopped out.

"Anytime. Try to have a little fun if you can, and text us when you land."

Us being her and Sadie. Thanks to a shitty home life when I was younger and my having severed all ties to my blood relations, Lyn, Sadie, Chase, Jax, and Grayson were my family.

I grabbed my bags from the back of her car and headed inside. It was the middle of the week, so the only people here were other business travelers. Going through security was fast and painless, aside from the fact they made me guzzle my coffee or I'd have to throw it away. Within a few minutes, I was heading through the terminal toward my gate.

My feet slowed when Luke came into view. He was leaning against a pillar, flipping through his phone, looking as gorgeous in profile as any other time. The flutters in my stomach spread, dancing across my skin, tingling in my lips, and lingering every place he'd touched or kissed.

When he looked up and flashed me a lazy smile, it was tempting to swoon and faint away.

This had to stop. As much as part of me didn't want to ignore what happened, I had to, or I'd never get any work done again.

I waved back and joined him at the edge of the gate waiting area.

The corners of his eyes crinkled when his smile grew. Did they always do that? *God*, I was screwed if he was even cuter than I'd realized. "Smart thinking, grabbing coffee here," I nodded at his cup.

"You could do the same," he said.

"Probably not a good idea. Lyn hooked me up, but I couldn't bring it past security so I chugged it."

Luke winced. "I don't know if I should be sympathetic or impressed."

He knew my friends. Both Sadie and Lyn had been my *dates* for various company functions and parties. I didn't care for the big gatherings, so they made sure I put in my time.

Silence lulled between us. That was normal. We'd known each other for years. So why was I staring at my shoes and thinking of excuses to walk away?

"What kind of a seat did you get? On the plane?" Luke asked.

I hadn't checked. Where did I put my phone?

Luke laughed lightly. "Stop, Anne. Front pocket?"

"Oh, right." I angled said pocket toward him. When his fingers brushed my hip through denim, I sucked in a sharp breath through my teeth.

His lip twitched, but he didn't pause, extracting my phone and unlocking it.

This wasn't normal, was it? Most people didn't let their friends and significant others have their phone lock screen codes, let alone their bosses. Why had that never occurred to me before now?

He raised his brows as he stared at the screen. "5A."

"Are we next to each other?" Could I spend an hour and a half next to him on a plane? Of course I could. Best time to practice acting normal. And sitting in cramped seats, arms pressed together, fingers itching to intertwine—

"No. *Someone*"—he gave me a curious look—"got an upgrade to business class."

Oh. "Thank you."

"For what?"

"Your assistant made the reservations?" Speaking of which— Luke could have told me he'd gotten me the upgrade, rather than going through all this… whatever it was.

"Then she likes you more than me. I didn't tell her to do that." He slipped my phone back in my pocket. "I kind of wish I'd thought of it, but enjoy the seat. Think of it as a spot of good luck, which you deserve."

"Thanks." And now there was going to be awkward silence again. "So I've been thinking about the configuration of the inventory call stack." Technical work-talk—guaranteed to make any lull in conversation that much more boring.

He placed a finger under my chin and tilted my head up.

My breath caught. My mind froze. A tingle raced across my lips, and I resisted the urge to lick it away.

"We're not going to fix the game today. When was the last time you had a chance to read or watch something new? Take advantage of the next few hours of freedom," Luke said.

My tongue flicked across my bottom lip before I realized what I was doing. Could he hear my heart hammering against my ribs?

"Okay." I couldn't pull my gaze from his. Would he kiss me again? Bad idea anyway, but in the middle of the airport, when Chase could show up any minute? "I'll pretend to relax." I tried to act natural about moving out of arm's reach.

"Ladies and gentlemen, we're ready to begin boarding." A voice came over the loudspeaker and announced that they were now boarding Business Class rows.

Luke waved a hand toward the boarding ramp. "Go. Enjoy the leg room and amenities."

"If I have to." I gave an exaggerated sigh, accompanied by a smile.

I boarded, stowed my carry-on, and settled into my seat. I was in the last row before the curtain that separated our seats from coach. Who would be next to me? I wasn't up for small talk on the best days, and especially not first thing in the morning, on a flight I'd been reluctant to take.

Read. Interesting idea. Pulled up my books on my phone. Biggest problem—where to start. It had been way too long since I lost myself in a book.

I was torn between looking engrossed if someone sat next to me, and watching for Luke to pass by, without looking like I was watching. I'd scrolled through the first fifty or so books on my to-be-read list half a dozen times, before I realized I wasn't registering any of the titles.

One of the attendants announced they were getting ready to close the doors. No one had taken the seat next to me. My luck was even better this morning than I'd expected. I turned my attention back to my phone. What to read?

Someone brushed my arm, and a familiar clean scent teased me. It was like Luke's, but not quite. I looked up, to see Chase sliding into the seat next to me. Wait. Did Chase and Luke wear the same cologne? How had I never noticed that before?

"Nice of you to finally show up," I said playfully.

"It's all about making an entrance." He settled quickly and turned to halfway face me. "Glad you got my present."

His...? "The seat upgrade?"

"Yup. I figure you're overworked and don't want to be here, and I had the points. You might as well enjoy this a little."

What was it, with everyone telling me that today? "It's a perfect fit. Thank you."

Some of the tension drained from my neck, as I sank into my seat. Chase sitting next to me was pretty much Ideal Scenario Number One. He'd understand if I didn't want to talk. The silence between us wouldn't feel awkward. He'd be a perfect buffer. This trip was shaping up to be pretty decent after all.

"So what's up with you and Luke?" Chase's tone was casual. The plane pulled from the gate and headed toward the runway.

I choked on the air. "Nothing." My answer came out in a single syllable. I drew a deep breath. *Slow down.* "I mean, why would you think...? Nothing's up." I managed to enunciate every word.

"Mhm. Then you need to get that blushing thing under control."

I pressed my palms into my flaming cheeks. "I'm not blushing." Was I?

"Every time you see him or hear his name, since yesterday morning."

Fuck. I slid my hands to cover my entire face. Who else had noticed? No one, right? Chase simply knew me that well. "It was just a kiss." Or two. Or more. And a lot of groping. "And we're pretending it didn't happen." My already quiet words were muffled by my hands.

The plane started moving again, but I was too focused on Chase's lack of response. I glanced sideways at him.

His expression unreadable.

"What?" I asked.

He shrugged. "If you were looking to hook up with someone in the office, you could have come to me." He trailed a finger lightly along my jaw.

My breath caught, and my pulse hammered in my ears. "We didn't *hook up*." I wanted to laugh his words off as a joke, but *God* if he didn't summon every fantasy I'd ever had about Chase at once. "You? Really?"

"Ouch. Or anyone but him. But yes, me."

The plane lifted off. Chase tilted his head and brushed his lips over mine.

The bottom dropped out of my everything.

SIX

The pressure from the plane ascending combined with the surprise of Chase's kiss, squeezing my heart and fracturing the wall I didn't realize I'd built there to keep him out. The clenching was exquisite and startling.

I didn't know how to react. What to think, beyond *this is incredible.*

He broke the kiss, then dipped in for another and a quick peck, before finally pulling away. The intensity of his gaze sent another wave of fissures racing along the box around my heart.

"Annie? Say something." Chase's tone was a sweetly shadowed blend of command and concern.

"Me?" The question slipped out as my reality swarmed back into my thoughts. "You want *me* to say something." I processed his words. "What about you? Did you decide to do this overnight? And if not, seems like *you* should have said something." I wasn't upset, just confused.

The plane leveled out, and my stomach dropped again. What was going on in my world?

One corner of Chase's mouth tugged up in a half-grin. "I did. I've been flirting with you for years."

"You talk like that with everyone." It was true. No shame. Last week he practically wrote a soliloquy about how nice Grayson's ass was. "I mean something obvious." Apparently, I was a little dim when it came to the men around me and how they felt about me.

He glided his fingers down my arm, leaving goosebumps in his wake. "You're my sister's best friend. I thought it might be awkward."

"Except, no one cares about that but you."

"No?" He was studying me again with that penetrating gaze that wanted to burrow into my soul. "That hasn't colored the way you see me at all?"

Beyond the thoughts of, *he sees me as a sister and he'd never look at me otherwise*? I shrugged. "No." My denial was less than convincing.

He loosely gripped my fingers and ran his thumb along the back of my knuckle. A million tiny shocks of desire raced through me, and my mouth was suddenly dry. We got drink service on this flight, didn't we? Why was I even thinking about that *now*?

Because my brain was bottlenecked on the *Chase Hughes just kissed me* thing.

"I've been thinking about it for months," Chase said. "Rather, I've been thinking—daydreaming, fantasizing—about you for years. But I didn't know how to bring it up. We have the same friends. If things get awkward between us..."

Our friends would take sides. I didn't want that. But his assumption meant—"You expect things to not work out?" Were we breaking up? We weren't even dating. How did we go from *I'm interested* to *don't make our friends choose between us*? I was over-thinking things.

"I didn't say that." Chase's calm tone was in stark defiance of my racing brain. He let out a light laugh. "You're adorable. You know?"

"What?" Should I be offended? Complimented?

"My money says, right at this very moment, you're starting to run variables through your head. As many as you can grasp. What I mean. What all of this means. What happens next. It's one of the many things I adore about you."

Complimented, I suppose? "Why now?" I still wanted that answer.

"Can I get either of you a drink?" The stewardess interrupted.

Whatever kind of juice they had on hand and vodka. A lot of it. Too bad I had to be in the office in a few hours. "Coke."

"Cup of ice." Chase's gaze never left my face.

The stewardess handed us ice, and me a soda. I pressed the cool can to my face. It didn't sap the heat away the way I hoped.

"I'm kind of glad you and Luke didn't do more than *just kiss*." Chase was calm. Collected. "In addition to the whole *because I want you* thing. If you'd slept with him, you might not want anyone else. Like me."

—the hell did that come from? "I can draw a lot of assumptions from a statement like that, but my brain is already overloaded. Fill in the blanks for me."

"He and I ran into each other at a bar a few months ago. We talked. We drank. We ended up in bed together." Chase picked up an ice cube and dropped it again.

Fuck my imagination. Now I had a whole new wave of images to tease me. I knew they were both bisexual, but picturing them together… I should be jealous, shouldn't I? Hard to tell, with the want racing through my veins. "Not your best story, but better than one that ends with a bad pun."

"Ah, no. This story had a happy ending. Or a few. At least that night. The sex was great. He's an attentive lover." Chase traced a cold finger along my bottom lip. "I can compete, but you might not have given me a chance if you already knew what he had to offer."

How was I supposed to respond to that? "If he's so incredible, why was it only one night?"

"I couldn't stop thinking about you."

I gently pulled back from his touch. His words, his gaze, and his skin against mine sent a warm, fuzzy glow through me. They also made it hard to think, and there was more to his words than I saw on the surface. There had to be.

"Do you have that problem with every person you hook up with?" I asked.

"Yes. But I have an idea of how you feel about Luke—I've never missed the way you two interact—so it was stronger with him. Besides, I don't do a lot of *hooking up*."

"But the flirting?" I discussed my sex-life details with my girl-friends, but Chase and I weren't *that* close. I'd always assumed...

"Serious with you. Playful with our friends. There's no other flirting."

But... The gears in my brain snagged. Chase was friendly with everyone.

Not the same as flirting.

Maybe not. I'd convinced myself that he treated me like anyone else. Ever since I dated Shawn, and he'd convinced me everything I did was wrong, I'd had so much trouble trusting my gut, and I didn't dare make that mistake with Chase.

"My point is"—his voice was soft—"you and I are amazing together anyway. If you're interested in more, I'm here."

I was. Definitely. Totally. Mostly.

Why was I hesitating?

Because if we pursued this, it could ruin our friendship. And my friendship with Sadie. And anything I might have with Luke. There was no reward without risk. If things didn't work out with Chase, were we close enough we could recover? Besides, I didn't have anything with Luke. Not like that.

I might if we hadn't been interrupted.

So I'd test the waters with Chase. Not that I was dating Luke. It wasn't even an option. And with Chase... he was right that we had so many friends in common, I'd lose more than just him.

"I need to think about it," I said. More than I already had.

"Will you let me help you decide?"

I should tell him *no*, but curiosity won out. "How?"

"May I kiss you again?"

My heart swooned that he asked permission, and the way he searched my face sent goosebumps speeding up my arms.

"Yes," I said.

He slid his hand to the back of my head and gripped my hair enough to pull, drawing a gasp. He dipped his head, bit my bottom lip, and licked away the sting before crushing his mouth to mine.

Every inch of my body sang in response. I needed something to hold onto, and the only thing I could find was his shirt. I fisted the fabric, terrified if I let go, this would evaporate.

Chase tugged my hair harder, exposing my neck. He kissed along my jaw and up to my earlobe, to nibble.

"I know why you're hesitating," he murmured against the hollow behind my ear.

"Why?" I moaned as much as spoke.

He pulled back to look me in the eye, never letting go. "You're thinking about him. You don't want to let go of what almost was. At the same time, you can see the rift that would run through our group if..." He frowned. "But we'll be incredible together, you and I."

The hint of possession in his voice should turn me off, but it sucked me in deeper.

What would Sadie do?

Not make out with her own brother.

A giggle tried to force its way up, and I swallowed it. *If she wanted it, she'd tell him* yes. "Prove it," I said.

He let go of my hair to trace a finger along the shell of my ear, never dropping my gaze. Intensity simmered between us. When he kissed me again, it was gentler but just as enticing. "Challenge accepted," he said.

My pulse roared in my ears. What had I gotten myself into?

SEVEN

Chase plucked an ice cube from his cup and glided it over my heated, swollen lips. He drew a line down my neck and followed the wet trail with another of kisses.

"I have a head full of things I'd love to do to you," he whispered. "And I'm going to see how much of it I can get away with here." He popped the ice in his mouth and kissed me. Ice and heat shocked through me. I whimpered and leaned into the kiss, dancing my tongue around his and the rapidly melting ice.

Chase slipped his hand under my shirt and teased cold fingers up my stomach.

Anticipation, fear, and desire mingled in my veins and pulsed between my legs. Why couldn't I be a wears-skirts kind of person? I leaned in more, and rested my hand on his thigh for balance.

He groaned against my mouth.

When I stroked my fingers over the topography, his groan increased in volume.

I should pull away, but instead I slid higher, stroking his erection through his trousers. Cupping and teasing in response to his grunts and moans.

He worked his fingers under the bottom of my bra. The chill

was fading, but not so much I didn't feel the cool when he dragged a thumb over my nipple.

I had to be as wet as his cup of half-melted ice. I continued to tease Chase's shaft and tried not to squirm too much.

"Excuse me." A polite voice interrupted.

I broke away, my face as flaming hot as the rest of my body, to find the stewardess watching us.

"We've had a complaint." Her tone was kind and soft. "Could the two of you"—she gestured—"be less obvious? More discreet?"

"Of course." Chase never missed a beat.

I wanted to sink into my seat and disappear, as the woman strolled away. My desire had intensified, though. Was someone else watching us? What if another passenger was getting off to what we were doing?

Hot.

Fantasy was one thing, but public displays of lewdness got people arrested.

I couldn't look at Chase. "I'm going to read," I mumbled. I lowered my tray table to rest my arms on, so they wouldn't shake, and stared blankly at my phone.

I didn't process a single word in front of me.

"I meant everything I said," Chase murmured.

"So did I." Including the uncertainty.

Silence settled between us again. I should be reading. Or over-analyzing what happened. Instead, I was thinking about Chase's hands, roaming my body.

And Luke. What if he'd been the one to catch us? Would he have watched? Gotten off?

I squeezed my legs together as tightly as I could, but the action didn't do anything to sate my need.

Chase rested a hand on my thigh, under the table. "You're not really reading."

I shook my head. Did the fact that the screen had gone to sleep give me away?

"Keep pretending," he said softly.

What?

He undid my jeans.

I could barely hear over the roar of my heartbeat.

He dipped his fingers under the waistband of my pants. I had to slide down in my seat, to give him better access, and it was still a tight fit.

But Chase's fingers were long and slender, making it easier for him to glide them under my panties.

I was so turned on, when he neared my clit I arched into his touch. I glanced sideways, to find him watching me again. Still? Everything we were doing was hidden by my tray table.

He teased over my clit, sending a shudder through me with each pass. When he focused his attention on the swollen button, I dug my fingers into his arm, needing something to hold onto.

He stroked and circled and nudged me toward orgasm. I bit the inside of my cheek when I came, my ass rising out of my seat.

I dropped back with a breathless gasp, as Chase pulled away.

He sucked his fingers clean, one at a time.

God, this was hot. Had anyone seen us? I risked a glance around. As far as I could tell, no one was paying attention.

"Peaches. My favorite," Chase said.

Luke made a similar comment the other night. Was pussy tasting like peaches some sort of guy-thing I wasn't familiar with?

Getting away with getting off sent boldness through me. "When do I get to return the favor?" I asked. Terror mingled with the hope that he'd ask me to pay him back now.

"There's no favor to return." He was genuine. "This isn't tit for tat. I just wanted to see you come."

"Verdict?"

"Better than any fantasy." He smirked and tangled his fingers with mine.

My brain was going to be a chaotic wreck from here to eternity if he kept this up.

EIGHT

I was still processing, as the plane taxied up to the gate and stopped. Chase. And me. It didn't seem real, and at the same time, it was more vivid than anything. Partly because of the pleasant tingle that lingered on my lips. My fingers were intertwined with his and resting on the arm between us. Two hours ago, he was one of the gang. The sexiest one. The only one I fantasized about. But still, nothing more.

And now we were… dating? *Seeing where things go.*

The brush of his lips over my cheek was terrifyingly tender and sweet. "I'm at the vendor's site all day. Text me when you know your plans for tonight, and I'll squeeze myself in," he said.

"All right." There was a good chance he'd have been part of my plans anyway, but this was different. The night might not end with us parting ways at our hotel.

We were among the first to disembark, since we were at the front of the plane, and every few seconds, Chase brushed against me. I was a live wire of nerve endings by the time we reached the gate.

Luke appeared a few minutes later, his gaze flicking between us, one eyebrow raised as he joined us. "How was your flight?" His tone was casual. Same as always.

My cheeks were red, weren't they? Bright, tomato-colored… Now that Chase had reminded me I wore certain emotions on my face, I couldn't stop thinking about it. I started walking toward baggage claim, more to avoid their stares than anything.

Luke joined me, and Chase managed to wedge himself between us, to be by my side.

"Same as yours, but with better amenities." Chase squeezed my hand.

Did Luke see that? Would he know? Did it matter? If Chase and I made this all official and long term, Luke was going to find out anyway.

He and Chase really…? My mind was on other things on the flight, but now, with it flitting back and forth between the two men, I was imagining them together. With me. Without me.

"What about you, Anne?" Luke asked. "Good flight?"

Incredible. Hot. *You should have seen us*. There was so much possibility in that response. "It was good. The extra leg room was nice."

"Hmm. Cool." Luke wandered toward a newspaper- and gift-shop, and we drifted that way with him. He didn't dwell, instead falling into step on my other side and brushing his arm against mine.

Was that on purpose? Had he always made casual contact with me when we walked side-by-side? No. I would have noticed.

Then again, I'd convinced myself for years that neither of them was flirting with me. That Chase wasn't interested. That Luke was just extra friendly.

"Rumor is some couple up in Business Class was practically fucking each other. Did you see them?" Luke's question was calm. Casual.

If I'd been drinking, I would have choked. I could picture it in my head.

Chase traced his fingers over the back of my knuckles. "*Practically fucking* isn't accurate at all."

My body was on fire, and so was my face, but for very different reasons. I needed to find the closest hole to climb in and hide.

"Hmm…" Luke was saying a lot of that today. "I hope the show was good."

Chase chuckled. "You like a good show?"

"All depends on who the stars are."

"You would have loved this one," Chase said.

Forget the hole. I needed to yank both of them into a corner and do something hot enough to land us on a porn site. Embarrassment was fading, replaced with that rush I felt when the stewardess asked us to stop. The potential of both humiliation and someone else getting off to the sight of the three of us together lingered on my tongue. I could feel Luke's hands gliding up my chest, his lips on my neck. All while Chase worked his fingers lower, sucked on my throat—

"Annie?" Chase's tone implied I'd missed something.

I shook the fantasy aside. It was hard to walk and clench my thighs together at the same time, anyway. "Sorry—what?"

"Sushi tonight? Chase knows a fantastic place." If Luke was asking, was he going to invite everyone in the office?

I was turned on by the idea of an audience, but that was different than dinner with co-workers I barely knew outside of video conferences. "Work?" Wow, that came out dumb. "I mean, I'm not sure I know how to deal with a night off."

Luke tickled his fingers lightly along my arm. "I'm ordering you to take tonight off, as your boss, and the three of us will go explore the city for a few hours."

Yes, sir. The sassy retort froze on my lips. "Yes, sir." Maybe I shouldn't have said that out loud. Too late to take it back.

We reached the carousel for our bags, and Chase slid an arm around my waist.

The gesture was warm. Comforting. Possessive. Was I okay with that?

"I didn't realize the two of you were more than friends." Luke's tone was impossible to read. Then again, I'd been misreading it for a long time.

"We weren't. Were?" And now I couldn't speak. Did Luke think

I'd been making out with him even though I was with someone else? "Just friends. We were just friends before."

"We had a *conversation* on the plane." Chase's emphasis was distinct.

"Hmm."

I was starting to really dislike Luke's non-committal grunt. Mostly because I couldn't interpret it.

"Did it go better than the *conversation* you and I had?" Luke asked

Chase squeezed my hip. "She gave me permission to try to win her over."

"Then I want the same." There wasn't much room for misinterpretation in Luke's words this time.

That didn't stop me from asking, "What?"

Luke stepped in front of me and held my gaze. "I want permission to try to win you over."

Were they really almost-fighting over me? This wasn't happening. There was no way. I held up my arm and pinched. *Ow.*

"Anne?" Luke raised an eyebrow.

Chase dipped his head near my ear. "It's not a dream. I promise." The heat of his stage whisper danced over my skin.

"Dream-you would say that." I refused to be stunned silent, even as I struggled to process what was going on.

"There's a dream version of me?" Chase trailed his nose along the shell of my ear. "What else does he say? Would you like me to provide him with some explicit dialog for his next appearance?"

This was over the top. I loved the idea and the attention, but it was too much. Straight out of some imitation of an *Alpha hero always gets what he wants* romance novel. "You're both yanking my chain." That had to be it. *Including those kisses?* "There are hidden cameras?" *The kind that land us on Smut Central?* My brain needed to stop. "Will I see this on YouTube in the morning and have to pray it doesn't go viral?"

Chase spun me to face him, and cupped my cheeks between his hands. A whimper stuck in my throat at the intensity in his gaze and touch.

"I would *never* do that to you." He sounded hurt, but he wasn't as sparkling good and innocent as that tone implied.

"You told Sadie that Jax called her names, and you did it to keep them apart."

Chase dropped his hands, tilted his head back, and let out a frustrated groan, before looking at me again. "Ten years ago. *Fuck.* We all made mistakes in high school. I thought we were over that."

Luke grasped my hand, drawing my attention, and rested a finger under my chin.

I was learning to like that as much as I disliked his generic *hmm*.

"I don't know what he's up to, but I'm not willing to let you go that easily unless you tell me to leave you alone," he said. "The only thing holding me back was I don't want you to think—"

"That my job is on the line. I get it." That was the one thing I *did* understand. But this appeared to be exactly what the two of them said it was—these gorgeous men were fighting over me.

A barking laugh escaped my throat.

Chase and Luke stared at me, questioning expressions on their handsome faces.

"Care to share the joke?" Chase asked.

That was what I wanted to say to them. This was happening— except shit like this didn't happen in the actual world.

"Um… Okay. You can both try to win me over." It felt ludicrous, saying the words, but at the same time, I was looking forward to the ride.

"Good." Chase grinned. Gripping my hips, he pulled me back to him and crushed his mouth to mine.

A fresh wave of desire spilled through me. *God*, I loved everything about his kisses. How was this my life now?

NINE

My lips were still tingling when Chase stepped off the shuttle for his car-rental company.

"Looks like I need to up my game." Luke sounded more entertained than put out.

I fell into step beside him as we headed for our car. "Please don't."

"I don't understand."

"I can only handle so much smoldering intensity." I kept the teasing in my reply. We reached the car, and I set my bags on the ground.

Instead of opening the trunk, Luke turned to me. "And you're getting your fill from Chase?" Amusement overrode the hurt in his voice. He stepped toward me, and I backed up until I collided with a cement pillar. "You don't want to be pressed against the wall?" Luke grabbed my wrists in a single swoop and pinned them over my head. His body molded to mine. "Devoured, until your legs are weak and your voice is hoarse?" he growled against my skin.

I didn't fight my whimper. "I never said that."

"You sure?" Luke let go and put some distance between us.

Did. Not. Like. I wanted his body fitted against mine again. "I just don't want to lose the fun." I could do this. Handle the flirting and be normal around him. I'd been psyching myself up to do that for more than a day now. It came more easily than I thought. "All I'm saying is, give me as much Ryan Reynolds as Gomez Adams."

"So… masturbating with a unicorn?" Luke winked before turning away to load our things into the back of the car.

"I could get into it if that's your thing."

"I don't come in rainbows."

I laughed at the visual and his playful retort. "Probably good."

"Happy to prove it."

My brain stalled, but only for a heartbeat this time. I could do this. "Even better. Do you think if you ate a handful of Skittles first, I could taste the rainbow?"

He sucked a sharp breath through his teeth and shook his head. "The things you do to my imagination…"

Me? To him?

"We should get going." Luke opened the passenger door for me. "Otherwise, we may not make it to the office."

Responsibility warred with desire, as I slid into the car. "Office. Right."

We left airport parking and were pulling onto the freeway, when Luke's phone rang. Just a few minutes earlier, and I'd think the damn thing was trying to interrupt us.

He pulled it from his pocket and handed it to me. "Anyone important?"

"Scott." My gut sank. Did the company CTO regularly make casual calls to Luke? "Answering. Putting on speaker." I swiped as I talked.

"Hello." Luke spoke loudly and clearly.

"How far out are you?" Scott was usually friendly. Chatty. The way he cut straight to the point was less than reassuring.

His abrupt tone kicked my stomach into my shoes. "Just left the airport," I said.

"Good. You're both there. Something came out of Sacramento

today." Scott let out a long sigh. "Someone published the entire game plot, including our surprise ending, online."

"What? Why?" I knew why, but it was easier to ask than admit someone with access to that information—someone so close to this project—was trying to fuck us.

"Next steps." Luke had lost any hint of playfulness and was all business.

Hot.

"Chloe's already released five other variations in the same forums, to confuse things. Yoshi is handling everything else public-facing," Scott said. "Zane emailed you machine information. I need you to find out who this came from and deal with them."

"On it. We'll check in soon," Luke said.

Dread hung heavy in my limbs as we disconnected from Scott. As if missed deadlines weren't enough, now we were dealing with sabotage—espionage?—too. "Nice of someone to set up a welcome present for us." My sarcasm came out with more bitterness and less teasing than I intended.

"Yay." Luke scrubbed a hand through his short hair. "When we get in, Mike and I are going to talk. I need you chatting with developers. Keep it informal. Fast. Don't plan on getting a lot of your own coding done today."

"Right." I hated the idea of losing a day of work, but this was important too.

Luke rested a hand on my knee. The shock of heat was muffled by stress. "I'm glad you're here." He gently squeezed my leg. "No one else I trust more to get us through this."

It wasn't filthy or sexy, but it did summon a ball of warmth in my chest that spread through me.

We spent the rest of the drive modifying our plans for the week. I watched the scenery pass by in a hazy blur. I'd taken several trips out here, and always loved the scenery. Today, I couldn't see a lot of it.

Wildfires were tearing through the hills, not too far away, and the air was choked with smoke. We had summer fires in Salt Lake, but nothing this severe. I hated that so many of our programmers were dealing with the evacuation and the fear of losing their homes on top of a deadline and a visit from the boss.

We arrived at the building and headed straight for the floor where the developers worked. My first few times here, doing this felt awkward. Like walking into a stranger's home and making myself comfortable. But now, it was almost as familiar as walking into my own office.

The location Luke, Chase, and I worked in was Rinslet's international headquarters. Rinslet didn't have the same kind of massive campus that some of the bigger tech companies had, but they owned the entire building downtown, and it was one of the taller ones in the city. There was a little of everything on-site—cafeteria, gym, gaming room.

This was a satellite location for developers, so we only took up a floor. Everyone in the open-floor plan had their heads down and fingers flying over keys when we stepped into the room. A few people looked up, and then several more, and whispers fluttered through the air.

Luke growled softly. "Mike was supposed to let them know," he muttered.

"He's as busy as the rest of us." My defense came instinctively. I preferred to think the best of most people, but in Mike's case, I wasn't so sure that was wise.

"Hey, guys." Speak of the devil. Mike strode from his office, meeting us halfway. "I hope your flight was good. Glad you're here. Conference Room Gamma is set up for you to work in. You speak to Scott yet?"

Luke nodded. "You and I need to talk." He glanced at me. "You good?"

"Yeah." I was in my element here. There shouldn't be any hidden surprises, like my boss and my best friend's brother agreeing to compete for my affection.

I headed for the conference room and set up my laptop. I was getting ready to talk to the first person on my schedule, when my phone buzzed with a group text from Sadie and Lyn.

How was your flight? Sadie asked.

Shit, I forgot to text them when I landed. And I needed to tell them what had me distracted, too. How was I going explain this to Sadie?

TEN

I'm here. *I'm good. Sorry about the delay.* I sent the message.

In my mind, I added, *I would have replied sooner, but I was lost in the afterglow of your brother fingering me on the plane.* That wasn't going to work so great. It wasn't as though I intended to keep what was going on with Chase a secret, but Sadie, Lyn, and I shared all sorts of details about our love lives, and this one wasn't going to be so simple to dive into.

Did Chase already tell her? Probably not, but it was possible.

As long as you're all right, Lyn wrote.

Was I? I was a little confused, but the adrenaline racing through my veins, and the way my pulse whimpered every time I thought about either man, said I was pretty fucking good. *I am. And as soon as I get home, I have to tell you both something.* What if Chase *did* tell Sadie first? *It's a good thing, and I'm not keeping it a secret, so if you hear anything before then, just remember this is a story told better face-to-face.*

Yeah, I was that friend who typed the mile-long single text messages.

That's not fair, Lyn said.

Sadie's reply was only a second behind. *Especially with a lead-in like that.*

True. Hearing I had to wait for more info would drive me nuts, but I had to look Sadie in the eye when I told her. *I know.*

When are you free? Sadie asked.

No clue. Today is going to be nuts.

Facetime us, Lyn said. *First thing in the morning tomorrow. We'll be waiting.*

Sounds fair. TTYL

The rest of my day could go that smoothly, and I wouldn't complain.

I dove into work.

A few minutes later, Luke joined me.

There wasn't much conversation. Deadlines called, and we both had a long to-do list that had grown even more with this morning's security breach.

Time ticked away, punctuated by the clack of fingers flying over keyboards.

Was Luke staring at me? I looked up to meet his gaze.

"You're adorable when you're focused. Have you ever noticed?" He asked.

How was I supposed to reply to that? The attention was amazing, but it also felt almost like too much. "Have I ever noticed how I look when I'm working? Can't say I have."

"I'm pouring on too much, aren't I?" He scrubbed his face. "It's been killing me, to keep my distance."

I should be concentrating on my work, but I couldn't turn away from this. "Why now? Not-that-I-mind." I swallowed, trying to gather my thoughts. "But, why now?"

"That kiss the other night undid me. Everything was right in that room."

"Including the broken code?"

Luke's smirk was worth the joke. "Maybe not that part. But when I saw you with Chase in the airport, I had to say something. This can't be a total surprise. I've never completely held back."

Yeah, but thanks to my past, I didn't trust the little voice in my head telling me, *he's flirting.* I still didn't completely trust it. I shouldn't be bothered that Luke was laying the attention on so heavily, if I needed a flashing beacon to get me to listen. Then again, I'd seen such bold affection mean bad things in the past. "I wasn't sure."

"And now?"

I still wasn't sure. How fucked up was that? "I'm looking forward to the discovery stage." And I wanted to change the subject. If I lingered on Luke while I was in the middle of overthinking him, I'd say things I couldn't take back. "We need to shift the QA schedule on the Groundrim final boss. We have before Sloth City, but the components won't be ready first." Work-talk—my trusty conversation fallback.

"Where are you looking?" Luke pushed back from his laptop and came around to stand behind me.

"Here." I pointed at the project timeline and forced myself to ignore how close he stood. That with the dip of his head, he could kiss my neck.

"Hmm." He leaned in, resting his hands on the table and bracketing my arms. "Make the change. Let Ben know." Ben was our project manager.

"Will do." I waited for Luke to pull away.

He didn't.

Did he expect me to work while he watched?

"I wish I'd been there on the plane." Luke's voice shifted, taking on a low, gravelly vibe.

Not what I was expecting. "So you could have stopped us?"

"No." He snorted. "I would have helped."

My mind blanked. Coated in a bucket of white, there was nothing there. "You're not jealous?" Was I missing something about this *competition*?

He rested his head against the back of my mine. "I would have watched. I would have helped." His words hummed through and around me. "If there was a lock on the conference-room door, I'd bend you over the table right now, and find out if you're as tight as I imagine."

God, there was no way I could ignore the desire spilling through me. Could we wedge a chair under the door handle? "And now we'll never get any work done again." It wasn't the most awkward thing I could have said, but it made the list.

"Sure we will. Same way we always have."

"You've got a lot more faith in us than I do," I teased. I needed this conversation to take a lighter turn.

"I've got absolute faith in you." Luke still had that deep, soul-seducing tone as he pulled away and returned to his seat.

I was wrong to think Chase was the intense one. Luke was going to consume me from the inside out.

Someone knocked on the conference room door, and Mike stepped into the room. "Do you guys have a minute?"

Sure. As soon as I dislodged my heart from my stomach. What if he'd done that two minutes earlier? Did I look guilty?

"What's up?" Luke sounded much calmer than I felt. I needed to learn that trick.

Mike pulled up a chair at the far end of the conference table. "We just got an email." He looked at me. "Are you all right? You look flushed."

Fuck. "I'm fine." I gave him a weak smile. "Long night. Distracted today. Email from whom?"

"Zane. Says he tracked down where the original upload came from. It was one of our remote build machines."

Zane was head of cyber security. The fact that he was handling this personally, rather than giving it to someone on his team, was another reminder of how critical the event was. I shoved the flirting from a moment earlier into a box, and opened my email. There wasn't much more information there than Mike provided. "So we still don't have anything."

"We do." Mike winced. "We have several other indicators that point to Billie. Logins. Change management."

That didn't seem right. "Zane doesn't mention those."

"We've been… uh… lax with security." The hesitation in Mike's tone hung heavy in the room. "With the tight deadlines. The crunch. Some things slip."

Nope. Still didn't buy it. His story had holes.

"You're sharing login information?" Luke sounded as skeptical as I felt.

Mike shook his head like a bobble in an earthquake. "No. Of course not. Not passwords or anything. But someone is on the machine, and they let another dev hop on to look at shared work. And Billie… She's been off lately." He looked at Luke. "Hitting on a couple of the guys. Making everyone uncomfortable with certain jokes."

Mike's biggest excuse seemed to be *we don't like following protocol*, and if that bit everyone in the ass, I was going to be pissed. But his story felt more *off* the longer he talked. I knew Billie. She'd been with the company for a couple of years, and she was top notch. She was also reserved and mostly kept to herself. I had a hard time seeing her as being on the giving end of sexual harassment, intentional or not.

But if Mike felt uncomfortable with her, was it my place to judge? "You talked to HR?" I asked.

He never looked at me. "It's not a big deal. But if she's taking things too far…"

"Why would she go from dirty jokes to corporate sabotage?" I was missing something.

He kept his attention on Luke. "*You* wanted information about the situation here. I'm providing it."

"Answer Anne's question," Luke said.

I appreciated the support, but not that it had to be offered. If my face was red now, it was thanks to the irritation flickering inside.

Mike rolled his eyes. "I don't know why Billie would fuck us all out of our jobs because we didn't like a few of her pussy jokes. Maybe you should ask her."

"You're the one making the suppositions. I'm asking you." I let anger slide into my tone.

"And I gave you an answer. What are you pissed about?"

Being ignored. Talked down to. Hearing another female programmer take the blame out of the gate. Was I in the wrong?

The moment the question popped into my head, I wanted to flatten it with a mallet, but it was here now and it wasn't leaving.

Would I have put up the same kind of opposition if he'd been talking about one of the guys on the team? Did that make me the bad guy?

"That's all I needed to know." I kept the self-doubt out of my retort and stared at my screen, trying to force my brain to stop sabotaging me.

"Thanks for the info. Keep us both posted," Luke said. "Wait," he added, when Mike reached for the door. "Anne's right to ask."

"Of course she is." Mike left.

I liked that Luke had my back, but now that I was questioning things, his support got tacked onto the list. Why wouldn't he take my side? He was trying to fuck me.

He would have backed me up anyway.

But he's been watching me a lot longer than I realized. Because I'm shit at reading a situation.

Not true.

Isn't it?

Best thing to do when my mind was plotting to undo me like this was focus on coding. Something I tended to get right, because I could follow a list of rules and not have to interpret anything. No more people decisions for me.

ELEVEN

My nagging brain plus an early morning flight plus no sleep last night sank into my bones. As the clock drew closer to five, I felt like I'd been compressed to preserve bandwidth, and parsed incorrectly on the other side.

The fun with Chase and Luke this morning felt like someone else's life.

My phone buzzed at the same time as Luke's chimed, and we executed a perfect ballet of reaching for the devices. It was a group text from Chase.

Would you rather stay in?

I'd drop a lot for their company, either of them, even before this, but I wasn't up for exploring the city. If I turned him down, would the fun end?

"I'm not going to answer on your behalf, but I also won't be offended if you tell him *yes*," Luke said.

"What about sushi?" I spoke the words aloud as I typed them. Was that silly? Luke would read my reply, but he was also sitting in the room with me.

Chase replied seconds later. *They deliver. Besides, you've had a long few days, and my money says you don't want to go out. I don't care where we are, as long as I have your company.*

That was sweet. Almost cheesy, but in a way that warmed me from the inside out. *Okay. Let's stay in.*

Meet you both at the hotel, Chase wrote.

Luke and I finished work with minimal conversation. The pauses were comfortable, like what I was used to, as long as I didn't think too much about the night ahead. Every time I started down that path, I ran into so many questions, my brain stalled. Did they really expect me to choose between them? So far, it didn't feel like it. How did this work tonight? I was used to dinner with either of them, but together as more than friends...? What was I supposed to tell Sadie and Lyn in the morning? Was this a good idea?

I had to shake it all aside, or I'd freeze up from indecision and doubt. Or worse, I'd pick an answer to each question, and it would be the wrong one.

Chase wasn't at the hotel yet, but we needed to check in anyway. There was only one person behind the counter, so Luke let me go first.

I gave the desk clerk a friendly smile and my name.

She typed. And then some more. A line creased her forehead. "I'm sorry—can you spell your last name for me again?"

"Fortier. F. O. R. T. I. E. R. And it's *Anne* with an *e.*"

"Like the show?" She smiled.

"Exactly."

She typed a bit more. "I'm sorry. I don't see a reservation for you."

No big deal. My name wasn't in there quite right or something. "Maybe *Anne* without an *e*? Or my last name is wrong?"

She shook her head. "We don't have reservations for any *Annes* tonight. Regardless of spelling."

"Is there an issue?" Luke joined me.

"She can't find my reservation." I wasn't near panic, but I was getting concerned.

He frowned. "Look under *Luke Rider.*"

The desk clerk worried her bottom lip. "You're not in here either."

"We are. My assistant made the reservations yesterday." Luke grabbed his phone, jabbed the screen a few times, and showed it to her. "Here's the confirmation email from our travel agency."

She looked between phone and computer, typing some more. Clicking. "I'm sorry. That information isn't in here. And we don't have any available rooms. We're full up because of evacuations and such. I'm sorry."

Luke clenched his jaw, and tension ran through his frame. When he looked like this, he was almost scary. A starkly abrupt reminder of the Marine past he never talked about.

He stepped away with a glance at me. "Let me make some calls."

The travel agency was closed for the day, so we split up the list of nearby hotels and started making calls. I got the same answer with my first three, and it didn't sound like Luke's luck was any better.

Chase arrived, and his smile when his gaze met mine chased away the stress.

"What's going on?"

Luke's groan of frustration echoed around us.

I gave Chase a brief rundown of our lack of accommodations.

He held up his index finger. "Don't go anywhere." He approached the desk and exchanged words, ID, and a credit card with the woman who hadn't been able to help us. Her frown vanished by the end of the conversation.

I understood how she felt.

Chase joined us again and handed us each a keycard.

"Must be nice to have all those frequent-traveler points." Luke's tone was light, with the slightest twinge.

Chase gave him a dry smile. "Not as nice as you're assuming. They still don't have any extra rooms, but I have double queen beds, and the couch pulls out, so all three of us can share a room. If you're interested."

"I'm in." My reply slipped out without thought. I'd spent a large portion of my teenage years sleeping at Sadie and Chase's. Luke's raised eyebrow made me wish I could take the words back.

"Me too." Luke shrugged. "I'm not missing out again if anything happens."

"Sleepover." I tried to toss the word out with careless abandon, and not think about whether it sounded silly or not. And I definitely wasn't thinking about the implications of Luke's reply.

Just kidding. I totally was.

"I don't have enough hair to style, but I'll rock the flimsy teddy," Luke said. "This includes giggly pillow fights, right?"

Chase rolled his eyes. "That's not how a sleepover works. We're going to need a lot of pizza and to expect not to sleep."

"That's not a sleepover; that's my life." The teasing made it easier to ignore my trepidation about what this might become. These were the same two men I always laughed and joked with. Just because they'd shifted our relationships in the last few days… "Besides, I was promised sushi."

Luke bowed deeply. "And sushi you shall have, m'lady."

Chase grabbed my bags before I could, and we headed upstairs.

The room was one of those business suites with a separate bedroom and a reasonably sized living room.

Luke tossed his bag near the sofa as soon as we walked in the room. "I'll take the couch."

"That doesn't seem fair. Shouldn't we draw straws or something?" While I had no idea what to expect from tonight, it was nice to know he hadn't just assumed we'd end up in bed together. Sweet, even.

Chase opened his mouth.

"Nope." Luke cut him off. "It's Chase's room, that he was kind enough to share, and neither of us is letting you sleep on the couch, Anne."

"That's true. I was going to say that. He just beat me to it," Chase said.

It still didn't feel right. "Am I allowed to argue this logic?"

They both shook their heads, and Chase put my bags in the

bedroom. "Ordering the sushi," he called. "Tell me if there's anything you won't eat."

"Pretty sure everyone here's fine with any sort of meat," Luke said.

That was true, whether he was talking food or sexual preference, and the way things were going today, I assumed both were legitimate topics.

We made small talk and caught up on each other's days, while we waited for food to arrive. No one sat next to anyone, which felt odd. But cramming three people onto the couch so we could all be together, or any combination of pairing off also seemed weird.

How was this supposed to work?

Dinner was more of the same. When we were done, we drifted into the bedroom, to watch TV *someplace more comfortable*, but that left the awkward question of who was supposed to sit where.

I'd never dated two guys at once before, especially not at the exact same moment. Was this a date? Was this three friends hanging out?

"Three people in one tiny space, sharing a single bathroom. Just like college." Chase's comment was a welcome distraction from my questions.

Luke raised an eyebrow. "Including the sexual experimentation?"

"I'd pretty much moved onto the *doing* rather than *experimenting* by then," Chase said.

"I'm more of a late bloomer." I let the reply roll casually off my tongue. It wasn't a secret in our inner circle that I was bi, but I dated mostly men, so sometimes claiming anything other than *straight* felt like I was an impostor. "I never even thought about it until Shawn." It didn't matter how much time had passed. His name was rancid on my tongue.

Chase's distorted expression mirrored my bitterness. I didn't want to ruin the evening with bad memories. Why did I bring up my ex?

"Who's Shawn?" Luke looked between us.

Chase mimicked spitting. "A fucking asshole."

That's what everyone said back then, too. I wished I'd listened to my friends, rather than the boyfriend who ran my ego into the ground. "A guy I went out with." I didn't want to leave Luke hanging, but I wasn't going to linger on details. How little information would let us move back to more fun topics? "He used to tease me about the kind of porn I like. Would ask me all the time if I was a secret lesbian who was going to leave him for a woman. After he and I broke up, I started talking about it with…" Another confession. What was up with me spilling so many secrets tonight?

Luke and Chase both leaned in. "With whom?" they asked at the same time.

"A friend. We're talking about experimentation, right? She helped me figure a few things out." There. Conversation was back to neutral. We could have fun again.

Chase frowned. "Wait. Not Sadie. Please say not Sadie."

"Why? Because you still think you can say who your sister hooks up with?" I tried to keep the defensive tone from my voice.

"No. Because then the story isn't spank-bank material."

My cheeks heated to flaming. He was… to me? "It wasn't Sadie. It was Lyn."

Luke whistled. "He's right. Definitely fantasy material."

"That's not fair." My retort slipped out before I could stop it. Why? Because I'd been trying for so long to *not* fantasize about either of them? "You get new visuals, and I don't?"

Chase smirked. "You've got a better imagination. Picture me with whomever you'd like."

"No, she's right. Fair's fair." Luke crushed his mouth to Chase's.

TWELVE

The way Luke kissed Chase wasn't a simple peck on the lips. It was one of those hungry, all-consuming kisses I felt just from watching. The kind where I knew exactly why they were both groaning and breathless.

When they broke apart, Chase growled. "I'm definitely in for that."

"Totally hot and masturbation-worthy." I fanned myself.

Luke turned his attention back to me. "What other fantasies do you have?"

"Well... I have one, but it's risqué. Almost taboo in today's society."

Both guys leaned in closer.

"A full week off work without being called in, and eight hours of sleep on every one of those nights," I said.

Chase licked his bottom lip. "I always suspected you had a filthy, kinky side."

Luke tossed up his hands. "Too much for me. You're way out of my depth."

"What did you have in mind?" I asked with a laugh.

"I'll show you how it starts." Chase grasped my fingertips and tugged me to my feet. He cradled my face. His kiss had the same intensity as those we shared on the plane—soft but insistent and all-consuming. He nibbled my lips. My jaw. My ears and neck. The drawn-out attention sent goosebumps racing over me.

All while Luke watched. If he was enjoying this even half as much as I liked seeing the two of them kiss, that made the whole thing even hotter. It didn't matter that Chase kept his kisses above my shoulders; my entire body was a live wire.

I didn't know how long we stayed pressed together, but when he pulled back he wore a lazy grin. "That's how the fantasy *starts*."

"It's a fair appetizer." Luke stepped forward.

My gaze dropped to his crotch without thought. When I saw the outline of his erection, it took a moment to look up again.

He was smirking. "My fantasies tend to be more direct. We start with the main course."

"Which is?" I was enjoying this game, especially with Luke looking at me like I was dinner.

He pressed his hand to my throat, applying just enough weight to nudge me back against the wall. He crushed his mouth to mine and his body to mine and devoured my moans and gasps. It was only a kiss, but the way we fit together, the way my body molded to his, the way his hard form teased every inch of me drew me to life. It was intense and terrifying and incredible. Especially when he squeezed his thumb in, making my head light.

I gasped for more when he pulled away. He glanced at Chase. "Do you have a comeback?"

"I'm enjoying the show too much for that."

"*That's* one of my fantasies." It was easier to admit it when someone else said it.

Luke's grin was dangerous. "Being used and fucked for an audience who gets off on your pleasure?"

His phrasing made me tingle everywhere. "Yes."

Luke guided me to the widest space of empty floor between the foot of the beds. The way Chase watched me and Luke still gripped my neck, combined with their lingering kisses on my skin, had an insistent pulse throbbing between my legs.

Luke moved to stand behind me and glided his hands up my sides, under my shirt. His palms were hot and rough. "Arms up."

I complied, and he tugged my shirt over my head. Technically, my bra wasn't any more revealing than a bikini top, which Chase had seen me in more times than I could count, but this felt different. My heart hammered against my ribs.

Luke pushed my jeans to the floor, and like that, I was standing in the middle of a hotel room in nothing but a bra and panties, while two gorgeous guys stared at me.

The lust and desire filling the air were almost tangible. I couldn't remember ever being more aroused.

Luke unsnapped my bra and slid it down my arms. In a move so fluid I barely registered how he did it, he tugged my hands behind my back and had them bound with the lingerie.

He slapped one of my ass cheeks.

I sucked in a sharp breath through my teeth. Not what I expected.

"Is that a good gasp or a bad one?" he asked.

"Definitely good."

Luke alternated sides, slapping one butt cheek then the other, each smack reverberating through the room. The sound was as much a turn-on as the lingering sting.

He glided his hand lightly along the curve of my ass. I was torn between closing my eyes and sinking into the abruptly gentle touch, or watching Chase watch me.

Luke slipped his hand between my legs from behind and pressed into the crotch of my panties, drawing a new moan. He teased through fabric until I was swaying with his touch. He shoved the cotton aside and slipped two fingers into me without warning. "*Fuck,* baby doll. You're soaked. You like a little filth in your life?"

"Yes." My reply came out timid and breathy. The sensation of having something inside me was delicious.

"Sweet, sweet Anne." He pumped. In and out. In and out. Deeper with each thrust. "I guess it's true what they say—the nerdy ones can be extra dirty."

Could I be? I never had been before—not with anything but

what I watched online—but Luke's tone and Chase's gaze made me want to bend to their will. "I'll be whatever you want."

"Mmm… I like the sound of that." Luke withdrew, and I whimpered with disappointment. "What if I want you to beg?"

"Please?" I poured my desperation into the word.

Luke didn't touch me, but his breath caressed my neck. "*Please what?*"

"Please make me come?"

Luke and Chase both groaned.

"Since you asked so sweetly…" Luke slipped his hand between my legs again.

I moaned when he found my clit. I was so wound up, it didn't take much circling and stroking, to draw me to orgasm. Waves of pleasure crashed over me, and I ground into his hand until it was too much and my body jerked away.

Luke pressed into my back, one hand on my stomach, keeping me stable when my legs wobbled underneath me. He shoved his sticky fingers into my mouth. "Tell me how good you taste, baby doll."

"So good." My words were muffled by his fingers. I'd never understood the fascination with this, but right now it was better than candy. I sucked greedily, driven by his groans of encouragement.

Chase stepped up to kiss me. Our tongues mingled with each other and around Luke's fingers. So apparently this *could* get hotter.

"Seems I can only watch for so long," Chase murmured between licks and kisses.

"I'm as happy to have you here as over there," I said.

"I know I said earlier you didn't owe me, and you don't. But since we're talking about fantasies, on the plane—and several other places throughout my life—I was absolutely dreaming of your lips wrapped around my cock." he said.

I stared at Chase with wide eyes and licked my lips. Did that look sultry? I hoped so. "Okay."

"Kneel on the corner of the bed." Luke's tone left no room for argument.

I did, then I crawled toward Chase and, holding his gaze, grabbed his zipper between my teeth and tugged it down.

The gravel in his moan was intoxicating when I kissed along the hard outline in his trousers.

He freed himself, and I flicked my tongue over the head of his cock, before taking him into my mouth.

Looking up at him as he watched me sent a fresh rush of need pulsing through me. I licked and sucked, using his grunts as cues.

When he knotted his fingers in my hair, holding me in place, I gasped. He struck the back of my throat. I bit back the gag and relaxed around his length.

I heard the tear of foil. A condom? A moment later, Luke glided his cock along my slit, startling me and cranking my arousal higher. He slipped up and down a few times, before gliding inside me. "Fuuuuck." He gripped my hips tightly. "I love seeing you like this. Flushed. Wet. Sucking on a thick cock while I'm buried balls deep in your cunt. So fucking sexy."

His crude words were as enticing as any touch and spurred me on. I wanted him to fuck me, fill me up, and whisper filthy things in my ear forever, while he called me *baby doll*. I shouldn't like the nickname, but the way Luke said it, I wanted to be his everything.

I rocked between the two men, falling into a haze of ecstasy. The pace picked up. Luke pounded harder. Chase struck the back of my throat with every thrust, though he had his fist wrapped around the base of his cock.

"*God*, Annie. I'm so close." Chase pulled back, stroking his shaft.

I stared up at him, desire and desperation coursing through me. "Come in my mouth?" I pleaded.

That earned me another pair of grunts that felt like the most delicious praise, and Chase forced himself between my lips again.

A salty spurt hit the back of my throat, and then kept going. The noises Chase made, sharp and punctuated, were a million tiny fingers dancing over my skin.

He knelt to kiss me, licking himself from my lips. He reached a hand between my legs. When he found my clit, my body shuddered away, still tender.

Luke covered Chase's fingers before he could withdraw, and used both their hands to stroke my clit.

Orgasm rushed up fast, tearing a scream from my throat and flooding my entire body. I clenched around the shaft buried inside me. I felt like all of me opened up.

Luke's grunts grew punctuated then stuttered, reaching a frantic pace, before he slowed to a stop. We all sat there, panting. The cool air kissed the sweat from my skin, and Luke trailed his tongue up my spine, doing the same.

"I think you left a wet spot," he muttered.

I'd never done that before. "Sorry."

"Never be sorry for that." Chase was studying me with adoration that made my pulse kick up again.

"I guess we'll have to use the other bed." Most of the growl was gone from Luke's voice, but I still heard the undercut.

My dreams were going to be filled with wet, sticky sex and *baby doll* for a long time.

THIRTEEN

We cleaned up and collapsed in the other bed.

I felt more exposed than I was used to. Pinned between Luke and Chase was the perfect way to be. I kind of loved this feeling of being vulnerable but safe with them. Like I could let my guard down here.

And the happy fuzziness in my brain was blocking out most of the *but what now?* questions that had nagged me all day.

"You're not really going to sleep on the couch, are you?" I asked Luke.

"As opposed to…"

If none of us moved, things would be perfect forever. "We could all sleep here. Like this."

"It's a tight fit." Chase squeezed my hip. The gentle gesture felt possessive. And perfect.

"That's what she said." Luke grinned.

I laughed. Nothing had changed, except that we'd all just had the dirtiest sex I'd ever been part of. Just a teensy, tiny, tremendous thing.

Behind me, Chase shifted. "If you both want to stay here, I don't mind. We'll just have to snuggle close."

"Yes, please." That sounded so completely right. Even better than a week of regular sleep.

Luke kissed the tip of my nose. "Is this what you had in mind when you said *sleepover?*"

"It will be going forward. Past sleepovers for me have involved a lot more talking and a lot less fingering." Not counting the experimentation with Lyn.

Chase sighed heavily. "Fantasies dashed."

"What fantasies?" Luke looked past me. "You were in the same house when these things happened, as I understand it."

"Yeah, but that was no man's land," Chase said. "I was *not* allowed in that part of the house when the girls were over."

They'd confessed their long-term attraction. I could do the same. "I never would have minded."

"See? You miss one-hundred percent of the shots you don't take," Luke said.

Chase made a gagging sound. "Did you just motivational-poster us?"

"It *was* kind of creepy." I had to agree. "Can't you say that in a funny voice—maybe Jerry Seinfeld or something—and take the edge off?"

"Out on the edge, you can see all sorts of things you can't see from the center." Luke finished the phrase with a stoic look that was disrupted by his trying not to smirk.

I knew that one. "Vonnegut? You're full of wisdom tonight."

"He's full of something." Every time Chase spoke, his chest hummed against my back.

Luke tucked a strand of hair behind my ear. "Adoration, horniness, and fuck-you-till-you-screamitude."

"You didn't exhaust your supply with the last round?" I was pleasantly sleepy.

"Hmm…" Luke screwed up his face. "Gorgeous woman in my arms, and my naked cock pressed against your bare stomach? Easy supply to replenish."

I smirked at the twitch against my abdomen.

"Wait. You're buying this? I can do motivational quotes too," Chase said.

I only had so much appreciation for that sort of thing, even wrapped up in two men and post-coital bliss. "Please don't. Let's just say I don't like him because of the quotes; I like him in spite of them."

"I could serenade you instead." Chase sang the first few stanzas of "Twisted Transistor" by Korn, in the sweetest baritone ever.

"Hauntingly disturbing." I did like his voice, though. In fact, everything about this evening was pretty much perfect.

THE FAINT STRAINS OF "HEATHENS" by Twenty-One Pilots infiltrated my dreams and dragged me awake. I forced myself to sit. The only custom ringtone I had, because Lyn, Sadie, and I all had the same songs for each other.

"'S'wrong?" Sleep lined Luke's question.

"Nothing. Call from my friends. I need to get this." What was I supposed to tell them? Would they hear the shower running in the background? *Oh yeah, that's Chase. No big deal. Hey, did you know your brother is hung like—*

No reason to give them that level of detail. I'd be surface-level honest.

I raked my fingers through my hair, and pulled on a camisole as I dug my phone out of my purse. "Hey," I finally answered.

My best friends' faces smiled back at me. "We wake you?" Sadie asked.

"It's only six here. I'm surprised you're up before ten," I teased.

She stuck her tongue out. "We were promised secrets. Now that we're face-to-face, spill."

"It's not a big deal." Saying that, instead of telling them made it sound exactly the opposite, didn't it?

A door squeaked behind me.

"Do you want to build it up some more?" Lyn asked. "Add a few more qualifiers?" Her tone was light.

I let out a nervous laugh. "No. So here's the thing——"

"Hey, guys." Chase pressed into my back. His chest was hot against my exposed shoulder blades.

My stomach dropped into my shoes, as I stared at two faces working their jaws. This wasn't the way I wanted to tell them. "There was a fuckup with our reservations, so Chase let us crash with him."

That was innocent enough. Except the memories summoned by his fingers dancing along my waist were anything but.

"That was why you forgot to tell us you landed?" Was Sadie's tone flatter, or was I just expecting it to be?

The tiny image of me in the bottom right corner of my screen showed Chase, waving. "That was our fault." His tone was light and casual. "We distracted her by telling her how desperately we want her."

Really?

"*God,* could you not?" Sadie's retort reminded me this was normal for us. Chase had been doing this to me for years. He'd make a flirty comment, she'd tell him to stop, and I'd write it all off as Chase being Chase.

Except I knew better now. They hadn't been throwaway comments on his part.

"Wait. *We?*" Lyn said.

I glanced at Luke, who was sitting in bed, watching the whole exchange silently.

"Do you... Should I...?" I didn't know how to phrase my question.

Luke nodded. "I trust them to be discreet." Rinslet had a barely-existent fraternization policy, but a manager fucking a direct report was still frowned upon.

I turned my camera toward him, and he wiggled his fingers.

"Is that... *Score.*" Lyn's enthusiasm sent pleased embarrassment rushing through me. "Is this a dating thing?"

This was awkward from both directions. My friends had metaphorically walked into the bedroom the morning after, before the guys left, and plopped down on the bed to ask for details. And the guys stuck around to listen. "Kind of. Yes. I mean, not like Sadie's thing."

"A test drive. I get that." Lyn sounded completely unfazed.

"Sadie?" I asked. Her silence and flat expression had me worried.

She shrugged. "You grew up together. Isn't that weird?"

Even though her question mimicked my earlier thoughts, defensiveness filled me. "So did you and Jax."

"True." Sadie's tone wasn't as convincing as I'd hoped. "I get it. I mean not really, because eww… but I guess if I weren't related, I could see the attraction to Chase. And your boss? Score." Her smile was a relief.

"That's what I said," Luke called.

This wasn't bad. Much closer to best-case scenario than worst. "So we're good?" I asked.

"As long as no one hurts anyone's feelings, we're fine." Sadie winked.

"And also, as long as you make time for us still between work and your fuck boys," Lyn added.

I grinned. "Deal. Talk to you soon." I disconnected and dropped my phone back in my purse.

Pleasant shivers raced over me when Chase nuzzled my ear. "Feel better, now that you have Moms' permission?"

"Could you not?" I mimicked Sadie's words from earlier, my tone as light as my mood.

Luke climbed from the bed to join us, and stood in front of me. "I like the idea of being a fuck boy. It's got a ring to it." He lifted my chin, and I met his gaze. "You were right yesterday."

"About what?"

"It's going to be hard to get any work done today."

My smile grew. The silly one that had flitted in and out since last night. "We'll manage. You have faith in me."

"Smart man." Chase settled his hands on my hips.

This was perfectly delicious. I could handle being sandwiched between the two of them over and over and over. "We don't *have* to go into the office, do we?" I let disappointment mingle with teasing.

"You probably should." Chase planted a row of kisses up the side of my neck.

I tilted my head, to give him better access, careful not to break away from Luke's touch. "Easy for you to say. You're not going with us."

"This went so much better than we planned." Luke murmured against my lips.

My laugh faded as his words sank in, dragging ice through my veins. "*Planned?*"

FOURTEEN

B ehind me, Chase stopped moving. He felt frozen in place.
Luke pulled back to study me with concern.

"What do you mean, *we planned?*" Nagging whispers about potential definitions chewed at my thoughts, but I wasn't going to make any assumptions. I wanted to hear the truth. It would be fun. Funny, even. And then we'd go back to playful kisses and taking too long to get ready for work.

Chase moved into view, a reassuring smile on his face. He couldn't hide the hesitation underneath. "Nothing. We've talked before about how we're both attracted to you. *Planned* isn't really the right word for that."

"No, it's not." My concerns were growing, rather than rushing away. Shawn lied to me so many times when we dated. Cast so much doubt back on me. Made me question myself—my feelings. I never saw it until we broke up.

Was I missing it again?

Chase was a friend. So was Luke. They wouldn't—

"*Planned* is the right word for it." Luke sighed. "Calling it anything else is bullshit."

Nope. Nuh-uh. I would not jump to conclusions. "What is *it?*" I looked at Chase. "Tell me straightforward-like. Don't wrap it up pretty."

Chase pinched the bridge of his nose.

"When hooked up, your name came up," Luke said. "I'd tell you I don't know how, but you were there in every other tangent. It came out that we both like you. Care about you. Would like more than friendship."

That was sweet. So why did it taste rancid? "Okay?"

"I admitted I was holding back for the same reasons you hesitated—our shared friends." Chase pulled on a pair of trousers over his boxer briefs.

"Luke was hesitating because he's my boss." An explanation I was sick of hearing. Not because it was an invalid reason, but I didn't see a way around it, and that obstacle nagged at me. None of this eased how much the word *planned* bothered me. "And?"

Luke stood with his feet shoulder-width apart, hands clasped behind his back. "I had another reason for waiting, but it's related. You're not going to be working for me much longer."

They couldn't fire me, could they? "After everything I've done? All the hours I've put in? I'm on the chopping block?" I mean yeah, our game launch had been the worst in the company's history and I was a team lead, but I'd tried. My heart hammered against my ribs, and my breath came in short gasps. This wasn't—

"*No.*" Luke was emphatic. "No one is firing you. I promise. The opposite. You're not supposed to know this, but after the game launches, Scott wants to move you into a Design Director position. He's just waiting."

The wheels in my brain spun freely, not snagging anything. Not processing anything. Promotion. Not working for Luke, but with him. Recognition for the months of long hours. Having a say in the direction of games. My dream job. "Basically, everyone's just… waiting?" More motivation to finish the game. Like I needed another reason.

"Exactly." Luke's smile was tentative.

I should leave things as they were. This was a happy outcome. I mean, until I had to pick a guy, or things didn't work out with either of them, but there was no reason to go into dating assuming the relationship would fail. "But that's not what you mean by *we planned.*"

Chase winced. "We agreed neither one of us would pursue you until we both could. He made a move early, and I didn't want to miss my chance."

"And?" I wasn't hearing anything bad, per se, but they radiated guilt. The backstory was nice, but it didn't answer the original question. And why did Luke's phrasing make them look like they'd been caught with their dicks out?

"We may have made a bet about which one of us could win you over." Luke grimaced with each word. "The prize is you."

They made a wager, and I was the reward? My jaw dropped. Apparently that was a thing that really happened. I tried to find a response, but anything I would have said would sound more like a low keening than words.

"It's not like what you're thinking." Chase reached for me.

I stepped back until I collided with the dresser.

"It was a stupid way to phrase things." Luke hadn't moved from his at-ease stance. "I care about you. Not a stupid bet."

"Yeah, but you agreed to it anyway. Not only that, but you meant it enough that you still think of me in those terms." My voice came back, fueled by anger, hurt, and disbelief. "I can't— You really — A fucking bet? Am I supposed to be flattered that you think I can be won and traded? Spoiler alert—I'm not."

Chase took a step toward me. "Annie."

"No." I held up my hand, index finger out, as a warning. I saw two choices—curl up in a ball and sob for the next decade, or swallow this horrific feeling and go back to work. I wouldn't pretend none of it had happened, but I would ignore the giant pit in my gut that enjoyed any part of it. "Don't call me that. Don't touch me. Don't come near me. Guess what? You both lose."

"Please. I'm sorry." Luke's posture softened, but he kept his distance.

I grabbed a change of clothes from my luggage and focused on keeping myself from shaking. From breaking. Was the room part of their plan? This trip? The seat upgrade had been. How much didn't I know? "I'm going to shower. And when we get to work, I'm going to pretend nothing's different. And Jamie is going to spend the day finding me a new room."

"All right," Luke said.

I stormed into the bathroom, slamming the door behind me. I barely managed to get my clothes off before stepping under the shower. The water shifted from lukewarm to too hot, and I didn't care. I needed the sound to drown out any sobs that slipped out with the tears streaming down my face.

FIFTEEN

My eyes were clear and my resolve was steel when I emerged from the bathroom, ready to confront the day. Chase was gone.

Seeing Luke sent a wash of uncertainty through me.

"Anne..."

"Nope." I couldn't say more. Wouldn't bend to the doubt.

He sighed. "Give me fifteen minutes, and we can head into the office."

A little more time to compose myself. I'd passed that first hump of looking Luke in the eye again. I could do this. I just had to treat him the way everyone else did. Not like a friend or a crush or more.

I hadn't been here long enough to unpack much, so gathering my luggage didn't take time. A tiny thing to be grateful for that didn't make me feel any better.

Luke was my boss. That was it. He'd reminded me many times in the last few days.

Chase was probably going to be harder to shove aside, but I could focus on one thing at a time. After work tonight, I'd go back to my own room and probably not see Chase again until the week was up.

Easy peasy.

Another wave of sobs bubbled up in my throat, and I clenched my fist until it passed. I wouldn't cry over something like this. Last night was fun. I misunderstood the purpose, but now I knew, and I hadn't technically lost anything or anyone.

Not really.

Only two people I considered friends.

But once I recovered from the shock, we could be friends again.

Maybe.

Just not anything more.

An ache pinged behind my ribs.

I could do this.

I didn't give Luke more than a glance when he finished his shower. Partly to drive home my anger, but as much to keep my resolve from crumbling.

Luke tried a few times to initiate conversation, but I didn't say more than was needed.

Rain drowned the world as we drove into the office. It mingled with the smoke in the air. Usually, I loved the rain, but today the news said the high winds and lightning were increasing the fire spread and risk.

There was probably some sort of metaphor for my current situation in there. I wasn't going to think about it.

As we approached the building, I boxed up my hurt inside steel and ice. I'd spent years pretending I wasn't attracted to Luke. I could live on the other side of the coin, too.

We arrived before half the office, but Mike was already here.

Luke grabbed his attention as we walked in the door. "I need a room where I can meet with some of your people today without disturbing Anne."

"Sure. I'd like to be in those meetings," Mike said.

Made sense. They were Mike's people

Move you into a Design Director position. Luke's news echoed in my thoughts. I should be celebrating that. Doing giddy mental dances every time I thought about it. But I was stuck in the emotional mire instead. With Luke holding meetings, I'd have a while to ponder.

That was good, unless I thought myself into a pit I couldn't climb out of.

Luke nodded at Mike. "Get me a room. I'll include you on the invites."

I turned away and headed toward my—our—temporary office. I was halfway down the hall when I heard Mike.

"Anne. Hold up." He jogged to catch up with me.

I gave him my practiced smile. "What's up?"

"Are you all right?"

"Totally fine. Why?" I was more out of sorts than I thought, if Mike noticed. He'd never struck me as an observer of people.

He shrugged. "Just an impression. I know everything is stressful right now. Trust me, I know. If you need an ear from someone who gets it…"

I wouldn't be talking to him. I forced my smile to reach my eyes. "Thanks. I appreciate it."

Maybe I'd misjudged him. From every other time we'd ever spoken.

I set up my laptop and tried to dive into work. After a few false starts, I managed to lose myself in admin tasks.

"Hey." Luke's tone was quiet when he interrupted a few hours later. "Lunch?"

I shook my head and kept my eyes on my screen. I'd walk down the street and grab something quick when he was gone. The more time I could spend engrossed in my work, the less I had to think about how Luke and Chase used me as a prize in a dick measuring contest.

"Before I go, Jamie's been calling around off and on all morning. She hasn't found any rooms yet, but she'll keep trying," he said.

I didn't want to keep her from her work. True, this was part of her job, but— "Don't worry about it." My voice was raw. "I'll sleep on the couch."

"A—"

I glared at him. "The couch is fine."

"All right." Luke left again.

I let out a long sigh and dropped my face into my hands. I hated this. Why did they have to… Why couldn't they have just… They could have just told me.

Then again, I could have done the same, instead of making assumptions and swimming in fantasy for so long.

That didn't make what they'd done any more right. I couldn't forget that. They'd bet me as a prize.

I turned my attention back to my laptop.

Well, *attention* was a loose term. I wasn't focused on anything. The email from Zane was a welcome distraction.

Rumor was, more than a decade ago, before the company was even known as *Rinslet*, he'd hacked their network and distributed a release version of a game weeks early.

He'd been hired to keep people like him from doing the exact same thing, and while this situation wasn't identical, I wondered if it ate at him that it happened under his watch.

His email might as well have been in a foreign language. I understood enough to know it contained computer names and IP addresses, but the rest escaped me.

I called him on my cell phone, in case I needed to wander to someplace more private. "Tell me what I'm looking at."

"Someone, presumably from Team Percival, hopped almost every development machine in the building, to connect and upload that content."

That didn't make any sense. Rather, I understood what he meant, but not why anyone would do it. "Indulge me and let me talk through this?" I said.

"Sure."

"Typically, a person hops connection points to hide their location." The concept was, as I understood it, to use one internet connection to get to another and another and another, until it was difficult or impossible to find out where they'd started. "Which means they wouldn't want all those points in the same place, and they'd prefer unsecured or at least less secure spots to connect to."

Zane clucked. "Typically."

"So why do things this way?" I knew the answer, but I didn't want to believe it.

"Because they either want you to know it was them, or they want you to think it was someone very specific."

That was what I was afraid of. "Don't we have security to prevent this?"

"Security only works if people aren't sharing passwords."

I wanted to ask my last question least of all. I saw the answer in his message, but maybe he'd tell me I'd interpreted things wrong. "Who does it point to?"

"Wilma Clayton."

Billie. The woman Mike indicated. One of our best Percival devs. It couldn't be what it looked like. But unlike people, data didn't lie.

If I told Luke about this, would he fire her on the spot? "I need time to investigate," I said. "Leave this with me?"

"I understand, though I don't like it. I am going to force that entire team to change their passwords, right now."

That made sense. "What do I need to do?"

"Email everyone. Tell them they'll be locked out of their machines in five minutes. They can get back in when they change their passwords."

I was already typing. "Done. I'll keep you posted on the Billie thing, I promise."

"Be right about this, Anne."

I wanted to give him a confident *I am*. The best I could manage was, "Talk to you soon."

Seconds after I sent the message, I had a reply from Mike.

What do you think you're doing? This is my team. You can't make calls like this. Are you an idiot, or just trying to steal my job?

The harsh words sank under my skin, and I was typing a reply before I could process. *I'm sorry. The decision needed to be made right away. I didn't mean to step on your toes.*

I hit *Send* and sank back in my chair. I'd made a mistake, but was it in asking Zane for more time, or in cowering with Mike?

L uke didn't take issue with my decision to force the password change. *I trust you.* His assurance didn't soothe me the way I think he intended. Why couldn't I trust myself?

On the drive back to the hotel, Luke called Chase. Such great pals, they decided which of them got to date which woman and had each other's numbers.

Luke put the conversation on speaker, *to make sure everyone was on the same page,* and told Chase finding new rooms was a bust, so he'd have roommates again tonight.

So much for avoiding Chase.

I didn't say anything. I didn't know if it would be worse if I let the anger flow and wanted to take it back later, or forgave them when I wasn't sure that was the right thing to do.

With Shawn, every time we fought, he'd insist it was my fault. For saying the wrong thing. For overreacting. For making him mad.

I'd figured out after that wasn't the case, but my fucking brain still wavered on how to spot when I was interpreting things wrong. Especially here and now, with *them.*

Back at the hotel, I set up camp on the couch, pulled on my

headphones, and opened my laptop. If that didn't say, *leave me alone,* I didn't know what would.

Chase returned a short while later and stopped in front of me with a warm smile. "Hey."

I pointed at my headphones and stared back blankly.

"Annie…"

It didn't matter that my music mostly drowned him out. I saw his lips move. Saw them form my name. Heard his voice in my head. I clenched my jaw and stared at my computer screen again, refusing to look up until I saw his legs pass by and disappear into the other room.

I had to get over this, and now was as good a time to start as any. Work would distract me. Hopefully.

When I was talking to Zane earlier, I'd put the pieces together that, if someone used internal passwords to make their hops and release our spoiler info, they could have just as easily used Billie's info to frame her. The thought had nagged me since that conversation, and it was the biggest reason I hadn't looped Luke in yet. We should have fired Billie the moment I had the information, but my gut said not to.

My gut also said Luke would have listened to me, if I'd asked for time. But my gut lied a lot. What if I was wrong about Billie? What if I told Luke, and he fired her anyway, but she didn't do it?

I hated keeping this kind of secret, even though he'd lied to me. His sin wasn't corporate-espionage level; it was just Anne-is-gullible-and-fun-to-play-with level.

I didn't know where to start, to prove anything about Billie one way or the other. Her other work? On-network activities?

Like I'd done so many times in the past few months, I found myself staring at the version control system—the way we kept track of who was making changes to the code and what changes they'd made, in case we needed to roll back to something previously over-written. This had very little to do with leaking a series spoiler, except that we'd split the details up between teams, so no one had the full picture.

Sure, someone could put the pieces together and figure out the full story—a lot of fans had done that—but a direct script excerpt? Something no one had full access to, unless they had administrator-level rights to source control? Which would include a person with their manager's password?

Had *Mike* been in here, poking at things?

I stared for hours, but nothing clicked. It all looked normal. Billie had accessed a large number of files, but they were all ones she should be working with.

My gaze drifted to the computer clock, and when I saw it was almost nine, my stomach growled. There were no answers for me here tonight. Maybe when my head was clearer.

Time to grab some food then pretend I could sleep.

I closed my laptop, set it on the coffee table, and pulled off my headphones. The moment I could hear the world again, the faint sound of the TV in the other room rushed in to meet me. It would be so easy to walk the ten or twenty feet to the bedroom, and talk to Chase and Luke. But I couldn't. What if I did that, and I set myself up for more of the same?

The sound of a door opening drew my attention, and I looked up to see Chase emerge from the bathroom. I traveled my gaze up his body, over gray sweatpants and his bare chest, to his damp hair and captivating stare. God, he looked good. The past rushed back in a wave of longing and desire, of staying with Sadie and always hoping for a glimpse of something like this.

Fuck, that hurt.

"I really am sorry. Talk to me, please," he said.

I wanted to. Wanted it so desperately that part of me was willing to accept and agree with anything he said, to make things right. That was the problem—I'd cave, and they'd think they could do something like this again. The way Shawn used to.

I shook my head, grabbed my purse, and walked out of the room. My heart dove into my empty stomach with a *thunk*, and my brain warred with itself. I was being unreasonable. But I wasn't. But I was. But… I grabbed my phone, more out of habit than because I wanted to look at it.

There was a text and a missed call from Sadie. *Call me. Stat.*

It was an emergency. I'd been moping in my own thoughts all night, and she needed me. I dialed her number, and pressed my phone to my ear as I stepped off the elevator.

"Hey," she answered cheerfully on the first ring.

"Hey. Are you all right?" I wandered over to a tucked away corner of the lobby.

"Yeah. Are you?"

What? I settled onto a cushion that let me press my back to a pillar. "You're the one who sent an emergency message."

"You're my emergency," Sadie said. "I'm worried about you."

Realization spread through me, drawing a sad smile. "You talked to Chase."

"He didn't give me details. He just asked me to tell you he was sorry. Said you wouldn't hear it from him."

No. My thoughts revolted. I didn't like the idea of someone playing messenger on my behalf. "I heard him fine."

"What happened?" Sadie sounded concerned.

Which—of course she was. I might doubt Chase and Luke's motivations, but Sadie was my best friend. My sister. "Apparently, there was more to this whole *hitting on me* thing than he or Luke disclosed up front." I laid out the conversation from this morning for her. Bile coated my throat when I got to the part about the bet, but I made it through the whole story without falling into tears of frustration.

"Basically, Chase and Luke went out, and it didn't go anywhere because they both like you, and they talked about that." The way she said it made the whole thing sound simple and trivial.

Wasn't it?

I bit the inside of my cheek, to collect my thoughts before replying. "They discussed competing against each other to win me over. They made a bet. And they never bothered to tell me."

"Telling you kind of invalidates the bet, right?" Sadie laughed.

I didn't know how to respond. She was agreeing with every part of me that said I was being dumb.

"Jax and Grayson talked about dating me, before they approached me," she said.

"Jax and Grayson were already a couple, and they didn't talk about you like you were some sort of prize to be won. They didn't establish rules. Contest terms. A bet, about who could steal your heart first. Chase and Luke might as well be cashing in skeeball tickets for me. I don't even know if they like me or just liked the idea of the competition." The moment I spoke the words aloud, they latched onto a fear I hadn't given a name. Now it was real. And gut-wrenching.

"I think you're exaggerating. And of course they like you, Sadie said."

Was I? Exaggerating? Why did I feel justified in my reaction in that case? "This is exactly why I should have turned Chase down. I knew everyone would take sides." My gut had been right about that. "I didn't think…" The next words were harder to say. "I didn't think you'd be so completely on his. I thought you'd give me a little bit of—"

"I'm not completely on his side. I can hear in your voice that you're miserable, and this morning you were so happy, you were almost singing."

"They used me as the wager." I must not be making myself clear. What wasn't I saying right? "If I tell Chase this is no big deal, that my feelings on the matter aren't important as long as he *didn't mean anything bad* by it, how's that going to help me feel better?" I'd love an answer, because she was right. I felt like shit.

"That's not—"

"What you meant. Right. Silly Anne, misinterpreting things. Blowing her feelings out of proportion." The retort scraped through me like razor-bladed claws. It spoke to so many of the accusations Shawn threw at me every time we fought.

"That's not what you're doing."

"Forget it." I didn't trust her to say any more, or myself to hear either of us correctly. "Chase is *actually* family. I get that." I almost sobbed on the words. "I understand. Bye."

The instant I hung up, my phone rang again. Sadie.

I ignored the call.

And the next three, as I walked back to the elevator.

Her text came in as I stepped into the waiting car. *Call me back, please? Talk to me?*

Maybe she was right about what she'd said on the phone. Everyone was saying *please* and *I'm sorry*, and I was ignoring them.

But Shawn did that to me so many times—ignored my concerns and insisted if I didn't accept an apology, it was my fault. Who was I supposed to trust? The friends who'd always been there for me, or myself?

It shouldn't be a choice I had to make.

SEVENTEEN

I wasn't looking forward to spending another morning commute of not talking to Luke. Especially if it was followed by us, working in the same room together and not saying anything.

He was my boss. I still had to discuss business with him. That wasn't a big deal.

I also needed to tell him about my findings from yesterday. "I talked to Zane. He traced the leak back to an account." I kept my tone cool and conversational, as Luke drove toward the office.

"Who?"

"Billie."

This was when Luke would stop being so nice. Tell me I'd fucked up. That I was an idiot. Ask why I'd kept things from him. Why Billie was still working for us.

Luke glanced at me. "What do you think?"

All of my defensive responses lodged in my throat. "I don't think she's responsible." I reached for reasons why not, but I hadn't found anything concrete yet.

"Okay. I can't hold the dogs off forever, but I can give you until the end of the day. You don't have to give me a new name, but I do need a direction to point Zane in, if this isn't it."

Tension I didn't know I'd been holding drained from me, and I sank back against the seat. "Thank you."

"Fuhgettaboutit," he said, in a near-perfect Tony Soprano voice.

It would be so easy to laugh. To have fun with this moment. I just had to forgive him and pretend twenty-four hours ago—or rather, the events that led to the revelation of twenty-four hours ago—never happened.

I wouldn't be tossed around emotionally like that. Never again.

This felt different than Shawn's emotional manipulation, though. But I couldn't put my finger on how or why.

We arrived at the office, set up in the conference room, and dove into work. The bulk of the sound in the room was fingers, clacking on keyboards. The air didn't feel as heavy as yesterday. Maybe the smoke outside was clearing up.

My phone rang a little after noon, and sourness coursed through me. It was Lyn. Would this be a repeat of last night?

I couldn't shut everyone out of my life, and I'd curl up and wither if I pushed away another friend. "I'll be back." I managed to keep my voice steady as I pushed back from the table.

Luke nodded, watching me with an expression I didn't want to recognize as concern.

I took the stairs down, to organize my thoughts to the rhythm of my shoes, hitting concrete. When I stepped outside, the sunshine hit my face and sank into my soul. I paused outside the door and drank in the warmth.

This was a building on a block of assorted businesses, so there wasn't a lot of space to loiter in, but I found an empty patch of sidewalk away from the entrance, near a tree, and dialed Lyn back before I could fall into the fear that this would go badly.

"Hey." Lyn managed to pour sympathy into the single syllable. "How are you doing?"

"Depends on what you've heard."

"That Chase was a dick. That Sadie misses you."

I sighed and blinked back the sting behind my eyelids. "I don't want to make you take sides." I couldn't stand losing another friend.

"Are you hurting?"

So much more than I wanted to admit. "Yes. But don't hate anyone because of me."

"Because of *Chase*." Lyn's correction was emphatic. "Did he tell you this is your fault? It's not."

"No. He never said anything like that." In fact, neither Chase nor Luke had. They'd been trying to apologize.

"I don't hate anyone. I want you to be all right."

A lump formed in my throat. Such simple words, and they were choking me up. "What if I'm wrong to be mad, though? What if the only reason it's a big deal is because I'm making it one? If I let it go and moved on, everything would be fine."

"Fine for whom? What does your gut tell you?" Lyn *tsked*.

Lies. Always lies. "To be mad. To forgive them. I don't know anymore."

"So listen to it."

I rolled my eyes. "If you're trying to be helpful, you're not." So why was my frustration sapping away?

"You're fighting your instincts right now. I know you. If you stop telling yourself you're wrong, and start believing you're right, it's going to help."

"So I'm wrong to think I'm wrong?" I chuckled dryly.

She laughed. "I suppose yes, I am saying that. If you were home, I'd wrap you in a big hug. Until then, hug yourself and trust yourself. I do."

So did Luke. He'd said so more than once. "If you insist," I said.

"I do. How can I help?"

"I think you already have." I couldn't explain how, but I was feeling a little better. She made sense, even with such a short exchange. Lyn was amazing like that. "Thank you."

We chatted a minute or two longer, made plans for the weekend, and then she had to get back to work. I needed to do the same, but I wasn't ready yet. I had to sort out the wash of emotion clogging my thoughts. I leaned against the tree, eyes closed and face to the sun, until I heard a car.

I looked to see Chase parking a few spots away. I expected a clench in my gut, and there was a small one, but it was tempered by being happy to see him.

He approached, a plastic takeout bag hanging from one arm, and a drink holder with three cups of soda in the other hand. "Authentic Russian food. You can either eat with us or take yours and go somewhere else. I'll understand either way."

"Did you and Luke plan this?" The question popped out without consideration. I needed to know.

He shook his head. "I wanted to see you, and I thought this might get my foot in the door."

"Food. You thought you could bribe me with lunch."

"Not *bribe*, but sate. You always forget to eat, Annie."

True. "Lunch sounds good." And I could eat in the same room as them. I'd spent the last few hours with Luke. I didn't have to talk to eat.

Chase's smile was brighter than the sun and twice as soothing.

We rode the elevator back up and found Luke exactly where he'd been when I walked away. He smiled too, when I moved my computer to the side and accepted a takeout box from Chase.

Chase had gotten me *pelmeni*—dumplings filled with meat. We didn't have a lot of variety in Salt Lake, but Lyn was eternally trying new dishes and comparing them to the local places as experiments for her café, and we got to be her taste testers. These weren't quite as good as hers, but I was biased, and they were real close.

"I don't think I've ever had Russian food before. This is good," Luke said.

"The people who own the place are this great older Russian couple. Political refugees."

Not something I heard very often when it came to other continents. "Like, former KGB or something?"

Chase's smirk said he had a story to tell. "Like Romanovs."

What?

"It's my understanding that's just a name these days." Luke looked as surprised as I felt.

"Not to the people who hold it." Chase leaned in. "*Never* tell a Romanov they're just a name. So this man's grandmother, back when the wall came down, saw the balance of power shifting and decided it was time for her family to fill the vacuum."

And I questioned *my* decisions. "Bullshit."

Chase held his hands up. "Honest to God, this is the story they tell. So Babushka had acquired a long list of friends in her life—she was everyone's mother or sister or best friend—and she'd convinced several of the oldest and the youngest that it was time to rise up."

I could almost picture that in my head. And I could see Chase spinning a similarly compelling argument, if he decided that was what the world needed.

"Since we've never heard of it, I'm guessing that didn't go well." Skepticism filled Luke's voice.

Chase wasn't deterred. "It was going better than you might think. Problem was, one of the women in her rebellion-to-be was married to a KGB agent. This girl would have freaked if he tossed her surrogate babushka in a Gulag—"

"Not a thing anymore in the eighties," Luke said.

Chase rolled his eyes. "Send her to Siberia, then. Whatever. So I'm taking a little bit of artistic license."

I suspected he was taking a lot, but the story was entertaining, regardless. "What happened next?"

"So Mr. KGB went to the actual grandson." Chase looked pleased that I asked. "Told him what she was up to. He actually sounded concerned. She'd organized hundreds of potential-rebels through all the people she knew. KGB agent gave this man and his wife a choice—take Grandma and leave the country, or she would be arrested. They weren't as impassioned about the cause, and Mr. KGB offered them the paperwork they needed to get to the US without hassle, so they packed up their belongings and their grandmother, and left."

It was a good story. Had all the right elements—a heroine I could root for, an extended family who cared, and a sympathizer within the system. "How much of that is true?"

"That's the tale they tell. Who am I to question it?"

I laughed in spite of myself.

Even Luke was smiling. "You do know some incredible stories."

"Funny how none of them are about you." I didn't mean it to be an accusation, but as I said it, I realized Chase rarely told tales about himself.

Chase shrugged. "I'm an open book. You already know all my secrets."

"Obviously not." I hadn't forgiven the guys yet, and I wasn't letting anyone off the hook for a few dumplings and a fairytale.

"She's right, you know," Luke said.

Chase sank back into his seat. He radiated confidence, even when he was being poked with doubt and criticism. How nice would that be? "As if you'd say otherwise."

My insides twisted, and Shawn's voice echoed in my head. *It's your fault you're fighting. If you'd been nicer, he wouldn't have to say those things.* God, I hated that voice so much. Why couldn't I ignore it?

EIGHTEEN

I *wish you didn't make me…* The mental Shawn-voice faded as Luke held my gaze.

"If she was wrong, I'd say so. That doesn't happen very often, though." Luke was talking to Chase, but he was focused on me.

"Fair point." Chase's agreeing with Luke silenced the voice even more.

I didn't want to think about me. "Tell us a story about you."

This was when Chase would bite back. He'd tell me *no.* To stop. That I was stupid for pushing the issue.

"When I was fifteen, I was at Jax's. One of the rare times I spent more than a few minutes at his house," Chase said.

I didn't know this story. If I did, it wasn't in this context.

"Something was peeking out from under the corner of his bed, and I was curious. New comic? Naked chicks? The glossy cover and hint of colors made me think it was the latter, so I tugged. *Nope,* none of the above. Naked dudes. Alone. With each other. With the biggest cocks I'd ever seen. Not a single woman to be seen anywhere, and trust me, I looked. I stared at those pages and had no idea why they made my skin so hot."

Luke looked like he was trying to hide amusement.

I'd expected if Chase shared a story, it would be something lighthearted and flippant. That wasn't where this was headed.

Chase shook his head. "Jax came back from wherever he was—grabbing something out of the basement, or who remembers—and the instant I saw him, I shoved the magazine under the bed and ran back home. I was so embarrassed by my own reaction, I didn't talk to him for days."

"Is that why you pushed Sadie away from him?" I couldn't imagine, and the timeframe didn't line up.

Chase huffed out a laugh. "No. That was something completely different. I didn't understand how the pictures made me feel. It took me a while to process. That it didn't mean Jax was interested in me. That I could like girls and boys. That I could be turned on by them and still daydream about you." He locked his gaze on mine.

Heat flooded my face, and I turned away. I didn't want to feel better around him and Luke, but I did. This was how it always went with Shawn, though. Wasn't it? We'd fight. He'd apologize and be sweet. We'd start over.

Why did this feel different? Not so littered with landmines?

We wrapped up lunch, and Chase left us to work. He'd convinced our vendor to accept our new deadlines and requirements, and was off to try to sign someone new while he was in town.

I only had a few hours left, to keep Billie from being fired. She probably had no idea—at least I hoped she didn't. My mind was clearer than it had been since we arrived, and now was the perfect time to go back over all the information I had.

Big problem was, I didn't have any more idea of where to look than yesterday. I stared at the source control, willing it to give me answers. All those files, ones Billie *should* be working on, checked in at seven. Eight, Mountain Time, since that was what my computer was set to, and those times made sense. We'd all been working late hours, and checking a file in at seven at night was nothing, comparatively speaking.

My brain clicked, whirred, backed up, and replayed what I was looking at.

Those were morning timestamps. "When did the leak happen? What time?" I asked Luke.

He half glanced at me. "We were on the plane, so… between eight and nine?"

"Our time."

He nodded.

"You ever talk to Billie before ten?" Now I had his full attention.

"Mandatory meetings, but no, not really."

It couldn't be this easy.

Why would someone do that? I'd asked Zane.

Because they either wanted you to know it was them…

Or were arrogant and didn't think they'd be caught. Not what Zane had said, but I could see it. I dialed him on the speaker phone between us.

"This is Zane."

"It's Anne. I need some information."

Luke was ignoring his laptop and watching me with curiosity.

"Shoot," Zane said.

This wasn't going to pan out. I'd need to go a different direction. "Who was in the office before eight—seven local time—Tuesday morning?"

"Mike Mejia, Jon Shepherd, Greg D'Angelo."

Not a long list, but I didn't expect it to be. "Dropping a list of dates in messenger. Looking for a common name among them." I gave him ten dates that fell before we had big code breaks, including the major one that first delayed our launch, months ago.

While Zane typed, I forced myself to breathe. I didn't dare look at Luke. I didn't need another layer of stress added to this.

"Mike." Zane spoke with certainty.

"Thanks. I'll keep you posted." I hung up.

I finally turned to Luke again when he sighed. "What are we looking at?"

It was too obvious. Too easy. Why hadn't we seen it before? Because we didn't want to think one of our own would turn on us. This project meant everything to all of us.

"Mike is behind a lot more than a leaked ending," Luke said.

Maybe. "It's all circumstantial, and we'd have to do an audit on the code, to see if there's more to it than meets the eye. But the leak… signs point to him. What next?" I'd been taking stabs in the dark to get this far. "You can't just fire him, any more than you fired Billie."

"True, but I can talk to him. Do you want to be there?"

"Do you think I should be?"

"I think I'd like your opinion on the matter, but ultimately it's up to how comfortable you are with the whole thing."

I didn't want to look Mike—or anyone—in the eye and ask if they were involved in trying to destroy our project. But I had to know. If one of them was responsible, I had to ask him *why*.

"I'll be here." However, I would let Luke do most of the talking. I needed to absorb. Take my cues from him. Make sure my shitty instinct didn't speak out of turn.

Luke called Mike in first. If we felt like he was okay, he'd be involved in our conversations with the two people on his team. My gut told me he was where we needed to start, and that made me nervous.

"Hey." Mike smiled when he walked in the room. He settled into a seat a few down from Luke and never looked at me. "Manager pow-wow? We gonna discuss before Ms. Fortier pulls another power play, like yesterday?"

"Something like that." I couldn't hide the sarcasm in a retort I didn't mean to say out loud.

Mike didn't so much as flick a glance at me. "I understand that someone without a lot of experience makes bad calls sometimes. It's not her fault. But yesterday's stunt is going to cost us days of sifting through the fallout. Days we don't have."

Fury mingled with doubt. I hadn't fucked up, but that didn't stop the Shawn-voice from asking, *Didn't you?*

"No, it won't." Luke's tone was hard. "Anne made the right call, and no one's life fell into a downward spiral because they had to change their password."

Mike pursed his lips. "You're the boss, which is why I'm here. What can I do for you?"

"We're looking at the storyline leak that happened the other morning," Luke said.

Thank God he was stern and cool, because my doubt was clashing hardcore with my knowledge.

Mike nodded. "The information that came from Billie's account."

"It looks like that on the surface, but we don't think she's the culprit. Which is why Anne made the call she did yesterday." Luke's expression was marble. A Greek god, carved wearing a modern wardrobe.

Mike maintained a faint smile, but it didn't reach his eyes. "I'll talk to her about our security protocols and get something written up with HR. I suspected she was sharing her login information, to make her job easier."

He was awfully quick to cast blame in a specific direction. My irritation grew, drowning out anything else.

Luke shook his head. "I'll take care of that. Thank you. I'm more interested in the fact that the leak happened before she entered the building. Early enough that only three of you were here at the time."

The way Luke was handling this was sexy. I'd like to think I could be as direct, but I'd probably waver. Especially with the way Mike was blocking everything with misdirection.

Mike shrugged. "I assume she logged in from the VPN."

"The leak came from within the building. Internal IP address, not a VPN connection." I was tired of this. Mike had flaws, but he wasn't stupid. There was no way he thought we were buying his story. Did he want to be caught?

The asshole still didn't look at me. I slammed my palm on the table, sending a sharp *smack* through the room and making him jump. Good. Arrogant fucker. "We need to know you're not responsible for the leak." My voice was harder than I expected.

Mike finally turned toward me with a snort-laugh. "You sure do like to jump to conclusions. Why would I do that?"

"I don't know. Why?" I bit back. His confidence made my doubt return. Why were we doing this? He couldn't be guilty.

Mike narrowed his eyes. "I suspect whoever did it found out what a bullshit ending we're about to be fed, and wanted the world to know how badly you fucked up."

"*Chloe* has known how this series will end since Game One. And it's a good fucking ending." Now I was getting defensive and swearing. I needed to yank my emotions back in, but I couldn't. "It's incredible. Just because your tiny, homophobic, incel brain—" I snapped my jaw shut, but I'd already gone too far.

Mike's infuriatingly subtle smile was back. "It's bullshit, and people like you are the reason the industry—this company—are in decline. You vapid—"

"*Enough.*" Luke stood.

"*Why?*" Mike mimicked my earlier question. "People like her are the reason—"

Luke stepped closer to Mike and leaned in, palms on the table, silencing him. I'd never seen Luke look so terrifying. Or so incredible. He stared down Mike, their faces inches apart, but never touched him.

"Anne, call Zane. Tell him to lock down all the machines in the building *now* and completely remove Mike's access. When you're done, explain to everyone that they'll be allowed back in soon, and ask them to please stay at their desks until I can talk to them. I'm going to make sure Mike has his belongings and see him to his car."

I wanted to say *yes, sir* and salute. Luke's presence evoked that kind of reaction in me. His command of the situation was fucking sexy. "Will do."

"I'll fucking sue you and this entire company for this." Mike glared daggers at Luke as they left the room.

I made the request with Zane when they were gone. As I headed into the main room, I heard a quiet wave of *what the—?* roll through the cubicles.

"Everyone sit tight. We'll explain soon," I said.

No one heard me. Even the people sitting closest to me didn't look in my direction.

"Excuse me." I raised my voice.

Heads turned toward me, but not many. The volume in the

room grew, as more and more of them stood to talk, and saw Mike boxing up his things.

"What's going on with Mike?"

"Are they firing all of us?"

"This is bullshit. After all the work we've done?"

The questions and fear grew louder with each passing second. This needed to be under control. Why did Luke make me do this?

Because he trusts you.

Right.

I climbed on the nearest desk, ignoring the *creak*. It held. "*Hey*," I shouted.

Two dozen people swiveled to face me at once, and embarrassment flooded my cheeks. I might be bright red, but I was going to do this.

"No one in this room is being fired. Not today, and God willing, not at all." This wasn't what I was supposed to say, but if I didn't do something, there was going to be a revolt. "Mike is no longer with the company. I know many of you consider him a friend, and this is never the way we want things to go. But Luke will explain everything in a few minutes."

"What happened?"

"Why can't we get into our computers?"

"I have unsaved work."

The shouts came from multiple places in the room, making it difficult to tell who most of them were from.

"Mike is a good guy."

"He was set up."

"You can't fire him because you're incompetent."

The last one sent ice spilling through my veins. The noise was reaching a volume that buzzed in my head and made it difficult to think.

NINETEEN

Billie stood next to me, stuck two fingers in her mouth, and released an ear-splitting whistle. "*Hey*. STFU and listen to the boss."

Did she really just say *STFU?* I liked her more than before and could see exactly why Mike didn't. He probably hated that some woman had the nerve to speak her mind. His loss. I gave her a grateful smile and turned back to the room. "Yes, Mike's been let go. You all know Luke is a full-transparency kind of guy, and he'll fill in the details. As far as I know, no one else needs to be concerned. We just need you to sit tight for a few minutes, until Luke is back."

More murmurs rolled through the room, but they were of curiosity, not anger. The group's fear faded.

When Luke returned, he didn't offer much more information, but said as soon as he had clearance from Legal he'd explain more. It calmed people down, but I doubted anyone would get much programming done.

I was emotionally numb by the time we got back to the hotel. Between a fun lunch with Luke and Chase, and the turmoil with Mike, I didn't dare feel anything. I shrugged off Chase's offer for dinner later, and settled into my little corner on the couch, my head-phones on.

Minutes ticked away on the clock, and I wasn't focusing. I tried pulling up a movie, but it didn't hold my attention. I avoided social media, because I didn't want the reminder that things weren't right with Sadie.

I wanted to be talking to my friends again. When I took off my headphones, voices drifted to greet me.

"… without Anne," Luke said.

"And when she's talking to us, we'll include her. This is about you and me." That was Chase.

What were they talking about?

"We were stupid to even consider it," Chase said.

"I think we've figured that out already."

Chase choked off a laugh. "I mean, in addition to the obvious *this was probably a bad idea*. It's killing me, to have her not talking to me."

"Same."

I shouldn't eavesdrop. I stood to join them and interrupt, but curiosity kept my feet glued to the floor.

"What would have happened if things went the way we thought?" Chase asked. "We both try to win her heart, and she picks one of us."

Anger tickled my senses at the reminder that *betting Anne's heart as a prize* was a real thing. I'd rather be dryly amused that they hadn't considered the potential consequences—any of them sooner.

"To be honest, I never thought beyond a future with her." Luke sighed. "She'd end up with me, so there was nothing to consider."

"Except you're wrong. She'd pick me. We know each other better."

Nope, anger was winning out.

"Fuck, we're assholes." Did Luke sound genuinely remorseful? Then again, hadn't both of them before now, too?

"You know, I don't want to see you miserable almost as much as I don't want to be miserable," Chase said.

That was convoluted. I stepped up to the doorway and coughed, to draw their attention. "I'm not choosing either of you." The meaning behind the words, that I'd lose them both, clenched around my heart.

From the way one corner of Chase's mouth tugged up, he didn't reach the same conclusion. "That's my point. If you and I are together, I don't have an issue with you and Luke being together too."

"I'm on board with that," Luke said.

I was too. Or I would be, if this one argument hadn't had so much fallout. "Too bad this was over before it started." I didn't know how I kept my voice from shaking, because the statement threatened to rip me apart. I couldn't talk to them anymore. I turned away.

"Anne." Luke's tone made me pause. "Do you ever wonder if you're doing the right thing?"

A shiver ran through me, and I resisted the urge to hug myself as doubt poured through me.

"This isn't me being passive aggressive or telling you you're wrong. You're not." Luke was kind. "I saw how you reacted to Mike. I felt your doubt, wondering if you were wrong. I've been there. I wouldn't be begging for your forgiveness if I didn't realize I'd fucked up. But I'm asking if you've got that voice in your head that belongs to someone else. The one that makes you question everything."

He was trying to manipulate me. To trap me into saying something I didn't want to. "Doesn't everyone?"

"No. But a lot of people do." There was an ache in Luke's voice that I rarely heard and never for more than a breath. "*I* do."

Did I dare ask? "How?"

"My first few weeks of college, I struggled to integrate. Mostly because I'd just come out of Afghanistan and was adjusting to things like sleeping in beds. Then I met the RA in my dorm. Gorgeous man. Sweet. Sure, we fought sometimes, but that was always my fault. He said so."

Luke stared past me, as if he was lost in a memory. "He was caught for dealing Adderall and blackmailing several of the people in the dorm. When he went before the disciplinary board, he convinced them it was my idea. He got us both kicked out of school."

I knew Luke didn't graduate. A lot of people at the company hadn't, because Scott valued skill in his developers more than a degree. I'd never imagined it hadn't been Luke's choice. I didn't know what to say.

Luke let out a shaky breath. "He apologized. Told me he was worried about his career. I understood, right? Besides, if I'd been more attentive to him, it never would have happened."

I knew this story. Not the details, but the ex-boyfriend's accusation. "But it wasn't your fault." I felt stupid, saying that. Luke had obviously figured that out.

He shrugged. "I'm lucky that I'm smart. It was enough to get me an internship at Rinslet, even without the degree. I wouldn't be here if it wasn't for Scott."

That wasn't fair to Luke. "You wouldn't be here if you weren't intelligent and talented."

"That too." Luke grinned. "It's taken a lot of time and a bit of therapy to understand it wasn't me; it was him who was the problem. I still hear his voice, though."

"I know, Sadie knows. We all saw that Shawn did the same to you." Chase finally spoke. He turned from me to Luke. "And I'm sorry you went through that. I only know what it looks like from the outside, and that's hard enough. I can't imagine being in it."

My friends had tried to tell me then, and I'd pushed them away. Even if this wasn't the same situation, I didn't want to shove my friends out of my life again. "It's different."

"Because you recognize that it happened? Because you got out? Because he was right, and you're still wrong? Why?" Luke asked.

I didn't know how to answer his questions. I wasn't sure what was up or down anymore.

Luke frowned. "This bet? I was wrong to make it. Chase was wrong. You're not wrong for feeling anything you feel about it."

I didn't know how to sift through my thoughts anymore. They

were a jumble of chaos. "That's sweet of you to say, but... you're wrong." I cut off my laugh at the twisted irony of my statement. "Good night."

TWENTY

"Annie." Chase's tone stopped me in my tracks. "Don't spend another night on the couch. Take one of the beds. Better yet, stay and talk to us. If I have to promise I'll never tell you again how gorgeous you are, to get you to talk to me, I will."

I turned, scrunching my nose in distaste. "I'm not good with that."

"Which part of it?" Sincerity radiated from his expression. "How about, I can still shower you with compliments, and you can go back to pretending you think it's harmless?"

How did I ever do that? "None of what's happened this week gets undone. I want our friendship back, but I can't forget."

"Good. Because not all of this was bad," Luke said. "Not to me."

I leaned against the doorframe and jammed my hands in my pockets. "It only took the one bad thing to sour it all. But I won't forget the good either."

"If you want another apology, I'll give you one. Over and over." Chase looked so sweet. The boy next door. The guy I would have given my heart to years ago, if this were a movie.

I didn't want more apologies. "I get it—you're sorry. I can't say *it's okay*, because it wasn't. But I do forgive you." When the words rolled out of my mouth, they took a huge weight with them that I hadn't know I was carrying. God, that felt good. It couldn't be wrong if it was this much of a relief.

"Sure you don't want one more apology?" A hint of playfulness leaked into Chase's question. "Me, on my knees at your feet, worshiping you?" He stood.

Luke grabbed the back of his shirt and yanked him back to the bed. "That's not an apology; it's oral sex."

"The two are frequently the same," Chase said.

"Not when we're apologizing for objectifying her."

I couldn't help my smile as I pulled out a chair from the desk and sat. "I could stay for a little while longer. It's not like I was getting anything done, all the way out there in the other room."

"You haven't eaten yet, have you?" Chase was abruptly serious.

I shook my head.

Luke raised his hand. "Question. I've been wondering this for a while, and I can finally ask—what's your obsession with feeding Anne?"

Obsession…? I'd never thought about it like that before.

"Did you consider tackling that asshole you fired today, when he came at her verbally?" Chase asked.

Now I knew what they'd been talking about when I wasn't listening. War stories from the conference room.

Luke looked at me. "I not only considered it, I ran a split-second list of pros and cons, and I'm still tempted to find him and punch him for the way he treated you."

The protectiveness in his body language and words made me feel gooey inside. "People say things like that to other people all the time." Shitty, but true.

"But he said it to *you*." Luke told me before turning back to Chase. "What does this have to do with food? Did someone beat up Anne's food once?"

"You okay with me telling this story, Annie?"

Chase's question triggered a rush from the past when I realized what he was asking. I was touched that he wanted my permission.

"Here, yes. Nowhere else." Everyone who mattered, except for Luke, already know about this part of my life. I didn't know if I could tell the tale myself.

"Annie's a fairytale princess, but Grimm got her origin story a little mixed up."

"I buy it," Luke said.

I'd never thought about my life that way before. "I'm not."

"Her mother passed away and left her to be raised by an evil stepfather." Chase slid into storytelling mode with his typical ease. "Down to the fact that he was the perfect member of the community in public. Everyone loved this dude."

"Ah." Luke frowned.

The wounds from my mother's death were old—I was only nine when it happened—but they still ached like a broken bone on a cold night. The memories of how my stepfather treated me were fresher, because I'd been stuck with him through my teen years. He was the reason I'd spent so much time at Sadie's.

"Half the time, the asshole didn't care where she stayed. That's why Anne's part of our family," Chase said. "The rest of the time, he needed proof that he was a loving father. For parties, social events—whatever. So she'd have to go home for a few weeks at a time."

A shudder raced through me, and I hugged myself. It was harder than I'd expected to dive back into this.

Luke furrowed his brow. "Are you all right?"

"I'll stop. You don't need to relive this." Chase looked concerned too.

"It's okay. Keep going, or you won't get to the happy ending." I had to remember the story had one. It was one of the things that kept me from falling into darkness when I looked back on that part of my life. "I wasn't abused or anything. Not physically. But there were a lot of nights I went to bed hungry, and to school the same way the next day. I learned to push through it."

Chase was shaking too, but his looked more like barely controlled anger.

"When Chase realized what was going on, he went out of his

way to make sure you ate," Luke said in understanding. "Hard to compete with that."

"I thought you both agreed this wasn't a competition. Besides, I lo… ike you for different reasons." That was almost bad. I didn't want to linger in the dark anymore. "Anyway, if Disney ever writes a gamer geek princess, they totally stole the idea from my life story."

Chase relaxed a little, but he still sat stiffly. "Can you imagine Pixar basing something on our lives?"

"Pretty sure I've seen that on Smut Central." Luke's cheer sounded forced.

The conversation drifted toward light and playful, but the long week caught up to me earlier than I expected. I stayed awake as long as I could, but the next thing I knew, I was waking up fully clothed and tangled with Chase and Luke.

There was a text message waiting for me, from Sadie. *Please talk to me. I'm sorry.*

Chase rested his chin on my shoulder. "Don't be mad at her because of me. She's your sister."

Anne's part of our family, his words from last night rang in my thoughts.

"Go call her," Luke chimed in. "We've got time."

I didn't want company for this conversation. Luke and Chase would give me privacy, but I needed a little extra space. I grabbed my key, made sure I was presentable for the public, and headed into the hallway. I walked as I dialed and waited for Sadie to answer.

"I'm sorry," she said when she picked up. "For diminishing your feelings, for telling you that you were wrong, and for giving you a bad haircut."

"Way to take the *oomf* out of any speech I had planned." Not that I'd had any idea what to say. "And you haven't cut my hair since eighth grade."

"It was a really bad haircut. I'm really sorry."

I stepped into the lobby when the doors slid open. "It hurt. A lot. What you said, not the haircut." I planned to forgive her, but she wasn't walking away without me saying my bit. "I've always looked up to you. Even now. And to have you dismiss me like that…"

"Why?" Sadie asked. "I'm touched, but I'm a shitty role model."

"You never hesitate or doubt yourself."

Sadie laughed dryly. "I doubt myself all the time, and I make my share of mistakes."

"But it doesn't stop you from *doing*. You always act." I leaned against a nearby pillar, tucked away from view.

"And you're smart about the decisions you make. You think things through. You weigh the consequences. Don't be me. I love you for you."

Same thing I'd told Chase and Luke last night. "It sounds pretty smart when you put it that way."

"Because I'm brilliant," Sadie said. "Forgive me, please?"

"I do."

"Good." Cheer slipped into her voice. "As soon as you have days off again, movie marathon. Your choice. I'm buying… whatever we need."

"It's a date. Talk to you soon." I felt better as I disconnected. It sucked, not talking to my friends.

My concerns from the flight were back. If this was how badly friendships could deteriorate after one argument with Chase, what would happen if we hooked up again and our relationship went even further south? I couldn't handle that.

I headed back upstairs, and the guys and I rotated through the shower, getting ready for our days. The one thing I wouldn't miss about this trip was sharing a bathroom.

My goal for the day was to find out how much additional damage Mike had done. I had a strong suspicion he was behind a few of the delays we had with programming, but if I could prove it, it would also give us a direction to go toward fixing things more quickly

I settled in to work next to Luke, in the conference room. It was bittersweet, swapping conversation and jokes with him like we'd always done, but knowing that more was possible if I was willing to risk it. I didn't know if I was.

Based on what we found yesterday, I asked Zane to have his team compare all the timestamps from when files were modified from this building, versus when people were in it. He had a list to me by midmorning, and I started working my way through it.

New problem—for every file change on the list, the history that came before it had been deleted. There was no way to roll back or recover anything that was changed.

Fuck. I sank back in my chair, pulling my attention from my screen, and blinked to clear up my dry eyes. When I looked again, Luke was watching me.

"Something wrong?" I asked.

He shook his head. "Enjoying the view. How about you? You're stumped on something."

"Yes."

He tugged my hand from where it rested near my laptop, and brushed his lips over my fingertips. "Magic kissing mojo?"

I started to laugh, but revelation stopped me short. "*God*, you're incredible."

"I know. What's up?"

I actually had the answer. "Get me access to the deleted change logs."

"If I had that power, I'd do it in the heartbeat. But auditors only. You know the rules."

"Oh." I slumped again. The rule made sense, specifically in instances like this. If someone could erase things and then erase the proof they'd done it, we'd be fucked.

Except, what good did any of that do, if I couldn't restore things?

"I can get you screenshots or an export of the logs," Luke said. "Just not access to the software itself."

And if there was something to fix, we could go through the right channels to restore it. "I'll take that. Duh."

"Sorry. Wasn't thinking. I was distracted." Luke winked. "One extract from Internal Audits coming up."

By early afternoon, I had a list of everything that had been changed—presumably all by Mike, based on a ranting email he'd sent us this morning—down to the single quote. What Mike had done was randomly tweak modules after they passed final QA. Over and over, across different nodes and projects. More than half the time, it was a female developer's work—a neat feat, considering he only had four working for him.

The cheers from both Team Percival and Gawain, when I told them how much time we'd just saved, probably could have been heard without a conference line.

"You're brilliant," Luke told me when we finished the update call.

I flushed under the compliment. "I didn't do it all myself. *Magical kissing mojo*, and all that."

"No, this is all on you. Fantastic job."

Months' worth of stress faded away, as I started to work through my own list.

Now, if only my personal life could be as simple as restoring a few corrupted files from the past and overwriting the mistakes that came after.

Except, had hooking up with Luke and Chase been a mistake? Any of it? That little voice said it was, but I didn't feel like that was the case.

TWENTY-ONE

That night in the hotel room felt like the when we'd checked in. The way things always had with Chase and Luke, before everything fell apart. Dinner, laughing, and having fun. I didn't even try to keep track of the tangents, as long as I could follow them and each hop made sense.

"Annie and I are Dance Dance Revolution champions. As in, *official*," Chase said.

Luke looked impressed. "DDR? No shit. Like *Scott Pilgrim* level?"

Chase gave a short barking laugh. "He wishes he was as incredible as us."

"I had no idea."

"There are a lot of things you don't know about me." I wanted to keep my tone serious and somber, but I was enjoying myself too much. Funny how frequently that was a state of mind for me around these two.

"We all have a lot to learn about each other. But I'm not opposed to stripping away a single layer at a time, until I can see it all." The way Luke dragged his gaze over me, I felt it in my core.

Chase adjusted himself on the bed. "There's a lot of innuendo there. Does that mean we're transitioning from learning about each other to sex?"

"That's a real weak transition." Not that I minded. With the hurt gone, my mind was happy to linger on our first night here. The need. The want. I swore my brain was whimpering *use me*.

Chase shrugged. "It comes with a strong follow-up. That's got to count for something."

"Are we keeping count now? Inches? Orgasms?" With each word, Luke ticked off another finger.

"I thought you two weren't competing."

"It's always a competition when it comes to sex," Chase said.

Luke leaned in closer, mouth inches from mine. "Not if my filthy baby doll doesn't want it to be."

The words flipped a switch, and my every nerve ending sparked to life, looking for stimulation.

"Wait. Are you competing with me about who's right?" Chase asked. If he had any idea what was racing through my head, he was an asshole. A glorious, tempting asshole who was dancing his fingertips down my spine, and talking as if this were the most casual thing in the world.

"You two are ridiculous." My voice was breathy, giving me away. If the flush to my skin hadn't done so already.

Chase kissed the shell of my ear. "But we're well hung."

"Are we talking length or girth?" Luke asked.

"If you're going to insist on keeping count, I'm strictly looking at number of orgasms."

"That sounds like a challenge." Chase teased up the bottom of my shirt to brush my skin.

Luke hadn't touched me yet, but the way he watched me… "Where do I submit my application?" he asked. "I like to think I work well within a team environment. As long as I'm in charge."

"I think the application process should involve a talent show." I was going to make them work for this at least a little bit.

"Would you like to be restrained or just worshiped?" Luke asked.

Either. Both. And then some. They were making it hard to draw this out. "Without using me as a prop."

Chase stood and tugged at his zipper.

"Without using anyone's genitals as a prop." I added quickly.

Chase pouted. "You're taking all the hard out of this."

Luke knelt at my feet and grasped my fingers. "There once was a proper lady. Who moaned when her boss called her *baby*—"

"Is that a limerick?" I was laughing. "It's horrible."

"Thank God you stopped me, because I had no idea how to get from there to you kneeling and begging."

"You didn't have a problem with it the other night." Chase didn't sound upset. "Are you sure I can't just show you how talented I am?" He reached for his zipper again.

I shook my head. "That's not part of the application process."

"What do you bring to the team, Ms. Fortier?" The way Luke said my name grasped a moan from my chest and tried to extract it.

I painted on my best *innocent* face. "I'm adorable."

"You are," Chase said. "But if we're taking team applications, everyone has to prove themselves."

"Let's be honest, the competition is pretty weak right now." I had no idea what I'd do that would be better.

Luke pulled me to my feet and set me in the middle of the room, like he had the other night. This time he left my clothes on, at least for now. "All right, DDR champion, you can dance. Show us your moves," he said.

Yeah, right. "I don't dance; I follow a series of arrow prompts on the screen."

"I think he's onto something." Chase sat on the edge of the bed, full attention on me. "Dance for us."

I had no idea what to do, so I swayed my hips and hugged myself in a slow, I hoped hypnotic rhythm. It kept their attention, so I must have been doing something right.

"You call that your *Sucker Punch*?" Chase asked playfully.

He was referencing the movie, and so was I. "I prefer *Baby Doll*."

"Me too. And I like the dance. It's got potential. I'd like it better if you took your top off." Luke's tone implied more command than suggestion.

I stripped my shirt off, never pausing in my *dance*. The pair of hungry gazes on me was fuel on the fire simmering under my veins.

"Jeans next."

I spun my back to them as I undid the button and zipper, then shimmied the denim down my legs, my ass straight up in the air. I turned to face them again. No idea how my basic pink bra and blue panties were drawing that kind of attention, but I reveled in it.

"What do you think?" Luke was looking at me, but I was pretty sure he was talking to Chase.

Chase tilted his head, looking me up and down. "Stunning, but still too many clothes." He crossed the room, pulled out a chair from the desk, and moved it next to me. "Lose the underwear and take a seat." His tone was more playful than Luke's, but no less enticing.

Luke snapped and pointed at the chair. "You heard the man."

I did and was happy to comply. It was easy to keep up the not-quite-dance while stripping off my bra and panties, but there wasn't much seductive about sitting.

"Spread your legs. Show us that incredible pussy," Luke said.

There it was—the tingle of desire. I trailed my fingers up my thighs as I pushed them apart. It felt incredible, to be exposed like this. To be the focus of their desire.

"No." Luke clipped off the word when I traveled my hands toward my core. "You can touch yourself everywhere that feels good, except there."

My laugh was strained, but I could tease a little longer. Or was he the one doing the teasing? I skipped over the center of my pulsing need and moved higher, dragging my nails lightly across the back of my neck. Gliding my palms over my breasts. Lingering to squeeze my nipples.

Chase had shed his pants and freed himself, and was stroking while he studied me. He was so hard. So thick. I wanted to taste and feel him.

I slid my hands down my stomach.

"No," Luke warned, when I drew too close. He'd removed most of his clothes, too, and his erection stood straight up, lonely and tall.

I nodded. "I could help with that."

"You will, baby doll, but not yet. You're busy with yourself."

Which was fun, but my body ached for more. I scratched up the inside of my thighs, then moved back to my breasts, to play harder this time. Rolling my nipples between my fingers until my body was clenching from need, and I couldn't pinch hard enough.

My chest heaved from holding back. "Please?" Begging worked last time, and I liked the way it tasted. Being vulnerable for them. Letting Luke control how quickly things went.

"Tell me what you want."

"You. Both of you." My plea came out breathless.

Luke gripped his shaft and dragged his thumb over the head. "No. But you can make yourself come."

Fucking right, I could. I dipped my fingers between my legs, sliding two inside me and arching into the penetration. It wasn't the same as one of the guys, but it was still incredible. With my other hand, I found my clit. There was no more buildup or tease. I rubbed frantically, grinding against my touch, my hips thrusting in desperation.

I melted against the hardwood back of the chair, head tilted back and eyes closed.

"Watching is nice, but I can't keep my distance anymore." Chase's words blended with the fuzz in my head, rather than disrupting it.

And then his lips were on mine. His fingers at the back of my head, holding me in place.

When he pulled away, I opened my eyes to find him watching me with a look that stole any breath I had left.

"*God*, you're gorgeous." His words rumbled over me.

Luke was next to him and had rolled on a condom when I was otherwise distracted. He gripped my wrist loosely and drew my fingers into his mouth, to suck them clean one at a time, while Chase teased along my chest and arms.

Luke tugged me to my feet, slid behind me, and pulled me with him when he sat. His cock slid inside me, stretching me out and making me moan.

Chase stood in front of me, lightly stroking himself.

I was hungry for more of what I'd had the other night. Losing myself in the pleasure of being filled. I leaned forward enough to lick Chase's tip. Swirl my tongue around the sensitive skin. Let my senses dance to his groans.

He thrust into my mouth.

Luke teased me gently. A barely there touch over my breasts, my nipples, and my thighs. It was a new kind of torture, on the opposite end of rough. Faint and almost ticklish. It felt as good as everything else we'd done, though.

When Luke started to thrust in me, the movement jarred Chase from my mouth. He picked up on his own. I watched, fascinated and aroused, as he yanked his shaft, his eyes half-shut.

There was a power in knowing he was doing that because of me. That even though he and Chase dictated what we were doing, I had the ultimate control.

The jerk of his hips and staccato grunts said he was close. He shuddered, as sticky white ribbons squirted across his hand. My chest. A splash along my leg.

Luke gripped my throat, and pulled me into him, increasing pressure and the pace of his hammering in me. My head swam, light and giddy. Wrapped in pleasure.

Chase knelt between our legs, and I whimpered at the sight. He licked along my slit, and had to be tasting Luke as well.

Fuck, this was hot.

Chase focused on my clit, sucking and writing the most erotic sonnets with his tongue. Ecstasy enveloped me, encasing me in a climax that rippled through me, starting with the clench between my legs and tingling all the way to my fingertips.

Luke was grunting too—I was vaguely aware of that incredible sound. Slamming against me harder. Frantically. His voice raw. His grip on my thighs tight. The shudder of his orgasm rumbling through him and into me.

As we slowed to a stop, I swore the world around us did the same.

"Everything about you is fucking incredible, baby doll," Luke murmured against the back of my neck.

God, I just wanted to live in this bliss forever.

And ignore that teensy nagging insistence that I could never have this again.

TWENTY-TWO

A girl could get addicted to waking up sandwiched between two men. But as consciousness rushed in, so did the reminder that this ended today. Especially when Chase extracted himself to shower. He had an early flight out. Luke and I would spend a few hours in the office before we left.

Luke dragged a finger over my lower lip, as he lay next to me in bed. "What's with the pout?"

"I'm going to miss this."

"It doesn't have to end."

But it did. The realization I had yesterday, when I was talking to Sadie, wouldn't leave me alone. "Not talking to you two sucked. This has been fun and incredible and a whole huge list of adjectives, but that just means the longer we drag things out, the worse it hurts when things don't work out next time."

"What makes you think that's what's going to happen?" Luke asked.

"It might, it might not. But odds are higher on the *might* side." I hated the reality of that. "With Lyn, we made friendship work after. I need that from the two of you—your friendship."

"You have it. Always." Luke brushed his lips over my forehead, then pressed his forehead to mine. "I'm going on record as saying I want more, but I understand why you're holding back. I'm here if you change your mind."

I nodded, and pulled away before I could sink into the comfort and lose my resolve. I sat with my back to Luke and hugged my knees to my chest.

Silence settled between us. When the shower shut off, the bed bounced from Luke getting up. "Do you want to go first?"

I shook my head. I needed more time to collect myself. That seemed to be my mood of the week.

"I won't be long. Then you can hop in." Luke grabbed clothes from his bag and headed into the bathroom as soon as Chase stepped out.

Chase studied me when he entered the room. "You okay?"

"Just gathering my thoughts. Telling myself I can do with you what I did with Lyn."

He frowned. "I don't think Lyn loves you the same way I do."

My breath caught at the confession. The declaration. "Chase, I can't—"

"It's okay." He crouched in front of me and cradled my cheek. He traced his thumb along my skin. "I'm not trying to guilt or force you into anything. I'm here for you, however you need. I always will be." Chase's sincerity ached more than if he'd laughed the whole thing off.

"I know." And I did. Even when we were fighting, part of me always knew I had him.

He pressed his lips to my forehead, and my heart clenched. "I have a plane to catch. I'll see you back home."

I nodded, not trusting anything that might come out of my mouth.

LUKE and I wrapped up at the office. There wasn't much to do, besides tell the team they were awesome and to keep up the good work.

We headed to the airport and boarded our plane without issue. Our seats were next to each other this time.

I settled into the window seat, and Luke took the spot next to me. One of my least favorite things about flying was figuring out where to put my arms so I didn't bump into rowmates, but I liked the connection that danced between us when his forearm rested against mine.

We didn't say anything as the plane taxied. I was becoming a master at ignoring anything uncomfortable about silence with Luke, but that didn't mean I liked it. The dip in my gut as we left the ground was now tied to the memory of the first time Chase kissed me. I was going to call it ButterfliesPlus. I should trademark that.

"You thinking about the flight in?" There was no accusation in Luke's question.

I should tell him to please kindly step the fuck out of my head, but I didn't mind that he knew me well enough to ask. "I'll probably never fly again without thinking about that, even if it did turn out to be a mistake." The last bit felt obligatory, but it also didn't feel true.

"Do you really believe that?"

Not even close. I wanted to. Logically, keeping Chase and Luke at arm's length was the best way to avoid all-around heartbreak. It was also the best way to avoid any potential we all had together. "You're going to read into this, and I wish you wouldn't, but I can't stop you. Would you really be okay, being with me, if I was with Chase too? If I picked both of you, instead of one or none?"

"Yes." Luke's reply came without hesitation. "I'm really okay with it."

I flexed my fingers on my knee, twitching for something to grasp. Needing to ground myself. When Luke tangled his fingers with mine, a shock of warmth and surprise raced through me. I could pull away, but this was comforting. It was right. I didn't want to resist.

How long would it take us to get back to *normal*? Did I even want to?

We kept the conversation to work-related topics for most of the flight, planning cleanup, laying out next steps, and daring to dream about when we were finally done with this game. I appreciated both that Luke stayed away from personal topics and that he rarely let go of my hand until we landed.

Compulsion and experience meant we checked our work email while waiting for our luggage. The world didn't stop turning because we were in the air. Most of the messages I had would wait until I was back at my desk, but the meeting request from Human Resources made me frown.

"I've got to meet with Scott." Luke sounded as confused by his meeting as I was. "I can drop you off at home."

I showed him my phone. "I'm heading straight to the office, if you don't mind me hitching a ride that way."

"That's fine." Luke's frown deepened. "Any idea what it's about?"

"I was going to ask you."

We could toss all sorts of speculation around, but we'd have answers when we were done with our meetings.

Dana, the Human Resources Director, led me into her office moments after I arrived, though I was early. She closed the door behind me, gestured for me to sit, and did the same. The concern etched on her face made me uneasy.

"How are you doing?" she asked kindly.

It didn't sound like a casual greeting—not with that tone—but I didn't have any other context. "Good. A little jetlagged. Looking forward to sleeping in my own bed."

"I understand." Her chuckle sounded forced, and her smile didn't reach her eyes. "It's always nice to come home."

"Yup. Sure is." I was a master at awkward silences by now, but she had a reason for calling this meeting. "What can I do for you?"

Dana leaned in, eyeing me with sympathy. "You're familiar with our company's sexual-harassment policies? And you know that you can always come directly to me, if you're not comfortable going to your manager? I don't want you to ever feel like you don't have a voice."

Super weird. Tension cranked through me. "I realize." It would have to be a fairly significant level of harassment, for me to something like that, but I didn't really deal with it in this job. Mike was the worst, and he was gone.

Dana looked less comfortable with each passing second. "The employee that was terminated the other day, Mike Mejia, was apparently guilty of more than you realize. He forwarded me some information this morning, and while I don't know how he obtained it, the content has me concerned for your wellbeing and happiness."

"Okay…? I don't know what you're looking for, so you need to tell me what you're concerned about."

She leaned back to look at her monitor, and clicked her mouse.

"If there was a lock on the conference room door, I'd bend you over the table right now, and find out if you're as tight as I imagine." Luke's voice was hollow, coming from her speakers, as if recorded on a poor quality mic.

All the blood drained from my head, leaving my thoughts spinning and my skin cold. I'd never fainted before. Would this be a first?

"Is there more?" My voice cracked on the question.

"No." Dana's face was bright red. "Was he talking to you? The company supports you. Rinslet is on your side, as am I. You don't need to put up with this."

"I'm not putting up with anything." How much could I say? We'd broken the rules, and I had to admit that, to keep Luke from getting in trouble, but this could get us both fired.

Was she looking at me with pity? "There won't be any repercussions for you if you want to come forward, but you don't have to. He was completely out of line. He's being dealt with."

"Wait. As in, right now?" The words sank in, and my panic spiked.

"Yes."

The meeting with Scott. *Fuck.* I wasn't letting Luke get fired for sexual harassment. At least, if we went down, we'd do it together. "This isn't right. It's not what it looks like." I stood and walked out of Dana's office.

"Anne, come back. Please."

I ignored her. I couldn't think of anything, except that Luke was about to be punished for us having fun. The elevator up to the executives' offices took an eternity. I cut a straight line to Scott's office, and didn't pause when his assistant tried to stop me. When I pushed into the room, Luke and Scott swiveled their heads to look at me.

"You can't fire him," I said.

TWENTY-THREE

Scott gestured to the farthest chair from Luke. "Have a seat. Do you want me to ask him to leave the room?" Scott nodded.

"No. Please don't." This was bad. Another consequence. This one possibly unrecoverable.

Scott looked at his watch. "You didn't talk to Dana for long. Did she explain the situation to you?"

"Yes. Can't we say the recording doesn't exist, since neither of us gave permission?" I spared a glance at Luke, who didn't look nearly as concerned as I was.

"This isn't court," Scott said. "The fact that the recording is illegal doesn't change what's on it. We're pursuing Mike for a number of legal reasons, but that also doesn't change this circumstance. Do you understand how this looks?"

According to Dana, it looked like Luke harassing an employee. "Yes, but it's not like that," I said.

Scott pinched the bridge of his nose. "I've heard this story before. I've told this story before. Luke's already given me his side of things, and it's exactly what I expected. He told me he abused his position and crossed a line, and none of it is your fault."

"Why the fuck would you do that?" I'd smack Luke in the arm if he was sitting closer.

"To protect you," Scott and Luke spoke at the same time.

I crossed my arms over my chest and sank in my chair. *Idiot.* Lovable, sexy, protective idiot.

Most of the time, it was easy to forget Scott had been running this company in one form or another for two decades. He tended to look and act as young as any of us. Today, the lines around his eyes and mouth were evident. "This is where you tell me it's not his fault; it's all on you. That he didn't threaten your job, and you were out of line."

"Are you serious?" I stared at him blankly. "Why would I do that?"

"Like I said, I've heard and told this story before."

"Then you're an idiot too." *Shit.* I didn't mean to say that out loud.

Scott raised his brows and stared at me.

I really called the head of our company an idiot. And I wasn't even done talking. "It was consensual. All of it. There was no power struggle. There was some seduction, but really, it's no fun otherwise." I could shut up anytime now, please. "None of that's your business. Point is, I'm not going to tell you it was all my fault, and it's not all his fault. We're adults, and we both knew what we were doing."

Luke looked like he was trying to fight a smile. Nice to know my babbling in vague terms about our relationship was funny to him.

Scott was still watching me. "Are you done?" he asked.

"Yes," I said sheepishly. "Please don't fire me. Or Luke."

He stared at me until I wanted to look away, but I didn't.

"I still can't have you reporting to him, if you're doing what this recording implies." Scott furrowed his brow. "No, wait. There's no implication there. It's really straightforward."

I'd like to curl up in a ball and die now. "We're not doing *that.* Not anymore. Not that it's any of your business."

"The details aren't. The *one of my managers is sleeping with his employee* breaks our rules."

"You're dragging this out a bit much." Luke finally spoke. "It's starting to look dickish."

What?

Scott's face cracked into a smile. "I could see that."

"Is there a punchline here?" I wasn't going to be someone's joke, especially after everything that happened this week.

Scott turned back to me. "This was supposed to wait, but circumstances being what they are... I can't lose either of you, but I also can't keep the report-to structure the same. Anne, I'd like to offer you a director position. You can't step into your new duties until this game is out the door, but if you accept, you report to me, not Luke, effective immediately."

It didn't matter that Luke had warned me this was being considered; actually hearing Scott make the offer stalled my brain. I had the sense not to ask things like *what?* and *are you sure?* But most other mental functions left me.

"Anne?" Scott prompted.

I shook off the shock. "Okay. I mean, *yes please*. That is... I'll take it? Whatever it is I'm supposed to say."

"*Yes* will do fine." Scott chuckled.

We talked over a few more details, and he promised me an offer letter on Monday.

"Go home, both of you. Details are none of my business." Scott fixed me with a pointed glare. "Take the weekend off. You've both earned more, but that's the best I can give until the game is in players' hands."

Exhaustion and relief flooded me, making my limbs feel like lead, as we headed back to Luke's car.

He pointed us toward my house. "Do you want to celebrate?" he asked.

"Yes, but no. Maybe something small. I want to save the big one until I'm actually doing the work."

"Sounds fair."

"This doesn't change anything else between us." I hated saying it, but the point needed to be pounded into the ground a few more times, apparently.

Luke twisted his mouth. "I didn't figure it would."

What else was there to say?

TWENTY-FOUR

When Luke dropped me off, he insisted on carrying my bags inside, even though I argued that I'd be fine. The *thanks, see you Monday* we exchanged was one of the most awkward things ever, and I'd just had HR play audio of my boss telling me he hoped I was tight when he fucked me.

I closed the door behind him and sank to the floor. The last week made me intensely aware of how empty my house was.

Fortunately, friends were just a message away. I sent Sadie and Lyn a text, letting them know I was back and that we should hang out tomorrow. Celebrate my not-quite-yet promotion. They understood when I said I needed tonight for self-care.

I showered without having to work around anyone else's schedule. That was nice. I yanked on my most comfy T-shirt and PJ bottoms, without worrying about who might see me in them. And I pulled my damp hair back from my face in a terrycloth headband.

None of the motions distracted me from missing Luke and Chase. My actions didn't convince me I was making the right decision by pushing them away. I could call, and they'd probably make time for me. Both of them.

Why was I fighting this?

What if I'm wrong? What if people get hurt? What if I get hurt?

But what if I was right? What if being with them was right? What if the last couple of days were a glimpse of how incredible things could be, despite setbacks? Didn't it count for something that I loved them?

Love. My own admission caught me off guard. It was true, though.

My phone buzzed from its spot on the table next to the door, startling me. The text from Sadie said *knock knock.*

A heartbeat later, someone knocked, giving me my second heart attack in so many seconds. It would be Sadie and probably Lyn. So much for self-care. Not that I minded the company.

I opened the door, to find Chase and Luke on the other side. Hello, Heart Attack Number Three. Especially with the way they both looked me over.

Chase held up a plastic bag with steam condensing on the inside. "Dinner? You got Sadie's message, I assume?" His gaze had stalled on my chest. So he was behind the *knock knock* text.

"You're going to bribe me with food, so you can stare at my boobs?" I asked playfully.

"Food... Money... Promises of amazing orgasms..."

Luke shook his head and tugged on my hair. "I like this look on you."

"You like any look on her," Chase said.

"Truth."

I stepped aside to let them in. "Explain?" I meant to say, *to what do I owe this unexpected but wonderful visit,* but my brain and mouth were out of sync.

"We figured, if you were planning on staring blankly at the TV tonight, and we were planning on staring blankly at the TV tonight, we could do it together." Luke made everything sound so reasonable.

"At my house." Duh, me.

Chase grinned. "You're the one with the amazing theater room."

"Which you talked me into." Why was I arguing? I was elated they were here. It was perfect.

"Not that you needed a lot of convincing," Chase said.

Luke grabbed the takeout bag from him. "And we brought dinner."

"Which we covered already." I set the food on the table next to my phone. "That's it? *We're here to watch TV?*" I'd be okay with that, but given how much I wanted me-time an hour ago, I wanted all the us-time I could have. How had I convinced myself, even for a day or two, that I'd be okay, ignoring the connection I felt with them?

"We're also here to win you over properly this time." Chase grasped my fingers and stroked his thumb over the back of my knuckles. "By telling you up front that we've talked about this, and you don't have to choose, but we're hoping you will and it will be both of us."

My heart skipped, and I let out a soft laugh. "So win me over."

Luke rested his finger under my chin and tilted my face toward him. He brushed his lips over mine in a touch so feather light, he took my breath with him when he pulled back to hold my gaze. "I love you. I don't know long I've felt this way. Is it cheesy to say, *since the first time I talked to you?* I think it's true. I want you in my life. By my side. We make an incredible team. And an even better three-some. Especially when you're caught between us, holes filled, moaning in ecstasy until your voice is gone."

Heat flooded my face.

Chase saved me from having to think of a response, by moving behind me and wrapping his arms around my waist. He nibbled my ear. "I *can* tell you exactly how long I've loved you. My fifteenth birthday, when you wore that gorgeous sundress to try to get what's-his-name's attention. *George? Bob? Dickhead?*"

"You've been holding out on me for more than ten years?" I didn't know if I should lean back or forward. Luke had a point— me, pinned between the two of them, was pretty perfect.

"I know *now* that I've been in love for a long time. Back then, I just knew you gave me awkward boners and I couldn't stop daydreaming about you."

"Hmm… yeah. That's *true* love." Despite my sarcasm, I struggled not to laugh. "This is how you win me over?" It was working. I was hooked on both of them.

Luke jerked a thumb at the food. "Did we mention dinner?"

"And there's the whole *confessions of love* thing," Chase added.

I couldn't hold the poker face any longer. "I love you both too. I can't shove that aside or pretend it doesn't exist. It takes too much effort, and I'll miss out on too much."

"Exactly." Luke pressed his mouth to mine softly at first, then deepened the kiss into something demanding.

I draped my arms around his neck, drawing my nails up his skin, and sinking into everything.

Chase trailed his lips along the top of my back, to my shoulder, nudging one of my top's straps aside. "Food's going to get cold." He didn't sound concerned.

"Fuck the food." I managed between Luke's devouring my composure via my lips.

Luke bit my bottom lip. "I'd rather fuck you."

"That's good, actually. I don't want to walk into the kitchen, to find you with your dick in a box of Pad Thai." It'd be funny… but also disconcerting.

"Unless that's your kink." Chase glided his hands under my top, to rest his palms on my stomach.

Luke's chuckle was muffled. "If it's got more spice in it than the cinnamon in apple pie, I'm not sticking my dick in it."

"I'm spicy." They made me feel like I was, the way my skin lit up every time they were around.

Luke kissed the tip of my nose. "You're scorching. But more like peach pie."

There it was again. I pulled away to look him in the eye, without breaking the connection to either man. "What is it with peaches? Is that a guy thing?"

"It's an *us* thing," Chase said.

Luke almost looked apologetic. *Almost.* "One of the things we talked about, regarding you—what your pussy would taste like."

Should it sting, to be reminded of what they'd done? No. They apologized. I forgave them. "You know now."

"I do. And right now I'm very much in the mood for more of the same." Luke hooked a finger in my waistband and snapped the elastic. He kissed down my chest, hitting my bare stomach when Chase pushed my shirt up.

Butterflies danced inside when Luke knelt in front of me. He might be the one on his knees, but I was happy to surrender full control to his whims.

TWENTY-FIVE

Luke dragged my clothes down my legs. His lips on the inside of my thighs—the rough scrape of his five o'clock shadow—burned over me. He followed a slow, indirect path that made me squirm in anticipation.

Chase kissed from my shoulder up to my neck. He scraped his teeth over the sensitive skin and sucked. I couldn't squeeze my legs together, but every other bit of me clenched at the tantalizing sting. The little girl in me giggled, and a laugh slipped out.

"What's so funny, Annie?" Chase asked between bites and sucks.

"Chase Hughes is giving me a hickey."

I felt him smirk. "And that's just the start."

Luke licked over my slick skin, and my laugh melted into a moan. He pressed his face into my pussy, devouring me, groaning against my skin, and sliding up to my clit and back down several times. He thrust his tongue inside me.

God, that was incredible. I swayed on my feet, into his attention, careful to never break away from Chase.

Luke moved his fingers to my clit and played while he devoured me from the inside out. With Chase's hands on me and Luke's tongue inside me, the drawn-out pleasure was delicious.

My pleasure built slowly. Each time I started to clench, Luke eased up.

Until he didn't. He pressed in hard on my clit, and orgasm ripped from me. I ground into him, breathless and needy, until it all became too much and my body shied away.

Luke stood, pressing me back against Chase and keeping me upright. They were so warm. So safe. So completely fucking amazing.

"You're wobbly, Annie." Chase's tone was playful.

"Proof the two of you are incredible at what you do."

Luke nibbled my earlobe. "We have a stunning medium to work with."

"I hope you don't think we're done, because *God*, I want to fuck you." In a single, impressively fluid swoop, Chase lifted me into his arms.

I laughed at the sudden tilt of the room, hugged his neck, and buried my face in his chest. He carried me into my room and set me gently on the bed.

Both of them stripped out of their clothes and rolled on condoms. It wasn't some sort of fancy dance, but I enjoyed the show regardless.

Chase knelt between my legs and kissed a lazy path up, to my lips. He claimed my mouth, swallowing my sighs as he glided the head of his cock along my slit.

He slid inside me with a long groan that felt as good as his thickness. My body lit up in response.

He thrust at a slow pace, pulling out almost to the tip, before plunging deep again. "How are your legs?" he asked.

Pinned to my chest. "Better."

"Good." He gripped my hips, hitting marks Luke had left and sending sharp stings of pleasure racing over my skin. Chase rolled onto his back, bringing me with him, only slipping out for a second before impaling me again. He glided his palms up my chest, to cup my breasts. "You're my absolute favorite sight. Always. But especially when you're flushed and smiling."

My skin heated at the attention.

"Just like that." He smirked.

I didn't care that he set a slow pace. It felt good to have him buried in me.

Where was Luke?

Chase dragged his fingers up my back, pulling me into him, and the mattress shifted.

Slick, cool fingers teased along my ass. There was Luke. He nudged my rear opening.

It felt different. Not bad, though. "I've never…"

Luke pressed his mouth to the hollow of my neck, behind my ear. "I told you I wanted to fuck every hole, baby doll. Do you want me to stop?"

"No." If I relaxed both my body and my trepidation, his touch felt good. "But be gentle?"

"For this, all right."

More cold slid over my skin. I didn't have lube in my house, though I would in the future. "You planned this."

"I hoped it." Luke barely penetrated me with two fingers. "I was a Marine—always be prepared."

"Those are Boy Scouts," Chase said.

"*You're* a Boy Scout." Luke's tone was teasingly defensive. "I mean, yeah. I think you're right."

My laugh mingled with a sigh. Luke pulled his touch away, but Chase was tracing his thumb along my slit, bumping my clit before gliding away again.

Luke nudged my ass again, this time with the head of his cock. "Relax," he said gently. "You're going to want to clench. Focus on doing the opposite."

Chase distracted me with licks along my chest, as Luke pushed into me an inch at a time. Slowly. Coaxing me. The stretch—the new sensation—was agonizingly delicious.

"You good?" Luke asked when he was fully inside.

I nodded.

The rocking between them was slow as well. A cautious buildup toward the incredible. Mild discomfort melted into pleasure, flowing over and through me.

As the speed of everything increased, my orgasm held back. Unsure what to make of this new combination of touches.

Chase finally focused on my clit, circling and rubbing. Harder. Faster. Pushing me past that edge of uncertainty to tumble into a ravine of intoxication. I dug my fingers into his arms when I came.

He moved his thumb to my mouth, and I sucked hungrily. Climax lingered, holding me in that cloud of pleasure.

I lost track of who came when. The room was a chorus of grunts, screams, and then heavy panting, as we slowed and struggled to catch our breath.

When Luke slid out of me, I felt like part of me deflated. He pressed against me, though, keeping me from missing his presence.

Chase softened inside me and slowly withdrew as well. "I was worried you wouldn't hear us out."

Luke kissed along the back of my neck. "I wasn't."

"Really?" I raised my brows, though only Chase could see.

Luke nipped at my shoulder. "Not really. I was terrified of losing you."

"You didn't." I couldn't imagine being this close to one of them and not the other. How did this happen in just a week? Or was that why I'd never dared admit either of them was flirting with me? Because it would mean choosing?

It's because you're dim, and you're wrong.

It was easier than it had ever been, to tuck away the Shawn-voice. It didn't belong here. "Though I'm grateful you didn't make me choose."

"Me too," Chase said. "You would have picked, but you would have always felt like something was missing."

Luke snorted. "You mean picked me."

I rolled my eyes, but I was laughing. That would probably become a new regular. "Doesn't matter now, because you both got smart."

"Damn straight." Chase tilted his head up, to brush his lips over mine, then rolled me onto my back.

We cleaned up. Or rather, they insisted I stay where I was, and they cleaned themselves and me up, then served me dinner in bed.

Pretty sure they didn't plan this part, unlike the double penetration, because my being fed hot wings while surrounded by fluffy bedding, and trying not to giggle at the fun, was messy.

Which I loved. Then again, I loved all of this.

"ALL MY FRIENDS ARE HEATHENS—"

"Your friends are calling." Luke talked over my ringtone.

Last night, I slept better than in ages, and we'd all been awake for a bit this morning, but there was the sex, and the lying around, talking about breakfast, rather than actually getting it.

"I'll get it." Chase climbed from my bed. He looked gorgeous and very naked.

Speaking of— "They're probably on Facetime." I didn't move to stop him.

"You get it." Chase tossed the phone to Luke, who was still covered by blankets, and pulled on his boxers.

Luke swiped to answer. "This is Anne's phone. She's tied up at the moment—"

"Not literally." I poked my head into the frame, loosely holding the sheet over my chest. My hair was a mess. They'd seen worse.

Chase dropped back into the bed, on the other side of Luke. "Ladies."

Sadie covered her eyes and peeked out through her fingers. "We'll call back when you're not busy. This afternoon?"

"Probably a good idea, and that'll work." I laughed.

"But you owe us details," Lyn added.

Sadie screwed up her face. "Eww, no. No details."

"She can censor the story and just include the important bits about me," Luke offered.

Nope. I was going to be selfish about my men. "They're mine— the guys and the details. Sorry, not sorry."

Sadie rolled her eyes. "You can keep them."

"Lucky bitch." Admiration filled Lyn's voice. "Let's do lunch

later. Bring your boy toys. We need to grill them. Question, not—
You know what I mean."

"Question us about what? You already know us," Chase said.

Sadie shook her head. "Apparently not."

This was going to get circularly silly quickly. "'Kay. We'll send lunch details."

"You'll get distracted and forget," Lyn said. "We'll send lunch details, and if you're late, we'll assume you're fucking."

"La la la la la." Sadie mimed covering her ears.

That goofy grin was back. The one I had the day we arrived in Sacramento. "Love you both. Later." I hung up.

Chase took the phone from me, turned it off, and tossed it to the foot of the bed. "I believe we were discussing breakfast?"

"Anne à la mode?" Luke nuzzled my neck.

This was so right. The perfect fairytale ending, for this twisted princess.

EPILOGUE

I t took four more months to get the game in the hands of our customers, even with all the code Mike tried to get rid of, and another two months to make sure everything was stable.

But here I was, in my new office, with my finally-official *Director* title. I sank back into my executive chair, a permanent smile on my face.

Billie had stepped into Mike's job in Sacramento, and now that I'd been promoted, she was leading both teams, though several of our developers were moving on to pre-production games. I was heading up one of those new projects, and while it wouldn't hit market or so much as tickle gamers' thoughts for years, I was so excited to have a say in it.

My office was a lot like Luke's, but in a different part of the building. A huge *CONGRATULATIONS* sign hung from the top of my whiteboard, and my trashcan was filled with paper plates, cake crumbs, and empty soda cups.

My desk was mostly clear, but a figurine of X, courtesy of a miniature sculptor Lyn knew, lived between my monitors.

And Luke sat in the chair across from my desk. "How do you like the new digs, Bosslady?"

"Digs?" It was weird, me being in the Director's chair and him on the other side of the desk. "They're swell." Weird, but amazing. Then again, everything with Luke and Chase was amazing. I was seriously smiling all the time.

"You usually say *swell* when things aren't."

Fair point. "This time, they're actually swell. I love the new place. I'll make you come to me sometimes now."

"You call, I'm here."

At the sound of a knock, we both looked up. Chase stepped into the room and closed the door behind him. He was subtle about twisting the lock, but I'd seen it done enough times that I didn't miss it.

"You heading home yet?" he asked.

"Nah. I like it here so much, I thought I might move in."

"Can I have your theater system, then?" Chase asked.

"What?" I feigned hurt. "You're not going to come live here with me? In my perfect new office?"

"Say *yes* now. She's going to spend half her life here anyway," Luke teased.

Chase sighed and came around to my side of the desk. "I don't know. I bet you don't even get 4K on those monitors."

"I do." Perk of the job—high-end gaming rig. "But fine. You can go live in my big empty house, all alone, and I'll stay here, in my cozy office, with Luke."

"Whoa. I never said *yes*." Luke moved to stand next to Chase. "I have my own cozy office."

I pouted.

Luke tugged my bottom lip down. "Speaking of awkward segues… I've been thinking that I don't like going home to separate beds. Ever."

"I don't think there's room for all three of us in here, and Chase obviously thinks my screens are too small." I knew where Luke was heading, but I wanted one more jab of fun.

"Your globes are exactly the right size." Chase dropped his gaze to my chest. "But I'm sure we can find plenty of ways to entertain ourselves here."

"Fine. I'll spell it out. I was thinking someplace besides the office," Luke said. "As in, all three of us living together in the same place."

Yes was on the tip of my tongue. "Did you have a specific place in mind?"

"I figured we'd all want a say in that. Maybe new memories in your place. Or a new place that's ours. It doesn't matter, as long as I get to come home to the two of you at night."

I looked at Chase, who grinned and said, "I'm in."

"Me too." I was going to be high on giddiness by the end of the night. Did that count as intoxication? Now I was being silly, too.

"Except for one thing…" Chase looked away.

"What thing?" I didn't like his hesitation, but he was up to something.

He nodded across the room. "I was hoping to try out your new couch. See what kind of *bounce* it has."

Me too. "You can do that anyway."

"Yeah?"

"Sure," Luke said. "You stay here, sleep on the couch, and we'll go celebrate."

Chase turned and covered Luke's hands with his own. Pressing in, he crushed his mouth to Luke's.

I groaned along with them. They didn't kiss often, but it was becoming more regular. "I can leave both of you here, if you need some privacy."

Luke stood, never breaking the kiss, and used his body to nudge Chase back. They finally split apart.

"Don't you dare go anywhere." Luke's tone was playfully threatening.

I was up for that challenge. "Or what?"

"I'll spank you."

I stood, placed my palms on my desk, and stuck my ass out. "Big words, big man."

Luke's palm connected with my backside before I'd registered that he moved. The *smack* that echoed through the room mingled with my gasp. We shouldn't do this in here, but that didn't stop us at any point in the last few months.

He tugged at my hair, pulling my head back. "Stay," he growled in my ear.

I whimpered. There was no room for argument. Not that I would argue. "Yes, sir."

"Good girl." Chase leaned in and kissed me hard. He caught my bottom lip between his teeth when he pulled away.

This was fun. A little kinky, a bit risky, and a lot of the most amazing anything I ever could have hoped for.

Fourteen-year-old me never would have believed me, if I'd told her when she was drooling over Chase, that this was our future. Then again, twenty-three-year-old me never would have bought that I'd be spending nights in sexy-boss's bed. But it was all real. *Our* future. All three of us together. And nothing could be more perfect.

ASKING FOR IT

ONE

My friends and my business were the two things I loved most in this world.

They were also currently the two things causing me the most frustration. I was heading to my favorite all-night bookstore—could it still be a favorite if it was the only one?—in an attempt to take my mind off both.

I wasn't sure I could enjoy the trip through my guilt, though. I'd blown off my friends' invitation to spend time with them and their guys, by telling them I had to deal with my shop. Now I was here instead.

For years the three of us were Sadie, Anne, and Lyn. Three Musketeers. Peas in a pod. All sorts of cute phrases for things that just fit perfectly together. But things had changed since they landed themselves in long-term relationships. It wasn't that they'd cut me out of their lives, but each of the was with two men, and most of that group consisted of our inner circle. Hanging out with them meant watching the flirting, the googly eyes, and subtle intimate touches. And now I was Lyn The Third Wheel. Seventh wheel? Either way, I was the spare, in the trunk for emergencies, but other-wise, on the outside looking in.

That analogy was crappy on a lot of levels, but no one was around to hear it, so I wasn't going to fix it.

I wouldn't wallow, though. They were happy, and I was genuinely glad to see that. Sometimes I just wasn't in the mood to be immersed in their gooshiness.

All right, I was a teensy bit jealous that they each had two guys. I'd never had a problem getting laid. It was easy to hide my insecurities and extra pounds behind a mask for one night, but longer than that and both became evident.

Not wallowing. Not wallowing.

My night would be filled with enjoying a good book, and coffee made on someone else's espresso machine.

The bookstore-slash-coffee-shop was nestled in a part of Sugar House where old and kitschy met new and trendy.

This was one of the original buildings in the area, and I loved the way vines crawled along the stonework outside. Inside had a similar feel, with solid bookshelves extending in every direction, and an eclectic collection of wrought iron and carved wood in the café.

I liked to wander when I came in here. There were certain sections I always hit up—romance, sci-fi fantasy, and manga—but I wanted to stroll past all the books, make sure I didn't miss any or leave any lonely.

There were people in almost every aisle, reading, browsing, and lingering. It was a gorgeous sight.

I'd stay in the stacks for hours if I didn't have to be up early in the morning. I wanted to buy everything that caught my eye. With all my spare money going back into Java Loading, my anime gaming café, I had to limit myself to only a few books.

Selections in hand, I paid, and made my way to the adjoining coffee shop. They had a new salted caramel, extra espresso, with a mocha whip drink that looked incredible.

And it was probably a billion calories. I got the no-caff, no-sugar, no-fat macchiato instead.

There was one free table left. Score. I took my drink and settled in to read. The chatter washed over me, making the scene in my book, where the heroine meets the hero in a crowded train station, feel more real.

"Excuse me," a seductively deep voice said.

I glanced up from my book to find the owner of the voice watching me with starkly pale green eyes framed by black hair. *Hello, sexy.* "May I help you?" Some nights I might flirt with him, but I wasn't in the mood tonight.

"I'm Fred, this is Barney." He jerked his thumb at the guy with him. Who was just as gorgeous. *Fred* looked more professional, in a button-down shirt with the sleeves buttoned around his wrists, and *Barney* was in a faded concert T-shirt and battered jeans.

The serious one and the clown. Interesting, but not unique, combination. Stupid names. "I'm Betty." I could play along with whatever their game was until they were gone. Especially for the view.

"Told you she was a Betty." Barney nudged Fred. No surprise, Mister Concert T-shirt wasn't as reserved, but he was just as nice to look at as his friend.

Fred pursed his lips, but turned a smile back on me. "We're sorry to interrupt. There are no more free tables. May we share yours?"

It was a polite enough request. I gestured to the chairs next to me. "Help yourself."

Fred nodded at my book. "It must be a good book."

"It's one of my favorite series." It was the new issue of *Spring Popcorn*. The artwork was Japanese inspired, but the artist was local. The two main characters were male best friends who refused to admit they were in love. She had a stunning grasp of the male form, and the way she alluded to their will-we-won't-we physical relationship was almost hotter than seeing it in vivid detail.

Almost. My imagination was happy to fill in the blanks. The same way it was doing right now with Fred and Barney. Hell, they could be the stars of the comic. Or my life. I didn't have any issue slotting them into a fantasy or two, where I was the middle in a Bedrock sandwich.

"No spoilers. I'm two books behind," Barney said.

He was reading this? "Then you probably don't want to know that Haru turns into a dragon halfway through this one, to save everyone from the Nazi invasion." I kept my tone serious. The series was strictly contemporary, with no magic, so I half-hoped he'd know I was teasing.

His grin was worth the joke. "I'd better catch up, then. Especially if there's a little bit of dragon-on-best-friend action."

"That's a disturbing image." Disturbingly intriguing.

Barney winked. "But you're totally trying to figure out the logistics anyway."

"Busted." I was enjoying this more than I'd expected.

Fred nudged his friend. "We'll let you get back to it. Thanks for letting us intrude."

I'd read a while longer, and if they got too loud I'd go. Right. Like I could focus with two mister hotties sitting right here.

They kept their voices low enough that I had to strain to hear them, even though they were only a few feet away. Sounded like they were from out of town, but loving the city, and hoping to see more of it while they were here.

I wasn't reading anything, despite trying my best to look like I was. I tried to block them out and pretend they weren't impacting my universe with their manga-come-to-life looks and politely low conversation. It didn't matter how hard I stared at the page in front of me, I wasn't processing any of the words.

A tickle bubbled in my throat, and I reached for my coffee. When my fingers collided with the cup instead of grasping it, my gut sank. I'd missed.

Iced coffee splashed everywhere. Down my shirt. Over my slacks. On their shoes.

"I'm so sorry." All my composure vanished, and I fumbled for napkins to mop the table.

Fred plucked my purse from the floor before the creeping puddle reached it, and my panic surged harder until he set the bag on my now-empty seat.

"Excuse me," Barney hollered at a nearby employee, cranking my humiliation higher. "Can we get a mop over here?" He left, and returned a moment later with a stack of napkins. He handed me several. "Take care of yourself. We've got this."

"Thank you," I mumbled, and started patting coffee from my once-white top. The liquid suctioned my clothes to me, clinging to my boobs, every fat roll. The sooner I got out of here, the sooner I could tumble backwards into humiliation. Until then, I was going to be collected.

I looked up to find Barney staring at me.

"Enjoying the show?" I hid a wince at the aggravation that slid into my voice.

He looked up, meeting my gaze unflinchingly. "Quite a bit." There was a sincerity and heat in his reply that scorched my already hot skin.

"Sorry about him." Fred elbowed Barney. "His filters don't always work right."

Barney didn't look fazed. "She asked, I gave her an honest answer."

"While she's all sticky and covered in coffee." Fred started undoing the buttons on his shirt. "Take this."

I held up a hand to stop him. Not that I would have minded the show. "I'm okay, really." I didn't look cute in a guy's shirt, the way some girls did. It would probably fit, but I wouldn't drown adorably in it. "Besides, we can't both be showing off our assets. People will get the wrong idea about this place."

"Do they have coffee shops like that? They should," Barney said.

If they were going to pretend this was no big deal, I could summon some phony self-assurance. Sex, fake confidence, and self-effacing humor had been my shield most of my life. "The kind where they spill your coffee on you instead of letting you drink it?

Barney looked me over again. Every time he did that, I swear I felt his gaze. "Assuming *they* is *you*, do I get to lick it off after?" he asked.

Was he hitting on me or making fun of me? It didn't matter.

The coffee was drying and my clothes were getting uncomfortable. "I'm sorry about your shoes. Thanks for your help, but I need to get home."

I turned away, eager to escape the embarrassment and confusion.

TWO

I was halfway to my car, when I heard, "Betty." Fred jogged up next to me. "Wow, that really does sound weak."

"It really does." I looked at him with raised brows, it probably wouldn't if it were my name, but it didn't escape me he still didn't offer his real name.

Barney joined us. "If you get in your car now, it gets covered in coffee too, and you have an uncomfortable drive home. We're staying next door. Walk over with us, and you can clean up in my room. Borrow something dry. Be on your way."

"Wow, that's…" I had no words.

"Super generous, right?" Barney winked. His *cute* was becoming *creepy*.

Fortunately, it helped me grab an answer. "A unique, but not super convincing way to get me to come back to your room."

Fred shrugged. "You're the one who spilled the coffee."

I didn't appreciate the reminder, but he said it without accusation or cruelty. He almost looked hurt at my tone. That hardly seemed fair. "Then this *isn't* a ploy to get me to join him in his room?" I asked.

"His room, my room. It absolutely is." Barney grinned.

It should have occurred to me to wonder before now, which of them was hitting on me? I'd say Barney, but Fred was working awfully hard to keep me happy. He was either one hell of a wing-man, or...

No. There was no way it was both of them. Because that was what I'd been fantasizing about, and getting it would either be too much of a coincidence, or a cruelty when it went badly.

"But more people than you think tend to balk at the idea of two men from out of town trying to pick them up at the same time." There was a trace of humor in Barney's voice.

I pinched myself. Ow. Nope. I was still here. I did it again. Still hurt. Still didn't change the sexy dual scenery.

"What are you doing?" Barney asked.

"Trying to figure out what kind of dream this is." *Are you a good dream, or a bad dream?* The voice in my head sounded like the good witch from the Wizard of Oz. Maybe I'd dream of yellow brick roads next.

They chuckled, and Barney's smirk melted to something less cocky. "Since you don't seem interested, I'm making a genuine offer to let you clean up, which will be followed by a genuine offer to buy you a fresh cup of coffee after. And then we'll try again to seduce you."

"That sounds like a lot of trouble to go through for the woman who just spilled coffee all over herself." My brain wanted to say *chubby girl*, but I'd let the insult gnaw at me from the inside, rather than exposing it to them. "You could have let me walk away and found someone—" cuter, thinner, and less abrasive "—else to win over."

"If we'd been interested in someone else, we would have approached them instead." Did Fred sound... wounded?

A guy like this—like them—could smile at any other woman and have her. If he was hurt that I wasn't falling for the charm, he may be more concerned with hearing *no* or *yes* than who it came from. But he hadn't struck me that way up to this point. If I'd gone to the bar instead of the bookstore, I probably would have accepted their offer. I'd have been there for a hook-up, and they seemed sincere enough.

Except for the fake names.

They were cute. They were flirty. I did hate being covered in coffee.

And if it was so easy to lie to me about who they were, they were hiding other things as well. "I appreciate the offer, but I'm going to call it a night, gentlemen. I hope the hotel elephant shower has hot water, and that the stone houses aren't too drafty when you get back to Bedrock."

Barney laughed.

Fred gave me a short bow. "Yabba dabba doo, Betty. Maybe we'll run into you again before we leave town."

"Maybe." Unlikely. I'd probably avoid this bookstore for the next couple of weeks, specifically to keep that from happening. I was socially awkward that way.

There was a whisper of regret in my mind telling me stories of what could have been as I drove toward home. I couldn't help but replay the conversation in my mind. I was used to pick-up lines that reached *hey baby, let's fuck* without much hesitation. *Fred* and *Barney* actually made an effort. Plus, they were hitting on me *together*.

I'd made the right decision walking away, but everything about their attention painted a little smile on my face that didn't want to leave. Their company was fun while it lasted, and it had been a while since I walked away from two attractive maybe-hookups, and felt good about myself.

I parked around the back of my house. My café was up front, and took up the entire ground floor of the converted Victorian home. The rear stairs led up to the bedrooms and living area on the second floor.

I'd gotten the house for an amazing price in auction. Low enough I could pay cash, and still have a little—very little—left over for renovations.

Until about a year ago, I'd always operated in the black. But I took a risk based on how well business was going, and secured a large loan to upgrade a lot of my equipment. Renovations slowed business enough both during and after, that I was struggling to pay that new bill.

There was an envelope slipped through the mail slot when I stepped inside. As I skimmed the formal notification on city letterhead, my heart sank.

A request for a zoning change had been filed, to remove residential properties from my area.

I'd had to fight to get my housing here to begin with. I couldn't afford to move to a new place now.

THE SUN WAS SHINING, the birds were singing, and okay, it sounded cliché, but I felt great in the morning. Sleep gave me enough sanity to know I could deal with the zoning issue just fine when the hearing happened in six weeks, and I still had warm fuzzies from the attention I got from Fred and Barney last night. I didn't mind blocking out the doubt, since it was a snapshot in time.

I put on one of my more fitted tops. It was sunny yellow, to match my mood, it did great things for my cleavage, and it mostly hid my tummy. I'd be standing to bake a lot of today, and wearing an apron, so I didn't have to worry about the space between the buttons gapping apart when I sat.

Living above my shop made for a convenient commute. In under a minute, I was in my gorgeous, big, industrial kitchen. Stainless steel appliances lined the walls, including three double-sized ovens opposite a massive fridge. In the middle stood a large island— half stainless steel, half butcher block. I loved this place, even if it was part of the reason I was struggling to make ends meet.

Today it would help pay for itself. I'd started taking on catering jobs to supplement the café's income. Tomorrow would be my biggest event yet. One hundred each cupcakes, bagels, croissants, and chocolate chip cookies, for the Digital Media company town hall.

Anne had teased me about working for the enemy—she was a game Director for DM's biggest competitor, Rinslet. But she's also told me if I happened to overhear any corporate secrets, she was happy to be my confidant.

She'd been joking. Mostly.

I set a pot of coffee to brew, and prepped my workspace for the pastries I needed to make for the shop this morning. Two hours later, I was on my third cup of coffee, and was setting the day's sweets under glass in the café.

Violet, my store manager, would be in soon to open up.

Time to get down to the big order. In my dreams, I was making enough money to hire more bakers. People I trusted as much as I did Violet to do their jobs without constant supervision. For now, the task of baking was mine.

I had a rhythm to my work that let me manage multiple batches at once. There was always a temptation to sample the goods, especially with me having skipped breakfast, but more coffee kept my stomach from growling.

The familiar ringtone that Anne, Sadie, and I all used for each other reached my ears. I pulled the call up on the tablet I kept on my counter, to find Anne grinning at me.

"You're baking," Anne said as a greeting.

I grinned. "What gave it away—the apron or the kitchen?" The happy note from last night still lingered in my thoughts. I turned back to my work, knowing she wouldn't mind.

"I'm just perceptive like that." Her tone was as bright and sunny as the weather. She'd had a long run of stress at work, but since a few things fell into place, she was a lot more like her old self. It was nice to hear. "Real quick, so you can work, girls' night out this weekend?"

Just the three of us? "Totally up for that."

"Yay. So, what has you humming?"

Was I? "I'll share details, but not until we're face-to-face. This weekend, probably."

"I'm never going to live that down, am I?" Anne laughed. When she'd first hooked up with her guys—as in her boss and Sadie's brother—she put off telling us by saying she'd rather have the conversation face-to-face.

"Maybe someday. Just not today." I turned to find her pouting at the camera. Too adorable. "All right, I'll spill. Otherwise you'll think it's a big deal, and it's not. I got hit on last night, and while it didn't go anywhere, it made me feel good."

"You're being vague with your pronouns."

No. Just with my counting. "Because it's not a big deal, because it didn't go anywhere. Text me details for this weekend."

As I resumed working, I tried out the humming again. I liked that. I kept a tuneless song flitting around me as I worked on cupcakes. Those needed to bake and cool first, so I could decorate them while everything else was cooking.

It might have been nice to lose track of time, but with a timer on each step, that wasn't happening. Still, the next couple of hours passed quickly.

"There's someone here to see you." Violet's cheerful voice startled me as I was stepping away from the oven.

Not the best timing, but not the worst either. "Do me a favor, keep an eye on those." I nodded to the oven. "If I'm not back in twenty-five minutes, take them out?"

"No problem."

I dusted the flour from my apron before hanging it up on its hook, and headed out into the main shop.

Fred and *Barney* were standing near the front counter. They were dressed differently than last night, both looking gorgeously sexy in suits that accentuated their sturdy builds, ties that my imagination wanted used on me, and flat expressions that growled *don't fuck with us.*

My stomach turned in on itself, and every muscle in my body tensed. How did they find me? Did they follow me home?

THREE

I'd pushed my luck for far too long, making a habit of one-night stands with strangers I met in bars. And now the one time I'd picked a bookstore instead, I'd managed to run into not one, but two creepy stalkers. If I screamed, Violet would call the police. The thought didn't reassure me the way I wanted it to.

"What are you doing here?" I kept my tone steady, despite my creeping fear. "Did you follow me home last night?"

Fred frowned. He had the nerve to look offended? Now? Or was that his normal look? "I'm looking for Jaelyn O'Driscoll. Are you she?"

How the fuck did he know not only my name, but all of it? "May I tell her who's asking?"

"Owen Samson." He extended his hand, and nodded at Barney. My already churning gut plummeted into my feet, and I knew he was going to say, "and my associate Kingston Ryder."

Fuck. Fear bled into irritation. These were the two assholes who had been trying to buy out my business for several months. And last night I'd considered going back to their hotel? Worse, I'd enjoyed their company.

I crossed my arms rather than shake his hand. "I'm still not interested. Now that we've covered that, I have a huge catering order I need to get back to. I trust you can find your way out as easily as you found your way in."

"Sharp wit *and* dangerous curves. You're destruction in a stunning package." Kingston used the same flirty tone he had as Barney.

Why was a sliver of me still enjoying him? Still sending shivers of desire through me while my brain begged me to indulge a fantasy. "If I'd realized last night that you're the kind of men who can't take *no* for an answer—"

"We have a new offer for you, and it's a good one," Owen said.

I clenched my jaw at being cut off. If I screamed, I'd look irrational and unreasonable, even though they were the ones who kept coming back after I turned them away. It was tempting to scream.

Kingston's smirk didn't improve my mood. "Not as good an offer as last night."

And now he was mixing business with pleasure? Implying screwing him was better than… whatever this was?

Then again, this was irritating the hell out of me, so sex probably would be better.

Bad libido. Stop.

Owen sighed. "Don't listen to him, he forgot to put his dick away. We're here on business. Nothing else."

"Something we agree on." I gave them a thin smile. "This is absolutely nothing, because you're leaving."

"Five minutes." Kingston's tone and posture changed like a switch had been flipped. His playfulness disappeared behind an intimidating mask of seriousness.

This was why I hadn't recognized their voices last night. Kingston was always the one to call me, to negotiate, and this voice was different than the flirty, carefree one he'd approached me with in the bookstore.

I could reinforce a third time that they needed to leave. But if I heard them out, and their offer sucked as much as I expected it to, I'd have blocked off more of their avenues for arguing. I hated knowing they could control the conversation this way, but I was going to close every loophole they could find, until they heard me.

"Five minutes. I won't start a timer, but make it fast, and make it good."

I shouldn't have phrased it that way. *We always take our time, and it's always good.* I swore I could hear Kingston's voice in my head.

His lips twitched, and I pursed my lips, daring him to take the accidental innuendo outlet.

Owen elbowed him, and his serious mask was back in place.

"May we do this in your office?" Owen asked.

No, because my body was still reacting to them. It didn't matter that it shouldn't be. We'd stay in a public place, where it was easier to remind myself that everything about them right now was pissing me off.

Even admit the memories of how nice last night was. How they'd looked at me. How sincere and complimentary they were…

"Out here is fine. Did you know who I was yesterday?"

"No," Kingston said quickly. "The only Jaelyn we know is the curvy avatar."

Call me Lyn. I swallowed the offer. Only my friends called me Lyn.

He was talking about the woman in my shop's logo. The cute one with the generous hips and breasts, and a waist I'd never have. She looked like me as much as she looked like any voluptuous brunette. I went out of my way to keep my own face off social media—I hated pictures of myself. I didn't even let Sadie post me on her different pages.

But Owen and Kingston were the same. I'd dug into them a lot in the past year. They identified their company with names and a logo. I'd never been able to find a single picture of either of them. I'd assumed they were rich old assholes who didn't understand social media.

Turns out they were rich younger assholes, who probably understood more than they let people know.

"What's this proposal and why is it so much better than the previous ones?" I asked.

Owen pulled an index card from his jacket pocket. "Ten percent over the previous amount." He needed notes to tell him that?

"Wow. That's *so* much better." I let the sarcasm spill into my retort. "Answer's still *no*. Wow, that didn't even take one minute. Have a nice da—"

"There's more," Kingston said smoothly. "And fuck, you make it hard. To behave."

I was getting real sick of them talking over me, especially since that pause in his phrasing was intentional. I was as mad at the part of me loving the flirting as I was at them. It would be so easy to slide into a playful comeback. A lot more difficult to forget who they were, in order to do so. "You were saying?"

Kingston's smirk was back. Sexy, arrogant jerk. "Most of the cafes we bring on are happy to take our money and step aside. We made a mistake assuming that was what you'd want to do as well."

Thank you, Captain Obvious. I swallowed my retort. The sooner they finished their spiel, the sooner I could get rid of them.

"You built the place, you love the place, I get that." Kingston sounded sincere. He was good at faking it, apparently. "I understand that more than you might believe."

"That's not a high bar." I couldn't help myself.

The corners of Owen's mouth twitched. "You keep the property. The new amount is only for the business. We'll rent the shop space from you, ask you to keep running the place, and double your salary. The only thing that really changes is we acquire your business's debt, you'll have access to our suppliers, and we'll put our sign in the window next to yours. This remains *Loading Java*, it simply comes a subsidiary of Kingu Kafes."

It was an implausibly sweet deal. On the surface. It was tempting to say *I'm in*. It would solve the letter from last night. It would solve a lot of things. It was also too good to be true. I had questions—the same ones they'd never answered in the past. For instance, how were they going to afford to be so generous, when I could barely keep the place operating the black?

"For that kind of money, you could set up your own shop. Why are you so focused on mine?"

"You have a customer base, a solid brand, and reliable product,"

Kingston said. "Competing with you thins the local market as well as our chances of succeeding."

That made sense. "And your solution is give me a lot of money, and beyond that, everything is business as usual." It wasn't quite that cut-and dried though.

Kingston nodded.

Owen looked more hesitant.

"Until you decide you don't like how I do things, and you override me by either firing me or buying me out." With as starkly as we clashed now, I didn't suspect that would take long.

Owen furrowed his brow. "We don't plan on—"

"My answer is still *no*." It felt good to be the one talking over him. "I run my café the way I do, because I like having this control. This is my business. My investment. My passion. Thank you for your time. See your way ou—"

The loud blare of the fire alarm cut me off, shrieking so sharply it threatened to pierce my eardrums.

FOUR

Smoke. Now that I wasn't distracted, the heavy smell hit me hard. I rushed to the kitchen. My only priority was finding the source and shutting it down.

Violet was already at the oven, muttering and pulling out smoldering trays of cupcakes. The panic in her expression grew when she saw me. "I'm so sorry. I had a customer, they kept me longer than I realized. I'm so sorry." Red splotched her cheeks and deep creases marred her forehead.

She was typically too detailed and aware to let things like this happen. The freaking out she was doing right now was rare.

"It happens. It's okay." I was stressed too, but I didn't blame her. "I need you to shut off the fire alarm. Call the fire department and let them know there's nothing wrong. Clear people out of the shop and open all the doors." As I talked, I ticked off the list in my mind. Lists made me calmer. "Anyone currently here gets a $5 gift card for their next visit. Put a sign on the counter that gives everyone 5% off pastries for the rest of the day, as an apology for the smoke smell. Do you have all that?"

Violet nodded.

I knew she would. She was my store manager for a reason. "You all right?" I softened my tone. "This isn't a big deal. No one got hurt. Everything will be all right."

"Okay." Her smile was weak, not hiding the lingering stress. She headed toward the alarm shut off.

As soon as she left the room, I sank against a nearby counter and let the panic overwhelm me. I'd already had a long day with baking and everything else. This would only add another hour or so onto the end of my day, if everything went perfectly, but I was going to be exhausted by the end of the original schedule.

Emotion indulged, I breathed in and out slowly several times to force it away. I turned to grab my apron.

When I saw Owen and Kingston near the kitchen doorway, I jumped in surprise, and my heart lodged in my throat. Why did they follow me?

I didn't have the time or patience for this. I tugged on my apron, never making eye contact with them. They'd seen me crack, but they wouldn't see me break. "Something I can help you with, that we haven't already discussed to death?"

"Actually, we'd like to help you." Owen was calm. Smooth.

No, really. I had zero time. "Are you going to magic a hundred chocolate and vanilla cupcakes out of thin air."

Kingston smirked. "Sort of."

I was learning to love-loathe his sexy, smug face. Was that a thing? I was making it a thing.

"I did two years at a Cordon Bleu school in Massachusetts. You tell me what you need done, and I'll do it," Owen said.

Of course he had. Mister sexy, rich businessman was also a baker. I'd read it on his profile on his company's site, but I figured it was just words to give their investments in cafes some credibility. I looked at Kingston, waiting for a similar boast. "And you?"

He shrugged. "I did two years of being a short order cook. I can follow instructions like no one's business."

"Why would you help me?" I didn't understand.

"Because you're sexy and stressed." Kingston's flirting didn't seem to be just for show. He slid into it without hesitation.

I shot a glare at him. "Try again."

Owen had probably been the straight man for as long as they'd known each other. "Because you're catering under a label we're trying to purchase, and at the end of the day, we'd rather its reputation stay solid."

That actually made sense. "This isn't going to change my mind."

"Didn't think it would. Clock is ticking?"

And I loathe-loved Owen's gorgeous perfect way of looking good and being rational and saying all the right things at the wrong time.

I pointed. "Aprons are behind you, sink is behind me. Wash up. You're going to get your suits dirty. And you realize I'm just using you for the manual labor."

"Worth it." Owen had already pulled off his suit coat and hung it out of the way. He rolled his shirt sleeves up, exposing an intricate Celtic knot tattoo trailing up the inside of his arm.

I'd never been an arm girl before, but strength and surety in his movement made me want to whimper in delight. I turned away before I could imagine him pinning me to the wall by my wrists and running his lips over—

Nope. I was on a deadline, and he was one of the assholes trying to buy my dream out from underneath me.

They'd offered to help, and if they were competent, I was going to take it. "The bad cupcakes need to be thrown out, and the pans cleaned."

Kingston grabbed the first muffin tin. "Master dishwasher at your service."

I wasn't going to let them do anything that could slow me down more, but with the extra I'd made of certain items, that still left me with a list of tasks. "There's dough for croissants in the walk-in, in big plastic containers. Start kneading a batch." Might as well get Owen moving on those, since they'd take the next most time. See if he was worth what he said.

"You got it, boss." He vanished into the fridge, and reemerged with one of the tubs of dough.

We worked for the next couple of hours. They picked up every task I gave them without complaint, and by the time afternoon rolled around, I was ahead of schedule rather than behind.

I'd be out of here long before midnight, the scenery was stunning when it was quiet… My day was looking up after all.

"Who delivers the best food around here?" Kingston's question was the first non-baking one anyone had asked since we dove into work.

I needed more information to respond, though. "Pretty much anything is available on one of the apps."

"I'll rephrase that. We need to eat, what do you recommend?"

That they not watch me eat. My schedule didn't allow for meal breaks on days like this, but I wasn't up for stuffing my face in front of them anyway. "Depends on what you're in the mood for."

Owen paused in his bagel shaping duties, and held my gaze with a penetrating stare. "What do *you* want? You can't say *nothing.*"

"Why not?" Maybe they hadn't caught on yet, I didn't respond well to being told what I couldn't do.

"Because you're swaying on your feet. You can't run on coffee alone."

I could and I had. But arguing with them would make this into a big deal, and I didn't want that. "There's a great Chinese place just a couple of blocks away. They have fantastic pork soup dumplings." The owner was as white as anyone, but he'd gone to Hong Kong on a Mormon mission, decided he liked cooking more than the faith he'd been raised in, was trained by a local master, and came back to open his own restaurant.

"That sounds great." Kingston pulled out his phone.

"Menu and phone number are in the binder on the counter." I pointed. "I'll have the side salad with ginger dressing." The twin looks of disbelief I received were almost accusatory. "I'm not that hungry."

My bitch of a stomach chose that moment to growl and betray me.

Owen raised an eyebrow. "I'll have what she recommended."

Kingston called in the order, which included three helpings of soup dumplings, plus my salad. Either I did a fantastic job upselling the food, or he was assuming and ordering for me. I wasn't going to make a fuss out of it. If one of them was going to eat it, fine. If they tried to give it to me, that was their mistake.

We worked until the food came, then set up a space away from the work area, with three stools pulled up to an island.

Sure enough, Kingston slid me a bowl of pork dumplings, along with my salad.

I pushed the extra food back. "This isn't what I ordered."

"But it's what you wanted," Owen said.

He was right, but I didn't appreciate the assumption. Just like that, a morning of peace evaporated, and my irritation was back. Half at them, for going against my wishes, and half at myself for being too stubborn to take the food.

FIVE

Kingston nudged the dumplings back toward me. "If you keep eating rabbit food, you'll damage those curves."

I clenched my jaw. Jokes about my weight were at the top of my *things I hate* list. Go figure. But that wasn't what he'd done.

He was watching me with a *look* again—one that set my blood on fire. The food *did* smell good, but I didn't like that they'd ordered for me when I told them not to. "I'm good with the salad. Now you have leftovers for later."

"No fridges in our hotel rooms," Owen said. "The food stays with you unless you want it to go to waste."

They were backing me into a corner, the way they kept trying to do with buy-out negotiations. And I wasn't making a big deal out of this. I moved the box to sit outside my arm. I'd have Violet take it home or something. "Fine."

I plucked cucumber slice from my salad and nibbled it far longer than I needed to. The dumplings looked good and smelled better. Why did they have to force my hand?

Kingston wielded his chopsticks with ease as he took a bite of food. His groan was a low, throaty rumble that sent pleasant shivers racing over me.

Own was using a spoon, and his moan was just as tempting. "You're right. This is incredible."

Jerks. They were doing that on purpose.

"I know you're not hungry"—Kingston sectioned off another bit on chopsticks—"but you have room for one bite." He held the food out.

I could eat that and be delicate, and then we could drop the entire conversation. I leaned in and took the food offering. As I licked my lips, I earned another groan. I was going to bake under the intense heat of Kingston's gaze.

I must have been bright red as I turned back to my salad. It didn't look as appetizing now that I had the other flavors on my tongue, but this was about pride and proving a point.

"Would you like another bite?" Owen teased his fork near me.

This was just mean. "I'm fine."

"You look a bit put out."

"But you still look *fine*," Kingston said. "I'll agree with that."

The flirting was going to get old. It hadn't yet, but I was sure it would. "I'm not that girl."

"What girl?" Owen put his spoon down.

"The one who says she doesn't want anything, and then eats half her—" I couldn't say *date* or *boyfriend* "—dining companion's food. Besides, I have my own, which was thoughtful, if not presumptuous, of you."

"Fuck, you're stubborn." Kingston sounded amused.

"Says the man who refuses to take *no* for an answer."

"If you want the food, eat the food. It's not like you care what we think," Owen said.

"And *you're* infuriatingly logical."

Kingston laughed. "Isn't he, though? That's why he lets me do the negotiating. People want to come to the bargaining table with their hearts, not their minds, regardless of what they say. You, for instance, are looking at our offer mostly based on your heart."

"I told you this was my passion. You don't need a psychology degree to figure out I'm not turning you away because of the money." I didn't care for being analyzed, even if I was doing the same to them. But Owen had a point, too. If I didn't care what they thought of me, why was I hesitating to eat? And now I'd done the one thing I didn't want to—made a big deal out of the food.

"I'm not doing this because you're right. About anything." I set my salad aside, grabbed a pair of chopsticks, and plucked a dumpling from the broth.

"Of course you're not." Owen kept a straight face.

Kingston was smirking though.

It was a good thing they were leaving at the end of the day. They wreaked havoc on my mind and body, and part of me wanted a lot more of the same.

I really wanted the focus off me and my dietary choices. Always, but especially now. "How long are you two going to be in town?" That was polite and gave me information at the same time. It would tell me how long I needed to hide and avoid them.

The glances they exchanged were impossible to interpret.

"Is it a secret?" I asked.

Owen opened his mouth.

"Yes." Kingston talked over him. "At least for now it is."

"Ah." Not that it was really my business, but it was an odd thing to not want to discuss. "Then, how about that gorgeous weather we're having? Or are your thoughts on that a secret too?" I kept my tone light.

"It *was* a secret, but then the press caught wind, and social media started talking, and now *everyone* knows I think the weather is perfect right now." Kingston finished with an exaggerated sigh, and the corners of his eyes still crinkled with laughter.

If he weren't gorgeous and rich and completely on top of the world, I might start to think the steady stream of humor was there to mask an insecurity.

"Speaking of the gorgeous weather—" Owen looked like a light bulb had just gone off in his mind —"we're meeting a few friends up at Strawberry Reservoir on Sunday. They've got a huge cabin up there. You should come with us."

Besides the fact that the invitation was completely out of the blue, the lake meant water meant boats and swimming and most likely people in bathing suits. Not for me. "Why?"

"They come from some of the more influential families around here," Owen said. "In politics. In money. It's a good chance to make some connections."

"Also, they're fun. Otherwise, what's the point?" Kingston added.

That still didn't answer my question. "I'll be clearer. Why *me*?"

"You're smart. You're an excellent businesswoman." Owen ticked off bullet points.

I stared at him blankly. "Which doesn't translate to *come hang at the lake with us and meet our rich friends.* You barely know me."

Owen raised an eyebrow. "We're still trying to make you a business partner, and this is a good excuse to get to know you in a social-but-professional environment."

And there it was. His answer didn't bother me the way I thought it should.

"Some people think it doesn't matter who you know, but it does. Use this to your advantage," Kingston said.

I hated the idea of owing anyone or calling in favors, but Kingston was right. Their reasons for introducing me didn't have to be mine. "Don't suppose any of your friends are connected to the city council." As in, could they put me in touch with someone who could help me with my zoning issues?

Not that I'd skirt the system that way, but I'd feel a little better about my upcoming hearing if I knew someone.

"As a matter of fact, yes," Owen said.

"Sounds like fun." I was making a mistake, accepting. But they were here on business, and had made no illusions about it. I doubted they had any false ideas about why I'd join them anywhere else, either.

The conversation drifted back to barely-there small talk. We finished lunch, and dove back into baking.

"The limited edition poster you have for X-10, in the café." Owen shaped out bagels like a pro. "We called in every favor we could think of, and couldn't get one of those. How'd you manage it?"

Kingston rolled his eyes. "He's a fanboy. Don't get him started, or he'll never stop."

"What did you think of how it ended?" My question was leading. A lot of the *fanboys* had a problem with the way the X franchise had wrapped up. In the final game, the hero confessed his love to the man he'd been sent to execute in Game 1, but whom he saved instead.

If Owen fell into that category, maybe it would be enough to tell my libido to calm the heck down and stop drooling over him.

"Loved it." Owen's excitement shone in his gaze. It was the most emotion I'd seen from him. "That ninth game shook my faith, but 10... *Wow.* I should have seen it coming, and I didn't. Brilliant. Appropriate. Possibly my favorite game ever."

I'd pass the praise along to Anne, but why couldn't he have been an ass about the whole thing? "It is pretty good."

"And the poster?" Owen asked.

I shrugged. "I fucked one of the developers."

Kingston looked impressed. "I hope he was worth a poster."

"*She* is worth a lot more than that. But we make better friends than lovers." Why had I gone out of my way to bring up what Anne and I used to have? To prove to them I was desirable, or to remind myself?

Neither of them looked fazed. Bonus points to them for not casting judgement, though a hint of jealousy might have been nice.

"So, is X's relationship based on you two?" Owen's question was light and playful.

Anne wasn't involved in the writing, just the programming. "Well, she did pretend to execute me once, in order to save my life. Slid her cart racer into mine, to push me out of the way of a blue turtle shell. But we didn't swear vengeance on the legions who did it."

"No?" Kingston leaned against a nearby counter, palms rested on the butcher block top. "Because that's some pretty serious shit."

"Everyone gets a little power hungry when they're playing a

mushroom driving a cartoon car. He lost anyway, so I suppose fate stepped in on our behalf."

Chase could be a sabotaging asshole in Mario Kart, but Anne loved him and he was Sadie's brother, so we forgave him the competitive streak.

"So are you a Princess Peach kind of player? Toad?" Owen asked.

"Donkey Kong."

Owen's eyes grew wide. "You know how to control that slide?"

"Better than anyone, especially if they try to pass me in the corners."

"Brutal." Kingston sounded appreciative. "That's sexy."

I flushed at his sincerity. Not used to not having a comeback, I turned my attention back to making buttercream frosting.

The only way I had to measure time was by how much we got done. I was still surprised when Violet poked her head in.

"Store's locked up," she said. "Do you need anything"—she glanced at the men—"or do you want me to stick around at all?" Her implied meaning *are you all right alone with two strange guys* was clear.

I gave her a reassuring smile. "I'll be okay, thank you. Enjoy your night."

She gave me one last wave, and was gone.

Owen offered to help decorate the cupcakes. That was a little more control than I wanted to give up, but I also wanted to finish. I made him prove himself by piping on a piece of wax paper, and was impressed with the results.

We worked for a couple more hours, putting the finishing touches on everything, and boxing it all up.

"Last one." Owen added the box of cupcakes to the stack, and turned to face me.

He had two almost perfect smudges of chocolate on his forehead, that made him look like he had double eyebrows and was very surprised. I bit my lip to hide my amusement, but a laugh slipped out.

"What did I miss?" He raised an eyebrow. That made it even funnier.

Kingston joined in the laughing. "Chocolate on your face."

"Where?" Owen frowned.

I shouldn't keep laughing, but I couldn't help it. "Your forehead. Here." I crossed the distance between us, and smudged the frosting away with a towel.

"You think that's funny?" Owen's tone was threatening, but he was smiling too.

"A little, yeah."

He booped my nose. "There. Now you have chocolate on your face too."

"You jerk." I reached to wipe it away.

Owen grabbed my wrist. "Leave it. It looks cute."

A shiver of desire ran through me at the heat of his grip, and when I met his gaze, my breath caught at the intensity staring back.

Now would be the perfect time to pull away. But my body was too focused on the heat flowing between us and the faint scent of his cologne mixed with sugar, to get the message.

SIX

I forced myself to act, dipping a free finger in the extra frosting, and aiming a touch for Owen's cheek.

He captured my other wrist as well. His grip was more solid and tantalizing than my fantasies promised, and now my brain was skipping ahead to the part where he'd pin me to the wall—

"What are you going to do now?" Owen's tone was teasing mixed with challenge.

Whimper and beg him to lift me on the counter and take advantage of me? "Pout?" I jutted out my lower lip.

Kingston had gone quiet. Was he watching? Enjoying or irritated?

"That's not a deterrent." Owen pulled my frosting covered finger into his mouth.

When he traced circles over my skin, licking it clean, that whimper escaped.

His smirk was another layer of delicious. He dropped that wrist, still studying me. "Next plan?" He asked.

I nodded at my still captured hand. "You got chocolate on my wrist, too." I'd stop short of asking him to lick every inch of me —probably.

A touch met the small of my back. "Save some for me." There was Kingston. He grasped my fingertips.

Owen let me go to reach past me and grip the back of Kingston's neck. He crushed his mouth to Kingston's in the sort of all-consuming kiss that made my lips whimper for a hint of the same.

I think my gasp was as loud as Kingston's when they broke apart.

Kingston chuckled softly and bit his bottom lip. "I meant the gorgeous lady's chocolate frosting, but that's pretty good too."

Just. Wow.

The way they interacted with me, with each other, told me they were practiced at this two-guys-one-girl thing. Not that I expected to be their first. I was here for the physical gratification. The show between the two of them was an added bonus. Were they more than friends? They must be with a kiss like that.

When Kingston licked the sensitive skin along the inside of my wrist, my questions faded into the background and I moaned. That felt better than should be legal.

"Good?" he asked with a grin. His composure had returned.

Mine hadn't. Any answer I could come up with felt weak, so I settled for nodding.

He increased the pressure of his tongue, alternating between licking and sucking, until goosebumps raised over every inch of me, and my nipples strained against my bra, wanting to feel this for themselves.

"Did you plan this?" My doubt was a bitch for trying to ruin this moment.

Owen twisted his mouth. "Which one of us?"

"You seem to work together pretty well, so both or either?"

Owen dipped his finger in the frosting again, and trailed a line down the side of my neck. He leaned in and dragged his tongue up the same curve, stopping with his lips on my earlobe. "Did we plan for you to burn dozens of cupcakes?" he whispered. "To have a deadline. To be willing to accept our help. To be so much fun to talk to, on top of being sexy as fuck?"

When he put it that way…

He caught my earlobe between his teeth, and tugged before pulling away to look me in the eye. "No. But if I had, I couldn't have hoped for better."

"What if I kick you out right now, with a terse *thank you*, and that's that?" I wasn't going to do that. They were delicious and there was nothing wrong with a physical, no-strings outlet to relieve stress, if that was where this was going. It didn't even matter that they were my rivals. It wasn't like I had to look them in the eye on a daily basis.

Kingston turned me toward him. "Then you kick us out. It was still a good day." Damn him for saying the right thing. "Are you telling us to leave?"

"No."

He was close enough I could see a faint dusting of flour in the dark stubble on his jaw. He fiddled with the top button on my blouse, tugging the fabric aside.

"Good. Because I can't help but wonder, what you'd look like in just this apron." He was making it difficult to remember why I didn't care to have them in my life. He scraped my skin with a fingernail, stealing my breath.

I took the apron off. Was that better, or worse? "You're not finding out today." I kept my tone playful.

"What if"— He trailed a finger along my chest, following the curve of my shirt, dipping into my cleavage —"I want to see what you look like with nothing on at all? I've been fantasizing about unwrapping you since last night." He dipped his head next to my ear, hot breath caressing my cheek. "If I drag my tongue over your bare skin, do you taste like salted caramel?"

Absolutely not. That was ridiculous. "Only one way to find out." My response came out breathy. My pulse hammered in my ears at my own challenge—this kitchen was public. A lot of people got off to the idea of getting caught, but it was one of my top fears. Was there a phobia based on that?

Focus. Two gorgeous men were showering me with compliments and kisses, this was my place, even if it was in the business part of the building, and no one else was here now.

Kingston undid one button and then another, until my blouse hung open.

And there was another surge of insecurity; in this brightly lit room, my less-than stunning body would be on display.

He tugged the fabric open, exposing bare skin and breasts straining against pale satin. The way he raked his gaze over me, I suddenly felt like a goddess.

"Fucking gorgeous." Kingston slid his hands up my sides and his lips down my neck. He kissed along my collarbone and down to the top of my breasts, teasing his thumbs over the cups.

Owen trailed his fingers lightly up my spine, almost enough to tickle, but the sensation was too tantalizing to pull away. He unclasped my bra with a deft twist. The tension that fell away was nothing compared to the anticipation that replaced it.

With double the attention, it was easy for me to fall into the physical. Owen kneading one breast while he nibbled on my neck and shoulder. Kingston drawing a nipple into his mouth to suck and lick.

The attention drew on, building the desire that raced over me and wrapping me up in the illusion of being wanted. Needed. I didn't care that they'd done this before with anyone else. It meant they knew where to touch to make me moan and squirm. Their touches were a delicate ballet of hands and mouths, and my body was the stage.

Kingston ran a hand down my back, over the curve of my ass, to my leg, and pulled my leg to his thigh. He slid a knee between my legs.

Without Owen there, chest and erection pressed into my side and hip, I wouldn't have the balance for this.

Kingston pressed his leg higher, against my mound, and I ground into him. A new point of contact drew another sigh from me. The way he groaned into my skin, still worshipping one nipple then the other with his mouth, cranked my need higher.

I had to feel more. As much as I could. *Everything.* I dragged my nails down Owen's chest, to his hard length. When I cupped him through his trousers, he jerked into my touch with a dangerously delicious moan. He was hard and thick, pressing into my palm as I stroked him.

Kingston let my leg down, and raised his head as he knotted his fingers in my hair. His dark eyes sparkled with promises of mischief.

I could drown in that look.

He brushed his mouth over mine. "Better than salted caramel." He nipped my bottom lip. "Better than anything salty or sweet." He tightened his grip in my hair, tugging hard enough to draw a gasp from me. "Better than anything." He kissed me hard.

My mind sang and whimpered and begged for more.

Kingston undid my slacks, and slid his hand under the waistband, over my panties, teasing me through fabric.

I gripped Owen tighter, and he bit my shoulder.

The sting of pleasure and pain was new to me, and incredible.

Kingston kissed along my jaw up to my opposite ear. "I fell asleep last night dreaming of fucking you. You were incredible then. You're better in real life." His whispered words, the flattery, were more effective than poetry.

"Do you have condoms?" I wasn't so far lost as to skip important steps, but I was getting close.

Kingston pulled back to meet my gaze again. He wore a dangerously hungry smirk as he extracted a condom from his wallet and held it up between two fingers like a prize.

In a disruption of hands, and my nervous giggle when my pants got stuck on my shoes, my clothes were shoved to the ground and kicked aside.

I unzipped Kingston's trousers, reveling in his throaty gasp when I wrapped my hand around his shaft. He bit his bottom lip, looking like it took immense effort to pull away and roll on the condom.

Kingston's hands on my hips, he guided me to a nearby stool, and nudged me to sit. I didn't like the absence of Owen's touch. I was greedy to have both of them embracing me again.

And then he was there again, half-supporting me, turning my head to face him so he could claim my lips.

Kingston slid between my legs, which parted eagerly, and dragged the head of his cock along my slit, teasing until I whimpered against Owen's kisses.

When Kingston pushed inside me, spreading me open and stretching me out, I let out a muffled gasp. He worked to a steady pace, thrusting enough to build my pleasure, and bring it to a heady ledge. He dropped his head to my breasts again, to suck on a nipple.

Owen worked a hand between us, down my stomach, to find my clit. He circled the swollen button, faster, harder.

Climax surged through me without warning, splashing around me. Consuming me. I clenched around Kingston, lost in orgasm, my body shuddering away when Owen's touch became too much.

More. The insistence was louder now, rather than being sated. I fumbled my way through unzipping Owen's slacks, and freed him. The noises they made, the attention they gave me, the scents of sugar and sex, were better than the finest liquor, going straight to my head.

Kingston increased the pace and intensity, slamming against me, inside me, striking the right spot and breathing new fire into a fading orgasm.

I stroked Owen in rhythm with the pump of Kingston's hips. Gripping tighter as another wave of pressure built inside me.

Owen covered my hand, setting the pace, not letting up even as I came again, tumbling into the sea of sparkles that danced behind my eyelids.

Twin grunts, staccato and wrapped in climaxes of their own, filtered into the haze I floated in. Fingers dug into my hips. Warm sticky fluid covered my hand.

The world slowly swam back into focus as we slowed and stopped. Owen was behind me, holding me upright, and Kingston had his forehead buried in the crook of my neck.

It would be a little while before I wanted to move from this spot. The impulse was there to cover up. At least grab the apron Kingston said he wanted to see me naked under.

But it was easy to ignore the thought, nestled between them.

"So…" Kingston kissed along my shoulder. "You'll take a look at the contract now?"

Ice raced through my veins, freezing my entire body.

Owen's groan was a different one than he'd been making all day. This sound was less sexy and more disbelief.

I forced myself to move. To extract myself from the pile of limbs, and grabbed the apron. It wasn't enough. I needed a dozen layers of clothing between me and them. "Get out." I bit off the words.

They were both already on their feet, straightening their clothes. Buttoning and zipping up.

"I didn't mean it like that," Kingston sounded apologetic.

Which was bullshit. At least I could recognize that now.

"Please." Owen studied me with… pity?

I didn't want his fucking pity.

"Let me explain—"

"Listen to me." I interrupted Kingston with bitten off words. "Don't talk. We're done. Get. *Out.*" I spoke through gritted teeth. I refused to break in front of them, no matter how desperately I wanted to shatter into a million pieces.

SEVEN

The catering for Digital Media consumed enough of my brain that I could ignore yesterday, and what happened with Kingston and Owen. But as the event wound down and exhaustion sank into my bones, my brain was free to skip along any path it wanted.

By the time I got back to my apartment above the shop, my thoughts were berating me full-force.

I fell for the guys' bullshit, less than a day after they lied to me about who they were. It hurt from my toes to my hair follicles, that I'd let down my guard even a little. What was I thinking?

I was an idiot. Sex didn't equal a connection and neither did good conversation. A lot of people knew how to get along.

But this was different.

Was it? If I hadn't enjoyed their company, I wouldn't have screwed them. The day was fun, the sex was good, and I got to try the whole two-guys-at-once thing. Honestly, I'd expected disappointment, but that was good—*really* good—so I could check that off my non-existent bucket list.

It was sorted then. I'd had fun, no one used anyone, even though apparently that was what they'd been trying for, and it was time for

309

me to move on. I hadn't been an idiot after all, just made a few naive assumptions.

My thoughts didn't get the memo, though. Through the night and into the next morning, I was treated to replays of Kingston's kisses and Owen's touches and two skilled lovers savoring me like the most delicious delicacy.

As I made pastries for the shop, ghosts teased me with memories of them both working in my kitchen. Of the synchronicity we'd achieved. Of how good they looked in aprons, with their sleeves rolled up.

This wasn't working for me. I didn't swoon over one-night stands. Especially when they turned out to be assholes.

That must be why I couldn't move on. I'd resigned myself to the fact that most guys I hooked up with were either desperate and horny, or looking to fulfill some fuck-a-fat-chick fantasy, though they rarely said so.

But Owen and Kingston did it to get at my shop, and they never tried to hide that fact. It made me feel like merchandise. The extra two dollars spent to get ten dollars in free shipping.

"Do you have a minute?" Violet startled me from my staring off into space.

I shook away the haze of thoughts, and caught sight of the clock. Shit, the pastries. "Yeah. What's up?" I rushed for the oven, and pulled out the Danishes with plenty of time left to prevent another yesterday. I needed to stop spacing out.

"So, Anne is like a big deal over at Rinslet, right?" Violet asked.

I turned to face her. "She'd tell you not really, but she is." I'd take any chance I could to brag about my friends' accomplishments.

Violet lingered in the doorway, tangling and untangling her fingers. "I've got this friend, Luna, who's an amazing programmer. She's seriously top notch. But she's having trouble breaking into... well... anything. Sorry, *breaking into* was a bad phrase. She can't get anyone to take her seriously. I was wondering if Anne could give her some tips?"

"I'll ask and let you know, but probably." The answer would be *yes*. Anne loved to help other women get a foothold in development, but it wasn't my place to speak for her.

Violet grinned. "Thank you. I'm gonna open shop."

This was the life I'd built for myself—the life I wanted—with my café running smoothly, and friends who could count on me. I wouldn't let a pair of pushy—sexy, talented, intelligent, incredible in bed—strangers occupy space in my mind

While I worked, I called Anne on speakerphone. I wasn't in the mood to be on camera, even for her.

Her cheer when she answered made me smile a little, and the small talk helped more. I needed to get Owen and Kingston out of my head and telling her would help.

"Violet wants me to ask you a favor." I explained the same thing Violet had told me. Business first, and then I could expose a portion of my gullible soul.

"I'd love to help." Anne was cheerful. "Oh, idea. Would you be okay with them joining us Saturday night?"

"Of course." My answer slipped out without thought, and then my brain caught up. I was absolutely happy to help Luna out, and it wasn't as though we'd planned anything more than dinner. But I hadn't seen Anne and Sadie alone for a couple of weeks. "If Sadie is okay with it."

"She will be," Anne said.

As okay with it as Anne was. Because co-opting our girls' night out meant neither of them had to give up any more time with their men. I hated the bitter thought. "Cool. Let me know for sure, and I'll tell Violet."

"Are you okay? You sound... sad." Anne's tone shifted in an instant.

I smiled at my kitchen, to force the same feeling into my voice. "I'm great."

"You sure?"

"Positive."

"Okay. Call me if you need to talk, and we'll see you Saturday night."

My expression slipped the instant I disconnected. Anne was busy with work. Her shorter hours meant no weekend work, not that she had unlimited time.

Why was her time with me so much easier to surrender than her time with her guys?

Probably not a fair question—that wasn't why Anne made the request.

Was I sure?

I WAS PRACTICED at bottling my hurt and redirecting it into work. I didn't quite have the same willpower when it came to other things, and the next morning, my order from my dairy distributor included a tub of cherry-chunk, brownie batter delight ice cream. Which I spent the next two nights making an unhealthy dent in, as a dinner replacement.

By Friday night, I'd eaten way more than I intended to, but that didn't stop me from serving up another big bowl. I put a banana in there—that made it healthy, right?

I was binge-watching Project Runway, waiting for the inevitable moment when the token Plus Size model would be eliminated, when an unknown number rang through on my cell phone.

Not unusual, since I used the phone for business. I summoned my inner customer service persona, and swiped to answer. "This is Jaelyn."

"Don't hang up, please."

All the ice cream in the world couldn't suffocate the hurt Owen's voice summoned. I was too frozen to speak or disconnect. If I said anything, I wouldn't be able to hide how I felt, and he wasn't worth the tirade that wanted to push past my lips.

"Lyn?"

"My friends call me Lyn, you don't." I kept my voice steel. "I'm not signing your contract."

"That's not why I'm calling. I want to apologize."

"There's nothing to apologize for. We all know what happened. I would have preferred to know up front I was part of the business transaction, so I'd know I was a whore." I winced at the emotion that leaked into my words.

"Technically we were the ones exchanging sex for what we wanted. But we weren't—"

My fury spiked. "Are you actually mansplaining *my own feelings* to me?"

"I'm sorry. That wasn't my intent." Owen sounded sincere. Then again, he had yet to sound otherwise. "And sex plus a business proposition wasn't either. I didn't go into that thinking *If we fuck, that'll make negotiations easier.*"

"Uh-huh."

"Neither did Kingston. He's a good guy."

Why hadn't I hung up yet? Because he didn't get to see how pissed off I was. "He is your business partner." Friend? Lover? I'd never actually clarified that, but it didn't matter. "It might not be a great relationship if you didn't think highly of him." I bit back my thoughts about Kingston trying too hard, in order to hide his insecurities. "Let me guess, he just has a hard time separating business and pleasure. Did you know who I was at the coffee shop?"

"No."

"Really." My tone was back to flat.

"I swear to you."

A clipped laugh slipped out. "Your word doesn't mean anything to me."

"That's fair." Owen let out a long exhale. "Listen, forget the pitch. Come up to the reservoir with us this weekend."

Seriously? My disbelief and distrust couldn't crank any higher. "Why?"

"You'll like these people, not just as connections, but as people. And I had fun the other day, we'd like to spend time with you again."

Uh-huh. "What's your end game?" I didn't understand any of this, including why I hadn't hung up yet. Oh, right, because I wasn't letting him see that I cared.

"As in, what am I hoping to achieve?"

"Exactly that. Is this the next attempt to lull me into a false sense of security, and then dump another *you won't want to turn this down* pitch on me? Tug at my emotions to get me to play?" My experiences said that was the only reason for someone to keep trying this hard to win me over—they wanted something.

"Do I strike you as a *tug on emotions* kind of guy?" Owen asked flatly.

Mister Infuriating Logic? "No."

"My *end game* is spending more time with you. And as Kingston would say, enjoying the view. We'll pick you up at six Sunday morning."

"I haven't said yes, and I'm not up that early on a Sunday anyway."

"You are, because you bake everything fresh the same day."

Logical prick. I did still want to meet his friends. It may not do me any good, if this was some sort of cruel prank—my gut curdled at the idea mixed with memories. But if he was sincere, I may have a way to easily take care of this zoning thing, and if it was a joke, they'd never know they had any impact on me. I knew how to grin through the worst.

"Are you in?" Owen asked. "I should warn you, we're not giving up on your café, but I'll find a different way to convince you, and it won't involve tricks or sex or asking over and over again."

"I'm curious to see how what you think will work." And I was ready to turn him down, regardless.

"Me too. Sunday at six?"

He wasn't getting the best of me. Telling him *no* felt like the easy out. I was going to make them work for a result they weren't going to get. "I'll be ready."

EIGHT

Saturday night, Anne was already at the restaurant when I arrived five minutes early. So were Luna and Violet, but they stood several feet away from Anne.

I tugged them all together, and made introductions. I'd met Luna a few times, but she tended to be quiet unless she was talking about topics she was passionate about.

Sadie showed up just a few minutes later. "Oh, come on," she called lightly as she approached. "I was even on time. Do you know anyone else who's not early to everything?"

"Fashionably tardy is one of your charms," I teased.

Sadie stuck her tongue out at me and flipped me off. "Two minutes early is not late."

"Come on." Anne grabbed my arm. "I skipped lunch. I'm starved."

"How did you skip… Oh. Chase is out of town, isn't he?" I put the pieces together. She needed a Chase in her life to keep her fed, she was so skinny.

That was the last thing I needed in mine. A man who wanted me to eat more. Lunch with Owen and Kingston rushed back, rapidly followed by the memories of amazing sex, and asinine things said after.

Tomorrow was only to make connections.

We were shown to a table, and conversation was stuttered as we ordered drinks and food. I wasn't in the mood for Sadie and Anne to give me *looks* for getting a salad, so I indulged with quesadillas, and asked for a box, so I could put half of it aside immediately.

As our food arrived, things relaxed.

Anne and Luna slid into more technical conversation, filled with terms I only understood in the loosest sense. They were swapping programming stories and, from the laughs, jokes in a literal different language.

I'd never seen Luna this interactive. It made me smile that she and Anne were getting along so well.

"You obviously know your shit. What do you need me for?" Anne dipped a fry in enough ranch dressing to drown it, and popped the food in her mouth.

"I can't get anyone to talk to me. Like, interviewers and such." Luna pushed her food around her plate.

She could be some serious competition for me when it came to picking-but-not-eating.

Anne tilted her head and studied Luna. "What's your specialty?"

"Network security." Luna's enthusiasm for high-level java jokes vanished beneath a soft voice.

Violet nudged her. "She's the best. Seriously. She did this thing with my VPN… Am I allowed to tell them about that?"

Luna nodded. "Only them."

"She did this thing where… hell, she basically rewrote it, and now I can watch K-Dramas as they air."

"You don't speak Korean." Not that I was aware of, anyway.

Violet grinned. "No, but I can infer a lot from what's happening on the screen."

"Jealous." Sadie's tone was playful. "You can hook me up, Luna? Pretty please with sugar on top?"

Pink dotted Luna's cheeks, but she smiled. "Sure."

"I can talk to our security guy, see if he has any referrals for you," Anne said.

Luna's eyes grew wide. "No. That's okay. Taurus is… I mean, really, it's fine. Don't worry about it."

I wasn't understanding this conversation for entirely different reasons than I didn't understand the programming one. Rinslet's head of network security was Zane. "What's Taurus?"

"Never mind." Luna ducked her head. What I thought was quiet before was practically shouting compared to her volume now. "I wasn't sure what I was hoping you could do for me, but don't worry about it."

I looked between Luna and Anne. "What did I miss?"

Anne paused, burger halfway to her mouth. "Zane was an old school hacker, and he went by Taurus."

"He's-the-best. Probably. Definitely." Luna's jumbled reply sounded defensive.

Pieces clicked in my head. How didn't I see it sooner? I loosely followed cybercrime, because I had to make sure my café was safe. A few years ago there was a huge FBI takedown that no one was talking about outside of those circles. A young woman who had supposedly written a piece of malware that brought an entire sector of the college system to its knees. "You were behind *Project Fail.*"

"I wasn't *behind* it." And now it looked like Luna was trying to vanish inside herself. A move I was intimately familiar with. "I didn't mastermind it or anything. Someone paid me to do a job, it was a challenging one, and… I'd like to say I didn't know any better, but really my ego won out in the end, and I convinced myself it would be okay, mostly because I wanted to prove to myself I could do it."

"Oh. Wow." Anne sounded awed. "That was you? You've got *mad* skills."

"I'm not doing that anymore, I swear," Luna said. "I've done good things since then, I promise. But now that past is linked to my name, and no one will talk to me."

"I'll ask around—without dropping names, and let you know what I find out, Luna," Anne said.

We drifted into silence as everyone ate, then Sadie turned to me. "Anne said you were all smiley the other day," she said.

Oh yeah, that. "Couple of cute guys at the bookstore were friendly and flirty. Nothing big, just the kind of attention that makes a woman smile." I stopped short of saying when, since I'd blown Anne and Sadie off to make that trip. I'd rather not get into details anyway, since thinking about the next day summoned a jumble of emotions that made my gut churn and my food suddenly unappetizing.

Sadie looked skeptical. "*Friendly and flirty*? Tell us more."

"There's nothing else to say, really. You don't want a play-by-play of them asking about my yaoi." My smile looked real, but I was being devoured from the inside-out.

Sadie's expression said *I really do*, but she nodded. "That's fair."

I might tell her and Anne later, but definitely not when anyone else could hear. It took me a long time to learn to open up to them, and even now there was a tiny nagging, every time I brought a problem to them, that said I was either being a bother, or was stupid if I couldn't figure out the solution on my own. Did I think the same of them? Of course not. My low self-esteem loved the boost of knowing I could help someone else.

"Ooh, speaking of"—Violet was suddenly excited—"what ended up happening with those two guys the other day? The ones who came into the shop. I'm surprised they haven't been back. Disappointed, really. They were *hot*." She made a sizzling sound.

"They were assholes." I needed to change the subject, but was drawing a blank. My brain had chosen to focus on the parts of that day that didn't bother me—the kisses, the touches, the fun…

Sadie leaned in. "There were guys? Since when does asshole matter if you're only looking?"

She was throwing my own logic at me, damn it. I had a counter, though. "They're the guys who keep trying to buy my shop."

"And they had the nerve to approach you in person?" Anne's cheerful demeanor slipped. "You want I should hunt them down?"

It's okay. We talked. We fucked. They're still assholes, but I was an idiot, so it's not their fault. I wanted to spill, so badly, but not in front of Violet and Luna. They were sweet enough, but they weren't my inner circle. "No, but thank you. It's one of those too-weird-for-fiction stories. There was a disaster while they were there, they helped, and at the end of the night"—they showed their true colors—"they promised to back off on the *we want your business* thing." The lie tasted as bad as the memory.

"They've been calling you for more than a year," Sadie said. "Why would they back off now, all the sudden?"

They wouldn't. I shrugged, not having a better response.

The conversation shifted away from me, and kept going for a few hours. As the clock crept toward ten, my tomorrow-plans loomed like a big, daunting beacon in my thoughts. I hated to be the one to leave first, but I needed to at least try to get some sleep before tomorrow. I pushed back from the table. "I hate to do this, but I've got an early morning. Are you all okay if I cut out early?"

"We'll be fine," Sadie said.

"What she said." Violet nodded at her.

Everyone was friends with everyone. Awesome. I looked at Sadie and Anne. "I'll call you Monday."

As I headed to my car, I heard footsteps running to catch up with me. "Lyn." Anne grabbed my arm to stop me. "Early morning? What's up?"

"Nothing. I promise." *Everything.*

Anne tugged me away from the restaurant entrance, to sit on a bench around the side of the building. "Tell me," she said.

"I slept with them." The instant the confession slipped out, I braced myself for the judgment. Not because Anne ever had, but there was a first time for everything. "I mean, not slept, but there was sex, but first there was niceness, and they were so complimentary, and we were having fun, and then they ruined it. I'm such an idiot."

"You're not." Anne twisted her fingers with mine and squeezed gently.

I dragged in a deep breath. "I am. Because that's where I'm going in the morning."

"For more sex? I mean, if you're gagging them first… then they can't ruin it, right?"

A laugh slipped out without my permission. "They know the Millers. They're going to introduce me. I'm going so they don't know they pissed me off, and so I can make friends with people on the city council. Not for sex."

"I can still hurt them for you, if you want."

"I'm good, but thank you."

Anne squeezed again. "I don't want to see you hurt. Ever. Pretty sure you told me something similar not too long ago, and it works both ways. If you're okay with all of this, then that's fine. But you're not an idiot. Do you have this under control, or do you want me to yank you out of it?"

I appreciated having the options. "I've got it under control." And the more times I told myself that, the truer it would be.

NINE

Leaving the restaurant before everyone else didn't help me when I got home; I tossed and turned most of the night.

When my doorbell rang in the morning, I was on round five billion of *what the hell am I doing?* The question hadn't stopped me from stuffing a swimsuit, towel, and change of clothes—none of which I intended to need—into an oversized bag, along with a bottle of Sauvignon Blanc, to go with brunch, or just picnic-style drinking in general.

I answered the door to find Kingston kneeling on the front step, head bowed.

He didn't look up. "I'm so, so sorry. Please forgive?"

Was I more embarrassed for him or me? I was at least a little curious if he could see up my denim skirt. "Please get up."

"I'd make a joke about being up just because you're here, but no erection humor until you forgive me." He stood, putting him a few inches above eye level instead of tantalizingly below.

"Where's your other half?" I wasn't getting dragged into fun with him. No witty banter. No teasing.

Kingston patted his legs and chest, his back and front, and his left and right shoulder. "All of me is here."

"I meant Owen."

"Ah. He's in the car. Said watching me humiliate myself in front of you once fills out his lifetime quota."

I wasn't going to forgive him just because he was goofy and cute. "Anyone can grovel."

"But how many people do so willingly?"

I pursed my lips and stared at him.

"I'm sorry about the other day. Sincerely and honestly." His serious tone replaced the playfulness, and he held my gaze. "It may surprise you to hear this, but I don't always read a room right, and sometimes my jokes fall flat."

"If that's your idea of a joke… Has it ever in your life been appropriate to fuck someone and then tease them about it being for business?"

He shrugged, and pulled off *sheepish* with flair. "It's never come up before. You're unique in a lot of ways. Forgive me."

"Are you going to give up on trying to make the deal?"

"No."

The honesty was refreshing. I didn't like his answer, but I wouldn't have believed him if he said anything else.

"And fair warning in that same vein," Kingston said. "I'm hoping if you spend time with us, you'll see what a good idea this partnership is."

"What you're proposing isn't a partnership." It was pretending to let me stay on in a management position until they didn't like my feedback. I would only have the power they assigned me, that they could take away just as easily.

"Semantics. But I swear to you, cross my heart, hope to die, stick a needle in my eye swear to you, sex is not part of that equation. Anything physical is its own separate thing."

He wasn't talking past tense. But he was still being honest.

"In that case, I should be up front and say the only reason I'm going with you today is because"—someone's fucking with my zoning… I wasn't going to tell him that, in case he decided to use it as leverage—"you're right that it's good to make connections."

Kingston offered his arm. "That's fair. Shall we?"

My body wanted that contact again. That heat I felt every time he touched me. My heart and mind knew better. I Ignored his arm and fell into step beside him as we walked to the SUV waiting at the curb.

Owen smiled as we drew closer, and offered a cheerful "Morning," when we were within earshot.

"Morning." I tried to keep my tone and expression cool, but my smile was as genuine as it was hesitant.

Kingston held open the front passenger door for me.

"I'm fine in the back," I said.

"Take the seat." Kingston gestured. "He and I see each other all the time. If you're up here, it'll be harder for you to pretend you're not part of the conversation."

Called out on an intention I hadn't vocalized to myself. "Fine. Thank you."

We settled into our seats and hit the road. This early on a Sunday, there was no traffic, and we were on the freeway heading east in less than ten minutes.

"Are the two of you from Las Vegas originally?" I asked. It was where they opened their first store, and I'd rather lead the conversation toward them then let it drift back to me. If I gave them the right opening, they had the kind of egos that would let them talk for hours about themselves.

"No," Owen said.

I waited for more. So much for my brilliant plan and observations. It was early, though. I'd come up with something else to draw them out.

Kingston leaned forward, resting one arm on the center console between Owen and me. "Vegas was a twenty-first birthday present from my mother." Some of his cheer had vanished. This wasn't the business-voice I heard on the phone, but it wasn't his standard light-heartedness either. Odd way to sound when talking about family.

My parents were amazingly supportive, but I understood not everyone's were. I heard the same tone from Anne when she delved into her past.

"Fortunately"—Kingston's cheer was back, like flipping a switch

—"I got to take my best buddy, and we tore up the town." He slapped Owen lightly on the arm.

"Ah. A fun-filled weekend of strippers, free booze, and high roller suites?" I kept my tone playful.

Owen laughed. It was a throaty joy that danced over me with temptation. It didn't matter that I barely knew him, I suspected that kind of amusement wasn't typical for him.

Which was fortunate, given how much I liked it.

"*Birthday Trip* is a code word for business trip, in this case. I was supposed to…"

When Kingston didn't finish the thought, I glanced at him to see if I'd missed something. He'd leaned back in his seat, and was sitting with his face just out of my view.

"… find some direction," he finally said.

What made him hesitate? Did I want to know *that* much about them?

"We stumbled on a little gaming café," Owen said. "Most incredible thing we'd ever seen."

Kingston resumed his leaned forward position. "That's where we went instead of all that stuff you said. We spent days on end in that place."

I liked the visual, Kingston in a faded concert T-shirt, Owen in a button-down with the sleeves rolled up, both of them hunched over computers in someone else's shop, kicking ass in something multi-player.

"What's with the smile?" Own asked.

Was I? "You're not my typical customers." Why didn't I just tell them the truth? *I'm fantasizing about the two of you having fun, and it's both completely non-sexual and makes you even more desirable.* That was why.

"I think you'd be surprised. But this was also ten years ago." Owen was sliding into the more casual tone I'd heard from him when we were baking together.

They were either supremely confident in their plan to win me over, or capable of letting down their walls a lot more easily than I did. What would it be like, to be so comfortable with existing? I shook the deep thought aside. "I know how the story goes from here—you spend time in the shop, you think *this is wicked awesome,* and set up your own place to drive the guy out of business."

"Ouch. And no." The look Owen gave me was withering.

"He was already going out of business, which we found out after chatting him up," Kingston said.

A process I was becoming familiar with. The two of them were practiced at the *chatting someone up* experience. "About twenty minutes, then?" Please let this joke land better than my previous comment.

Kingston grinned. "Young and not nearly so experienced, remember? More like an hour."

I laughed.

"The shop owner mentioned things were failing." Owen picked up the story. "I was straight out of cooking school, and every one of my business ideas centered on baking, so I tossed out some ideas about fresh baked sweets."

"He liked what we had to say, but wanted to move onto other things." The way Kingston dove in, it felt like they'd rehearsed this story. They probably had, but the two of them still had a dynamic that was nice to watch. "He's an old school, hard core gamer who didn't like the direction of the industry, or that his shop couldn't make it as-is."

"So he sold it to us." Owen glanced at Kingston in the rearview mirror.

What was that look? Questioning? About what?

Kingston shrugged. "Everyone already knows, she might as well too." He focused on me. "I did it to piss off my mother. She'd told me to make something of my life, and I intended to prove I could do that through gaming. Not as direct a route as some people take, but I'm happy with the outcome."

"And the rest is history and listed for the world to read on our website." Owen wrapped the entire tale up with a nice neat bow.

A story like theirs didn't end so abruptly, though. I could ask for more info—it was tempting—but I didn't want to delve into the innermost details of their private lives. I wasn't here to get to know them on a friendship level, just to learn enough to protect myself and my own shop.

"So are the two of you…" What was I doing? This was the exact opposite of not delving into their private lives.

Owen glanced at me. "Are we…?"

It wasn't that I had a problem asking *are you a couple*? They'd played tonsil tag in front of me, so it was a reasonable assumption. "I'm wondering if your partnership goes beyond business. Beyond friendship."

Silence.

I glanced between them. "Is this another of those *secrets* like how long you'll be in town?"

"No. Rather, it's not something we talk about a lot, but it's not a secret," Kingston said. "It's just not as cut and dried as a label."

"Also, I don't want you to take it wrong when I say the kiss the other day was as much for your benefit as ours," Owen added.

Curious. "Now you have to explain."

Kingston drummed his fingers on the center console.

"You said you had a friend, the one who got you the X poster, and the two of you make better friends than lovers." Owen seemed to be measuring his words. "It's kind of like that."

Kingston silently flattened his palm on the leather. "*Kind of.* I dated this woman, years ago, who thought it would be hot to see two guys together. That was the first time we…"

"Shared." Owen picked up the thread without pause. "There was kissing, more, between Kingston and me. It was good."

"Good isn't exactly a screaming endorsement. And doesn't quite line up with that kiss I saw." It had been incredible for me, and I'd only watched.

"He's understating things," Kingston said. "Tell me you're surprised. She and I didn't last long—she was jealous of my relationship with Owen—"

"Seriously?" I shouldn't be any more surprised about that than Owen being minimalist in his description. But it had been her idea.

Kingston playfully tapped Owen on the arm. "I was glad it showed early. My friendship with Owen is one of those things I'm not sacrificing. We've got an occasional with-benefits thing going on. We lean into the passion when it feels right for the situation."

"You were reading yaoi, you're an X fan, the kiss added to the moment." Owen made it sound like a reasonable step in a business plan, rather than an intense, shared moment.

Right. "But it was totally spontaneous." I kept my sarcasm light.

"We didn't discuss it first, if that's what you're implying." Kingston almost sounded wounded. He didn't have the right.

But I liked the idea that they were in-tune enough with each other that a kiss could be spontaneous, and my imagination was running rampant with fantasies of them together. Especially given how easily they talked about being friends-with-sometimes-benefits.

"You're not jealous, are you?" The faintest hint of concern ran through Kingston's voice.

I'd wonder if I'd imagined it, but his tone wasn't hard to read.

"We're not dating." I had to remind myself as much as him. "But no." Kind of turned on. Okay, a lot turned on. Letting that truth slip out was a gaping chasm of a line that I wasn't crossing with them.

TEN

The cabin was rustically beautiful, as I expected from a group of twenty to thirty something trust fundies. In the middle of a forest clearing, set back far enough from the lake to be private, but close enough to have its own dock, and make swimming and boating convenient.

The interior defied the log-cabin look, with tile floors, stainless appliances, and high-end electronics. I wasn't judging—it looked comfortable, and it was hard to complain about that.

Kingston and Owen introduced me to the six other people there. Half had just come back from an unsuccessful morning of fishing, and the other three were arguing over how many ingredients could change in a drink and still have it be a mimosa.

The morning passed in a blur of fruit plates and idle chatter. The more time that ticked away, the further I drifted toward the living room walls.

I should mingle. This wasn't a large group, and I *was* here to make connections. The way everyone had split off into packs of two or three made it difficult to know where to gravitate, so the edge of the room got my company.

"Mind if I share your wall?" Owen startled me when he

brushed my shoulder and leaned back next to me. He handed me a cold bottle of water. "I'm sorry for assaulting you with so many names at once. It's a lot to keep track of."

I took a long swallow of water. The icy cold froze my uncertainty. I looked up to find Owen watching me. I turned away before eye contact could become more. "It's fine. I'm good with names."

"I should have guessed that. Let's see… you give each one of them a nickname, and associate their real names with whomever you've decided they are?"

I didn't like being pegged so easily, even if it was exactly what I was doing with everyone else in the room. "Maybe."

"Care to share?"

"No."

"Why not?" Kingston seemed to appear from nowhere, and planted himself between us and the rest of the room.

"People never appreciate the instant judgment, even when there's truth to it," Owen said. "So many want to categorize everything around them with neat little labels, but apply one of those labels to them…"

It was both terrifying and enticing that he understood where I was coming from. "What he said. And if I picked the wrong trait to focus on with your friends, I'll find myself walking home."

"Never." Kingston didn't look fazed. So, status quo. "But people, am I right?" He rolled his eyes, but never stopped smiling.

I gave an exaggerated sigh. "It's true. Life would be so much easier if it came with anime narration that explained every single intent and power—"

"In excruciating detail?" Owen pushed away from the wall to look at me. "You want a diatribe about everything except the one thing that matters?"

"Which is?" I had to know.

"*I like you, let's fuck*," Owen said. "When was the last time you heard anyone say that in an anime who wasn't cast as the overbearing love interest?"

"I've all but said that, what does that make me?" Kingston asked.

Far more appealing than he should be. "The enemy," I teased. "I take back what I said. Endless grandstanding and super villain monologuing suck."

Kingston rested a finger under my chin and raised my gaze to his. "You don't get out of it that easily. I like you. Let's fuck."

Heat flooded me, and I broke the connection. It severed the spark flowing between us, and I instantly wanted that feeling back. "You like my café. We're not going to screw. And you're definitely not what snap judgment says you are. Neither of you."

"Is that good or bad?" Kingston asked.

I didn't know yet. "It's certainly interesting."

"I'll take interesting. Life can always use another surprise." Condensation had formed on Owen's bottle, and when he tiled his head back to drink, several drops ran down his chin, over his throat, and dampened his shirt enough to tease.

Kingston dragged his thumb over Owen's chin, wiping away some of the water.

Thirsty took on a literal form as I suppressed the desire to lean in draw my tongue along a similar path. I had male friends who were close to the point of playful flirting, and I'd never seen them do anything that intimate. "Not all surprises are good." I pressed my own water bottle to my cheek. Dribbles hit my chest, and both their gazes followed. I wanted to turn in on myself and hide, but I pretended not to notice.

"Agree to disagree." Owen looked me in the eye again. "Even the bad kind of unexpected leads to change and growth."

I couldn't argue that, but it didn't make me like the idea of bad surprises any more than I had thirty seconds ago. "Change can be scarring." Sometimes those scars were invisible. I certainly went out of my way to hide mine.

"Come join us." Peter interrupted, saving me from my thoughts, and pulled us into their group of two. "We want your opinion on this start-up coming out of Phoenix. The newest *we'll beat Facebook* site."

They didn't want my opinion, or Kingston's it seemed. They were mostly interested in what Owen had to say. I wasn't surprised they ignored me, but how surprised would they be to know Kingston had more to offer than he let on.

We moved between groups for several hours. Lunch was an informal buffet of more fresh fruit. I was grateful for that on a lot of levels. And by that afternoon, I found myself in a lawn chair, in a small clearing a bit back from the lake. The trees blocked the sun, and the cool breeze was enough to tease the heat from my skin.

Owen and Kingston were with me. They hadn't left my side much, which was odd since we were here to see their friends, but I was grateful at not being left to fend for myself. What was I thinking? I wasn't the kind of person who mingled and made connections.

We had company, though, and it was exactly who I needed it to be. Ravyn had been my favorite person to talk to so far, aside from my not-dates, and her brother Ramsey was on the city council.

"What do you do, Lyn?" Ravyn asked.

Enjoying her company didn't mean I'd completely shed my discomfort in this group. I didn't want them to see they intimidated me at all. "I'm an entrepreneur."

"She owns *Loading Java*," Ramsey said.

Ravyn gave him a curious look. "How do you know that?"

"I saw the zoning order come across my desk."

He was definitely the guy for me to meet. This day wasn't a mistake after all.

I glanced at Owen and Kingston, both looking relaxed, gorgeous, and frequently focused on me. I had a hard time thinking it was a mistake anyway, no matter how much I shouldn't be fantasizing about them. It wasn't like I was planning a future with them, though. I simply liked the memories of all the different things they did with their fingers… tongues… other extremities.

"I've always wanted to drop in there, and I'm not sure why I haven't. Why a gaming café?" Ravyn set her beer on the ground, and scooted forward on her chair. The way she leaned in, elbows on her knees, pressed her breasts together. Stunning view. I wasn't sure if I wanted to stare, or wallow in envy.

The fact that no one else gave her a second glance was odd, but not bad for my self-esteem.

"For the prestige and fame." I tossed out the joke lightly. *Please don't let it fall flat.*

Kingston snickered.

Ravyn and Ramsey smiled.

"You may be in the wrong business," Ravyn said. "Only reason I know these assholes is they're friends with Ramsey."

"They're not big L.A. Players?" I feigned shock. "They told me they were invited to *every* party in Hollywood." Except I hadn't had a clue what they looked like until they walked into my shop.

The teasing earned me more chuckles. I liked having a similar sense of humor to these people.

"Property values in L.A. are outrageous. We're not going near that place." Leave it to Owen to pick the reasonable retort.

Another thing that made him sexy.

And I could stop drooling over them any time now, please. "I love gaming, anime and baking... and I found a way to do all three." My story sounded a lot like Kingston and Owen's. Instinct braced me for a jab or two about *of course you love baking, it shows.*

"I need to stop by at some point," Ramsey said. "What's your specialty? Like, if I have to order just one thing off the menu, what do I get?"

"It's all good." My inner fat-girl was still on alert for the jokes. *Of course you like it all.*

Ravyn slapped him on the leg. "She's not going to sell if she thinks it sucks, dummy."

Ramsey shrugged. "Of course not, but she's got a favorite. Don't you?" He looked at me.

"The chocolate croissant. Messy, but worth it." And the creation I was proudest of. The recipe took a lot of trial and error.

"Messy as in, chocolate everywhere? All over your fingers...?" Kingston wiggled his eyebrows.

I fixed him with a warning glare, and braced myself for a surge of bad feelings associated with sucking chocolate off fingers. But everything that led up to his damning question at the end of that night was still a pleasant memory. "All over."

Ravyn cleared her throat. "I was thinking it was too cold to go in the water, but someone needs to cool off."

"You can't take the heat of this package." Kingston gestured at himself.

I was certainly struggling with it.

Ravyn rolled her eyes, stood, and offered me a hand. "Do you want to walk away from this testosterone fest, or stay and be worshiped?"

"They're not—" Not me. I was never the center of that kind of attention.

Ravyn pursed her lips. "They are."

"I could use a drink." I stood as well.

Ravyn gestured toward the cabin, and we headed into the kitchen. She grabbed two lemonades from the fridge and handed me one.

"How well do you know them? Owen and Kingston?" I tried to sound casual. I sipped my drink to hide any fidgeting.

"They've been friends with Ramsey for years. I see them every few months."

I both did and didn't want to ask my next question. It would be obvious why I wondered, but since Ravyn already made the comment about worshiping, it wasn't as though she'd missed the attraction. "Do you know…" How should I phrase this? "Do they ever mix business with pleasure?"

"No." There was no hesitation in her response. "I mean, I guess it's possible, since I don't know how they spend their downtime, but I can't imagine Owen *ever* crossing that line. He doesn't even like to call in favors."

"They never do." Ramsey's reply came from the kitchen doorway. "I'd bet a hedge fund on that. Kingston blurs a few lines, but—if you don't already know this, you haven't spent enough time with them—their business is their world. They'd never jeopardize it."

I understood the sentiment, but was I doing exactly that to myself, by being here?

ELEVEN

By the end of the night, as we were saying our *goodbyes*, I'd decided to forgive Kingston for joking that sex meant I'd sell my business to them. It was a lot less stressful to go back to enjoying the scenery and the conversation, at least for the next hour or so drive down the canyon.

After that, it wouldn't matter. Our time together would be done.

When we reached the SUV, Kingston playfully tugged my arm toward the back seats. "Let Owen chauffeur."

"That seems a little odd." Didn't it?

Owen shrugged. "No odder than the two of us in the front seat and Kingston alone in back. Keep each other company."

As we headed toward main roads, an unexpected sadness surged through me, clenching around my heart.

"Why the frown?" Kingston tugged a thumb over my bottom lip.

The intimate touch caught me off-guard, but soothed me. Did I dare say out loud what I was thinking? It would be rude to hide it. "I'm not ready for the day to end."

Insecurities twinged inside. Was it stupid to admit that?

The corner of Kingston's mouth tugged up. "It's not over yet. Don't waste the drive pouting."

"What would you suggest instead?" I asked.

He trailed his fingers up the inside of my thigh, and fissures of need sparked under my skin. "You look gorgeous in this skirt." He wasn't answering my question, but I could be patient. "I swear I had a *Basic Instinct* moment every time you crossed or uncrossed your legs today."

"Except, I'm not a killer." I knew where the compliment was going, but it was tinged. "Or… whatever. I've never actually seen the movie."

"The important thing is, you're *way* more attractive than Sharon Stone." Kingston's fingers crept higher, nudging my legs apart.

I shook my head. "I'm not."

"Disagree." Kingston moved his hand further up the inside of my thighs, and my skirt crept higher.

That same nervous *we're in public* fear was back. But it was dark, the windows were tinted, and there was no one else on the road.

Kingston brushed a light touch over my panties, and I gasped.

"Is that a *keep going?*" He asked.

Was it? Just a few days ago I was furious with him. With both of them. Was I willing to dive into a physical situation again? Kingston told me up front, his goal was to prove they were likeable business partners.

Did that include the sex?

"Lyn?" Concern crept into Kingston's voice.

I was spread-legged, skirt bunched around my hips, while one man drove and another teased me. "I don't want this to end like the other night." I kept my voice firm, trying to make the words sound like a command more than a terrified confession.

"I don't either." Kingston eased his hand back, resting it on my knee instead. "This isn't… It's sex. Not business."

That simplified things. Didn't it? I glanced up at Owen. "Are just going to drive and pretend there's nothing going on back here?" I tried to keep my tone light.

"I'm not pretending anything." He briefly met my gaze in the rear-view mirror. "I'm listening to and enjoying every second of it."

Being watched wasn't my thing. Not even by whomever I was with at the time. So why did the fact that Owen was the watcher—listener—raise goosebumps everywhere?

"How many times have you done this?" I asked. The situation was too well orchestrated.

Kingston squeezed my knee. "This specifically? You'd be my first. You get to pop my fooling-around-in-the-back-seat-while-my-best-friend-drives cherry."

I did want it. *Him.* Twice with the same fling broke a rule I'd rarely had to consider, but it wasn't as though we'd make a habit of this. I could think of the drive home as a chance to rewrite the ending of our last hook-up.

After tonight, I wouldn't put myself in a social situation with them again. Easy to do given they didn't live here.

I summoned the boldness that acted as my shield when I went to bars, covered Kingston's hand, and slid it up my leg again. "Yes. Keep going."

"Face me." He lightly slapped the inside of my thigh.

The teasing sting made me sigh. I shifted in the seat, one knee bent between us and the other foot on the floor.

Kingston leaned in and kissed me so lightly, I felt his breath on my skin as much as his touch. "Nope, not enough," he growled.

He pressed his weight into me when he slanted his mouth over mine. I half-reclined against the door and my body molded to his. He deepened the kiss, drawing it out until I felt the tingles all the way to my toes.

Kingston trailed his fingers down my chest, and followed the same path with his mouth, passing my skirt, and skipping the pulse of need between my legs, to tease along the inside of my thighs instead.

I writhed under the playfully light touch, shifting my hips to bring me closer to his mouth.

He chuckled against my skin, and pressed a palm into my stomach to keep me from moving.

It was the most delicious torture.

Kingston finally moved back up, to scrape his teeth over the crotch of my panties.

I whimpered.

He hooked his fingers in the elastic, and dragged the lingerie down my legs. When he dragged his tongue up my slit, I gasped and my hips bucked, needing more.

He devoured me with a hunger that made my pulse scream. Licking along my slick skin, diving his tongue inside me to taste my inner walls. Groaning as loudly as I was. He moved his fingers to my clit.

My entire body jerked in response.

The longer he stayed between my legs, the more the outside world fell away. My breath came in pants, and I gripped his short hair, needing something to hold onto and not wanting him to stop.

I came hard. My hips bucked, and my entire body tensed for a moment, before I slumped back with a happy sigh.

Kingston climbed back up my body, and dropped his mouth on mine again, kissing me hard, sharing my taste with me.

I wasn't ready for this to end. I reached below his waist to trace the hard bulge in his jeans. His muffled moan against my mouth was electricity sliding over me. Still teasing his erection, I pressed my body into his, to push us both upright, until he was sitting and I knelt next to him.

The more intently I stroked through denim, the louder he groaned. I liked that sound. The hum against my lips.

I liked orgasms as much as the next person, but I enjoyed giving as much as receiving. There was a unique rush in seeing another person get off, especially when I was helping or even better, responsible.

I dragged down Kingston's zipper and freed him. His skin was hot against my palm as I stroked. When I lowered my head and flicked my tongue over the head of his cock, he sucked in a sharp breath through his teeth.

Incredible sound, and delicious motivation to take more than a taste. I took him into my mouth, sucking, licking, and pumping.

Each jerk of his body and growl of pleasure was an invisible touch, dancing through over me.

He reached under my chest, between my legs, staying away from my still-tender clit, and sliding along my slick skin.

Desire, the volume of his moans, and the ambient need drove my pace. I lost myself in sounds and sensations as he thrust against the back of my throat. I whimpered when he slipped two fingers inside me.

The angle and sensation weren't right to make me come, but I liked the feeling of penetration. That combined with the jerk of his hips spurred me on.

"Lyn." Kingston's voice was gravel. "Gorgeous. I'm too close." He tried to nudge me back.

I was wrapped in the moment and didn't want to stop.

He slid his fingers higher, to my clit, and a shudder of *too much* mingled with *don't stop* and stalled my brain.

Another orgasm rushed over me, flashing a rainbow of stars behind my eyelids. I gasped in the pleasure, until my body jerked away from his touch.

Kingston's chuckle was self-satisfied as his hand fell away.

I was lost in the haze of climax, and not done with him yet. I resumed stroking and licking. Bobbing my head. I wanted to taste him. Hear that enticing sound he made when he came.

And it was loud. His grunts increasing in volume as he thrust against my face.

I didn't pull away as he finished. When he finally slowed to a stop, I licked him clean.

I knelt upright.

Kingston captured the back of my neck and crushed his mouth to mine. There was no tender sweetness here. He consumed me, diving into the kiss like he was as desperate to be close as I was. This kind of intensity and need could burn me alive, and I'd love every minute of it.

When we finally broke apart, I was breathless. Flushed. Just plain happy.

"That was possibly the single hottest thing I've ever heard." Owen's comment startled me.

Kingston kissed my forehead and squeezed my hand. "I have a singularly hot partner," he said.

I'd almost forgotten Owen was here. That we were driving down the freeway at seventy miles an hour. That anything else existed. I wanted to be embarrassed, but a new layer of pleased wove with everything else, that Owen had been listening.

After we straightened our clothing enough to sit, I leaned into Kingston for the rest of the ride home, ignoring the whisper in the back of my mind insisting I was going to miss this. It was a fling like any other, and this was my chance to burn the good into my mind, and let it keep me warm until the next hookup.

When we turned onto my street, I forced all the emotion from my veins.

Owen opened the rear SUV door, and offered his hand. I accepted, but Kingston wrapped an arm around my waist before I could leave, and pulled me into his chest.

Owen grabbed Kingston's wrist, stepped close enough I felt his heat, and pressed Kingston's hand to the front of his jeans, to cup a bulge that was visible even in the dim lighting.

Hot.

"This is what the two of you do to me." Owen's even tone was a new caress that made my mind whimper and beg, and he hadn't touched me.

This was *friends with occasional benefits?* Because there was no way it was purely for my enjoyment.

"What are you going to do about it?" Kingston's retort was borderline bratty challenge.

Owen raised an eyebrow, and focused on me. "If I didn't have an early flight, I'd fuck this stunning woman and make you watch."

Yes, please. Though, *early flight* sounded like an excuse. I wouldn't be hurt. The three of us were screwing. The two of us? Owen had been there, watching, and for all I knew, that was how he sated an attraction to Kingston that neither of them wanted to label. But the fact that I didn't know proved what we all had was nothing more than sex. "So that's my answer?" I kept my tone light. "You're leaving tomorrow?"

"*He* has an early flight. You're not getting rid of me that easily." Kingston's breath was hot on the back of my neck.

Owen dropped Kingston's hand to squeeze my fingers. "Technically, neither of us is leaving for good. We want a shop here because we're moving here. I'm making a few stops at our other locations around the country, then I'll be back. You're not getting rid of us so easily."

But they weren't a couple, moving across the country together.

You don't have a shop here. If I brought that up, we'd be talking business as it related to us. I didn't want to spoil a second night in a row that way.

My brain was already racing ahead, though. Never seeing them again felt bad. Having to avoid them in the same city could be worse.

Because I was a novelty and a fetish. I was screwing out of my league, and I couldn't pretend otherwise much longer. Meeting their friends today reinforced that point too distinctly.

Worse though, I was starting to like Owen and Kingston. That was stupid and terrifying. "I won't keep you. I have an early day anyway." It was tricky to extract myself from their embrace with any manner of grace, but I managed to get my feet planted on the pavement, and put distance between me and them.

Kingston hopped from the back seat and reached for me.

I stepped away from him. "I had a lot of fun today. Thank you."

"Us too." His smile didn't reach his eyes.

That wasn't hurt. There was no way it could be.

They'd leave and go enjoy their lives, pretending whatever they wanted about their relationship with each other, and I hoped the next woman enjoyed it as much as I had.

TWELVE

R aindrops slamming against my window woke me about two minutes before my alarm went off. It was gorgeously gray outside. I love the rain, but thank goodness it held off until this morning.

Yesterday lingered in my head as I got ready for the morning. As much as I wanted to file things in a *Pleasant Memories* folder, and move on, I couldn't get the highlights out of my head.

I grabbed a sweatshirt that hung low enough to cover my ass, so I could wear leggings. It didn't matter that it was one of the hottest months of the year—rain meant cool weather, which meant I could be comfortable and hide inside my clothes at the same time.

As I did the morning's baking, my mind was free to drift to Kingston and Owen. Every time I yanked my thoughts away from them, and tried to ponder anything else, even repeating my favorite recipes, the men meandered their way into my head.

I needed to occupy my mind more intently. I was doing a podcast today with *Roxie's Face For Radio*. That would distract me from missing men I barely knew.

If the situation were different, if Owen and Kingston weren't trying to push me out of this place, I'd go out with them again, if they asked.

Not that they would. Which was good, because I wasn't a long term girl. Not for guys like them. Once they settled down, they'd end up with trophy wives, probably occasionally help each other jerk off in the hot tub, and attend parties like the one this weekend, but stuffier.

Did I really think that little of them, that they'd live their lives for money and public image?

I had to. Believing anything else was dangerous

I wrapped up my morning baking, chatted with Violet for a bit, and headed out to Roxie's.

I'd been on her show a few times since Sadie introduced us; it was always a lot of fun, was great promo for Loading Java, and didn't require me to be on camera. Roxie's staff animated every episode.

The recording was fun, but when it was over my thoughts were free to drift back to Owen and Kingston.

That needed to stop.

Pouring myself into work for the rest of the day helped, and by the time I climbed into bed, I was exhausted enough I slept hard.

Tuesday morning the guys were still vivid in my thoughts. Seriously, what was up with my brain? I didn't linger on one-night stands.

Throughout the day, every time I talked to someone, performed a basic task, glazed Danishes, my brain would wonder what kind of commentary one of them would have. Kingston with a joke. Owen with a reasonable observation.

Who did that? Got hot and bothered over a guy who couldn't take life seriously and one who saw the world through a completely structured lens? Logic wasn't sexy.

Yes it is.

Sigh.

Wednesday was more of the same, but Roxie's podcast with me aired that morning, so having it playing in the café gave me a new point of focus.

Distraction didn't last long, though. If anything, my missing-the-guys feeling was getting more intense, rather than fading.

This was why I should never see a fling more than once. Give me a little attention, and I lapped it up and whined for more like a lovesick puppy.

The rain was back that night, and the white noise of falling water helped soothe my fractured thoughts. I wanted extra comfort this evening, so I pulled on my ultimate wrap-me-up-in-a-hug outfit. It was a kitten onesie Sadie gave me for my birthday. She made it herself, which meant it fit perfectly, and was super soft and comfortable.

My phone rang and I glanced at it. Only friends got to talk to me this late.

Owen's name flashed on the screen.

I swore my heart started panting.

Send him to voicemail—that was the only answer.

I grabbed the phone and hit *Answer*. "This is Lyn."

"Can I call you Lyn? Are we friends now?" His voice was huskier than normal, like he was tired. Which must be why he was more playful than I was used to.

I let out an exaggerated sigh. "I guess I'll allow it tonight." It was easy to keep the teasing in my voice—I was so much happier to hear from him than I should be. I almost didn't care if he was calling to make a buy pitch.

Almost.

"In that case, Lyn, I called to tell you I caught the show today, with Roxie. You sounded fantastic."

My heart lapped up the simple praise, and my mind had lost any ground in the *stay removed* argument. It was going to make one final push anyway. "Did you tune in to make sure I *represented your future brand appropriately?*"

"Is that what you want me to say?"

"Do I strike you as a *tell me what I want to hear* kind of person?" I playfully turned a version of his question from the other day back on him.

He chuckled. "Not even close. I turned it on to hear you—hand to God. If Kingston had told me you had such a sexy voice, even without the visuals..."

"You're one to talk." I didn't mean to let that slip, but this was too easy. "Pun not intended? Was that a pun?"

"If you stretch your imagination a little... Or a lot."

"I've got a pretty vivid imagination." Right now, for instance, it was whispering completely inappropriate things in my ear, in Owen's voice, while it pictured his fingers trailing over my body.

"I usually don't, but... Anyway, you sounded good."

What had he been going to say? "You can't leave it at that. But what?" I asked.

"It's not business related."

"That's not dispelling my curiosity."

"You were warned." The way he said *warned* added a new layer to the fantasy, that somehow led to my ass being slapped. "But my imagination runs rampant when I'm talking to you."

Me too. Great, my brain had sided with my body and heart now. "I was warned." This was when I should call it a night. Thank him for tuning into Roxie, and hang up. I lay back in bed, phone to my ear. "How's... Where are you today?"

"Chicago. It's windy. You also don't strike me as a *let's discuss the weather* kind of person."

Only if I had to, and it was one of the last things I wanted to be doing with Owen. "Make a lot of assumptions about the kind of person I am?"

"No more than you make about me."

Touché. "What else have you assumed?"

"I assume you're in bed, wearing something that makes you look delectable— *Fuck*, I wasn't going to say that."

Heat flooded me. Flirt or shut him down? "No take backs." Like I was going to give myself any choice. "And you're right. My pussy is on display for anyone to see who walks in the room."

Nothing.

Did I just screw up big time?

"Show me." Owen's tone left no room for argument.

Which made me specifically want to argue, even just teasingly. "I don't send pictures of myself to *anyone*. But maybe, if you asked really nicely, I'd consider a neck-down shot?"

"I'd rather see your face."

"That doesn't sound like begging."

"Please." He even made a request sound like an order.

I grinned in my empty room, at the smooth retort. "Those are my rules." If I dragged this out too long, the punchline wouldn't be funny. It might not be anyway, but I was willing to take the chance. "I guess I can make an exception for you, because you sound sexy when you're tired." I was getting bold. I tugged up the hood of my onesie and snapped a picture from the chest up. "Sent."

More silence greeted me. Then Owen chuckled. It was the kind of laugh that flowed over me like skilled fingers, raising goosebumps everywhere. "Absolutely stunning," he said. "Most gorgeous pussy I've ever seen."

"Right?" My smile grew.

"You're lucky I don't have a furry fetish, or I'd be jerking off right now."

My breath caught. Yeah, I'd opened the door with a pussy joke, but... "You mean that wasn't the plan?"

"The plan was to call and tell you I caught you on the show, make small talk, and then wish you a good rest of your evening."

"Except you're not a small talk person either."

"I'm really not."

One of the things that made him attractive beyond the *wow he's hot* level.

"I genuinely want to know how Chicago is," I said. "Do you have any free time when you make these trips? What will you do while you're there? Any places I have to see?"

"You're good at that."

At asking questions? Here was another one. "Good at what?"

"Not talking about yourself."

I hadn't intentionally steered the conversation away from me. Not this time. "I wasn't——"

"My point exactly." Owen sounded playful. "Have you ever been here?"

"No." I could stop there, but it wouldn't hurt me to offer a little more personal information. "Vacation when I was little was camping in Jackson Hole. I always said I'd travel when I got older, but first there was no money, and now there's work."

"You take vacations, though."

"Work, and still no money. And no, time off isn't really a thing I do." Had I just walked into a trap? Thanks, brain, for picking now to ignore the flirty fun. "Is this where you tell me if I sold to you, I'd have both time and money?"

"This is where I describe the scene from my hotel window, since you can't be here."

"I'd love that."

There was a pause with shuffling and what sounded like a sliding window or door in the background. "I've got a view of the river," Owen said. "The skyline here isn't like in Salt Lake, here you can see forever on a clear day. But from my room, it's more like a corridor lined with buildings and bright lights, cut out of black velvet, with a plush carpet of water running down the center."

The verbal tour would be fantastic on its own, but in Owen's voice it was almost foreplay. "You make it sound amazing."

"It is through the right lens. Add it to your bucket list."

"Is that an order?"

"You don't strike me as a *take orders* kind of woman."

I wasn't. "For the right person…"

"The right person wouldn't demand it of you." He was so reasonable.

I could talk to him forever. Though, one of us would lose our voice, and then the other would, and the conversation would be reduced to heavy breathing… Heat raced over my skin at the idea of the ways I could touch myself, to breathe heavily for him. "Says the man who ordered me to send him pussy pictures."

"An order you argued with, despite planning on doing it anyway."

"Busted." I laughed.

"I should let you get some sleep."

Oh. Such a simple, thoughtful statement, but it hurt. The pain was a good reminder that I shouldn't be flirting with him, given the business nature of our relationship. "Probably a good idea."

"One more thing, though."

This was where he'd make his pitch. Because why not end the conversation on a down note? "All right?"

"I'll be in New Orleans in a few nights, if you'd like a remote tour."

My heart body-checked my brain and slammed it out of the ring. "I'd love that."

"It's a da—eal. Sweet dreams."

"'Night." I set my phone on the nightstand.

My brain had recovered. Was this part of the pitch? Kingston told me flat out that their goal was to convince me they'd be good business partners.

The ache behind my ribs desperately wanted that call to be what it looked like on the surface—friendly and flirty. But I couldn't believe nothing hid underneath.

THIRTEEN

Thursday night, Kingston slipped through the café front door as I was locking up. His hair was damp, and hints of the next wave of storm dotted his shirt. He fixed me with a smile that he must think was irresistible.

He was right.

"We're not open, sir." I rarely closed shop, but that was how the schedules fell today.

He didn't look deterred. "Perfect. Then you're free to hang out. I'm taking you to dinner."

I raised my eyebrows at the assumption. "Since when?"

"Since…" He looked at his phone "I assume about two minutes from now."

"What happens in two minutes?"

"I convince you to say yes."

Arrogant bastard. I should be annoyed. The best I could summon was cautious. "Is this all part of your plan to prove to me what a good business partner you'd be?"

Kingston searched my face. "Does that get you to join me?"

"No." It would put an immediate end to the conversation. Which was best for everyone.

His grin was back. "Good, because I didn't want to lie about my intentions. I want your company for the night."

My heart did a happy skip-jump-hop at the sparkle in his dark eyes. "I don't know."

"What would it take to convince you?"

"How long is left on the clock?" Why couldn't I keep myself in check around these two?

"Let's call it *Time's Up*, for simplicity's sake." He pocketed his phone. "I promise you a night you'll never forget."

An easy guarantee, given how hard it was to get them out of my head anyway. "All right. You're on." I swore a chorus of singing forest animals broke out in my skull.

When he offered his arm this time, I nestled my hand into the crook of his elbow. Light raindrops pattered on us as we strolled down the front walk to his SUV rental. He opened the passenger door, and made sure I was seated, before hurrying to take his own seat.

Rush hour traffic was thinning, so we were on the freeway within minutes, which was when it occurred to me that we were heading toward the mountains. Park City? Did he think a fancy dinner would leave a bigger impression on me? "Where are we going? Or is it a surprise."

"Kind of, not really? My original plan was a picnic in the mountains, but since it's raining, it'll have to be an in-car one."

Damn-it-all, now I was swooning again. "I haven't been on a picnic in forever." Not a real one. For months after I bought my property, it was nightly picnics.

"No time?" Kingston asked.

Owen must have told him what we talked about last night. That made the most sense, but for some reason I didn't think that was the case. "How'd you guess?"

"I've been where you are. Where operating in the black become the single consuming goal in life."

"I thought this wasn't about a sales pitch," I teased.

"It's not. I'm making a simple observation. I'm capable of those, too." The shift in his voice was something I couldn't name.

"Never doubted it for a moment."

"How about this—If I intend to make you another business pitch, I'll warn you first."

That sounded convenient. "Like, a big flashing beacon?"

"A verbal one. Along the lines of *whoop whoop, warning. Incoming sales pitch. Whoop whoop.*"

I laughed. "I *would* appreciate the heads up."

"It's a deal then. Otherwise, anything we talk about, shop related or not, is us getting to know each other. Period."

"Why?" It was a simple question, with a complex background. I didn't understand, if he wasn't trying to win me over for business, where was all the effort coming from?

Kingston glanced at me, then steered us across three lanes of freeway to pull onto the shoulder and stop. The light traffic was a savior, but the rain was pouring down now, making it dark as night out here. This hardly seemed like a safe place to have a conversation.

He put on the emergency flashers, shifted in his seat to face me, and gripped my chin enough to hold my gaze to his. "I get the feeling you don't always listen to me."

His touch didn't hurt, but the accusation did. He commanded attention. There was a strength and intensity in his fingers that made my pulse roar.

"I hear everything you tell me," I said.

"But you're not actually listening." The power that spilled from him stole my breath. "Pay attention. You're intelligent. Funny. Gorgeous—head to toe and *every* bit in between. I'm here because I want to get to know you. Period. No qualifiers."

I couldn't grasp a response. The best I could manage was to stare back with wide eyes.

"Are we on the same page now?" he asked.

I nodded.

Kingston's grin was back. The flipped switch between serious and playful was almost as disconcerting as the way my body reacted to him. "Good." He crushed his lips to mine, and spent several seconds licking, nibbling, and dancing his tongue around mine.

I was breathless when he pulled away.

"Picnic awaits." He pulled back onto the road.

Should I be scared of the mercurial moods? I didn't get the impression he'd hurt me, or that he'd even consider it. What I did see was an alternate version of what I did. I hadn't wanted to admit such a sexy, self-assured guy could be dealing with any sort of insecurity, but he was hiding something under the humor. Not about me, but about how he wanted the world to see him versus how he thought it did.

"Tell me about you," Kingston said.

I had a practiced pitch I could give to most people when they asked this question. If Owen had asked me directly last night, he'd have gotten the same thing. "I was raised in a happy, lower middle-class family, went to private school—"

"Uniform? Plaid skirt, white shirt, knee-high socks?"

"Khaki's and polo shirts."

"Don't destroy the fantasy." Yup, playful Kingston was back. "That image is going in its own folder in my brain."

"I own one. A short plaid skirt." Why did I say that? Because I loved this attention, duh.

He licked his lips. "Even better. Sorry to interrupt, fantasy saved, please continue."

I'd been thrown out of the rhythm of my story. "Umm… dance in high school"—I almost stalled on the memory, thanks to my derailed train of thought, but I bit back the negative association— "community college, Associate's in business, office manager work while I saved my pennies, and then I found a cheap house up for auction, which brings us to here."

"I feel like there are some pieces missing in that story."

"I could say the same to you." I meant as far as his tale about how they'd bought their first shop.

"You *were* listening."

Of course. Listening and my self-doubt clashed, but I heard what he said. "I told you so."

"So I caught up on *Spring Popcorn*. There are absolutely no dragons or Nazi's," he said.

I was grateful he didn't press my omission of information. "No? Maybe I read a different version."

"The one in your head?" His tone was teasingly accusatory.

"Exactly."

We slid from *Spring Popcorn* to other manga and comics, our favorite TV shows and books... It was easy to talk to him. I suspected as much, based on our previous conversations, but there was some doubt with us talking one-on-one. I liked that we had so much in common, and that what we didn't wasn't an obstacle.

He drove us into Big Cottonwood Canyon, navigating the roads with practiced ease. He wasn't intimidated by mountain driving.

We parked a way back from the main roads, in a wooded clearing. The scents of dirt, pine trees, rain, and the faint hint of Kingston's cologne were borderline arousing.

He shut off the engine. "I may not have thought this through one-hundred percent."

"Oh?"

"My plan was that we'd eat in the back of the SUV, but we still have to get back there."

"I don't mind getting a little wet." Why didn't I realize how that sounded *before* I said it?

"So I've seen."

I shook my head, but couldn't hide my amusement. "Wet in the rain. See?" I opened the door and stepped out.

The rain was coming down a lot harder than I expected, and my shriek ended in a giggle when I was soaked within seconds.

"You're right, wet is good." Kingston was by my side.

From his gravely tone, I expected to find him staring at my chest, but his gaze was fixed on my face. Raindrops pelted me. My hair clung to my cheeks. None of it mattered, because I couldn't turn away from the way he watched me.

No one had ever looked at me like that before. Like I was the only person he could see. Like I was his sole focus.

Kingston brushed my hair off my face, and his mouth over mine. His kiss seared my soul. I almost expected to see the rain evaporate before it hit us. It was just a kiss, but it tingled through all of me.

I whimpered when he broke the sweet, intense kiss. He pressed his forehead to mine. "Dinner?"

"Isn't that what we're doing out here?" My half-joke came out breathless.

"You're more like dessert, but we can have that first, if you want to be stripped down—"

"No." My response came down more forcefully than I intended, propelled by the chill that raced down my spine. Hello, unwelcome and traumatic memory. "That is… Not out here."

He tangled his fingers with mine. "Okay. Dinner."

I was grateful he didn't ask *why*? I couldn't relive that moment enough to talk about it. It already haunted my dreams too often.

FOURTEEN

Kingston raised the rear door as a temporary shelter from the rain. There was already a blanket unfurled in the back of the SUV.

"We'll get your blanket all wet," I said.

"The blanket can be washed." He moved the quilt to the edge of the SUV, so we could sit with our legs hanging outside, then grabbed a cooler from where it was secured near the seats, and pulled it forward as well.

Kingston extracted a tray of fresh fruit and cheese. It looked delicious.

Which must be why the nagging in my head asked *Does he think I need more fruit?* Now that the edges of old wounds had been exposed, my insecurities could rush back. I tried to argue with myself that fruit was all I ate at the cabin, and I made a fuss about the salad the first day I met the guys.

"Why fruit?" I forced out the neutral question.

He plucked a large strawberry from the mix, and traced it along my bottom lip, drawing a gasp from me.

"Take a bite," he said.

I did. There was really no dainty way to bite into a strawberry so big, and juice dribbled down my chin.

Kingston leaned in and dragged his tongue up, licking the mess away. "That's why," he murmured against my lips.

He was toeing into dangerously perfect territory. Making it difficult to remember if I had reservations about liking him. Lulling me into security.

"I won't look nearly as sexy eating cheese." I needed to lighten the mood.

"All a matter of opinion."

I held a cheese cube up in the air. "Really?"

He drew my fingers and the food into his mouth, licking along the pads of my skin, before pulling away, taking my breath with him.

"Let's just say the chocolate frosting event left an impression on me." He brushed his lips over mine. "Laying you out and eating dinner off you may have become a favorite fantasy."

I couldn't… but my imagination said I certainly could let him do something like that, just not out in the open. I squeezed my thighs together, but it didn't suppress the throb. "Something to try later."

"I was hoping you'd say that."

I didn't know how to follow a line of conversation like that, so I stuffed a few grapes into my mouth.

"You're no stranger to the picnic lifestyle." Kingston joined me in eating.

"When I first bought my property, I did a lot of blanket-on-the-floor meals."

He tilted his head and studied me. "I'm intrigued."

"It's not a super fascinating story. I bought the house in auction, and I was certain I had enough left over for the renovations. I'm smart, I could figure out how to do the work myself, with videos and such." I laughed at past me's naiveté. "I was so very wrong."

Kingston shook his head. "Yeah, a lot of that stuff isn't really a one-person job."

"Especially if you don't know what you're doing." I could admit that. Now. "So I was putting all of my money into sheetrock, tile, and appliances, rather than furniture, but I couldn't install any of it."

"You obviously figured something out."

I got lucky. That was all there was to it. "I was at the fabric store, torn over upholstery, and this cute pink-haired girl introduced herself." Sadie basically adopted me.

"Ah, the extrovert swoops in and makes themselves at home in the introvert's life. I love that kind of story."

I didn't have to ask which he was. "I don't suppose you have a similar tale about Owen."

"There was math involved, rather than fabric, but finish your story first."

Math. I was definitely curious. "One of her friends came from a family of contractors, and he knew how to do a lot of what I needed. She got them to provide the manual labor, a few of them installed my network, and we pulled everything together into Phase One of Loading Java. I still went way over budget. I slept on an air mattress, with none of my own real furniture, for a long time. A couple of them even worked for me for free until I could afford employees." I owed Sadie a lot. And Grayson. And Anne, Jax, Chase…

"Your friends are good people."

Fewer things were more true. "They are. You'd like them."

"I look forward to meeting them."

Were we at a *introduce me to your friends* point in our relationship? Since I'd already met his, it seemed so.

We talked some more, put away the food, and kept talking. I lost track of time as the rain slowed to a drizzle.

A gust of wind tore through the night, and I shivered at the sudden chill.

"You could always strip out of those wet clothes," Kingston said.

The casual suggestion didn't hit me as hard as before, but I still wasn't up for any nudity outside of my own home. "I'm fine."

He crawled back into the SUV, and grabbed something from the back seat. "Come here." He crooked his finger.

I joined him, and sat next to him when he patted the vehicle. He wrapped us both in a fresh blanket.

"Better?" he asked.

Warm. Safe. Comfortable. Pressed against him? It was pretty much heaven. "Better."

Silence settled between us. It was as comfortable as leaning against him. How screwed was I, that I wanted to make a habit of picnics in the rain with Kingston?

"We almost lost our first shop, too." His voice was subdued.

"What happened?"

He sighed. "My mother was upset that I'd invested in such a piece of shit idea. She cut me off. Disowned me." The pain in his voice was like a knife through the heart.

"I'm sorry."

He shook his head. "It's okay. I mean, it's not, but… what are you going to do, right? Anyway, we were out of cash, and we were determined to make the thing take off. Every cent we made from the shop went back into it. We'd work the café all day, and then go to second jobs at night. Owen was cooking, and I was washing dishes. Working at a restaurant had the added bonus of free food. No air mattress, but we did have a shitty motel room with only one bed."

"Wow." I wanted to say I couldn't imagine, but I had a pretty good idea. I hadn't been close to starving, but it was rough in the beginning. "You spun it into something big, though."

"We did. And there's a lot of satisfaction in that."

I wanted to ask if he ever repaired things with his mother, but was that appropriate when a relationship ended that way?

"I still don't talk to her," he said, as if reading my mind. "It doesn't matter what we've done with the place, to her it's still not a proper way to earn a living. When I figured out nothing I did would be good enough, I severed ties."

"I'm sorry. I wish I had something better to say."

Kingston kissed me on the forehead. "You mean it, and that's what matters."

As we settled into silence again, drowsiness pulled my eyelids shut. I struggled to pry them open again.

"Hey." Kingston shook me gently. "Come on. I'll take you home."

Embarrassment coursed through me. "I promise it's not you." Or rather, it was, but not in the way falling asleep on a date looked. I was letting my guard down around him.

"How much sleep do you get at night?"

"Enough." Four to six hours.

He climbed from the SUV and helped me do the same. "Not enough," he argued. "But I'm flattered you trust me enough to sleep here."

I did. That should be a scary thought. It wasn't, though.

He kept an arm around my waist as he walked me to the front of the vehicle, and made sure I was settled inside.

I didn't mean to doze on the way home, but the next thing I knew, we were parked behind my house.

"I'm a lousy date." My voice was gravelly from being woken up. "Falling asleep on you over and over."

"You're the best date I've ever had."

When he said things like that, my insides melted. "I'm not so tired I won't remember that in the morning." Did that make sense? I wasn't sure.

"Good." He brushed his lips over mine. "Thank you for tonight."

He waited until I was inside, and then drove away.

I leaned against the back door, and stared at the ceiling. I wanted more. Another night with him. Another kiss. Another fuck. Another anything.

At the same time, that sales pitch was still looming. It didn't matter that Kingston wanted to get to know me, or that Owen had called just to talk... It didn't change their ultimate goal, and it didn't change that I'd pick my business over anything in this world except my friends.

There was a looming expiration date on Kingston and Owen's being in my life. There was no other way to look at things.

FIFTEEN

My next couple of days were disrupted by fantasy enhanced memories of Kingston, especially any time I was in the kitchen.

My dreams were mostly of Owen whispering in my ear in that deep, seductive tone. He wasn't always saying sexy things, sometimes it was as simple as *Willis Tower lights up at night, and it's the most amazing display of technology meets art.*

When Owen called me on Saturday night, anticipation tightened in my belly just from seeing his name on the screen.

"Hey, Kitty Cat." His voice and the nickname caressed my senses.

Were aural orgasms a thing? I was starting to think so. "Hey, yourself. We've moved on to pet names now?"

"Pet, Kitty Cat, I get it." He chuckled. "You ever send anyone else a picture of your fleecy pussy?"

"Never once."

"Then you're only *Kitty Cat* to me. I like the exclusivity of that." He was starting off strong.

Not that I minded. Maybe I should. But it felt amazing to just hear him, that he'd called, that this was so easy to slide into... I couldn't take issue with any of it. "You're definitely a club of one."

"Question for you. Where have you always wanted to visit?"

"Tokyo." I didn't need to think about my answer. "I want to see a real cosplay café, and wander a city that's amazingly huge on the inside, but still has a connection to nature farther out. Don't suppose that's on your list of places you'd set up a shop." Why would I ask that? Because Even though I'd barely known them more than a week, I was reaching a point where I couldn't picture them not in my life.

Owen's laugh was light. "It's on my to-visit list. Not sure I want to consider the cost of doing international business, or of property there, but I'd definitely take a vacation or three."

"Take lots of pictures." I pushed out the casual words instead of the *make sure you take me* that wanted to force its way out. "How's New Orleans?" Best to change the subject now, before I said something I couldn't take back.

"I have a confession to make."

I didn't call to give you a tour. The flirting is just to loosen you up for business.

It was easier to ignore my doubts than I expected. "I'm listening."

"I don't ever do touristy things when I travel for business," Owen said. "But I wanted to give you more than just a description of the view from my hotel, especially since I'm facing a brick wall, so last night I agreed to go on a ghost tour with the couple who manages the shop here."

"You did that *just* for me?" I was flattered, and only a little skeptical.

"Absolutely."

"You didn't enjoy it at all."

"It was ludicrous. Superstition, hokey myths... Fuck. You don't believe, do you?"

I was amused by his sudden concern. "I'm not sure. Maybe, maybe not. But that doesn't answer my question. Did you enjoy it?"

"Technically you didn't ask a question. But yes, it was entertaining as hell."

I settled onto my bed, back against the headboard and pillow in my lap. "Tell me about it."

I listened as he described the buildings, the legends, and some of the ghosts who were said to haunt the various stops they made. He gave vivid details of the architecture and folklore, but seemed to have an instinct for not lingering too long on any one thing.

I was captivated. Though honestly, I probably would have been captivated if he'd read me a croissant recipe.

"And there was a tarot reader at the end of the tour. I had to pick a card, of course," he said.

I grinned. "Of course." I'd always been fascinated by tarot cards and fortune telling. Luna could read them, and she'd had me pick a card a few times, but I was firmly in the *it may or may not be real* camp. "What card did you get? What does your future hold?"

"Three of swords," Owen said. "Apparently it has something to do with romantic betrayal."

As in, I'd betray him? A shiver ran through me, and I hugged the pillow. "That's haunting."

"Good thing I don't believe." Owen sounded unfazed. "Fuck. Don't tell Kingston I'm talking shit about this stuff."

Curious. Not enough to wipe the tarot reading from my mind, but a good distraction. "Okay, one, why not, and two what makes you think I'm talking to Kingston?"

"Because he told me. And because he *does* believe."

Somehow I wasn't surprised that they held such a deep-seated belief in opposition, but were friends in spite of it. "The two of you are close." *Duh.* But were Owen and I close enough he'd give me more of an answer than before about his relationship with Kingston?

"I love him." Owen said the words with all the assurance of a man who wasn't terrified of being called less-than-masculine. So, so sexy.

But did he mean the same thing I heard? "When you say *love*, is this a romantic thing or more familial? Have you told Kingston?

Because what the two of you have is a little more than *occasional benefits*."

Owen sighed. "That's a lot to answer at once."

"And best done with emotion, not logic," I teased.

"Ouch."

"Another emotion. Good job." I made sure my tone conveyed playfulness rather than trying to shut him down.

Owen chuckled dryly. "Yeah, the two of you bring that out in me. But... I don't have the kinds of answers I think you want. I love him. I'd do most anything for him. I've never specifically used those words with him."

"Maybe tell him, instead of making excuses to be with him through a third party?" Given I had been—was still?—that third party, was I talking myself out of... something more? Of all the things I was worried about when it came to them, that wasn't on the list.

"I don't make excuses," Owen said. "If I want sex, I ask for sex."

So I'd seen. The heat of memory flushed my skin. "Sex, yes. You're very skilled at sex and asking for it. I meant the rest."

Another sigh. "This is going to sound melodramatic, but Kingston and I saved each other."

Interesting detour, but I didn't mind. Each glimpse into their pasts made them more real. More desirable. If I asked for details, I'd be another step closer to having to admit they were more than just casual fun. "How'd you meet?"

"Math."

The same thing Kingston said. It was nice to know their single word stories matched up.

"Is there more to it than that? Is this a *Math Saves* kind of public safety warning?" I teased.

His breathing shifted for a heartbeat, a heavier puff. I pictured him on the other end of the line huffing out dry amusement. "His parents paid me to tutor him in math when we were in junior high. Except he didn't need it. He wasn't actually failing, but anything less than an *A* was disgraceful to them, and he understood it, he was just bored, and didn't want excelling to damage his *I don't give a fuck* reputation."

A young Kingston putting more effort into what people thought than a mark on a paper? Easy to believe.

"I was the brooding smart kid no one wanted to approach back then," Owen said.

"I know that feeling." I'd been a lot the same. *Resting bitch everything.*

"But Kingston looked past that. He sort of... adopted me."

The extrovert bringing the introvert into their fold.

"He brought his grades up," Owen continued. "To prove I was doing what his parents wanted, and so they'd keep paying me." A pause. It ticked on longer than a breath or two "It was what we both needed at the time. He's a good guy and he deserves good things."

I didn't know how to interpret that. "It feels like you're directing that at me."

Another pause.

It would be nice if I could say Owen's hesitations didn't mean anything, but he was measuring his words. Each time the silence drifted in like this.

"I am." He finally spoke. "He and I... What we have works. You're a good thing, Kitty Cat. Amazing, in fact."

Now I was the one who had to consider my next words. Instinct wanted to say *no I'm not.* Few people reacted well to a compliment shut down like that, but especially these two. "Thank you?"

"I'm glad the two of you are hanging out. I should let you go before it gets too late. Sweet dreams."

The abrupt wrap-up ground through me, stealing any questions I had. "You too."

I disconnected, but sleep wouldn't be my friend tonight. I was too caught up in analyzing the intricacies of the conversation with Owen.

SIXTEEN

My phone chimed early in the morning. I'd think it was Anne, but it was the default tone, not our custom one.

You up? The name on the screen said *Persistent Asshole*.

The label I'd given him when he was calling every few weeks trying to buy my business. I should update that to have his real name. *Depends on who this is ;)*

My phone rang seconds after I hit *Send*.

"Your concierge and tour guide for the day," Kingston said the instant I answered.

Maybe I wouldn't change the name on his contact, though I might add a smiley face at the end. "What if I have other plans?"

"Cancel them. What I have for you is a million times better."

"Which is...?"

"A surprise."

Nope. "I don't do surprises."

"Oh." He managed to encompass *deflated* in a single syllable. "In that case, I have a friend in management at Digital Media, and he's screening their new game for a few people."

It wasn't strawberries in the rain, and it was *fraternizing with the enemy*. But it did sound fun. Besides, I wanted to see him and I wasn't actually doing anything else. "Is it any sort of conflict of interest that some of my closest friends work for the competition?"

"Was it when you catered for DM?"

No. "I take a non-disclosure agreement seriously."

"Then it's not a problem now. I'll pick you up in thirty minutes, and we'll get breakfast first." He made the decision sound so simple.

But wasn't it?

Thirty minutes was both way too much time, since I was already up and dressed for the day, and not nearly enough to sift through my entire closet for a different outfit that looked sexy-cute without looking like I was trying too hard.

A skirt was tempting, especially the plaid one hanging in the back, but not in front of other people. Especially not people I did business with.

I settled on a sun dress that flared out under my breasts, and a crop sweater. Mickey Mouse ears decorated the dress—I would be the perfect blend of playful and professional.

My doorbell chiming saved me from second-guessing the decision. I grabbed my purse and phone, and headed downstairs to answer.

When I opened the door, Kingston whistled. "My memory always understates how gorgeous you are," he said.

"Thank you." I'd need to practice accepting praise, if they were going to keep showering me with it. When did I make the shift from questioning everything kind they said to believing they meant it? Was I letting my guard down too quickly?

As we drove to breakfast, my phone chimed again. *That* was one of my friends. "I should turn this off," I muttered, swiping at the screen.

"I don't want you to miss anything important."

And I wasn't up for talking to Sadie in front of Kingston. "It's a friend. I'll call her back."

"I don't mind."

"I don't want them to know I'm with you." Why did I say that? I could have gone with *really, it'll wait*. But I had to be honest instead.

Kingston's expression shifted to disconcertingly neutral. "Why not?"

Because they looked out for me. That I was out with *him* might not be easy to understand. I didn't want my friends to judge me. Not that they ever had, but they'd never seen me do something like this. "Last time I told them about you, you were the asshole who wanted buy my shop, and slept with me to get to it."

"Except I didn't, and they're not going to know otherwise until you tell them." He was frowning now. It was better than no emotion, but it still hurt to see.

"I'm sorry. You've been honest with me from the start—except that whole fake name thing—this is all coming out wrong."

His frown relaxed. "Happens to the best of us."

"If you're sure you don't mind..."

"You telling your friends I'm not actually an asshole? I'm pretty sure." Now the teasing was back.

Telling Sadie meant admitting this was more than a fling, but not saying anything hurt Kingston. I didn't want to do that, because I cared that he was happy. Maybe this *was* more than a fling. A fling with a guy whose best friend loved him. With said best friend apparently trying to push us together. How did this get so complicated so quickly?

I called Sadie back.

"Hey." She was cheerful. "Stopped by your place and you were gone. Are you busy today?"

"You know it's ungodly early on a Sunday, right?" I teased. Anything before ten was a foul thought to Sadie.

"I'm aware." Her huff was playful. "But last week you seemed sad, and I haven't heard from you since, so I'm checking in with you."

The concern warmed me. "I'm good." Her bringing up last week was the perfect segue to where I was, but more stuck in my throat.

Kingston rested his hand on my knee, sending a shower of sparks to mingle with my hesitation.

"Are you sure? Do you want to hang out? I miss you," Sadie said.

I did adore her. "I'm... rain check? I'm on a date."

"Is that code for *I woke up in a stranger's bed and I don't know how to get out of here without a fuss. Save me?* Say *yes* and I've got your back."

Because I didn't date. "No. An actual date."

Kingston pulled into the parking lot of a diner, and shut off the engine.

"Is that why you're not calling us?" Excitement bled into Sadie's voice. "Tell me all about him. No, wait, you're with him now. Tell him you need friend approval. Not that you do, but I want to see this guy that Lyn is willing to call a *date*. Do you like him? Of course you do. How did you meet him?"

She didn't expect me to answer all of her questions, but the last one was the most important. I glanced at Kingston, who was watching me, then tried to force my thoughts into some semblance of order. "You know how I told you about those guys who want to buy my shop?"

"And the sex? And the assho— oh, no. Lyn."

Was that disappointment? Judgment? "Yes." I switched the phone over to FaceTime. Sadie wouldn't filter herself and I needed that right now. I showed her Kingston.

He grinned and waved. "Kingston. Asshole Extraordinaire, at your service... Holy shit, you're *Sadie Sews*."

"Not relevant. What did you do to my Lyn?" Sadie demanded.

"Well... I screwed up, I begged for her forgiveness, and then I begged again to spend more time with her. Do you have any idea how amazing your friend is?"

Sadie shook her head. "Better than you do."

"Fair point, though I'd like to move up a little farther on the scale."

It was odd to hear me talked about this way. A girl could get used to the indirect praise.

"He's cute." Sadie was talking to me again. "Does he know if he hurts you, there's no place in the world he can hide from us?"

"He does now, and he would deserve it," Kingston said.

Grayson walked behind Sadie, then paused. "Who's the hottie?" He asked.

Sadie gleaned back. "Lyn's new manservant."

Sadie, Anne, and I teased each other and their boyfriends all the time, but that was inner circle stuff. Did I want them drawing Kingston into the same?

"Ready to serve at Her Majesty's whim." He fell into it so easily.

What if he fit in with us? What if Owen did? They'd have to, for me to stay with them. Was I thinking about long term with them? No. I was living this day today. "Anyway," I said. "He made nice, we're good now, and he asked first if I was free. I'll call you tomorrow and we'll figure something out?"

"Yes. Definitely yes." Sadie was emphatic. "You have so much to fill me in on."

And with any luck, I'd figure out at least some of it before we spoke again.

"That went well. It seemed to go well." Kingston tangled his fingers with mine as we headed inside. "You tell me. Did that go well?"

"She didn't threaten to send the cops, so..."

"Good thing I never plan on hurting you."

Except for that whole looming matter of him and Owen wanting to buy my shop. And Owen being in love with him... Did Kingston feel the same? Would he if he knew? *Did* he know?

Gah. Too many questions, and I just wanted to hang out and have fun.

We were seated, and ordered coffee. As soon as the waitress left, Kingston leaned in. "I can't believe Sadie and Grayson know you."

"Grayson did half the wiring in Loading Java." I wasn't surprised he knew who they were. Sadie had a huge online following with her costume design, and Grayson was a popular game streamer. Even if Kingston only followed one of them, they frequently appeared on each other's channels.

Kingston tapped his index finger on the table rapidly. Odd twitch. He huffed out a breath. "I heard... The two of them... Is it true?"

"Is what true?"

"She's married to him and his boyfriend."

It had been a gorgeous ceremony. Held in my back yard. "It's true."

Kingston shook his head.

"What?" I asked.

"Nothing. Or rather, I'm processing. In a good way."

I wasn't going to read into that.

Ha, I totally was. I could make so many assumptions regarding why Kingston cared if Sadie was married to two people. The obvious one for most people would focus on my relationship with him and Owen. But my brain revolted at the thought. Not because I didn't like it, but because it was so implausible.

Wasn't it?

I stashed the familiar insecurities about me being undesirable, and dove into the now instead. Breakfast—the conversation and attention that went with it—was fun. So was the unofficial demo with Kingston's friend from DM. I even got my name on the demo copy list, to give me promo for my shop.

By the end of the day, I wasn't thinking about anything but how much I enjoyed spending time with Kingston.

He walked me to the back door at my place.

"Do you want to come in?" I had things to do before tomorrow, but I didn't want to give him up just yet.

He brushed his lips over mine in the most agonizingly sweet kiss. "Desperatcly."

I unlocked the door.

"But I won't," Kingston said.

My heart ground to a halt, slamming into my ribs with a painful *crunch*. I couldn't hide my frown.

"If I come in, I'm going to want to kiss you. And undress you. And kiss you some more, until you're writing in pleasure and your legs are too weak to stand."

Me too. "Is that bad?"

He shook his head. "I don't want sex to define whatever happens next."

"That's sweet." Disappointing, but also reasonable.

"I was hoping for *noble* but I'll take *sweet*. I'll still leave you with something, though." He wrapped one arm around my waist, gripped the back of my neck, and crushed his mouth to mine.

My body molded to his hard frame. Everywhere we made contact, despite there being layers of clothing between us, my skin scorched with need. His erection dug into my stomach. Desire throbbed between my thighs. This felt so… *real.*

Kingston broke away with a groan. He dragged a thumb over my lips. "I'm going to be gone for a few days, fetching some things from my old place. I'll call you as soon as I know when I'll be back."

"I don't drop everything for just anyone." Did that sound light? Carefree?

"I'm special."

He really was.

I nodded. "I'll talk to you then."

He brushed his lips over mine again. "Don't forget about me while I'm gone."

"I'll try not to." Not that I ever could. Whatever happened, Kingston was a permanent part of my memories.

SEVENTEEN

Sadie and Anne were supportive and happy for me when I gave them more details about what I'd been up to with Owen and Kingston. I shouldn't have expected otherwise, but my self-esteem was a massive bitch whenever she felt tiny.

Weeks passed, and summer melted into not-quite-summer at an agonizingly slow rate. My days went the same as always, with me getting up early to bake for the shop, and working all day. But my nights were marked by if I got to talk to Owen, or go out with Kingston. When neither was available, I went to bed early and let pleasant dreams of either or both men keep me company.

It didn't matter that Owen and I limited our conversations to *friendly* topics rather than *romantic*, or that my dates with Kingston never ended with more than a kiss. I'd never felt so adored. I'd never enjoyed anyone's company so much outside of Anne and Sadie.

One Friday night, a little more than a month after I first met them, I was talking to Owen. I'd hesitated to bring up *Kingston* and *love* again, on the off chance it put an end to these conversations. Apparently I was a little worried after all.

Owen was on the last leg of his trip, and had already described several parts of Atlanta for me. The conversation drifted where it would, and I wasn't in a hurry to hang up, even though I had to be up early. I wanted to know why, out of all the degrees Owen could have pursued with his knowledge and interests, he chose a cooking.

"I love too cook." He made it sound so simple. "And I wanted to go into the restaurant business. For me, school was one of my steps. Why an anime gaming café? The real reason, not the flippant answer you gave Ravyn and Ramsey."

I wasn't willing to admit this to many people, but it felt okay to tell Owen. "It combines my three favorite things… Anime, gaming, and food, in case that wasn't clear."

I could have guessed you love food. My insecurity spoke in his voice. But those scars were far older than he was, and he didn't deserve to fall under their scrutiny.

"It's scary how much we have in common," he said.

"I know what you mean."

"Have you got your pussy on display tonight?" Owen's tone was playful.

I smiled at the memory. "No, but I am laying here in nothing but panties and a camisole."

If he said *show me,* I didn't know what I'd do. There were some things I wasn't willing to commit to photo.

Silence.

What was he considering?

"Tonight, I want the guided tour." His voice had dropped an octave. "Put me on speaker, lay back, run your hands over your body, and tell me how every single bit of it feels."

I set my phone aside. I'd never done anything like this before, but for him, I wanted to, and I wanted the moment to be perfect. "Where should I start?" I couldn't hide the quiver in my voice.

"Over your top, your breasts. I want to hear your gasps as you tease yourself through the fabric."

I glided my hands up my torso, the way he told me to, moaning when I brushed over the more erogenous bits.

"Fuck." Owen's voice an octave lower was even better. "Are your nipples hard? Tell me how it feels."

Hesitation lodged my reply in my throat, but the compulsion to please Owen won out. I teased the nubs, my shirt rubbing against them and adding extra friction. "They rock hard. It feels so good."

Good enough I kept playing. Moaning. Not trying to bite back any noises that wanted to slip from my throat.

"Top off," Owen said.

I stripped off my cami. "Done."

"I wish I was there. I can picture your gorgeous breasts. Pale skin. Delicious nipples. What it's like to draw one into my mouth, and suck until you whimper."

Memory mingled with now. "I'm licking one." I pressed my breast up and flicked my tongue out. "And pinching." Being in the moment made it easier to describe things. I rolled a nipple between my fingers, gasping with each touch. "It's not as good as your mouth, though."

Owen grunted. "God, I can almost taste you. I'm so hard right now. Keep playing, Kitty Cat."

I did—twisting and rolling—how long did he want me to do this for? It felt good, but it wasn't enough. "I'm squeezing my thighs together." My confession came out breathy. "I want more."

His guttural, "Hmm..." rolled over me. "Slide your fingers between your legs. Tell me what it feels like."

It felt like I wanted him here, those solid arms pinning my hands above my head while he pounded inside me. "I'm wet. Slippery. My panties are... useless."

"Take them off. I want you naked in bed, thinking about me."

"Done."

Owen's chuckle was gravel. "Spread your legs. Imagine me kneeling between them."

"Like I could think of anything else right now."

"There are so many nights I wish you and I had..." Owen trailed into one of those pauses. Instead of making me nervous, it built the anticipation, because I wished the same. "I'm stroking my cock," he said. "Imagining sliding inside you. You're so fucking tight. Slick. Perfect."

"I'm using my fingers." I pushed three inside myself. "It's good, but not the same."

"No toys?"

I had plenty, but they would stay in the drawer for now. "It's not the same. I want to get lost in the fantasy of skin on skin."

"*Christ.* Me too. Make yourself come, Kitty Cat. I want to hear the incredible sounds you make."

Usually when I masturbated, I didn't have the patience to hold out. But if I lasted longer, I kept Owen on the phone longer. I slipped between teasing my clit and dipping my fingers inside me. I lost track of talking and myself in the sensations, and letting them tear noises from me.

I held out as long as I could, but I hovered on the edge of orgasm, and had to push myself over. When I came, I let the cries and moans fall into the room, until my throat was dry and I was spent.

"Fucking hell, gorgeous." Owen grunted as much as spoke. "I'm fisting my cock and stroking so hard it aches."

I relaxed back into the sheets, and listened to his noises. Boldness, carried on post-orgasm bliss, filled me. "If you were here, I'd wrap my lips around you, then beg you to come inside me."

"*Jesus.*" The noises Owen made were guttural. Almost primal. His breathing grew stuttered, followed by a rapid series of grunts, and one long one.

And then silence.

"You still there?" he asked roughly.

"Yes."

"I wish you were here instead."

I physically felt that sentiment. "Me too."

"You're incredible."

I didn't know how to respond. Another compliment, and I didn't want to ruin the warm fuzzy glow. "How did you know?" My question was breathy.

"Know what? That you're incredible? It's pretty obvious."

Thankfully no one could see how bright red I must be, flushed from the string of kind words. How to phrase my question? "You didn't ask for pictures this time."

"You don't like pictures of yourself."

"That's true…"

"Don't misunderstand"—Owen's voice was throaty, rasping over me—"I love that photo of Kitty Cat Lyn. But I don't want to push you away. Never, but especially tonight." Did his voice catch?

"When *will* you be here? I want to actually feel you next time," I said.

Empty air.

No. Nonononono.

"I fucked up." Owen's regret sent fissures of doubt through me.

My blood curdled. I wouldn't jump to conclusions, no matter how loudly my brain was screaming that this was it. This was when the betrayal happened. "Not what a girl wants to hear after sex, even the long-distance kind."

"I want to be there. Have you here. Something that lets me touch you. But…" His sigh opened the chasm of doubt wider. "Kingston likes you. Adores you. I— I should let him tell you that but it's context. I told you I'd do anything for him."

I didn't know how to react. My thoughts were split between terror of this being a charade and fear of it being more. Being what my heart hoped for. "Okay?"

"I was supposed to keep my distance. Be the good, supportive friend. His wingman. Let things go where they would with him and you." The husky, deep sound of Owen's voice, the one that sent goosebumps racing over me, was back. "And instead I'm falling for you. I don't want to take you away from him. I want you both— wow, that sounds even better aloud than in my head."

My heart plummeted into my shoes. *I want all of that too*, the words jammed in my throat. The lack of response that came out instead had to be the worst thing I could have done… aside from maybe laughing.

Owen bit off a dry chuckle. "Do you know how many logic holes exist in this relationship?"

"This isn't a relationship." I cringed at the words. Nope, that was worse than keeping my mouth shut.

"First of all, ouch. Second, anyone you interact with on any sort of ongoing basis is a relationship. You're making an assumption."

Not so much, given what he'd just confessed. "Logic holes?"

"Well, I was going to tell you three people don't stay together long term, but since you don't see what we have as *that*, there's no point." He didn't sound bitter, but his hurt was piercing.

"I had an almost identical conversation with one of my best friends before she married her boyfriends. Plural." I shouldn't be presenting counterpoints, not after the way I basically shut him down, but my heart was racing ahead of me, asking *what if?* What if things did last with them? What if everything either of them said was sincere. What if we could have warm fuzzies and fun sex and incredible conversations all the time, forever?

"I bet the three of them trust each other."

"Implicitly."

Owen sighed. "Let me rephrase my statement. Three people don't stay together long term when they don't trust each other."

I do trust you. Except when this conversation started, I'd been waiting for the other shoe to drop. Expecting this would be the end of *us*.

"You're not going to deny it," Owen said.

If only I honestly could. "If I lie and tell you *Of course I trust you,* that doesn't help the situation."

"I see."

"But I want to." That was easy to say. Out of all my stalled answers, this one was as direct and real as I got.

"Yeah?" His sadness faded. "What's it going to take to turn that into *I do?*"

Was his phrasing on purpose? Almost always. "You're doing everything right." Easier to admit than I expected. My past said they were full of shit. That there was something they were hiding from me, and it was going to destroy me. But that wasn't based on them. I might not like some of the things they'd approached me with when we met, but as far as I knew, they'd been honest since. "I guess... time. I need time, and that's on me, not you."

"I'm willing to keep going and see what happens next if you are. Kingston will be too."

Terrifying thought. Letting them into my life more than ever before. This was risk versus reward, and they were an incredible reward. "I am."

EIGHTEEN

Every few months, we did a Cosplay Saturday theme in the café. The staff wore costumes, and we encouraged the customers to do the same.

It was a huge business day, especially since a few of our staff liked school uniforms—the men and the women—and fans would come just for the sexy-cuteness of those outfits. People would also stop by to see the spectacle, then end up staying for coffee, sweets, and sometimes gaming time.

I never dressed up. I played the *I'm the boss, I don't have to* card.

But today, I felt good. There were a lot of days like recently, but after talking to Owen last night, I was light as air.

I finished the morning's baking, including the extra for antici-pated business, then headed upstairs to change. I pulled the plaid skirt from the back of my closet, paired it with black Mary Janes, white knee-highs, and a button-down white shirt. The finishing touch was twin braids.

As I descended the back stairs, Anne's, "Holy hotness, gorgeous," greeted me.

"Hey, you made it." I skipped down the last few steps to greet her. *Damn* I felt good.

Anne gave me a noisy kiss on the cheek. "Glad I didn't miss it."

I stepped back to look her over. "Someone's out of costume."

"No, I'm not." She put her arms out and twirled. "I'm inconspicuous extra number seventy-two."

"Very specific. Why not sixty-nine?"

Anne snorted. "Because once you realize the flaws with actually doing that, the joke isn't as funny."

"You didn't think of it."

She grinned. "I didn't think of it. Forget the skirt, I love this mood on you. These guys are really good for you. When do I get to meet them?"

Heat flooded my cheeks thinking about them. "They really are incredible. Owen will be back soon."

"So… give you two weeks straight of fucking, and you might be able to make time for me?" Anne teased.

"It's not…" *that kind of relationship*. But last night it became that with Owen, and while Kingston and I hadn't slept together again, we were pushing the boundaries of what could be called *no sex*. A teensy bit of me said I should be concerned about that, but I believed him when he told me why he was holding back. "I'm sure we'll need a break long before two weeks is up, to eat and stuff."

"Uh-huh."

Anne stuck around to help with the day's rush. Our other friends filtered in and out as they were able. The event was a bigger success than we'd ever had. A few more of these, and I wouldn't be worrying so much about paying the bills.

My friends took off as the crowds dwindled. My staff and I were in the process of gently shooing people out the door when a pair of arms wrapped around my waist.

"I never would have skipped class if you'd been there," Kingston murmured, before nibbling on my earlobe.

I leaned back into him. This felt so good. So right. "You skipped class? You scoundrel."

"Scoundrel? I do say, m'lady, I'm a scoundrel of the worst sort." His accent was bad enough, I couldn't identify it.

"What sort is that?"

"The sort who's hopelessly smitten."

My breath caught.

"Can your staff finish without you? We need to talk." Kingston's question was a blanket over my warm fuzzies.

Now my voice was gone for a different reason. I nodded toward the kitchen. He took my hand and led me into the other room.

I spun to face him as soon as we were through the doorway. "What's up?" I struggled to keep my tone light.

"We have a problem."

Was this it? I'd all but stopped waiting for the other shoe to drop, but I knew they still wanted this place. It was probably even more attractive after a day like today, and Kingston had promised me a warning before he pitched me again. The thought was there, but I struggled to believe it. "What kind of problem?"

"I talked to Owen this morning," he said. "I adore you so much, and I wasn't sure what to think when he brought you up."

Adore—the same word Owen used. I was pretty sure that was on a similar level as *love*, but I didn't dare read anything into this. "Do you talk about me a lot?"

"Yes. But he never tells me anything private you've told him, and I'm the same."

"So, what *are* you talking about?" This conversation wasn't going the way I expected. It could still fall apart, though.

"We talk about how incredible you are."

I smiled in spite of myself.

"And that's the problem," Kingston said. "I'm not letting you go without a fight, and neither is he."

But Owen and I talked about all three of us... But if he didn't share that part of the conversation with Kingston... This was making my head hurt. "If you could cut to the point, I'd love that, so I don't panic over what you do or don't mean."

Kingston smiled. It wasn't an arrogant kind of smirk, it was gentler. "Neither of us is willing to give you up, and both of us have too much invested in our own relationship to destroy that. So, when he gets back, all three of us are going to talk and figure out how we all fit together."

He didn't mention Owen's more-than-friendly feelings toward him. Had they talked about it? I wanted to know—possibly needed to—but it didn't feel like my place to bring it up.

"Sometimes you sound like him. All logical and stuff." I should have seen this coming. Owen and I had the beginning of this conversation. He was right, I needed to trust them more. Now seemed like a good time to actively work on that.

"I'll take that as the ultimate compliment." Kingston closed the distance between us, rested his hands on my hips, and pressed his body to mine.

I gasped into the kiss and draped my arms around his neck, locking my fingers together. Voices drifted in from the other room, but it was easy to block them out when I was wrapped up in Kingston.

"I was thinking"—his words hummed against my lips—"we could recreate that first night in here. I know it's only the two of us, but you've got frosting on hand…"

"I like the way you think. Everyone will be gone soon."

He dragged his nose up the side of my neck. "Why wait?"

A new flavor of discomfort crept into my veins, tugging on an old memory. "Because there are people out there. Someone could walk in here any moment."

"That's part of the fun. The thrill of the danger." Kingston fiddled with my buttons, undoing one.

My stomach recoiled at his touch. The sounds on the other side of the door turned to raucous laughter in my head. I pushed him away and stepped back. "I said *no*."

NINETEEN

My words came out more forcefully than I intended, but I was glad for the distance. Cool air rushed in, but it didn't soothe my nausea. I rebuttoned my shirt, hiding more skin than I had before.

"Okay. We'll wait." He studied me with concern.

I shook my head and stepped back farther, but the actions didn't stop the past from forcing its way to the front of my mind. The memory of— The laughter. The pointing. The humiliation. I choked on a sob. Why did this still have this impact on me?

"Lyn." Kingston kept his distance. "Talk to me?"

I couldn't tell him this. No one in my current life knew this story. Not Anne or Sadie…

He extended his hand. "Whatever's going through your head right now, it doesn't make me care about you any less. Whatever your reasons for telling me to stop. I'm sorry I didn't get it sooner. Tell me what you're thinking?"

If I kept locking this away, I gave it power over me. I did want to trust Kingston, and this was a big thing. The worst he could do was laugh and agree with the people who… I frowned. "Can we go upstairs?" To get away from the people, and give me time to collect my thoughts.

"Of course."

I headed up first, uncomfortably conscious of whether or not I cared if he could see up my skirt. This was a man I was falling for, though. He had never been anything but adoring. Kind. Attentive. This wasn't the same as what happened back then.

I'd repeated *this isn't the same* enough times that when we reached my apartment, I could breathe again. I locked the door behind us. "You can sit." But I had too much nervous energy, so I was going to pace.

Kingston lingered nearby.

"So..." I laughed nervously as I exhaled. "This is probably stupid."

"Don't do that. It bothers you. It's not stupid."

Why did he have to be so sweet?

I clenched my first and forced my tongue to loosen. "I told you I used to dance." I could do this. It wasn't a big deal. "I was still the chubby girl in the group, but I was good." The words weren't going to stop until I finished. "I always danced without anything on under my tights, to avoid panty lines. A lot of the girls did. My boyfriend at the time—"

Bile rose in my throat and I swallowed it back. He wasn't just my boyfriend, he was also my first everything. Kiss. Making out until the car windows steamed up. Sex...

Kingston watched me, concern on his face.

Thankfully he didn't interrupt. I might not be able to finish if I lost more momentum. "He found out, and he thought it was hot. That's what he told me. I believed him. I believed everything he told me. We were doing a performance at school. In front of the entire auditorium. He rushed the stage, yanked down my bottoms, and exposed me to every single one of my classmates." I nearly gagged on the memory. "For the next two years, until my parents finally caved and moved me to a different school, every time I walked down the hall, someone would shout *Hey, Fattie Bush*." Not the most creative taunt, but so painful to teenage me.

I forced myself to look at Kingston. The story was out there, it didn't control me, and I wouldn't cower away from the consequences.

His fists were clenched and his mouth drawn in a straight line. "I'm sorry. No one deserves that, but especially not you. I swear, if I ever meet that asshole, I'll pound his dick into the dirt with a baseball bat."

The force and venom in his voice startled me, and I had to admit, seared away my blanket of doubt. "You'd go to jail for that."

"Worth it. There are a lot of things I'd do for you."

I ducked my head.

He placed a finger under my chin, forcing my gaze to his. "So, no public stuff. Nothing that risks us getting caught. I won't ask again," Kingston said. "But I will ask if I can stay tonight. You can keep the skirt on—and everything else—all night if it makes you feel better. I'm not assuming sex, I just want to be here, to hold you."

I laughed, to keep tears from escaping. "How are you so perfect?"

"I paid a witch two buttons and some pocket lint when I was five, and here we are." He took my hand and led me to the couch. "I'm happy to watch movies with you, or talk, or anything, as long as I get to hold you."

I curled up next to him tucked my feet to the side, and rested my head on his shoulder. When he draped an arm around me, I actually felt small. Safe. How did he do that?

We put on the newest Marvel movie, because we'd both only seen it twice.

Kingston trailed his fingers through my hair. "Since we're spilling secrets—not that mine is the same type as yours, but it changed my world—I talked to Owen today."

I frowned. "So you mentioned."

"About more than you."

I figured. He's your business partner. This was about something else, though. Kingston had let me get through my story, I'd do the same for him.

Kingston's hand stalled. "I was jealous when he said he was

falling for you. Jealous both ways. You got something from him I've wanted for years, but never realized it until he told me. And then he said he loves me, and I said it back."

If this were an anime, this was the moment where I'd go pale like a ghost and get a giant sweat bead and know that I'd lost them both. After being terrified of exactly that for weeks, for different reasons, why wasn't the fear there now?

I sat up, needing to look Kingston in the eye for this conversation. "And?"

"It doesn't change how I feel about you." He cupped my cheek and searched my face. "I don't want to keep anything from you, but I don't want to push you away, either. I meant everything I said earlier. And you're not surprised or freaking out. Owen told you already."

I leaned into his touch. "It's kind of obvious, even with as little time as the three of us have spent together. But he also told me his half. Not yours."

"And you're still here."

"It's my house."

Kingston rolled his eyes, but he was smiling. "Tell me what you're thinking."

"I'm thinking it's more of a revelation to the two of you than to me. I'm thinking I'd be a little hurt"—I didn't want to hold back. I wanted to be honest with him—"a lot hurt, if I lost you because of it. Either of you. Actually, it's kind of a relief."

He kissed me lightly. "Every time I think you can't get more amazing... So you think you could date both of us, while he and I are figuring things out with each other?"

Pretty sure that was what I'd been doing. It was nice to let myself put the label on it. "Looking forward to it. If we're having this conversation now, what are we supposed to talk to Owen about tomorrow?"

"Not sure I plan on talking much the next time I have both of you in a room together." He laid a series of playful nibbles along my bottom lip. "And we're missing the movie."

"Spoiler alert—the good guys win," I teased.

Kingston nudged me to lean back into him. "It's always about story more than the conclusion," he said.

I couldn't agree more.

I was aware of the good guys getting their asses kicked badly for the first time, and the next thing I knew, Kingston was shaking me gently.

"Hey." His voice was soft. "You missed the post credits scene."

I'd missed everything else, too. I forced some of the sleep from my eyes and sat up, mostly to stay conscious. "I keep falling asleep on you. You must think I'm the worst."

"Twice is hardly a habit." He stood and tugged me to my feet. "And I think you're the best."

"You're lucky you're cute, or I wouldn't let you get away with the endless flattery."

He tugged me toward the bedroom. "I'm lucky about a lot of things. *Cute* does make the list. I'm guessing it's more comfortable in here."

"It is. But I'm not sleeping in this." I fumbled with the buttons on my blouse. Great, I was too tired to undress myself.

"Here." Kingston kissed my knuckles, then gently pushed my hands aside. He removed my blouse and skirt, and draped them over the back of a nearby chair. "Bed. Now." He pulled back the comforter to expose the sheets.

I lay down. "Yes, sir."

I was half-aware of Kingston stripping off most of his clothes too. Shame I wasn't more awake to enjoy the show.

He slipped into bed behind me, wrapped his arm around my waist, and pressed into my back. "Sweet dreams."

When I opened my eyes again, it was because sunlight was streaming through the window and warming my face.

Kingston had an arm draped over me and was pressed against my back. A specific part of him pressed harder than anything else, into one ass cheek.

A woman could get used to waking up like this. How selfish was I for wishing there were one other person here with us? Then it would be perfect.

"Good morning, gorgeous." Kingston's breath was hot against my shoulder.

I snuggled back into him. "It really is. Good, I mean. And morning too. I'm gonna stop talking now. At least until after coffee."

He laughed. "I have a better idea. Do you have any whipped cream? Chocolate sauce?"

"Downstairs. In the mood for sweet coffee?" I'd never seen him take more than cream and sugar before.

"Not quite. I want breakfast."

"Do you want anything with the whipped cream and chocolate? Waffles? Pancakes?"

Kingston kissed my shoulder. "You."

"Oh." Heat flooded my cheeks.

He untangled himself from the sheets. "Don't move."

"But—"

Kingston stepped into view. He was only wearing boxers, and *wow* that view. He held up a warning finger. "I'll be right back. Promise."

When I heard my apartment door open and close, I raised my eyebrows. He was actually going downstairs dressed like that. Insane. And loveable.

Was I actually thinking the *L* word about Kingston?

Yes. I couldn't put it into that little three word sentence, but… I couldn't deny anymore that thinking about him or Owen made a happy flutter in my chest.

Kingston returned quickly, proposed toppings in hand, and a bath towel draped over one arm. "Will you trust me?" he asked.

"I do." Saying that felt so good.

He tugged me to my feet, grabbed his shirt from the back of the chair it was draped over, and folded it over my eyes.

My heart hammered against my ribs at the loss of one sense. I strained my ears for any sound. The texture of the carpet against my feet was a sharp contrast to the sunshine on my cheek and the cool air on my arms.

When Kingston trailed his fingers up my spine, I sucked in a sharp breath. "You can stop me any time." His voice was low and seductive.

I licked my lips, but couldn't find a response beyond nodding.

He stripped off my bra and panties, leaving me exposed and blind.

A spike of panic gripped my lungs.

His lips along my bare skin soothed me again. "Lay down."

At least I could climb into my own bed in the dark. But the texture was off. Rougher. The towel he'd fetched pressed into my bare skin. So many sensations I felt every day, but never paid attention to.

And we were just getting started.

The pause and absence of any sound or contact cranked my anticipation as much as the air on my exposed skin.

Lips brushed over mine, and I sighed. Cool liquid hit my nipples and I shifted to a gasp. The syrup flowed and pooled over my skin, and my pulse raced at the sensations.

Kingston dragged his tongue up my breastbone in a lazy path that teased around my breasts, up to my collar bone, and back down again. When he finally closed his mouth over one nipple, I whimpered.

He devoured one breast and then the other, licking me clean as if he were being graded and wanted a top score. A pause in his attention was punctuated by the hiss of the whipped cream can, and a new feathery light brush against my skin.

Then his mouth was back. Sucking and nibbling until I was clenching the sheets and whimpering.

"I love watching you." His words hummed against my skin. "Always, but especially when you're turned on. Your skin gets this stunning pink tinge. The way you bite your lower lip… *Christ* you do wicked things to me."

"Me? To you?" My laugh faded into another moan when he drizzled syrup down my stomach. A flash of self-consciousness vanished when his mouth followed the trail without hesitation.

He covered me in an alternating pattern of chocolate, whipped cream, and open mouthed kisses, over my hips, my thighs, and spreading my legs to lick along the inner skin.

I didn't know how much of the wetness pooling from me was syrup and how much was desire.

When he finally dragged his tongue along my slit, my hips bucked and I ground into his face. He plunged his tongue inside me, and my body gyrated in time to his attention. His thumb on my clit, circling and rubbing, over and over, time to his hungry licking, pushed me to orgasm.

Kingston eased his thumb away when I started to clench around him, then pressed back in again, drawing out my climax. Coaxing me until I was writhing in pleasure.

I collapsed back against the sheets with a breathless gasp. The darkness was comforting now. A way to sink into the mini tremors still tickling my senses.

The weight of Kingston's body covered mine. His kiss tasted like chocolate, whipped cream, and me, and was sloppy. Hungry. Uncontrolled.

"I need to be inside you," he managed between nibbles on my lips.

"Yes. Definitely yes."

I heard the tear of foil—a condom—and Kingston pushed my legs farther apart to kneel between.

It was so easy to lose myself in sensation this way. How good he felt sliding inside me. Gripping my thighs. Pushing my knees to my chest. And then pumping at a frantic pace.

He struck that sweet spot that yanked me toward orgasm again, and I clenched around him, clenched the sheets in my fists, clenched my toes when I came.

His grunts reached that delicious crescendo that meant he was close too. I'd missed that sound. It was more enticing that my favorite song.

The entire world seemed to pause when he slammed those last few, frantic thrusts against me, and then stopped.

He rested his cheek on my chest as we caught our breath. I had no idea how long we lay like that, but it didn't matter. This moment was as perfect as anything could be.

Kingston finally moved to strip off my makeshift blindfold, and kiss me. "I made a mess." His tone was playful and not the least bit apologetic.

There were traces of chocolate on us, on the towel… some had gotten on the sheets. I didn't care. I smiled and kissed him back. "I guess we need a shower."

"You're not going to get clean if we take one together."

"Then it'll have to be a long shower." I paused as the word flowed easily, waiting for that mental voice to remind me not to get too attached. To point out this would be over soon.

That nagging reminder wasn't there. I could imagine this lasting forever.

TWENTY

I spent most of Sunday in bed with Kingston, and it was incredible. Not just the sex, though that was amazing, but his company and everything about the day.

The only thing that would have made it better was Owen being there. How was this my life, that I not only had that option, but there was so little angst between the three of us to agree it was a good next step?

I hated to send Kingston home Monday morning, but we had work. The fact that Owen texted and said he'd be back tonight instead of tomorrow made parting more bearable.

I didn't try to ignore the anticipation of the evening as I baked for the day. *We need to talk* had never been more appealing.

It was my day to balance the books from the week before, and we'd done even better at Saturday's event than I realized. I'd be making an extra loan payment to the bank this month.

A little before noon, I grabbed myself some lunch—I'd probably had more pastries in the last month than I should have, but today seemed like a good day for another one, to help with paperwork.

Just after two, there was a knock on my office door, and Violet poked her head in. "Do you know Ramsey Miller?"

"Mhm. Why?"

"He's here to see you, and he asked for Lyn."

I pushed back from my desk. "I met him a few weeks ago. Nice guy."

"He's really not." Violet scowled.

Weird. "Fill me in, after I talk to him."

Violet followed me out to the café, where Ramsey sat at one of the tables.

He grinned and stood when he saw me. "Hey. How have you been?"

"Good." *Fantastic. Incredible. Amazing.* "You?" I wasn't close enough with him to give him any more than a polite answer, no matter how much I'd enjoyed his and Ravyn's company.

"Good. Good. Normally we have a constable deliver these, but I wanted to say *hi* and try the coffee and chocolate croissant— amazing but the way." He handed me an envelope.

Nervousness whispered at the edge of my mind. "Constable? Am I in trouble?" I forced a light laugh.

His chuckle sounded genuine. "Nothing like that. The zoning hearing on your building has been bumped up to Wednesday. Not that you're going to fight it, but notifying you is a formality."

"Why wouldn't I fight it?" My blood was icing over in my veins.

Ramsey's smile slipped. "Because you're selling? Making things *official* with Kingston?"

My gut flipped in on itself. I should have skipped lunch. "Did he tell you that?"

"Not in so many words, but he never stops talking about you. He did tell you I was pushing— *Fuck.* He didn't tell you."

I couldn't speak. Where was my wit? My venom? Why wasn't I biting back?

"Didn't tell her what?" The fury in Violet's question mirrored what I felt.

Thank the heavens for Violet.

Ramsey set the letter on the table. "I shouldn't say anything else."

"Finish the thought." I found my voice, and forced it out through a raw throat. I was fucking scary when I was pissed off.

"Kingston filed the petition to change the zoning. When the request came in today to push the date up, I figured it was because the two of you are... He would have told you... *Fuck.*"

My world spun. I was going to be ill. Would projectile vomiting on Ramsey be more humiliating than what I'd been through in the last month? Were Kingston and Owen laughing about this right now?

"You're such a raging fucking tool." Violet's voice grew in volume as she stepped toward Ramsey. "I always knew, but this... You fucking asshole. People like you are the reason the system—"

I settled a hand on her arm, and used the pause to find that same ice to force through all of me. I wouldn't break. Not in front of him, and sure as hell not in front of Kingston and Owen when I confronted them. I picked up the notice from the table. "Consider me served. Thank you for letting me know. I'll be there."

"I really am sorry." Ramsey sounded sincere.

Like I was ever buying that kind of bullshit again.

"If you were sorry, you'd take it back," Violet said.

He fixed a glare on her. "It doesn't work that way."

"Why not? Can *I* call in a favor? You sadistic fuckhole." Violet was yelling now.

I tightened my grip on her arm. "It's okay. Let him leave. I do have a favor though, Ramsey."

"If I can," he said.

"Don't tell Kingston we talked?" I kept my tone sweetly submissive. "I don't want to cause any ripples between us."

Ramsey's smile wasn't so confident now. "Of course. I'd rather not step between that anyway."

"Thank you." I was calm now. At least on the surface. What raged underneath... I was saving that.

TWENTY-ONE

I vanished into my office again. As soon as the door swung shut behind me, tears of frustration and disbelief tried to force their way out.

I wouldn't cry. I wouldn't fall apart. They weren't worth that.

It took far too long to collect myself, and then I sent Kingston and Owen a message. *Excited about tonight.* Thankfully bitterness didn't carry across texts. *Can we meet at one of your hotel rooms?*

Kingston's answer came in seconds later. *Mine. Miss you. See you then.*

I clenched my fist so tightly my nails dug into my palm, and summoned more calm.

Miss you too. See you then. I could pretend to care as well as they could. At least for the next couple of hours.

I wrapped up work a little early, to get ready. It was tempting to wear something I could hide in. The baggier the better.

They didn't get to see me shrink away, though. I would never again hide from someone trying to humiliate me.

I dressed in one of my more flattering shirts. Something that gave me nice cleavage. Took the attention away from the trouble spots.

Fat. You mean the fat. Call it what it is.

I wouldn't fall into that pit. Not tonight. I couldn't afford to.

Doesn't matter what you wear. They don't care. This was all a joke for them. You're a joke.

No. I forced the taunting aside.

On the drive to their hotel, I kept the music loud enough to drown out my thoughts. It took more will than I had to climb from the car, take the elevator to their floor, and walk down the hall to Kingston's room.

I forced myself to breathe when I knocked.

Kingston opened the door with the biggest, sweetest smile ever, and the careful wall I'd been building all day almost shattered. He stepped aside to let me in, and the instant the door closed behind us, he spun me to face him.

I planted a palm on his chest, and shoved him back, stepping farther into the room to find that Owen was there too. Perfect. I could sever both ties at once.

"What's wrong?" Kingston looked hurt.

Good. Fuck him. Or not. Never again, in fact. "Are you familiar with zoning laws in this city?" I was still cool. Calm. Ice.

"Shit." Owen's exclamation almost undid me. "You were supposed to tell her."

I focused a deadly sweet smile on him. "Tell me what?"

"Depends on what you know." If Kingston was trying to sound flippant, he failed.

I was glaring by the time I turned his way. "It shouldn't. You should have told me from the start. But that would ruin the fun, wouldn't it? Sorry, let me back up. Did you know the zoning on my building is being challenged?" I felt no satisfaction when Kingston winced. "I talked to Ramsey Miller today. He stopped by to tell me in person, because the two of you are such great friends, that the hearing to decide if they'd kick me out of my house or not had been moved up to two days from now. At your request, just like the original filing was."

"What? No." Kingston managed to sound genuinely surprised.

I wasn't. He'd been lying to my face about everything for more than a month. "You didn't file for a zoning change?"

He grimaced. "I did, but I figured I still had a few days to fess up."

"And by then it wouldn't matter? Because you'd have suckered me into thinking you care?" My retort held a sharp edge. "Maybe you shouldn't have pulled strings to move up the hearing date, in that case."

"I didn't do that. I promise."

I let out a barking laugh. "Oh, then it's okay. We're okay. None of this matters."

"Kitty Cat—"

"Don't." I whirled on Owen again. "Don't call me that. And don't think you can use logic to convince me this isn't a big deal. You fucked me. Both of you. To get to my shop. This was the plan from the start, wasn't it? Pick me up at the bookstore—"

"We didn't know who you were," Owen said.

I looked at Kingston. This was going to give me whiplash. "Didn't you?"

"Hand to God." He had the nerve to raise his fucking hand.

I shook my head in disbelief. "Like that means anything coming from you. Like I trust a single word you say. It's just a complete and total coincidence that I got the zoning change notice the same night you *found* me in the coffee shop? And the next morning you *just happened* to walk into my café, when the pick-up didn't work? You figured, fuck the fat chick, and she'll do anything we ask?"

Anger bled onto Kingston's face.

"I promise you—"

"Or was this a fetish?" I cut Owen off again. I could probably scream at Kingston all night, but if Owen started talking, if he was reasonable, I didn't know if I'd have a counter. I wouldn't be shut down. "A game, maybe? Let's fuck the fat—"

"Stop." Kingston's voice was hard. "Don't call yourself that."

Seriously? "Fuck you. You don't get to say what I do. I can call myself fa—"

"No. Because you're not." Kingston was definitely mad. Good. "You're intelligent. You're fun. You're gorgeous."

"I'm gullible. I'm easy to lie to. I'm desperate for a connection. Why don't you say what you're really thinking?" Why did this hurt so much?

Owen reached for my arm and I jerked away with a glare.

He held up his hands and kept his distance. "You'll probably take this the wrong way, but your shop isn't worth what you're accusing us of."

I barked in disbelief. "Is there a right way to take that?"

"No one's shop is worth that. Why would either of us, let alone both of us, spend a month leading you on, for a little café?"

"*Wow*, you're shit at apologies. Or do you just want to twist the knife a little more? The deception isn't complete until I'm bleeding?"

Owen's expression was blank, but if I looked close enough, I swore I could see a barely controlled emotion under the surface. "You know me better than that."

"Do I? Is the two of you *falling for each other* part of the game? A way to draw me in? A way out? *Sorry, Baby, now that we have what we want, we love each other. Bye.*" Even as I spit out the sarcasm, I knew that last bit wasn't true. But if it was real, other things they were saying may be too, and I couldn't accept that.

Owen pulled off a spectacular imitation of hurt mixed with anger. "The only reason to do what we did, either of us, with you, is because we love your company. Not as in your business, but spending time with *you*. I was genuine—we both were. I love everything about you."

"You don't get to say that to me. Not now. Not ever." I was shredded from the inside-out. "You lied to me the moment you approached me. You didn't even give me your real names. I should have known everything after that would be just as much bullshit. I should have—" I choked off a sob. *Don't break. Not here. Not in front of them.*

I forced myself to breathe. To look calm, despite crumbling.

"This charade, joke, whatever it is, it's over. Don't set foot in my store again. Don't call me again. We're done."

I spun on my toe and stalked toward the door. It was tempting to bump Kingston with my shoulder on my way past, but I didn't want to feel him ever again, even for that.

"Lyn." Pleading hung heavy in his voice, hitting my back. "Please. I love you."

Thank God he couldn't see me. I didn't pause as I walked out of the room, down the back stairs, and to my car. I made it out of the parking lot, and all the way to the bookstore before I had to pull over. I couldn't see the road through the tears streaming down my face.

How could I have been such an idiot?

TWENTY-TWO

I didn't sleep that night. I tried, but the dreams were torture. A blend of school and now, people—Kingston and Owen—laughing at me. Stripping me bare. Exposing me to the world.

I gave up around three in the morning, downed half a pot of coffee, and made my way to the café kitchen. Now seemed like as good a time as any to bake new recipes for customers to try.

I burned the first couple, staring off into space. That made the taunting in my head worse.

With some more coffee, I was ready to go.

I lost track of time as I lost myself in cooking. Whenever my stomach growled or my eyelids drooped, more coffee.

"Lyn?" Anne's concerned tone drew me out of my haze.

I instinctively painted on a smile when I looked up at her. "Hey. What are you doing here? It's the middle of the day." It was, wasn't it? Sun was streaming through the windows, and not low in the sky.

"Violet called me. She said something happened yesterday, and she's worried about you."

"I'm fine." My voice cracked. "Just tired." A shudder ran through me, and tears tried to force their way out.

Anne pulled up a stool next to mine, wrapped an arm around

my shoulder, and pulled me into her in a half hug. "Why didn't you call?"

"I don't know. I didn't want to be a bother. You have your life. Your guys. So does Sadie." Tears were flowing freely again. I didn't want to be crying. Why couldn't I stop?

"We're always here for you."

They shouldn't be. I made this mistake. It wasn't their responsibility to drop everything and console me for being blind. "They used me. They told me up front that they were going to win me over as a business partner, and I pushed my doubts aside. I thought it meant more. I'm such an idiot."

"You're not." Anne shifted and pulled me closer, hugging me tight. "This isn't your fault."

"But it is. I knew who they were, what they wanted, and I pretended what we had was something else."

"If it was me that this happened to, would you tell me it was my fault?"

"I don't know."

"But you do," Anne said gently. "You know and I know this isn't on you. They lied. It's not up to you to read between the lines every time. You have to trust people sometimes, and it's their fault for breaking that trust. You're more than that. You deserve better."

I wasn't sure I agreed with that last bit. I leaned into her, sobbing and unable to grasp more words.

She held me until I was done, then got me a damp paper towel to wash my face, and something to drink.

"What are we doing tonight?" Anne asked.

"I'm going to curl up in a ball and vanish." The crying was inevitable, but it didn't help me feel better.

Anne stood and tugged me to my feet. "Then I'll stay with you while you do that."

"If you're here, then technically I haven't vanished." I followed her upstairs, lacking the strength to protest.

"Then I guess I can't let you vanish."

The words were enough to tug more tears loose. Would I ever stop crying?

Anne loaded one action movie after another, always picking those with no romance. She ordered pizza, but I couldn't stomach food. I nibbled a couple of bites to keep her happy, and couldn't manage more.

She fell asleep, head in my lap, around midnight. I gently moved her aside to make some coffee. If my dreams were going to be the same as last night, I wasn't having it.

By the time the sun rose, I'd numbed the pain enough to do something resembling functioning. Anne offered to go to the zoning hearing with me, but I shooed her off to work. She was busy, and I refused to let her miss two days in a row because I'd given my hea—

Made a mistake with who I trusted.

Neither Kingston nor Owen was at the hearing. Because no one showed to argue for changing the zoning, and because I had my paperwork in order to show why it should stay as-is, the request was dismissed.

Arrogant idiots. All that trouble for nothing, on their part.

Unless Kingston never intended to pursue it after we got close.

I couldn't believe that. Refused. It was the only way to cling to any bit of sanity.

As I was leaving, Ramsey caught up to me.

"Hey, I heard you guys split," he said.

I smiled too brightly. Toning it down meant falling apart. "Split implies what we had was real." Was it better or worse that I said with so much enthusiasm and cheer?

Ramsey shook his head. "I'm glad things went your way. I love the café, and you shouldn't have to change how you do business."

"Thank you." I was too much sunshine, but I couldn't lower the glare. "Can I do anything else for you?"

"I wanted you to know, it wasn't Kingston who pushed the hearing up. I assumed, and I shouldn't have. The clerk said it was one-hundred percent a scheduling issue."

"That's fine. I need to run. Have a fantastic day."

Ramsey's smile was weak. "You too."

I was numb. I wasn't thinking about Kingston and Owen. The only way to get through this was to stay icy until the pain receded.

On the way home, I stopped at the grocery store. The ice cream called my name, and I'd forgotten to sneak in an order with my supplier. But I still hated that I ate so much last time. I grabbed a box of sugar free ice pops instead. Those would hit my sweet tooth perfectly, and keep me from getting dehydrated from the coffee I also stocked up on.

Every time I dozed off, as the night wore on, the nightmares rushed back. That coffee was a lifesaver.

I was more alert on Thursday. The world around me was in focus, and all I had to do was keeping looking forward. And drink more coffee.

Friday was more of the same, but I was up for getting back to the books. I wouldn't let my café crumble from neglect, after keeping it out the hands of… assholes.

I logged into my banking portal to make my extra loan payment —it still felt good to be able to do so, as long as I ignored the memories of how that night ended.

My loan balance was at zero.

Odd.

Software glitch? All of my other accounts looked right. I could check back in a few hours, but a quick call to the bank would clear things up.

The woman who answered was cheerful. She probably meant to sound pleasant, but the sincerity grated on me. Did she mean it? What was she hiding from the world, under that brightness?

I couldn't go through life questioning everyone who sounded like they meant something. "Hi. I'm calling because my loan balance isn't showing correctly on the website." I gave her my name and account number.

"I can check that for you, hang on." The clacking of keys filled otherwise dead air. "Miss?"

"I'm still here."

"Your account is fine. I show the loan paid off. I'm not sure why it's not reflecting that for you, but give it a few hours—"

"I'm sorry." I couldn't have heard her correctly. "I didn't pay off my loan. I wish I had, but no."

"Oh." More clacking keys. "Can I put you on hold for a moment?"

"Of course."

I didn't want to deal with this today, but it was better than what I'd been mired in. At least this was a problem I could confront head-on. Something I could get a solution for.

After a few minutes, the hold music vanished. "Jaelyn?" Miss Cheerful was back.

"Yes?"

"There's no mistake. We received your check, drawn from Kingu Kafes, for the full balance this morning."

Fuckers. "That's right. I forgot they were sending that today. I'm so sorry to take up your time."

"It's fine. Is there anything else I can do for you?"

Castrate the last two men I slept with. "No, thank you so much." I disconnected.

I was so livid, I was seeing red. Apparently that was a thing. My anger had me swaying on my feet. How *dare* they? I could call and scream, but I wanted to look them in the eye and ask them *what the actual hell?* They couldn't buy their way into my life any more than they could fuck their way into my café.

I made it to their hotel and was hammering the side of my fist on Kingston's door before I registered confronting them in person wasn't the best idea for me right now. They probably weren't here anyway.

When Kingston answered the door, surprise on his face, my stomach crumpled. If it hadn't been empty, I might have vomited on his shoes.

"Lyn." He sounded relieved.

I was angry. And tired. But mostly angry. I shoved past him, stalling for a heartbeat when I saw Owen was there too, sitting at the desk. "What are you doing?" I demanded.

"Working?" Leave it to Owen to be understatedly direct.

I wasn't in the mood. The room was wobbly—did anger do that? "With my loan. You can't just go around paying off people's loans. If you thought I was pissed about being fucked to get into my good graces, large sums of money I didn't ask for, in addition to the sex, aren't going to help."

"This isn't about sex," Owen said. "It's not about your shop, or our business. It's a gift. There's no lienholder. We don't have any claim to anything you own."

Kingston moved into view and stood next to Owen. "We want you to be successful and happy."

"Oh, okay. Sure." Sarcasm bled into my retort. "And I'm supposed to believe that? How do I know this isn't a way to get back into my life?"

"It's not. I'm telling the truth. Why do you have such a hard time believing we like you for you?" Owen's typical calm demeanor was buried under a frown.

My brain stalled on his question, and I forced the gears to start turning again. "But you didn't tell me the truth." That was the problem. The root of all of this.

Kingston pulled out a spare chair. "Sit, please? We'll talk." When I shook my head, he stayed standing "I'm sorry I put off telling you about the zoning. But that was the only—"

"The only lie? That and the names? One of the very first things you said to me when we met face to face? *Barney*? Your track record speaks for itself." Maybe I should take the chair. Four nights of no sleep was catching up to me.

"I'm sorry," Kingston said. "*We're* sorry. It was a dick move anyway, but I hate that it was done to you."

I wasn't hearing that no-fault bullshit. "That *you* did it to me. This wasn't a generic fluke; *you* made it happen."

Owen sighed. "You're right, we did."

"Ravyn and Ramsey told me you don't call in favors." I focused on him. Or tried to. He was kind of fuzzy around the edges. "Guess I was special?"

"You are special. There were no favors." Kingston looked blurry too. "I filed a request for a zoning change. Anyone could have done it."

"I tried to have it pulled after we met you. I would have used a favor for that, but Ramsey couldn't make it happen. We had to let it go to hearing," Owen said.

I should shut this down and go home. Why was I here? "Goodie for you. You did something cruel, and then couldn't backstep it. Boo hoo."

Owen's frown deepened. "I'm sorry. I miss you."

Why did he have to sound so sincere? It made me want to punch something.

"Give us another chance," Kingston said.

"How many chances do I give you?" Darkness licked the corners of my vision. I was definitely wobbling. And so tired. "I think I'll take that seat now." My world went black.

TWENTY-THREE

Why was I in a hospital bed? An IV running into my arm?
Everything in my brain was fuzzy. I'd been furious at Kingston and Owen. Yelling. Wobbling.

Someone kept asking me questions. My head throbbed as I tried to make sense of the memories. Was I taking any medications? Any allergies? When was the last time I ate? That was easy. Days ago. Unless coffee counted.

"…leave when we… answers." Owen? He was shouting, but I couldn't make out all the words. Owen shouted?

"…deserve answers… what you did… Fuck you both." That was Anne. She sounded pissed.

"I'll help you find the door." Luke's voice was more distinct. Or carried better. Or I was becoming more aware.

The pain shooting through the back of my neck said the latter was definitely the case.

"*No.*" Kingston's reply was easy to make out. I could picture him stubborn and squaring off against Luke's six-foot-two of imposing former Marine. I wasn't surprised Kingston didn't back down.

"Sirs, please."

I didn't know that voice.

"Tell Lyn," Owen called.

"No." And that was Sadie.

Was the entire world here? For me? What had I done? I didn't want this attention. I wanted to curl up in a ball and vanish.

A beeping noise sounded next to my ear. Great, now what?

A nurse appeared by my side almost immediately, looked at something near me, then at me. "It's a blood oxygen monitor. I need you to take a deep breath."

"Why am I here?"

"Take a deep breath." She was sterner this time.

I complied, mostly to get this part over with.

"Now exhale slowly, and repeat," she said.

I didn't have the patience for this, but after several excruciatingly slow inhales and exhales, the beeping stopped.

"I'm Joy. What do you remember?"

"I'm not sure. It's all jumbled."

Joy nodded. "A sign of exhaustion. Keep breathing. Your friend told 911 that you passed out. In the ambulance, you told the EMT you hadn't eaten or slept since Monday."

"I was delirious. I didn't mean that." Crap, I didn't want to be stuck here. I started to sit. The alarm went off again.

Joy nudged me back gently. "Your blood tests show low potassium and some other nutrients, and you're dehydrated, so I suspect at least some of it's true. Keep breathing, or I'll have to put you on oxygen."

I made a show of taking and letting out several deep breaths.

"Good." She smiled. "Your friends don't know what happened —privacy laws—and I can't let them all in here at once. Who do you want to see?"

"Can I see two of them? Sadie and Anne. Purple hair, and blonde?"

"All right."

A moment later, Anne and Sadie appeared in my doorway, and then I was wrapped in hugs.

"We were so worried." Anne squeezed me tighter. "You're okay, aren't you?"

I was going to cry again, at their concern, and I didn't want to. Aside from that I was okay. "I'm fine. How did you know…?"

Sadie made herself comfortable next to me on the bed. "Kingston slid into my DM's. Said he didn't know how to get hold of any of your friends. I waited until I was here, and knew you were safe, and could look him in the eye before I told him what I thought of him."

"The yelling in the hallway?" I put some pieces together.

Anne nodded. "Luke is out there standing guard. What happened?"

"Long story. I had to see them about something, I was more tired than I thought…" Shit. The shop. "I need to get home. There's baking to do. Other work."

"The doctor's not ready to discharge you," Joy said from the doorway.

Sadie leaned into me. She did a decent job of making pinning me down look like a hug. "I already called Violet," she said. "The café will have to go without pastries for a day. It'll be okay."

"No. I can't. I—"

"Stop." Anne's voice was sharp. "You can. You will. If you're good, maybe we and the doctor will let you do a little work on Monday."

Sadie pulled out her phone. "Now, call your mom. Tell her you're all right."

"You told my mother?" Another person worrying about me who didn't have to.

Sadie pressed the phone to my ear. "You're in the hospital. Of course I told her."

"Hello?" Mama sounded concerned.

And now my heart was cracking at her voice. Did exhaustion make someone cry about everything? "Hey, Mama."

"Jaelyn. How are you? What's wrong? Your friend told me you were in trouble. I'm trying to book a flight out there now.'"

As much as I wanted to see my parents, I didn't want them paying last-minute flight prices. "I'm okay. I promise. I'll get the doctor to tell you so, too, if you need to hear it."

We chatted for a few more minutes, and I promised her I'd eat and sleep more, and convinced her not to change their vacation schedule for this. I'd see them in a few months. She asked for Sadie, and I handed over the phone.

Sadie's replies were mostly *yes* or a variation of it. By the time she gave me the phone again, my curiosity was at capacity.

"What did you tell her?" I asked my mom.

"To take care of you, and not to leave your side, and that if this happens again, we're hopping the next plane there."

"Yes, Mama."

"Love you. Dad loves you. Be safe."

I smiled. "Love you both too." I disconnected.

The doctor came to talk to me, and I told him it was fine if he did so in front of Anne and Sadie. I regretted the decision when he brought up the not eating or sleeping thing. He refused to discharge me if I was going home alone.

"That's not a problem," Sadie said, before I could argue. "I'm moving in with her for at least a couple of weeks. She won't be alone."

I gave her my best *excuse me?* look.

She shrugged. "I promised your mom. I have to. Besides, you take care of us all the time. You listen to us. You feed us. Over advice and hugs and support. We're here to do the same for you. Always. You just have to ask, or in this case, you don't even have to do that."

More tears stung my eyelids at the warmth that raced through me. I really did have the best friends in the world.

WHEN SADIE and I got back to my place, she set her bags in her old room. "You didn't change much."

"I haven't gotten around to it." It wasn't that I cared if she knew I missed her, but I was already taking up her time. I didn't need to be clingy or sound like I was pulling a guilt trip on top of that.

"You missed me." Sadie grinned. She grabbed my hand and led me into the kitchen. "Sit."

I pulled up a chair at the kitchen table. "You have your own life." Weak comeback.

"That you're a part of. Where's all the food?"

"I have plenty of food."

Sadie pulled a half-empty box of rice cakes from the cupboard, and a mostly full box of ice pops from the freezer. "Do you make sandwiches with these?"

I clenched my jaw. The last thing I wanted right now was a lecture on my eating habits.

Sadie grabbed her phone. "Pizza or Chinese?"

"Pizza." Not Chinese. Not again for a long time. The pit in my chest ached at the thought. How many other memories had been tainted?

Sadie made a few more swipes, than dropped into a chair across from me. "Ordered. You're in idiot, by the way." She met my gaze unflinchingly.

What was I supposed to say to that? Only I got to call me names. "Excuse me?"

"You heard me."

Because I'd fallen for the bull Owen and Kingston fed me? "What happened isn't my—"

"It's not your fault, I know. I agree. The stuff with those assholes? Not your fault in the slightest. "The not eating? The shutting us out so you're *not a bother*? That's on you."

Unbelievable. "This is your idea of supporting me?"

"You're one of us, Lyn. You're not a burden or a third wheel. We want you in our lives because we like you for you."

I didn't care for her plucking thoughts out of my head that were meant for me alone. "That's not what this is about."

Sadie raised her brows. "Isn't it?"

"No." Maybe a little?

"I'm not trying to be mean," Sadie said. "But I'm not taking back what I said."

"You called me an idiot." Like I hadn't done the same to myself countless times.

She didn't flinch. "*Idiot* was harsh, but I needed you to listen. You can be heartbroken. Take all the time you need to heal. You deserve so much more than being led on. You're worth more than that." She sighed. "My point is I wish I could show you what we see in you."

I didn't know what to say, and I was tired of feeling. "I'm going to lay down until the pizza gets here." I pushed back from the table.

"Wait." Sadie grabbed my wrist before I could walk away. She stood and threw her arms around me and squeezed tight. "You're amazing and wonderful and smart and successful and beautiful and so many other words that would take me all night and into next week to list. No one, not even you, should be allowed to tell you otherwise."

I didn't know what to do besides hug back, and fail to swallow past the lump in my throat.

THE FIRST THING I did Monday morning was drop a check in the mail, for a normal loan payment amount, addressed to Kingu Kafe's corporate offices. I couldn't pay them back all at once, but there was no way in hell I was taking anything from Kingston and Owen, especially money.

Sadie became my shadow, going so far as to get up when I did, and make me breakfast. I'm pretty sure she would have force fed me if I hadn't eaten voluntarily. With her company, it was easy to distract myself from my thoughts.

On Friday, a letter arrived from Kingu Kafe. My torn up check was inside, along with a note written in simple block letters. *The money was a gift. Non-returnable. We miss you. Owen.*

I used a baking blow torch to light the entire thing on fire in a steel bowl in the café's kitchen, while Sadie watched.

"Are you going to send them another one?" she asked.

It was tempting. "What do you think the odds are they'll send it back the same way?"

"Is either of them as stubborn as you?" Her question was kind.

I twisted my mouth in disbelief. "Do you remember who they were before…" The playful retort turned to ashes in my mouth. *Before they decided to stop asking to buy me out, and moved to using me instead?* "I'm done dealing with them."

The next week, I fell back into more of my routine. Except, every time I thought of Kingston and Owen, my heart cracked.

Though technically, I was almost always thinking about them. I missed them so desperately. My mind and heart never stopped arguing over *I love them* versus *they lied to me. About something huge.* Even worse, I never knew which part of me would take which side.

Violet, Sadie, and I were sitting around the café after it closed, taking our time cleaning up for the evening. Sadie would probably head back home in a few days. Which was fair, her husbands missed her, like I would when she was gone.

She and Anne already had a schedule worked out, to make sure I *behaved*. I'd assured them that was unnecessary, but I did appreciate the concern.

Violet finished putting up the last of the chairs, save for those we were sitting in, and joined Sadie and I at a table near the counter. We were discussing the café's next Cosplay Saturday, and whether we should have a set theme, with Sadie providing costumes. Something I was happy to spend a little extra business money on, for both her and my employees.

"You're dressing up again." Sadie wasn't asking.

And there was another shitty memory. I exposed so much more of myself than my body at the end of that day. "No."

"You were glowing last time," Violet said.

"Because—" an attractive man told me I was pretty. "No."

Sadie scowled. "You rocked that skirt. You put so many of my peers to shame."

"But not you." I let a hint of bitterness into my retort.

"Including me. You were a goddess. And it wasn't because some guy was here."

"No, but it was because some guy lied about how he felt about me, and I believed the bullshit."

"Did he?" Sadie countered. "I know he kept something from you. But that doesn't mean he lied about all of it. And if he did, fuck that guy. His faults don't change how incredible you are."

"A lot of my kids struggle with who they are versus who the world tells them they should be." Violet's statement came out of nowhere. Her *kids* weren't actually her children—she volunteered at an LGBTQ+ shelter for teenagers when she wasn't here.

I had no idea how she found the time for all of it, but I understood being driven to keep busy. "I can see how that would be a common theme." I was missing a connection between her statement and our conversation. "Do they… turn to cosplay?" How idiotic did I sound right now?

Violet smiled. "Sometimes. Everyone copes differently. A lot of them, when they lose the support of people who were supposed to love them, because the kids don't meet that pre-defined mold, don't know where to find the line anymore between a forgivable slight and an unforgivable action."

"Ah." She was talking about me. "I'm fat. I'm insecure. I screwed out of my league. Not even in the same ballpark as someone's parents turning their backs on them for who they love."

"I don't pass judgment on the severity of the hurt, only that people hurt. You and they both blame things on being who you are, and it's not your fault."

I saw where she was coming from, but I disagreed. "It's not—"

"The same?" Violet finished for me. "How many times in your life have you diminished your pain, because you don't think you've earned the right to feel?"

I didn't have a response, beyond *you don't understand*, and something told me that wouldn't cut it. This wasn't as bad as trying to take the opposing point against Owen, but it was close.

I missed Owen. An ache throbbed behind my ribs. Shouldn't I be numb to that now?

Violet studied me. "Nothing? You can say whatever you're thinking. I'm listening. I'll hear you."

And now Kingston was in my head, too. Telling me he wanted to get to know me for me, not to take my business. I gasped on a sob. Why couldn't I stop thinking about them?

I shook my head, unsure how to process any of this. It hurt, and someone was the cause of it. I let it happen. "Why can't I make this empty pit in my chest go away?"

"Sometimes life hurts." Sadie covered my hand with hers.

I knew that, but, "I was hoping for a more actionable answer. I thought they were sincere. They sounded… It felt…" *Real*. Even now, I swore the connection between all of us was real.

"Some people are good liars, and some people just make mistakes," Sadie said. "It's not always easy to tell which is which."

Violet nodded. "I agree. But here's the thing, I've rarely seen you happier than you were last Cosplay Saturday. During the day, in that gorgeous outfit. Not like someone hiding or hoping if they played by the right rules, things would be okay. You opened up. If you got to that point because of Kingston, that's one thing he did right. But you're that person even without him."

"And that was part of the problem." A *big* part of the problem. I opened myself up to them. "I don't want to believe they did this maliciously." Now that I was talking, my jumbled thoughts from the last few weeks spilled out without much order. "But of course I don't want to. What I want doesn't change what is."

"People can make mistakes and learn and grow," Violet said.

"And sometimes people make a bad judgment call, because they make mistakes, not because they're bad people," Sadie added. "And sometimes people who have been hurt have a hard time accepting that others love them for them, without ulterior motive."

I glared at Sadie. "I'm starting to think you're not on my side."

"Then you're not paying attention." Sadie didn't flinch. "Maybe they used you, maybe they didn't. You assumed the *probably* awfully fast, and I'm trying to tell you it's not the only option."

I scrubbed my face, and blew out a noisy breath through my fingers. "I don't know what to do." I *wanted* to undo the bad, and only have the good. "Sometimes I have this almost irresistible impulse to talk to them again. Not to forgive them, but just to hear their voices." Sometimes. Every waking moment. Whatever. "That's a bad idea, isn't it?"

"It might be. There are times when it's best to avoid the people at all costs who hurt us. Other times, reaching out is the only way to heal." Violet was making good use of her therapy training. Of course she was putting it back on me to make a decision.

I was grateful for that, and at the same time resented it. I wanted an easy answer. "Those people we should avoid… do they change their business plan for the person they hurt, to avoid doing it again? Do they pay off hundreds of thousands of dollars in debt, without demanding something in return?"

Violet shook her head. "There's always a price attached to anything from the *avoid them at all costs* people, no matter how generous the act looks."

"I can see why you let her run things." Sadie leaned her head on my shoulder. "She's smart. I don't have quite such eloquent words, but Violet is right that you were happy with them. You were *you*. I'm sure they won't be your only chance at that, and I'm not saying they weren't wrong. I don't know if I could forgive them. I want you to do what will hurt you the least now, and later."

"Me too. Go figure." I let out a short laugh.

I still didn't have answers, though. And I still hurt, both thinking about how Kingston and Owen lied to me, and thinking about how much I missed them. But at least I had my girls, and myself, even if Sadie was pushing this whole agenda of self-worth pretty hard.

TWENTY-FOUR

I sat in the front passenger seat of Anne's Ford Escape, staring at the shop across the street from us. The sign was an alteration on the original Kingu Kafe logo, to remove the heavier anime elements. The banner underneath said *Grand Opening*.

Sadie leaned forward from the back seat. "It looks basic."

"It's just a coffee shop. It doesn't have to be more than basic," Anne said.

We should turn around and go home. The thought had taunted me for the last hour, as we drove up here.

I'd heard rumors that Kingu was opening a new shop, and I tried to ignore the chatter. It hurt that they'd gone through with it anyway, but it was their original plan—open a new location here, regardless of if it was mine or a different one.

The invitation that arrived in my mail was probably meant just for me, given that address was hand lettered, and so was the brief note inside, in the same handwriting as the note from Owen returning my check weeks ago.

I wanted to be surprised at the personal invite and at the details of this place. Nearly fifty miles from my shop, in a different county, and it wasn't an anime gaming café. Like Anne said, it was just a coffee shop.

The part of my brain that had been listening to Sadie said this was more proof they cared about *me*, not my shop.

Their parking lot was packed, which made sense. They had a name, even if they were only serving coffee. But them putting up a place like this was no more competition for me than a Starbucks would be in the same location.

I'd gone back and forth since about whether or not I wanted to come.

"We can go home," Anne said. "You saw."

But now that I was here, I wanted to see *them*. Of course, that would lead to wanting to talk to them, which could lead to… what?

If they'd been using me for my shop, and they brushed me off now, at least I'd know. If they liked me for me…

"I want to see what it looks like inside." I had no idea anymore what was a mistake. "But I'll stay in back. I just want to see what they've done, and then we'll go."

The interior was beautiful—anime meets abstract. Owen and Kingston's influences were evident in the decor, borrowing from what I'd seen of their other shops, but it was also its own unique design. If someone told me the shop owners were usually my competition, I wouldn't believe them.

When my gaze fell on Kingston working the register, any thoughts about my environment vanished in a surge of longing tinged with pain. He was smiling, chatting, and sexier than I remembered.

Which was saying a lot.

I dragged my attention away long enough to search out Owen, but I couldn't find him. So, I stared at Kingston some more.

"Do you want to go talk to him?" Sadie asked.

I shook my head, despite the *yes* screaming in my skull.

Anne nudged me toward a just emptied and wiped-down table in the back of the dining room. "Sit. We're going to go get drinks and coffee, and then all three of us can agree that it's not nearly as good as yours is."

"What if it is, though?" I asked.

"It's not," Sadie said.

I was going to be waiting at least a few minutes, given the line. Perfect time to stare at Kingston while he was too busy to notice. Was that pathetic? The chubby girl stalking her crush.

The gorgeous curvy woman staring at a man who cares about her. The correction in my head was in Owen's voice.

"You're the most stunning thing in this room." This Owen voice was external, and made butterflies dance in my stomach. I looked up to find him standing next to me. "I told Kingston you'd show."

My heart slammed into my ribs so hard, I could only hear him. "You think you know me that well?" I managed to keep my voice steady anyway.

"Parts of you."

If this was Kingston, the comment would be followed by a comment about how intimately he wanted to explore more parts. "Oh?" It wasn't my best comeback, but I still didn't know how I wanted to react to them.

"We *very* briefly considered using this as a chance to give you a huge, public apology."

I hated that idea.

"We agreed you wouldn't appreciate it," Owen said. "I was surprised Kingston saw things my way."

Because Kingston had been listening when I spilled my heart and my secrets. He hadn't even hinted that he might use my past humiliations against me. The opposite, in fact. "Did he tell you why?"

"A very reasonable *taking this public forces Lyn's hand and that's wrong.*"

"He didn't tell you anything else?"

Owen shook his head. "If you shared anything with him, it's between you and him until you tell me otherwise."

"Until. You assume—"

"Nothing," Owen said. "I'm not a *make assumptions* kind of guy."

"You assumed I'd show up here today."

"I knew you would. It's different."

I rolled my eyes. I was enjoying this so much, and it was the most basic banter. "You're an arrogant asshole."

"So, I've been told. But I knew you would be here, because if our roles were reversed, I'd have shown up. You saw what you wanted to, does that mean you're leaving?"

"Yes." Was I pleased or slightly terrified that he knew me so well?

"Give me two minutes of your time?"

I wanted to give him all my time, but there was a little catch inside. One tiny doubt that was loud enough I couldn't ignore it. I didn't want to be hurt again. Especially not by them. "I'm pretty sure you've already taken at least that much."

"Please."

"One minute."

He grabbed a napkin from the canister on the table, wrote *Reserved* on it in the most perfect block letters, and set it down.

I followed him through an *Employees Only* door, down an empty hallway that led us away from the excitement of the café.

We stepped into a back office and he closed the door behind us.

I wiggled my fingers, not sure what to do or say. "So what—"

Owen cupped my cheeks in his palms and crushed his mouth to mine. The intensity in his kiss re-broke my heart. Or maybe that was the walls around it shattering. Either way, it was the most delicious agony. Why hadn't we done more of this before? I wanted all his kisses. Forever.

I summoned what little willpower I had, and pushed him back. "I can't—" what? I didn't know what I could or couldn't do. I reached for the door.

Owen loosely. grabbed my wrist.

I could break away, but did I want to?

"I can only speak for me, because Kingston would be upset if I stole his moment," Owen said. "I'm sorry about what happened— what we did. I'd take it back. I tried, and it wasn't an option. I can apologize over and over, and do better next time, if you let me have that chance. I've never met *anyone* like you. You fill a void in my life I didn't know was there. I love you."

That was definitely my heart falling into a million pieces. "You don't get to say that to me. Not now."

"You being pissed off doesn't change how I feel, but I don't say it to manipulate you. You know me better than that."

Did I?

Yeah, I did. Damn it.

"Good luck with the new shop. Not that you need it." I reached for the door again.

This time Owen didn't stop me from leaving.

TWENTY-FIVE

When I got back to the table, Sadie and Anne had returned with drinks and pastries.

"Got your note." Sadie held up the *Reserved* napkin. "Not your handwriting, though."

Was I flushed? Scowling? My brain and heart were a jumbled mess.

"Did you talk to Owen?" Anne asked.

I nodded.

"It went that well?" Sadie's question was a discordant blend of flat and teasing.

I shrugged. "I don't know. It wasn't bad. It was… kind of really good."

Sadie toed an empty chair toward me. "What are you doing back here?"

"I don't know. About any of it. Still." I sank into the chair. I had my answer, knew what I wanted. Why couldn't I embrace it?

Because part of me still argued I wasn't worth this kind of hassle.

But you are. I didn't know if that was Owen, Kingston, or even Sadie arguing with me.

Damn it.

We sat and chatted. Anne and Sadie never asked if I wanted to go, but they did both feed me sweets. They had six that looked incredible—cheese, cherries, chocolate, more chocolate, mint, and a fruit tart—and insisted we had to sample all of them.

They also insisted my baking was better. They were wrong. Owen's recipes were different, but they were just as good as anything I made. I wasn't surprised or upset about the confirmation.

More than an hour passed. We were taking up valuable table space, and I didn't know what I wanted to accomplish. We should go.

"Lyn?" Kingston's voice drew my attention. He stood a few feet away, watching me with an unreadable expression. "I thought you left."

"Holy shit, Fattie Bush, Lyn, is that you?"

My gut curdled and the world around me slowed to a crawl. The new voice was one that still haunted my dreams. I looked up to see Samuel, my ex-boyfriend from school. The horror in my veins matched Sadie and Anne's expressions.

Kingston radiated a rage I'd never seen before. He followed my gaze, and in a single, fluid motion, grabbed Samuel by the collar and pinned him to a nearby wall.

"What the fuck did you just say?" Kingston growled.

Samuel held up his hands and twisted, but didn't break free. "What the fuck? This isn't about you."

"It is." Kingston drew back his free arm and landed a fist in Samuel's gut.

Samuel doubled over with a gagging gasp.

"Brutal." Sadie sounded awed.

"Sexy." So did Anne.

Humiliating. Or was it? It was definitely stupid.

Samuel stumbled away, muttering something about suing the store until it crashed and burned.

"You just destroyed your café, Day One." I wished I could be as impressed as Sadie and Anne. I was grateful, though. Was that wrong of me?

"You sound too much like Owen. I say there's no such thing as bad publicity. I have to handle this—don't leave." Kingston flashed me a smirk, and was gone.

I missed that look.

"Tell me you're not swooning at least a little on the inside," Sadie said.

I faced my friends again. "I thought you were on my side."

Anne fiddled with the paper sleeve on her coffee cup. "We are. Never doubt that. And sometimes that means telling you you're wrong. You haven't taken your eyes off him for more than a few minutes at a time. I'm surprised he snuck up on you."

"He just risked his entire store to stick up for you. Do you still think he wants anything from you besides *you*?" At least Sadie was consistent in her argument. "Do you really want to leave?"

I wanted this to be better. The hurt wouldn't magically evaporate, but I believed that Owen and Kingston were sorry. That they wanted to move forward. And Owen was right—their actions were only worth it for someone who mattered to them. None of this was worth their time unless they actually cared about me. "No."

"Sorry about that." Kingston was back, apron gone, and a baseball cap pulled low. "The leaving you alone, not the other thing. I won't apologize for shutting up that loudmouth fuck. Anyway, I need to make myself scarce. Join me?" He nodded toward the same door Owen took me through earlier.

I was out of arguments. I followed him into the empty hallway, along with Sadie and Anne.

"You're staying?" Kingston asked. "I'll drive you home."

I was staying. I turned to my friends. "I'll be okay."

Anne nodded.

Sadie stepped past me, and stopped when she was toe-to-top with Kingston. She was at least a head shorter, but she focused a frighteningly fierce glare on him. "You met Luke? The Marine?"

"I did," Kingston said.

"If you hurt Lyn again, at all, if you make her doubt anything, what Luke could do to you will pale compared to what I will." She spoke with so much assurance I didn't doubt she would make good on the threat.

I loved my friends.

"I don't doubt it for a second." Kingston was serious. "And I'd deserve it."

"Damn right you would." Sadie squeezed my hand. "Call me if you need me, Lyn."

I was smiling in spite of myself. "I will. Thank you."

Anne and Sadie left.

Kingston offered his arm. It didn't matter that we were probably only walking the short distance to the café office, I fitted my hand in the crook of his elbow. More of my doubt flitted away at how right the contact felt.

Owen was already—still?—waiting in the office, when Kingston pulled us inside and shut the door.

Kingston dropped to his knees. "I'm so sorry." He looked the way he had the day we went up to the lake. "I miss you. I want you in my life. I'd do anything in my power to make this right. Just tell me what. Jewelry? A lifetime supply of whipped cream? Beat up another ex-boyfriend?"

After all the angst, was I going to cave so easily? "I don't want *things*."

"Neither do we," Kingston said. "But I don't know what else to offer. You stopped talking to us. I don't know how else to show you how much you matter, than to give you everything. And I would. Do you want the coffee shop?" He pulled a key ring out of his pocket, and started working one key free.

I covered his hand, biting back a whimper at the shock that raced through me. "I don't want the coffee shop."

"I want something," Owen said. "I know I don't have a right to ask, but I want it anyway."

I didn't want to guess what he'd say. "What?"

"Time. And you."

Damn it.

"That's two things," Kingston said. "I thought you were the math guy."

Was he seriously...? Of course he was. Humor to hide insecurity. The same way I used bravado to hide mine.

"I was so close to trusting you, but..." I sighed. "But I want to. Trust you. I miss you both, too, and I want us to work, but..." What?

Owen moved closer, gripping my fingers and running his thumb over my knuckles. "I'll say it over and over, we both will, and we'll keep proving this is about you. About how we feel about you, until you know it's true."

Kingston stood and gripped the back of my neck. The possession in his touch sparked through my entire body. His kiss stole my breath. My thoughts. Everything. The harder he pushed, crushing his mouth to mine, the further I fell into him.

He didn't have to do anything but kiss me, to light my senses on fire and leave me whimpering for more.

He rested his forehead against mine. "I only kiss one other person like that."

Right. They loved each other. I'd seen it with that first kiss. I heard it in the way they talked to and about each other. And they treated me the same way. "All right. I'll give you time."

"So, we're free this afternoon," Kingston murmured against my lips.

"You're not free." Every inch of my body screamed *more*. "You're opening a brand new store. You won't prove anything by walking away from the event."

"That's not what this is," Owen said. "We don't usually attend our own Grand Openings. We're only here to see you."

Kingston tugged me gently toward the door. *"As I was saying,* we've got a room in the hotel next door, so we could be up here during construction. If you'd like to come over and—"

"Wash off the non-existent coffee?" I asked.

"I was going to say *fuck*, but if we're using euphemisms now..."

I smiled. Wow, that felt good. "You have a little more wooing to do"—but not much—"before I say *yes* to sex. But *no* to the euphemisms."

"What?" Kingston sounded shocked. "You don't want my pulsating rod deep inside your love tunnel?"

I laughed.

"You'll be lucky if she wants you within ten feet of her, when you talk like that." Amusement marred Owen's serious tone.

Kingston brushed his lips over mine. "That does make me really fucking lucky, it's true."

"You're impossible." So was this entire situation. But it felt right and real. *They* felt right and real.

TWENTY-SIX

The walk across the parking lot, to their hotel, was agonizing. Mostly because I wanted us to have privacy.

Owen unlocked his room and let us in. The instant we were closed off from the outside world, Kingston tugged me into his arms.

I pressed a finger to his lips, and nudged him back. "I'm not that that easy, and we're not done talking yet."

He pouted and watched me with wide, puppy-dog eyes.

Disturbingly sexy.

"What would you like to talk about?" Owen sounded reasonable, but his hand was under my shirt, fingers gliding up my spine.

Talk? My brain stalled. "I… You… Before this all fell apart, we had something else to discuss." Was it smart to put this back on them? Pretty sure they only had one thing on their minds right now —me. Not that I had an issue with that.

"Technically we already talked about that." Kingston traced a finger over my bottom lip. "We both want to be with you. In a long-term way. And in a *God, I missed you and you look amazing*, way. But to the first, we don't have a problem sharing you. How do you feel about it?"

Not the most eloquent phrasing. "Sharing me? Like I'm a pastry?"

Kingston dipped his head to trace his tongue up the side of my neck. "With extra chocolate syrup," he whispered in my ear.

Pleasant shivers raced over me.

"Dating. Seeing what comes next. Falling further," Owen said. "Three ways. Kingston and I are exploring things, too. God, I want you to be a part of it."

I did to. I wanted to melt into them and stay here forever. "I'd be hurt if you wanted otherwise, and I'm tired of hurt."

Owen spun me to face him, and cupped my face between his palms. "I'm tired of it too. We're going to make things right."

There was no hesitation or tenderness in his kiss. He dove in, devouring my mouth and my moans. Bruising my lips. Pressing in until the rest of the world fell away. I could stay wrapped in him, in them, forever.

"I promise all the teasing and foreplay next time." Owen's gravelly turned-on voice was even better in person. "But right now, I need to feel you. Tell me I can fuck you."

I wanted that too. "Yes."

When he yanked up my shirt, something ripped.

I didn't care. I loved the hunger and frantic abandon as much as I loved the way I was pressed between the two men.

Kingston's hands roamed everywhere my skin was exposed.

Owen alternated between kissing me and tearing at our clothes as though neither of us could get naked fast enough.

And then there was nothing between us. Owen's skin was hot against mine as he used his full body to push me back to the bed. He straddled my thigh, one knee between my legs, grabbed my wrists in his hand, and pinned them above my head.

This blew fantasy out of the water. Especially when he crushed his mouth to mine, and dragged a row of nibbles down my jaw, to suck on my neck. He pressed his leg higher, into me, giving me something to grind against.

Kingston knelt next to me on the bed. He'd lost his clothes, too. He cupped my breasts and flicked his thumb lightly over one nipple.

As I whimpered, an amazing reality drifted in to wrap around us. They were here with me because they liked me. Not for some fetish or just to get laid or to steal what I'd worked for.

This was my life. Not a borrowed night. Not something that would end in the morning, or later tonight, or in half an hour. I got to discover what happened next, after the incredible sex. And I already had a good idea it would be amazing.

Which made every touch that much more intense.

Owen let go of my wrists to straighten up and roll on a condom, and moved completely between my legs. My anticipation surged when he nudged my opening. I arched my back with a moan, pushing into him, when he penetrated me.

"Fuck." His groan was breathless.

There was no more build-up. He pushed my legs forward, gripping the back of my thighs, and slammed inside me at a frantic pace.

Kingston continued to devour my neck. My shoulder. My nipples.

I reached out, needing him to be more a part of this, and gripped his shaft. He adjusted to give me a better angle.

A new spark of ecstasy sped over me when Owen pressed a thumb to my clit. He pushed me to the edge, then eased back, never letting up on his thrusting.

Orgasm slammed into me, and everything shifted to vivid. The touches. Sounds. Scents. It was all high definition and all consuming.

I was still wrapped in the sharpness when Kingston pulled away. He kissed the outer shell of my ear, and whispered, "Play with your tits."

I moved my hands to my chest. Squeezing. Pinching. Tugging. Kingston knelt next to my head, cock in his fist.

"I love seeing you like this." His words were punctuated with grunts as he stroked himself. "Laid out. Flushed. Stunning and caught up in pleasure."

"Me too. I mean…" I hoped he knew what I meant.

Owen gripped my legs tighter, thumbs digging into my skin. He shifted the angle enough that each new thrust struck something deep inside. "I can't…" He panted. "You feel too good. I can't hold out."

I clenched around him in response.

I knew those staccato grunts. The fast, stuttered sound of his orgasm. That drawn out final groan before he paused, then relaxed. He resumed a lazy, out almost to the tip then back in again pace. Then slid his cock higher, to tease my clit.

I was too sensitive. It was too much. But I didn't want to pull away.

Kingston spilled a warm, sticky stream across my chest, covering me with ribbons of cum.

The sight, the moment, Owen's touch, their pleasure, drew me to climax again. This one drawing out until my entire body shuddered.

I struggled to catch my breath as I collapsed back on the mattress. Owen leaned in to kiss me. More gently this time, but it was still just as amazing. "Don't go anywhere."

Not that my legs would let me even if I wanted to.

Kingston kissed me again, everywhere. He didn't try to avoid the mess as he lightly teased his tongue over my nipples. Each lick sent another shudder through me, until I had to nudge him away.

When Owen returned, he tugged Kingston up, and crushed their mouths together. Oh, wow. The woman who walked away from that, from what they had, was an idiot. I didn't know if I wanted to whistle or groan at the ghost of sensation that rushed through me.

They broke apart, and Owen used the wet washcloth he'd fetched to gently cleaned me up. A moment later, both of them collapsed on either side of me on the bed. Owen pulled me back into him.

Kingston studied us with one eyebrow raised. "I'm going to allow it. But only because he was gone for a month, and then I got him to myself for a month after that."

"Allow it?" I let the disbelief slide into my question.

"Yes." Kingston brushed his lips over mine. "If that's all right with you."

Owen kissed along the back of my neck. "Whatever my Kitty Cat wants, she gets."

"Oh, there's got to be a story behind a nickname like that." Kingston lay on the pillow facing me, and rested a hand on my hip.

I shook my head. "It's not a great one."

"It's a fantastic one," Owen countered. "And it comes with a picture."

"I used to come with pictures," Kingston teased. "Probably won't be doing that again for a while."

I appreciated the sentiment, but didn't buy it. "You're implying you're not going to jerk off to porn anymore?"

"Is it porn of you?" Kingston's face lit up. "Or are you watching with me? I could get into that."

Owen's sigh was heavy and exaggerated, his breath caressing my back. "You're impossible some days."

Kingston smirked. "But you still love me. Go figure."

"I think you're both perfect," I said.

"*You're* biased. But also brilliant. And right." Owen kissed my shoulder.

One phone in the room chimed, and then another seconds later. "Do you have to get that?" I wanted the answer to be *no*.

"They'll wait." Kingston didn't make any hint at moving.

And then the rings sounded again, one and then another. And again, seconds later.

"One of you should get that." I didn't want to be jostled, but it was probably urgent.

Owen kissed my bare shoulder. "Not me. Let the Punisher do it."

"Fine." Kingston rolled out of bed, and fished his jeans from the floor to grab his phone from the pocket. He jabbed the screen, then listened for a moment, before sighing. "Dylan is freaking out. Our social media manager." He looked at me. "The internet is blowing up that one of our employees assaulted a customer."

"One of your employees?" I raised my brows.

Kingston dropped back onto the bed. "There's video."

Of course there was. I frowned.

He tapped my nose playfully. "Don't look like that. I'd do the same thing again in a heartbeat." He swiped his phone again. Ringing echoed from the speaker when he set the device in the middle of the bed.

"Thank, God. It's about time you called me back. What did you do?" The woman who answered the phone sounded panicked.

I would be too.

Kingston's sigh was exaggerated. "You saw what I did. The asshole deserved it. I'm not sorry."

"You're going to give me a heart attack. Before I'm thirty. I want to live to see thirty," Dylan said.

Something told me this wasn't the first time she'd dealt with Kingston's impulsiveness. Anne and Sadie had been right earlier—I liked that it was about me this time. Was that wrong?

"We have an official company statement." Owen sounded more professional.

Dylan's laugh was strained. "Thank you. I'm listening."

Owen pursed his lips and furrowed his brow before speaking again. "While we don't condone violence, we also abhor any level of bullying or degradation. The employee in question will be disciplined, and the customer is no longer allowed in any of our establishments." He was good. "Make it sound pretty, and send it to me for approval."

"On it, Boss. Keep him on a leash for the rest of the weekend? I'm going to have my hands full with this."

Kingston looked at us with a hungry grin. "Won't be a problem." He disconnected.

"The employee in question." I repeated Owen's phrasing, amused at the idea of anyone trying to discipline Kingston. "Would you really put him on a leash?" Could I get into that? Owen dominating Kingston? Without a doubt.

Owen shrugged. "Kingston's right that this isn't bad publicity.

Some people will boycott the café. Others will come in specifically because of what he did. He'll never work there again, regardless. The leash idea does have possibility."

Kingston flopped onto his back, laying his head on my thigh. I loved everything about the casually intimate contact. "Given there's no leash in the room, does anyone want strawberry crepes?"

"They're not even in the same category, and it's six in the evening." Why was I arguing? Those sounded amazing.

"Lemon and blueberry, then." Kingston rolled to look me in the eye, never breaking contact. "You've never had breakfast for dinner?"

"More times than I care to admit." Then again, I hated admitting to anyone that I ate anything besides lettuce. It was odd for me to throw out a comment like that so casually, but I liked knowing that it was safe.

"Whatever you would like," Owen said.

I also liked knowing he meant that. "Crepes sound wonderful." In fact, all of this was wonderful. I meant what I told them about wanting time to rebuild trust, but my heart had already surrendered, and I was pretty confident they'd be gentle with it.

"When you smile like that, it looks whimsical. I love that look," Kingston said.

Me too.

Owen sat, and pulled me upright too, so I was leaning against him. "Care to share what you're thinking?" he said.

What was I thinking, besides *hehe, sexy men like me.* I forced my thoughts to assemble. "The night I met *Fred* and *Barney*, I was a heartbeat away from a pity party, because my friends were drifting away from me, to be with their men, and I was going to be alone forever."

Kingston opened his mouth.

I silenced him with a look, before he could deny or correct past me's assumptions. "Turns out I never lost them. And now I have my two guys, too. Life is pretty freaking amazing."

"It really is." Owen brushed his lips over mine.

I glanced at Kingston. "You were saying?"

"Nothing you didn't already. You do have us, eating out of your hand... off your stomach... licking everywhere..." He rattled his head. "And it's fucking incredible."

And it would only get better. I had no doubt.

EPILOGUE

S ix Months Later

A PAIR of kisses was my favorite way to wake up in the morning, and today was no exception. It was the perfect way to drift into a new day.

Owen and Kingston were wavering on long-term housing, so they were still living the hotel life, and still sharing a room. But most nights all three of us ended up in the same place. Last night though, they showered me with kisses and apologies and told me they had things to take care of early.

I'd been bummed, but I trusted them. Completely. It was an amazing feeling.

I finally let my eyes flutter open, to them on either side of me. They were fully clothed compared to my flimsy T-shirt and panties. That hardly seemed fair. "I thought you were busy."

"We are. Get dressed." Kingston defied his own words by draping an arm over my stomach. "I'd say wear that, because yummy, but we're going out."

"Out where?" I wasn't motivated to move anyway, pressed between two warm bodies, but even less so if a surprise was involved.

Owen stood and tugged my hand. "Vacation."

I couldn't go on vacation. "I have too much work." There was planning to do. Schedules to rearrange—

"Taken care of." Owen was probably as good as reading my mind. He brushed his lips over my fingertips. "You have to let this happen sometime."

Kingston rolled to the side and stood, before taking my other hand. "Everything will be fine."

In the past few months I'd hired another baker and a few more café employees. I'd taken test days off, and things could run on their own. Violet was more than competent. But the idea of walking away from my baby for more than a day terrified me.

They were right. Time to dive in. I forced myself from bed. "What do I need to pack?" I asked as dressed. It had taken time to get used to being in various stages of undress around them, but now it felt natural.

"Taken care of," Owen repeated. "Sadie came by while you were working yesterday.

"Already taken care of," Owen repeated. "Sadie came by while you were working yesterday."

I pursed my lips. "You're making me regret giving you keys."

"No we're not. You ready?" Kingston said. "I swear you won't regret this. I wouldn't do that to you. We wouldn't."

"All right." I wasn't really ready, but they were going to talk me into it eventually.

My world went black when a blindfold was fitted over my eyes. "Uh…"

I could navigate my house, including the up and down, on a pitch black night with my eyes closed, but I was still nervous letting them lead me downstairs. Kingston held my hand until I was seated in a vehicle. Owen's Jeep based on the height, and the faint scent of *New Car* air freshener.

The three of us talking was a nice distraction as Owen drove, but it didn't erase my anxiousness. Each time I reached for the blindfold, one of them grabbed my hand.

The car stopped, and the engine shut off.

"Now you can look." Kingston pulled away the blindfold.

We were in a parking garage. From the signs outside the window, it was long-term airport parking.

"Okay…?" I wasn't surprised by this bit, since Sadie had packed my bags, and it was too cold for camping. Besides, Owen didn't like roughing it any more than I did.

"Kingston wanted to keep things a surprise until we landed. At our final destination," Owen said. "But changing planes, taking you through customs, and everything else required, all without you figuring things out or anyone asking questions… Let's just say even I couldn't figure out that logic."

"Customs?" Where were we going?

Kingston handed me a boarding pass. "Tokyo."

My heart did a happy little jump skip. "Really? I mean, duh, of course, the ticket says so, but… really?" I'm glad I didn't put up more of a fight this morning. So many firsts about to happen, both terrifying and exciting. *Tokyo.* "You've been planning this for months," I realized. Now I knew why Owen insisted I get a passport.

He shrugged. "Guilty."

They unloaded the luggage from the back of the Jeep, refusing to let me carry any of it. If anyone besides Sadie had packed for me, I'd insist on checking everything before we went any farther, but she probably had me more than prepared.

There were only a couple of other people on the shuttle to the airport. Owen tangled his fingers with mine as he sat next to me.

Kingston was on my other side, and kept an arm wrapped around me. "Odds of joining the Mile-High Club?" he asked in a soft, playful voice.

I loved the idea, but it also scared me. I wasn't sure I was there yet. "Ask me again on the trip home."

"I will. Believe it." Kingston kissed me on the cheek.

We reached Terminal 1, checked our luggage, made it through

security without any hassle, and grabbed coffee before reaching our gate.

With caffeine pumping through my veins, and some of my excitement settling, my brain was firing on all cylinders again. I had a surprise for them, too. I'd been saving it for our six-month anniversary, but that was only a few days off, so telling them now was just as good.

I never imagined I'd be the person who celebrated every relationship milestone, but we'd made a big deal out of every month together, and it hadn't gotten old yet.

Then again, everything about our relationship was still fresh and amazing.

"I need to show you something." I grabbed my phone and scrolled through images.

Kingston rested his chin on my shoulder. "Dirty pictures?"

"Seductively sweet pictures?" Owen asked.

"Both." Not really. At least, not at all in the way they meant. "I've been thinking…" Now that the words were on my lips, it felt like a presumptuous assumption. But I trusted them. I knew what we had, and how real it was.

The reminder was enough to propel me forward. I showed them my screen. It was a mock-up of the Loading Java logo—the brunette perched on the edge of the coffee cup—but she wore their crown. "I know I only bring my shop to the table, and my recipes, but—"

"Yes." Kingston cut me off.

"Only if we're completely equal partners," Owen added. "You have as much say in any decision as we do."

"But only if we get your recipes. You did say that. Promise me." Kingston's voice was light.

I couldn't hide my smile. "I did say that."

Kingston twitched in his seat, half standing, then sitting again.

"Do you need to pee or something?" Owen asked.

Kingston rolled his eyes and flipped Owen off. "I want to go down on one knee," Kingston said. "But… public."

My smile grew. "I'd be okay with it, just this once, but only because you warned me."

Kingston dropped to one knee in front of me. I'd seen this twice before, but this time he wasn't apologizing. He grasped my fingers. "You're my universe. I love you more than anyone, and I every day I thank any god who listens that I found you. I can't imagine not having you in my life. Our life. You're the perfect addition. Nothing would make me—us—happier than to call you partner in everything. Business. Life."

My breath caught. This was half a heartbeat from… "You almost make it sound like you're proposing."

"I'm not. Not yet. That's the next surprise, two nights from now at the base of Mt Fuji."

I caught my laugh when I studied his face and saw how serious he was. "Now it's not a surprise."

Kingston shrugged. "You don't like surprises."

"If you're not asking yet, I'll save my *yes* until then." I looked at Owen. "Does he speak for you?"

Owen gave me a half smile. "Only sometimes. He's more eloquent and personable than me, so I'm just going to kiss you and remind you that you and I love each other, so this makes perfect sense."

"It really does." I brushed my lips over Owen's, then leaned forward to kiss Kingston. "I love you both so much."

A small smatter of claps erupted around us, and I flushed that we'd drawn a small audience. I had no idea what anyone thought of the fact I was kissing both men, but screw anyone else's opinions.

"You can stand now," I murmured to Kingston.

His grin grew. "I know. But one of my favorite things is being on my knees at your feet."

"Get up ." I tugged him to his feet with a laugh.

This was more amazing than I ever thought I'd have. Than I even believed I deserved, a year ago. I was excited for Tokyo, this business partnership, and spending the rest of my life with these two incredible men.

EPILOGUE 2

Owen
   I'd had as many lows as highs in my life, but the notable highs soared above anything else. Meeting Kingston. Meeting Lyn. Watching their joy and awe and excitement as we touched down in Tokyo.

Together, it was hard to argue with them when they wanted to see the city *now* instead of sleeping first. But the fact that Lyn couldn't stop yawning as she insisted she was fine, because she'd slept on the plane, made it easy for me to veto.

Touring the city with them was incredible. Tokyo was on my bucket list anyway, but it was that much better seeing it through their eyes.

As the sun crept lower in the sky, Kingston was checking his phone more and more often. Sexy, fidgety fucker.

"Do you have something else you'd rather be doing?" Lyn asked playfully after check number twenty-seven.

Kingston pocketed his phone. "I was thinking… sleep off this jet lag some more? Or at least back to our place, and rest for a few hours."

This was as close to subtlety as he got. I adored it. Since he gave his *let's be together forever* speech in the airport, I'd convinced him to let me do the talking once we got back to our rental.

"I could rest for a few hours." *Rest.* As if that was going to happen.

Lyn looked between us with a smile. "I already know what's going to happen. You already know what I'm going to say."

Kingston slipped one hand into hers and one into mine. "But it's not official until it *does* happen."

"I agree." Besides, I had a surprise still—one I suspected Lyn would be okay with—that carried the weight of a second ring nestled away in my luggage.

Lyn's sigh was exaggerated. "All right. Let's go back, so I can find out what this big not-surprise is that you're proposing."

I shook my head at her word choice, but mostly because I didn't think of it first.

We'd opted to rent a more traditional guest house rather than a hotel room. When we stepped inside, Lyn's mouth fell open. "Wow." Her voice was soft as she took it all in.

It was as beautiful in person as online, but I was more interested in watching her as she explored every room, through sliding doors, to discover the futon in the bedroom, her attention lingering on stunning inked artwork.

While she and Kingston explored, I took the excuse to slip a box with two rings into my pocket.

"It's amazing." Lyn finally looked at me.

I couldn't see anything else. "Yeah, you are."

Pink flushed her cheeks. I loved that look on her. I loved any look on her.

Lyn ducked her head. "If you're not careful, I might start to like surprises."

"You're going to love this one. I promise." I grasped her fingers and tugged her closer.

"This one's not really a surprise, though."

If I wasn't careful, I'd break my stern façade too soon. "Trust me."

Kingston watched us both with a sexy smirk that said he had

answers no one else did. Time to prove him wrong. I cupped his cheek and held his gaze. The warmth and affection that looked back was tinged with a hint of shock, and took my breath away.

"Every day, I'm grateful I met you," I said to Kingston. "It took me longer than I should have to figure it out, but I've loved you for years. You're my opposite. The perfect partner in everything. My best friend."

"And I keep you from being wound too tight." His playful retort caught.

I smiled. "And that." I turned to Lyn, drawing her fingers up to kiss the tips. "And you. You're sunshine, you're warmth, you're so much I need that I never knew I was missing. You compliment both of us. I can't imagine not knowing you. Not having you in my life— our lives. Because I can't imagine there not being an *us* that involves you, me, and Kingston."

This wasn't what I'd planned to say, but as happened frequently, I had to adapt when one of them turned big, adoring eyes on me. I had to let go of both of them to tug the rings free, but it wasn't enough time to regather my thoughts.

"I don't care what we call what we have, as long as there's a promise of forever. I want—need—you both in my life." I opened the box.

Lyn clapped and squealed with delight. "Yes. That's what I'm supposed to say, right? Because *yes*. Always yes."

"You sneaky bastard," Kingston said. "Me too."

I raised an eyebrow. "You have to say it."

"Yes." His smirk was back.

I slipped Lyn's ring on her finger first. The bands were both simple, black titanium. "Anne helped me size it. We can pick something more vibrant if you want."

"I don't want. It's perfect." Lyn threw her arms around my neck and kissed me hard. Her body molded to mine, the perfect amount of soft and yielding mixed with insistence. Just like her.

When Kingston cleared his throat, I let Lyn go and turned to him. "Feeling left out?" I teased.

"I want a ring too." He held out his left hand, ring finger isolated.

I slipped his band into place, dropped the box, and gripped the back of his neck, holding him captive.

His grunt of surprise was intoxicating. I crushed my mouth to his and dove my tongue past his lips to dance and tease around his tongue. Sparks practically sizzled from us. I was so glad I'd stopped denying what this was.

When I finally let Kingston go, he stood there for a moment, eyes half shut and mouth half open. He shook his head and turned to Lyn. "Me too. I already gave my pretty speech. But you, me, all of us. Partners in everything?"

"Yes. Of course. Always." Lyn nodded.

Watching them kiss was as delicious as participating. An incredible blend of chaos and beauty, wrapped around each other. It was enough to make me hard.

Lyn gripped Kingston's fingers and mine when they broke apart. "I want to ask something too." Her tone was shy. Seductive.

"Anything." As if I could deny her.

Her blush was back. "I want to watch the two of you celebrate your engagement."

Because she loved to see me with Kingston, and always flushed when she asked. "We can do that."

Kingston

I'd never looked too closely at my relationship with Owen. Digging past the surface, to the shared hook-ups, the sex even when there wasn't another person there, was the kind of thing that could end friendships.

I didn't dare do that.

Then Lyn came along…

And now here I was, on my knees, with my best friend's cock in my mouth, while our girlfriend watched.

I'd never been so turned on. Submitting this way, tasting Owen, and hearing Lyn's gasps.

I was surprised when Owen pulled back. He tugged me to my feet, and gripped my chin. The possession in his gaze stopped my heart.

"*God*, I want to fuck you." His voice was low and commanding.

I nodded toward our luggage. "You know where the lube is."

I stripped off my clothes and crawled toward Lyn, who had her shirt and bra pushed out of the way and was watching with her tongue caught between her teeth. I absolutely got off on her getting off on watching us.

Her eyes grew wide, and I was stalled by Owen's hand on my throat. He pulled me upright, so I was kneeling, back pressed into his chest.

"I'm not done with you." He growled.

Fuck. Here I thought I couldn't get any harder. I was pretty sure Owen secretly delighted in proving me wrong, even when he didn't know what I was thinking.

Owen bit my shoulder and I groaned at the sting. Desire screamed though me. Every muscle in my body tensed in antic-ipation.

I grunted in surprise when the cold lube hit my skin, but I adjusted quickly as Owen glided slippery fingers along my ass. He teased my opening, penetrating just enough to taunt me.

My dick stood at attention and begged for the same. I was willing to drag out the agony a little longer, to make this last.

Owen pressed his other palm into the small of my back, urging me forward, until I was on all fours again.

He inched his cock inside me. We'd done this enough that relaxing was second nature, and the anticipation of the tight fit, of being stretched out, cranked my pulse to full speed.

The futon shifted, drawing my attention to Lyn. She wriggled out of her pants and stripped off her shirt, not taking her gaze off us for more than a few seconds at a time. I loved that sight. The rise and fall of her chest. The flush in her skin and gleam on her lips as she licked them.

I was torn between using both hands to support myself, and reaching for my cock, where it hung aching to be touched.

When Owen reached around to grip my shaft, I groaned at his possessive touch. He yanked hard. Fast. As if demanding I enjoy the moment. And I did. My breath came in short pants as he pumped me fast, but rocked inside me slowly.

Lyn slid three fingers inside herself, dropping her other hand to play with her clit. She was as captivating as she was captivated, making me wonder where to focus. Especially when those intoxicating whimpers started falling past her lips.

Owen moved his hands to my hips, gripping hard and pounding harder. He was done holding back, which means his patience had run out.

Was I smug about that? About pushing him to the point where physical gratification was his core goal? Damn right I was.

But I was out of patience too. I fisted my own cock, choking and stroking. Faster. Harder. In time with Owen's thrusts. Spurred by Lyn's mewls. My body tensed at the sensory overload, and reveled in it.

My balls tightened. Stars danced behind my eyes. Pressure built inside and release hovered just out of reach.

And then Lyn made the amazing gasping sound that meant she was coming. Her face screwed up. Her hand moved at high speed. Fuck, she was gorgeous when she was lost in climax.

I came hard, shudders racking my body. Jizz coated my hand and splattered the blanket. I didn't want to stop, especially with Owen still buried in me, but my energy faded as skin became hypersensitive.

Owen's grip tightened. He was going to leave marks. Good. His grunts were louder than Lyn's. Roars of ecstasy in the open room. His rhythm increased to high speed, then stuttered to a stop.

He kissed along my spine as he pulled me upright, and reached around to cup my softening cock. The *mine* in his touch was implied.

And I was. I belonged to him. To her. The three of us were incomplete without each other.

We cleaned up, changed the comforter, and collapsed in a pile on the futon. Lyn buried her face in my chest, and Owen draped an arm over me, pinning me in place.

This was status quo for us, and I had no complaints. "So, when we get home... house shopping?" I liked sharing a room with Owen, but I was tired of living in a hotel. I was even more tired of those nights when Lyn ended up in a different place than us.

"Are you going to buy me a nice one?" she asked.

I loved that she was comfortable asking. "Whatever you want."

"Hmm..." Her consideration hummed against my skin. "I kind of like where I am."

I would have made a face, but she wouldn't see it.

"Kind of?" Owen asked.

She kissed my chest. "Okay, a lot. It's near my friends. I know it's not big or grand, but it's mine. It could be ours."

So much for giving in easily to us buying her something huge.

"It doesn't have to be grand, as long as we're all there." Of course Owen had to be reasonable.

I let out an exaggerated sigh. "I don't know if you're being sappy, or just yourself."

"Both. Are we talking about moving into Lyn's place?"

Lyn rolled away enough that she could see me and past me to Owen. "It's a little cramped for billionaire life."

"Pretty sure I offered to fix that." New place. Huge house.

Owen squeezed my hip. "The property next to yours is for sale." Of course he knew that.

I liked the idea. "It's a longer commute, but not by much." I studied Lyn. "You don't have to decide tonight, but we're not going anywhere without you."

She grinned. "Damn right, you're not."

I kissed her nose, and leaned back into Owen. This was so perfect, and I was so fucking lucky. To have Lyn. To have Owen. For all of it.

———

RUNNING FOR IT

ONE

There's one thing the stories about Cinderella never mentioned—any prince who threw a ball and invited the entire city, just to find his bride, knew exactly how to appeal to the public.

The way Ramsey Miller worked the socialites in the Hotel America ballroom, with a warm smile here, a handshake there, and the occasional kiss on the cheek, was *Prince Charming*, brought to life.

He'd bleached the copper out of his hair—I assumed because blond polled better than auburn, or something ridiculous like that. He looked incredible anyway, wearing an easy smile and a suit made to accentuate his strong arms and torso.

I turned my attention back to my other guests, which was the reason I couldn't fault Ramsey too much for sweet-talking everyone tonight. This was *my* event, and even I intended to schmooze a little.

I'd rather have the check-equivalent of everything donated to the fundraiser, from the food to the hotel itself. But people had paid a good price for the meal, and would drop even more during the silent auction.

A trending hashtag always drew in more money than simply asking people to write a check. An event like this would ensure the kids who needed a place to stay, the residents of the LGBTQ+

shelter I ran, would have food and clothes, plus a little more, for the next several months. Nights like tonight produced ninety percent of the money that kept us afloat.

My sister never had this choice, which I still regretted years later. At least this way other kids like her would.

It wasn't my shelter—I hadn't founded it or anything—but over my years of volunteering, people had come and gone, until I was responsible for more and more. I wasn't technically even in charge, but we'd never been able to find a replacement after our last head left, so I did the job. Tonight, that included raising funds. Tomorrow, it might mean I was making lunch. Every day was a new experience.

"Violet." Lyn joined me near the wall, where I was recharging before my next pass through the room. "Amazing turnout."

"It really is. Better than I could have hoped for." When I wasn't working at the shelter, I managed Lyn's anime gaming café.

She was a great boss and good person, and these days, she practically glowed with happiness. At least a little bit of that had to do with her boyfriends—yes, plural. She had two, and I couldn't even imagine one making me that happy. I liked her guys, but they happened to be close friends with Ramsey, which was the only reason he was in my life again.

Lyn handed me a champagne glass with bubbly amber liquid in it. "Sparkling grape juice," she said. "How are you holding up?"

I loved *doing*. Working. Making a difference. Helping people. However, I preferred to do so behind the scenes or one-on-one. "Drained. But it's worth it."

"How appropriately direct." Lyn laughed lightly.

I smiled. "And true. The reminder keeps me going."

"I get that." Lyn nodded across the room, at Ramsey. "Do you need me to run interference?"

Even though he was around more often, Lyn did a good job of making sure I could be somewhere else when he came into the café. I think she misunderstood my reasons for wanting to stay away— not that I'd gone out of my way to set the record straight.

It wasn't that I didn't like Ramsey, though I tended to get defensive when he was around. It was that I remembered how good things were when I was with him. I adored the person he was behind closed doors. I even had fond—*scorching*—memories of those occasional nights we'd shared the bed with his best friend.

But he wasn't the same person in public. He was plastic. Fake. Working the world with a smile, a handshake, and the occasional kiss on the cheek.

"I'm good," I said to Lyn. "He's another guest tonight, and the last thing he wants is to draw attention to our past." It was the last thing I wanted too, but I wasn't going to wear a mask, in order to achieve it. I'd be polite, but I refused to be fake, even here.

Lyn gently squeezed my arm. "I'm going to find the guys. If you need anything, wave or holler or quack really loudly."

I chuckled. "I will." We both knew I wouldn't. I had this under control. My gaze drifted back to Ramsey, who gave me a tentative smile when he saw me. I turned away, not able to ignore the way my pulse kicked up.

Yup. Totally had this under control.

As Lyn melted back into the crowd, I swallowed the last of the sparkling juice, wheezing at the burn of bubbles down the back of my throat. Time to go thank more donors.

In my off-the-shoulder satin dress, and shoes and clutch dyed the exact same sapphire blue, I looked like I belonged with these people, in this world of crystal and sequins and diamonds.

But my dress was off the clearance rack, and my best friend, Luna, and I had turned our hands blue dying the accessories.

I was so out of place.

The politeness and platitudes flowed, as I said *hello* to one person after another.

"You've done a fantastic job with this event. You're so efficient."

"Those poor kids. Someone needs to show them love. They're lucky to have you."

"Did you put this entire thing together? I need to hire you to plan my next event."

I never quite knew what to say in return.

"Thanks. When our robot overlords take over, I plan to be their favorite human."

"They should thank the genie I told I wanted to spend my life helping people. I freed her after that."

"I run on caffeine and fresh day-planner pages. Are you sure you can afford my rates?"

All of it said in jest, though from the expressions I got in return, most of the people here didn't do *jesting*. The best responses I got were giggles and *you're silly*.

When I was dating Ramsey, I jokingly referred to myself once as Laffy Taffy. Frequently stale, just a little off flavor, and always ready with a horrible pun.

He'd corrected me. Told me I was more like saltwater taffy. I was sweet, fun to unwrap, came in the best flavors, and was his favorite.

"You're a hard woman to track down. Most popular person here."

Hunter's voice behind me promised real conversation and summoned memories I liked to ignore. The kind that sent delicious shivers running down my spine, along with the ghost of his fingertips over my skin. Because those times when he'd joined Ramsey and me...

"Everybody wants a piece of me. What can I say?" I winced as the words passed my lips. He was totally going to take that wrong. I spun to find him standing there with Ramsey, and a tribe of butterflies leapt to life in my stomach.

"Can't say I blame them." Laughter danced in Ramsey's green eyes. His presence made my heart whimper.

Hunter was just as breathtaking. Dark hair. Strong jaw. Long, skilled fingers.

I swallowed the lust surging through me. "Thank you for coming this evening, gentlemen. Your support means a lot to the kids."

Hunter snorted in disbelief. "Did you just feed us a prepared line? Who are you, and what have you done with Violet?"

"I learned it from watching you." I smiled sweetly. "Thought I'd communicate in your language." Which was what I needed to remember. I'd pushed them out of my life because after a while, the stark difference between their public and private personas became too stressful to be around.

"Don't we feel special?" Ramsey's tone was playful. "I won't hold you up. We just wanted to say *hi* and congratulate you on a fabulous event."

I turned up my smile. "Thank you. I'm going to pretend you mean that."

"I do, Ta—" Ramsey shook his head.

Taffy. The pet name tugged at my heart. I didn't do *phony* with anyone, and I'd just about reached my limit here. "Enjoy your evening." I walked away before I could say something I'd regret in the morning. Like, *Maybe we could try again.*

I tried to get back into the mingling, but every time I turned, I either saw Ramsey or Hunter, or was disappointed that I didn't.

This wasn't great.

As the event wound down, Hunter joined me again. "Fair warning. Don't jump to conclusions; Ramsey promised to behave."

My stomach lurched. "What does that mean?"

"Can I have everyone's attention?" Ramsey's voice carried from the center of the ballroom. He stepped onto a chair.

What was this? Morbid curiosity kept my feet frozen to the ground.

"Violet has been thanking each of you individually, but I want everyone to know how grateful I am—*she is*—that you're all here tonight. This is such an important cause, and your support means the world to these kids." Ramsey commanded attention without even trying, and looked and sounded good doing so.

But— "This isn't so bad."

"Excuse me. Hi." A woman stepped up next to him. "Hello." She waved at the crowd.

Hunter sighed, and when I looked at him, his jaw was clenched.

It wasn't over.

"Ramsey's too humble to say, but I'm hoping I see even half of this generosity when I call each of you for campaign donations."

She laughed lightly. *Tittered*—I finally understood what that word meant.

Did she just— Who the hell was this woman, hijacking my event? Was she really begging for funds for Ramsey's State Senate campaign, now?

"Thank you, Debbie." Ramsey's voice was tight. "But Violet doesn't need us hijacking her event. That's the peak of tacky." Though he sounded cool. I saw the anger flashing in his eyes. But if she were a member of his staff, saying more would make him look bad.

"Violet…" Hunter was apologetic.

I yanked away from his hand on my arm. "Nope. Don't bother. In fact, tell Ramsey it's lovely to see nothing has changed." I let disappointment spill into my retort. I needed this kind of visceral reminder of why I kept him at arm's length.

TWO

If there was a mood for so-completely-unsurprised-I-couldn't-be-angry, that was me. At least, that was what I tried to convince myself of, as I sat at a table in the back of the ballroom, working through numbers and paperwork for the night. My shoes sat next to me on the table, taunting me with their cruel heels and the torture they'd done to my feet tonight.

The hotel staff had cleanup under control, and technically this could wait until morning. But it was going to take me a little while to shut off my brain, to keep it from focusing on the moment I was pretending I didn't care about, so I might as well get something done while I was here.

The chair next to me slid out, and the familiar scent of ice and musk greeted me. I wouldn't give Ramsey the satisfaction of looking up.

"How's my favorite workaholic?" His voice was warm.

I grabbed my handbag and opened the side pocket.

"What are you doing?" Ramsey asked.

I handed him a small make-up mirror. "Letting you talk to your favorite workaholic."

"She's got a point." Hunter dropped into a seat across the table.

Nope. I wasn't getting sucked into banter with them, especially not after what happened earlier. "Have a good evening." I closed my tablet and stood to leave.

"Wait."

Ramsey's hand on my arm stalled me as much as his request.

He rose as well. "Let me apologize." The playfulness was gone.

I shook my head. "Please don't. Not if it's going to happen again." And it would. "I'm not mad. I should have expected it."

Ramsey tightened his grip. "It won't. I was furious Debbie did this. She's fantastic at her job, but she's also new and doesn't know all our rhythms yet. I've talked to her. It wasn't right of her to hijack your event, and I'm sincerely sorry."

"Okay." I tugged out of his grasp and crossed my arms. This was where I should leave, so why was I still here? Because all night, my defenses had been slipping. He'd taken steps to fix things, and this wasn't specifically his fault. "So… how have you been?" I hid my wince at my weak question.

Hunter smiled. "Small talk. I think you broke her."

I stuck my tongue out at him.

"Don't offer unless you mean it." Hunter winked.

I rolled my eyes but couldn't hide my amusement. Sticking around put me in a tough situation, though. Hunter was right that I hated small talk, but I didn't want to get sucked into a real conversation with them either. *Just leave.* "I caught Ravyn's latest comic. I love where she's taking the series." Ravyn was Ramsey's twin sister.

"She got the imagination in the family," Hunter teased.

"I don't need talent when I'm this good looking." Ramsey gestured at himself. "Besides, you weren't complaining about my imagination the other night." His gaze was on Hunter. Were they flirting with each other?

I'd seen them together in the bedroom—the whole friends-with-benefits thing Ramsey and I had with Hunter—but not *together,* as in a couple. "Any secrets about where the story's going?" I asked. "Insider information?"

Hunter covered his ears. "No spoilers."

Damn them, I was enjoying this.

"You'd rather talk about my sister than about me?" Ramsey's hurt was exaggerated.

"I figure that'll get me more answers than asking about you." Catty? A little.

"I'll tell you anything you want to know," he said.

I couldn't ignore his sincerity. Then again, that had never quite been the problem. He had always been genuine with me, but the mask he put on for public consumption was a different person, and I didn't like watching him flip that switch.

"Do you still play?" I asked. It wasn't a secret that he could play guitar, but he didn't tell anyone that when he was younger, he wanted to be in a metal band. He composed music, and Hunter wrote the lyrics.

"I do. In fact, we've been working on something for a couple of weeks. Stress relief."

"Can I hear?" The question was out before I could consider that I was falling into this conversation and enjoying it. I wouldn't take the request back, though. I always enjoyed their collaborations.

Ramsey leaned in, mouth near enough my ear I felt his breath on my skin, and sang. The lyrics were angsty, and his voice had that rough edge so many metal singers wished for. When Hunter sang as he stood, picking up the harmony, chills raced down my spine.

"I love it. It's heartbreaking and beautiful."

Hunter worked his jaw, then shook his head.

"What?"

"I was going to say, *Your face is heartbreaking and beautiful,* but I wasn't sure how you'd take it."

I ducked my head. *Your-face* exchanges were typical for us back in the day, but the comment flustered me.

"Not used to seeing you at a loss for words," Hunter said.

"I hope you're pleased with yourself." Great. Now *I* was starting to get flirty.

"Whoa. My best friend and my ex? Not. Cool." Ramsey's tone was light and playful, with zero trace of offense.

Any time I'd seen Ramsey in the past few months, Lyn or

someone else was around. Having witnesses made it easier to stick to my resolve to keep my distance. But now, no one else was here.

This was half-fun, half-awkward, and all-enticing. Did I want to fall into it, or walk away? "You know you'd watch." Fall into it, apparently, because now those tantalizing memories were back, refusing to be ignored while they sent desire spilling through me.

"He absolutely would," Hunter agreed.

Ramsey hadn't moved away from me since he finished singing. "I don't know. It's *so hard* to picture myself in that situation." He pressed into my back. "A person never really knows what they're going to do, until the situation actually presents itself."

Hunter made a lassoing gesture—Jr. Rodeo Champion three years in a row—and mimed pulling himself closer to us. He wrapped an arm around my waist and dipped me. My squeal of surprise vanished when he paused with his lips a breath from mine.

My pulse hammered in my veins and roared in my ears.

Ramsey cleared his throat. "I don't think I could watch." His tone was impossible to decipher.

"Never bothered you before." Hunter righted me, taking his time before pulling away.

Ramsey grasped my fingers and tugged, to spin me into his arms. He gripped the back of my neck and held my gaze. "Watching definitely wouldn't work for me. I'd have to participate."

I was one hundred percent heat and desire. "If you're not careful, I might think the two of you are serious." My voice came out thicker and huskier than I intended.

"What do I have to do to convince you we are?" Ramsey asked.

My breath caught. Goddess, I could drown in that gaze.

"I've got a room here for the night." His voice was low. "Bed big enough for three."

"We're not getting back together." I had to put that out there now, before I lost all grip on my senses.

Ramsey hovered his mouth near enough mine I felt his breath on my skin. "Tell me you don't still feel that spark."

"Just one night." I was reminding myself as much as them.

"Not *just.*" Hunter was at my back. "It'll be so incredible you won't forget."

I never had. I rose on my toes, to press my lips to Ramsey's.

He gripped my neck harder, and crushed his mouth to mine. I gasped in disappointment when Ramsey broke away too quickly for my liking, but he didn't let me go.

He pressed his forehead to mine. "We should continue this conversation upstairs," he said in that same growly voice he sang in.

The sound and sentiment were a skilled touch, sliding over me. "If you insist."

The three of us left the ballroom, walking side by side but not touching. I'd be wounded by that, but there was no reason to announce a casual hookup to the world. Besides, the anticipation that roared through me was wonderful at helping me ignore most everything except what came next.

The elevator ride up was quiet. Cool. From the outside, three friends sharing a car up to their respective rooms. The stroll down the hallway was the same.

Ramsey opened the door with a sleight of hand so smooth he would have made most magicians jealous, and let us in the room. I caught a glimpse of sprawling luxury, before his hands were on my cheeks and my back was against the wall. He kissed me hard, devouring my moans and clinging to me like I was his oxygen. Or that was me, arms around his neck and nails digging into his shoulders, clinging for all I had.

THREE

I lost track of one kiss flowing into the next and then another. At any other time, I could deny how much I missed this—how much I missed Ramsey—but not now. This was familiar. Delicious. Everything.

When Ramsey let me go, I didn't have time to flounder, before Hunter was tilting my head in his direction. Claiming my lips. Knotting his fingers in my hair. I swore sparks danced everywhere he touched. He and I had always connected—that whole friends-with-benefits thing—but tonight, it felt more intense.

Maybe I was making more of this than I should be. On the other hand, my memory had understated the feeling of Ramsey's fingers gliding up my arms. His breath on my skin. Hunter's teasing growl, as he licked a line up my neck.

Ramsey slid my zipper down my back one agonizing tooth at a time. "I missed unwrapping my favorite candy." He drew his mouth up my shoulder to my neck, and then to nibble on my ear. "You taste even sweeter than I remember."

"My second wish from the genie. *Make me candy flavored.*" It didn't matter that I hadn't had that conversation with them earlier; they ran with the reference.

"Your face is candy flavored." Hunter caught my bottom lip between his teeth.

I laughed. I'd missed both of them, not just Ramsey. "One of the things I like about you. You're not going to follow that with, *So's my cock. Want a taste?*"

Hunter rolled his eyes. "Tacky. Besides, you already know it's more of a cherry flavor."

"It's true." My teasing faded into a surprised gasp when something fitted over my eyes.

Ramsey pressed his lips into the hollow behind my ear. "Since you're only here for the night, let's make the most of it." He pushed my dress to the ground, leaving me blind and exposed, in nothing but a strapless bra and panties.

My anticipation was back, spiking my pulse and making my head fuzzier than any champagne could. Fingers grasped mine and tugged, all other contact falling away. I didn't hesitate to follow. I trusted whoever led me to do so safely.

Another pair of hands rested on my hips and pulled me to a stop. My bra fell away, and my panties were pushed to the ground. Cool air kissed my dampness, and my heart hammered against my ribs.

"On the bed. On your back." Ramsey set my hand on the edge of the mattress, so I'd know where it was.

I didn't make any excuses or apologies for loving the way he took charge in the bedroom. The last few years apart, the arguments since—they all fell away as I did as commanded.

Silence settled into the room, blanketing me in desire and raising goosebumps everywhere. With no sight, I strained my ears for any indication of where they were. Of what came next.

Hands grabbed my wrists and pinned them above my head.

Ramsey's lips on mine drew a light moan. I didn't need to see, to know who was kissing me; he was more demanding, serious, and eternally clean shaven. He followed a lazy path down my chest. He paused to flick his tongue over my nipples until I squirmed against Hunter's grip, then continued his journey downward.

Ramsey kissed over my stomach. Lower. Dropped to kiss my leg near my knee.

It didn't matter how much I struggled or groaned; I wasn't getting free. The anticipation was delicious.

His journey back up was more excruciating. He bit the inside of my thigh, and I groaned at the spike of pleasure mingled with the sting of pain. When he finally reached the focus of my need and dragged his tongue up my pussy, my hips rose off the bed, wanting to be closer.

Hunter cupped my breast and kneaded it, rolling a nipple between his fingers.

Ramsey licked feverishly, gliding up to my clit but not making contact, before driving his tongue deep inside me. He tasted and teased, until I was whimpering, before he finally wrapped a finger on either side of my clit, and sucked the swollen bud.

I came hard, pressing into his mouth. He didn't let up, even after I slumped back against the mattress. He dove two fingers inside me, still tracing the alphabet over my clit, pushing me past discomfort and into another orgasm.

Hunter's grip fell away, and he pressed his lips to my shoulder. "You good?"

I nodded. "So good." My throat was raw. Had I been screaming?

Ramsey slid between my legs, the friction of flesh on flesh dancing through every hyper-aware nerve ending. He nudged my opening, then thrust inside me, stretching me out as he buried himself to the hilt.

My breath came in shallow gasps, as he glided out to the tip before thrusting back in and working to a steady rhythm.

Hunter pressed his cock to my lips, and I parted to let him in.

Ramsey picked up the pace, until he slammed against me hard and frantic. Hunter didn't stay in my mouth much. Their groans and touches were a new layer of eroticism, pushing me toward another climax but not over the edge.

Hunter's grunts shifted, and I knew he was coming. My body remembered all these sounds. Scents. Sensations. Tastes as that first salty spurt hit the back of my throat, and he emptied himself in my mouth.

Goddess, I'd missed this.

The mattress near my head shifted, and then by my shoulders and side, as Hunter moved next to me.

Lips wrapped around one of my nipples, and Hunter flicked with his tongue. He sought out my clit, teasing and coaxing while Ramsey fucked me.

I lost track of where one feeling ended and the next one started, as I tumbled into another orgasm. Ramsey's grip on my legs, his punctuated groans, told me he was there too.

My world spun in the best way possible, though the ride had stopped. I was lost in a cloud of post-coital amazingness.

Ramsey loosened the blindfold and tugged me onto my side, as he lay facing me. He kissed the tip of my nose. "Missed you, Taffy."

"I missed you too." It didn't change anything, but there was no reason to get into reality right now. We'd established rules before we started, and the world would still be waiting in the morning.

I WAS VAGUELY aware of the mattress shifting. This wasn't my pillow or my sheets, but I knew that scent...

"I'll talk to you in a few hours." That was Ramsey's whisper.

I reluctantly pried one eye open, to find a fully dressed Ramsey pulling away from Hunter and standing.

"What's wrong? What time is it?" Sleep slurred my words and my brain.

Ramsey moved to my side of the bed. "It's barely four. Go back to sleep." His tone was soft and kind.

"But—"

He brushed his lips over mine. "I have an early meeting, but there's no reason you have to be up yet. Sleep. Enjoy the room." He kissed me lightly again. "Last night was amazing."

Warm fuzzies flitted in my chest and wrapped me in warmth. I wouldn't ask if we could do it again, but the words were right there.

"See you both later." And Ramsey was gone.

What wasn't he saying? The desire to sleep, plus the lingering feeling of security, wouldn't let me focus on the question.

"Come on. I'm tired. You're comfortable." Hunter wrapped an arm around my waist and pulled me back into him.

The touch was familiar. Safe. Hunter had been a good friend and was a brilliant cuddler. It wasn't like I was going to make a habit of this, so it wouldn't hurt to finish out the night here.

"You're ringing." Hunter's sleepy voice dragged me awake again.

The numbers on the clock taunted my blurry gaze. "Your face is ringing." Not my best comeback, but it was five in the morning.

"That doesn't even make sense." Hunter extracted himself from the bed.

Your face doesn't make sense. Nope. I was awake enough now that no longer sounded clever. I sat up, took my purse from him when he handed it over, and extracted my phone.

Luna. If she were calling instead of texting, it couldn't be good. "Hello?"

"Violet? You need to get here now. There's water everywhere, and it's so hot, and—oh God—I don't know what to do." Panic rang heavy in her voice.

FOUR

I adored Luna. She was my best friend and frequently my link to sanity. She wasn't always great under pressure, though.

One of last night's shelter volunteers called in, and as she frequently did, Luna offered to step in. She was more of a night owl, especially since she was having trouble finding a steady job in her field, so she promised it was no problem.

"Luna"—I kept my tone kind but firm—"take a deep breath. What's going on?" *There's water everywhere,* sounded far less serious than, *There's blood everywhere,* so I wasn't ready to panic.

Luna sighed. "The boiler broke. Or exploded. Or something. What do boilers do? It's leaking. The basement is flooding. Why is the water a nasty color? That's not normal. The kids are freaking ou—"

"*Luna.*" This was so not what I needed this morning. Not that it was her fault, or that I wanted something like this on any morning, but today I'd hoped to spend a couple more hours wrapped in warm fuzzy memories before I had to face reality. "The water shut-off valve is under the stairs, in the wall. Turn it off. Have Oliver help you if it's stuck. I'll be there in twenty minutes."

"Okay. And Violet? Thank you." She already sounded less panicked.

I smiled at the genuine gratitude. When I disconnected, I found Hunter watching me with a mix of amusement and concern.

"I'm guessing whatever that was, it means you don't have time for breakfast," he said.

An ache of regret pinged in my chest. "No. Crisis at the shelter." I climbed out of bed and paused, suddenly hyper aware of my lack of clothes. What was I doing? He'd held me down and fucked my face last night, and I cared if he saw me naked this morning?

Apparently so.

He didn't seem to have the same hang-up, as he stood at the foot of the bed gloriously naked.

Goddess, he was handsome.

I forced aside the sudden burst of modesty, and gathered my clothes. My panties were a wreck, but I could go without. The strapless bra would be less than comfortable, but it would do for now. "*Fuck*," I muttered when I grabbed the dress.

"What's wrong?" Hunter had pulled on a pair of boxers. That was moderately better, but no less distracting.

I held up the dress. "Not exactly made for flood clean-up, and I don't have time to go home." I didn't care if anyone saw me in last night's clothes, but wet, skin-tight satin would be impossible to work in. Worse, if it ripped, I'd expose my panty-less ass to a house full of teenagers.

"I got you." Hunter rummaged through a suitcase near the bed.

The last thing I wanted was to be in something of Ramsey's. "I'll be—" I stopped when Hunter straightened and handed me a Westminster College T-shirt and a pair of jogging shorts.

Ramsey went to the U, like any proud local boy whose family's name was on at least one of the school's buildings. I know—I met him in college. I was there on an academic scholarship. He wasn't.

These were Hunter's clothes.

Only slightly less awkward, and far more curious, but I needed something. "Thank you." I took the clothes from him and tugged them on. They were a few sizes too big, but drawstrings on the shorts kept them up, and a knot at the waist of the shirt prevented it from turning me into a human sail.

"I thought this was Ramsey's room." That he was only in for one night.

Was that hesitation? "It is," Hunter said. "But we've been doing a lot of strategy planning for the primaries, so I made myself at home."

Sounded reasonable, but I felt like there was more to the story. An unformed question tickled my tongue.

My phone chimed. The text from Luna just read, *SOS. It's getting worse.*

"I need to go." I grabbed my purse. "Where are my shoes?"

We spent a moment searching for them, but they were nowhere to be found.

How did I lose my shoes? It didn't matter, since I couldn't work in the heels anyway. I'd buy a pair of slippers in the hotel gift shop and borrow someone's shoes when I got to the shelter. I was out of time. "Thank you. For *everything*."

Hunter squeezed my fingers. "Any time. Good luck. Call me if you need anything."

"I will." I wouldn't.

On the elevator ride down, I raked my fingers through my hair and pulled it back into a ponytail. It was early enough the lobby was nearly empty. Fortunately, I had the day off from Loading Java because of last night's event, so I didn't have to let Lyn down by calling in.

I dialed the emergency plumber as I drove, and made arrangements to get someone out to the shelter in the next couple of hours.

Any other calls would have to wait until I saw the actual damage.

I pulled into the small strip of asphalt on the side of the building —aka the *parking lot*. Luna's car was here, along with a few belonging to the residents. There wasn't room for more.

The shelter was actually a converted pair of houses, some of the oldest in the city. A polygamist had built on the adjoining properties for his two wives, with a corridor connecting the homes, so he could more easily split his time between his families.

The main house was on the corner of the block, and that was where the entrance was, as well. I walked in, to find the main common area strewn with mattresses, water pooling around each, creating a series of mini lakes on the hardwood.

"The basement is flooded," Luna explained. "So I had the mattresses brought up here."

We were more crowded than normal due to the cold weather, so there were temporary rooms downstairs.

I couldn't complain that she'd started on cleanup, even if the results weren't quite ideal. The situation was shitty, regardless. I pointed at a couple of older teenagers. "You, haul these outside and stack them near the dumpster." I singled out another lurker. "Grab the mop, ring it out in the bucket, and get as much water as you can."

The bulk of the damage would be in the basement, but I needed to do a quick tour of the rest of the house, to make sure every room that needed attention got it.

The main floor was common area, with several tables, chairs, and sofas, for people to gather and be social. The other house held the kitchen and dining room.

It was the top two floors that made this shelter different from the larger, state-funded ones. The smaller, original bedrooms were still intact and slept two people each. I did a quick survey of the individual rooms, careful not to invade any more of the residents' privacy than I needed to.

Since we only allowed minors here who had left home or had been kicked out due to their sexual orientation or identity, we wanted to give them a new home. A place where they could go without worrying for their safety, so they could get back to life and growing up.

That also meant everyone helped out, because this was their home.

My sister, Eva had been ten years younger than me, so I was

gone and out on my own before she hit her teens. She and I hadn't been close enough for her to come to me when she started struggling with her sexuality.

Instead, she'd gone to our parents. The people who should have protected and loved us. They sent her to conversion therapy, and less than two weeks in, she'd taken her life.

I never forgave them or myself. But at least here, these kids would have the kind of acceptance she hadn't.

The upstairs was undamaged by today's event. A few of the rooms looked like hurricanes had blown through, but that was status quo. A chill was setting in, though, and an overall musty smell permeated the building.

I told everyone to bundle up, to grab clothes from next door if they needed layers, and promised the heat would be back soon.

"How can I help?" Jesse—one of our older guys—leaned against his doorframe. Dark circles were under eyes that bugged out when he tried to hide his cough. He'd been sick for a couple days but refused to rest. There was always something more he felt he *had* to do.

I pointed him back into the room. "You can get some sleep. I'm ordering you."

His chuckle faded in a cough. "You ever take your own advice to slow down and let others help?"

"Nope. And when you're in charge, you can exempt yourself from the rules."

"If growing up means working myself to the bone, no thanks," someone behind me said.

I turned to kindly shoo them away, but they'd already run off.

Basement next. I took a few deep breaths, to steel myself for what I'd find, and headed in.

The water was almost up to the bottom step.

I hollered four names and handed out more tasks. "Grab some tarps from the toolshed. One goes at the top of the stairs, one out under the pavilion. Two of you haul boxes up the stairs and set them on the first tarp, the other two finish taking the boxes outside.

The moment you're done, out of the wet clothes and into extra layers, to warm up."

I hated asking them. If any of them got sick because of this, I'd feel so bad. But the work needed to be done quickly.

While I picked my way through the basement to make sure I hadn't missed anything, cold biting into my ankles, I called the place we got our beds from. They'd have replacement mattresses for me in a couple of days.

It was too long—we were already past capacity—but yelling wasn't going to magically increase the available supply.

My phone rang, and I answered. The plumber was running behind. Go figure. I had a basement full of water, and he had more important things to deal with.

I could call other places, but I'd worked with this one enough that I trusted them and they gave us a good rate.

"If you have a sump pump, you can start getting the water out before I get there," he said. "I'll do it once I arrive, if you haven't, but this will make things go faster."

"Where am I supposed to get a sump pump?" I was asking myself as much as him.

"I-bet-Oz-has-one." Luna's rush of words startled me, and I spun to find her standing at the bottom of the stairs. Pink dotted her cheeks, probably not all from the cold.

Cole—he only let Luna call him Oz—had a hard exterior and a soft heart. He'd been a huge name in tech more than a decade ago, but decided he was tired of the grind. One of his rentals had a lot of basement-flooding problems because the property sat on a water table.

He was also a beast of a grump with almost everyone but Luna. Who would be happy to call him, based on the way she was biting her bottom lip.

"I'll get started on water removal," I told the plumber. "Get here as soon as you can."

The plumber sighed. "You should know, if anything big is broken, I can't start work today anyway. Your boiler is so old, there's a good chance I'll need to order parts. It's going to be a couple of days."

So I had a house over full of people, without enough beds and with no heat.

Wonderful.

FIVE

I made some calls, to get space heaters. It took calls to five different places to find enough heaters, but I secured them all.

"Cole's here." Luna practically lit up at the sound of an old truck parking on the street.

I followed her around front. Cole's pickup was an ancient Chevy with a hardtop, with as many parts replaced as were original. I waved at Cole, and he gave me a terse nod. His gaze flitted past me quickly, to land on Luna. As he turned back to his pickup, I swore I saw the corner of his mouth twitch.

"Brought some stuff." He opened the camper shell and tailgate.

He pulled out a couple of giant fans.

"Eep." Luna squealed. "You're amazing. Basement is soaked. Wet carpet everywhere. Does that sound dirty? Didn't mean it that way. Promise."

Cole glanced at her with a raised eyebrow, then grabbed more things from his truck. A bucket, some PVC pipe, and what I assumed was the pump. "This is temporary. It'll get you cleaned out. Let you know when I'm done," he said.

"Do you need help? That's a lot of stuff." Luna was already reaching for the bucket.

Cole moved it out of her range. "I got it."

Luna didn't look wounded by his gruffness. "Okay."

"I could use some help." I felt bad pulling her away from Cole, with as excited as she looked, but this was best for all of us. "I need to sift through the stuff that's under the pavilion."

"Of course." Luna had recovered from her earlier stress, and I assumed it had something to do with the well-muscled, grumbly man standing a few feet away.

"Find me when you're done," I said to Cole.

He nodded.

Luna waved at his back, as I gently tugged her toward the yard. When we got there, she nodded at my T-shirt. "Westminster?"

Last night rushed back to me in a poofy cloud of pleasant memories. It tugged along a reminder that my past with Ramsey and Luna was messy. I was torn between giving her all the naughty details, the way I normally would, or keeping them to myself because of *who* they involved. "I didn't make it home last night," I confessed.

Luna let out an exaggerated gasp. "Was he cute? Well hung? All of the above, I'm sure. Probably smart."

"All of the above." I pointed her toward a box. "If it's salvageable, set it on a table. If it's unrecognizable, throw it out. If you're not sure, ask me. We'll decide. How'd your interview go yesterday afternoon?" Probably didn't end in a job, since Luna hadn't called me, but that didn't mean it went badly. Few interviews resulted in on-the-spot offers.

Shit. I shouldn't have mentioned her search for jobs. That would tie back to Ramsey, as well. But I did want to know, and between yesterday's event and this morning's crisis…

"It was all right." Luna's tone implied it wasn't great. "I got through all the questions. They seemed really impressed with my credentials and my test results."

"But…?"

"But then one of the interviewers asked me if I was *that* Luna. It's not a common name or anything…" Her shoulders slumped, and she dove back into her work.

Luna was a brilliant programmer. Yeah, I was biased, but it went beyond that. When we were in college, Luna had worked with a professor to build a *cure* for one of the most malicious pieces of malware the internet had seen in about five years. Her code had saved hundreds of schools that had been held hostage billions of dollars.

The problem was, the last virus that was as bad, a few years earlier, was hers. She hadn't done it maliciously. A lot of people might not believe that, but I knew Luna. She'd done it because someone said, *Hey, I bet you can't do this*, and she said, *That sounds like fun. I bet I can.* She'd done it for the challenge, never stopping to think someone would do evil things with it.

When various international law enforcement agencies caught up with her for the earlier code, that was what she became known for. No one cared about the good she'd done since.

"I'm sorry, L." I wished I could do something for her.

"I expect it. When it goes better, it'll taste so much sweeter. And it will go better." She shrugged again. "Don't think you can dodge the question. Does your Westminster boy know you're a U girl?"

"Lots of people wear Westminster shirts, not just alumni. And none of them care where I went to school." The entire box I was looking through was clothing, caked in mud. Cheaper to replace through donations, than to get these back to wearable again. I carried it to the *toss* pile.

When I turned back to Luna, she was watching me with wide eyes, her mouth in an *O* shape. "You hooked up with Hunter." Her voice echoed off concrete and aluminum.

"I di— What? Why would you say that?"

"Because you're making a big deal out of a T-shirt, and he's the only reason you would."

"I'm not making a big deal out of anything. I didn't even mention it." I couldn't deny her guess though. I couldn't lie to Luna.

"Mhm." Her serious expression melted to a grin when she opened a box of books and flipped through a few without any pages sticking together from water damage. She moved each clean book with reverence, giving the pile an isolated spot on the table. "Does Ramsey know?"

I sucked on my teeth, searching for the right way to say *definitely yes*. She knew I'd been with both of them before. My breakup with Ramsey had directly and specifically coincided with Luna's legal issues.

"I see. That sounds fun. Was it fun?" Luna's question was strained.

My heart sank. "I'm sorry. It wasn't— I shouldn't have— It's not like it's going to happen again." I'd discovered early on in dating Ramsey that I struggled with his two halves—public and private. I was willing to overlook it most of the time, especially when we first hooked up. The sex was amazing, the conversation was amazing, *Ramsey* was amazing. So what if he'd been raised to be polite in mixed company?

"Why not?"

The question caught me off guard, and I struggled to wrap my brain around it. "We broke up." It was the not-so-polite, upper-class company Ramsey kept that I started to have an issue with. The off-color jokes were nothing new. When we were in college, Luna and I spent a lot of time at parties, and I'd heard plenty of crude jokes and comments about my various body parts.

The more time I spent around friends of Ramsey's family, the less tolerable they got. The worst part was Ramsey would laugh along with them.

"Because of me." Luna stopped sorting. She was frowning now. "You still care about him. You miss him. You go out of your way to prove to yourself that you don't, but you do. And it's because of me."

"No. What happened with you was a catalyst, but it wasn't the cause. I should have left him long before that." Things started to deteriorate when the jokes turned toward me. My decisions.

"That's a sexy piece of ass. You plan on sharing her before you make her yours forever?"

"You ever worry she spends so much time with those *kids?"*

"You oughta lock her away before she starts thinking she can change the world."

Those were the nice things. What hurt the most was that Ramsey never shut them down, and he actively worked to keep me from doing so. He'd apologize at home. *They don't know any better.* He never wanted to hear that they might if he told them or let me tell them.

And then Luna was arrested. The people around Ramsey never said her name, they didn't even know her, but her case was high profile in the business world.

"This is why you get them pregnant early. So they don't get all uppity."

"No way a pretty little thing like her was smart enough to do this."

"Face like that looks better with something in her mouth."

"Too bad she'll turn in prison. A woman like that needs a good man to straighten her out."

When I went off on them, Ramsey had to physically drag me from the room, apologizing for *my* behavior. After we left, he was sorry. It wasn't enough. I told him I couldn't do that anymore. He said I couldn't ask him to pick between me and the people who could make or break his career.

"It definitely wasn't your fault," I repeated to Luna.

She fiddled with a damp fringe on a pillow. "He's gotten better. Making a stand. Building his campaign on fixing some of these things. He was at the fundraiser."

"It's too late." My reply came out with less force than I intended.

We were finishing up the box sorting, when Cole came out and said he was ready to set up fans. Luna jumped to her feet to help him, and I let her.

I tried to ignore my inner war over Ramsey, as I found places for the new mattresses and set up the space heaters that were delivered. We were past capacity. I hated turning people away, but we couldn't take anyone else in.

When the plumber finally showed up, I breathed a sigh of relief. He spent about half an hour in the basement, before telling me he had to call someone else in.

That couldn't be good.

I stuck close, as he took his associate first through the basement and then through the rest of the house. It was hard to hear them, with their heads bent together and the whispered words, but they made a lot of notes.

When they turned back to me, they wore matching grim expressions.

"The boiler can't be fixed," the plumber said. "The best way to heat the place is going to be installing central air, especially in this climate, with this setup. The problem is, the house isn't built to support the ductwork."

"So… what do I need to do?" A nagging thought in the back of my mind was starting to panic, but I couldn't give it my attention.

They exchanged looks again, and the plumber handed me a tablet. "This is a breakdown of what we recommend. You're welcome to call around for other estimates. I understand. The thing is, the house isn't livable as a shelter as it is. If you can't bring it up to code in a week, we'll have to file to have the building condemned. And while the work is being done, we can't have anyone living here."

This couldn't be happening. What was I going to do? Fundraisers like the one last night brought in operating capital, not the kind of money it would take to renovate or get a whole new building. And even if we could raise the money, we had to deal with where the kids would stay until this place was overhauled or a new place was ready.

I needed time. Ideas. Money.

Connections.

Damn it. I needed Ramsey.

You're doing this for the kids, repeated in my head as I pulled up his personal number. The one no one had, except his closest friends and family.

"Hey, Taffy." The smile in his voice sent pleasant shivers racing down my spine whether or not I wanted it to. "Long time no talk."

The hint of playfulness should make this easier.

It didn't.

"Hey." I dragged in a deep, silent breath. *This is for the kids.* "I... um... I-need-a-favor."

Silence.

Was this where he'd tease me? Give me grief about coming groveling, when I swore I'd never be one of those people who used their connections?

"Anything. What's wrong?" Damn him, for sounding concerned.

"I'm at the shelter. A city inspector just left." I'd keep this clinical and factual. More for my sake than his, since I was the one dreading this conversation. "He's condemning the building. I know you can't fix unsafe construction, but... I don't know what to do." It hurt to admit that. This call *was* my plan, and it was the best I had.

"I've got you covered. Give me the night, and I'll call you back tomorrow morning."

This would be okay. He'd help me figure things out. "Thank you."

SIX

I woke up to a string of alerts on my phone, all with the shelter's name, as well as messages from another of the shelter volunteers. *There are cameras outside. A news van. What do I do?*

What?

I clicked through to the first alert. Local news, running a story about the shelter. About it shutting down. About all of these kids becoming homeless for a second time.

Every story was a flavor of the same.

This wasn't what I had in mind when I asked Ramsey for help.

I replied to the text. *Remind them the kids can't be on camera.* The last thing we needed was to get in trouble for exploiting minors. *Otherwise be polite. I'll let you know as soon as I have answers.*

I dialed Ramsey next. I was going to be cool, icy even, while I got to the bottom of why he thought this was the way to go.

"Taffy." He was chipper when he answered.

"What the fuck did you do?"

"Good morning, Ramsey," he said in a falsetto supposed to be me. "How did you sleep? *Goddess*, that one night we had together reminded me how much I love your cock."

I growled. The teasing used to be fun, but not now. "I have you on speaker. The cameraman wants to know if you're really that well hung." My words came out with more of an edge than Ramsey's had.

"Hmm. Be honest with him."

Fucker wasn't supposed to call my bluff. "You don't want that," I said.

"I'm not any more insecure about my dick size than you are likely to be talking to the press while you bitch me out."

I clenched my teeth. "You knew it would piss me off, and yet you called them anyway. What happened to talking in the morning? Making a plan together?" I pulled on clothes. Thankfully, I'd showered last night, to get rid of the swamp-water smell that permeated me.

"We're talking. I assume we'll be planning soon. I didn't ask you, because you would have said *no*."

I put him on speaker and set the phone on my bathroom counter, so I could yank a brush through my hair. "If you knew I wasn't going to like it, you shouldn't have done it."

He *tsk*ed. "You and I both know putting something in the public eye, exposing it, is what gets it attention. If you didn't think that, you wouldn't hold the fundraisers."

"So you couldn't have said this to me when we spoke last night, *before* you arranged it? I'm not unreasonable." I didn't have time for much makeup. A touch of lip gloss, a feather of mascara, and I was good.

"Time was critical, and I had to make a decision or miss the opportunity."

"Which was it, Ramsey?" I made my way to the kitchen. We had coffee at Lyn's place, and it was free, but I needed a kick to get me there. "You didn't have time to ask me, or you figured it easier to ask forgiveness than permission?"

"A little of both. Hang on. Tell them I'll be there in fifteen. Yeah, it's her." His last two statements were distant, as if he'd pulled the phone from his ear. "Sorry about that. Hunter says *hi*."

Suspicion snaked through me, and I set the empty coffee pot on the counter. "Fifteen minutes to what? Where are you?"

"The shelter. Someone needs to be available to talk to the Local 13 Morning Crew about what's going down. Get here in the next ten minutes, and they'll speak with you instead."

"*Fucker.*" I cut myself off, hanging up on him.

Irritation pulsed in my skull, as I abandoned the idea of coffee, grabbed my purse, and walked out the door. Ramsey had a point that people pulled together for an in-their-face cause, but he'd backed me into a corner. He knew I hated this kind of shit— preening for the camera, pretending to be someone I wasn't—and he'd manipulated me into it regardless.

Fury and frustration poured through me, as I drove to the shelter. I told my phone to send Lyn an apologetic text, saying I was going to be late, I was super sorry, and I'd explain when I got in.

Hopefully, voice recognition sent the right note. With my luck the last few days, it told her I was running away to Aruba, and to fuck off.

True, that didn't sound anything like what I'd said, but who knew?

When I got to the shelter, it wasn't as bad as I'd feared, though it still wasn't great. A single news van sat out front, and none of the kids were around. The parking lot was full, though, so I had to park across the street. The neighbors must be hating this, and they didn't need another reason to complain about us.

"Violet." Hunter's call drew my attention. He was on the other street-facing side of the main building, waving me over.

The cameraman, reporter, and Ramsey weren't too far from him.

"There she is." The reporter was a large Hawaiian man who called himself Kool Kahuna for the cameras. He and Ramsey approached me, wearing twin grins, while the camera stayed behind. "Pleasure to meet you." Kahuna shook my hand vigorously.

"Same. I'm a huge fan." It was true. I'd learned to hide *star struck* when I was dating Ramsey. The after-parties he got us into at

Sundance helped a lot with that. But Kahuna was a friendly, cheerful presence on TV, and rumor was he was just as kind in real life.

"We only have a few minutes until we're live again, so if you want to join us, we need to make this quick," Kahuna said. "You ever do live TV before?"

I shook my head. "But I'm not bad at beating stage fright."

He nudged Ramsey. "You spend any time with this guy, and that's a given. Am I right? So this is a little different, since it's live. There are no retakes. No do-overs. But it doesn't matter. We'll have fun with any flubs, and I make them all the time. You stall for any reason, nudge my foot, and I'll step in. Ramsey asked me not to mention that this was a GLBT shelter, so we're only calling it a youth shelter. I'm going to ask you basic questions about what you do here. Keep names out of it. Any questions?"

"I don't think so." I was still processing the current information, and my missed coffee that was so far away. I was grateful they were keeping the full nature of the shelter out of things, not because I was embarrassed, but because the last thing these kids needed was some new hate group showing up on their lawn, protesting their existence.

"Great. Producer says we're on in sixty. Love the look by the way. *Down to earth* is perfect. Lighting's best on this side of the house. Let's go." He jerked his thumb back toward the camera.

Ramsey stepped up beside me as we walked and dipped his head near my ear. "You look amazing, by the way, and I'm glad you made it."

I was still pissed at him, and he hadn't earned the privilege of a response.

The next two hours passed in a blur. Kahuna made it easy to forget the camera was there, and I didn't have to fake any of my answers. All of his questions were focused around getting me to talk about what a great place this shelter was—what a good opportunity it was for the youth.

We had about fifteen minutes between each shoot, and we used it to relocate to different parts of the shelter and make sure we were cleared for filming. At the end of each segment, Kahuna would give the same spiel about the shelter being threatened and looking at relocating, and provide a website address where people could donate if they wanted to help.

A little voice in the back of my mind pointed out Ramsey never once mentioned his campaign. He was there as support and another person to bounce conversation off. It was true Kahuna introduced us both by name each time, but he gave no other context.

When it was all over, I was exhausted, but in a good way. I thanked Kahuna and his staff profusely as they packed up, and then the shelter was quiet.

I still had to deal with Ramsey. Maybe I could just go to work and pretend he wasn't here.

He stepped in front of me, charming-as-fuck smile in place. "Before you yell at me—"

"I'm too worn out to yell," I said. "You already know what I'm going to say."

"Okay, then before you walk out, there's a Part Two to this plan."

We were going to do this after all. "The plan you promised we'd make together? The one you dumped on me out of nowhere anyway? This could have gone so much worse."

"But it didn't."

I clenched my jaw and stared at him. What was I supposed to say that I hadn't delved into a dozen times with him before?

"I'm sorry." Ramsey's expression softened, and so did his tone. "The producer is a friend. He called me early this morning, said their scheduled show cancelled, and asked if I wanted to do an around-the-town kind of piece for my campaign. I immediately thought of you and the kind of positive exposure this would be for the shelter. I had to give him an answer right away."

It was a reasonable explanation, except— "And then you manipulated me to get me down here."

"I couldn't have you shut this down. Wouldn't you have?"

Probably. And it would have been a mistake. "This wasn't the right way to get this done. You should have given me the chance to decide for myself. Did you see I went along with things when it came down to it? Even without you pulling my strings?"

"Yes, and I'm sorry."

"Don't." I spat. "Don't apologize if you don't mean it."

SEVEN

He reached for my hand, and I stepped away from his touch. He frowned. "I do mean it. I should have told you the entire story from the start. I did what felt right at the time, and I see now it wasn't."

I shook my head. *Easier to ask forgiveness than permission.* Such bullshit. Just not usually Ramsey's form of bullshit. If he did something, it was because he knew he was right, no regrets.

"What did you want to tell me?" I shouldn't hear him out, but I was shutting down my heart, so it didn't matter. He'd talk, I'd say *no,* and I'd go to work.

"Part Two. I can make it happen now, but I didn't want to pull the trigger before talking to you."

I narrowed my gaze. "That's what you were going to tell me before I yelled at you?"

"You didn't technically yell," Hunter said. "And we came up with this while we were waiting for the cameras to show up."

"*Hunter* came up with it. But he's right." Was that pride in Ramsey's voice?

I checked the clock on my phone. "Five minutes? I promised Lyn I'd still be in this morning."

Ramsey rolled his eyes. "She'd let you take the day off. She wouldn't even ask questions."

But I'd hate letting her down. I twisted my mouth, waiting.

"I'll give Dottie a call," Ramsey said. "We'll do a fundraiser in Vegas. Like a pop-up event. Tomorrow night it's there, and at midnight, *poof*—it's gone."

Ramsey's grandmother insisted we call her Dottie, rather than *Dorothy* or *Mrs. Miller*. And she'd done a lot of charity work, and her events made the one last night look like a children's party.

I adored her. She'd reached that age where she was willing to say *fuck it* to what anyone thought, and do things her way. However — "You can't put an entire event together in a day."

Ramsey grinned at the challenge. "Day and a half. I'll call her right now, if you say *yes*. She'd love to do this for you. I'll have the plans for your approval by tonight, and we'll fly out there tomorrow afternoon."

"I can't…" My protest died in my throat, as my gaze landed on the faces pressed to the windows, watching us. I didn't have a choice.

"You're not giving up control; you're delegating. Everything gets your sign-off, down to the caterers and brand of shrimp, if you want." Ramsey knew me too well.

I had a week to find these kids a new place to go, and no funds for it. "All right. Let's do it."

"Perfect." Hunter clapped.

It was adorable.

Ramsey's grin was more assured. "Dinner tonight, as an apology and to discuss strategy?"

"Is this a dinner for the press?" I couldn't help the question. He might not have used this morning to campaign, but now he was donating his valuable time to youth in need. Perfect photo op. I hated that I had to consider the possibility before I gave my answer.

His pleased smugness vanished in a blink. "This is dinner for us."

"No. I can't do this again." I'd almost prefer this were a press dinner. Then Ramsey would be on his best behavior, and I'd see

Media Ramsey in action rather than Alpha-Sweet, Sometimes-Nerdy Ramsey.

"It's dinner with friends." Hunter chimed in. "I'll be there too."

He was *so* not a deterrent.

"You have to eat, we have to eat..." Ramsey dangled the thought like the reasonable and honest proposal it was.

That didn't mean I had to eat with them. I did need to approve those plans for tomorrow night, though. "Okay. It's a work dinner. We discuss the event tomorrow."

Ramsey raised an eyebrow. "We'll pick you up at six. Get you home before it's too late, because I assume you'll work tomorrow, even though you're about to host a massive fundraiser in another state."

"You assume correctly."

Ramsey stepped closer, and I backed away again.

"I'll see you tonight." I tried not to look too awkward, waving. I wouldn't hold up to a drawn-out *goodbye* and who knew what else. There was no telling what I'd agree to next, especially with my body whispering, *One little farewell kiss wouldn't hurt.*

Lyn's café—Loading Java—was only a few miles from the shelter, and even in morning traffic, I was there in under ten minutes. I rushed inside, past our standard line of early customers, and into the kitchen, where Lyn was grabbing a fresh round of pastries.

Thankfully, she was alone. I'd walked in on her with one of her guys a few times, and while I'm pretty sure she was more embarrassed than me, I wasn't in the mood for unexpected smooches this morning. From anyone.

"I'm so sorry." I grabbed my apron from its hook and tied it in place. "I'll help with morning rush, and then I'll explain." And ask for a day or two off, out of the blue. The idea of dumping that kind of surprise on someone curdled my gut. I'd be letting Lyn down. I *hated* that. Maybe I could miss the party.

But then I was letting someone else beg for money on my shelter's behalf, and I couldn't do that, either.

"Don't worry about it." Lyn was kind. "You looked good this morning. We had it on in here."

Heat flooded my cheeks. "Thanks."

We made it through the morning rush with the practiced efficiency of our well-matched crew. When we hit a lull that looked like it would last at least a few minutes, I pulled Lyn aside.

I explained to her what happened last night with the inspection. And what Ramsey's plan was. "So I may need to take off early tomorrow, and take the day after as well," I said. "I'm *so* sorry. I wish I could give you more warning. I'll ask if anyone can take my shift—"

"It's okay." Lyn sounded like she meant it. "You're doing something important, to you and for others."

I still felt guilty. "But—"

"I get it. Learning to relax and take time off gets easier with each day you take off, though."

I didn't want it to get easier. "I never want to feel right letting people down."

"You're not letting me down. And don't worry about covering your shift. Owen will do it."

"Okay. Thank you." I was out of arguments.

"If you need anything besides a pop-up Vegas party, let me know," Lyn said. "I have *connections* too. Mine are just less public."

I smiled at the offer. Lyn's friends had helped her remodel this building. I was happy to put them on the payroll to help with mine, as well. "Ask them to be on standby. Whatever comes out of this, I'm going to need a lot of help."

I went back to work, but I couldn't stop thinking about tomorrow. And tonight. Every time *dinner with Ramsey* popped into my head, a giddy little beat danced behind my ribs. It was foolish, but knowing that didn't stop my heart from hoping otherwise.

I spent far too much mental energy on *what should I wear tonight*, as the hours at work ticked away. Especially since when I got home, I didn't know.

My apartment was a simple one-bedroom, with sparse decoration. It suited my needs, and I rarely was here long enough to do more than sleep and shower.

The little black dress in the back of my closet called to me, and I tried to ignore its siren song. I'd bought it because *every girl should have at least one*, and I needed to replace the half-dozen I'd had that reminded me of Ramsey.

The new one hadn't done what I wanted it to. I was wearing a black leather mini when I met Ramsey, and that night, as well as the many others we were together, he could do a whole lot to me when I was in a little black dress, and no one around us was ever the wiser.

Need pulsed between my legs at the rush of memories, and I squeezed my thighs together. Little black dress? Bad idea.

Which must explain why I tugged it from my closet, pulled it on, and accented it with matching heels and thigh-high stockings. At some point, I'd have to admit to myself I wanted this. Wanted him. That having him around in more than a passing-hello way made my pulse skip rope, and I was okay with it.

Being honest about that didn't change the nagging voice, asking me, *What happens when he forces me to choose between him and how we act in public again?*

He'd apologized and I'd avoided him since because I knew spending time with him would break my resolve.

I pinched the bridge of my nose, to stem the flow of conflicting thoughts. It didn't work.

The doorbell ringing did the trick, though.

I grabbed my purse, gave myself one last glance in the mirror, and tried to pretend I wasn't hurrying to answer the door. The way Ramsey looked me over, eyes wide and lips pursed in a silent whistle, didn't erase my frown. He and Hunter were dressed casually, in T-shirts and jeans. Though Ramsey's look was more expensive than my dress.

"Ah. It's that kind of night." I forced a chuckle. "Give me five, so I can change."

"Don't you dare." Ramsey grabbed my wrist before I could turn away, his rough grip sending a fresh wave of desire through me.

I sucked in a sharp breath through my teeth, and gestured down with my free hand. "I'm not—"

"You're fine. Better than fine. *Fuck.*" Ramsey finished with a low hiss.

At least the dress had the desired effect. I handed Hunter his freshly washed clothes. "Thank you for these."

He handed the shirt back. "Pull this on."

"It doesn't really match."

"It's perfect. Trust me." His smile was more friendly than hungry, setting an odd contrast of tone. He jerked his thumb behind him. "You'll see the rest outside. Come on."

I pulled on his T-shirt, feeling silly as it hung down almost as far as my dress. I trusted him, though.

We headed down to the parking lot, where Ramsey's Cheyenne waited in a visitor spot. Not that I'd ever seen it before, but it was the most ostentatious-but-practical-for-the-weather thing here. The locks clicked off with a flash of lights, and Hunter headed for the back of the vehicle. He emerged after only a few seconds, holding two suit coats and ties.

That was so familiar, it muted my muddled emotions around Ramsey and my dress. Both men slipping on the ties over their T-shirts, then shrugging into the jackets was less expected, but it did even things out with my modified outfit.

Ramsey held the front passenger door for me, and grasped my fingers for balance as I stepped up in the seat. Hunter passed me a tablet between the seats, from the spot he'd settled into behind me. There was a bullet-point list on the screen that had to be his.

"This is what Dottie has planned for tomorrow. If she needs a decision from you, it says so. If you have veto power, it says that too. Some things had to be set in stone from the start, like location, so I apologize you don't have 100% control." Hunter leaned in to indicate specific list items. With him this close, his aftershave teased me, and softer memories flitted in my thoughts. Of great conversation. Of curling up next to him and falling asleep. Of so many things.

What was wrong with me?

EIGHT

As Ramsey drove and offered running commentary, Hunter went down the party list with me.

"It all looks good." I handed the tablet back. "I'm struggling with the whole gala-overnight thing. Will this really work?"

Hunter huffed a laugh. "Of course. Think of the viral potential. You get a message that says *Pop-up Party in Vegas, to Support LGBTQ+ Youth*. You know that the biggest and best will be at the Luxor, and like Cinderella, it all turns back into a pumpkin at midnight. You want people to know you were there."

Well, *I* didn't care if people knew I was there—not for the reasons he meant—but I got the point. If word got out, if we drew a quarter of the expected donations, I could fix up the shelter. I didn't know what I'd do with the kids while repairs were taking place, but I was working on that. I twisted in my seat, to look at Hunter. "I love it. Thank you."

"Anything for Ramsey's favorite lady." His smile warmed me to my core, but something about his words made my brain stutter.

I couldn't grasp the thought, so I let it go for now.

A short while later, we pulled into a strip-mall parking lot and picked a space in front of a local diner that specialized in ice cream. If you weren't happy with that, they had burgers as well.

"Classy," I teased. "Perfect." The three of us came here all the time in college. Even though Hunter went to a different school, he was Ramsey's roommate then, and hung out with us even outside the bedroom. I'd never minded, because he respected our alone time, and I liked Hunter.

The only other diners inside were a single family, who looked to be finishing up their meal. It was a Monday night in the middle of winter—not a lot of call for ice cream.

The waitress gave us a lingering glance and smirked when she arrived at our table. "Love the outfits." She was sincere. "You know what you're having?"

Same things we always had. Ice cream on a brownie for Ramsey —extra cherries on top. Two scoops of whatever caught my fancy in a waffle cone, and a banana split for Hunter.

As she left, a new thought occurred to me that I was surprised hadn't before. "This is a formal affair tomorrow night? Or will I show up in my blue satin to everyone dressed in parachute pants and leg warmers, like it's the 80's?"

"That's an oddly specific visual," Hunter said. "And not at all what we planned. There's still time to change things if you'd like."

"Definitely not." I didn't have time to shop, but I had the formal wear on standby.

"Let me take care of the dress. Don't pack anything but toiletries."

I stared blankly at Ramsey, trying to convey, *Do you even know me?* with a gaze. "Like I'm not going to pack for any possibility. Is this so you can make sure I look appropriate?"

"You always look appropriate." His assurance was smooth. "But I want to surprise you."

I frowned. I hated surprises.

"I know. But this one will be good. I promise," Ramsey said.

An awkward lull settled between us. It was worse because we'd never had trouble with conversation in the past. Even the silent moments always felt right. The family on the other side of the dining room left, giving us the entire place to ourselves. Our ice cream arrived, and we dug in, while I tried and failed to ignore the glances Hunter and Ramsey kept exchanging.

This was too much. "How's the campaign going?"

They both looked surprised at the question.

"You really want to talk politics over ice cream?" Hunter asked.

There was no reason. I already had a good idea of what their politics were. "I'm looking for more of a *how are you feeling about the race* kind of vibe."

"I'm set to win the primary." Ramsey's confidence was no surprise.

"Big plans for when you win the general election?" I was pushing him in a specific direction. He'd been groomed by his family for this path. Known for years that he'd do this. So we used to play a game that took things to the extreme.

"Equality." Hunter ticked off one finger. "Prison reform. Schools."

I didn't want a list of public talking points. "This is me. You can give me the *real* dish. No matter how over the top it is." I wanted more fantasy—the *whatever his heart desires* kind not the *tie me up and fuck me* kind. Though…

I shook the second notion away but couldn't get rid of the rush of heat it brought with it. The point of this game was to pick *anything*, no matter how ridiculous. Comic-book-level stuff. Better.

"Ah." Recognition flashed in Hunter's eyes. He nudged Ramsey. "She wants to know how you're going to *Batman* the place, Bruce Wayne."

Ramsey rolled his eyes. "Don't joke. You know how I feel about Batman."

We did. "That Christian Bale was the pinnacle—"

Hunter joined in. "And no one else could ever reach that bar," he said in unison with me. We finished with giggles.

"Don't knock the Dark Knight." Ramsey looked stoic. "He's always watching. Knows when you're sleeping. When you're awake."

Hunter looked like he was struggling to keep a straight face. "That's Santa."

"Who hurt you, that you can't tell the two apart?" I asked with mock concern.

Ramsey stuck his tongue out. "You have to get a lot more naked if you want the illicit details of how I feel about pain."

The heat was back, setting fire to my skin and lighting up my imagination. I had to get back to the fun conversation, so I could get rid of the phantom sensation of Ramsey's palm—his belt, my hair brush—smacking into my ass.

I held my spoon toward Ramsey, using it like a microphone. "So, Councilman Miller, if—*when*—you're elected, what are your plans for cleaning up crime in the city?"

"Giant robots." There was no hesitation in his response.

I wasn't at all surprised, and I knew where he was going with the answer, but that didn't stop a giggle from slipping out. "As in *Robocop*? *Terminator*? You know Skynet destroyed humanity. While that's technically a crime deterrent, I don't think it's what your constituents are looking for."

"Vibrators and toasters are three percent of the voting population, and all voices deserve to be heard." Hunter rambled off the fake statistic with complete seriousness.

Ramsey cleared his throat and adopted a serious look. "You're not thinking big enough. *Giant* robots. As in, the Grandaddy Gundam, RX-78."

I adored this side of them. The geeky, fanboy side that they didn't show anyone. "Don't mechs tend to destroy cities, Councilman?" I asked.

"Well, actually"—Hunter adopted his best *I'm on the internet and an expert* voice—"you'd find the damage was far worse if you let the monsters roam free. The mechs keep more of the city from being destroyed, even if they themselves are complicit in the destruction."

I laughed and shook my head in disbelief. "Spoken like a true politician. I'm not sure the threats to Salt Lake are Neon Zeos." I said the name wrong on purpose, with a lilt of teasing in my voice.

Ramsey clenched his jaw.

I stared at him, eyes wide and innocent. "Is something wrong, Councilman?"

"It's Neo Zeongs. And you know that."

Another laugh slipped out. Goddess, this was familiar and good in the best possible way, and I was way past wanting it not to. "Maybe."

"You're such a brat, Taffy."

I shrugged in agreement. "What are you going to do? Bend me over your knee and spank me?"

"Aww." Hunter pouted. "I want to be spanked."

My brain slid to a halt.

Ramsey placed a finger under Hunter's chin and raised his head to meet his gaze. "Of course. She hasn't earned it. You just have to beg."

Heat spilled through me, and I struggled to catch up. Not only was the exchange flat-out adorably sexy, it was also anything but friendly. Yesterday morning, ungodly early, replayed in my brain. Me, waking up, still hazy, to find Ramsey saying, *I'll talk to you in a few hours*, and giving Hunter a *goodbye* kiss…

Fuck me. I was such a blind idiot. "You two are together." The words came out louder than I intended. Ramsey glared at me and I clapped my hands over my mouth. A glance around us said no one was paying attention to the silly friends in the corner booth.

My heart dropped into my shoes. I was letting myself fall into a *what if* fantasy with Ramsey, and he was in a relationship. I was a side dish. Not even what Hunter had been to us in the past, because he was a friend. I was just the ex.

"You didn't think to mention this—I don't know—two days ago?" Before I climbed back into bed with them. Before I stood on the edge of the *delusion* rabbit hole and considered jumping in, headfirst?

They exchanged a look, and Ramsey gave a slight shake of his head.

Hunter turned back to me. "We don't tell anyone, which you probably noticed."

"You just made sure everyone saw you at one fundraiser helping kids like you, and you're fast-laning another, and you feel like you have to hide who you are?" I wasn't accusing them; I was genuinely curious.

Ramsey sighed. "There's a difference between supporting a cause and being the cause. You know that. If I came out, the focus would be on my gayness—because you know I wouldn't be bisexual to the media—and not what others needed."

That was surprisingly altruistic and painfully realistic. "Imagine the kind of role model you'd be."

"An amazing one," Ramsey said. "But I'm not the only one I'm thinking about." He looked at Hunter. "Maybe someday I'll—*we'll*—get there, but not yet. I'm a rich white boy, who's played straight my entire life. Letting my money and other, more experienced individuals speak is more helpful."

I wanted to argue that this was another version of his public face versus his private one, but I understood not outing people before they were ready. For all the acceptance out there, just as much bigotry still existed. And it was sweet that he was worried about Hunter in that way.

Hunter tugged one of my fingers, drawing my attention. "What happened after the party? We don't make a habit of that."

"God, no." Ramsey shook his head.

Of course they didn't. "Because it would look bad if it got out."

Hunter raised an eyebrow. "Because that's not the lifestyle either of us wants. I don't care if other people open their relationships, but I'm selfish with my guy."

My guy. So much possession in the simple phrase. And my jealousy was skyrocketing. Then again, they hid what they had, and I'd always made it clear I wasn't interested in being someone different in the bedroom than I was out of it. They hid their relationship so well, I felt bad for Hunter. I'd hated having to fake-smile when I was with Ramsey, and he had to fake-everything.

I shut off all my *what happens next* fantasies about Ramsey. "Thank you for the ice cream. It was fun hanging out again. See you tomorrow?"

"You're taking this wrong." Hunter settled a hand on my bare knee, startling me.

"What happened after the party wasn't a mistake." Ramsey tangled his fingers with mine. "It's not what we planned, but there are no regrets. You're not just a warm body."

Hunter squeezed my knee. "You're Violet."

"I don't know what that means." But I wanted to, so desperately, just based on the pair of simple touches.

NINE

R amsey dropped a large bill on the table and tugged both Hunter and me to our feet. "You wanted to go home. Let's get out of here."

"I *want* to finish this conversation." I reluctantly pulled my hand away and crossed my arms, mostly to keep temptation at bay.

Ramsey held my gaze, never letting go of Hunter. "So do I."

I tapped my toes inside my shoes, as my brain followed a series of possible outcomes based on hope, experience, and cynicism. I couldn't argue that this was a private conversation, but there was no one here to eavesdrop, unless the staff got bored with their gossip about their co-workers. Having this conversation in the car meant I couldn't look them in the eye while we talked, and I needed that. Going to someone's house meant the temptation of clothes coming off, given the topic, or disappointment I shouldn't feel if the clothes stayed on.

"Talk to me now," I said.

Ramsey sighed and raked his fingers through his hair. "This is not the way I wanted things to go."

"Sorry you can't control every single little bit of life."

He raised an eyebrow. "You talking to me or yourself?"

I opened my mouth to retort, and he held up a finger. "I'm not trying to pick a fight," Ramsey said. "Sit back down, at least?"

"Fine." It was a reasonable request, given I was refusing to leave without answers. We took our spots around the table again.

Ramsey leaned in, but there was no contact. "You know I miss you. I've never hidden that."

And yet, you're with someone else. I swallowed the retort. Did I expect him to wait for me, when I'd made it clear we weren't happening? Especially if he had a chance with Hunter?

"Two nights ago was amazing," Ramsey said. "We had a long talk after." He indicated Hunter. "You and I are good together, Taffy. We need to try again."

And I was the idiot who wanted to. Fortunately, I didn't have to decide. "Hunter said he didn't want an open relationship."

"I don't. This isn't open. It's for you alone, and we'll talk about what that means if you're interested," Hunter said.

Exclusive offer. Limited time only. Step inside for details. I stifled a barking laugh at the rush of random thoughts and stood again. "I can't..." Couldn't what? Give him a part of me again. As much as I ached to pursue this topic. "I'm gonna catch a bus home. I'll see you tomorrow." Fuck. I had to see them tomorrow.

I needed to make sense of my thoughts before I could look them in the eye. The jumbled mess in my brain wouldn't do at all.

I strode toward the door.

"Violet." Ramsey's call hit my back, as I stepped outside.

The cold blast stung against my hot cheeks, but I didn't pause.

"Violet." Ramsey had caught up to me now, his voice near enough he didn't have to shout.

I still couldn't look.

He grabbed my arm as we passed his SUV, and he spun my back to the vehicle so I faced him. We stared each other down, as my desire warred with fury over how he'd restrained me. I swore sparks raced between us. I could step closer, but I'd be hard pressed to move away, the way he had me boxed in.

Ramsey let go of me and moved away a few paces. "Don't take the bus." His voice was flat. "Let me drive you home."

I'll be fine. "All right. Thank you." I climbed into the back seat before he could offer another option. Hunter was his boyfriend. They should be sitting next to each other.

No one said anything, as Ramsey pulled onto the main road. With as little production as possible, I took off Hunter's shirt, folded it, and handed it to him.

"Thanks." His voice was impossible to read.

This wasn't what I wanted. I wasn't upset at either of them. Maybe I should be about the way they'd hidden their relationship— I would have liked to know that before I climbed into bed with them —but in a certain light, I understood.

So what was my problem? Why couldn't I talk to them or even look at them?

Because I *did* still want something more with Ramsey, and my reasons for leaving him hadn't changed. I was immensely jealous of Hunter. Was this what it had been like for him? Occasionally being invited into our bed? Having to watch from the outside, the rest of the time?

There are no regrets about what happened. Ramsey's words snuck into my thoughts.

I didn't regret it either. I wanted more of it. If I had them drop me off tonight, and kept this conversation closed, would I regret that?

"What you're talking about..." My voice came out wobblier than I wanted, and I licked my lips. I hadn't wanted to do this without being able to look them in the eye, but I'd rather that than not doing it at all. "It's not like what Lyn has with Kingston and Owen."

The three of them loved each other. They were happily exclusive. Hunter was a friend, but he wasn't more, even if it was tempting to think of him as the competition.

"I don't know what it is," Ramsey said. "I want to see you again —date you, before you tell me I can already see you. I'm not going to ask that you don't see anyone else, even if I want to. That's not fair of me, because I'm not giving up Hunter."

It sounded straightforward. Could I do it? I was more torn on the letting-Ramsey-back-into-my-life thing than I was about sharing him with Hunter. "It doesn't erase the problems we had before."

"We'll work through those," Ramsey said quickly.

I fiddled with the hem of my dress. The short, flared skirt I'd worn specifically for him. I tapped Hunter on the shoulder. "And you're okay with this?"

"I already have the guy. Hard to argue with the position I'm in." He glanced back at me.

Fuck it. "All right. Let's give it a try."

We pulled into my apartment parking lot, and Ramsey opened the back driver's side door for me. As I swung my legs to the side, to climb out, he moved in, pinning my wrist to the seat. He slid between my legs, the fabric of his trousers teasing my thighs.

He licked a slow line up my neck, to my ear. "Tell me you didn't wear this dress for me."

"I did." My anticipation was back, whimpering for more. It was different, knowing Hunter sat in the front seat, where he could watch but it wouldn't be easy for him to participate. What did he think of this?

Ramsey let go of one of my wrists, to move his hand under my skirt. He teased the elastic of my underwear. "And yet, you wore panties."

"Never stopped you before."

"And it won't stop me now." Ramsey glided his finger along my skin then lower over the lace. He stroked along the crotch, pressing enough to tease, and drew his mouth to mine, claiming my lips in a series of hungry pecks.

"What about Hunter?" I asked between kisses.

"I rarely mind a good show." His voice from behind me was husky. "And I always enjoy you two."

A good show. We were in the visitor parking of an apartment complex, half hanging out of an SUV, and anyone could walk by.

The thrill of getting caught, putting on a show for a random stranger, made my pulse race. But, "Are you worried about being seen. You being you?" It never stopped Ramsey before, but who knew now?

"No." His reply was hot against my neck. He shoved my panties aside and slipped his fingers to my clit. "I'm not whipping out my dick, just giving my date a goodnight kiss." He teased lightly.

"While your fingers wander," I managed between gasps.

He dipped lower, gliding inside me to thrust over and over. "Exactly."

My hips swayed to his touch. My breath came in short pants. We might not be visible to most people, but Hunter knew exactly what we were doing. That made me clench with need.

Ramsey withdrew his fingers and moved back to my clit, stroking hard this time. Drawing tiny circles. Pressing and teasing and nudging me to teeter on the edge of climax.

"Come for me, Taffy," he growled into my neck.

My laugh was shaky. "I don't do that on demand. That's not how this works."

"No?" Ramsey worked faster. "What if I tell you once you're inside tonight, I'm going back to Hunter's." He pushed me closer. Orgasm was just out of reach. "I'm going to fuck the hell out of him, while this moment is still fresh in our minds."

Yeah, that was pretty fucking hot. I bit the inside of my cheek to keep from crying out as Ramsey's words and touch sent me topping into ecstasy. Every inch of me shuddered with the release of desire, and I ground into his touch until I was spent, and my body shuddered away.

I rested my hands on the seat behind me to keep myself upright.

Ramsey pressed two slick fingers to my lips and I drew them in, greedily sucking myself from his skin. He kissed me around the touch. Around the licking. Sharing my flavor. His tongue dancing with mine and around his fingers.

We finally broke the kiss and he rested his forehead against mine. "I wish I could take you home with us tonight. I can, can't I?"

I wanted to. So desperately. "I have to work in the morning, and I won't get any sleep if I go with you."

"No, you really won't." He pulled away with one more kiss. "At least let me walk you to your door."

I couldn't argue that request, and I really couldn't ignore how badly it sucked to stay here after they left.

Only a few days back in my life, and I was already completely smitten with Ramsey again. I was so fucked. In more ways than one.

TEN

I was always grateful I'd been born with the *multi-task like a boss* gene, but this morning, more than ever. As I worked through my routine at Loading Java, a portion of my mind was focused on last night. The conversation with Ramsey. What we agreed to. What came after.

Those thoughts wouldn't be dissuaded.

In the midst of all that, I made a series of calls to local extended-stay motels. Whether the shelter moved to a new building or was just remodeled, the kids would need someplace to stay in the interim. This was the best temporary solution I could come up with. A couple of the volunteers would be on hand at all times, like they were now, and we'd make the situation work.

I breathed a sigh of relief when I found a motel willing to reserve an entire floor for us for the next two weeks. It was a great starting point.

The hours both sped by and crawled at a snail's pace. I was in the back room, doing inventory on teacups, when I heard a voice boom from out front.

"I'd like to speak to the manager. Now." Hunter's tone wasn't nearly as threatening as the words implied it should be.

A silly grin bounced onto my face, and I didn't try to stop it as I stepped into the shop. "What can I do for you, sir?" Besides question why he was alone.

"How much for… you?"

I was surprised he asked that in front of customers and other employees. Then again, he wasn't Ramsey. I clucked. "You can't afford me."

"I'll buy you lunch."

I screwed my face up, pretending to consider the offer. "In Las Vegas?"

"Sold." He grinned. "You ready to go?"

"Thirty seconds." I ducked into the kitchen, to grab my purse and duffel bag. It didn't matter that Ramsey told me not to pack anything; I still had a few changes of clothes and an emergency dress, just in case. I joined Hunter, and we made our way out to his car.

"Ramsey's sorry he's not here himself," Hunter said as he held the passenger door for me. "He's stuck in a meeting. He'll meet us at the airport."

I understood that. It was disappointing to not see him now, but I would soon enough. "No big deal."

Hunter took his place behind the wheel, and we were on our way.

"I'm curious," I said. "What does a campaign manager do?"

He navigated lunchtime traffic downtown like a pro. "You manage Lyn's place. What do you do?"

"Inventory. Scheduling. Opening and closing the shop. Anything Lyn tells me to."

"There you have it."

We both knew the work wasn't that basic. "Anything Ramsey tells you to? Is this a paid position? Volunteer? Do you get paid to be his boyfriend?"

Hunter shot me a half-dry, half-amused look. "Volunteer. Never question that I serve him for free." There was a hint of teasing in his voice.

"That's fair. And don't give me a glossed-over answer like that. You know I need details."

"Something I adore about you." He merged onto the freeway. "But details always depend on the situation. I make sure all the parts are clicking *behind* the scenes, so he can focus on *the scenes*. I do the hiring. Scheduling. Inventory—banners, buttons, shirts. Whatever he needs that he's not thinking of, because he's focused on other priorities."

Impressive. I let out an exaggerated *that's so sweet* sigh. "So dreamy. I know most people think details are boring, but the way you talk about them is so sexy."

He tapped me lightly on the nose. "You don't have to win me over. I'm already there."

"I wasn't even thinking about that. I'm serious. I like a guy who has a grasp of how many *Miller for Senate* T-shirts are in the back room."

"I can't tell you that off the top of my head or anything."

"Uh-huh." I let the disbelief drip from my retort.

Hunter sighed heavily. "Seventeen small, thirteen medium, thirteen large, and two XL's. New shipment will be in Thursday."

"See?" I asked playfully.

Hunter shook his head, but he was smiling as we pulled into the airport. He opened his mouth, and his phone rang, cutting him off. "You okay if I take this?"

"Of course."

I listened to Hunter's half of administrative details. I'd meant what I said—most people would find this boring, but I adored how on top of things he was.

As he talked, he turned the car toward a part of the airport I wasn't familiar with, and parked us in an empty lot.

Security was nothing like I was used to. We were in and out in just a few minutes, and walking out the gate, to climb a short set of stairs to a small jet.

I stalled in the plane's doorway. I'd never seen something like this in person—it was straight out of the movies, with the leather and wood and so much space for an airplane. Yeah, Ramsey and I had traveled a few times when we dated, and I thought First Class was opulent. But this was the family jet, and he hadn't had access to it back then.

I guess he'd *earned it*.

"Hey." Ramsey's greeting jarred me from my awe. "Sorry I had to meet you here."

Hunter stepped around me. "'S'all good."

"Totally fine," I said. Sometimes work demanded a little extra time and responsibility.

"Hey, handsome." Ramsey tugged Hunter in for a long, heated kiss.

That he reached for Hunter first stung, but *Goddess* was it amazing to watch.

Ramsey let Hunter go, and turned to me. "I'm glad you're here." His voice was low and smooth. He brushed his lips over mine, lightly enough to tempt and tease, then deepened the kiss. Desire sang over and through me, all the way to my core.

I'd missed this feeling so much.

Ramsey stepped back. "Lady and Gentleman, take your seats. Let's go to Vegas."

I settled into a spot that was more comfortable than my living-room furniture. This would be a short flight, so there was no reason to take advantage of the amenities. However, it was tempting to at least see what kind of secrets a plane like this held.

As we taxied toward the runway, my phone rang. "Sorry. I forgot to turn it off."

"Go ahead and take it." Ramsey waved a hand. "No restrictions here."

Talk about decadent. "Hello?"

"Is this Violet?" the woman on the other end of the line asked.

"It is."

"This is Tawna, from Extended Stop Motels. We talked earlier?" Her voice was timid, which it hadn't been earlier.

"Of course. What can I do for you?"

"I got a call from corporate, and they had me cancel your reservation."

Disappointment sank into my bones. This had been the only place on my list that even talked to me. No one wanted to rent an entire floor to a group of kids. Too much liability. "Did they say why? Is there anything I can do?"

"They said there were insurance issues. Problems with legal guardianship. Liability concerns."

I clenched my jaw and turned away from the two sets of eyes watching me. "Those are just a bunch of phrases. They don't mean anything." They did, but I couldn't let this reservation fall apart.

"I'm sorry." Tawna's voice was tight. "I'm happy to let you stay here, but this came down from corporate. It's out of my hands."

It wouldn't do me any good to yell at her. "I get it. Thank you." I dropped my phone into my lap and scrubbed my face, letting a long breath out through my fingers.

"What's wrong?" Ramsey's question was all concern.

If I left this until tomorrow, would it give me enough time to find a solution? I'd need at least that long, to think of what to try next. "Nothing. I've got it." My hands muffled my words.

"Would you have it faster or less painfully if we helped you brainstorm?" Ramsey asked.

Yes. No. Maybe.

Warm hands grabbed my wrists, and Ramsey pushed them into my lap as he moved into the seat next to me. "Talk."

"If I don't, will you stop asking?"

"Nope."

As I told them what was going on, it was impossible to hide my frustration. Sometimes, talking through something presented answers, but this time, I drew a blank.

Hunter had his phone out. "Give me thirty minutes."

"I can't." I shook my head.

Ramsey squeezed my hand gently. *"Can't* what?"

"Can't keep asking for favors. I owe you both too much."

Hunter stared at me with disbelief.

"That's not the way this works." Was that hurt in Ramsey's voice?

Who was he kidding? "That's exactly the way this works."

Ramsey placed a finger under my chin and turned my face toward his. "This isn't *tit for tat*. We're not keeping score. You're a friend who needs help, and Hunter can help. If one of us needed something, you'd do the same."

"What would you need from me?" I wanted to take back the question as soon as I asked it. Mostly because I hated feeling like I couldn't contribute—and what was I offering them in return, for everything they were doing?

"You know better than that," Hunter said. "If you don't, I'm telling you now. Money and connections get a lot of things done, but not everything, and frequently not the important things."

There was an underlying thread in his voice I couldn't identify.

"So, I've got this." He dialed.

My *thank you* was muffled by his talking to whoever picked up on the other end.

I listened intently to his half of each conversation, trying to tell how things were going. It didn't work. He briefly explained the situation each time, followed by short, pleasant answers, and then he'd hang up.

The fact that he kept making calls made my heart sink. We landed, and he was dialing more people. We were getting in the car, when he *whooped*. "Got it."

The car was big enough that two bench-seats faced each other in back. Ramsey slid in next to me, and Hunter took the spot across from us. Everything about his expression and posture said *pleased*.

"Eight-plex in Sugar House. All of them two-bedroom, two-bath," Hunter said. "The new owner had everyone move out because he's remodeling, but the bank held his financing. The place is empty for at least two months, and your kids can stay there. No charge. He'll write it off as a donation."

"You're the best." I leaned across the divide, to give him a *thank you* hug.

"I wanna be the best." Ramsey's pouty voice was exaggerated. He wrapped an arm around my waist and yanked me into his lap.

I squirmed more than was needed to get comfortable, feeling him half-harden underneath me. "You are the absolute best."

"Mhm." He scraped his teeth over my neck. "At what?"

"Everything? What are you looking for?" I teased.

Ramsey bit my shoulder hard enough to draw a yelp, sending a spark of desire through me. "Something sincere would be nice," he growled.

"No one hurts me like you do." That sounded bad. "I mean that in the best way possible."

"Mhm," he repeated, settling his hands on my hips and moving me into my own spot.

Had I offended him?

ELEVEN

R amsey leaned in, to hover his lips near my ear, his warm breath teasing my skin. "You need a little pampering, in case there's more agony later," he said in a stage whisper.

"I have no idea what that means." Was it supposed to be sexy? Threatening? I was pretty sure it meant he wasn't offended by my comment.

He chuckled. "I thought it was a clever segue, but maybe not. You have an appointment at the hotel salon in about"—he looked at his empty wrist—"fifteen minutes."

If pressed by the right person, I had to admit I missed this part of dating Ramsey. The part where certain things that I considered luxuries and he considered necessities were paid for by default. I'd have to be pressed hard, though, because even admitting it to myself made me feel selfish. "If you insist."

"I do."

We reached the hotel, and Ramsey gave my hand a quick squeeze and promised they'd see me in a few hours, and a member of the staff showed me to my appointment.

The stylist yanked the scrunchie out of my hair with a sigh. "At least it's not elastic. Says in your appointment notes you can do whatever you'd like, as long as you don't cut more than a couple of inches off."

Because of course Ramsey sent instructions. Those weren't as specific as usual, though. "I could have you dye it blue?"

"In the amount of time we have? Yes, if you want to destroy these gorgeous curls."

I didn't. "I trust you. Make me look like a princess, going to a ball. More Meghan Markle than Cinderella," I added as an afterthought.

"You got it, hon."

The next few hours were almost enough to make me forget the looming party, from having my scalp massaged, and my fingers and feet soaked and rubbed. The stunning blue polish… I didn't even have to ask. I hoped the color raised a few eyebrows.

When I handed my personal stylist a tip, she gave me a keycard with a room number.

"I'm told your things are already up there," she said.

"Thank you, for a wonderful experience."

I checked my phone as I took the elevator up. How was it already four? The party didn't start until seven, but I couldn't walk in there—couldn't let guests arrive—without looking everything over first. And now my nervousness was back.

I stepped into the kind of hotel room I thought only existed in movies. The living room was bigger than my entire apartment, with three couches, white carpet, and gold everywhere. A door at the far end led to a bedroom, that I assumed was equally as overwhelming.

Ramsey was waiting, already dressed for the night in his tux. *Goddess*, he was breathtaking.

"You look incredible. And you probably want to get downstairs ridiculously early," he said. "Hunter will meet us there."

"You know me so well. I'm feeling a little underdressed, though." I gestured down.

Ramsey reached for a long bag hanging on the back of a nearby door. "Clothes off."

I raised an eyebrow, and he stared back at me with a look that said, *Argue with me. I dare you.*

It was tempting, but the clock was ticking, and if I pushed back, we'd be here for a while. Oh, and I'd mess up my hair. But the way Ramsey was watching me, with barely hidden desire, I didn't care.

"Can we pretend I argued, and you can punish me later?" I asked sweetly.

He huffed. "I guess."

I kicked off my shoes, then stripped off my shirt, intently aware of how he watched my every movement. "How much is everything?" I asked.

"Everything is *everything*." Ramsey's tone was hard.

Right. Desire roared over me, as I removed my jeans, my bra, and finally my panties, leaving me naked and on display in the middle of the room.

Ramsey closed the distance between us, stopping far enough away I couldn't feel his heat, but I could reach out and touch him.

Self-consciousness wanted me to cover up, but I fought the impulse.

He dragged a finger along my jaw, down my neck, to my arm, and lower, to grasp my fingers. He kissed the tips. "Love the blue."

My entire body was probably flushed pink, but I didn't dare look.

Ramsey smirked and returned to the dress bag. He unzipped it, to reveal swaths of black underneath. It was a stunning gown. I'd never worn anything so elegant.

He unzipped the dress and beckoned me with a finger, as he removed the dress from its hanger. "Arms up."

"I—" didn't have any panties on.

"Yes?" He watched me with that look of challenge again.

I put my arms up. "Nothing."

Ramsey moved behind me, to slip the dress over my head. He slid his palms down my sides, smoothing out the skirt even though it mostly fell to the floor on its own. He zipped up the back, sucking everything into place. Looking down, I could see the scooped neck, the skirt with a slit almost the hip, and the off-the shoulder short sleeves.

I wanted to see the whole deal from a better angle, though. I stepped toward the three-way mirror, and Ramsey grabbed my arm. "Not yet."

I heard some light shuffling and a faint *click*. The cool touch of metal met my neck, and I looked down to see a strand of diamonds and sapphires that fell to a stop right in the middle of my cleavage. The light danced off the gems in tiny rainbows.

"It's only a loaner." Ramsey trailed his fingers down my spine. When he took his hand away, the weight of another chain rested on my back. "Now you can look."

I moved in front of the mirror and gasped. I really did look like a princess, including the stunning back necklace that was undoubtedly worth more than the sum of my worldly possessions. After a few spins, so I could see myself from every possible angle, Ramsey joined me.

He rested his hands on my shoulders, just below the sleeves, and pressed into my back. "You're breathtaking."

I really did look incredible. "This sets a new bar in the little-black-dress department."

"I don't mind." Ramsey dragged his lips up my neck, to rest in the hollow behind my ear.

I met his gaze in our reflection. We were straight out of a fairytale.

"The last few days have been a whirlwind, even by our standards." He moved his hands to my hips, holding me tight. "I want to make sure you're still okay with what we talked about last night."

"The dating again, or the fact that we're explicitly non-exclusive?" My non-answer was a stall, and it shouldn't have been. I should have been able to say *absolutely* without hesitation.

"I was thinking the latter, but now that you ask, both."

I frowned. This was when I should move away, but I didn't want to lose his touch. "I want to be okay with it."

"But you're not."

"I don't know. I'm not *not* okay with it. It feels like it's worth seeing through."

Ramsey pressed his lips to my neck again, letting the kiss linger.

"I feel it's worth it too. When we get home, we'll have some alone time, just you and me. Catch up. Actually date."

I leaned more of my weight into him. It was a lovely suggestion. "When are you going to have time for all of this? Me. Hunter. Alone. Together. Campaigning."

"When are you?" he countered. "Loading Java. The shelter. You're about to move into either a massive remodel or a construction project…"

Touché. "I'll figure it out."

"Exactly." Ramsey tangled his fingers with mine and pulled us from the mirror. "I almost forgot…" He pulled a shoe box from the dresser.

A pair of stilettos sat inside, with straps that wove in a crisscross over the foot and had ridiculously long leather laces.

He set them on the floor. "I'll tie you up."

"Frequently." I laughed and let him slip on the first shoe. He wove the laces up my calf and tied them a few inches below the knee. With the slit in the dress, only a hint would show when I walked. It was the perfect subtle touch.

Ramsey secured the second shoe and stood. "Those, you can keep. In fact, only the necklace has to be returned tomorrow." He held out his bent arm. "Shall we?"

I hooked my hand near the crook of his elbow. "Let's."

Our path took us downstairs and out back, to a set of tents. It didn't look very fancy from the outside, but stepping into one was like moving into an entirely different world. I had no idea how they put chandeliers in the middle of a tent. Crystal lined the tables. There was silk and linen everywhere.

"It's stunning." My awe tumbled past my lips.

"Isn't it, thought?" Hunter joined us. He looked me over, brows raised. "Though… no competition. You look incredible."

"Thanks. Ramsey has good taste."

Hunter nodded. "So much truth there. You ready for the grand tour, to set your mind at ease?"

If the main hall looked like this, I wasn't too concerned about how everything else looked, but I did want to see for myself.

For the next hour or so, Hunter led us through to the kitchen and the staging area, and gave us a sample of the hors d'oeuvres.

It was all amazing. I grasped for words but couldn't find them.

"You okay?" Ramsey asked.

"I can't believe you made all of this happen. Because I asked." It was so much.

He settled his hand on the small of my back. "Of course I did. *You* asked. The cause is as important as it gets as well, but…"

I kept my mouth shut, waiting for him to finish the thought.

Hunter leaned in. "But you are and always have been at the center of his universe," he said softly.

Was that envy I heard in Hunter's voice?

"Ah. Violet."

I cringed at the woman's familiar voice, but pasted on a flat expression before I turned to face her. "Debbie." I extended my hand. "Good to actually meet you." For all I knew, she was a nice person, and the other night really had been an honest mistake.

Her grip was too firm, and her hands hot and dry. Her smile looked painted on. "Same. Will we be seeing a lot of you, going forward?"

"Absolutely." Ramsey spoke before I could consider the appropriate answer.

Why wasn't that my default reply?

"Fantastic." Debbie's smile was as fake as the little rhinestones glued to the roots of my nails. She gave all her attention to Ramsey. "I need to borrow you for some photos. I promise to return you intact when I'm done."

"No problem. I'll catch up with you two soon." Ramsey was cool and professional, as he walked away.

That was new. Sure, he wore a mask in public when we dated, but he never shied away from contact. Small affections. Except the equation was more complicated now. Did that devour Hunter—having to hide who he was? Who they were? I already didn't like it.

"Debbie seems nice." I couldn't think of anything else to say.

Hunter looked at me with surprise. "Really?"

"Shouldn't she?" So I wasn't the only one she rubbed wrong.

"To each their own. I'm not a fan, but she's the best at her job."

"Being pushy, possessive, and bitchy?" I should have kept the thought to myself, but Hunter wouldn't mind.

He laughed. "Getting people elected. Never doubt for a moment that I'm the queen of possessive and bitchy in Ramsey's life." His tone was light, but it tugged on his comment from earlier, about me.

"I'm not trying to move in on your relationship." There were more people now, so I kept my comment vague.

"I know." Hunter steered me to the edge of the room, away from the staff. "I also know when Ramsey sets his sights on a goal, he doesn't stop until he's met it. His sights have never left you."

Ramsey'd moved on, though. "But you and he…" Weren't just close, they also shared bits of their life I'd never be a part of.

"Yeah." Could Hunter read my mind? Or did he recognize both halves of the equation? "And I believe him when he tells me how he feels about me. But there's always a sliver of envy and resentment."

"For me?"

"I assume the question is rhetorical, but yes."

Hunter's statement gripped me hard. I didn't want to be that stumbling block in someone else's relationship. It made me feel dirty and uncomfortable, and the fact that Hunter had been part of the sex made it worse. Had I been fucked a guy who didn't like me? Who didn't want me around? But he'd assured me it was fine. "You said… about the last two nights… Was that…" A lie for Ramsey's sake?

TWELVE

"**W**as I being sincere?" Hunter filled in my unfinished question with a very different response. "Absolutely. That's what you wanted to ask, right? Because you don't assume I'd use you."

Not that I was going to admit to now.

Hunter sighed and leaned his weight against the wall. He tugged on my fingertips and held on as our arms hung between us. "Just because I'm jealous you're a permanent part of my boyfriend's life, doesn't mean I don't like you." His voice was almost a whisper. "I'm a complex individual, capable of feeling more than one thing at once."

"Do you want me to not do this?" Awkward phrasing.

He shook his head. "I would have said so, if that were the case."

"But—"

"First of all, backing away from something you want isn't any more *you* than it is *Ramsey*. You're giving it another try because you feel something for him."

"Yes." I almost felt guilty admitting it.

"And second, you're not responsible for how I feel. You can't second-guess anything outside of what I tell you."

I wanted to argue that I could try. That instinct and reading beyond the surface—seeing the subtext—was necessary in their world.

Hunter pushed away from the wall, pulling me with him. "How about this? I enjoy your company. I like the way Ramsey lights up when you're around. All of that outweighs the jealousy. I mean that. You don't have to dig through it for a double meaning. I'd rather have you around than not. But whether you decide to stay with Ramsey—to hang out with me—has to be based on what you want and what we all agree on. Not on what you think one of us might want that we haven't said."

That was a lot to absorb. "You're so fucking reasonable sometimes."

"I'm reasonable all the time. To a fault. Besides"—Hunter leaned in so his mouth was near my ear—"you're the only woman I've ever enjoyed fucking, and *gods*, do I enjoy it."

I smiled past the flush in my veins. "You're such a charmer."

"Junior League Champion, three years running."

And now we were back to being *us*. I was good with that. The teasing wouldn't silence my inner nagging over his confession, but I appreciated his honesty. "Of charming?"

"Of everything, I assume. I'm the full package, babe."

"You most definitely are."

We chatted until guests started trickling—and then pouring—in. Ramsey still hadn't returned. I recognized a handful of people, but for the most part, this was all new territory. Hunter seemed to know everyone, though. He introduced me to one person after another, always with a one- or two-sentence snippet about them, to help me remember who they were.

"Violet. Hunter." Dottie's familiar call came from behind.

We turned to find Ramsey's grandmother approaching, wearing the warmest smile of anyone in here. She wasn't a frail old granny. She was as tall as Hunter, in her heels, and unlike most of the women here, she wore a tailored suit.

She gave me a quick hug and a kiss on the cheek. "I was so happy to hear your name when Ramsey called me. I've missed you."

"Same." I meant it. I didn't know my grandparents, but Dottie always treated me like a member of the family.

"I'm glad you're here, too." She greeted Hunter with the same hug and kiss. "Where's my Crow?" That was her nickname for Ramsey. She said his parents had missed out by naming one child Ravyn and not naming the other in kind. Especially since, like a crow, Ramsey always insisted on being heard.

Hunter gestured broadly. "Your guess is as good as mine. Publicity photos, I assume."

Dottie raised an eyebrow and looked at me. "Does he realize this is your event, not his?"

"Not his doing." I assured her.

"He's perfectly capable of telling the media hounds *no*." Dottie squeezed my hand. "When you see him, tell him I'm looking for him. And I hope I'll be seeing more of both of you."

A call pulled Dottie away, and Hunter and I were left to mingle again. The shoes Ramsey picked out were amazing, but not for standing in for hours. After I was certain I'd talked to everyone at least twice, I begged off to a quiet corner, to sit for a little bit, with Hunter for company.

That was where Ramsey found us. "Hey." He pulled out another chair across from us, frustration etched on his face. "Debbie set up an interview and didn't tell me first." He looked at Hunter. "Don't worry. I've told her this not-warning-me-first shit doesn't fly."

But he'd done the interview anyway, because he couldn't turn away the perfect press opportunity. I didn't have to ask if that was the case. The fact that he'd vanished for several hours said it all. I almost wished my brain defaulted to *maybe he was* with *someone*. It wasn't a concern, though, even before he was with Hunter. I'd always been more worried about Ramsey's love for the cameras than whether he was fucking around.

"Dottie was looking for you." Hunter didn't sound any more forgiving than I was inclined to be.

"I found her. Thanks. I really am sorry." Ramsey's expression softened.

Hunter nodded. "I knew what I was signing up for."

Somehow, I'd managed to forget. Or at least diminish the memories until they felt insignificant.

Ramsey turned to me. "It's a universal apology. To both of you. How are things going?"

"I met the CEO of Insignia Oil. He stared at my tits the entire time he told me what great taste you had in causes. But at least I wasn't the only one objectified. The woman brought in to fix the Digital Media problems loves Hunter's ass in those trousers."

"I'd have a hard time arguing with either of them." Ramsey's light tone said he wanted to laugh this off and move on. "I really am sorry, Violet. I've been trying to nail this interview down for months, and it just happened to fall tonight."

Hunter's snort was soft. "Go, Debbie."

Ramsey twisted his mouth. Watching them not-argue was almost worse than arguing with Ramsey myself. "And?" Ramsey asked.

"I'm interviewing more people the day after tomorrow," Hunter said and looked at me. "I can fire her if I find someone at least as good to take her place."

That seemed fair. "You dropped almost everything, to make this happen. I can't fault you that one or two things couldn't be pushed, especially if you didn't know about them."

"So we're all good." Ramsey stood.

It seemed that way. I didn't feel any lingering animosity.

"Do you want to get out of here?" he asked.

The idea of leaving definitely made it better. "Can we do that?"

"Things are winding down. The doors close in less than two hours. Dottie has her own *Hunter*, who set all of this up with the staff, and will make sure it all comes down." Ramsey made it sound so easy.

Hunter pushed away from the table and tugged me to my feet. "It's a fair point. I vote for leaving."

"I really feel like I should stay." This was my party. I should be here until the end.

"What are you going to do if you do stay?" Ramsey asked.

"Be here?"

He grabbed my other hand. "Not a good answer. Give me something more concrete than, *I have to help*."

"Isn't that enough?" I didn't have anything else.

"Nope. They've got this covered." Ramsey led us farther from the crowd, toward a rear exit.

We took the elevator up to the same floor as earlier. And stopped in front of the same room. I'd never even thought to ask if we were all staying together, though I hoped so. Would that be an issue if someone dug into Ramsey? People did that in politics, right? Had he reserved three separate rooms, to only use one?

"You two looked good together tonight." Ramsey's comment interrupted my rambling thoughts. "Like you were having fun."

"We were," I said.

"Someone had to keep the guest of honor company, while you were occupied," Hunter said. "Besides, Violet's way better to talk to than most of those assholes."

"Fair point." Ramsey opened the door and let us step past him. "I feel like I should make it up to you." He spun on me the moment we were all inside, pressing me to the wall with his body and trapping me in place.

I knew this look. This posture. The heat and playfulness in Ramsey's gaze. The possessiveness. My pulse raced in the most delicious way, but I was going to poke the bear a little more. Especially after he'd vanished for so long. "No need. Hunter kept me satisfied."

"Really?" Ramsey slid two fingers into my mouth, and I sucked instinctively. "So you don't need me?"

I shrugged, unable to say much with my mouth full.

The sound of fabric tearing filled the room when Ramsey ripped the slit of my dress with his free hand. He dropped his wet fingers to tease my bare pussy. "So I should just let the two of you go at it?" he asked, as he slipped between my folds.

His closeness and touch, and the threat in his voice made me slick with need.

"I should sit back and watch, while he slides his fat cock in your tight, wet pussy." Ramsey dipped his fingers inside me, and I thrust into the penetration.

I couldn't find my voice, as he pumped in me. When he pulled out, I felt empty, and I wanted more. This time he shoved his fingers, slick with my juices, in Hunter's mouth. Watching Hunter suck him clean made me squeeze my thighs together.

"I think I like that idea." Ramsey's voice was low and suggestive. "Letting Hunter spill his load in you. Licking you clean after. Tasting both of you, while you writhe against my tongue.

I was pretty sure that was a submissive kind of thing, but there was nothing submissive in Ramsey's posture or words.

"Would you like that, Taffy? Me, between your legs, sucking Hunter's cum from your pussy?"

I licked my lips and nodded.

Ramsey turned to Hunter.

"I do like fucking Violet almost as much as I like seeing you on your knees," Hunter said.

How was this the hottest thing I'd ever been involved in, when we'd barely crested *foreplay*?

THIRTEEN

Hunter traced his thumb along my jaw, holding my gaze, and our conversation from earlier rushed back.

He dipped his head, lips millimeters from mine. "I meant all the good things. I want you here," he murmured so softly I barely heard him, before claiming my mouth in a soft kiss. Hunter wasn't rough like Ramsey, but his intensity and deliberate movements were their own kinds of arousing. He lay barely-there kisses along my bare shoulders and chest. Up my neck as he removed the necklace and set it aside. He let his nails glide lightly down my spine as he unzipped my dress and let it fall to the floor.

Goosebumps covered every inch of my completely exposed body. I was on display in nothing but my lace-up heels, and *fuck* it made me wet.

Hunter moved to my front, to kiss down my chest, over my hips, along the tops of my thighs. The slow burn was excruciatingly delicious. He unlaced my shoes one at a time, barely touching my calves, and had me step out of the heels so he could set them aside.

The only contact he made was with not-particularly erogenous bits, but I was slick with need, and my chest heaved with each breath of anticipation.

Hunter stood and brushed his lips over mine. He gripped my wrists and raised my hands to kiss my palms. "Can I trust you not to touch anything? Not even yourself?"

"You're asking a lot, but I'll do it for you," I teased. My desire was amplified by Ramsey's silence. I couldn't see him, but he was here watching everything.

Hunter let go of me and put some distance between us. He was as methodical about undressing himself as he had been me. Tie off first and set aside. Cuff links safely on the dresser. Belt whipped out with just enough snap to send a pleasant shiver down my spine. Shirt untucked and unbuttoned.

This was the most low-key, seductive striptease I'd ever seen, and Hunter did it all while watching my flushed and naked body. When he stripped off the remainder of this clothes, he was already hard, his cock thick and long and standing at attention.

He moved in for another kiss, as soft and simple as before, but he pressed closely this time, his bare skin searing against mine.

I reached to stroke his erection as it dug into my stomach, and he clucked.

"You promised no touching." The calm warning in his voice was like fingertips dancing over my skin. He caught my wrists, grabbed his tie, and bound my arms in front of me.

Sexy, but ineffective. "I can still do plenty like this."

Hunter gripped the knot and lead me by the writs to a nearby chair. As he sat he draped my arms over his shoulders, then grabbed my hips, guiding me to straddle his legs.

I felt like I was barely balanced, but he held me steady, guiding his dick between us rather than inside me. He didn't stop me from grinding into him. Letting his cock slip along my wet pussy and tease my clit. The build left me lightheaded. Desperate. If this were Ramsey I'd beg. It may not get me what I asked for, but it would up the ante.

Something told me Hunter had a specific plan, and it would be worth riding out.

He half-prompted half-lifted me enough to penetrate me, gliding in easily and stretching me out. When he was buried inside, he hit that perfect spot that tingled from my toes all the way to my finger-tips. He reached between us to tease my clit while I rocked against him.

I was already near bursting from the build-up, the pressure of his touch, his cock in me, the way he raked his gaze over me, drew me to a fast, hard orgasm. I clenched around him, wanting more.

As he eased away from my clit, he increased the pace, slamming inside me, drawing out my climax until the world was a blur and my head was lost in clouds of pleasure.

Hunter crushed his mouth to mine, nipping my lips and sucking on my tongue. His restraint was gone. He dragged his mouth down my chest, to scrape his teeth over my nipples until it stung, then moved back to my lips. "I won't last long," he murmured between grunts. "You feel too good."

With all this build-up, I'd lost all sense of time anyway. And I was going to beg after all. "Come inside me. Please."

"Fuck. Fuck, yes." Hunter grunted and gripped my hips hard. He pounded me. Harder. Faster. He was close. And then his stuttered gasp told me he'd come too, spilling inside me.

The frantic need tapered, slowing and then stopping as we did. Hunter rested his forehead against my chest, his heavy breathing matching mine.

That was incredible. *Wow.* Anticipation still hummed through me, though. More waited for me. Could I handle more?

And then Ramsey was there, naked and knotting his fingers in Hunter's short hair. Yanking his head back and kissing him hard.

Hunter twitched inside me, even as he was softening.

Yeah, I could take a bit more.

Ramsey unbound my wrists and gently took my hands. "Can you stand?"

I wasn't sure I could talk yet, and I might be wobbly on my legs, but I could manage. I nodded, and let him help me to my feet.

He fisted my hair, yanking my head back and drawing a whimper from me. He kissed me hard, before sucking down my neck to bite the soft skin where it met my shoulder. "Every time you look in the mirror"—he growled—"every time you brush your fingers over that tender skin, remember who put this here."

"What about when it fades?" Thankfully my voice came back in time for me to sass.

"I'll have to replace it before then." Ramsey lifted me into his arms, carried me the short distance to the bed, and set me in the middle, moving pillows to prop up my head.

Ramsey knelt between my legs and forced them apart. His rough kisses up the inside of my thighs said the teasing was done. This was hungry and desperate, and when he dove his tongue into my pussy, my hips bucked and I thrust into his face.

It wasn't only that his touch was enticing—that would leave me panting anyway—but knowing he was tasting Hunter on me. That he was licking me clean like I was the most delicious delicacy.

Ramsey took his time, sucking, devouring, until I was writhing against his face and whimpering. When he glided higher, to wrap his lips around my clit, a fresh shock jolted through me. I screamed when I came, gripping the short strands of his hair tight, and holding him in place until his touch was too much.

Ramsey moved up my body to claim my mouth in a messy, slippery, tantalizing kiss. Goddess, we tasted good.

He pulled back and his fevered gaze met mine, stealing breath I didn't think I had left. He pinned my knees to my chest and pushed inside me. It was a fast, frantic fuck. Skin slapping against skin, moans mingling in the air, and gasps of desire.

I shouldn't have another orgasm in me, but there it was, yanking me into the most delicious oblivion of stars and galaxies dancing in front of my eyes.

Ramsey spilled inside me, gripping the backs of my thighs hard enough to bruise. It was all part of the bliss, and I didn't want to come back down.

When the frantic pace slowed again, then stopped, the haze remained, wrapping up my thoughts while Ramsey covered me with playful kisses. He vanished for a few seconds, and returned to clean me up, tenderly wiping away a mixture of juices.

He fell into the bed next to me, and Hunter joined us. It was one big, warm pile of adoration, I felt theirs for each other as strongly as I felt my own.

I was so glad I'd decided to do this—to give Ramsey and me another chance. I'd missed this feeling. This closeness. Obviously the sex, but everything else too. Ramsey's presence. His company. Pretty much everything about him.

Except for that one thing that drove us apart last time. That thing I refused to name tonight, because in this room I could pretend it didn't exist. As long as tonight lasted, everything was perfect.

FOURTEEN

I wasn't a pass-out-immediately-after-sex kind of person, but it usually numbed my brain. Tonight, though, as I lay curled up with Ramsey and Hunter, I didn't want to fall asleep. This moment was perfect, and in the morning, it wouldn't be.

"Do you turn into a pumpkin in the morning?" Ramsey asked.

It was a silly, poorly-phrased question, but I knew him well enough to recognize the meaning mirrored my thoughts. "Lyn made me take the day off, so I don't have anywhere to be tomorrow.

"We should go be tourists." Hunter didn't sound tired either.

Just the thought of walking made my feet ache. "Not in those heels."

"You have other shoes," Ramsey said. "In fact, I'd bet you packed clothes, even though I told you not to."

"I'm not taking that bet. It would be a poor way to start off a night on the strip, gambling on a loser."

Hunter raised a hand, worked his jaw, then dropped his hand. "I'm not sure that makes as much sense as you think."

"But you got my meaning."

Ramsey sat up, tugging both of us with him. "Let's go. Get

dressed." He was already on his feet. He grabbed his trousers and a tiny box fell out.

"What's that?" Hunter's suspicion amplified my ambivalence.

"It's from Dottie." Ramsey opened the velvet wrapped box to reveal a stunning ring nestled inside. The cluster of diamonds was as big as my thumb. "It's been in the family forever. She wants me to give it to the person I marry." *Person.* His wording may have been gender neutral, but the ring wasn't.

Even if it were, it was only going to fit one finger at a time. "It's pretty." I tried to keep my tone light.

"Uh-huh. Stunning," Hunter said flatly as he pulled on his jeans.

Ramsey snapped the box shut again. "What was I going to tell her?"

I didn't have that answer, but I suspected if we kept this up for any amount of time, we'd need to figure it out.

Hunter took the ring from Ramsey, and shoved it in his pocket. "I'll make sure it gets put in a safe."

We finished dressing, and headed down to the strip. When we stepped outside, the magic that had started to evaporate, the pocket of the world I wanted to stay in as long as I could, was bright and vibrant again. I loved the lights of Vegas at night. I loved that even at one in the morning, there were people everywhere.

And as Ramsey wrapped arms around both our waists, I loved that no one knew us. There were no expectations for how any of us had to act.

"Where to first?" I was happy to just look. Wander. Escape with them. I was even willing to ignore my aching feet to have a few more hours of this.

"You know what I've always wanted?" Hunter leaned into Ramsey, nudging him into me and pushing all of us in a new direction. "Okay, not always, but let's call it that."

I had a few guesses, but no concrete idea. "Chocolate covered strippers?"

He laughed. "Definitely not. This relationship has the perfect number of dicks in it. I want my boyfriend to win me a prize at Circus Circus."

"Ooh, me too." It was childish and ridiculous and I loved the idea.

Ramsey snorted. "Not sure what makes you think I'm capable of that. Hunter's the athlete." He led us through the front doors of Circus Circus anyway.

"Ramsey Miller can do anything he sets his mind to." Right now, I had no doubt.

"Ooh, I like that as a campaign slogan. We should have Debbie put that on all your pages," Hunter said.

We followed the signs that said *Arcade* past slot machines, tables, and restaurants.

Ramsey shook his head. "Fuck Debbie."

"Do. Not." Hunter's voice went hard.

A giggle slipped past my lips without my permission, and I bit it off. We were still joking, weren't we?

Ramsey and Hunter both laughed, and I joined back in. This was like being drunk. Great, now I wanted to drink. No reason I couldn't. No one was relying on me to be sober tonight. We'd already done the *absolutely scorching* sex thing.

We pulled up short in front of the arcade, and the laughter stopped. No lights were on, and the security gates were down.

Hunter pouted. That was adorable.

"Apparently I can't do everything." Ramsey was almost surprised. "Oh, I have a better idea." He looked at Hunter. "You know that thing you said you wanted to see?"

Hunter shrugged. "The life sized Gundam in Japan?"

My laughter was back.

"With Violet," Ramsey said, pointing us back toward the main floor.

Wait. What?

Hunter shook his head. "She'd never."

"I'd never what?"

"She might if we put a few drinks in her first." Ramsey kept talking as if I hadn't said a word.

Which I didn't appreciate. "Given what the two of you just did to me—with me, in me, on me—I don't think I need to be drunk for much."

Hunter sucked in a sharp breath. "You say that."

"You're killing me. You know that, right? I'm dead with curiosity..." I trailed off when we stopped at the edge of a pit, next to a Texas Hold 'em table.

"We'll start small, have a couple drinks, and work our way up." Ramsey finally looked at me. "Hunter thinks you could compete. I tend to think he's right."

I thought that too, when I was winning one hand after another against friends. But Hunter was right about something else. "I'd definitely need to be drunk to believe that. This isn't just for laughs around the kitchen table."

"Nope. It's better." Ramsey pointed me toward a chair. "Five hundred in chips," he said to the dealer.

What? "I can—"

Ramsey crushed his mouth to mine, cutting me off and stilling my thoughts.

I sighed when he pulled away.

"You can." He nudged me until I sat.

I bid the minimum allowed with the first hand. Just me against the dealer. When I won, I left the money on the table for the next round, and Ramsey handed me a whiskey sour to celebrate.

The wins kept adding up until they didn't. I frowned when I lost hand number nine.

Ramsey rested his hand on the back of my chair. "You've still got chips. Might as well play until they're gone or you're tired of the game."

"But the two of you—

"Are fascinated," Hunter said. "Keep playing."

So I did. I lost track of how many hands I won or lost. Sometimes the chip pile was almost nothing, and others it was intoxicatedly large.

The drinks kept coming, too. Until I was making more mistakes than I should be. Until I was giggling more than I should be. Until more people were joining the table, because we'd flown past late night and into early morning.

My head was light and I was giggling maybe more than I should be, but the guy who had joined about five hands ago? Totally bluffing, and I was going to win big.

I put all my chips on the line. Not that I had a bunch left, but if I won, I'd be close to the five-hundred dollar mark I started at.

He flipped his cards, and I frowned.

Nope. He hadn't been bluffing.

"C'mon, Taffy." Ramsey tugged my sleeve.

I sighed in resignation, but it had been fun. When I stepped from my stool, my head swam. Oh, pretty lights. I stumbled and Hunter caught me with a laugh.

"We need coffee." He leaned as much weight on me as I did him as the three of us made our way to the main floor.

Ramsey tapped Hunter lightly on the nose. "See why I love those smarts? That's why he runs things. Always on top of the details."

"Love. That's sweet. You two are an adorable couple." I swayed my hips, and something hard bit into me when I bumped into Hunter. "Is that a… something benign in your pocket, or are you just happy to see me?"

"Only you, Taffy, would use a word like benign while you're completely drunk," Ramsey teased.

"I'm not drunk. You're drunk." I was a little drunk.

Hunter nudged me upright to reach into his pocket. "Oh." His tone went flat. He was holding the ring from Dottie. "I wasn't supposed to bring this with me."

"You know what sucks most about that thing?" Ramsey was suddenly sad. "I'm expected to use that. I can't hand it to Ravyn, who'll look amazing in it no matter who she marries. I'm supposed to fall in love with some woman who doesn't mind the trophy life wife—" his laugh was sad "—wife life, and who we like each other enough to exchange rings." He watched Hunter the entire time he spoke.

I felt bad for him. For them. "When you put it that way, it would be easier for Hunter and I to get married." I meant the comment to be funny. To lighten the mood. I was met with two blank stares. "I know. I'm not saying that. I'm just saying, no one's watching us like they watch Ramsey."

"Must be nice." Ramsey sighed.

Sunlight struck my face, and I pulled the covers over my head to block it out. My head throbbed in protest at the sudden movement.

"Did we… step in front of a train last night? This morning?" Hunter's question was as sluggish as my thoughts.

Ramsey groaned. "What is that beeping?"

"Your phone. Pretty sure," Hunter said.

My gut lurched up, then down, then in a circle over and over. I was less than delicate untangling myself from the men as I raced into the bathroom. As I was emptying the contents of my stomach, my hair was pulled back. Ramsey gently rubbed my back.

When I was spent, I sank back onto the floor, and prayed for the room to stop spinning. Thankfully no one had turned on the lights.

Hunter handed me a glass of water, and returned to leaning against the wall and rubbing his forehead.

Ramsey sat next on my left, mimicking my knees-to-the-chest posture.

"Neither of you look violently ill." I was a little jealous of that.

Hunter rolled his neck. "We drink casually more often than you. But God, it's been a long time since I got black-out drunk."

Ramsey slipped his right hand under my left. "Oh, shit." He held both up.

I looked down to see Dottie's ring on my finger, and my stomach curdled again. "I'm just holding this, right?" Snippets of early this morning trickled back.

"Maybe the two of you should get married. Imagine how much that eases concerns about sneaking around." Ramsey sounded sad.

Hunter's face was illuminated by his phone as he scrolled

through. His string of *shit, shit, shit* got louder the longer he stared. "I don't think you're just holding it."

"I'm not agreeing to this," I argued.

Hunter tilted my chin and met my gaze. "Please? Marry me?"

When we'd gotten to the chapel, they wanted a marriage license, and the courthouse wasn't open yet. Did that stop us?

"Hang on. I know a guy." Ramsey already had his phone out.

I swallowed hard as my gut threatened to revolt again. Holy fuck. I'd married my ex-but-not-boyfriend's boyfriend.

FIFTEEN

This would be fine. Between Hunter and I, we could plan anything, and Ramsey was a master of executing those ideas —even when we were too drunk to think right apparently. This didn't even require a complex plan. "We can get it annulled? Do we even have to do that much? We can just ask the chapel not to file the paperwork? No one but us knows about this."

"About that..." Hunter was still staring at his phone. "These photos? They're on the *Miller for Senate* social media pages.

"How—" Ramsey was on his feet in a flash, bolting back into the bedroom. "*Shit.*" His shout echoed through the entire suite.

I pulled myself up to sit on the edge of the tub. Given the situation, this seemed like a good place to talk about it.

Ramsey returned and handed me my phone. "So, you know that interview I did last night?" He was uncharacteristically sheepish.

"Yes..." I was torn between checking my phone now and flushing it before I saw if I was caught in the fallout. I wouldn't be able to think until I knew, though.

"I saved some photos from the interview to a shared cloud folder. And I saved the wedding photos to the same place, so Debbie shared them."

As Ramsey spoke, I saw the text from Luna. It just said *congratulations.* There was no *!!!* No :) In Luna speak, it said *fuck you.* "No," the word tumbled past my lips. She thought I'd hidden this from her.

"I don't care where you accidentally put them. Debbie had no right." Hunter's anger grabbed my attention again. He jabbed his screen hard enough I wondered if he was cracking the glass, the brought the phone to his ear. There was a short pause. "Save it." He clipped off the word. "No part of my personal life crosses into Ramsey's campaign… I don't give a fuck what you found there… Bullshit. You knew better… No. Don't do *anything* until you hear from one of us." He disconnected and swung his arm as if he wanted to throw the phone. Then pressed it to his hip, as if looking for a pocket.

Right. We were all still naked. I pushed to my feet, legs shaking from uncertainty rather than hangover. "I'm going to get dressed." I walked past both of them. The numbness in my mind was going to vanish any minute now. The panic would set in. I'd rather be wearing clothes when it did.

I yanked on panties. A bra and T-shirt. Jeans.

Numbness was still there. I sank onto the edge of the bed.

Ramsey and Hunter were shirtless, but at least they'd tucked away the dangly bits. How distracted was I that I didn't care if their dicks were hanging out?

"We have to undo this." I was stating the obvious, but I couldn't find anything smarter.

"It's not going to be that easy," Ramsey said.

I started at him as if he were speaking a foreign language. He must be, because the words coming out of his mouth didn't make any sense. "It's very much that easy if Hunter and I both agree. I had a friend go through a no-fault divorce. We sign some paperwork —a lot of paperwork—and we're done."

"Or, we could stick to the plan we made last night." Ramsey was still speaking in gibberish. "The one where this makes things easier."

I blinked several times, until he was a blur, then squeezed my eyes shut and watched the sparkles behind my eyelids. I finally looked at him again. "This is what I'm hearing—*we got drunk and did something stupid. Let's all lie to everyone and tell them we meant it.* Do you remember why you and I broke up?"

"Vividly."

"And you're asking me to lie to the entire world—not just a few cameras—and tell them this entire thing was on purpose. You want me to stay with Hunter because... Why? Not that I dislike you, Hunter, but marriage?"

Hunter puffed out his cheeks and sucked them in when he sighed. "I get it. No explanation necessary."

"That makes one of us, because I need to know why you're not taking my side."

"There are rumors about Hunter and I," Ramsey said. "People are noticing what we are. The rumors are quiet now, but they're getting louder."

I was clearly missing something. "So own it. "Maybe it's time—"

"This marriage isn't a big deal." Ramsey sounded like he believed that. "I'm only asking that you play along until we—"

"Figure out how to spin a divorce?" I didn't appreciate being talked over. "If it wasn't a big deal, you wouldn't be asking me to play along."

Ramsey frowned. "Please, Violet."

I couldn't... What was going on? "If you ask me to do this, to pretend I'm married to someone I wouldn't otherwise choose, for your political career, and I do it? That's the end of us." I hated the words, but I meant them. I wouldn't out Ramsey and Hunter, but what they were asking me to do was a personal line I wouldn't cross just so he could be elected.

"He's not doing it for his campaign." Hunter's voice was quiet. "He's doing it for me."

Was it possible to drink oneself into an alternate dimension?

"Are you sure?" Ramsey asked.

Hunter nodded.

"Fill me in. *Now.*" Before this drove me over the edge.

Hunter pressed his back to the closest wall and turned his gaze to the ceiling. "It took me a long time to figure out my preferences, and I'll be honest, I didn't put a lot of thought into it when I was younger. My parents are religious, and so was the community I was raised in. If you think *hetero* is the default assumption, multiply that by one-hundred and press that weight on a kid whose entire world expected *great things* from him."

I'd seen that before. I'd heard it from more than one of the kids in my shelter. There was what most people experienced just from existing, and then there was being paired with the opposite sex from the time a kid was old enough to walk, for appearances. For *isn't that cute? Isn't he such a lady killer?* Moments.

"Anyway." Hunter sighed again. "Fast forward through a couple of decades of denial that I've told my therapist about so you don't need to hear it, and a series of events that forced the pieces to fit, and I realized I'd been in love with my best friend for as long as I could remember. Telling Ramsey was the most frightening thing I'd ever done."

I couldn't be jealous of that. Not of the pain or sincerity in Hunter's story.

"Fortunately that went well," Ramsey said and squeezed Hunter's hand.

Hunter's mouth twitched in an unformed smile. "He went with me to tell Mom, and that was the second scariest, because she'd always been my biggest supporter." His frown was back. "She dropped a bombshell on me, too. Assured me first she still loved me. All the stuff a parent is supposed to say, but Dad had been diagnosed with Pancreatic cancer less than a week earlier. *This will ruin your father*, she said. *You know how he is.*"

"I'm sorry." My sympathy felt ineffective, but I didn't have anything else to offer.

Hunter tugged his hand free from Ramsey and crossed his arms. "He only had six months to live. Mom begged me not to send my father to his grave knowing his only boy was queer."

Goddess, my heart was breaking for Hunter.

"Dad's still with us, thank God." Hunter's smile didn't reach his eyes. "But he hasn't recovered, he's simply holding on because he's a tough bastard. And every chance my mother gets, she reminds me, *begs me*, to keep the secret just a little longer."

I couldn't believe I was considering going along with this, but the reasons had changed, and I'd heard variations of Hunter's story—seen the negative fallout—too many times to fault him for his decision. "How long are we talking?"

"After the elections, Hunter will be out of the public eye. No scrutiny. No one is going to notice or care if he quietly divorces, and his parents will think he gave marriage a try." *After the elections.* Ramsey wasn't talking about the primaries.

"November?" I couldn't hide my disbelief. "It's *January*."

"November is the worst case scenario, right Ramsey?" Hunter's voice was pointed. He didn't want to be married to me any more than I did him. "We're not going to stop looking for solutions. All I'm asking is that you work with me on a plan that doesn't involve having papers drawn up *right now*."

Money and connections get things done, but frequently not the important things. Hunter's words from the plane bounced into my thoughts. Something neither he nor Ramsey ever did, remind me of the favors they'd done for me in the past. I was going to do this. Please don't let me regret it. "Okay. But the ring?" I held up my hand. "I can't wear this." It was Ramsey's ring for fuck's sake, and now that it was on my finger, I could admit to myself I'd hoped it would end up there. But not like this.

"Of course not," Hunter said quickly. "We'll get you something more appropriate to us."

"You can't tell *anyone* this isn't real." Leave it to Ramsey to drive home how important the facade was.

More pieces of reality sank in. "But our friends…" Shared friends, thanks to Lyn's relationship with Owen and Kingston. "When Hunter and I *break up*…"

"We'll tell them this is why there's been friction between you and me, because of you and Hunter." Ramsey had figured too much of this out too quickly. "But on this trip we talked, and we're all friends again. And then you'll have an amicable break-up."

Which would make it harder to be with Ramsey after. This was such a fucking mess. "I have to tell Luna. I won't lie to her."

"I'm fine with it as long as she will be," Hunter said.

I still didn't know if I was.

SIXTEEN

Talking to Luna, making things right with her, was my top priority. I sent her a text, *We'll talk as soon as I get home. This afternoon. I'm sorry.*

Her reply was instant—*it's fine.*

All lower case. Period at the end. She was furious with me.

Hunter had a slew of messages to sift through, and a lot of them were from family who wanted to know more about this mystery *Violet* woman. The one from his mother said *Not Ramsey's ex-Violet.*

My other texts and voicemails were more happy sounding than Luna's. Various versions of *Congratulations.* Lyn's made my stomach churn all over again. *You should have asked for more time off. It's not a big deal. Take a honeymoon. Enjoy each other.*

No, no, no. I already hated walking away from work with short notice yesterday and today.

We don't want to make a big deal out of things. It's why we kept things secret. As I typed, I shared the message with Hunter and Ramsey. Hunter was doing the same so we knew that we weren't giving anyone conflicting information. This was one reason lying sucked so much.

Lyn replied. *It's okay. Take the days. At least the rest of the week.*

I couldn't. That would devour me. *Please don't make me do that. I'll be there tomorrow, like I'm supposed to.*

Lyn's *Fine. I can't force you to not come in* wasn't as fatal sounding as Luna's, but it still made me frown.

Ramsey didn't have many messages, especially considering the news went out on his accounts. One was from Kingston, asking if Ramsey was okay with Hunter and me, and one was a voicemail from Ravyn. Ramsey played the short snippet for us.

"Really?" Ravyn's tone was flat.

She wasn't buying it. Smart woman.

As we packed, rode to the airport, and got on the plane, the conversation was all *next steps.* Tension tightened in my neck and throbbed in my skull with each new thing I had to do or remember. Any peace I'd achieved over the last day was gone, and I just wanted to curl up in a leather plane seat and sleep for a billion years.

We'd tell people a story that was mostly-true, but still had to open with a lie. Hunter and I had been together for a while, and that was why Ramsey and I clashed. Partly because of my past with Ramsey but largely because he'd hated keeping my relationship with Hunter a secret.

When my barking laugh slipped out at the last bit, Ramsey shot me a withering glare. I shrugged. "At least own it with those of us who know better."

"So, Violet should keep her apartment." Hunter interrupted before Ramsey could counter. "But she'll need to move in with me. We can take our time, but anything you need, I'll have brought in," he looked at me.

"And when people ask *why now?*" I couldn't imagine anyone would buy this story.

"Vegas, especially the party, made the two of you see how tired you were of hiding the truth and keeping your distance, so you let impulse take over." Ramsey's immediate answer wasn't a surprise, but at least his flat tone said he didn't like this arrangement either. "You meant to tell your families and friends first, but someone leaked the news.

Ramsey raked his fingers through his hair. "Fame is fleeting if you're not pursuing it. If your relationship isn't constantly on display, people will forget."

"Our friends and family won't forget. And not many will understand if it looks like I went from you to Hunter and back to you."

The longer we lived this lie, the harder the break-up would be on everyone around us. The harder it would be to find my way back to Ramsey without questions. Yeah, I went years without seeing him, but twenty-four hours ago I was excited to be giving us another try.

"This gets shittier the longer I think about it." Hunter couldn't have echoed my thoughts more perfectly.

"We'll find a solution fast," Ramsey said. "We'll keep our explanations brief. Stay low-key."

I didn't believe it. "You're not capable of low-key."

"I am for the two of you." Ramsey's sincerity would have meant more if this entire conversation were about anything else.

We landed in Salt Lake far too soon for my liking.

Hunter would take me to Luna's, and then back to my place to pack enough to stay at his.

When we reached the house where Luna rented the basement, I asked Hunter to drop me off. "I need to have this conversation alone."

"I get that. I'll be at the coffee shop a few blocks down. Call me when you're ready to go."

I nodded. Before I could climb from the car, he grabbed my hand and tugged me back.

He pressed his lips to my forehead. "I know this is a universally bad idea, but there's no one I'd rather be accidentally married to. We'll figure this out fast."

"Okay." I couldn't think of anything better to say.

I heard his car drive away as I headed up the side path and down the stairs to Luna's door. I knocked, and waited.

There was no answer, but Luna's car was in the driveway. The curtains in the tiny window next to the door moved. Probably not the wind.

I knocked again. Still nothing.

I sent Luna a text. *Please talk to me.*

I'm not home, she replied.

The exchange would have made me smile if I weren't so stressed. *I didn't say I was at your apartment. Please let me in. I'll explain.*

You don't have to explain to me who you love.

As I read Luna's reply, I heard the deadbolt *thunk*. The door opened, but there was no Luna. I stepped inside.

"Congratulations." Luna's flat tone startled me. She swung the door shut behind me. "I would have gotten you a wedding present if you'd ever even bothered to mention you were dating him, let alone in love enough to get married. But I'm sure your boyfriend—husband—will shower you with all sorts of gifts."

"It's not real." Goddess it felt good to say that. I turned to find Luna standing with her back to the door and her arms crossed.

Her frown deepened. "What's not?"

"You have to promise not to tell anyone, and please don't be mad at me. Please." The day's stress weighed me down and made my voice crack.

Luna's expression softened. "I promise I won't tell anyone, and I won't be mad." Her tone was kind. "What's not real?"

I collapsed on the couch. "This all stays between us."

"Always."

I didn't know how far back to go. Too much had happened since that first charity dinner, leaving a smear in my memory. "So... Ramsey and Hunter are a couple, and they don't want anyone to know, because Hunter's dad doesn't know he's gay—bi? Pan?—and Ramsey and I were going to try dating too, not exclusive, cuz of the whole Hunter thing, and all three of us were good with it. And then last night we had way too many free drinks and decided it would be a lot easier to keep all of our secrets if Hunter and I got married and the news got leaked and now we have to figure out how to do damage control and end this thing without too many people getting hurt and Goddess, I am *never* drinking again."

Luna studied me with sympathy. "It's my fault, isn't it?"

"What? *No.* How would this be your fault?"

"Ramsey told you what he did for me, and he forced you to do this in return?"

Apparently my day could get more fucked-up. "What did Ramsey do for you?"

"Oh."

Not the answer I wanted. "Luna?"

She perched on the arm of the couch, feet on the cushion next to me, and stared at her fingers. "I don't know for certain it was him, but I don't know who else it could have been, so I always assumed he did it to win you back."

"*Luna?*" Had I missed the Alice-in-Wonderland-style *Drink Me* label on those drinks last night?

"Remember when I was arrested, and my plea bargain and sentence were so much more lenient than we expected?"

Pieces were clicking for me. "Yeah..."

"My public defender and the ADA implied they'd heard from a friend that I wasn't a risk. They recommended the judge go light on me. That happened two days after you broke up with Ramsey and was exactly the opposite of what I'd been threatened with up to that point."

"You never told me."

Luna finally met my gaze. "I figured you knew. Why would Ramsey do that unless he was using it to win you back?"

I didn't know. Unless he really did it just to help Luna.

"If you want me to keep this quiet, I will," Luna said. "You don't have to explain yourself, I know you have a good reason for it. But I'll help you find a way out. Also"—she ducked her head—"I'm sorry in advance." Her last words were quiet.

I couldn't handle any more surprises today. "What did you do?"

"I called Lyn."

"And?"

"I told her we should throw you a huge surprise party, to celebrate your wedding, and surprise you as a thanks for *your* surprise."

It was no mistake she'd said *surprise* three times. I hated surprise parties.

Luna shrugged. "I was *really* mad." She must have been.

"It's okay. I promise to act surprised. It's no big deal." But it was one more thing to deal with. I sighed. "I don't know what to do. I made these promises, I had a good reason, but… this sucks."

"You could get stuck with a worse guy than Hunter." Luna offered a weak smile.

It was true. "But I don't want to be *stuck* with anyone."

"Do you want to ask the cards?" Luna was already looking at the shelf where she kept her favorite tarot decks on display.

I didn't believe in the mysticism, though there was no reason to stop Luna from doing so. I was willing to admit that more than one of her readings had opened my mind to new possibilities and given me direction I wouldn't have seen otherwise. "Sure. Can we do one of the pretty decks?"

Luna grabbed a manga tarot, and led me to the kitchen table. She handed me the cards. "You know how it works. Focus on your question, shuffle, three times, and then cut the deck and hand it back."

My question may be too vague, but it was the best I had. *How do I get out of this?*

I handed Luna back the deck. "Hunter and Ramsey are together."

"Not anymore apparently." Luna's retort was dry but amused. She looked at me with a frown. "Sorry. Inappropriate."

"Everything about this is. They're not out—obviously—and they're keeping it a secret because of Hunter's family, so I agreed to help them keep the secret, because all I could think about…"

Luna frowned. "Was Eva, I know. And you really don't have to explain."

"I owe you at least that much."

Luna gave me a soft smile, then laid out the cards—one, then three, then one.

I frowned at how many were upside down. That didn't seem like a good thing. And one was The Fool. That had to be bad. "You usually only give me 3 cards."

"This is for clarity. I have a feeling you need some of that."

I really did. "Okay, tell me it's not as bad as it looks."

"It's never as bad as you think it is," Luna said. "And neither is this. The situation or the cards." She pointed to the first one. I knew enough about the images and numbers to know it was the Three of Wands. "The question we're asking this card is, what aren't you seeing clearly? Yes, you've made some choices, you've set things in motion, but that doesn't mean your story is done. You still have time to decide—which you excel at—and write the ending. You still have time to make it good, instead of bad."

"That sounds hopeful." One thing I could always count on Luna for was seeing the silver lining. "But what about him?" I pointed to the upside-down Fool."

"That's you."

I scowled. "Thanks."

Luna gave a light laugh. "It's still not bad. You're the hero of this story, and your intuition will guide you. But you've got a lot of doubt, which is fair. You've let fear take the reins in the past, but you can still follow your heart toward an answer."

That was almost sappy. And left me with a strange blend of hope and confusion. "Give me more." The next card was the Seven of Cups, inverted.

"Yes, ma'am. You're looking for a solution to let you be at peace with the current situation—"

"I'm really not. I want it over with."

Luna looked at me with her eyebrows raised. "Over is still a solution, one of many. And you have *so many* choices here. But you can't have your cake and eat it too. Some are fantasy, some are realistic, and some will destroy you. Don't let your fears and daydreams get in the way of what you're truly capable of."

I didn't have *that* many choices. Stay with Hunter and live the lie, or divorce him and let him deal with the fallout, since the entire world knew apparently already knew about our mistake.

"You're questioning me." Luna didn't sound upset.

"I'm not. The cards, maybe."

She smiled. "You don't *have* to listen, but try not to write it all off too quickly." She pointed to the next one, an Eight of Coins, also upside down. "You can still influence the situation. You haven't lost control."

That was the most comforting thing I'd heard today. "Okay…?"

"This is your chance to master something you're already good at, but it's going to take work, and it's going to hurt. Don't settle. Don't let yourself get dragged into the unfulfilling. Push past the pain points, and you'll be happier and stronger for it."

That just sounded like smart life advice. Or painful life advice. Then again, I was a bit of a masochist.

"What's the last one?" I asked. Besides an inverted Knight of Swords.

Luna sighed and tapped the card lightly with one fingernail. "Probably Ramsey."

That wasn't fair. "I have to be a fool and he gets to be a knight?"

"I already told you The Fool isn't bad. This though… has the potential to be destructive." Her voice got quiet toward the end.

I hated the sound of that. "You said there were no bad answers."

"I said it isn't as bad as it looks. Things can still go wrong if you let them. But this is all about possibility and potential. Your knight is committed to the truth. His truth. He's focused. Driven. He'll do anything to support his own agenda, but he doesn't have a strategy, and he can be rigid and inflexible."

"That doesn't sound like Ramsey at all," I couldn't help my sarcasm.

Luna met my gaze. "You can still influence things. You haven't lost control."

"But it's going to hurt." I'd heard everything she said.

"Probably. But you'll come out the other side better for it."

That other side was far enough away that I wasn't comforted.

SEVENTEEN

Now that I was alone, I needed to think. Clear my head. I walked the few blocks to where Hunter was. Nothing had changed by the time I arrived; go figure.

As I approached I saw Hunter at the back of the dining room, on his phone, tablet set up in front of him. Was it wrong to be jealous that he'd found time to work? Maybe I should be grateful I'd married such an efficient man.

I wanted to roll my eyes at myself.

When I walked inside, he looked up. Like I'd flipped a switch, he set his phone down, and packed up his things as I approached. When I reached the table, he was on his feet, greeting me with a warm *Hey*, and a long, sweet kiss that was a heartbeat too long and too short both at the same time.

"I thought you were going to call me." He still sounded like the Hunter I knew. Kind. Polite.

"I needed to think."

"Did it help?"

I shook my head.

"Do you want coffee? Anything." He asked.

"No. That's the last thing I need." This was going to take some getting used to. Not his behavior—he wasn't acting much differently than I was used to—but my mind asking how I was supposed to act, with every single exchange. It wasn't like there were cameras in here. We weren't on display. But, best to get in the habit now.

"But if you have things to do, I can..." wait? I had a schedule to keep as well. "Have Luna drop me off." Was that the right response?

"Nope. I'm good to go." He wove his fingers through mine.

Holding hands as we walked out to his car was the most awkward thing we'd done so far. He was the gentleman I expected, opening the passenger door for me and making sure I was settled before hurrying to the driver's side.

As he sat, he didn't start the engine.

"Are you sure you don't have more to do?" I asked, hating that this disrupted two afternoons.

"I cleared the rest of my day for you, sweetie."

I winced at the awkward pet name.

Hunter furrowed his brow. "Babe?"

"That's a hard *no*."

He screwed his face up in thought. "My little flower blossom of sticky sweetness."

My laugh slipped out on its own. That felt nice. "Definitely not. Violet is fine."

"Violet it is." Hunter grasped my fingers to kiss the tips, then started the car and pulled us into traffic.

"You can just drop me off at my place," I said. "I have to do a few things before I pack, so I'll take my car. Meet you at your condo later."

"I really did clear my day. I'll go with you."

"I'm not going to run away."

Hunter smiled. "Hadn't considered it for a moment. But the longer you leave me alone with my thoughts, the bigger I realize the rock and hard place are that we're stuck between."

"Same."

"Settled." He navigated afternoon traffic with ease. "Where to first?"

"I need to stop by the shelter and tell the kids to pack, so they can move into the temporary place."

He turned down the next street that took us in that direction. "Done."

I didn't have the strength to argue the escort, and I didn't mind his company, so I settled in for the ride.

When we reached the shelter, I worked for several minutes to gather the kids, and was met with one *give me a minute* after another. I didn't want to let my impatience show, but my brain was ticking and I couldn't help but fidget.

Hunter squeezed my hand. "I've got this." He stuck two fingers in his mouth, and let out an ear-splitting whistle that the neighbors probably heard.

Impressive.

The sound of footsteps echoed back, all rushing toward us, accompanied by several people asking, "What was that?"

Double impressive.

"Is this everyone who's home?" I asked when most of them were gathered. There were only a couple of kids not here.

I was met with nods, but gazes were fixed on Hunter. Time to get this over with. "All right, here's the deal. We need to have some major remodeling done, and you're all going to a new place for just a little bit, while that happens. If you pack up, the bus will—"

"Is this the new ball and chain?" Someone asked

Another voice chimed in. "He's cute for a shackle."

Order was gone.

"Why haven't we met him before?"

"He's famous, right?"

"Does he know any basketball players?"

"Movie stars?"

"Is he good in bed?"

"Hey, Violet, my gaydar is going nuts over your new husband."

A fist squeezed my lungs, and I fought to breathe. I couldn't lie to these kids. "Pack your stuff." My words came out sharper than I intended. "This is all personal." I tried to soften my tone. "You can talk to any of the other volunteers if you have questions. I'll be right back."

I headed outside as fast as I could without looking like I was running.

"Violet." Hunter's voice hit my back.

I couldn't stop. I couldn't breathe. I couldn't—

He grabbed my arm and spun me.

I tried to gulp in the air, but it didn't work. Was this a panic attack? I was going to pass out. What the fuck was I doing?

"Hey." Hunter cupped my cheeks and forced my gaze to his. "Focus on me. Nothing else."

"That's the problem, isn't it?" My reply was shrill. "The focus is on you. Nothing else."

He didn't flinch. "Focus on my face. My voice. Climb out of your head, and live out here for a few."

I did what he said, pouring my attention toward his touch. His calm presence. "I can't do this." I managed to keep my voice steady. "I can't lie to those kids—to everyone. Nothing personal toward you."

"I get it." Hunter studied me. "Do you want me to call a lawyer? We'll tell everyone the truth right now."

If we did that, he'd have to deal with the fallout. Letting Ramsey down. His parents.

"What about... everything?" I floundered for a better word. If I backed out, I let him down, and I reneged on a promise. That was at least as bad as what we were doing now. "Why isn't there a third way to do this?"

"Maybe there is."

"How?"

"If there's one thing dating Ramsey taught me, it was how to keep a relationship private. We don't have to do this in front of the cameras. If you want a third option, an in-between point, that's it. We do this, but privately."

I couldn't see it. "You live a public life."

"*Ramsey* lives a public life. Most of our day-to-day isn't together. You and I will be the same."

But that wasn't the problem. "I don't give a fuck what the public thinks. What about the people we care about? Your parents will want to meet me. Lyn's throwing us a surprise party—surprise by the way, you didn't hear that from me."

"Do you want out?" Hunter's question was sincere, free of any accusation.

That *people we care about* included him. If ended things now, I definitely let him down now. If I didn't, I let other people down later. "I don't know."

"Then work with me to sort out the cleanest way possible to do this."

"Yeah." Did I have a choice? I was a slave to my own sense of responsibility.

I shut off my mind as best I could, to muddle my way through the rest of the conversation at the shelter, then through packing some essentials at my apartment. At Hunter's condo, he showed me the guest room. Told me the place was as much mine now as his, and to make myself comfortable.

I didn't see that happening, but that would be the case anywhere I went, not just here. Since I wasn't ready to unpack, I spent the next several hours doing shelter work. Calling contractors, getting estimates, making sure payments would clear until the money from these two fundraisers hit the accounts.

When Hunter knocked on my open door , my eyes were dry and my neck ached from me sitting on the bed to work, but I'd managed to forget the world for a while.

Now it was back.

"I'm going to pick up dinner," he said. "What're you in the mood for?"

My stomach grumbled at his question. Had I eaten today? "A lot of anything? Whatever you're in the mood for." I climbed from the bed to find my purse and give him cash.

"I was thinking burgers. And it's on me."

Yup, I was definitely hungry. And not letting him carry me. I handed him a twenty.

He refused to take it. "Let me. I'm not asking. I'll be back in a little bit."

"But—"

Hunter turned away.

Rude. I sank onto the edge of the bed as the front door opened and closed. Now what? I'd lost the groove I was in, and now my mind had time to wander.

"Hey." Ramsey stepped into view.

Or not. Every circuit in my brain shut off, leaving me with no idea of what to think or feel. "Hey."

"Hunter said you're having a hard time." He crossed the room to stop a short distance from me.

"Do I assume anything I say to him, you'll hear?" The question came out more sharply than I intended. "It's been a long day."

Ramsey sat next to me, and his leg pressed against mine. "He didn't tell me what you said, just that you were struggling. He's worried, and so am I. I think I'm allowed concern, as your boyfriend." His tone was light.

It still weighed heavily on me. "I'm coping."

"I know what you're—"

"You don't have any idea what I'm going through. Lying to people is your life."

There was no response. I glanced sideways to see him frowning.

"I'm sorry." I hadn't meant my words to be so harsh.

"No. You're right. There are maybe three people in the world who I let see me. What else am I supposed to do?" Ramsey asked.

"You could stop pretending in front of everyone else."

"It's not that easy."

I wanted it to be. There were few things I wanted more than for Ramsey to be able to bury the mask. "What would happen if you did? If you came clean about everything? Or even just some of it? About Hunter." About me.

"My career would be over."

I couldn't deny that was a likely outcome. "If you keep on this path, the persona becomes the rest of your life. You're city council now, and you're already hiding something big. State senate is only a step or two from DC. Any secrets you have at that point, will have to be buried so deep they'll devour you."

More silence.

I sighed. "You're tired of hearing me say it, and I'm tired of saying it."

"I'm scared." His voice was so soft, I wasn't sure I heard him right.

I wasn't going to ruin the moment by asking him to repeat himself. I held my breath, not wanting to miss what came next.

"This is who I am," Ramsey said.

"Not to me. Not to Hunter."

"This is what I've worked for. It's the thing I know. It's how I make a difference in the world."

"If you want to help, what you did in Vegas? That's help. Not empty promises you may or may not be able to keep, but bringing funds and positive attention to places that need it."

He shook his head. "But that's not where I am right now."

My shoulders slumped. Here we were again, in the same place as when we'd broken up. There was less yelling this time, and I was more willing to admit it was going to hurt like hell to lose Ramsey. But it had been a day, and I was already cracking. "What I told you in Vegas, that if you ask me to do this…"

"That it's over for us." He sounded resigned.

"And I know I made this choice. I'm here because I said I would be, and I'll see things through with Hunter. But…" My throat ached. I didn't want to reach for the next words. Thinking them, vocalizing them, would make them real.

Ramsey twisted on the mattress and placed a finger under my chin. "I love you." Sincerity bled from his words.

And it almost tore my heart apart. Of course the bastard would pick now to say that. "I love you too." So much. "But the life you live? I can't. I can't sign on for years or even months more of lies. Even when the wedding issue is fixed, there are still more. Will you keep pretending you're single? Finally come out? Tell the world you're with one of us and ask the other to hide? I can't do that.

Hunter deserves better that that. I don't have a problem with you seeing both of us, but the secrets? I can't be a part of that."

"I'm not going to stop trying to make things right."

I shook my head. "Only one thing makes this right."

"There has to be a compromise, and I'm stubborn." Ramsey dropped his hands to my hips and tugged me toward him.

I clenched my jaw. "You think now is the time for sex?"

"No. But let me hold you for a little while."

I wanted to push him away, but I also wanted to climb into his lap and never leave. I leaned into him and pulled his arms around me. I wanted to cry, but the tears weren't there. Why did this have to hurt so much?

EIGHTEEN

Getting up early, so I could open the cafe, was the most familiar and normal thing I'd done in days. Stumbling bleary-eyed through unfamiliar rooms, and a shower... not so much.

My plan was simple. I'd be out of here and on my way to work before Hunter woke up, and I'd send him a text letting him know I'd be home late, which would happen even if I weren't avoiding him. No need to for awkward conversation. For pretending I didn't ache over my break-up with Ramsey last night.

The pit in Hunter's eyes last night, when I told him why I'd rather eat somewhere they weren't, had been bad enough.

I liked plans, and this one was straightforward.

Except I had to pass by the kitchen to get to the front door, and the light was already on.

"Coffee?" Hunter asked.

I steeled myself—now was a good time to practice for the rest of the day—and turned to find him leaning against the far kitchen counter, next to the coffee maker. "I'll grab coffee at work." My tone was light and pleasant.

"You doing okay?" he asked.

"I'm good." I was so, so not good.

"No. Really. How are you?"

I sighed. "We're not performing for anyone in here; you don't have to do this."

He raised an eyebrow. "Are you talking to me, or yourself? You know I genuinely care."

"I do. I just…" Another sigh. I'd have to get that under control too. "I'm running on determination and if I stop, I'll stall."

"You have to process."

I leaned against the door with my arms crossed, more to hold myself in than to keep him out. "If I do, I'll crumble. I won't be able to stop fixating on how fucked up this all is."

"All right." Hunter sounded as unhappy with the conversation as I felt. He grabbed a travel mug from the counter next to him. "Take the coffee anyway? I don't drink mine the same way you do, and it would be a shame to dump this." He crossed the room to hand me the stainless steel.

Warmth sparked in my stomach, and a resigned smile slipped out. I took the mug from him. "All right. Thank you. By the way, I'll be home pretty late tonight."

"Is it something I said?" His laugh was weak.

"No. I promise. Even if I weren't here, doing"—I waved my free hand in lieu of words—"I'd have to work late. After Lyn's, I have a bunch of shelter work to do, and it's easier from there."

"That's fair. Be safe."

I nodded. It felt odd walking out the door. It wasn't like I was going to give him a goodbye kiss or anything, though.

When I got to work, I found Lyn in the kitchen, as was typical in the mornings. She'd already been up for hours, baking for the day. She looked surprised to see me. "I kind of hoped you'd call in, and take me up on that offer for time off."

"Do you even know me?" It was a struggle to keep my teasing from sounding forced.

Lyn arranged croissants in a neat row in a wire display basket. "You just got married."

Right. "And we're planning something big"—it wasn't really a lie, the big thing was just more like *divorce* than *honeymoon*—"but he has obligations, I have things I can't let slide. Trust me, things are still intense at home." Suffocatingly.

Lyn handed me the basket. "Hunter always struck me as a good guy."

"He really is wonderful." The truth was so much easier than bullshit. "I'm gonna prep to open." I walked back into the main shop, placed the croissants on display behind glass, and got to work.

The rest of the day was long, but uneventful, and I was worn out when I got *home* that night. The small lamp left on in the living room, even though Hunter had gone to bed, made me smile. I shut everything off, and as I climbed into bed, I let exhaustion take over my mind.

The next morning, Hunter was up and waiting, with coffee, when I got to the kitchen. I wanted to tell him he didn't have to do this for me, but when I'd dated Ramsey—my heart ached at the name—Hunter had always been up this early.

"Still a morning person?" I asked lightly. "And thank you." I took the coffee he handed me and sipped cautiously. Perfect temperature.

"I am until someone makes me stop. And, sorry to get all business on you first thing in the morning…"

My sliver of disappointment wanted a friendly, no-pressure chat, but *business* was probably better. "It's fine."

"Will you be home for dinner tonight?"

"Is there something on the calendar? Are we expecting guests?" I hadn't been told and forgotten. Had I? Dinner with his mother was tomorrow night, but I'd set aside time to dread that after work.

"The question is exactly what it is." Hunter almost looked amused. "If you're going to be here, I'll plan on enjoying your company."

Oh. There was that spark of warmth again, bigger this time. "That sounds nice. I'll be here."

My mood was lighter than in a few days—charcoal instead of pitch black, but I'd take it—as I headed to work. Once there, things ran the way they should. The way they always had. It was soothing to fall into the familiar routine, including my weekly, mid-morning meeting with Lyn to talk schedules and ordering, and just check in.

Elle, one of the bakers Lyn had finally hired as backup, on Owen's insistence, poked her head into Lyn's office. "Ramsey is here for you."

His visiting wasn't unusual—though the knot that formed in my stomach at his name was tighter than I was used to. He was a fan of the chocolate croissants, and stopped by a lot to chat with Lyn.

She looked at me as she stood. "Do you want to hide back here? I don't know how things are with—"

"Sorry, no," Elle said. "He's here for Violet."

My blood ran hot and cold at the same time. Pretty sure that wasn't good for me.

"I can tell him you're busy." Lyn looked concerned.

So, so tempting. I stood anyway. "It's okay. I've got this." When I saw him, the way my feet threatened to stop without my permission, maybe I didn't have it after all. A pang of hurt and longing gripped me. When we'd gotten back together, I had a fantasy I hadn't dared vocalize even to myself. That if he and I made things right, if we were back together, when he came in here he'd greet me with a long kiss, and no one would bat an eye.

That wasn't happening.

His smile was a poor substitute for more, but I'd take it. I stopped close enough to be polite, but far enough to try to keep temptation at bay.

"Hey." His greeting was as casual as his posture.

Fucking bastard. Would it be worse if he could hide how this was impacting him, or if his stance was genuine. No, I knew better. He missed me too. "Hey." I couldn't fake it as well as he did.

"Can we talk someplace?"

Out here is fine. That was what I wanted to say, so I wasn't sure why, "The storeroom?" came out instead.

He nodded, and followed me. The room was barely big enough for two rows of shelves, and freezer against the back wall. I had no idea why I locked the door behind us.

Ramsey raised an eyebrow. "If this is your office, I need to talk to Lyn about giving you an upgrade." His tone was light.

"What, you don't like the place?" I swept my arm to gesture to everything. "I decorated it myself. And I have fast access to the chocolate stash." I patted the freezer.

"I *am* a little jealous of that. I— Oh my God." Ramsey's gaze stalled on the top of the shelf dividing the room. "Is that the new Wing Zero Custom?"

So freaking adorkable. Damn it. "They came in a week ago. Lyn was supposed to tell you. I asked her to make sure she got you an extra one when she placed her order." I sat on the freezer. This should keep some distance between us.

He stepped closer, between my legs, and settled his hands on my knees. "You're sexy when you feed my Gunpla fascination."

My entire body lit up like a Christmas tree, and my heart hammered against my ribs. It would be so easy to say I didn't mean the other night. To take it all back. He'd accept that. "I'm a married woman now." My retort came out far flirtier than I intended.

"To my boyfriend. And your husband knows I'm here." Ramsey slipped even closer.

The conversation with Luna popped into my head, maybe as a way to distract me from Ramsey, or simply my brain's screwed up sense of humor. "Do you remember when Luna was arrested."

"You're kidding, right?"

Fair point. "She says someone pulled strings to get her a reduced sentence. She told me that yesterday. Do you know anything about that?"

Ramsey twisted his mouth. "Should I?"

"She thinks it was you. Was it?"

There was a long pause before Ramsey said "Yes."

"Why didn't you ever tell me?"

"I did it because it was the right thing to do. Luna didn't deserve that situation and I could help. I didn't tell you because I didn't want you to feel obligated for… anything."

"Thank you. A few years late, but thank you." I poured the sincerity into my words. While secrets were status quo for Ramsey, he loved recognition as much as he did anything. It must have devoured him to keep this to himself.

"Now that we have that out of the way…" His voice was low, with a hint of growl underneath. He tilted closer, angling his mouth toward mine. "I miss you, Taffy."

I swore my heart paused. It took all of my willpower to plant my palm on his chest and stop him. "Nothing's changed."

He sighed and straightened, but didn't move away. "How are you?"

"Fine."

"No, really."

"Perfectly all right. I'm still keeping everyone's secrets."

He traced his thumb along the seam of my jeans, near my knee. Did he know he was doing it? "This is me you're talking to. No secrets in here, and I'm worried about you."

"Did you bring me a solution that doesn't force you and Hunter out before he's ready? That doesn't hurt anyone we know?"

"I'm working on something, and those aren't just words. But everything I've come up with so far is going to hurt Hunter."

Aside from stepping out of the spotlight and letting us end things quietly. But that wasn't Ramsey, and it never would be. I was okay with that, until the fakeness came into play.

His hands inched higher on my thighs. "Ravyn stopped by my office to tell me she knows this entire wedding thing is bullshit."

"That sounds like her." I let a tiny smile slip out.

"Kingston keeps asking if I'm all right with losing you."

Odd. I barely knew Kingston, and really only through Lyn. He hadn't lived here when Ramsey and I dated, so the first time I met him and Owen was when they tried to buy Lyn's shop. "Why would he think you aren't?"

"Because he's heard me talk about you." Ramsey made it sound like the most obvious answer in the world.

"Ramsey…" I was short on protests or the desire to use them, but I needed to.

"I know. It still doesn't change anything." His hands were on my hips now. "I had to see you today. I had to tell you..." He sighed and pressed his forehead to mine.

I couldn't pull way, and I struggled to find my voice. "Tell me what?"

"Everything. So much more than I can put into words."

Like the other night, when I'd told him we were done, I didn't want to pull away. "I have to get back to work." Such a simple phrase for something that was so hard to say.

Ramsey let go and stepped back. "Yeah. I'll see you around."

I sat on the freezer for who knows how long after he left. It didn't help me collect my thoughts any. I finally hopped to the floor and tracked Lyn down in her office to finish our meeting.

"Close the door," she said.

Odd request, but I did and settled into the seat across from her desk.

"Do you remember the remodel?' Lyn flipped her pen between her fingers. She was staring at her computer.

"The one where you gutted half the store and expanded? Vaguely."

"And that I had cameras installed almost everywhere except the kitchen, for insurance reasons."

"Of cour— Oh." Reality slammed into me. Including cameras in the storeroom.

Lyn frowned. "Yeah. Oh."

She'd seen me cuddled with Ramsey. "It's not... I mean... Hunter knows." I was so bad at keeping these secrets.

"It's not my place to tell you how to live." Lyn's expression softened. "To say what kind of relationships you should or shouldn't have. As long as all of you are on the same page, I don't have to worry about who I let down by either telling or keeping the secret."

I didn't know what to say, and I hated that.

"You're not just an employee, you're a friend," Lyn said. "I want you to be all right."

"Me too."

"As all right as those people around you."

I clamped my jaw shut again. It was a convoluted way to say it, but she didn't understand, the people around me came first. I wasn't ready to get into that argument with Lyn.

She tapped her pen against the desk. "I don't bring up that I saw you two to make things weird. It's a warning. If you're hiding something, and I found out in just a few days, other people will too."

"I know."

"Do you? Owen and Kingston work hard for their anonymity, and it *is* work. Ramsey. Well…"

Ramsey was exactly the opposite.

"Trust me, I'm very aware." But this drove home the point.

NINETEEN

I actually slept Saturday night, though it was more a collapse of exhaustion than it was a peaceful thing. I woke up early Sunday, despite not having to open the café, and I was grateful to leave half-formed dreams behind of letting everyone around me down. Of our worlds crumbling when the truth came out.

I sleepwalked my way through a shower and dressing. My schedule was busy, even with the day off from one job. The first contractor was coming by the shelter today to start ripping out carpets and any Sheetrock with mold damage.

Hunter was in the kitchen already. I shouldn't be surprised at this point.

"I'm not interrupting your morning moments of peace, am I?" I rarely had enough time in the morning to stop and enjoy the solitude, but when I did, I wanted solitude.

"Not at all." He slid a mug of coffee and a bowl of oatmeal across the counter. "I heard you in the shower, so I made extra breakfast."

I had to admit, the best part of being married to Hunter was that it was Hunter. I settled on a kitchen stool. "If you're not careful, I'll get used to this. You're spoiling me."

"Nothing wrong with that." His smile was easy. Calming. Didn't reach his eyes.

I stalled with a spoonful of oatmeal halfway to my mouth. "What's wrong?"

"Trying to decide when it's best to break the news."

I dropped my spoon and it clattered against the edge of the bowl. Fortunately it didn't send oatmeal flying, but I wasn't sure that was a priority. "Probably best to just tell me at this point."

"I talked to Mom a few hours ago. They've asked her to stay another month, and she wasn't able to get through until now to tell me. She can't make dinner tonight."

Relief flooded me. "I'm... sorry?"

"No you're not."

At least I was consistent and obvious. "I'm sorry it seems to have you upset."

"I'm ambivalent. I didn't want to look her in the eye and play this game, but whenever she stays out longer than planned, I worry about her. She pushes too hard for others sometimes—she's a lot like you."

Except I'd never ask my child—only son or not—to lie to their other parent about their sexuality, simply to keep the peace. "Hmm."

"Don't judge." An edge slipped into Hunter's voice.

"I didn't say anything."

"You think very loudly sometimes."

I didn't have a response so I shoved some rapidly cooling oatmeal into my mouth instead. But it wasn't really a lot to chew around, so the bite didn't take long. The mood in the room had cooled too, so I might as well ask what I was thinking. "When we do have dinner with her, are we really going to sit through an entire meal and lie to her? What happens when this ends? Will you and Ramsey hide things forever? How will she feel when she finds out otherwise?"

"I don't know. I don't have any more answers than you."

Silence settled between us. It wasn't awkward, but I still had a desire to fill it with anything to keep my mind from tripping over all the *what if* scenarios it was coming up with. Problem was, those same topics were the only ones I could think of.

I thanked Hunter for breakfast and headed to the shelter. Deconstruction turned to scheduling more appointments, turned to making the budget work with fresh damage found under the carpet.

When my phone buzzed with a new text, I realized it was after eight at night. No wonder my eyes were dry and my neck ached.

You all right? The message was from Hunter.

New guilt. I should be much better at processing it, based on the last week. *I'm fine. Just lost track of time. I'm sorry if I made you worry.*

It's okay, as long as you are.

I am, I wrote. *I'm not sure when I'll be home, though.* It was both nice and a new kind of stress having someone at home waiting for me.

I got home a little before midnight. Tomorrow was going to be a long day. Hunter's bedroom door was closed, but he'd left a lamp on for me in the living room.

Sleep sucked that night, and I didn't hit that sweet, deep-slumber part until right before my alarm went off. I hit *snooze* far more times than I should have, and panic mingled with the lingering traces of bad dreams as I got ready.

As I was stepping into the shower, my reflection caught my attention and I spun. The person who stared back had dark circles under a glare of accusation. The Violet in the mirror almost screamed with accusation.

I shoved the self-loathing down and finished as quickly as I could.

Hunter was in the kitchen—at least something was pleasant about my morning. "I wasn't sure if I should wake you." His voice was kind. "This will have to do instead." He handed me a coffee to go.

The simple kindness clawed at my throat and tears pricked my eyes. Was I really getting emotional over coffee? I forced a smile. "Thank you."

"I can tell it's a bad time to ask, but you'll be more upset if I don't."

My insides clenched. "What's up?"

"Are you still up for the fundraiser tonight?"

I forced out a laugh, but I couldn't believe I'd forgotten. The reminder was in my calendar that I hadn't had time to check this morning, and I hated that the event slipped my mind. Those stupid, useless tears were threatening again. Goddess, I needed sleep.

"Of course." I smiled too brightly. Faking it for strangers would be a lot easier than with our friends.

I made it through the day thanks to heavy doses of caffeine and sugar, but I was ready to crash when I got home. It would have to wait. A new dress hung on the back of my bedroom door. Nothing as elegant as I'd worn in Vegas, but it was still stunning.

If I were less tired, I might be amused that Hunter and Ramsey were better at picking dresses for me than I was.

Events like this—fundraisers for whatever candidate Ramsey or his family was schmoozing at the time—had always been my least favorite part of dating him.

I doubted that being at one tonight, watching him from across the room as he smiled and laughed and flitted from person to person, would make the evening any better.

The instant we stepped from the car in front of the country club, even as the valet was pulling away, Hunter was by my side, offering his arm. I hooked my hand in the crook of his elbow, and he covered it with a long, tender kiss on the lips.

It may have been for show, but it felt natural.

When we stepped inside, Ramsey was the first person I spotted. The way Hunter's hand tightened over mine, I suspected I wasn't the only one. He leaned in close, mouth near my ear. "You got this?"

I nodded, fake smile in place as if he'd just whispered the sweetest thing.

So many people congratulated us that I lost count. I smiled through every guy with a version of *you got yourself a real looker* and every woman saying *so sad you're off the market now* imaginable.

As soon as anyone turned away, it was a different story. I'd learned a long time ago that listening to the background chatter at these things was toxic at best. Tonight it was impossible to ignore the murmurs.

Do you think it's real?

It won't last.

I always thought Hunter Sorenson was… you know.

I was tempted on several occasions to pull away and tell people exactly what I thought of their gossip. But Hunter's subtle grip kept me in place, and reminded me at the same time I wasn't alone in this.

Seeing Ramsey was still the hardest though. His handshake for Hunter and kiss on the cheek for me were the most fake things ever, and he made both look more genuine than anyone else here.

Then Ramsey was swept away again. Each time he tried to approach us the rest of the night, someone stepped in his path.

Turned out I still hated these parties.

The ride home was quiet. I didn't know if Hunter was respecting my exhaustion or if he was as conflicted about the evening as me.

When we stepped inside, I muttered, "Good night," and turned toward my room. Being so close to security, to solitude, was shattering the walls I'd had up all day. The reinforcements I'd put in place for this evening had already splintered.

"Violet." Hunter's voice was weak.

I couldn't. I walked into my room without looking back. With the door closing me off from the world, everything inside me crumbled. Everything I needed to do, everyone I needed to help, look out for, lie for, all pressed in on me until I couldn't breathe.

I stripped off my dress, and grabbed a nightshirt.

The fist around my chest clenched tighter.

I sank to the edge of my bed before my legs could give out. The thigh-high stockings and lacy underwear weren't me. Not like this. What was I doing?

Tears stung my eyelids, and I scrubbed them away with the back of my hand. I tugged on my shirt. Yanked off the first stocking.

A sob tore from my throat, and it loosed the tears I was fighting. And then I was wailing and gasping for air.

"Violet?" Hunter pounded on my door.

I bit the side of my fist to muffle myself, but I couldn't stop crying.

"I'm coming in," Hunter said and walked into the room. He sat next to me on the bed, and wrapped his arms around me. The comfort was perfect, which made me cry harder.

He was the one thing about this entire situation that didn't suck, and getting away from him was the one thing that was going to make it better.

He didn't ask what was wrong. Not that I could have paused long enough to answer. He simply held me until the tears were dried up, and my throat was raw and my eyes ached.

At some point, he tucked me in, but I didn't want him to leave. I grabbed his arm and tugged him next to me under the covers. I don't know when or how I fell asleep, but when I woke up Hunter was still wrapped around me, protecting me.

I opened my eyes to find him watching me.

His eyes crinkled at the corners when he smiled. "I promise I'm not staring at you while you sleep, like a creeper. I just woke up."

"You say that…" I wasn't in the mood to laugh, the weight of everything hadn't lifted while I slept, but he was making me feel better. "Think we've found the latest sleep fashions?" I gestured down to me in my T-shirt and single stocking and him in a button-down with boxers.

"Something tells me Paris won't be knocking down our door."

"They're missing out."

Hunter brushed a strand of hair from my forehead. "Do you want to talk about it?"

"I really don't have anything new to say." I was sick of sounding like a broken record every time I spouted off *we need to fix things*, and nothing was going to get better if the situation stayed the same.

TWENTY

It was easier to let the days blend into each other, to run on auto-pilot, than to let my mind wander. If I focused on the tasks I had to do—cafe, shelter, home, repeat, I could get everything done that I needed to, without breaking.

As Thursday at the cafe wound to a close, concern set in. Tomorrow was supposed to be a cafe day off, but Lyn had asked me to come in for a few hours in the afternoon to help with inventory. I'd been torn between jumping at the chance to stay busy, and the fact that I hadn't had time to go visit the kids from the shelter all week. The other volunteers were available in the new place, but I missed the kids.

Keeping distracted and helping Lyn had won out.

When I got back to Hunter's and stepped inside, he and Ramsey were on the couch, sitting close heads bowed together.

They both looked up at the same time.

I hated that I'd interrupted whatever they were doing. I hated even more than seeing Ramsey ached so much.

"I didn't mean to interrupt," I said quickly, before either of them could pick the direction of the conversation. "I'll be in my room."

"You don't have to scurry away. It's your house too." Hunter was kind.

But it wasn't really.

"Stay, Taffy." Ramsey managed sweetness and command perfectly with those two words.

And I couldn't do it. Not here. Not where I was should be able to let down my guard and relax for at least a little while. "Why? So Hunter and I can practice being the perfect couple for an audience? Do you want to make sure we're cuddling and kissing properly?" The words fell with more exhaustion than venom.

A shadow passed over Ramsey's face. "I really don't. Not when I'm not a part of it."

"Stay, please." Hunter's request stopped me from tumbling down the rabbit hole of examining Ramsey's response. "Keep us company. You're not intruding."

The longer I lingered in this room, the harder it was to make my feet carry me away. I wanted to spend time with them. I'd been enjoying Hunter's company, and I'd never been good at turning away from Ramsey. Even the fact that I'd ended things with him before we ever really restarted didn't make it any easier to ignore how I felt.

"All right." It was easier to say than I wanted it to be. I headed toward the chair next to them.

Hunter stood. "I'll grab you a drink." He approached me and planted his hands on my hips to make sure we didn't collide. The assisted side-step put me closer to Ramsey, who wrapped an arm around my waist and pulled me to sit on the couch next to him.

The entire thing happened so fast I barely caught every step. I let out an amused huff. "I'd be upset that the two of you just handed me off like a football, if that hadn't been the smoothest thing ever."

"That's the point," Ramsey said.

I rolled my eyes, but I wasn't interested in relocating. It was comfortable next to him.

Hunter returned quickly, and handed me a glass with ice and orange juice.

I didn't know anyone who drank juice this way, especially at night, but it was exactly what I was in the mood for. "Thank you." I took a drink, and set the glass on the coaster Hunter had provided. "I really didn't mean to interrupt."

"You aren't," Ramsey assured me. "In fact, we were just talking about you."

"That makes me nervous."

Hunter shook his head. "Because Ramsey's being an asshole with his phrasing. Remember the first time you and I met?"

There was no way I could forget that. "I thought I was going to die of embarrassment." It was when I started dating Ramsey. Hunter was supposedly gone for the weekend, so Ramsey and I were fucking in the living room of their apartment. Hunter had canceled his plans, and walked in on us.

"Nothing to be embarrassed about." Hunter settled on my other side, sitting sideways so his shin rested against my thigh and he faced us both.

"I'm not now." Not with Hunter. I couldn't even say when it became as easy for me to be nude—more—around Hunter as it was around Ramsey, but I had no issues with it now. "I was then. Why were you talking about me?"

"I was so happy to finally meet the elusive *Taffy*. The instant I saw you, I knew I was right about you being good for Ramsey."

Ramsey shifted forward, to perch on the edge of his seat. "You never told me that."

"Was it my ass or tits that helped you draw that conclusion?" I was teasing, but given those were probably the first parts of me Hunter had seen, I was curious.

Hunter smiled. "It was the fact that you were in our apartment. You were the first partner he'd brought home in more than three years of living together."

"Oh." Realization sank in. When I'd met Ramsey, he hadn't even given me his real name the first night. It didn't take me long to figure it out it was because *Ramsey Miller* was as much a brand as a name, and he planned to be a much bigger one going forward, and the last thing he needed was to earn a reputation as a guy who had a propensity toward orgies. "But you said… you'd already drawn conclusions about me. What first made you think I'd be good for him?"

"When he washed that shitty black dye out of his hair." Hunter winked.

"*Hey*." Ramsey was indignant. "I'm a sexy fucking brunette."

"You're sexy. Period," Hunter said. "As a brunette… you're just trying too hard."

I liked the playful exchange. The honesty was a welcome relief and the ease of the banter was familiar and comforting. "I've always been partial to your natural auburn," I said to Ramsey.

"He lightens it because blond polls better."

"*Ha*." I wasn't surprised by Hunter's confession. "I so called that."

Ramsey clenched his jaw, but amusement danced in his eyes. "Not sure I like being ganged up on this way."

"Violet never complains about being double teamed."

I flushed at Hunter's words. "Not once. I think you might like it if you give it a try, Lollie." That was the name Ramsey gave me the night we met. He'd also given me a horrible pick-up line to go with it. I hadn't called him that since, but tonight it seemed appropriate.

Ramsey's growl was almost primal, and in a flash he straddled my legs and pinned my wrists to the cushion on either side of me. "I think I'm happier being on top." He was as much playfulness as threat.

"You sure?" I teased. "Because that's the perfect position for Hunter to ride your ass."

Ramsey raised an eyebrow. "You'd like that, wouldn't you?"

Now that the images were in my head, both men naked, the groans each of them made when they were turned on, and Hunter entering Ramsey from behind… Desire pulsed between my legs. "Yeah, actually."

"I don't top." Hunter nudged Ramsey's shoulder.

Ramsey let me go and rolled back into his own seat, landing with a chuckle. "Life is a lot better with all three of us."

Such a simple statement, but it threatened to send me into a spiral of regret and doubt. I didn't want that.

"Remember that weekend at Timpanogos?" Hunter's question kept me here.

I was happy to linger in the pleasant memories. "When you made me watch the entire *08th MS Team* series?"

"*Made* you?" Ramsey laughed. "What we *made* was your world a brighter place, for the experience."

I couldn't argue that, but it had more to do with the company than the show. "It's idealistic."

"Your face is idealistic," Hunter said.

"*Gee, Ramsey.*" He'd summoned that fake-Violet voice. "*Thank you for improving my life forever with Gundam.*"

This was so ridiculous. And twice as fun. "I've got much better curves than a Zaku."

Hunter shook his head. "No one has more perfect curves than a Zaku." He managed to say it with a straight face.

"They're perfectly symmetrical. Fantastic for engineering," Ramsey agreed. "But I prefer my people with a little softness."

I looked between them with disbelief. "I can't believe you're comparing me to a giant robot. And they're not even the good guys."

"But you still come out on top," Ramsey said as if it were obvious.

I couldn't help but take the conversation back a few minutes. "Unlike Hunter."

"Nice." Hunter laughed.

"At the time you said you enjoyed the show." Ramsey was still in serious mode.

I had a counter he'd appreciate. "Iron Blooded Orphans is a far more poignant moral examination of war."

Ramsey stared at me in surprise. "We never watched that with you."

"You watched without us." Hunter sounded just as shocked.

"All of it. Every single thing Gundam I could find, translated or not." I'd also made sure my favorites were available for the shelter.

Ramsey's smirk was all self-satisfaction. "We converted you."

But that spiral of sadness was back without my permission.

Tugging my heart and weighing me down. "I watch them because they remind me of you." I wanted to sound light and playful, but reality was back, slamming into my heart. "I don't want to be without you." But I couldn't be with him—them—either. I couldn't finish the thought out loud. "I'm gonna head to bed."

Ramsey grabbed my wrist. "Taffy."

I jerked out of his grip, unable to look at him.

"Violet?" Hunter was softer.

I couldn't do this. I walked away.

I bypassed the kitchen the next morning, and headed straight to the shelter without stopping to see Hunter. It wasn't that I didn't want to talk to him—it was the opposite. If I stopped and chatted, I'd remember the fun. I'd regret what wouldn't happen with Ramsey. I'd hate the reminder that this thing with Hunter wasn't real.

The last thought hit like a fist to the gut. It should have been an aftershock—no real impact—but I felt the sadness there as much as everywhere else.

Fortunately, there was more than enough work at the shelter to keep me busy. Administrative needs hadn't stopped for construction, and I had stacks of invoices, media requests, and messages for other various things to sift through.

My phone buzzed a little before lunch, and I grabbed it without looking up from my work. "This is Violet."

"Hey." Hunter's voice soothed me just like that, despite me not wanting it to. "Are you free for lunch?"

I could be. I shouldn't be. Did I almost miss the catch in his voice? "What's up?"

He sighed. "I got a call a little bit ago. From my dad. He's having a good health day, he heard the great news about his only son getting married, and he wants to meet my new wife."

"Oh." My insides twisted in on themselves. This was the last thing I wanted to do ever—look a dying man in the eye and lie to him about his son's relationships. "I have to work at the cafe this afternoon, but I can spare a little time." The words flowed out on their own. I'd stayed with Hunter because of this. It had to be done, no matter how much I dreaded it.

"When are you free?"

I wasn't getting anything else done until this meeting was over. "Now is good."

"I'll pick you up in about fifteen minutes. And Violet? Thank you." The genuine gratitude in Hunter's voice didn't erase my dread, but it did add a hint of sweet to the bitter taste in the back of my throat.

Since I was done working for now, I decided to wait outside for Hunter. The chill in the air sapped the heat from my cheeks, and I gulped in the fresh cold, trying to freeze my insides as well. When Hunter arrived, I hopped in the car almost before it stopped moving.

"Eager to get this over with?" he asked flatly.

Oh, there was more guilt. Wonderful. I couldn't lie, but the truth didn't seem right either, so I shrugged into my seatbelt.

"Me too." Hunter's voice was soft. He reached over and rested a hand on my knee, and the cold all rushed away.

We made the short trip in silence. The sign on the front door of the hospice facility said *Out of respect for our guests, please silence your phones*. I hated cutting myself off from the world, but it was polite, and we wouldn't be here long.

Inside the building looked more a high-end apartment complex than a medical facility. Rich wood paneling and plush carpet led us down a softly lit hallway, past widely spaced doors.

Hunter stopped in front of one and knocked. A voice that sounded so much like his called, "Come in."

We stepped into what would have been a large, nicely finished bedroom, if it weren't for all the monitors and wires surrounding a bed near the window. The man lying there, dwarfed by pillows and a heavy blanket, looked remarkably like Hunter. Older, with gray hair, and a bit frailer. But the face was the same. The kindness in his dark eyes was the same. Even his smile was familiar.

It would be sweet if I didn't know this was the man Hunter was hiding a part of his identity for.

They exchanged a couple words of greeting, and Hunter gestured to me. "Dad, this is my wife, Violet. Violet, this is Hunter Sr."

"Call me Dad, hon." He reached for my hand when I offered it in greeting, and pressed it between his palms. His skin was yellow and papery, but his grip and smile were warm and friendly. "I remember you. You were with Ramsey Miller for a while."

At least things were going to get awkward right away. I had no idea how to response. "Yes."

"I see." Hunter Sr. shook his head. "You know, I always figured you and he split because he was in love with my son."

Hunter coughed.

"But I can tell you and Hunter care about each other," his dad said.

Hunter reached for my hand and squeezed gently. "We do."

The simple statement rang with a clarity I hadn't had much of lately. We really did. For so long I'd only thought of Hunter as *Ramsey's friend*, but he'd been here for me. Still was. I was as terrified of him being gone from my life as I was Ramsey.

Hunter's dad pushed himself into a sitting position in bed. "Violet, hon, you've always seemed like a lovely person, so please don't take this the wrong way—"

Was there any other way to take a statement that started like that?

"—The last few years have taught me that putting off conversations means you may never get to have them, and this is one I need to have with my son." He looked at Hunter. "What the fuck are you doing, Junior?"

Hunter's wide-eyed expression reflected my shock. He worked his jaw. "I don't—"

"Anyone with half a brain can see how you and Ramsey feel about each other. I hoped you'd tell me at some point."

What was happening? My brain was glitching on reality versus expectation.

Hunter didn't look to be doing any better. "I'm not—"

"Going to lie to me, are you? You'd never send your old man to meet his maker on a lie."

"No, I wouldn't." Hunter's shoulders drooped, but the corner of his mouth tugged up. "And you're right. I do love Ramsey. He feels the same." The confession slid out on a puff of tangible relief.

I wanted to cheer for Hunter for being able to say it, but I was still struggling to process the unexpected situation. Would there be fallout from the confession? Screaming and name calling and accusations?

"I'm so proud of you." Hunter Sr opened his arms wide, and pulled Hunter into a warm hug.

Laughter and tears both bubbled up in my throat, spreading from the warm spot in my chest. The moment mingled with a flood of stories the shelter kids had told me. With memories of my sister. It was so beautiful in here, but so bittersweet.

"I'm sorry you found out this way, hon." Dad's voice was kind as he let Hunter go and focused on me. "It's best you know now, before you're with him too long."

I laughed through threatening tears and scrubbed my hand across my cheeks. He was apologizing to me?

"Did we break you?" Hunter Sr sounded concerned.

Hunter pulled me closer, and tangled his fingers with mine. "Probably just the opposite. Violet already knows how I feel."

His dad held up a finger, then snapped his mouth shut. "You know what? I don't want too many details there, as long as you're all on the same page. Why didn't you ever tell me? I've been waiting for you to *come out*, and then I hear you're married."

"Mom asked me—begged me—not to tell you. She said I couldn't send you to your grave knowing I was attracted to men. That it would hurt you so much."

"I raised you better than to think lies were the solution."

"You raised me to look good, and always have a woman on my arm. *Look at how handsome he is. He's going to break so many girls' hearts.* That's all I heard growing up."

There was an edge to Hunter's voice that I'd heard so many times.

His dad frowned. "You're right, and I'm sorry. Saying *I didn't know any better* doesn't change that, but it's the truth. I think I saw it when you were young, but I was scared. For me. For you. But everything you've done, I couldn't be more proud of you. As long as whomever you're with is treating you right, I don't care what's between their legs."

And now I wanted to cry again, and the acceptance in the room. "Thank you." I did mean to say the words aloud, and now two sets of eyes were on me. "If more kids could hear things like this…"

"What can I say? I'm incredible." Despite his frail appearance, he sounded as strong and confident as anyone I knew. "Whatever your reasons for doing this, Violet, thank you for being my son's friend."

"It goes both ways." It felt good to smile. To speak my mind. It felt *really* good. "And he's worth it."

"Come here." Hunter Sr gestured, and pulled me in for a tight hug. When he let me go, he did the same with Hunter, holding him for several seconds.

He pointed to a pair of chairs next to the bed. "Stay for a while. Catch me up. Introduce me to your *wife*. Tell me what's going on with you. With Ramsey."

This was the single most wholesome, warm moment I'd been a part of in a long time. As the three of us talked, the rest of the world slipped away. Dad had countless stories about Hunter. He was fantastic at bringing me into the conversation, too.

I loved every minute of it, not only for Hunter, but it was a reminder for me. Not every parent with a gay kid was an asshole. I wished my shelter kids, my sister, had this. It ached that they hadn't. But at the same time, the warmth that flowed between Hunter and his dad meant there were other families out there like theirs. With acceptance and love.

That filled me with hope.

As Hunter and I walked out of the hospice a few hours later, we were both smiling.

"I like your dad. He's—"

"Painfully direct and honest?" Hunter reached for his phone.

I did the same. "I wasn't thinking in those terms, but yes."

"He liked you too. He doesn't chat like that with just anyone." Hunter's bright smile wilted as he looked at his phone.

My *What's wrong* stuck in my throat as I saw a handful of missed calls and a texts, all from Lyn. "Shit." I'd blown through my start time for inventory. The nausea was back full force as I called Lyn back.

"Are you all right?" she answered, breathless.

Damn it. "I'm fine. I'm so sorry. We were talking to Hunter's father. I lost track of time. I'm so so sorry. I'm on my way now."

"*Violet.*" Lyn's tone cut through me. "It's okay."

"It's not." Fuck. I couldn't believe I was late for work.

"It really is. It's completely fine. It wasn't even…" Lyn sighed. "We aren't doing inventory. It was a surprise engagement party. Wedding party? It doesn't matter, because it's fine."

It did matter. Acid clawed its way up my throat. Had I known subconsciously, and blown it off? "I'm sorry."

"Stop," Lyn said harshly. "I get it. There's nothing to apologize for. You've been pushing yourself too hard. This isn't an offer anymore. I'm giving you the next week off. If you come into work, I won't let you."

The time off sounded wonderful, but the circumstances filled me with a rancid mixture of anger and frustration. "But—"

"I'll talk to you in a week, Violet. Please, don't worry about it. I'm not mad. I'm just concerned. Get some rest."

I dropped my arm limply by my side. How did I let this happen?

"Violet." Hunter's concern penetrated the shell wrapping around me. "Hey." He placed a finger under my chin and lifted my head. "Owen told me what happened. Come on. We're going for lunch."

"I don't…" have time? I'd cleared my afternoon for work. That I'd forgotten.

Hunter tugged me toward his car. "Come on."

I sank into my seat and let him drive. He pulled into a drive through and ordered us sandwiches. Thankfully there was no greasy smell. I don't think I could have handled it. We headed toward his place, and then drove past his street.

"Where are we going?" I managed to ask.

"Just a little farther."

Not an answer. I sank lower in my seat, arms crossed.

A few minutes later, we reached a ridge that looked out over the valley. It was a turn-off tucked away from the rest of the world, where we could look down on them, but no one would see us.

Hunter put the car in park and turned to me. He forced my gaze to his. "You can't keep doing this."

"Doing what?" I didn't like the harsh tone.

Lines creased his forehead and he searched my face. "Your friends, all of us, need you. Don't doubt that for a second. But what you're doing, stretching yourself thin like this, it's not good for you."

"I don't have a choice. There are things that need to be done, and I promised to do them."

"I get that. And you don't have to do them alone. The people around you will help. I'll help."

But I'd promised to see them through. The idea of dropping anything, the way I had with this afternoon's promise to Lyn, made me sicker. "People are counting on me. You don't understand."

"I do understand." He traced gentle lines along my jaw as he held my chin. "I've been where you are."

I clenched my mouth shut, and braced myself for a story that proved he didn't get it at all.

"When I started college, I was working with my mom's organization—volunteering. And then Ramsey got into student government. It didn't matter that he was at a different school, I had so many ideas to help him. I was balancing all of that with being a freshman. With a course load I'd been told was too much. I was running on less than four hours of sleep a night."

I winced at a story that could have been mine, but kept my mouth shut.

"Things started to slip," Hunter said. "Little things. I was late to an appointment here or there. I overbooked a few obligations. And then I let my mom down. And I missed getting some critical information to Ramsey. And it all came crashing down around me. I pushed so hard, I landed in the hospital for a few days."

"Ouch." I was sympathetic. Maybe he did get it. A little. "But that's not me. I'm not that kind of physically ill. I've got this."

Hunter's frown deepened. "You do. Right now you're keeping almost every ball in the air by yourself. How can I help?"

"I can't ask you to do that. These are my obligations."

"I'm not offering to do anything for you," Hunter said. "You tell me what needs to be done, and I'll do it."

"I… I can't."

He gripped my chin harder, and stared me down with a fierceness that stole my breath. "This is destroying you. I won't make a plan to ease up your workload, but you have to."

"The plan is, I'll take the week Lyn gave me, make sure everything else is in order at the shelter, and then I won't miss any more appointments."

"That's not what I mean."

It didn't matter. It was the best I had.

TWENTY-TWO

When I woke up in the morning, I almost felt worse than after that last hangover. The one where my world fell apart. My clock said it after eight in the morning. I didn't remember the last time I'd slept so late.

Besides Vegas.

I peeled myself out of bed. Every inch of me was exhausted. Things were strained last night with Hunter. We'd brought the sandwiches home. I ate with him, to prove I was taking his advice and trying to relax, but I hadn't known what to say.

As I stumbled across the room, something caught my eye. A folder sitting near my closed bedroom door. There was a Post-it note on top, with Hunter's neat script handwriting

Sorry I missed you before work. We'll talk about this, I promise. I wanted you to know they exist.

I opened the folder. The top page was a court document with Hunter and my names at the top, and *PETITION FOR DIVORCE* underneath.

So, there was that. I guess it made sense. We didn't have to hide anything from his family.

I didn't want to follow any trains of thought about the paperwork, and I didn't know what to do with myself. I told Hunter I'd make a plan, but I was so tired. My bed called my name, and I hated myself as I climbed back under the covers, but I also needed to lie back down.

My phone ringing dragged me back go consciousness. Somehow it was almost two in the afternoon. I forced the sleep away as best I could, and answered. "Hello?"

"Hey, Taffy." Ramsey's greeting danced over me, drawing me awake better than any coffee.

I should ask him not to call me that, but I was too happy to hear his voice. "Hey."

"I don't like the way we left things the other night. The way we keep leaving them."

I didn't either. "But I hate the alternative, too. Not the being with you part. Everything else."

"I get it. And I didn't call to rehash. We each know where the other stands."

And yet, neither of us was budging. "What's up?" I couldn't handle any sort of emotional or business conversation right now.

"I called to talk."

When people said that, it was rarely a good thing. "About…?"

"I don't care. Wow." Ramsey chuckled. "That came out wrong. I should say *anything*. I get to see Hunter every day, but I miss you. I had you back for such a short amount of time, and now you're just out of reach. I called to hear your voice."

My heart cracked. So much for not getting emotional. "You're not going to ask what I'm wearing, then?" I tried to tease. It was enough to lift my mood a notch.

"Now that you mention it…" Ramsey's smooth tone buoyed me further.

"Nope. Missed your chance." My playfulness slipped out more easily than I expected.

"Hmm…" His low hum rolled over and through me. "I'll tell you what I'm wearing. Suit. Tie. Wingtips."

And I had no doubt he looked sexy as fuck. "You're begging for it in an outfit like that."

"I don't beg. You know me better than that." Something clanged with Ramsey's voice.

Was that… "Why do I hear slot machines?"

"I just finished lunch with Dottie."

"In Las Vegas? Don't we have a thing tonight?" I shouldn't have said anything. Now I was dreading another fundraiser.

"We do. And I'll be back before then."

The conversation had taken a suspicious turn. "What so important in Las Vegas that you have to do it in person?" Did I have a right to ask that? I didn't care. Curiosity won out.

"It's a surprise."

I grasped for a response.

"I know you hate surprises," Ramsey said quickly. "I'll tell you about this one as soon as I'm able, and I promise it's good."

"I hope so. I can't take any more bad ones."

"I promise." Ramsey repeated. "I'll see you tonight?'

He and Hunter would be the highlight of my evening. "Bright and smiling on my man's arm," I said.

"*My* man. I'd only share with you."

I smiled. "Don't I feel special."

"You should. You always should. And I'm serious."

I stumbled over his meaning. "You're giving me permission to fall in love with my husband? So generous." My teasing felt flat.

"No," Ramsey said. "Even I can't stop something like that. I'm giving you permission to fuck my boyfriend."

"Did I mention how generous you are?" Despite parrying the comments, my mind was racing along the potential. Clinging to a desire I'd barely dared skim the surface of, as images teased me of being wrapped up in Hunter. Of admitting there was more of a connection to our sex. Of not having to assume he'd be gone in the morning.

Then the reality of last night brought the fantasy crashing down around me. "Pretty sure I've burned that bridge. He's asking for things from me I can't give."

"That doesn't sound familiar at all." Sarcasm laced Ramsey's reply. "You have your limits and he has his."

Was he really comparing my desire to not drop my obligations to his cavern of secrets? "But unlike me, his aren't reasonable."

"Hunter will do the impossible for someone he cares about," Ramsey said. "But he won't watch them destroy themselves. That's not unreasonable."

What happened to our angsty-light conversation? "I'm not—"

"Have this talk with him. But I know you'll work it out."

"How are you so certain?"

"Because I love you both, and I have excellent taste in people."

There were so many holes in that reply, I didn't know where to start picking it apart. I also didn't want to. "I don't have your confidence."

"So borrow some of mine." Ramsey's voice went muffled for a moment, as he talked to someone else, and then he was back. "I'm so sorry. I have to run. I miss you Taffy. Always when you're not around."

I shouldn't say it. The words would hurt. But holding them inside didn't make them any less painful. "I miss you too."

"We'll make this right, I promise."

I didn't know if we could, but as we disconnected I needed him to be right.

I sat on the bed for the longest time, staring at my phone. What was I supposed to do with my afternoon? If I checked in on the contractors at the shelter again, they'd probably bar me from the premises. I'd finished the month's paperwork.

Was it too early to get ready for the fundraiser tonight? It was a more casual event, so I didn't have to do the whole evening gown and heels thing.

Even though I was staying in the guest room, the bathroom was much larger than the one in my apartment. I'd been so busy, I hadn't had a chance to try out the large tub. It would be a shame to move out and not give it a whirl at least once.

Move out, the words soured in my gut, so I ignored them and ran a bath instead. The water was a half notch above comfortable when I dipped my hand in. *Perfect*. I stripped off my clothes and slipped into the water.

The heat wrapped around me, yanking me toward serenity. Was I really fighting relaxation? Hunter's and Ramsey's words bounced in my head, demanding I give them attention.

Why couldn't I just chill for a few hours? A question that extended far beyond the walls of this room and this moment.

I let Lyn down yesterday. Sure, it was a party, but what if it had been work? Or Luna needing something? Or a crisis with one of the kids? Not a basement flooding crisis, but the kind of crisis my sister had gone through.

If I pushed myself to a crash, to hospitalization, I couldn't be there for them.

Or yourself, I swore that was Hunter's voice in my head.

I sank lower in the water, until my head from the nose up was the only thing not submerged. If I relaxed now, what would happen? Anything worse than if I didn't?

No. In fact, if something did come up, I could probably deal with it better.

Why did admitting that feel like surrender?

I struggled with logic versus instinct as I soaked. After the bath, I took my time stripping off the blue nail polish from two weeks ago and doing my hair. Hurrying through either meant waiting, and either could be dropped if someone called.

No one did.

Hunter got home a little after five, and I was sitting on the couch with the divorce papers on the coffee table.

He looked between them and me. "You want to do this now."

"Did you think I'd want to wait?"

He shook his head. "Tell me what you're thinking."

So. Many. Things. I doubted he wanted a dissertation. Then again, Hunter would probably listen to me spew out every single thought I'd had since I woke up. "You first."

"I already had a turn." He crossed the room and stopped a few feet away, keeping the table and the paperwork between us.

"I can't just turn off my obligations."

"You don't have to. I'd never ask that. I want you to take the first step toward making sure you're as taken care of as everyone you're looking out for."

It sounded so simple. More when he said it than when I'd made the argument with myself. "If I stop..." What? The world hadn't ended today. I felt better rested than in weeks.

"You're not stopping. You're doing a risk assessment and re-prioritizing." Of course he had to make sense about it all.

Was I ready for that? "I think we got off-track. This is about the —" divorce. I couldn't say it, so I gestured to the paperwork.

"Agreed. We can't have one conversation without the other. Unless you're ready to sign that paperwork." Hunter's confident tone wavered.

He was holding a marriage I hadn't wanted over my head to force me to change who I was. No. That was the wrong way to look at it, and he'd made sure to say so.

"All right, I'll go first." Hunter came around the table and took the spot next to me. He cupped my face between his palms. "I don't think I'm ready to sign the paperwork. I'm not saying I'd propose— yet—if we had a chance to do things differently, but we didn't. *What if* isn't part of the equation."

Each stroke of his thumb along my cheekbone sent a fissure of comfort through me. He searched my face. "I've always liked you," he said. "You make Ramsey smile, but that's not the only reason or even the main reason. You're smart. You're witty. You're fun as hell to hang with. You've always been a good friend, and even though it meant I got Ramsey, I didn't like when the two of you split because it meant you were gone. But you're not competition. These last few weeks have forced me to admit I love you, Violet."

The words sang to my heart, and pulled a similar declaration to the surface. I opened my mouth.

Hunter pressed a thumb to my lips. "But I also won't watch you destroy yourself, because you think it's helpful to others." He let me go.

TWENTY-THREE

Hunter loved me.

But he wanted to change me.

No. He wanted to help me. If I let myself trip over the last few weeks, which I had to do to process this, I could see how bad things were. That this wasn't the beginning of a downward slope, I'd been plummeting toward the bottom of a ravine of taking on way too much before the boiler failed at the shelter.

I also saw Hunter, a bright spot of sanity and warmth in the midst of it all. Ramsey was there too. Just out of reach. I wanted more of both when I looked back, and when I looked forward.

"I love you, too." It was so much easier to say that than I expected. My heart fluttered just as much speaking the words as it did hearing them. "And I'm scared of making this change you're talking about, but I'm terrified of staying on the path I'm on."

Hunter brushed his lips over mine. "I'm here for you. Everything I said stands."

"And Ramsey?" It was an unformed question. It could mean a million things to either of us. "Technically he and I are still broken up."

"He didn't tell me what he's doing in Vegas, but he promised it would fix things. I trust him. Can we go back to us?"

We could. Now that I knew I wasn't trading one guy for another. "Yes."

Hunter's kiss was so tender, it was heartbreaking. Or the opposite. Was *heartmending* a thing? I was making it thing, because the cracks in mine were sealing and vanishing.

His feathered kisses along my lips and face and neck stole my breath. I didn't know what to do besides grip his shirt in both fists and hold on tight.

Kisses blended into more. Tentative touches up my stomach, under my shirt. Groping through my bra and teasing my nipples as I stroked his erection through his slacks. It was a drawn out make-out session that put any I'd been a part of when I was younger to shame. This wasn't desperate pawing, it was a methodical build-up of pleasure.

Hunter pressed his lips to the hollow below my ear. "Do you remember what I said about fucking you?"

"That you like it?"

"Such an understatement. Memories of being buried inside you and wrapped around you haunt my dreams."

I flushed at the strength in his words. "You're so poetic," I said.

"You expected anything else? I'm torn between spending the night devouring you, and the fact that we have someplace to be. If I ask you to join me in the shower, will it ruin your hair?"

I gave him a look that I hoped conveyed *ask me instead if I care.* "I'd love to join you in the shower."

Hunter led me into the master suite bathroom, which made the one in my room look tiny. The large walk-in shower only took up a small corner of the room, and there was plenty of space for two behind the glass. He turned on the water, and we stripped off our clothes.

He tested the water a few times before finally tugging me under the stream with him, and sliding the door shut to close us off from the rest of the world. He pressed his chest to my back to kiss along my shoulders and neck while he glided his hands up my stomach to cup my breasts.

"You've raised the bar on foreplay." My teasing was breathy. Each new touch was fresh and tantalizing.

"You deserve that and more."

As the water sluiced over us, Hunter glided his hands along my every curve, teasing and caressing until I was slick from the build-up.

He slipped his fingers between my legs, teasing my pussy, then hooked his hand under my knee to plant my foot on the seat in the corner. Yeah, he had a built-in seat in his shower.

I leaned forward as he dragged the head of his cock along my ass cheek, and then my slit. He penetrated me with a long groan that sent a shiver of delight through me. He didn't move inside me, though.

The water stopped striking my skin, and a moment later, he was holding the shower head between my legs. "Tell me when I hit the right spot," he said.

I guided the pulsating water into place, and a shudder ran through me as the steady stream hit my clit.

"Hold this in place." Hunter handed me the shower nozzle. He gripped my hips, and then he was pounding inside me. Hard. Fast. Digging his fingers into my water-slicked skin.

The combination of sensations built fast, after the slow path we'd taken to get here, and my body tensed in anticipation. Every muscle coiled, waiting for release. Needing it.

And then orgasm crashed around me, from my core, from Hunter's frantic pace. From everywhere. I clenched around his cock, lost in the pleasure, and milking him.

"Fuck, Violet." He squeezed me harder. The pounding reached frenetic, even as I let the shower nozzle fall away. Hunter spilled inside me, his groan loud and intoxicating when he came.

As he slowed to a stop, neither of us moved for several moments. Water struck our shins. He pressed his lips into my shoulder and pulled me back into him.

"You're incredible in so many ways, Violet."

I leaned more weight against him. "I could say the same to you. Don't take this wrong, but you're officially my favorite mistake."

"I love it." He laughed.

We took our time soaping up and rinsing each other clean. It was hard to move quickly when every other touch was followed up with a kiss. We finally managed to step out of the shower, and get ready for the evening.

The drive there passed in a haze of me thinking about how amazing this was. I almost managed to ignore the nagging voice reminding me I needed this with Ramsey, too, to feel complete. Did that make me greedy? I didn't care. I wanted them both anyway.

Tonight's fundraiser was in another convention room, in another hotel. The only thing that distinguished most of these from each other was the color of the tablecloths. Pink this time—a perfect match to my flush every time I thought about Hunter.

I clung to him from the moment we arrived. We looked like the perfect, loving couple. It came naturally to have him whispering in my ear. To laugh at his comments. To exchange little kisses. Tonight it was because of this fresh commitment we had, but even before, it felt right to be close to him. To fall into this role.

It took more than an hour for both us and Ramsey to be free enough to approach each other. As the three of us headed toward a less crowded part of the room, Debbie joined Ramsey.

If she pulled him away for hours again, I'd be so furious. I didn't care whether or not I had the right to be.

It didn't look like she was saying anything to him, but his flat expression spoke volumes given he'd been smiling and laughing all night.

"I need to speak with the three of you," Debbie said as soon as Hunter and I were within hearing range. "It's not a request."

Bossy much?

Ramsey gave a terse nod. "All right."

Did he know what was going on? This wasn't his *surprise* was it? If so, it was off to a shitty start.

We followed Debbie down the hallway, to an empty conference

room. She flipped on a switch, which illuminated just enough space to make things eerie, and closed the door behind us.

"What?" Ramsey asked sharply.

Debbie was focused on me, with a disgust in her gaze that made my skin crawl. "I can't believe you're a part of this," she said. "This marriage is a scam, and that's the least horrible thing about what's going on here. It's bad enough that Ramsey is hiding that he's fucking another man. But you? Absolutely disgusting that you'd demean yourself to hide their secret, given who you are. Do the kids at that shelter know?"

"Excuse me?" I could match disgust with anger, and then raise the ante to fury. "Did you—"

Ramsey settled a hand on my arm, and silenced me with a look.

"My personal life is none of your fucking business." His voice was hard.

"It is if you want to win this race, and the next one." Debbie stepped closer until she was in Ramsey's face. "This is the kind of bullshit behavior that makes losers, and I will *not* work for someone who's not interested in being the best."

Ramsey's expression went flat. "I see." His voice was stony. I'd rarely seen him like this—so furious he'd bottled the rage to use for later. "You're right, Debbie." There was no intonation in his voice. He was half a step from being a computerized voice. "I'll handle things tonight, and we'll talk in the morning."

Debbie blinked several times—was she surprised or something else? "Okay. I'll prepare a press re—"

"You won't do anything. We'll talk in the morning means we'll talk in the morning, and in the meantime, you'll keep all of your employment agreements in mind." Ramsey opened the door. "I assume you can find your own way back to the event."

"Yes. Thank you."

So that was what it took to shut up Debbie.

As she left, Hunter let out a long puff of air. "Wow."

Ramsey's chuckle was strained. "I'm done for the night. Think anyone would notice if we cut out early?"

"It's not your event," Hunter said. "No one will care."

"Are you sure she won't talk tonight?" How was I the only one worried about things falling apart if we walked away?

Ramsey nodded. "If she does, every Miller lawyer in the universe will be riding her ass. But worse, no one will let her work their campaign again. The *exposing us* threat is a bluff."

"How can you be so sure?"

"Because I've been watching this game play out far longer than I care for. Meet back at your place?" Ramsey looked between us.

Because it was our place. Hunter's and mine. The drive home would have been tense, if Hunter hadn't settled his hand on mine every chance he got.

Ramsey was already inside when we arrived. I wasn't surprised he had a key, but I did wonder how he got here so much sooner than we did. Hard to shave even a few minutes off a fifteen minute drive.

The instant Hunter closed the door, Ramsey crossed the room in a few long strides, grabbed a fistful of Hunter's shirt, and yanked him close, crushing their mouths together. They radiated desire and adoration.

I'd never watched anything hotter.

They broke apart with a duet of groans, but didn't move away from each other. Ramsey slid his hand to the back of Hunter's head, holding the two of them together. "I can't keep this up," Ramsey growled. "Two weeks is too long. There's no way I can stay away from you for nine months."

"Same." Hunter's reply was a bittersweet blend of need and sadness.

I should feel like an intruder right now. An interloper in an otherwise beautiful connection, but instead I was grateful to be a part of it. This didn't make me doubt what I had with either of them, and it reminded me they trusted me enough to let me be a part of it.

Still, it left my lips lonely and reminded me that Ramsey and I had a massive unresolved issue that kept us from having that.

Ramsey trailed his fingers forward to Hunter's jaw, brushing over his lips before finally dropping the touch and turning to me.

The intensity in Ramsey's gaze, the way he focused on only me, sparked through me. "I can't watch the two of you side-by-side and not be a part of it," Ramsey said. "You are so many amazing things, Taffy, but you're absolute shit at faking it."

"I'm not faking this." There it was. Telling Ramsey—confirming what he should already suspect—made my relationship with Hunter more real.

"Exactly." Ramsey flexed his fingers. He was so close, but didn't reach out.

I was both grateful and disappointed, because I wouldn't be able to tell him *no*. "So...?"

"You're right." The same thing he'd said to Debbie earlier, but in a vastly different tone. This was resignation and acceptance and hope. "I'm tired of this. Of missing Hunter. Of missing *you*. Of hiding who I love. Of trying to figure out what a future looks like if I have to tell more and more lies to keep our secrets. The public can accept who I am, or..."

"Or...? You'll move on? Just like that?" I needed to hear more. Right now, this was the chocolate brownie meant to sate a craving that was a day too old to be fresh.

Ramsey shook his head. "There's no *just* here. I'm resetting my priorities, and there are other places I can make a difference that won't require me to make this kind of compromise." He reached back to pull Hunter closer. "This decision isn't mine alone, though. I'm done asking the two of you to stay married, but I do need your permission to talk about us publicly. Otherwise, I'll leave your names out of it as much as I can."

"You'd better fucking not." Hunter's voice was hard. "You are *never* leaving my name out of your life again."

The two of them were *so* good together.

And I still hadn't been kissed. "What are you going to do? Tell the world *hey, I'm in an consensual relationship with a woman and another man. Accept it or suck it.*"

Ramsey laughed. A genuine, throaty sound. "Tempting, but I was thinking only if someone asked. I was leaning more toward telling the world I'm not straight, and that any other information about my personal life is that—personal."

"And if they push for details?" The way I was. This was too good to be true, but I really needed his commitment to the truth to be real. "If Hunter's name comes up? If mine does? If they want to know about our marriage?"

"Then I'll answer their questions. I won't lie. I need you back, Taffy." Ramsey traced a thumb over my bottom lip, drawing a soft gasp.

"I need that too." *Goddess* it felt incredible to say that.

Ramsey claimed my mouth hungrily, in an all-consuming kiss. He bit my bottom lip. Teased my tongue with his. Nibbled along my skin until my lips were swollen and tender and eager for more.

TWENTY-FOUR

"What was in Vegas today?" I asked Ramsey between hungry kisses.

He sank his teeth into my shoulder. "A new future."

"No." I groaned into the delicious sting. "No more riddles or surprises. How does it help us?"

He pulled away to look at me. "Tomorrow morning, Hunter is going to fire Debbie. He's going to do this as I'm holding a press conference to withdraw from the senate race."

"Oh." Not what I expected, but maybe I should have. Ramsey coming out was unlikely to end his career, but everything else about our relationship may not go over so well, and it wouldn't stay hidden if we weren't actively hiding it. "But… What about making a difference? Being made for this?" Every other reason he'd given me over the years for why he had to behave.

"I've been thinking about what you said. All of it, but specifically what you said about the pop-up event we did with Dottie. I talked to her today, to her lawyer, and financial adviser, about starting a charitable foundation to help shelters like yours. To bolster them. To build more of them. I'm going to head the entire thing, work my connections to grow it, and I'm hoping to God that

Hunter will help me with the administrative details." Ramsey finished with a satisfied grin.

"Well, apparently my boss is quitting his job tomorrow," Hunter said. "So I do have an opening in my schedule."

Ramsey turned his head long enough to give Hunter a quick kiss. "You're hired." Ramsey turned back to me. "That's the surprise. That's how I fix things. I'd do it anyway. You were right, it's how I can make a difference. But I'm hoping you'll stick around to see things in action. With me."

"I will." I couldn't fight my smile.

Ramsey gripped the back of my neck with a strength and possession that lit my soul on fire. "I love you, Violet. Every day you're not here, every day for the past few years, I've missed you." He drew his tongue up the side of my neck, to nip my earlobe. "I'm not letting you go again. Either of you."

"Is this a good or a bad time to tell you we decided not to go through with the divorce?" I didn't want to ruin the moment, but since we were implying long-term here, and I wanted exactly that, someone should bring it up.

Ramsey kissed along the shell of my ear. "I told you," somehow he made a whisper sound like a command, "I'll only share with you. With him. But you're both mine."

As he said *mine* he bit my neck. I'd be covered in marks soon, and the idea made desire throb between my thighs. "I love you too. Intensely. Completely. From now until forever."

"I want something from you," Ramsey growled against my skin.

"Anything."

"I want you on the couch, naked, fingering your pussy while I suck my boyfriend's cock."

I smiled through my flush. "You're such a charmer."

He tangled his fingers in my hair and tugged. "Damn right I am." He crushed his mouth to mine, stealing my breath. Pouring intensity and desire into the connection that flowed between us. "Naked and playing with yourself. *Now.*"

Ramsey let me go and I stepped away. I felt a bit silly taking off my clothes like this. Was I supposed to do something sensual? Dance? Just tearing them off all random-like didn't feel right.

I was deliberate about stripping my sweater over my head. When the knit material cleared my eyes, and I saw two gazes focused on me, confidence surged inside. I shimmied out of my slacks. Made a little show of taking off my bra and pushing my panties to the ground, and settled on the couch.

Hunter and Ramsey were still staring at me.

"Well?" I asked.

Ramsey shrugged. "Well?"

"You're supposed to be the show," I said.

He grinned. "Fair point." He turned back to Hunter and crushed their mouths together in a drawn-out, groan-inducing kiss.

I felt the ghost of fingers and lips gliding over me each time they moved against each other, and it clenched around me with desire.

Ramsey unbuckled Hunter's belt with a practiced flick of the wrist, and whipped it free from its loops with a sharp *crack* that sent shivers through me. Then they were kissing again. Bodies molded to each other. Mouths hungrily devouring each other's grunts. Ramsey gripping Hunter's erection through his pants.

The heat and intensity that flowed between them sparked over me. I was a part of that connection, and that was as enticing as every grope and touch.

I glided my hands over my torso, touching lightly enough to tantalize over my breast, my stomach, and my inner thighs. I wanted that feeling of skin on skin, but I wanted to draw out this moment of voyeurism.

Ramsey undid Hunter's trousers and lowered himself to his knees as he freed Hunter.

Hunter's groan, when Ramsey took him in his mouth, drew a similar sound from me.

Why did I have to get naked to watch the show? Did I care? Not really, given how incredible the watching was. Hunter half-closed his eyes and leaned his head back as Ramsey bobbed his head. Sucking. Licking. Stroking Hunter's balls.

I spread my legs and slipped my fingers to tease my opening and draw out the slickness. I spread my juices up and down, gliding along my pussy as Hunter's groans grew more stuttered. Less controlled.

I dipped my fingers inside me, and reached for my clit with my other hand. I pumped and stroked faster in time with the bob of Ramsey's head. I saw the tension coiling through Hunter. He was close, and I wanted to see his pleasure when he came.

Hunter's face screwed up, and his grunts were stuttered. He was fucking Ramsey's face harder and harder, until he paused. Shuddered. Sagged.

I let myself come, with Hunter's pleased posture burned in my mind. I closed my eyes and my head fell back as pleasure and climax wrapped around me. My orgasm tapered off, and I struggled to find my breath.

Hunter's mouth closed over mine, startling me. He was still panting too, teasing my lips as we gave each other life.

He broke away, and as Ramsey grabbed my wrist, I let my eyelids flicker open. Ramsey held my gaze as he sucked my fingers clean, each lick sending a shudder of delight through me.

When Ramsey finished, he moved my hand to his waist. "Take out my cock and stroke it."

His command and confidence stoked my need. I scooted to the edge of the cushion and did as ordered, freeing him. Wrapping my hand around his shaft. Holding his gaze as I stroked lightly. I teased my thumb over the head and smeared a drop of precum, and he shuddered.

Ramsey pulled my hand away and tugged me to my feet. "Do you remember the night we met?"

"Vividly."

"The one thing I desperately wanted that night was to pull you into my lap and fuck you." Ramsey sat on the couch, turned my back to him, and guided me toward his lap. As I lowered myself, he slid inside me. He wrapped his arms around me and pulled me into his chest, burying himself to the hilt and stretching me out in the best way possible.

He kissed along the back of my neck as he rocked inside me.

Hunter knelt in front of me and my anticipation spiked. He pressed his face between my legs licking me and Ramsey at the same time. Hunter teased my clit with his tongue and devoured my pussy while Ramsey built to slow, steady pace.

They both worked me, the pressure and pleasure building inside me, growing, blooming, driving my senses wild, until I came hard. I rode the wave of orgasm, enjoying every fresh sensation.

Ramsey pounded harder. Hunter pulled away and joined us on the couch, to press his lips to mine, sharing my taste with me. To kiss Ramsey. To tease my nipples.

Ramsey's thrusting grew to a frantic pace, pounding against me. His grunts and grip were familiar and right. He spilled inside me with a drawn-out groan.

As we all came to a stop, the world seemed to pause with us. No one spoke as we leaned into each other. I was happy to be still and enjoy the closeness of the men I loved.

We moved to the bedroom, to collapse in an exhausted but pleased pile on Hunter's bed. He and I each rested our heads on Ramsey's chest.

"So, the two of you..." Ramsey's voice rumbled through me. "Should I be jealous?" His tone was light.

"Mister I Don't Share Well?" Hunter scoffed. "Can you be anything but?"

I laughed. "This coming from the guy who said he wouldn't share his man."

"Ah." Hunter's bravado faded. "You remember that."

My smile wouldn't leave as I snuggled closer to Ramsey. "Yes. The two of us. The three of us, technically."

"I couldn't have planned it better," Ramsey said.

"Which is why you have me." Hunter propped himself up on one elbow.

I shifted my position enough so I could see him without straining. "While I see your point, you couldn't have planned it any better, either."

Hunter raised an eyebrow. "Oh?"

"Nope. Because it doesn't get better." I sighed.

Ramsey tilted his head up to kiss the tip of my nose. "You're a sap sometimes. I love it. Especially when it means you admitting I was right."

I snorted with laughter. "You were *so* not right. But things worked out in spite of that."

"Do I get to wear the ring?" Hunter's change of subject was blatant.

"Ravyn gets to wear the ring. I gave it to her yesterday, with Dottie's blessing. This way it stays in the family, and she can wear it no matter who she ends up with," Ramsey said.

"CoughBenCough." Hunter's words ran together. Ben and Ravyn were BFF's forever, the same way Ramsey and Hunter had been, and both of their families expected they'd end up together.

Ramsey clucked. "Don't let her hear you say that."

"You still weren't right." I'd let the subject drop now. I just had to get in one last word.

Ramsey shifted quickly, displacing me, and I squealed in surprise. He rolled enough to pin me to the mattress, his chest pressing into mine. "Take it back."

I stared back stubbornly. "Make me."

"Nope. Never." He tilted his head and brushed his lips over mine. "We're all here because this is where we want to be."

I wouldn't—couldn't—argue that. This really was better than I could have imagined, being back with Ramsey. Realizing how much Hunter meant to me. Life was incredible.

EPILOGUE

H^{unter}

SIX MONTHS later

There were a lot of things I loved about Violet. One of the simpler ones was the fantastic company she provided when Ramsey was on stage. This afternoon he was cutting the ribbon on the first of many new shelters his foundation brought to life.

Violet's hand was nestled in mine and her head rested against my shoulder, as we stood at the back of the crowed, watching Ramsey on a temporary platform in front of a motel that had been converted. For the last several months, I'd pushed around all the figures and paperwork and kept all the cogs moving to make it happen.

The house Violet managed was fantastic—small, structured and friendly—but it only held so many people. This place would give a similar experience to dozens more homeless youth who needed stability, shelter, and a home.

Ramsey was telling the audience something similar, minus the

Violet bits, but in snappier words that would make good sound bites and be highly quotable.

The faint smile on Violet's face was there more often than not these days. While Ramsey would insist in jest, probably, that it was because she was getting some incredible dick on a regular basis, I knew it was because she was getting better at how she took things on.

It didn't hurt either that my both of my parents had welcomed her and Ramsey into the family with open arms. When we finally had dinner with Mom, and didn't have to lie about the marriage being real, she and Violet got along splendidly. And Dad was still hanging on. Tough old bastard.

As Ramsey finished his speech and cut the ribbon, I tugged Violet away from the gathering and into an empty part of the shelter. It would be open for business next week, but for now, only certain parts of the building were available for photo ops. That was where Ramsey would be.

I'd rather steer clear of the cameras. I led her to the main administrator's office.

"You show me the sexiest things," she teased as we stepped into the room.

"Later, if you're good, I'll let you watch me create Excel formulas."

Violet laughed and pretended to swoon. "I'm not sure I could handle the heat."

I settled into the chair behind the desk and pulled her into my lap. She rested her head on my shoulder, palm resting on my heart. The only thing that would make this moment more perfect would be if Ramsey were here with us.

When Violet and Ramsey broke up a few years ago, when I finally let myself admit how I felt about him, I'd assumed we'd live a life that swung wildly between public and private. I didn't like the idea, but he was worth it.

This was so much better, though. So much more than I'd ever dared imagine. Married to an amazing woman. Committed to an incredible man. Giving others a chance at the same. If I'd wished on a magic lamp, I couldn't have come up with a more perfect scenario.

Ramsey

I took the press on a brief tour of the new shelter. Mostly the common areas. This was our experiment with this kind of project, and it went well. Starting tomorrow, we were spinning up several more projects like this, in larger cities around the country that didn't have many options for LGBTQ+ youth.

For the next forty five minutes or so, we took photos, I answered more questions, and the mood was light and cheery. My new press manager—Jake was as good as Debbie had been at getting the word out, and far less abrasive in the process—shooed everyone away.

I sent him home and went in search of Hunter and Violet. They hadn't told me where they'd be, besides *waiting*, but I could guess.

When I drew close to the main administrative office, I heard soft, familiar voices coming from inside. I summoned far more flair than I needed, and pushed the door open. "My best friend and my girlfriend. Wha—" My melodramatic exclamation trailed off. "You're cuddling."

Hunter looked up from Violet, who was sitting his lap. "You expected something else?" he asked.

"I expected you to christen the place. Fuck on the desk. Something."

Violet feigned shock. "But it's not our desk."

Hunter nodded, expression serious. "She's right. Isn't that kind of a creepy vibe?"

They were yanking my chain. They had to be. "Hotel sex is some of the best sex."

"This isn't a hotel anymore." Violet sounded serious, but her smirk was peeking through.

They were as much serious as they were joking. I loved it. "Right now it's mostly an empty building. The back of the Cayenne in the fast-food parking lot was more taboo than this place." That was a good fucking memory—a good memory of fucking? I'd watched Violet suck Hunter's cock. Fucked him while Hunter tasted himself on her lips. Watched her watching us as she pushed her new little black dress past her hips and fingered her pussy.

"It was after midnight, and the SUV windows are tinted." Apparently Hunter wasn't ready to let the joke drop.

I'd play along for about ten more seconds. "There are no windows in here and the door locks."

"But the door wasn't locked. Anyone could have walked in on us." Violet gave me a pointed glare, as if I were the case study for her point.

I was. "Which I think you wanted, since you didn't lock the door."

"Hang on, back up," Hunter said. "Are you arguing about the fact that we weren't having sex?"

"It's not an argument, it's an assessment."

Violet raised her eyebrows. "Of…?"

"Of which one of you I bend over that desk." I reached behind me and locked the door.

FIGHTING FOR IT

ONE

Anyone who said network installation wasn't sexy, never had the right scenery. And when it came to great views, it didn't get much better than Cole Denton, AKA Oz. As in The Wizard of.

Watching him lay cable—not a euphemism—along the bases of cubicles, so it could be connected and then hidden, was a thing of beauty. The way his back muscles flexed under his T-shirt… The deftness of his fingers as he crimped twisted pair… Wowza.

I was such a freaking dork. And proud of it. Best part was, Oz was too. Back in the day, he was top brass at Rinslet, one of the biggest gaming companies in the world. It was where he got the nickname, Oz. He preferred to be the man behind the curtain, making the magic happen.

He retired at thirty-five, and now, two years later, he'd founded an organization that offered tech apprenticeships.

"I was scanning the list of EdgeBite contestants this morning." I snapped another cubicle panel in place to hide wires. I preferred programming over manual labor, so I watched all the innovations, amateur or corporate, so I could dive into the tech as soon as the opportunity presented itself. "That they have a think tank out of Silicon Valley this year— Is that redundant, aren't they all?"

"No. They're just nosiest about it." Oz's tone was flat.

"Okay." I didn't mind the gruffness. He was one of those guys who was like that. I expected to carry most of this conversation, which I hated with strangers, but it was okay with Oz. "Anyway, one of competing companies has a new rendering algorithm that extrapolates from video and makes digital characters look real. Like, closer than we've ever been to the other side of the uncanny valley." The previews of their 3D models were *amazing*.

Oz moved a ladder under an open ceiling panel. "Up."

I climbed into the hole, leaned over to grab the bundle of cables from him, and headed for the next pillar to connect these. The first time he had me do this today, I'd teased him that he only picked me for the job because I was tiny and better at crawling through walls.

He'd given me a completely flat expression and said *Busted*. Anyone else would've thought he was serious, but I knew he was teasing me.

In my fantasies, his teasing took a much more physical form. He was still quiet in my imagination. Rough, intense, and working my body over with those skilled fingers, until I was sore and pleasantly spent. Then cuddling after.

Not that I ever expected that to happen in real life. He was a decade older than me, my mentor, and basically a tech god. I was a chatty, sunshiny noob to him, and I was fine with that.

"No comment?" I called down as I worked.

"They built the tech so they could make more realistic porn."

I grinned. These were the conversations I lived for with Oz. He had perspectives I'd never consider, and while they weren't always the most positive—okay, they really never were—I learned so much about the industry this way. "You assume. Besides, the internet is so vast thanks to porn."

Silence again.

I poked my head through the nearest opening in the ceiling tile. "No comment?"

"I'm your boss. I'm not talking porn with you."

When he offered to personally work with me as part of his

company's program, to give me next level training, I almost died. Mr. Smart, Sexy-as-all-get-out, was going to teach me new tricks, and make sure I didn't violate my probation in the process.

Wiring an office for CAT6 wasn't supposed to be on the lesson list, I knew this stuff, but there was a scheduling conflict and he'd offered me an extra five hundred bucks to help. I would've done it for free, but I couldn't afford to turn that down.

"You're my *mentor*, and I'm not asking about porn. I'm asking about the tech. They could've made it for other reasons."

"They could've, but they didn't. They pitched an investor friend. Disgusting pitch." Oz knew so many people in the industry.

I was both intrigued by his statement and wasn't going to ask for more detail. His definition of disgusting could be actual disgusting, in which case I'd rather not hear. If he was talking about a little kink, I'd still rather not hear. Best not to destroy the fantasy.

"Even if they did create it for that, it can be used for other things. Video games are only the start." Though they were what I was most interested in. I *super* was lucky that my best friend's previously ex-, now current-again-boyfriend had pulled some strings with my felony conviction. Gotten me a reduced sentence. Made sure I wasn't completely cut off from technology, especially not the way my *accomplice* was. But game programming and security was where I really wanted to be, and that had been out of my reach for the last couple of years.

The good news was I'd finished my probation a few months ago. My felony had been reduced to a misdemeanor. I'd be re-entering the industry in no time.

Oz's sigh carried the heavy weight of *why do you have to be so damn optimistic?* "3D renders that pass for real could put people out of work with training videos, digital tellers—"

"Any tech can put people out of work." I scooted to the edge of the nearby opening in the ceiling, grabbed the lip, and dropped down the few feet to the ground, rather than using the ladder. I was short, and I was nimble. "It can also create jobs. You can put the programming behind one of these to do training videos in places where there's no Cole Denton to offer apprenticeships for hands-on work. Or as an avatar for someone who's uncomfortable with their appearance for whatever reason. There's as much potential for good as for porn."

"This is why you'd make a shitty super villain." Oz's tone was flat, but amusement flashed in his eyes.

"I really would be bad at it. Why? Are you looking for a second?"

He raised an eyebrow. "Are you saying I *would* make a good super villain?"

I shrugged. Wiring was done except for the clean-up, but I wouldn't be the one to point out we could call it a day. "If the shoe fits..." And wowza they were big shoes. Was it true what *they* said about shoe size? "Think about it. The brooding tech genius who used to work for two of the city's best-known billionaires."

"Who left of my own volition. I don't have any issues with them."

"Exactly." I was making my point, and pleased.

Oz looked at me, waiting for me to expand on what he thought was a ridiculous reply.

I didn't have to hear the words; I saw it in his blank stare. "It's always the ones people don't expect," I said. *Duh.*

Oz shook his head in disgust. "In that case, what's my deal? If I'm a super villain, what do I want? Certainly not world domination."

"Um... vengeance." I should have worked harder on motive before making my declaration.

"For what?"

"For anyone who has the intelligence to create tech to change the world, but uses their powers to take advantage of others." Like the people who used me. Who set me up to take the fall for their plan. I shook the unpleasant thought aside.

"Like the people who used you." Oz being in my head was more comforting than creepy. "That makes me the good guy."

It really did, but I was making a point. "All villains think they're in the right."

The corner of his mouth tugged up. If he wasn't careful, he might smile. "If I were what you say, a genus mastermind super villain, I'd pick you as my second. Without question."

Was that a catch in his voice? My phone chimed before I could process. "Sorry. I forgot to silence it." One of Oz's rules was no phones on the job. I didn't usually have an issue with it, because Violet was the only person who called me, and she didn't tend to do so during business hours. I grabbed my phone, and the name *Graham* caught my eye. My pulse kicked up, and I hesitated over the alert. Now wasn't the time to read it.

"Luna?" Oz sounded concerned.

I shook my head, set the phone to quiet, and pocketed it. "Sorry."

"Don't worry about it, we're done anyway. You look like you've seen a ghost."

In a way I had. In college, Graham was my computer science professor. He taught me so much. He was also, as far as the law was concerned, my accomplice in the hack that made us both felons. That was one bit of probation pulling strings didn't get me around —I wasn't allowed to associate with Graham. No one cared that a few years after the law-breaking piece of code, before we were busted, we'd written another virus cleaner that stopped a massive piece of ransomware.

Did I completely lust after Graham? Yeah, but our relationship hadn't been like that. Did I have a thing for older men who were willing to share the secrets of the universe with me? Apparently.

Would I act on it? No. Sexy daydreams were nice, but knowledge was orgasmic. I'd started a search program to find him the instant I was legally allowed, so I could say *hi*. No other reason.

It also didn't escape me that I had an Oz in my life, just like my very favorite ever fictional redhead. Biggest differences between Willow Rosenberg and me? My college girlfriend almost landed me in prison, and if I was going to rock a corset, it would be microfiber, not leather.

"Luna?" Oz prodded again.

Right. "I know where Graham is."

"Hmm."

I expected that. *Everyone* in tech knew the sensationalized version of my story. Or they had. So glad that memory was fading for the public. Oz knew more of the details, but he didn't believe that Graham had nothing to do with setting me up, or sucking me into the scheme to begin with.

It had all been me. I couldn't resist the challenge, and I when I asked for his help, never telling him what it was for, he'd helped.

I was to blame, and I owed Graham an apology for squashing his career.

My fingers twitched by my side, wanting to grab my phone. Work was over. I could excuse myself and go get the details. Graham was probably in another state. Would I call? Text? Email? What was I going to say? I'd been asking that since I started the search, but I didn't have an answer yet.

"We're done for the day," Oz said again. "Go look, and I'll clean up."

I wanted to ask *are you sure*, but I didn't want to give him a chance to change his mind. "Thank you." I stepped to the side of the room, leaned against the wall, and pulled up the info. My heart leaped into my throat. Graham was still local. I could be there by bus in half an hour, that was how close he was.

That didn't mean it was a good idea to drop in unannounced. I didn't know anything about his life now. But looking him in the eye and apologizing was much better than a text. If he wanted me gone after that, I'd be on my way. Would he be indifferent? Hate me?

"Well?" Oz's question startled me.

I showed him the address. It spoke for itself.

"You're going over there?"

I nodded. That answered my question. My racing thoughts wouldn't slow until I did something about this.

Oz jerked his head toward the parking lot. "I'll drive."

"No. It's okay. You've got stuff to do. I won't ask you to chauffeur me around the city. I got it. I'll see you tomorrow. Thank you for everything." I was already sliding toward the door.

Oz grabbed my wrist, and a shock of heat spilled inside. "You didn't ask. You're not going alone."

I could argue, but I liked him looking out for me. Besides, if I was babbling at him, I could stay out of my own head on the trip, and we'd get there a lot faster. "Okay."

I loved Oz's truck. It was one of those big old Fords that had been around longer than me. He kept it in top shape, and it suited him perfectly. He gave me a hand up into the passenger seat, before taking his own spot.

My plan to fill the space with chatter failed. I couldn't stop my brain from the if-then loop it was stuck on over what I was supposed to say to Graham.

We got to the address on my phone way too soon. The building was an old house. Stepping inside revealed four apartment doors. Not an unusual layout for Salt Lake. The only reason my feet didn't freeze in place was I didn't want to hold Oz up.

I approached Apartment C, muttered two conflicting prayers for there to be no one home and for Graham to answer, and knocked.

The seconds ticked away. We should go. Locks clicked on the other side. We should have gone.

The door swung open, and Graham's wide-eyed stare landed on me. He looked incredible. Dark hair, penetrating gaze, and warmth in his hesitant smile. "Luna. What are you...? Not that I'm complaining, but why are you here? How did you find me?"

"I had a good teacher," I said shyly. "Probation is up. We can talk to each other again."

"Yeah. Who's the bodyguard?" He nodded behind me.

I glanced at Oz, before focusing on Graham again. "This is Cole. He's a friend."

"Just a friend?"

My heart hesitated but my mind spit out an immediate answer. "Yes." Impulse took over, and I threw my arms around Graham's neck. "I missed you. I'm so glad I found you."

"Me too." He returned the hug, squeezing tightly. His warmth, the scent of aftershave I still remembered years later, his voice—they were all perfect.

I should pull away, this wasn't the kind of relationship we had, but I didn't want to let go. Disappointment slipped through me when he finally released me and stepped away.

TWO

Graham jerked away from me and I realized Oz had a fistful of Graham's shirt and had pinned him to the doorframe.

What the hell? "*Cole.*" My exclamation came out tighter than I intended.

"This bastard ruined your life," Oz growled. "He manipulated you, he got you arrested, and I wouldn't be fucking surprised if he was grooming you from the moment he met you."

"*Whoa.*" Graham held his hands up, palms out. "Grooming? Never. Besides, you knocked on my door. What is this, Luna?"

Oz stepped between us. "You're talking to me, not her."

"Stop. Please." I rested a hand on Oz's arm. "This was never his fault. I sucked him in. You know that." He was one of the few people who was familiar with all the details.

Under my fingers, Oz's grip relaxed, but his muscles stayed tense. He let go of Graham and stood next to me. *Loom* might be a more appropriate word.

The disruption was nasty, but it didn't erase the warmth spreading through me from the hug. From seeing Graham again. And Oz's stance certainly didn't erase the fantasies dancing in my head. If Oz weren't here, a hug could've become a kiss, leading to roaming hands, stepping inside, clothes falling off—

"I was never *grooming* you." Graham held my gaze, yanking me into reality. "You were the most brilliant student I ever had. I wanted the best for you, and I still do."

A door opened and shut behind me. "Everything okay out here?" an older woman asked.

"All good, thanks, Gracie." Graham was warm and friendly.

She frowned, then headed out the front door of the building.

"Let's go inside and talk," Graham said quietly.

"Oka—"

"Nope." Oz cut me off.

I appreciated the concern, but it didn't seem to have been the best idea to do this with him. He had a point though that I should have this conversation in a public place. I trusted Graham, but I also hadn't seen him in a few years, and I was an optimist, not an idiot. "Coffee? I saw a place a few blocks away."

Graham cast a pointed look at Oz.

A billion scenarios had run through my head about this reunion, and this was nowhere in the bunch. "Can I talk to you outside?" I asked Oz.

He joined me on front porch, his arms crossed and an even deeper scowl than normal in place. "I don't care who approached who for help when you knew him. I don't trust him."

"You don't have to," I said. "But thank you for being here for me." It really was sweet. "And thank you for taking the time to bring me out here. I've got it from here."

"I'm not sure that's a good idea."

"I'm sure that's my decision." I smiled sweetly at him.

Oz sigh-growled. "I'll see you tomorrow. "

I waited until he was in his truck and had started the engine before heading inside. Graham was still in his doorway. "You've made some interesting friends."

"He's a good guy, I promise."

"Seems like it." Graham sounded sincere. "I understand wanting to look out for you. Coffee?"

We walked side-by-side toward the cafe. He was so close I felt the heat radiating from his arm. How did I restart this conversation? *How have you been* felt a bit weak, but what else was I supposed to say? Especially when I couldn't stop thinking about that hug becoming a kiss, then roaming hands, us slipping into his apartment to lose our clothes...

In the unlikely event that Oz wanted to stay and watch, that was even better.

"This isn't at all how I thought seeing you would go." Graham's tone was impossible to read.

He'd been thinking about me? About seeing me? "How did you think it would go?"

"I thought it wouldn't. I tried to keep you from finding me."

"Oh." My step faltered and my mood did the same.

"Don't take that the way it sounds. I hoped you'd moved on. Forgotten about me."

The man who taught me half of what I know? Who actually cared that the nerdy quiet girl wanted his input on a project? Would didn't dismiss me because of my awkwardness? Who starred in *so many* of my fantasies? "Like I could."

"When I saw you on my doorstep, I— What have you been up to?" He glanced at me with a sad smile.

I... wanted to sandwich you between me and the doorframe and kiss you until you couldn't breathe. I wouldn't ask him to finish the thought because it couldn't live up to my hopes. "Odd jobs here and there. Oz— Cole has taught me a lot about the hardware side of networking. Even if probation didn't keep me from doing real programming, no one wants to hire the girl who hacked the world. But I'm getting by. Life is pretty good. You?"

As we walked, his arm brushed mine and his fingertips skittered across the back of my hand. It was a little thing, but the light contact set my never endings on fire.

"I do a lot of private tutoring... A little... It pays the bills." Graham sighed.

The last time we'd spoke was at the courthouse before we

entered our plea bargains. Graham was convinced his career was over.

He'd recover. I had no doubt. But from inside the struggle, I understood how it could look bleak.

"Your friend is Cole Denton." Graham said the name with recognition. "You've got friends in a lot of interesting places looking out for you."

"It's nice." And it wasn't just Oz. My best friend, Violet. One of her boyfriends, Ramsey, was responsible for my reduced sentence years ago. Since Graham brought up Oz, it would be easy to gush, and I totally took that chance most of the time when it came to Oz.

Right now, I was here with Graham. A mind and man I'd looked up to for almost a decade. He wasn't my professor anymore. Hooking up with him wouldn't violate any ethics or honor codes. Optimism said he was as interested as me. Experience argued otherwise.

We reached the coffee shop, Graham held the door for me, and joined me in line. Did we look like a couple to the handful of other people here? Silver was peeking through around Graham's temples —how did he feel about being thirty-nine and going gray?—and I looked young for my twenty-nine. But if I kissed him, would anyone even bat an eye?

Would he return the gesture, or freeze up? Or worst of all, push me away?

I may have a slew of fantasies about people watching while we screwed, but I didn't know if making a move was a good idea, and I definitely didn't want an audience if it wasn't.

When we had a table, tucked away in the far corner of the cafe, I'd start simple. Ask if he was interested.

Or I'd chicken out completely.

We reached the cashier. "Quad shot mocha latte?" Graham asked me. "It's on me." He remembered what I used to drink.

Did my heart just start skipping rope? Darn straight. "Peppermint tea with sugar. I'm not young and dumb enough anymore to think I can drink espresso at night and still get any sleep."

"You're not even thirty, and you were never dumb." He turned to the cashier, repeated my order, and got himself a large coffee.

I'd been joking. He was so serious sometimes. Even that was sexy.

Graham took our drinks and handed me mine. Did I fixate on that moment when his hand brushed mine? Uh, *yeah.* My imagination was working overtime tonight, and I either needed to shut it up, or get it what it wanted.

We found a table away from everyone. He held out my chair and pushed it in as I sat, then took the seat across from me. A table between us. Was that intentional? Him being polite?

"How have you been otherwise?" I asked.

He studied me with eyes so dark I could swim in them, his sturdy jaw set in that way that said he was thinking. "Good. Surviving. You?"

"Same." I didn't want to do this meaningless banter. I wanted actual answers about his actual life. "Have you been doing any modding lately?" When we started talking, way back when, that was one of the first things we realized we had in common. Graham and I both got into programming by making mods for games.

Of course, it was a totally different beast back then. I was doing it so I could play Violet's PS1 games on my computer, since my parents didn't believe in game consoles. He'd gotten into rewriting games so he could change character appearances and scenarios.

Graham shook his head, an almost-smile tugging up the corners of his mouth. "That would be a violation of my probation."

"Uh-huh." Given how much tech had changed in the last three years, and the hoops I'd had to jump through to find him, I didn't believe for a moment he'd let himself get rusty. Besides, he loved the challenge as much as I did. "Tell me another story," I teased.

"Says the woman who tracked me down."

"I didn't start looking until our probations were over." Because I wouldn't have been able to stay away if I'd found him sooner. "And you did a fantastic job of hiding yourself for someone who's been obeying the rules."

"You found me, so I didn't do that great a job."

"Your words, not mine." My tone was playful. This was what I missed. Looking at Graham was nice, but the ease of our conversations… I'd craved that.

He let his grin break through. "I *have* been working on a theory, and I'd like your input."

"Of course." My excitement rose another notch. Whether he was talking about technology or something else, I was in for wherever the tangents took us.

"If a balrog ran a restaurant, where would he put it?"

Chibi Luna clapped with glee in my head. "Trick question?" This was a game we used to play all the time, spawned from the fact that the only things most Final Fantasy games had in common, were the name, the crystals, and the elementals. That conversation had become a challenge to fit all sorts of unrelated worlds together.

"Completely serious. Why?" Graham asked.

Because the answer was obvious. "Hell's Kitchen."

He groaned, but his smile never wavered. "And Luke Cage is his head chef, because he's the only person in the world the balrog doesn't accidentally set on fire?"

"They have a super low crime rate." I ran with the idea. "He's basically an unofficial Continental"—like in John Wick—"where no business is allowed on his grounds. Someone called him on the rule once, and he enforced it. No one's questioned his authority since."

Graham leaned in. "But he's got a soft spot for the neighborhood kids." Amusement and excitement bubbled in his voice. "They love his place at Halloween. Best. Candy. Ever."

Because a balrog chef would make the best treats. "Popcorn balls with a lot of cinnamon and a hint of habanero. Plus, he'd rock the decorations, walking that fine line between terrifying and whimsical." I could picture it, and the imagery made me laugh with delight. "The kids scream in terror when Mr. Balrog jump scares them, and they all love every minute of it." Everything about this made me giggle.

My laugh died when I realized how intensely Graham watched me.

"You look good." His serious tone was back.

Geez I wanted him to kiss me. Did he really think I looked good? That wasn't the kind of thing people said to just be polite. This was a key reason I didn't like small talk. I wanted to assume everyone was sincere.

"You look good too." The words tumbled past my lips. I couldn't take them back now. Screw this. I rose on my toes, leaned over the table, and pressed my lips to his.

When he didn't return the kiss, my blood ran cold and my face scorched flaming hot.

Before I could pull away, Graham slid his hand to my neck and held me captive as he deepened the kiss. He worked his mouth hungrily over mine, devouring my soft whimpers and licking away my doubt.

This blew fantasy out of the water, and it was only a kiss. The kind of toe-curling attention that made my blood sing and would keep me warm for a long time, all by itself. I gripped the edge of the table for balance. Were people watching?

If so, I hoped they enjoyed this almost as much as I was.

When Graham broke away, I gasped, and forced my jaw not to keep working. I licked my lips inside, like he'd done seconds before.

He let me go and sank into his seat. His frown was the frigid polar opposite of what I felt. "I'm sorry, Luna, I can't."

I stared at him in disbelief, waiting for him to finish the sentence. *I can't… wait to get you back to my place and get naked. I can't… believe we had to be apart this long.* Nope. He was done talking.

"You can't… be serious."

He raked his fingers through thick, dark hair. "I'm the last thing you need in your life."

THREE

My disbelief clawed toward something darker. "I can decide for myself who I do and don't want in my life."

"What about Tiff?" He held my gaze, unflinching, and my irritation inched closer to anger at my college girlfriend's name. "You're so sweet. Always seeing the best in people. I'm a disgraced college professor who may never teach again. It doesn't matter that my probation is over—the world sees what happens the same way your *friend* does. You need someone better—"

"*Stop*." I couldn't keep the edge from my voice. I was willing to overlook a lot of things. Give people the benefit of the doubt. But no one else got to tell me what was best for me. My parents did that to me in high school. Refused to let me skip grades or take early college courses. Told me to suck it up when I complained about being bored and then about being bullied. Pointed out again and again that if I was going to survive in *the real world*, it was best for me to learn to be like everyone else.

"This was a mistake." I shoved away from the table. My face had to be bright red from anger and humiliation. I needed to be anywhere but here. "You're right. I shouldn't have found you. Have a great life."

"Luna, sit down." Graham grabbed my wrist and I jerked away harder than I needed to, slamming my hand into a nearby chair and sending it skidding a few inches. The sting added to the growing lump in my throat. I stalked toward the door, not daring to look back. I had to keep my gaze focused on next steps. Reaching the sidewalk. Heading for the bus stop, which, thankfully, was nearby, and the bus was only a couple blocks away.

"Luna." Graham reached for me again.

I glared at him, pouring all my fury into the look. "Touch me, and I'll scream," I said evenly. I might scream anyway. Not really. Composure was important in public. But *wow* I wanted to lose control.

Graham stayed about a foot away. "I didn't mean——"

I slipped in my earbuds and turned away. As humiliated and pissed off as I was, I was still worried that if I let him explain, I'd believe him and forgive him. He was right—sometimes I was a shitty judge of character, and I didn't want any more hints that was true when it came to him.

The bus pulled up to the curb, saving me from having to pretend any longer that I could ignore Graham. I stepped on, and he let me go.

That shouldn't hurt. It was exactly what I wanted.

I took a seat at the rear of the bus, tucked away from prying eyes, and pretended to be involved in my phone. The screen wasn't on, and neither was the music. I couldn't stop replaying the entire coffee shop scene with Graham.

Did I overreact? I was as embarrassed as I was mad, but that didn't give him the right to tell me this was for my own good. Why didn't he just say *I'm not interested.* That would've hurt. A lot. But putting the whole thing on me.

And kissing me, first…

When I got home, I slunk into my basement studio apartment. The space was cramped, barely big enough for a full-sized bed and a desk, but it was cheap and I didn't take up much space. Violet had offered to let me stay in her apartment when she moved in with

Hunter. She'd let the lease auto-renew. I already owed her and her guys too much I could never repay.

I flopped down on my bed and stared at the ceiling. Speaking of Violet, I promised I'd call her when I found Graham. She'd make me feel better in an instant if I did.

I wasn't ready to feel better yet. I needed to process before I shared this with anyone, and especially before Violet insisted on hammering on Graham's door on my behalf, to tell him he was an idiot.

The next few hours passed in a zombie-like haze. I streamed *Fruits Basket* to remind me I wasn't the only clueless girl in the world who was attracted to an even more clueless guy, when there were plenty of other attractive men around me.

When I finally lay down for the night to sleep, I wanted to indulge in one of my favorite fantasies, with my favorite battery-operated boyfriend. An orgasm would make things better.

It was a scene I'd played out a billion times since Graham was my professor, and it never got old. I'd separated fantasy from reality then, and I could now. It would be easy to slide into the familiar scene.

A computer lab with just the two of us. We'd be working closer than we should be, and he'd push me onto a nearby empty space on a desk. Slide between my legs. Cup my face in his palms, and say, *"I'm the last thing you need in your life."*

Damn it. My frustration returned, bubbling inside.

I could deal with this. It was my imagination after all. I'd make a few alterations and it would become another of my favorite daydreams. The one where Oz walked in on us mid-screw, liked what he saw, and fucked my face while Graham pounded me from behind.

A good, hard, dirty round of everyone getting off, complete with the thrill of being in a public place.

In my mind, I rewound to before Graham opened his stupid mouth. While he was seconds from kissing me. The imaginary class-room door opened.

"I hope I'm interrupting," Oz said in that delicious tenor.

"I'm glad you have people looking out for you. I'm the last thing you need in your life," Graham repeated.

I yanked my pillow out from under my head, smothered my face with it, and screamed until I was hoarse and out of breath.

Stupid jerk had to go and think he was being noble and ruin everything.

I FELT BETTER the next morning. Amazing what a good night's sleep could do for clarity. Besides, I'd see Oz this morning, he'd sign off on me completing my apprenticeship, and then I'd stop by Loading Java and visit Violet and have ice cream and coffee for lunch. I was an adult; I could make decisions like that. I wasn't going to mix them together or anything. Though, if it was the right kind of ice cream...

I picked out a black pencil skirt, and a button-down teal blouse to go with it. There was no on-site work today, and this made me feel pretty and professional. I also paid more attention to my makeup than usual—blush, eyeliner, and lipstick, instead of just a dash of mascara and lip gloss.

An actual job may be out of my grasp right now, but I could dress for success. Tell myself if Graham could see me, he'd be sorry he was an ass.

Not that he deserved any more space in my head. Nope, I was banishing him from my thoughts. He was a silly little girl's silly little crush, and I was far too proudly weird to simply be called *silly*.

The outfit did more for my confidence than I expected, especially with the appreciative glances I drew as I got on the bus. The trip was spent sifting through job postings. I wasn't a convicted felon anymore, and I had wicked programming skills. I could own any of these positions.

I reached the building where Oz's apprenticeship company had its headquarters and headed for the entrance. The steel and glass structure was four stories of simplicity in the middle of an office park that was a lot the same. Oz's office sat on the first floor, near the rear entrance. The most understated suite here.

Few people had any idea he owned the entire business park.

The assistant working reception smiled at me when I walked in. "Cole is waiting for you. Go on back," Holly waved me down the hallway.

I walked the familiar, industrial grade carpet. This was the last time I'd do so as an *apprentice* and there was a sense of accomplishment in the thought. Oz's door was open, and I knocked lightly on the frame.

He glanced up from his computer, raised an eyebrow, and gestured to the table in the opposite corner of his desk. "Come on in."

I liked this room. Not just because it was his, but it had warmth. Personality. Richly stained furniture. Photos of his family on matching wood bookshelves—his parents, his sister, her kids. Him with all of them. There were also pictures of him with some of his former Rinslet colleagues. The only indicator in here that he had anything to do with the other company.

Oz stepped past me to close the door, then took the chair next to mine at a table big enough to sit four or five. He slid a manila folder to me. "This is your certificate of completion. All your finalized paperwork. It's been wonderful working with you, and I'm always available for a reference."

"Same. I mean, thank you. I mean..." *Sigh.* "You know what I mean." Such a dork.

Oz smiled. A rare sight, and as alluring as most everything else he did. "I do. Any questions for me about this?"

I shook my head. That was a safe way to answer.

"Then your apprenticeship is officially over." He stood and offered his hand.

I rose as well and shook it. His grip was firm and warm. When he let go, and moved a finger to my chin, my heart leaped into my throat.

He lifted my head and searched my face. "This feels like an

asshole move, doing this right after what happened last night." His voice rumbled over me.

"I don—"

Oz bushed his lips over mine, and my mind stalled. What in the what? He drew his thumb along my cheek as he cupped my face, titling his head to lean into the kiss. He was tender but unapologetic, the way he introduced his tongue to mine.

When he pulled away, I couldn't find my voice.

"Luna?"

"Wow." In my head, a chibi me was clapping and dancing and squealing.

His smile was back. "You're not going to slap me for waiting until there was another guy in the picture?"

Double what? He couldn't mean Graham. That assumption needed to be corrected post-haste. "There's no other guy."

"Sure." Oz still cradled my face—that felt so good. "There are days when you talk non-stop about Graham, and he never stopped looking at you last night."

Because Graham was the asshole. I frowned.

"What's wrong?" Oz asked.

I didn't want to get into this now, but I didn't want to hide anything, either. If Oz didn't like what he heard, it was better he have a chance to back out now. "There's nothing. I guarantee it. I kissed him last night."

A frown whispered across Oz's face and vanished behind his more typical mask of blankness.

"You're right." I needed to keep this brief. To not ramble. "I do —did—like him, and he pushed me away, *for my own good*." The idea still pissed me off.

Damn Oz's unreadable expression. He could've given me a *never mind*, or *good for him*, or *I'll kill the idiot bastard*. Instead, silence stretched between us.

Should I pull away? I screwed up twice in a row, didn't I?

"What did you do?" Oz asked.

"Told him he was a jerk and left."

"Do you have a problem with what I just did?"

That freaking amazing kiss? "Are you going to tell me you waited until now, for my own good?"

"I'm going to tell you that your probation is over, and so's your apprenticeship. I'm not your *boss* anymore, so it's no longer inappropriate for me to let you know how desperately I want you," Oz said.

Brain freeze. If Graham had done everything wrong last night, Oz was saying everything right this morning. I could kiss him, but I wasn't over the humiliation of the last time I tried that.

"I'm not an idiot." Oz traced a short path over my neck with his fingertips. "I don't expect that if you have feelings for him, they're gone. You don't need to swear forever to me, or even exclusivity. Yet. Keep a place for me on your calendar."

My tongue was stuck to the roof of my mouth. I licked my lips, trying to get them to form words, but it didn't work.

"Tell me what you're thinking." Oz's tone was one of command.

"I really want you to kiss me again."

He slanted his mouth over mine, and consumed me in a toe-curling, tonsil-tickling kiss.

FOUR

O z turned and nudged me, then lifted me to sit on the table, barely breaking our lip lock.

My skirt was too tight for him to push between my legs, but he fiddled with the hem as he rested his thigh against mine.

"Pinch me?" I whimpered against his lips.

He slid his palm over my bare skin, to between my legs, and pinched the tender flesh of my inner thighs.

I moaned at the sharp sting and the desire it sent spilling through me. "Nope. Not dreaming."

He chuckled dryly. "It's real. Is that the only reason you asked?"

"Yes. But it won't be the only reason next time." The pain had numbed quickly, but the tingle lingered.

Oz pulled away to tug at the edges of my blouse, near the buttons. "You always look incredible, but today you had to go and wear something that makes you easy to unwrap." He fiddled with the first button, teasing my skin underneath.

"I wouldn't say no." Did I sound desperate or sexy? Did I care?

Oz shook his head and kissed along my jaw, down to my collar-bone, stopping at the first button on my top, before pulling away, until the only contact he made was lightly grasping my fingertips.

"If I didn't have another meeting in thirty. I wanted to plan this better, leave us more time, but I was running out of it."

"Because of Graham?" I didn't like my ambivalence at his name.

"Partly. But also because I want to take you out. A date—so there's no question—and this is short notice, but it would be tonight. I had planned to skip the event, but a friend asked me to attend--"

"You need a date for something you don't want to go to?" That wasn't so sexy, but I was missing something.

There was his smile again. I could get used to that, especially if he only used it around me. "It's an industry thing. While I'd rather keep you to myself for the next several days, at least, this is a chance for you to meet people. You're brilliant and this can open doors for you."

The circuits met in my brain, completing the connection, and realization flowed in. "The Konsoles for Kids auction?" I couldn't think of anything else to say. The event was huge in tech. Some of the biggest names auctioned off rare collectibles to raise money for Primary Children's Hospital. Oz wanted to introduce me to those people? "I'm not great with the whole meeting people thing."

"You're great with me." He squeezed my fingers.

It was totally different. "I know you. You get me."

"And I'll be there with you. Admittedly, showing off the genius cutie who let me kiss her on my conference table, but this is about you, not me. It's a costume party, but a lot of people will be wearing normal clothes. It's a casual event."

Why was I hesitating? Because I didn't want a repeat of last night. Not that I was going to kiss anyone there except Oz, but I was plenty capable of embarrassing myself in other ways. This was a chance of a lifetime, though.

"Yes or no?" Oz asked.

"Yes." Saying it felt good. My shock was wearing off, leaving a hopped-up girl who'd had three quad shot mochas dancing in my brain and screaming with joy. "Yes, yes, yes."

Oz scooted me off the table and bent in for one more long kiss.

He brushed his thumb over my bottom lip before stepping away. "I'll pick you up at seven. I'd ask you to stay, but…"

"Meeting. I know. See you tonight." My voice tilted up at the end, and I hid my wince.

It took the last of my restraint to keep from skipping out of his office, down the hall, and outside. The instant I hit the sidewalk, several yards from the building, I let out a tiny squeal and clapped.

I had to call Violet. I needed to share this with someone. As I grabbed her number and listened to the phone ring, I walked past the bus stop. There would be another one.

"Hey." Violet's voice was bright.

"So glad you didn't send me to voicemail. We need to talk. Can you talk now? I can call back."

"Hang on, I'll go on break." Violet's voice grew muffled as she spoke to someone in the background. During the days she managed an anime themed gaming cafe, and in her free time—don't ask me how she managed that with two boyfriends—she volunteered at an LGBTQ+ youth homeless shelter.

I heard the faint sound of footsteps, and then a door closing. "Okay. What's up?" Violet asked.

I swallowed another squeal. Where to start? "So, last night I found Graham, and it was a *disaster*. I threw myself at him. He pushed me away."

"I'm sorry, L."

"No, it's okay. I'm over that." Or I'd put it behind me far enough it wasn't going to fuck with my mood now. "You know how my apprenticeship ended, and I knew something else would come along, but it hasn't yet? So, I was talking to Cole this morning," *talking. Ha.* "And he kissed me. Like full-on, tongue down my throat, made my toes curl… wowza. So good. And not only that, but he wants me to meet his friends." I couldn't talk fast enough. "Colleagues? It's not like a meet the family thing. But he wants to introduce me to people at the Konsoles for Kids auction. I don't know what to do. What am I supposed to wear? Oh, my God, Violet. Oz asked me out. Cole-freaking-Denton."

"I've got you covered," Violet said. "And I told you so." She did.

She'd tried to convince me more than once that the attraction went both ways. "As soon as work's over, I'll be there. Does that give you time?"

Aside from the fact that I'd be freaking out alone for the next couple of hours? "Yes. You're the best. Seriously."

"You'd do the same for me. Until I get there?"

"Yeah?"

"No coffee. No sugar."

I stuck my tongue out at the phone, but she knew me too well. "Yes, ma'am."

Even with the bus stopping every five minutes, by the time I got home, it wasn't even eleven in the morning. Violet would be here around three thirty. How was I supposed to keep myself occupied until then?

Washing my hair twice in one day was a bad idea, but I could shave *everything* from my armpits down. Wishful thinking? More like the power of positivity.

That didn't take nearly as much time as I'd hoped it would. I pulled on some basic underwear and a T-shirt, and spent the next few hours distracting myself with job hunting—sending off more resumes and sifting through listings. By tomorrow I may have a couple of names to drop or new people to reach out to, but no reason to ignore the existing opportunities.

Violet showed up right on time, which was still way too long for me. I let her in, and she handed me a garment bag.

"Lyn borrowed something from Sadie. You're going to love it," Violet said. Lyn was her boss at Loading Java, and Sadie—who was a brilliant professional cosplay seamstress—was one of her best friends.

I already loved it and I hadn't seen it yet. I hung the bag on the bar in the portable closet next to my bed and dragged the zipper down. Inside was a Japanese schoolgirl outfit—pleated skirt, short sleeved top, and kerchief. It was straight out of an anime. I loved it more now.

Even better, I didn't have to put on uncomfortable lace panties and bra. White cotton was appropriate, and I was already wearing my cutest set.

"Distract me," I said as I stripped out of my other clothes. Violet and I had changed in front of each other dozens of times. This was nothing.

"How?"

"I don't care." I unclipped the skirt from its hanger and pulled it up my legs. "Cute stories about Hunter. Ramsey's plans for world domination. Anything." The skirt rested perfectly at the top of my hips when I zipped it up. I moved on to the top.

Violet was waiting with the neckerchief. "We're adding new VR tech to the cafe. Lyn's converting a room, and we're getting the hardware straight from the manufacturer, the day it releases."

"Which means you're going to have it before release." Tech was the best distraction. It almost helped me sit still while we tied the accessories in place.

Violet headed into the bathroom, calling "maybe" over her shoulder. She returned a heartbeat later with a comb, hair elastics, and a scrunchie.

The hardware wouldn't be out for nine months, but the specs on it were unreal. I couldn't wait to get my hands on it. "I'll be your best friend if you let me play with it early."

"You're already my best friend." Damn her and her logic. She tugged the comb through my hair, and I felt her sectioning off pieces for a braid.

I already knew she was going to say yes, though. "Please, please, please, please, *pleeeeeeeaaaassseeeee.* If you say yes, I won't subject you to the detailed specs again."

Violet laughed. "You can tell me as many times as you want. I won't understand any more than I have so far. What you should do instead, is whisper those sexy nothings in Cole's ear."

"Not sure ARM processing is bedroom talk."

"With the two of you? Are you sure?"

"Fair point." It was pretty sexy that Cole would listen to me go off about things like that, and get it.

Violet set the comb on my desk and pointed me toward the mirror on my bathroom door.

As I took in my reflection, a girl with pale skin, a single braid of red, wide eyes, and way too much implied innocence stared back. "I look like jailbait." I was already going out with a man a decade older than me. Would this make him question that? I didn't care for the surge of doubt.

Violet met my gaze in the reflection. "You look fuckable, and of consenting age. Cole knows who he asked out."

"I'm supposed to be making business connections." I tugged at the hem of my skirt. I wanted her to convince me this was okay, because she was right, I also looked good.

Violet lightly slapped my hands down. "If they don't love you for your brain, they don't deserve you."

Even I wasn't the kind of optimist who could let that go unchallenged. "You know it doesn't work that way." A book wasn't always judged by its cover, but the odds certainly leaned in that direction.

"I know that it should. I won't be hurt if you want to wear something else, but I wouldn't have brought this if I thought it wasn't right." Violet's gaze, as she stared at me in the mirror, and her tone carried her sincerity.

I smoothed out the blouse and skirt. "I really do look good."

"*Duh.*"

I'd wear the outfit. There was plenty else for me to freak out about tonight anyway, like a first date with a man I practically worshiped, to meet his work colleagues and hopefully leave the right kind of impression on all of them that I didn't make myself even more of a pariah in the industry.

FIVE

Violet left fifteen minutes before Oz was supposed to show up. She gave me a hug and reminded me I was going to have an amazing night.

Fortunately, Oz was early, so I only had to panic with my own thoughts for about ten minutes.

On the drive there, I babbled. I didn't even know what about, but he listened and responded, like always. I was almost calm when we arrived.

The auction was being held in an event hall at the local convention center. A few people milled outside the doors, but most were in the room itself, which was decorated with neon and steel and looked so cheesy '80's. It was *brilliant*.

"Cole." A woman called from behind us.

Oz wrapped an arm around my waist as we spun. The gesture felt possessive, and I liked it. Especially when he pointed us toward a gorgeous brunette. She was probably Oz's age, and absolutely rocking a Wonder Woman costume. I'd never have the boobs and hips to pull off a look like that, but she owned it.

Her smile as we approached was warm, but something about it felt insincere. *No.* That wasn't the right word, but there was something under her expression that I couldn't pinpoint. "Didn't know if you'd make it," she said.

"Why would I miss an industry event, Judy?" Oz asked.

A scowl crossed her face but vanished in a blink. Was I projecting because someone pretty wanted my date's attention?

"This is Luna." Oz nodded, never letting go of me. "Next big name in gaming."

Heat flooded my face.

"I don't doubt it." She extended her hand. "I'm Judith—not Judy—Senior VP of New Product Development at Rinslet, Inc. Pleasure to meet you." Her handshake was firm.

"The pleasure is mine." Whatever vibe I got earlier must have been a fluke, because she was nothing but sincerity now. I liked her, and with a title like that, she had to have knowledge. "I'd love to pick your brain someday."

"Same." Judith jerked a thumb at the two men standing nearby. "Brandon, my Director of Sound Engineering, and Dustin, one of my top artists."

Brandon shook my hand then Oz's. "I didn't think the Wizard ever came out from behind his curtain."

"I make exceptions under the right circumstances." Oz's voice was tight, even for him. Where did the shift in mood come from?

Dustin's gaze was fixed on me. "You must be the right circumstances." The way he studied me, it was like he was hoping to figure out what was inside. He grasped my fingers and kissed the tips.

How was I supposed to react to that?

Oz tightened his grip and pulled me closer, and I was grateful. He looked between the two men. "Rumor is you have your fingers in new things, Judy."

Judith laughed lightly. "I do, but it's not either of these two. Rather, they work for me, but there's no fingering. How much have you heard?"

"No details, but if you're involved, I know you always want the best talent." Oz didn't look fazed by the innuendo.

"It's not that kind of opportunity," Judith said. "If it were, I'd move Luna to the top of my list."

Three more people joined us. The two men were dressed in sleeveless vests, similar to Brandon's, and the woman was in a platinum blond wig, a crop-top, and low-rise jeans.

"No Doubt?" I asked.

The new woman grinned and elbowed the guy closest. "Told you someone would get it." The four of them had matching spade tattoos, like an ace of spades, on their biceps. Pretty sure that wasn't part of the outfits.

Before we could do another round of introductions, someone else pulled Oz away.

So many people wanted his time, and he introduced me to every one of them. The names blurred together in my mind, but nobody questioned when I wanted their pictures to go with their business cards. I hoped I'd be able to sort it all out later.

Everything up for auction was in acrylic cases around the room, with reserves listed, and QR codes to scan and place silent bids.

"If it's not the wizard himself," a man behind us said.

I knew that voice. How? Oz and I turned, and I had to force my jaw to not drop open.

"Didn't expect to see you here." Scott McAllister was one of the two owners and founders of Rinslet, Inc, and an absolute personal hero. He was tall—then again, most people were to me—and built like a football player. His hair was graying around the temples, and he had that whole sexy silver fox vibe going on. "Who convinced you to step out from behind the curtain?"

Oz shook his hand. "Dorothy."

"She's good at that." Scott nodded. I didn't understand the reference. We hadn't met a Dorothy tonight. He'd never mentioned one before. Who—

"This is Luna." Oz pointed Scott toward me.

He turned a warm smile in my direction, and I barely had the brainpower to hold out my hand. If I were an anime character, my eyes would be huge right now, and I'd be swooning and thinking *he's so cool.*

"Hi." My voice squeaked out, and I hid a wince. "Nice to meet you." *Understatement of the freaking century.* Chibi-me was dying of stardom overdose.

"I've heard a lot about you." Scott's grip was warm and firm when he shook my hand.

The whispers around us seemed to intensify. My imagination was really working overtime. Oz had talked about me? To Scott. Fucking. McAllister? Geez, it wasn't about my crimes was it? This was where I should say *all of it good, I hope*, but my vocal cords had frozen.

My phone vibrated through my purse and against my hip. I ignored it. Violet knew where I was, and she'd wait.

"You're really the mind behind building a patch for one of the worst pieces of malware ever." Scott shook my hand a second time. "It's a pleasure."

If I died right now, on Oz's arm, Scott shaking my hand, I'd be happy. Dark thought. But not really. I was such a freaking fangirl. I found my voice. "The pleasure is definitely mine."

"Of course it is." Scott grinned.

Luna.

Did someone just whisper my name? More than once? Did endorphins cause hallucinations?

A woman a little older than me joined us, and Scott wrapped an arm around her waist. Her blond hair fell in soft curls around her face. She was the kind of elegant I'd never be, and she carried herself like she knew it.

Perfect complement to Scott.

"Cole. I heard you were here. Had to see it myself," she said.

"Hey, Kenzie. It's been too long." Oz's tone was more formal with her. Not in a bad way—more in a *we're not close* kind of way.

Scott squeezed her hip. They were adorable together. "Kenz, this is Luna."

"*Oh.*" Kenzie's composure slipped, and my gut plummeted. "Lovely to meet you." She was all smiles again."

"What was with the slip?" Scott's question mirrored the one in my thoughts.

"It really is lovely to meet you, I just surprised to hear your name." Kenzie frowned as she looked at me. "I say this because you're a friend of Cole's"—

That sounded *so* not good.

—"I'm the queen of composure, and I don't know if I could keep mine right now. All my respect," Kenzie said.

"Wait. What?" Was I just insulted? The words weren't delivered in a cruel way. Was she talking about the outfit? It was a mistake, wasn't it?

Kenzie reached for her purse. "You don't know. The anniversary article…"

My world was falling away, leaving me dangling in mid-air with no support. The whispers around us were louder than I'd realized. People were looking at us.

Kenzie handed me her phone. The headline on the screen said *10th Anniversary of the Hack that Brought the World to Its Knees.* A photo of me, complete with my name, was front and center.

The room spun around me. Now that I was paying attention to the whispers, it was clear what they were about.

Is that really her?

Fucking idiot.

They let someone like her in the door?

"I need some air." I broke away before I could hear anyone's answer, and cut a straight line for the nearest door, walking as fast as possible without breaking into a run.

SIX

Since we were a block from the dead center middle of the city, there weren't many places for me to escape to. I settled myself on a stone bench near a clump of trees, set away from the street, and breathed in the exhaust-filled air.

That didn't comfort me in any sense of the word.

Oz sat next to me, his thigh pressing into mine. "Hey." He covered my hand.

"Did you hear them in there?" I tried to keep the panic from my voice. People were supposed to forget about what I'd done. This was my chance at a fresh start. A new career. *Finally.* "They were calling me an idiot. A criminal. Worse." Things I didn't want to think about, let alone repeat.

"They don't know you. I do, and you're none of those things. Others will feel the same."

"I don't want to spend my time explaining myself, over and over. Especially if they've already decided I'm the villain."

"That's fair."

Panic was already fading, but it didn't leave me with any answers as it passed. "I know it'll be okay, it's just... It's a shock. I was putting this behind me."

"Do you want to leave?"

I didn't want my time with him to be over.

"Would you rather go inside again?" Oz asked.

"No. Please no."

"We can camp out here for tonight. I'll have someone bring a tent and sleeping bag." He sounded completely serious.

For all I knew, he was, and it made me smile. "I'm having a lot of fun with you. If we go, you'll take me home, I'll sit up all night, overthinking things and not coming up with solutions, and I don't want to go home to an empty apartment and be alone with my thoughts."

Oz tilted my chin up to look me in the eye. "So I'll go home with you, and you won't be alone." He brushed his lips over mine. "Because I'm having a lot of fun, too."

Back at my place, I realized just how tiny my apartment was when Oz joined me inside. I should've thought this through better.

"What's with the frown?" He asked.

"It's a little cramped in here."

He stepped closer. "I'll have to snuggle you close, then." A husky growl ran through his already deep voice. He teased the hem of my skirt, pushing it higher and tickling my thighs. "If I didn't already, this outfit would make me feel like a dirty old man."

"What if I like dirty older men?" I certainly did when they looked and thought like him.

"Lucky for me. Speaking of, did you ever fantasize about Graham? Have naughty dreams?"

All the freaking time. No way was I telling the man standing in my apartment, reaching his hand under my dress, that I diddled myself to thoughts of someone else.

"It's not a trap." Oz drew his mouth up the side of my neck, his hot breath sending goosebumps racing over my skin. "I want to hear what kind of filthy fucking thoughts you have."

"So, so many." Was it okay to say that out loud?"

He dragged a thumb over my bottom lip. "Don't stop talking now. How about me? What kind of things are you fantasizing about me doing to you?"

My eyes were wide and my imagination was inches away from hopping the tracks to be heard. I shook my head, unable to speak.

He pushed his thumb into my mouth, and I sucked instinctively.

"I'm here because I like the things you say and the way you think," he said. "What kind of things are you thinking about me with you. Tell me." There was a distinct thread of command in his tone.

"There is one I have a lot..." If I didn't say it, it was unlikely I could have it.

"See? Tell me. What kind of daydreams make Luna wet?"

My heart hammered against my ribs and my pulse raced. What if he thought I was a freak?

Then he wasn't for me? "That you're rough."

"Rough how?" He grabbed my wrist tightly, and I gasped

Here went nothing. "That you know it's okay to pin me down and take what you want. Fuck my face. Finger me until I beg to come. Stretch me out with your cock and fuck me until my legs don't work." Was that too much? "And then cuddle with me after."

Oz's smile was almost feral. Frightening and enticing. "Do you actually want that, or are you content with it staying fantasy?"

"I actually want that."

He moved his mouth to my ear, his hot break searing my skin. "You tell me to stop, and I will," he said.

"Okay."

Gentle Oz vanished as he shoved up my skirt and pushed my panties aside. He plunged two fingers inside me. "Fucking hell, you're wet." He pumped, in and out, sliding easily against my slick skin until my hips thrust in time with his movement.

My body swayed with the rhythm of hard and fast. I gasped in surprise when he pulled out without warning.

He shoved his fingers in my mouth. "Tell me how you taste," he ordered.

I spent my time sucking each finger clean, relishing his groans and my taste. "So, so good."

Oz knotted his fingers in my hair and yanked back my head. He crushed his mouth to mine. I could drown in the need that reverberated through me as he probed my mouth with his tongue.

"You really do." He groaned against my skin when he pulled away. "You do magical things with that tongue." Hand still in my hair, he forced me to the ground, undoing his pants with his free hand. He freed himself, and I whimpered at how big he was. Almost too big.

"This is what you do to me every time I think about you. Every time I hear you talk," he said. "And now I find out you've got a filthy mind hiding under all that sugar. I need to feel your dirty mouth on my cock." He pressed into my mouth without warning, holding me close, driving deep enough I almost gagged.

I'd never been so turned on. I wanted him to use me. To get off on me being his dirty little girl. To take what he wanted and make sure I got the same.

As he thrust against my face, I swirled my tongue around his thick shaft, relishing his taste and his groan. His movements grew shorter. His grunts deeper and more punctuated.

I met his gaze, eyes wide, not sure if I wanted him to finish now, and cover my face, or draw things out longer.

He let out a shuddering breath as he pulled away. My chin was wet with drool. My eyes watered. I needed more.

Oz yanked me to my feet again, and tore away my panties, leaving a rough burn where the fabric tore. He shoved his fingers between my legs again, but didn't penetrate me this time.

"Fuck, you're dripping." The gravel in his voice was enticing. "You're a filthy slut, aren't you?"

If he'd said that in any other circumstance, I'd be furious. The language was part of the play, though, and in the moment, it turned me on even more. I nodded my head. "Yes."

"If your teacher friend was here, and I made him watch, would that make you even wetter? I bet you practically come at the thought."

Geez, Graham watching us. Getting off on this as much as we were? "Yes."

Oz threw me on the bed and forced his thigh between my legs, prying them open. He pressed his knee into my pussy, and shoved my shirt and bra out of the way. He kneaded my breasts and pinched my nipples. Tugging hard. Twisting until the sting ached all over. Until my hips were bucking and I was grinding against his leg, desperate for more.

He dipped his head near mine. "Beg me for it."

"Let me come, please?" I was so fucking turned on.

He moved his hand from my breasts to press against my throat. "Make me believe you want it."

My head fuzzed and I floated into the clouds. "Please?"

"What would you have done if I felt you up in front of everyone at the party tonight?"

Oh, fuck. Just when I thought my pulse couldn't race any faster. "Let you."

"Because you like the idea of all those eyes on you."

I nodded.

"Say it."

My throat was so dry. I licked my lips. "At night, I finger myself to the fantasy of a roomful of people watching you fuck me."

"Because?"

"Because I'm a dirty, cock hungry slut." Things I'd only ever muttered in my own head. Things I didn't expect to ever say to someone else.

And the way Oz watched me, I'd say it again and again.

He tightened his grip on my throat and moved his other hand between my legs, to glide his fingers inside me again.

The penetration was incredible, but it wasn't going to get me off. My clit begged for attention and my thoughts were made of cotton candy.

"Finger me, please?" I *begged*. "Play with my clit until I come."

He slid his fingers out of me and up, to tease my swollen bud as he lightly choked me. I was teetering so precariously on the edge that it didn't take much to push me over into orgasm.

Climax racked my body, shuddering through me until my body was too sensitive to take anymore. I tried to pull away, but he didn't let up. I squirmed. This was too much, but it was also incredible.

Oz finally eased up.

I barely had enough time to draw a breath, before he rolled a condom on and thrust his cock inside me. He pinned my knees to my chest, gripping my thigh with one hand, and moving his thumb back to my clit.

He built to a slow rhythm, easing off each time I drew close to orgasm again, then pushing harder, both with the fucking and the fingering.

"God, your cunt's so fucking tight." He sounded like he was on the edge of losing control.

I squeezed around him, delighting in his groan.

He increased his pressure on my clit, stroking until I came again, clenching hard, spasming with him buried inside me. He thrust harder. Faster. Slamming against me with abandon. Pushing me deeper and deeper into pleasure.

I was lost in all of it when his stuttered grunts reached me, and he gave a few final thrusts, before slowing to a stop.

Our breathing was the only sound in the room for several seconds. Oz let go of my legs and rested his hands on either side of my head as he brushed his lips lightly over mine.

"You're so incredible," he murmured.

I might have blushed at that, but my skin must already be flushed and bright pink from the exertion.

He kissed me again. "Don't move."

I couldn't if I wanted to.

He vanished into the bathroom, and a moment later he returned with a washcloth. He was so gentle as wiped my face clean, and then moved between my legs.

There was no way we were both going to fit in my bed, but he made it work, pulling me into him and holding me tight.

I rested my forehead on his chest and danced my fingers over his skin, memorizing every texture and letting myself be wrapped in this cocoon of warmth and security.

"Is that a typical fantasy for you?" He asked softly.

"They run the gamut, but there are a lot of variations on that."

He kissed the top of my head. "So many things to learn about you. So many delicious, incredible things."

"You expecting company?" Oz's voice had that deep, sleepy sexy tone to it.

Amazing way to wake up. Too bad the knocking on the door got to me first. "Never. Probably Violet to take me to breakfast. Get the deets."

"Mmm." Oz pulled me tighter into him, his cock pressing into my ass and his palm teasing higher up my rib cage. "Too bad for her. I'm having you for breakfast."

"She'll understand." I didn't want to leave the bed yet, though. "What's the etiquette about texting my best friend, if she's standing a few yards away, because I don't want to get up?" Why hadn't Violet texted me? She always let me know when she was coming over.

Oz kissed me on the top of the head, and managed to extract himself from the sheets without disturbing me too much. "I'll tell her. Unless you have an issue with that."

"None at all." I liked the idea quite a bit. I reached for my phone out of habit, as he pulled on his jeans.

Yup, there was a text from Violet.

Oz crossed the short distance to the door, and undid the chain and deadbolt.

I opened the message, to find a photo of Oz's truck in my driveway, with a kissy face, a peach, an eggplant, and the words, *Call me later*.

That wasn't Violet on the other side of the door Oz was currently opening.

"Morning." Oz's voice was flatter than normal.

"Morning." *Graham.* "Let me talk to Luna. I need to apologize."

SEVEN

O z swung the door shut.

I should be mad that he did so without asking me first, but I didn't want to see Graham.

"Luna." Graham's voice was muffled as he knocked again.

He'd said he wanted to apologize.

Why did it matter? I had Oz now, even if I didn't, Graham had his chance. Though... I sat in bed, sheets pulled up to my chin, staring at the doorway. *Why not both?* My wonderful, pre-coffee, meme-driven brain asked. Oz specifically used the word exclusive yesterday. As in, we weren't.

Was that the stupidest thought ever to entertain after how amazing last night was? Maybe. Did that stop me from doing exactly that? Nope.

"Up to you," Oz said. "I won't be offended if you give him five minutes."

"Breakfast?" I offered weakly, not sure what I was asking.

"Can you promise me you won't be thinking about this very moment the entire morning if you don't talk to him?"

I could lie and promise that. But not really, because I was super bad at lying. "I'm here with you."

"If he hadn't pushed you away, would you have gone out with me last night?"

I had no idea if Graham would've been as amicable about Oz as Oz was about him. Though, given Graham's whole *this is for your own good* attitude, probably not. "I would've wanted to."

"If you want to talk to him, talk to him. I won't take it wrong. I meant the things I said yesterday."

I raised my brows as all the things Oz said rushed into my thoughts, carried on his heavy, seductive tone, including the part where he called me a dirty slut—in the best way possible—and said he wanted Graham to watch us fuck.

Great, now there was a throb of desire between my legs, because I'd do that in a heartbeat... after a lot of overthinking.

I climbed from bed and pulled on a T-shirt. "I'll talk to him and then I'm yours again."

Oz wrapped his arms around my waist before I could grab a pair of panties. He crushed his mouth to mine as he slipped a hand between my legs to tease his fingers over my bare, damp skin. He growled against my lips. "You're mine the entire time, but otherwise, I agree."

That shouldn't turn me into a gooey puddle of desire. It totally did. I dressed quickly and opened the door. Graham was still there. I kind of didn't expect that. Would he ask to speak with me alone?

He looked past me, and then met my gaze. "The two of you are just friends?"

"Things have changed." I'd rather do this in front of Oz. He sounded sincere when he said he was fine with it, and I believed him. But I didn't want any misunderstandings later. Besides, he made me feel safe. Not that Graham would hurt me physically, but he had the potential to do a number on my heart. "And yes, he knows what happened—and didn't—between us," I said.

"And he's okay with being your rebound guy?"

I scowled at the phrase.

Graham frowned and shook his head. "I didn't mean that."

"You did," Oz said. "And I'm okay with Luna and I defining our relationship, not you."

I wanted to get this bit over with. Yeah, there was an animalistic appeal in being fought over, but I hated conflict. Especially being at the center of it. "This is why you're here?"

"I'm here to apologize to you, and hopefully talk."

I crossed my arms. The physical barrier was to remind me I wouldn't listen to a weak apology that part of me hoped would be so good I couldn't ignore it.

"When you showed up the other day, when you kissed me..." Graham trailed off and looked past me toward Oz again. "Can we do this outside?" He nodded to the steps next to him.

There it was. I shook my head. "I'm good here, thanks."

Graham sighed. "I *have* missed you. I *was* staying away from you. I figured you'd moved on." His gaze flicked toward Oz again before landing on me. "But I lied when I said I hoped that was the case. I also wanted you to find me."

This wasn't an apology, and it wasn't tugging at all on that spark of hope that I had about anything to do with Graham. At least swooning chibi-Luna was still half asleep.

Why was I talking to Graham at all? I'd barely started things with Oz. Who was also right that I was still thinking about Graham. Damn my optimism that I wouldn't have to give either up. "I don't know what you expect me to say."

"When your pet bear said the things he did, he hit every doubt I'd had when I was your teacher," Graham said. "Touched on very fucking reason I kept my distance."

"This is crappy apology." I could swoon and daydream from now until eternity, but refused to imagine an *I'm sorry* when there wasn't one.

Graham frowned. "I promise I'm getting there. Cole's accusation reminded me of all the reasons I kept my distance, yes. But when the news hit last night, I couldn't stop worrying about you. Which meant I was thinking about you, about what originally happened, and about all the reasons it was hard for me to not tell you I was attracted to you. I'm sorry for what I said the other day. I shouldn't have put this on you. I do miss you, and I never should've used you as an excuse."

Graham rested a hand on my face and tilted his head.

He was going to kiss me. My pulse roared so loudly in my ears I couldn't hear anything else.

I placed my hand on his chest and stepped to arm's length, breaking his touch. Did I want the kiss? Unfortunately, yes. Did I also kind of want to see what Oz would do? Deck Graham, tell him to stick around and watch while Oz fucked me, or walk out the door without a word?

That last one terrified me. "Thank you for the apology." I kept my voice cool. "Was there something else?" I moved my hand from Graham to the door, ready shut him out.

"I know how to make this right. How to fix the bad press that story is going to generate."

"How?" Oz asked.

"This has been blowing up all night in the tech and education communities. I've been looking for my own name, and worried you were at home, falling into a panic spiral. I'm glad you were distracted." Graham's voice tilted at an odd timbre.

Oz made a low, frustrated growling sound I felt in the soles of my feet. "Do you ever offer a tl;dr version?" He asked.

"Context is important," Graham said. "Fine. This isn't going away. If it does, it could come back any time, as last night proved, and the only way to prevent that from being an ongoing threat is to deal with it. The world needs to see the real Luna. The kind of infamy you have, your last notable hack defines you. Ten years ago, you brought the world to its knees, and five years ago you saved it. The internet needs to remember the latter."

That was idealistic, even for me. "I didn't actually *save the world*."

"Schools and colleges versus government contractors? To most people, that's saving the world." Graham made it sound simple.

Oz stepped up next to me and settled his hand at the small of my back. "What you're talking about would have to be big, and even then, there's no guarantee it's going to overwrite what's already out there."

"Luna knows people who will help this go viral. Ramsey Miller. Sadie Sews. Grayso—"

"I don't know them." Okay, I knew Ramsey, but I'd met Sadie *once*. She definitely wasn't on the list of people I felt comfortable asking for favors.

"How do *you* know that, Graham?" Oz asked. "How long have you been watching Luna?"

"Violet is surrounded by people who live public lives. If Violet knows them, Luna knows them."

I noticed Graham didn't answer the second question. Did he avoid it on purpose?

"It may not work, but you know how the saying goes—the odds are better than if we don't try." Graham's tone was one of conviction. "The news hit last night, and while it won't vanish quickly it will fade. We don't have to shout louder right this second. As the original story gets softer, over the next week or so, we come in with something stronger."

"And you have the knowledge to make this happen." Oz's tone was flat with disbelief. "Luna can go to Sadie herself. To Grayson. To Ramsey."

The people around Violet really did lead public lives. I'd never thought of that before. But Graham was the right person to help with Graham's idea. Go figure. "It's not just about tossing the information out there and crossing our fingers," I said. "Going viral isn't a science, but there are reproducible elements that increase the odds."

"I never cease to be amazed at how much knowledge you retain." Graham smiled broadly.

Which didn't make me swoon at all. There may have been a rush of heat to my face, but that didn't mean I was enjoying any part of this conversation or wishing in any way that I'd taken more of Graham's other courses.

"Graham teaches how information travels, both behind the scenes and right in front of our faces." I hadn't taken the more advanced courses on The Psychology of Social Media, but I was in as many Gen Ed ones as I was allowed to cram into my schedule without disrupting my Pre Reqs. "One of his final projects"—for the course I couldn't get into—"was to create a piece of media and make it go viral."

Number of views were part of the grade, but just as important was how each element was utilized.

"I've learned a lot from seeing people do this over and over," Graham said.

Oz's cough was exaggerated. "In other words, you've made a habit of letting your students do the work, and you reaping the benefits."

I wouldn't say a felony conviction was a benefit of helping me.

"You never learned from the people you worked with? Who work for you? What a sad life that must be." Graham's derision was almost tangible. "Every student in that course has lifetime access to every project. The data, the theories, the execution. I don't hoard information. Would you like a list of references of what my students have gone on to do, using the things I taught them? I guarantee, you'll know their names. I also guarantee none of them leaves the kind of impression Luna does."

He was exaggerating, or everyone who'd ever met me would feel that way. My flush deepened anyway, running from my toes to the roots of my hair.

"This isn't my decision," Oz said.

Graham's idea was solid, and he was right. This wasn't going away. Someone would always know—always want to talk about— what I did ten years ago. I didn't like to think of myself as infamous, but I'd have to be blind to not see my own legacy. Every job interview where someone said *Aren't you the girl*.... Cases like last night, where someone like Scott McAllister recognized my name.

I needed to get ahead of things now, and Graham had the skills to help me do that.

"Luna." Oz's voice softened. "This is your future. Decide what to do next for you. Not for me or Graham or anyone else."

I didn't make decisions without considering the people around me.

"Imagine the challenge," Graham said.

"That was what got me in trouble in the first place." And a huge part of the reason I had to consider how it would impact my friends. But, *sigh,* the challenge of making this work—of doing it perfectly— really spoke to me.

Graham reached for me, then dropped his hand. "There are no dark or light powers, no matter what books and movies say. There's only what you choose to use your gifts for, and this is a good cause— you're a good cause."

I wouldn't describe myself that way, but what he was proposing was a good idea. And damn it, I did want to be challenged. Laying cable was a nice distraction, but digital penetration… "Let's do it. Where and when do we start?"

"The sooner the better." Graham looked at Oz. "My plan was to buy you breakfast."

I prayed Oz meant everything he said, about being fine with whatever I decided. I didn't want to lose or have to resent him because of this. I wasn't going to test those limits too much today. "I have plans this morning."

"Luna. A moment?"

I didn't know what to make of Oz's flat tone, and I didn't like the crevice of doubt it sent slicing through me.

EIGHT

I'd spent the last three years spinning my wheels and never getting traction. With work. With relationships.

And in less than forty-eight hours, everything was ramping up like someone had quadrupled the number of threads on the system that was my life.

It wasn't possible to move too far away from Graham in my apartment, but Oz and I did step out of ear reach.

"Last night was about getting you back on your feet," Oz said softly. "What he's proposing—will it help?"

I shrugged. "It's the only idea I have. It's also a really good idea. I also want you there—I want your input." The longer I thought about it, the more this entire thing felt reasonable.

"Do it. You and I have time."

"I hope so."

Oz tilted my head up with a finger under my chin and brushed his thumb over my lips. "Bring an overnight bag and come to my place after."

"Okay." Heat flooded me on a wave of happiness. I turned to Graham. "Let's do it."

We agreed on a place, and Oz told Graham we'd meet him there.

It'd be nice to take a shower, but mine was barely big enough for me. Oz and I finished dressing—which unfortunately meant he put his shirt on—and were on our way.

Oz kept his hand on my thigh when he wasn't shifting gears.

I texted Violet with a promise to call later. Or tomorrow. I wasn't sure yet. I checked my email, too, to make sure I didn't have any requests for interviews waiting.

There were already two replies to the resumes I'd sent out yesterday. Both said *We're not interested at this time*. They didn't even offer to keep my resume on file. Rude.

Graham was waiting when we arrived. He'd grabbed us a booth in the far corner of the restaurant—one of those that was a single half-circle wrapped around a table.

Oz slid in next to Graham and pulled me to sit next to him, sandwiching Oz in the middle.

Graham didn't look pleased as he put an extra foot between them.

We placed our orders, and Graham told the waitress to leave the coffee pot and expect that we'd need more. Was it bad that I liked that throwback to the old days, when we'd be in a random twenty-four-hour diner, talking code strategies until three in the morning and downing *way* too much caffeine?

"The basics." Graham pulled a leather portfolio from the seat next to him and opened it on the table to a blank notebook page. "This isn't just about getting Luna's name out there; we have to be smart about the details. Nailing the SEO. Ensuring the right click throughs…" As he talked, he wrote out neat columns across the top of the page.

So. Many. Schoolgirl flashbacks.

"How is this different than every other person out there who does the same and never gets seen?" Oz asked.

I knew this one, and the answer was so simple it didn't sound like a real reply. "Because we don't do it the same as every other person out there."

Oz raised an eyebrow and stared me down with amused disbelief.

Wowza that heated gaze made me squirm.

"It's like playing Street Fighter 2." Graham's voice held an edge. "Everyone knows that Abel's Infinite exists. The combo is programmed in. But it takes a whole new level of skill to hit the right buttons, under pressure, on purpose."

"And you can hit the right buttons," Oz said with disbelief.

Graham looked past him, to hold my gaze. "Every time."

Was he flirting with me? With my date…boyfriend? Bodyguard? … sitting between us?

Oz coughed to clear his throat.

Graham sank into his seat, but not before I caught his smirk. "In reality? I suck at Street Fighter. For the purposes of this analogy? Yes. I know how to lay out a web of the kind of genuine, interconnected links that search engines love. Every time someone searches for Luna's name, whether they want to know about the stuff we got in trouble for or see pictures of her sucking cock, our good results pop up first."

Was my face bright red? It had to be. Especially since I was fantasizing about Graham taking pictures while I sucked Oz's cock. Geez. "No one's searching for my name like that." My voice came out thicker than I intended.

"He's right." Oz nodded at my phone. "Look for yourself."

I pulled up a search app and typed my name in. There it was —*Luna Murphy suck cock* plain as day in the auto-complete suggestions. "Why…? Never mind." I was a woman in tech who just became a minor celebrity. It was tempting to see what kind of results the phrase returned, but I swiped away.

Another email came in, and I couldn't help but glance at the message from another company I'd sent my resume to yesterday. *We're sorry to inform you…*

My heart sank at another rejection, and I set my phone aside. "So… SEO. Click throughs. How do we make it happen?"

The waitress returned with three full coffee cups, two silver pots, and a bowl full of plain and flavored creamers.

"Keywords are great, but on a really simplistic level, other people talking about you, using those keywords, is the best. That's where your friends come in." Graham grabbed three French vanilla and dumped them into his coffee. "They're going to give us the kind of web that most companies pay huge money to build, with their existing networks."

I went straight for the sugar. Plain cream. "They're not my friends. I barely know them."

"I suspect you've left an impression. Oz has connections too, if he's willing to use them."

"Without question." Oz might look like a black coffee kind of guy, but he loaded up on as much sugar as I did.

Graham wrote out more notes on his pad. "You were at Rinslet when they were Cord. You know the original gang. Jordan has a huge fanbase."

Oz nodded. "I do and he does."

"Judith—"

"No." Oz clipped the word off. He exhaled slowly, nostrils flared. "This isn't her area of expertise."

I was asking him about that reaction later for sure.

"Why are you doing this, Oz?" Graham asked. "You were *just a friend* two nights ago, and now you're all in, for whatever Luna needs."

I downed my coffee too fast, ignoring that it scalded the roof of my mouth. I was going to need the extra energy if the tension between the two of them kept up.

Oz refilled my cup. "Fucking her didn't flip a switch. I was all-in before, too. Why did *you* show up this morning?"

"This is my fault. I need to make it right." Graham dropped his pen with a soft clatter.

Say what? "How could you *possibly* arrive at that conclusion?"

"When you hit my classroom, I was in my second year as a full-time professor, and my bosses were watching me very closely. I—" Graham sighed. "I was sleeping with the Dean of Computer Science's son when I was a TA."

"Imagine that." Enter Oz: Deadpan mode.

Graham shot him a glare. "He wasn't my student, but when we broke up, it brought a lot of extra scrutiny down on me. And then I met Luna." He turned to me. "And the first time I heard you dive into a topic you were passionate about, I knew I was fucked. Tiff had been a good friend—I thought—for a long time. I asked her to act as a kind of buffer. She wasn't supposed to fuck you. Especially not the way she did."

That was a lot to process. "I had no idea you knew her. You never said... Why didn't you ever tell me the two of you were friends?"

"Biggest reason, I was trying to keep my distance from you. I had no idea who she really was."

"And you never looked into her." Oz's *yeah, right,* was implied.

Graham shook his head. "That wasn't something I did with my friends. Especially in those days. Do you?"

I did. It had taken a lot of restraint on my part to not go full stalker on Oz. I came close a few times, but as long as I didn't have to crack any databases to get the information, it was considered public, and fair game, right? *Sigh.* Yeah, okay, I may have crossed a line or two.

But I wasn't in the habit of doing things like that when I started college, and while I didn't like that Graham never told me he knew Tiff, his reasons made sense

"You've got some sort of knight-with-a-tarnished-soul complex," Oz said.

"And you are...?" Graham asked. The waitress arrived, and he took plates from her, setting them in front of the right people.

Oz dumped a notable amount of hot sauce on his hash browns. "No tarnish here. I'm infatuated with an incredible mind and body, and the woman made up of it all, and I want to see her succeed."

Violet would tell me no one was Oz's level of kind and adoring without wanting something in return, but I was. I didn't do nice things on barter. Did that make me naive and get me in trouble?

Sometimes. Tiff was a great example. Was I happier with my decisions, regardless? With seeing the genuine and good in people? Without question.

I also wanted to keep this conversation on track. It seemed every time we swerved just a little, the guys slammed into each other's guard rails. I grabbed my phone to make notes of my own, and frowned at three more emails telling me *thanks but no thanks* to my resume. That was six total out of fifteen, all rejected before ten in the morning. That couldn't be good.

Nothing to do for it but move forward. "Next steps in this plan. What do I need to do?"

"You talk to every person you know, or who's connected to someone you know, who has a public presence. You ask for airtime, especially if they have a big social media following." Graham made it sound easy.

It couldn't possibly be. "What do I talk to them about?"

"Yourself. Whatever you'd like. Whatever they ask you. You can focus on what you did five years ago, creating a patch for the malware, if you'd like, but mostly talk about what you enjoy doing in your free time. Who you are."

Uh…yawn? "No one wants to hear that."

"I hate to say it, but I think he's onto something." Oz's demeanor changed in an instant. It was subtle, but I was skilled at seeing stoic lighten into reserved.

"I need a script, or a primer, or something." I babbled when I was under pressure. Or froze. Which would be worse?

"You really don't," Graham said.

Oz squeezed my knee. "You'll shine, no matter what."

I didn't see what they saw but arguing wasn't getting me anywhere. "It can't be as simple as getting on a few podcasts and livestreams."

"It's not," Graham said. "But that's your next step. Get on people's schedules, the sooner the better. While you're doing that, I'll put the framework in place to tie everything up. The SEO. The URL's. Send me your schedule as you have it, and then we'll move to next steps."

"Which are…?" Oz prompted.

Graham waved a hand. "Programming. Luna and I have it."

"I'll help." Oz wasn't asking.

"No offense—"

"Plenty meant, I'm sure." Oz's words were abrasive, but his tone and posture were still more casual. "I know my shit as well as you do, old man."

Graham scoffed. "You're seriously calling me old."

"I'm doing it facetiously. Who made an arcade reference in his analogy?"

"And who understood it?" Graham countered.

Was this where they'd finally come to blows? Was being watched over by two sexy, brainy men worth it if they were constantly threatening to fight?

Oz's chuckle caught me off-guard. "Guilty as charged," he said.

Did chest thumping just become bonding? Was that hot or a bit too caveman for me? I shouldn't be so fuzzy on the answer.

"If you've kept your skills fresh, we could use your help." Graham worked his jaw. "If you can follow directions." He seemed to add as an afterthought.

"Directions, yes. Orders not so much," Oz said.

"Big surprise there." Graham's tone was still light.

I liked the lighter mood, regardless the testosterone-fueled lead-in. My phone rang, and I grabbed for it. An interview? Maybe? I hit *Answer* before I registered that it was my Landlord's name on my screen.

"Hello." I kept my tone sweet, pretending I hadn't been mostly avoiding him.

"Luna. I was surprised to see your name in the news this morning." He wasn't nearly as friendly. "You're a convicted felon."

Frack. "I'm not. It was reduced to a misdemeanor, and even that's been removed from my record now."

"Now. You didn't disclose it when you filled out your application."

"You didn't ask." Was I wrong? Had he?

Oz held out his hand. "Give me the phone," he said softly.

"Look, you're consistently late on your rent, and now I find out you're a criminal. You have until the end of the month to get out."

What? All the coffee I'd had sank like a stone in my stomach. "You're evicting me?"

"I am. End of the month." He disconnected.

And now I was going to be homeless in three weeks. I dropped my phone on the table and my head into my hands as I sank in my seat.

"Did I just…" Oz was a man of few words, but not a man who was usually at a loss for words. "Did he kick you out for having a record?"

I nodded.

"He can't do that."

Graham sucked in a sharp breath through his teeth. "Actually…"

"Of course you'd know that." Oz sigh-growled. "Give me his name, I'll make this right."

I covered my phone without looking up, and slid it closer to me. "No." My other hand muffled my voice. Could I let Oz fight it? Call Violet and ask Ramsey to do something? Yes.

Was it worth the stress, to stay in a place where I wasn't wanted, and where friction and distrust had been building for months because I was late *a lot* with my rent?

No.

"Luna." Oz's voice was tight.

I finally looked at him. "Let it go." *Please.* I wouldn't ask, as much as I wanted to soften the request. He needed to know I meant this.

NINE

Graham cleared his throat loudly and the people two tables over shot him a glare.

I wanted to sink into my seat and hide forever. It wasn't so much the embarrassment factor as it was the cloud of tension that had been growing since Graham showed up this morning. The sun had just started to peek through that gray haze, and now the warmth was gone again.

"This just became mission critical," Graham said.

"Agreed." Oz clipped off the word.

The one thing they consistently agreed on was helping me. It was a starting point. "Graham said it would take a few weeks. This isn't something you can force."

"We can make some things happen faster. This is going to take more than an hour or two of coffee to plan though." Graham reached for the check.

Oz grabbed it first. "If you don't mind the drive, I have a good setup for that at my place. We can sit on the deck and get some sunshine."

I loved that idea. Oz's yard ran into the mountains and it was gorgeous up there. Besides, there was barely room for two of us in my place, and what I'd seen of Graham's, it wasn't much bigger. "Okay."

"Jeremy Ranch?" Graham raised an eyebrow. "I guess it's not as far away as some things."

How did he know— Because despite telling me he wasn't interested, he'd looked into Oz. I would've if our roles had been reversed.

Oz didn't look impressed. "Does that mean you don't need my address?"

"You'd probably better write it down so I have it." Graham slid his notepad to Oz.

We had our leftovers boxed to go, and Oz paid the bill, despite another protest from Graham.

Oz took me by my place again, to grab my laptop. The computer was a Christmas gift from Hunter, and was spec'ed out perfectly for the kind of coding I did. The nicest things I owned were from Violet and her guys, and I was forbidden from protesting because they were gifts. I loved the consideration behind them.

I jumped in the shower for the fastest rinse off in history, tugged on a yellow sundress that was perfect for summer mountain weather, and I was in Oz's truck again in under five minutes.

He leaned in and dragged his nose up my neck, both tickling and enticing. "You smell like Luna again."

"I assume that's a good thing."

"For now. We'll have to change that later when work is done."

Chibi Luna whimpered in my head, and it was possible my own tiny squeak slipped out.

Oz stole a kiss that was far hotter than it should've been considering it lasted half a second, and we were on our way to his place again.

As much as I wanted to sink into the simplicity of his hand on my thigh and the gorgeous drive up the mountains, the morning had raised a lot of questions, and as many were for Oz as Graham.

"Who's Dorothy?" My question popped out on its own, without any fanfare.

Oz glanced at me. "Ah."

That wasn't an answer. It didn't even mean anything. "Why did you shut Graham down when he mentioned Judith? Why are you really doing this—"

"Luna—"

"Do *not* give me the tl;dr versions of anything. I need context."

"Hmm." Oz downshifted as we hit the first steep grade up of our trip. "When we worked for Cord, when it was still young—when—we were, Scott and Zach went out of their way to bring in young, undiscovered talent. Most of us had never worked anywhere but McDonalds or bagging groceries. We certainly had no idea what a real corporate environment was like. And we were living our dreams."

I had no idea what this had to do with my questions, but I'd asked for context, so I was willing to wait through more talking than I usually heard from Oz in a full day. Plus, I enjoyed the sound of his voice and devoured any story I could about *back in the day*.

"Judith is Dorothy. I'm Oz, I used to call her Judy, it's—"

"A round about reference to Judy Garland, I get it." This wasn't nearly as scandalous as an emotional reaction from Oz implied it would be. I was relieved.

"She's the reason I was at the party last night, and never call her Judy, she hates it."

Okay, industry friends, then. Or... frenemies? Judith was polite. Friendly.

"She's my ex-wife," Oz said.

What in the what? The emotions that washed over me were muddied and dense. It wasn't like I thought Oz was a virginal saint, especially after last night, but we'd gone to a party at his ex-wife's behest? I didn't have a right to be jealous, but I was feeling something I didn't like.

He glanced over and squeezed my leg. "I'm assuming you still want context?"

"Uh... duh?"

"Don't make any assumptions until I get to the end."

Too late. "No more than I already have."

He shrugged. "Fair. All of us at Cord were also fucking around a lot. Pairing off. Grouping off. Even those of us who were *together* were openly sleeping with other people. It was all consensual. Not like what Violet has, because it wasn't closed up all nice and neat. The fucking was fun, but the flexibility of loving multiple people was what I liked. I'm not monogamous."

"You're polyamorous." Look at me, putting pieces together like a genius or something.

He nodded. "You deserve to know early on. I wasn't planning to keep it from you, but I had hoped the circumstances would be a little less... crammed in the middle of everything else."

This was where the jealousy should surge, wasn't it? Why was I assured instead? "Are you seeing other people now?"

"No."

"Will you want to?"

"Don't know. You've raised the bar on what I like in a person. I've been hooked on you for a while now."

I'd been drooling over him for ages, but that didn't stop me from looking other places. Like Graham. Not that what I had with Graham was anything more than obsession at this point. I didn't know what to do with this information. "Is that why you got divorced? Jealousy?"

"No." Oz's answer came without hesitation. "We had a difference in opinion about priorities, and in the end, she chose her career."

Ouch. "I'm sorry."

"It's fine." He sounded like he meant it and radiated the same sincerity. "This isn't a wicked ex story. I hated it at the time, but it's been more than a decade and the distance has given me time to appreciate her friendship, without the romantic attachment."

He made it sound simple. Except for the *more than a decade* part. I'd barely been legal for more than a decade. "Okay."

"*Okay?*" Oz echoed. "Did I break you?" Teasing slid into his question.

The lighter tone helped unstick my brain. "It's a lot to process, and it's not about tech. Not directly, anyway. People are more complicated than software, and I don't know what's expected of me in this situation."

"Don't think about it like that. I'm telling you so that you know, not to trick you or see how you respond. Though, I obviously hope you're okay with the entire thing."

"I think I am." Wasn't I? Logically, these should be warning flags. My new boyfriend—I liked the sound of *Oz is my boyfriend*—had a past of fucking his co-workers and was still friends with his ex-wife. But I didn't feel the issue. I wasn't concerned about it meaning bad things for us.

Maybe he should be the one concerned, because now I was wondering more than ever if I could have at least one night with both him and Graham.

The tiny lines Oz traced along my thigh with his thumb were comforting. "I do the apprenticeships, I rent out the inexpensive housing, because when I was in my early twenties someone gave me an amazing chance, and others deserve the same," he said. "You… You're this brilliant mind capable of so much. If you were ten years older, you'd have been one of the original crew. I'm glad you weren't, for your sake. You have access to so much more tech. Diversity. Freedom. But if anyone deserves a chance, it's you."

That stunned me to silence. And made me blush, I was sure. And was without a doubt, hotter than anything I'd ever fantasized about Oz saying to me.

"Besides," he said. Your intelligence is really fucking sexy, and *God* I love fucking you."

That was pretty hot too. "We have so much in common."

He chuckled. "Any other questions? I'll answer them all."

"I'm good for now." Really good. I could even ignore that my career was about to once again be over before it started. But that wouldn't be an issue, because we were going to fix things.

"Good."

We chatted about little things on the rest of the trip. He'd left messages for a few contacts while I was in my apartment. I sent Violet a text and asked her for the same.

We reached Oz's place, and Graham arrived a few minutes later.

It was cooler up here, given we were in the mountains, but the sun was high enough to strike my face and warm my skin.

"We should do this on the lawn, out back." Where I could see the little blue wildflowers and dandelions along the edges of the grass, that had significantly increased in number since I mentioned I liked them.

"We'll get glare on the screens," Oz said.

I shouldn't be out in the sun too much anyway. I'd burn. "We'll go inside when that happens. Or do you want me to beg?" I turned innocent eyes on Oz.

"So very desperately." Oz's voice dropped an octave.

Graham did that loud throat clearing thing.

I'll beg you, too. The offer died in my throat. Fantasy, meet the reality of rejection. Apparently none of Graham's actions or apology had erased that burning moment of humiliation from my mind. Go figure.

The tension flowing freely between Oz and Graham didn't help. The feeling had lightened in the diner, but the drive seemed to be enough to restore it to its original, thought-clogging heaviness.

"I'll grab a blanket," Oz said. "Give Graham the mini-tour and pick a spot outside."

I nodded. Impulse wanted to reach for Graham's hand, and tug him through the main floor of the house. What good was an impulse if over-thinking stopped it before it started? "This way." I jerked my thumb toward the rear of the house instead.

As Graham and I headed toward the yard, I pointed out the important things. "Bathroom's down the hall. Help yourself to anything in the fridge. Glasses are in the cupboard to the right of the sink." Oz gave me the tour once, and it had stuck in my head. It was terse but welcoming. I was still impressed he managed to pull off the combination.

We headed onto the deck. "Pick a chair. Power's there." I pointed to the outlets at the back of the house.

"You know your way around." Graham's tone was off.

He didn't get to be jealous. He'd pushed me away. Still, I didn't want him to not like Oz. I also wanted him to still want me.

"Everyone still dressed?" Oz called as he joined us on the deck.

Graham scowled. "You asked Luna to show me around and she did. The fuck kind of comment is that?"

The tension was back, hurrah. I stepped between the men, not because I thought they were might come to blows, but it felt appropriate to physically divide them.

"If you're going to keep poking and prodding each other for a reaction, I'm not going to do this." I wouldn't. I couldn't. "You're supposed to be the adults here. Act like it."

TEN

"Y̲ou're an adult, too." Graham's retort was tinged with frustration.

"In fact, you might be too old for him." Oz added.

I glared at Oz. "I'm not working with the two of you if you can't get along." They were going to suffocate me with resentment and distaste, especially since I was the focal point for them coming together.

"I'm fine with him." Oz shrugged.

Graham shook his head. "You keep saying that, but—"

"Enough." I wanted them both here, but we had to do something about the friction. I grabbed my deck from my bag, and left the rest of my things on the deck. They both knew I read tarot, though I'd never done it around them. "Leave your laptops here. We're going to ask the cards what it will take for the two of you to get along."

"I—" Graham stopped when I looked at him, and he set his laptop bag on the patio table. "Sure."

I understood that most people thought me consulting tarot cards was hokey at best and out right stupid at the other end of the spectrum. Oz and Graham had always accepted me. It was one of the reasons I adored both of them. Wanted to spend time with them.

Oz lay a large blanket on the back lawn.

I knelt on one side and gestured for them to take spots opposite me.

"How does this work?" There was no judgment in Graham's question, only curiosity. He sat with one knee to his chest, and the other leg stretched out.

I slid the deck into my hands and held it. What was I looking for? I wanted to resolve the conflict between Graham and Oz.

"On a really basic level, cards are drawn with a specific question in mind. Without that, the answers can lead to more confusion. Sometimes it's one card, and other times it's a layout meant to answer a specific type of situation." In this case, a single card wouldn't do, but I had a spread in mind that would help guide us.

Oz's legs were stretched in front of him and he leaned his weight on his wrists behind him. "And the spirits guide your hands?"

"Some people read that way, yes. I see it as the randomness of the universe giving me a little extra insight when I'm struggling to find my own." I shuffled the deck three times, then cut it.

"You look for advice in chaos theory?" Graham asked.

I repeated the main question in my head. *How do we resolve this conflict?* "That's as valid an approach as any."

Oz nodded. "I like it."

I laid seven cards out, four in a square and three more to the right, including an extra on one of the questions, to apply specifically to each man. Since they'd never seen this before, I would explain a little more in depth than normal.

I pointed to the first card, a Seven of Swords. "This one asks what's at the root of the conflict."

"And it's upside down, so that means bad, right?" Graham asked.

"It means the inverse of the card's original meaning."

Oz leaned in, studying the layout. "Like Bizarro Superman?"

"More or less." I was pleased they were showing interest and not just sitting there sullenly. I hated being placated, and neither of them gave off that vibe. "This one is about deception. Secret plans. And when it's reversed, it has to do with being hasty or impulsive when it comes to how we think." The meaning of the card flitted through my thoughts, swirling into how it applied to our situation. "Tiff tricking me ten years ago." My voice trailed off.

I knew my mistake was at the core of all of this, but I didn't appreciate the universe calling me out like that on step one.

"That feels deceptively simple," Oz said.

"Sometimes it works that way, and others it's not so direct." I pointed to the Six of Swords in the second spot. "This is what we can do to help resolve the conflict." A sigh rolled through me. "We need to focus on healing and moving away from the churn. You two need to understand that I brought this on myself. I was manipulated into it. Stop putting it on Graham." That was a stretch of the core meaning, but that was what they had to do in order to move on. "You can't change what happened, but we can repair it."

"Do you have every one of those memorized?" Graham sounded impressed. "That's amazing."

The compliment made me flush in the rising sunshine. "It's taken years of practice." I pointed to the next card. "This question is where is the clash in your perspectives coming from?"

"That one doesn't look like the others. It's an important one, right?" Oz asked.

Most people treated this like a party trick. The fact that both men were asking genuine questions warmed me. "Major Arcana, and yes. This is The World. It's a happy ending after a rough journey."

"There's no conflict in perspective there." Graham focused on me. "Who doesn't want a happily ever after?"

"The issue isn't wanting it, it's that you see each other as an obstacle to achieving it," I said.

Oz looked thoughtful. "That's true."

The next card, the Queen of Swords reversed, glared at me, accusingly. "Which leads us to what my role is in that conflict. You're letting your feelings for me drive you to bitterness, vindication, malice, and pessimism." The words hurt.

"What's wrong?" Graham asked.

I didn't want to be a catalyst for those things. "Introspection hurts sometimes." But that was why we were doing this, wasn't it? To move past the hurt.

"That one looks more positive." Oz pointed to the Ten of Coins. "It feels like success."

It was. "That card says what you should keep in mind as you work with Graham. It's hard-earned accomplishment after a difficult venture."

Graham snorted. The first derisive sound I'd heard from him since we started.

I didn't blame him in this case. "Cole has those things. Graham has been cut off from them, but that doesn't stop him from wanting the same."

"Which is reasonable." Graham sounded defensive. "I haven't exactly been a slacker in life."

"It's totally reasonable." I focused on Oz. "Imagine you were in his shoes. You'd decided to help the wrong person, and it cost you the future you'd built for yourself. You wouldn't begrudge him that, would you?"

Oz clenched his jaw. "You're not the wrong person."

"If I'm not wrong for you, I wasn't for Graham, either." I didn't realize that could be taken a couple ways until the words crossed my lips, but I wasn't going to clarify. "Speaking of..." I looked at Graham, and gestured at the Three of Wands reversed. "You've worked hard, and been on a tremendous journey, without having to leave home. Now that your probation is over, you see the things you worked for, the things you wanted, and you can't reach them. At the same time, Oz has a lot of them. Don't hold that against him."

"I can't just flip a switch and change the way I feel," Graham said.

"No, but you can make a conscious effort to see things from each other's perspectives." I studied the last card—the Queen of Cups, and mentally dragged in a deep breath. "You're both here because you say you want to help me. You need to work together."

How could I phrase this? "If you trust me—my thoughts, my intuition—then you need to trust that I'm okay with both of you."

Oz hovered his fingers over the cards, never making contact. "You make it sound simple."

"I know it's not." I looked over the spread one last time before gathering the cards and tucking them away again.

I needed to call Violet, if we were going to be here for a while. Let her know I was all right, Oz was amazing, and that I needed a favor or two. I wandered away from the blanket as I pulled up her number, but not so far that Oz and Graham were out of sight.

The tarot card reading was insightful, but that didn't mean I trusted them to play nice.

"Hey, Lucky Lady." Violet was cheerful. "Did Cole untie you long enough to say *hi?*"

Would he tie me up? Probably so if I begged. *Wowza* that was hot. I stashed the fantasy for future reference. "More or less. I got your text. Wanted to check in. And I need a favor."

"Anything. What's up?"

"I need to talk to Sadie. Grayson. See if I can be on their shows. Maybe Hunter can hook me up with people who want to interview me."

"Whoa." Violet's tone shifted to serious. "Yank the reins, L. Second of all, you're going to need to back up and tell me why, but first, you can't just do that. You can't launch into random requests, and pretend you didn't have that bear of a man you adore in your apartment overnight. You're still with him, aren't you?"

I looked over at Oz to see him staring back. Geez, I liked the way he looked at me. "Oz and Graham both."

"Uh, what?" Violet sounded amused. "You owe me so many details. What kind of story is there? A juicy one."

"No."

"Not yet, you mean."

This wasn't what Violet was implying, no matter how much I wanted otherwise.

"How was it? How was he?" Violet asked. "Them?"

"Just him." I was intently aware of Graham's gaze on me too. It wouldn't be hard to guess what I was talking about, even with only half the conversation. "And amazing." I didn't want to discourage Graham, but I wasn't going to hide that away for his benefit.

"Details when you don't have an audience. Or at least, more detailed impressions," Violet said. "Why do you want to be on Sadie's channel?"

I gave her a brief rundown of what Graham proposed and how we were approaching it.

"Everyone is going to be watching you, if you do this," Violet's teasing had melted to concern. "You can't do some things public and not all of them."

"You do."

She sighed. "True, but there's still a lot more of our lives out there than you're going to be comfortable with when it's you." One of her boyfriends, Ramsey, had been in politics, and still loved the spotlight. That meant she and Hunter caught the edges of it as well.

"My name is already out there. This way, I can control the narrative."

Violet *tsked*.

I rolled my eyes. "I know, I can't completely control it, but I can drive some of it." I had to believe that. "I've already been evicted over it." I hadn't meant to let that slip.

"No, L. It's okay. We have a guest room, and you're always welcome here."

I didn't know what I was going to do about the apartment situation, but I wasn't going to be comfortable living with Violet's guys. I liked them fine, but I wasn't close with them like I was her. "Can I let you know?"

She sighed. "Okay. I'll talk to people and get back to you. Do you want them to go through me, or call you directly?"

I'd much rather they go through Violet, but she'd take it on herself to become my *assistant* in this, and the last thing she needed was me piling more work on her. She did that just fine on her own. "Send them directly to me," I said. This was my project, and I needed to dive in headfirst. Hiding in the shadows except during interview time would only make the task more difficult. "And thank you."

"Always," Violet said.

We chatted for another minute or so before disconnecting, and I rejoined Oz and Graham on the blanket.

"Stay in one of my apartments," Oz said.

I shook my head. That was as bad as intruding in Violet's life. "That's how you make your money, and right now, I can't afford any place you rent." Not that he was running high-end condos, but I barely had the couple hundred a month for my tiny studio.

"I'm not going to miss it for a single unit, I promise. I'd offer to pay for your new place instead, but you wouldn't take that."

I shook my head. "No. I wouldn't."

"Then it's settled. We'll move you when you're ready."

I didn't remember saying *yes*, but it was one less thing I'd need to worry about now.

"I wouldn't have minded if you shared details." Oz settled a hand on my thigh.

Warmth seared through me at the touch and the light shift in topic. "I shared enough."

"I wouldn't mind details either." Graham's statement caught me off-guard. Before I could ask him if he was serious, he shook his head. "Did you see this new rendering algorithm they're hyping from EdgeBite?"

I could be disappointed at the rapid change in subject or I could be delighted that Graham wanted to talk about the same tech that caught my eye a few days ago. "Yes. The applications are so numerous."

"I'm sorry, did your bear just roll his eyes at me?" Graham looked at Oz with disbelief.

Oz's growl reinforced the nickname. "If you're going to call me anything, G-man, call me Daddy."

I wrinkled my nose in distaste.

"No?" Oz sounded surprised.

"*Daddy* isn't going to work for me." I didn't care what kind of nicknames other people tossed around, but that one didn't float my boat or tickle my pickle.

Oz shrugged. "What do you prefer? I've never cared for *Sir* as a general idea."

Possibly for similar reasons. "I already call you *Oz*." And while it wasn't a nickname I'd given him, I was about the only person who used it.

"You're a wizard?" Graham asked in disbelief.

Oz wiggled his hand. "I've got magic fingers."

Yeah, he did.

"And a magic wand, I assume?" Graham might be skeptical, but the antagonism that had been in his voice earlier was gone. His tone was sliding closer to the teasing he and I shared. "Because Oz wasn't that kind of wizard. Lupin, on the other hand…"

Oz raised an eyebrow. "Werewolf. Buffy. Fucking an adorable redheaded genius. I get it." He connected the barely-related dots in a way most people would puzzle at.

Graham looked as pleased as I was. Did Oz just slide into our *all things fictional are related* game without hesitation?

There was one problem with this whole line of conversation, though. "*Lupin* doesn't really roll off the tongue in the heat of the moment."

"I didn't roll off your tongue last night either," Oz said. "It was more of a lodged in your throat—"

"Seriously?" Graham's amusement faded.

"Definitely not." Oz studied him. "Especially not for you."

Graham furrowed his brow. "What?"

The play on words, on names, was a reach, but not a long one given we'd already edged into Harry Potter territory. I knew where Oz was going with the statement. "Sirius Black was a noble protector. I could see that in Graham."

"And he sacrificed himself." Graham was caught up.

Oz rolled his eyes again. "And he spent a lot of his life before that having fun and playing pranks. Graham doesn't strike me as a *prank* kind of guy. Besides, you're more of a Ravenclaw."

Graham scoffed. "I'm a Gryffindor if I'm anything."

I wasn't. Not even close. Like my not-quite-namesake, "You don't want to hang out with me in Ravenclaw?" I extended my lower lip in an exaggerated pout.

"You're not a Gryffindor. You picked knowledge over good," Oz said.

"I picked Luna."

Heated flooded me at Graham's simple statement. "You're implying that back then, when I came to you with the project, you would've said yes, even if I'd been asking for help debugging a basic Python routine?"

Graham searched my face. "The question is irrelevant. If you'd been asking for help with anything less than what you came to me with, you wouldn't be the you I'd pick."

And now I must be bright red.

Graham turned his attention to Oz. "I notice you didn't sort yourself. Are you going to claim you're a Hufflepuff?"

"Never got my Hogwarts letter." Oz made the answer sound obvious. "I was forced to become a hedge witch and whore myself out to grow my magic."

"Crossover alert." In the best possible way. I'd enjoyed this with Graham, but with Oz added to the mix, it was a whole new flavor of delightful.

"But a logical one." Graham was already weaving the two worlds in his head. I could practically see those sexy brain gears whirring. "In the UK, they find these magicians young and train them. But after the issues with Grindelwald in the US, revealing magic to so many people at once, the American Ministry locked down. They were more careful about how they approached wizards and witches."

"You've put a lot of thought into this." If Oz wasn't careful, he might start exhibiting distinct emotions beyond *grr* and *hmm*.

"And you haven't?" I asked playfully.

Oz's expression was stoic, but one corner of his mouth tugged up. "I haven't done an in depth analysis of whether or not Harry Potter and The Magicians take place in the same universe, no."

"Do you want to? Because we can go all night, and it's a lot of fun." And now my mind was tripping over all the things we could spend all night doing, and most of them involved fewer clothes, and far more tangible *magic wands*.

When Oz opened his mouth, I was certain he'd say *no*. His, "It's tempting," was a glorious surprise. "But we're not shipping Elliot with Draco."

I wrinkled my nose in distaste.

Graham looked horrified. "Elliot and Quentin forever."

"Finally something else we agree on," Oz said.

I was grinning like a loon. "I knew the two of you had more in common than me."

"We both have good taste. That's obvious." Graham was watching me with those dark eyes again. "You're proof of that."

"Again, I can't argue." Oz's phone rang, and he glanced at the screen. "I need to take this." Like that, he was unreadable again.

I wanted to yank him back as he walked away. I wasn't ready to surrender this moment.

ELEVEN

Oz stepped away to take what sounded like a friendly, let's-catch-up call with Jordan.

Probably time to get to work. "We need our laptops for this step?" I started to stand.

"Wait." Graham grabbed my fingertips.

It was a light touch, without assumption or command, but it stalled me. "What's up?"

"A moment of just your time?"

I nodded and sank back to my knees. Disappointment flitted inside when Graham let go of me.

"You seem happy with Oz. Already," Graham said.

You'd make me happy too. I didn't know how to say that without things getting convoluted. How did people propose things like that? *Yeah, I'm seeing the guy, but he and I are both cool with me seeing you, too.* It sounded simple enough, but would Graham accept it?

He might accept it more than the long silence I'd just let stretch between us.

"Right." Graham gave a brief shake of his head. "I'm sorry about what happened the other day. The things I said in the coffee shop. I realize I said the same this morning, but I want you to know even when there's not an audience, I still mean it. And I'm sorry for what happened back then."

He was still apologizing for the malware debacle. *Sigh.*

"I made those decisions, to do the coding job." I wasn't going to repeat this to him again. Not like this. "I came to you. I was compelled by the challenge. I hate that I sucked you in, but I've never blamed you."

"Don't hate the time we spent working together. I made my decisions too, and one of them was to spend more time with you. You really are a brilliant, amazing individual."

"Jordan and Chloe are in." Oz's voice cut through the moment. "Did I interrupt?"

"No." Like that, Graham shut down.

Boo.

"You sure? Because if you're confessing your undying love, I can come back in about five minutes." Oz sat next to me.

He had to know that implied anything but walking away.

Graham's exhale embodied frustration. "I don't understand this. You've got this one-of-a-kind woman, and you're joking about her with another guy?"

"You don't know me very well, so let me explain a couple of things," Oz said. "I'm the foil in any group. No one has ever said *Oh that Cole, he's such a joker.*"

Graham scowled and stood. "I need my laptop to start a calendar. You have dates for those appointments?"

Wait. Hear him out. Me. I swallowed the request. If Graham was closing the conversation off now, I wasn't in the mood for the rejection that would come with forcing him to listen when he wasn't open to hearing.

We fell into work. Scheduling. Planning. Never exchanging more than a few words at a time.

So much for the cards helping us work toward less tension. I wasn't doing days more of this. Did I want to put up with this for the next few weeks, or was I better off telling Graham that we could correspond via email and chat after today?

The thought of pushing him away, even if it wasn't far, made my insides curdle.

"Why teaching?" Oz's question came out of nowhere.

Graham stared blankly at Oz, seconds ticking away. He finally said, "Why did you ask?" His question held a suspicious edge.

"Luna's cards said you wanted success and fortune."

"I never used the word *fortune*." In fact, I'd specifically been careful with my phrasing because success meant different things to different people.

Oz shrugged. "Ten of Coins. Coins mean money."

"You're not possibly that simple." Graham had forgotten his work

"Pretend I am. You don't fall under that umbrella of *those who can't, teach*. You know your shit. What made you say *Fuck being paid what I'm worth. I'll teach.*"

Graham was back to the blank staring with no words.

That was super awkward. Like, chibi Luna sweat-dropping, waiting to see what came next.

"What?" Oz asked.

"I'm waiting for the follow up comment about corrupting students." Graham's voice was flat.

"I obviously don't have room to talk. I'm obsessed with the same woman, for probably very similar reasons."

Obsessed? Oz was obsessed with me? The power in the word rattled my thoughts. Was it wrong that I liked it?

"Success has a lot of shapes," Graham said. "For me, it includes helping other people achieve their potential."

And there was that sexy teacher vibe I adored in both men. Another thing they had in common besides me.

"Hmm." Oz grunted.

Graham scowled. "What is that? *Hmm?*"

"I respect that," Oz said.

Simple enough. They'd reached common ground without getting too snippy. Was it too soon to hope this was a trend? If so, I needed the animosity to lessen a lot faster.

Graham half closed the lid on his laptop. "What about you? You were one of the original crew, and most of them are still big names in some way. You vanished."

"I didn't choose the video game life. The video game life chose me."

I let a tiny laugh out at Oz's reply.

"Really?" Graham's flat question said he wasn't as amused.

Oz hadn't looked at a computer since we sat down. He was stretched out on the blanket, completely casual. "Cord recruited me. I fucked around there for a while, and like you, I wanted to be doing something that had more impact. I'd go into detail, but you've already checked up on me."

Graham shrugged. "I won't apologize for that."

"You sure?" Oz straightened and leaned in. "I can't needle you into feeling guilty? Because I'm getting the impression self-flagellation is your kink."

"Excuse me?"

"Do you get off on the degradation, or is it an act?"

Oz's question probably sounded strictly confrontational to anyone, especially Graham, but after last night, it held a deeper meaning for me.

The deep creases in Graham's forehead implied he wasn't impressed. "What kind of question is that? Do I beat off while I tell my reflection how shitty I am for the mistakes I've made? No."

"Would you do it while you watched someone else fuck the woman you adore? Would you suck his cock clean after he'd been inside her?"

Geez, this was making me squirm. I didn't want Oz to be so bluntly aggressive, but I also wanted to hear Graham's answer.

Red crept up Graham's neck to color his cheeks, and he clenched his jaw. "Are the rumors true, about the early days of Cord?" His question was calm, as though he were asking about the weather.

"There's a truth to most rumors. The degree of truth is the real question," Oz said.

Graham focused on me. "The rumors that a lot of your free

time—that entire original team—was spent in one giant fuckfest of an orgy."

I was grateful Oz had already told me this, or I would have choked on the air. Hearing Graham ask about it, not knowing how he felt, made it difficult for me to hold onto my composure, regardless.

"Yup." Oz *popped* on the *p*. "That's pretty solidly true."

Graham looked between us, his gaze landing on me again. "You're being quiet. What are you thinking?"

You first. I was looking longingly at the fantasy of having both men at the same time. Not a lot of people had patience, but I did. I'd waited for three years to see Graham again, though. And before that, several years just wondering if he noticed me. And now he was right here, skirting the edges of a conversation about sex.

Could I risk a replay of the other night? Did I want to deal with his rejection again? Believing Oz would be here regardless didn't help. They were two separate entities.

I had to know. "What if it was without all the stuff Oz just said. Without the humiliation." I liked that bit, but if it wasn't for Graham, I liked other things too.

"*It?*" Graham repeated. "Watching the two of you have sex?"

When he put it that way… "No. All three of us. Or him watching us." I had to force myself not to sound timid, amid the screaming in the back of my mind that said he was going to reject me again. Worse, if he was judgmental about it, I'd have to be mad at him again.

Graham lifted the screen on his laptop, lowered his head, and drummed his fingers on the keys, not really typing.

"Luna asked you a question," Oz said.

Graham looked around—everywhere but at us. "Are the cameras on a separate network than the one I'm attached to? Uploading to the cloud? This has to be a joke."

"You knocked on her door this morning." Oz was calm. "I already mentioned how I feel about that kind of joke, and how little do you know about Luna to think she'd pull a prank like that? What purpose would it serve besides cruelty?"

I hadn't followed the thought that far, but the notion soured my soul.

"That's not it." Graham sighed, and focused on me again. "You're okay with this."

"Yes." I'd given Oz more details, but that was as much dirty talk as anything, and I wasn't that comfortable with Graham. I'd like to be… "I like the idea of sex with both of you at the same time."

"I—" Graham worked his jaw. He shut his laptop completely, rolled onto his knees, and crawled toward me on the blanket.

When he brushed his lips over mine, my heart skipped with a bittersweet blend of hope and doubt. I leaned into his mouth.

He slid his hand to the back of my neck and deepened the kiss.

My heart hammered against my ribs, threatening to break free, and I whimpered.

As if spurred by the sound, Graham nipped along my lips, before licking away the sting and sliding his tongue into my mouth.

Fuck me, this was real.

TWELVE

Graham trailed his fingers through my hair and his mouth down my neck. This was tenderness blended with desire, like the perfect left of sweet meets tart cherry.

Not a single daydream I'd ever had about Graham came close to this. I needed to be a part of him. I nudged us both, my hands on his shoulders, my fists clenching his shirt, until he was sitting enough for me to climb into his lap and straddle his legs.

I was intently aware that Oz watched all of this, and that heightened my desire. He wanted to watch as much as I wanted his eyes on us, though I had no doubt he'd be happy to switch places with Graham as well.

Each kiss and touch from Graham, along my jaw, down my neck, around the curve of my ear, was delicate, as if he wanted to savor every moment.

"Are you sure this is what you want?" Graham murmured against the hollow of my neck, below my ear.

My chuckle was strained with frustration. "I'm sure, and I'm going to be offended if you ask again."

"I won't." He pressed his lips to the tender skin and traveled lower to drag his tongue along the exposed part of my chest. "I've always wondered what your freckles taste like."

"Always is a long time." A warmth brighter than the morning sun spread inside.

His light laugh hummed through my skin. "How about *far longer than I should have.*"

"What's the verdict?"

"Better than I ever imagined." Each time he shifted to kiss a new part of me, his erection pressed into me, hindered by the layers of our clothing.

The way he slid his palms up my thighs, pushing my skirt out of the way, was a stark contrast to Oz last night. Graham teased his thumbs under my panties, along my hips and waist. He moved his mouth back to my neck, sucking lightly at first, and then harder as I tilted my head to give him easier access.

I could make out with Graham all day. A different day. One where I hadn't waited years to find out what this would be like with him, and where we didn't have a captivated audience.

"I've fantasized about you for so long." It was easier to let the confession out than I thought. Oz's encouragement last night helped my courage, though I wouldn't tell Graham quite the same things about my desires. I wanted something different from him... and to not scare him off. "About you taking me on your desk, with people passing by outside. With that thrill of getting caught."

He glided his hands closer to the center of my need, brushing the edges of my pussy. "That would have been bad."

"In real life. But in my head, it's an amazing fantasy. Especially if someone wanted to watch. To get off to the sight of you fucking me." Like Oz was now. I could hear his heavy breathing mingling with ours.

"I've had a few of those daydreams myself," Graham admitted.

Hearing that added another spark to the already roaring inferno inside, licking at my skin. Wanting to be unleashed so it could consume us both. "Fuck me while Cole watches?" I let the pleading slide into my voice.

Graham let out a strained laugh. "You have so many hidden

layers." He promoted me to slide onto the blanket, then onto my back. "Let's peel away another one." He dragged my panties down my legs and tossed them aside, before kissing back up the inside of my thighs.

I squirmed at the light nibbles and scruff of his short beard on my skin. He didn't tease, as he reached my core, dragging his tongue along my slit. My groan mingled with two others and I arched into his touch.

He licked along my slick flesh, burying himself inside me, drawing up to my clit the back down again, like I was the most delicious ice cream. I moved to tangle my fingers in his hair, to draw him in closer, and Oz grabbed my wrists, pinning them above my head.

Oh geez. With Graham between my legs, licking, sucking, and tongue fucking me, and Oz keeping me from doing more than squirming, I was a bundle of nerve endings. Pleasure surged inside, inching toward climax.

Graham pressed his fingers to my clit as he probed my opening. I strained against Oz's grip, and he tightened his hold, fingers digging into my wrists in the most delicious way.

Orgasm spilled through me. My cries of ecstasy and pumping hips spurred Graham to lick and finger harder, devouring me until it was too much. Until my body shuddered.

Oz let go of my wrists and pressed tender kisses to each of my bare shoulders. "Fuck, you're gorgeous when you come," he whispered.

I flushed.

Graham pulled away, and I heard the tear of foil. He knelt between my legs, nudged my opening with the head of his cock, and slid inside me.

This wasn't a hard thrust, it was a slow, delicious stretch as I opened up to accept his length, stretching out with each inch, until he was buried to the hilt.

Graham withdrew to the tip, before plunging into me again, over and over, in an agonizingly delicious build to a steady pace.

Was I greedy for wanting more? I had two men watching and

helping me writhe in pleasure. I was going to take advantage of it. I rolled my head back to meet Oz's gaze. "I want to taste you."

That yummy, animalistic smile was back. He moved to kneel at the side of head, his cock in his hand.

Graham gripped my hips, pumping faster, when Oz pressed against my lips.

I opened hungrily, letting Oz in, swirling my tongue around his shaft as best I could, while Graham built to a frantic pace, slamming inside me.

I pushed down the top of my dress enough to expose my breasts, and kneaded, pinching my nipples, tugging for that extra spark of sensation.

Oz worked his hand faster along his cock, his grunts growing louder as his rhythm grew faster.

Graham moved his thumb to my clit, teasing the still tender flesh, coaxing while he fucked me hard and fast.

I didn't know where to focus. What sensation I wanted more of beyond *all of it*. I tumbled into overload.

A salty spurt hit the back of my throat when Oz came, but he didn't stay in my mouth. Cum slid down my jaw, another burst hitting my chest. My breasts.

I clenched the blanket in my fists as another orgasm stole my breath and my thoughts. Nothing existed around us, and at the same time I felt everything. Tasted it. Heard limitless desire in a duet of male groans.

Graham squeezed my hip tighter, his jerky movements stuttering to a stall, before he finished in a slow, winding down crescendo of movement and sound.

As everything stopped, I slowly became aware of the sunshine on my skin. The rustle of the wind in the trees. Grass poking through blanket and tickling my back. Graham's mouth on mine as he shared Oz's taste with me, kissing hungrily.

"God, you're amazing." Graham was breathless.

"Takes one to know one."

He laughed into the kiss and pulled away.

Oz brushed a loose strand of hair from my forehead. From this angle, he looked angelic. "Don't move," he said. "Either of you."

Not like I could if I wanted to.

Oz returned a moment later with two washcloths, tossed one at Graham, and took his time wiping me clean. A girl could get used to this kind of tender treatment. Ah, who was I kidding? I was already hooked.

We collapsed in a pile, my head on Graham's shoulder and Oz pressed into my back, arm around my waist.

The best thing about chocolate sandwich cookie ice cream was finding a whole cookie hidden away in the creamy sweetness. The most dangerous thing about chocolate sandwich cookie ice cream was finding one whole cookie, and following it to another, and another, until the entire pint was gone.

As I lay on a blanket on the grass, wrapped in sunshine and sand-wiched between Oz and Graham, I knew I was in the same kind of I'm-about-to-eat-the-whole-pint trouble. I was willing to just keep snacking on this sandwich cookie of us, over and over, until I was overstuffed.

Chibi-Luna giggled at my unintentional innuendo. Sometimes I cracked me up.

Oz trailed his fingers through my hair, as I listened to his heartbeat.

Graham lay behind me, hand on my hip and thumb tracing a short path back and forth along my skin. "You didn't look bothered by anything Cole said." Graham's tone was thoughtful. "The humili-ation. The self-flagellation."

If I told him what I was thinking, he could call me a freak. Say this was all a big mistake and walk away. With the sun beating down on us, and a soft breeze brushing my skin, the concern didn't hold any weight. "I thought it was hot."

"You did." Graham sounded surprised, but in a good way. "The idea of that turns you on?"

"Being used as a set of holes, and punished and told how dirty I am for the entire thing, while I choke on a thick cock and get covered in sticky bodily fluids? Yes." The next bit was the important part. Maybe I should've led with it. "In the heat of the moment, with someone I trust, as long as I know it's part of the sex and not real. And there's a lot of reassurance after."

Oz leaned up enough to brush his lips over the top of my head. "Doesn't she say the most brilliant things?"

"Hmm."

Wasn't that Oz's thing? I didn't like the idea of them both relying on the vague grunt.

"What is that? That *hmm*?" Oz asked.

Apparently he didn't care for it being used against him, either.

"It means I don't have an answer."

Graham was still here, so his hesitation couldn't be all bad, but I wanted that reassurance.

THIRTEEN

The three of us spent the rest of the day working and enjoying each other's company. Apparently all it took for Oz and Graham to get along were a pair of good orgasms.

Not that I blamed them. The experience left me wrapped in a pleasant ball of warmth. Graham's non-answers weighed on me, but his actions after made doubt easier to ignore.

It was almost nine at night when Graham stood reluctantly. "I should be on my way."

It wasn't late, late, but given he showed up at my place twelve hours ago, it had been a long day of work.

The break in the middle was pretty incredible though.

"You're welcome to stay," Oz said. "I've got room."

He had a way bigger bed than mine, that was for sure. Did I know because I'd had to sneak a peek at his bedroom more than once? Duh.

Graham shouldered his laptop bag. "Thanks, but no. This was a lot of fun, but I'm not going to make a habit of it."

Of... what? The statement didn't make any sense.

After Graham left, Oz tugged me into his lap and dragged his nose along the back of my neck. "I don't understand how anyone could resist making a habit of you."

Graham hadn't been talking about me. Had he? "I think he mean the three-person sex." That was a more reasonable alternative from the outside, but still not one I liked. "You're okay with what happened today, aren't you?"

"I told you I was." Oz's reply was kind.

"That was before it happened."

He wrapped his arms around my waist, and grasped my fingers. "I still have my doubts about Graham when it comes to me calling him more than an acquaintance. But if you like him, and he's not hurting you, yeah, I'm fine with it. And if you want me there for some of it, even better. Turns out I like watching you fuck. No surprise there, since I like watching you do a lot of things."

As we made our way to bed that night, Oz was wonderfully understanding that I wanted to skip the sex and just fall asleep with him wrapped around me.

I wanted to spend Sunday with Oz too, but we both had prior plans. Still, waking up to his kisses and someone else making me coffee was a luxury I could get addicted to.

He was driving me back to my place when his phone rang. He glanced at the screen for half a second. "It's Jake."

"I don't mind if you answer," I said.

Oz did exactly that. "Hey, Jake."

"Cole. How's it going? I need a minute."

"Sure."

I'd met Jake before. He placed Oz's people in new positions when their apprenticeships ended. I tried to busy myself with watching the mountain scenery. It was rude to eavesdrop, but it wasn't like I could go in the other room, and with the call on speaker…

"That woman you were introducing on Friday night. You saw the news about her?" Jake asked.

Me. I was *that woman*. I wouldn't assume this was bad news, except there wasn't any other kind about me out there right now.

Oz's jaw was set hard. "I did. I also know *the news* is tabloid hype."

"Funny how a piece of a——"

"If you wouldn't say it to her face, don't say it to me." Oz bit off the words. "I'd hate to have to kill a business relationship because you're a misinformed asshole."

Jake's chuckle was tight. "That's actually why I'm calling. I can't place your people anymore. I won't work with someone who supports the kind of loose ethics that young woman has."

Oh geez. I sank lower in my seat.

"You're wrong." There was no hesitation in Oz's retort. "About Luna. About the entire situation. But I'm glad you didn't hide it. You're right, we won't work together again." He disconnected, cutting Jake off.

I wanted to curl up in a ball and hide.

"This is on him, not you." Oz settled his hand on my knee.

The touch was comforting, but not enough to erase the situation. "You just lost a business contact because of me."

"No. He's gone because of himself, not you. You understand that."

"I guess." Not really. I heard the sincerity and command in Oz's words, but if this was Day Two of Luna is an Evil Mastermind, it didn't feel like it was going to fade into the background.

Oz squeezed my leg gently. "I'm here because I want to be. Because you're worth it. Not because we're fucking. Because you deserve more."

No one *deserved* just for existing. Not beyond the essentials. I didn't know how to argue that, though. "I guess."

FOURTEEN

The next few days were a slog of scheduling times I could meet with my friends' famous friends, and scouring ads for jobs and apartments.

Violet got me airtime with Sadie and Grayson, which went so well. They were friendly, made me feel at ease, and was about as perfect an introduction to this process as I could've hoped for.

Wednesday, Graham was taking me to meet his sister. This wasn't like a *let me introduce you to the family* thing. Though, there was a distinctly loud part of me insisting that in a way, it was.

Adrienne was an artist, and she was going to draw me, just a cartoon version, to use as part of my branding.

Who was I that I needed branding?

I was supposed to be myself. Which for me meant over thinking ten different outfits in a span of two minutes, until half my wardrobe, from cutoffs and a T-shirt to my nicest interview outfit, blanketed my bed.

I tugged a corset out of the back of the closet. Violet got this for me a few years back, for Halloween. It was pale blue and white, with gauzy, wire-framed wings. It was absolutely not the kind of thing that someone wore for the day-to-day. As I laced it on, and twisted this way and that in front of the mirror, it made me feel absolutely magical.

And now that I had that happy glow, I could put on something more practical. I was reaching for a T-shirt in the discarded pile that said *Gamer Girls Do It Better*, when someone knocked.

I opened the door to Graham.

"I'm early, I know. I…" His gaze fell on me and he trailed off. "Wow." He drew the knuckle of his index finger lightly up my bare shoulder, dropping his touch short of my neck. "It's always been hard to keep my hands to myself around you, but I don't know if it's possible anymore."

"Why would you have to?" I could be coy, but he was so freaking close and if I was going to spend more time with him, I needed some clarity. "I get it. Before, you were my teacher. Now, you're not."

"I don't know what you expect me to say, Luna."

There were a handful of things I wanted to hear, but there was one specifically that needed to happen sooner rather than later. "Stop with the mixed signals. You push me away for my own good. You want more. Oz is in the way. You don't want to keep your hands to yourself… There's no possible way you don't know I'm interested."

Graham reached for me, and I pressed my palm to his to stop him.

"If you do this, no more *but we shouldn't* after." I didn't know where the directness came from.

He gave a half smile and chuckle, twisted his wrist to break the contact between us, and rested his hand on my cheek. "That's fair."

He brushed his lips over mine and my heart skipped. When he pressed into me, pushing me back into the apartment, my body molded and yielded to his.

There was no tentative exploration like there had been the other day at Oz's. Graham didn't stop pushing until my back was to the wall. He dragged his mouth along my jaw and up to nibble my earlobe. "I'm not going to do any of that stuff you and he talked about."

I noticed he didn't say Oz's name. "You don't have to. My fantasies about you are different."

"There's more than just the *on the desk at school*?" Graham moved his mouth down to my collarbone, teasing his thumbs along the top of my breasts, above the hem of the corset.

Doubt whispered in. "I'm not the only one who's been... You've had..." Maybe I didn't want to know if he wasn't fantasizing about me.

"I can't count the number of times I've beat myself raw, to images of taking you, well, anywhere you wanted." He dragged a finger lightly over my nipple, drawing a tingle even though layers of fabric.

I sighed happily at the touch. "I love it when we're thinking the same things."

"Fuck, I wish we had more time right now."

"You were fifteen minutes early," I reminded him.

The sound that rumbled up from deep in his chest filled me with need. "Fifteen minutes isn't nearly enough time for what I want to do to you. I'll have to leave us wanting."

I'd been wanting for a decade. I also hated being late or keeping anyone waiting. I jutted out my lower lip.

He kissed the pout away. "What's wrong?"

"I hate that we can't just let passion take over and ignore the rest of the world."

"Me too. But I we have enough time for something." He teased his fingers under the waistband of my jeans.

I let out a light laugh at the combination of ticklish and seductive touch. "What did you have in mind?"

Graham flipped the button on my jeans and dragged down the zipper. "I realized the other day that I have a new favorite sight." He slipped his hand lower, under my trousers and over my panties. "Watching you come."

"I bet I look silly." How else was I supposed to respond to that?

He brushed his lips over mine. "You look stunning. Always." He slipped the crotch of my underwear aside, and drew his fingers lightly along my bare skin.

I parted my lips in a long moan and he leaned into swallow the noise, as he parted my folds.

The longer he kissed me and teased along my pussy, the slicker I grew. He slipped his fingers near my opening, and away again.

I rocked against his touch, desire building inside. The door was still open, and the noise of traffic drifted in, along with the distant chatter of people on the sidewalk. No one was going to come back here, but the possibility they might cranked my anticipation a notch higher.

Graham moved to my clit to circle the swollen nub. Wowza, he had skilled fingers. My breath came in short pants the longer he stroked me.

Orgasm crashed in, washing over and through me. Was I gasping? Screaming? I didn't know or care.

As my world slowly swam back into focus as Graham eased off, but my legs didn't recover so quickly. As I caught my breath, his pressing me to the wall held me upright.

My gaze landed on my digital clock, and reality whispered back in. We'd gone from early to late. "I don't have time to change."

"Never change. I like you just the way you are."

"You're a goof." I wasn't complaining. About any of this. His weight pressing into me, his erection digging into my leg, and the light mood in the room. In fact the only complaint I had was that we couldn't stay and play. "I meant my top."

"I want to keep the jokes going by saying something about him not being here. Is that appropriate? Am I allowed to joke about Cole?" Hearing that name pass Graham's lips made things even better. It was another barrier knocked aside.

"Depends on the joke, but you don't have to pretend he doesn't exist. This doesn't change what he and I have." More reality. "You realize that don't you?"

"I do. I'm still processing, but the fact that I get you—this— makes it easier. Don't change the top. You look magical, and Adrienne will work magic from the visual."

Heat flushed me at his use of *magical* and that it mirrored my thoughts.

Given neither of us liked to be late, with a little extra effort and reluctance, we peeled apart, and were on our way.

Apparently I'd already gotten addicted to Oz's frequent touch, because I was disappointed that Graham kept his hands to himself as we drove. Now that the initial making out was over, would this be awkward?

I didn't want that. I wanted to be the person I was when Oz asked me about my fantasies. When Graham was being wishy washy. This wasn't normal, was it? For me to slide into *okay, I'm seeing both of you now*, with so little hesitation.

Then again, when had I ever been normal? "How long have you known where I was?" I asked.

"I knew you stayed in state. Beyond that? Not until the other day. Following you would've made it harder to ignore you. Also, it's creepy."

Right. In movies it was romance. In real life it was stalking. "You just waited until a single night to learn everything about what I'd been up to."

"The things I want to know about you, I won't find online. I won't learn any other way than spending time with you."

Okay, that was super sweet. Like, chibi Luna swooning and melting kind of sweet.

"I did look up a lot about Cole, though," Graham said.

"Should I be jealous?" I teased.

Graham shook his head. "I think that's my line."

"I hope you won't be. Jealous, that is. I don't expect you to turn it off *now*, like flipping a switch, but if you could get there…"

He brushed his hand over mine, pausing to squeeze before moving back to the steering wheel. "How've you been? Genuinely. Not this fake bullshit most people expect."

"Good. I've been genuinely good. Finding work is tough, which means things like making rent are tough, but I have more than the necessities, and people looking out for me. You? You said private tutoring."

"I'm happy I get to keep teaching," Graham said. "And I

noticed you've kept up with tech. Despite… restrictions." He wasn't asking.

I'd all but confirmed that already. "What you're implying would've violated my probation. Are you wearing a wire?"

"You had your hands all over me earlier. You tell me." He navigated the streets with ease, taking us closer to the mountains and the edge of the valley.

"Well… there was something in your pants," I said playfully. "But it was pretty big for a modern listening device."

"Hard drives took up more space when I was made."

I couldn't help but snicker at his phrasing. "*Made?* Humans call that being born."

"I— Uh— What are you implying?" His defensive stutter was exaggerated.

I thought my implication was obvious. "Are you a Cylon?"

"N— n— *no.*"

I wasn't convinced, and I was struggling to hold my laughter back enough so I could speak. This was easy. Fun. Exactly what I missed about Graham. "If you are, you should know I won't betray the entire planet, no matter how good the sex is."

"So much for that mission." He sighed heavily.

"Wait. Don't let that stop you from trying. You can't give up that easily."

"I'm definitely not giving up. You already have the codes to bring down my defense system." His voice shifted to serious.

A knot formed in my chest at the abrupt shift in tone. "That was cheesy."

"At least I don't tell dad jokes. And you have to admit, it was sweet."

The best kind of sweet. "Better than chocolate…" I trailed off when he turned onto one of the roads leading to University parking.

"Are you okay?" Graham asked.

"This place has a lot of memories." I hadn't been back since graduation. Most of my college time was amazing, but those few mistakes—like the one I made with Tiff—were enough to spoil a lot of the rest.

Graham squeezed my hand. "I didn't even think to warn you, I'm sorry. Adrienne spends a lot of time up here in the art building, because she has teacher friends who let her use a studio. That's where we're meeting her."

"It's okay. I'll be okay." I had to get over it eventually. Didn't I?

FIFTEEN

We made our way to the Art building, and Graham led me to one of the rooms near the rear entrance. There was a woman near the front of the room, head down, attention focused on a drawing pad. I saw the resemblance to Graham instantly.

"Pst," Graham whispered.

She looked up and smiled when she saw us. "Hey." She gestured for us to join her, and gave Graham a hug when he was close enough. "Luna?"

"Hi." I liked her warmth.

"I'm Adrienne. So glad to meet you. I love your corset. Those wings are everything."

Yup. I liked her a lot. I spun so she could see my back. "Isn't the whole thing amazing?"

"I was going to say magical."

"That's what I told her," Graham said.

Adrienne tugged gently at one wing. "Magical Fae Luna. That's it." She returned to her chair and started sketching.

That all happened quickly. Not that I minded. No reason to stress about if she'd like me. If I'd like her.

Her pencil scratched across paper and she stuck her tongue out just a smidge while she sketched. "So you're the girl who got my big brother arrested."

My stomach plummeted into my shoes.

Graham coughed.

Adrienne looked up, eyes wide. "Oh my god, I'm so sorry. That came out wrong. I didn't mean—"

"How is she going to take that in a good way?" Graham's question was sharp.

"I was teasing, I promise." Apology rang in Adrienne's voice. "I didn't mean to strike any nerves. Graham's told me so much about you."

He had?

"And I have nothing but the deepest respect for you," Adrienne said. "You've done amazing things, and you're so brilliant. I'm honored to get to sketch you." She sounded sincere. She held up a line art, chibi version of me, complete with the wings on the corset.

The art, even though it was rough, was fantastic, and I'd said dumb things to new people plenty of times. I understood. "I can't believe you just drew that. I love it. Do you do this professionally?"

She blushed and returned to the drawing, this time with colored pencils. "I do 3D rendering for a commercial architect. But I'd love to work in games. Is that silly?"

"Not silly at all. Me too." Okay, now I liked her again.

"And I really am sorry," Adrienne said. "I don't blame you for what happened. Not even a teensy, tiny, minuscule bit. I know Graham blames himself. He's like that. White knight always coming to someone's rescue. He's been sticking up for me for as long as I can remember." She was a rambler too. Full respect for that.

I also liked hearing these snippets about Graham from someone else. "That's really sweet."

"It's especially useful when he comes to my defense at family dinners, when Mom and Dad are asking me when I'm going to meet a nice man, settle down, and give them grandkids."

I may not be ready for this conversation.

Graham chuckled nervously. "I have to take the heat off you, so I don't get it either."

"But now that he's got you, you've got at least five or ten more baby-making years than I do."

"*Adrienne*," Graham all but shouted.

I laughed.

"Oh, God, I did it again." Adrienne looked horrified. "It was a joke. I promise. I'm not usually this bad."

Graham sighed. "She's frequently this bad."

"Okay, so I am. I'm horrible at reading the room. Especially when I'm nervous. Always sticking my foot in my mouth. I didn't mean what I said; I just have a weird sense of humor."

"It's okay. I promise." And it was. There were few things I understood better than people thinking I was weird because I said things they didn't expect.

We chatted a little more while Adrienne added colors to the picture. I loved it even more now. It was me in my corset, wielding a deck of tarot cards.

She promised to digitize it and email it to me within the next couple of days. The three of us said our *goodbyes* and Graham and I left her to get back to her own art.

On the way out, I wanted to wander through the Computer Science building. Actually, I didn't, but I figured as long as we were here it was a good time to push past more of my discomfort. The school itself had nothing to do with what happened, other than being where I met Tiff. I'd learned a lot of wonderful things here as well as meeting Graham. I wanted to bring more of those moments to the front of my mind.

A voice filtered out from one of the rooms as well strolled down the hall. The sign out front said

Professor Erol

Ethics in Programming, Development, and Computer Science

Open to the Public

I grabbed Graham's arm and tugged him toward the door. "We have a little more time, don't we?"

"This isn't the kind of lecture you want to hear."

I twisted my mouth and stared at him, waiting for him to take it back. "I think is. This kind of stuff fascinates me."

"The topic, yes. The speaker? No. This isn't a *let's learn* kind of thing. I guarantee it's going to be a self-important man ranting about who should and shouldn't be allowed in computing. I worked with him, and I've never heard him do anything but."

I tugged Graham in the back entrance and into seats near the top of the amphitheater. "He's not going to just rant. I can sift through the opinions to hear worthwhile," I said. Ethics were subjective anyway, and this was free knowledge.

The lecture was only about ten minutes in, and Prof. Erol was wrapping up his introduction.

And then, as he launched into a diatribe about how teaching certain types of coding in school only led to malfeasance, my stomach dropped. I was watching a real life Professor Umbridge condescend to a room full of captive ears about the evils of the magic that was security programming.

When he used my name as an example, calling me a vile specimen of immorality, Graham actually freaking growled.

Graham half-rose in his seat and I yanked him back down.

"You were right." My voice was tight. "Let's just go." I wanted to be anywhere else. Now.

Graham clenched his jaw.

"Please," I begged.

Graham nodded, and we headed toward the exit.

"Does the truth bother you?" Erol's voice hit our backs.

Graham huffed, his nostrils flared, and turned to the stage. "The truth? No. The prejudiced meanderings of a misogynist? Quite a bit." He squeezed my hand.

While I loved seeing him standing tall, his voice booming across the amphitheater like the professor I'd fallen for, this wasn't the situation I wanted to see it in.

"Since we're speaking about you, would you like to provide a defense?" Erol asked. "Ladies and gentlemen, the sole reason the school updated our ethics policy a few years back. If you'll note the young lady on his arm, you can see he hasn't learned his lesson."

I wanted to curl up in a little ball and hide, but I stood there, expression blank, refusing to let this man beat me down verbally.

"I do have thoughts on the subject, yes." Graham's tone was firm. Confident. "If we start placing limits on innovation, we stop innovating. People need to be allowed to explore all possible avenues when they embark on discovery, and if we limit the scope of education, students will find the information somewhere else. Frequently without the structure and knowledge of an experienced individual to guide them."

Geez that was sexy. I was having flashbacks to that very first class I took from him, and why I'd been infatuated before we ever spoke one-on-one.

"Obviously, we need to use considerations and reason in each decision, but we need to provide the tools for others to do the same," Graham said. "Will someone use that knowledge for things we don't agree with? Always. That can't be stopped. But the negative can be minimized if we're guiding people rather than pointing them toward a shiny red button and telling them *do not touch*."

Erol's laugh was more like a barking pig. "Thank you for proving my point, Mr. Anderson. Give an otherwise intelligent man a bit of snatch and he's willing to abandon all reason. Which brings me to my next point—the proliferation of pornography on the Internet."

"That's not a valid counter." Graham's voice carried, but Erol continued to talk over him.

"Now that's a man who's never had good sex," a woman nearby said, just loudly enough for us and those around us to hear.

A few snickers rolled through the back of the hall.

I followed the comment to find Judith standing.

"You have something to add, young lady?" Erol was focused on us again, as Judith joined us.

"Ma'am, or Ms. Walsh will do fine, thank you." Judith's voice carried as well as either man's, and her presence commanded attention.

Chibi Luna was back in my head, swooning. *So scary. So amazing.*

"I see, Miss Walsh. Enlighten us." Erol sneered.

The corner of Judith's mouth tugged up. "*Ms.* But I understand your reluctance to accept peers who don't have a dick."

Between Judith and Graham, they expanded on what Graham opened with, crafting a compelling statement about growing knowledge rather than limiting it, and how prohibition is never the answer, even in schooling.

A pair of men in security uniforms approached us. "You need to leave campus." One reached for Judith.

She stepped away, eyebrows raised. "If I were to let you touch me, you wouldn't know what to do with me."

"We're leaving. That was all we wanted in the first place." I headed toward the door and prayed Graham would follow.

He fell into step behind me.

Judith joined us, on my other side. "Looks like we get an escort to the parking lot." She jerked her head behind us.

A glance confirmed security was following us.

This wasn't as humiliating as when I was arrested a few years ago, but it certainly summoned and attached itself to those memories. And once again Graham was involved, further sinking his reputation and career.

"You look good." Judith's compliment drew me back to the now. "Even in there, you looked good."

I gave her a weak smile. "Thanks."

"I don't believe we've met. I'm Graham Anderson." He extended his hand.

"Pleasure to meet you." She reached across me for the handshake. "Nice to see that like everything else he said in there, the parts about you were untrue."

Graham tangled his fingers with mine. "You know that from three minutes of stilted debate?"

"It's a lot more complicated than that, but that helps." Judith looked past him, to me. "How are you holding up?"

"Aside from the not being able to find a job, and the fact that the world runs on money, I'm great." I meant to say that bit in my head. Oopsie.

Her eyes grew wide. "You can't... Absolutely ridiculous."

"It's okay." I didn't mean to dump on her. Not only a stranger but a boyfriend's ex-wife—that wasn't convoluted at all. "Graham and Cole are helping me rebuild my reputation. I'll come out of things fine." And I would.

"So this is your Lancelot. The knight who thinks he's done you wrong and needs to make right for his queen." Judith's tone was one of respect. "I bet Cole loves you, Graham." Her voice twisted a notch.

"I hear your sarcasm, and I assure you he does not," Graham said.

"Regardless. Luna, give me your number. I see interesting opportunities all the time, and I'd be happy to drop your name."

I smiled. "All right. Thank you." The brief exchange made me feel a whole lot better.

As long as I could push aside the unpleasantness from the amphitheater, and the quiet whisper asking how much worse it would get before it got better.

SIXTEEN

I spent the next three days in one podcast and interview after another. At least it felt like it.

Between Hunter and Oz, they'd gotten me onto seven different shows. Since most were pre-recorded, I spent at least two hours in each studio. Add the bus rides to that, and I barely had time to sleep, with no time to see Oz, Graham, or Violet. At least I got to text them, and I was the goofy dork who scrolled through those messages over and over when I needed a mood boost.

I understood that the interviews were fluff pieces, meant to show the fun side of me, but that also meant I was repeating a lot of the same, with no real substance. I crashed every night when I got home, and dragged myself out of bed to extra coffee every morning.

This would be worth it though. The payoff. The success. Getting a job.

Even though the *thanks but no thanks* letters were stacking up.

I was grateful for Sunday morning. I'd see Oz and Graham today. Sure, it was to do more work—compare notes, regroup, and change any plans that required it—but I was still seeing my guys.

My guys. The term rolled easily through my thoughts and

warmed me from the inside out. I'd rather spend the day cuddling, but seeing them would help.

I grabbed a vibrant plum sundress from my closet, and tossed a light sweater with embroidered flowers over it. The colors were another accent to brighten my mood.

The instant I opened the door to Oz, he cupped my face between his palms and crushed his mouth to mine in a breath-stealing kiss that drew out my exhaustion and replaced it with comfort and adoration. He finally pulled away to press his lips to the top of my head.

"I missed you." His words sank into my skull and my soul.

The world was instantly a better place. "Same."

"Shall we?" He offered his elbow.

I grabbed my purse and laptop, locked the door, and hooked my hand around his arm.

When we reached the truck Graham was waiting on the passenger side, door open.

"Oh." That made me smile even wider. "I thought you were meeting us up there. Not that I mind."

He grasped my fingertips and kissed the back of my knuckles. "Change of plans. I wanted to see you now."

"Yay." I'd clap, except I didn't want to let go of him. "Three way date." I liked this Graham more than ever. Direct. Sweet. With me.

It was a snug fit with the three of us in the truck, but not uncomfortable. In fact, sandwiched between my guys was about the best thing ever.

My apartment was only a few minutes from the freeway, then Oz was taking us into the mountains, toward his place.

"Okay, so wait." I put more pieces together about Graham being here. Was he becoming okay with this entire arrangement? "Does that mean we're all friends now?"

"I'm hoping you and I are more than friends at this point," Graham said.

"But yes," Oz agreed.

The weight inside was lifting, leaving feathers and sunshine and joy behind.

The truck rattled and bounced with every bump, but Oz navigated the turns and inclines with practiced ease. "How do you feel about competition gaming?"

"I wouldn't do it myself." Random, weird question. I liked it. "It's cool that it exists, and with the right players and game, it's fun to watch."

"Judith called me last night—"

"Do you talk to her a lot?" Graham cut him off.

Jealousy poked me, but it didn't take much to shove it aside. Oz was here with me, not with her. Besides, I liked her, regardless of how brief our conversations had been, and I didn't want a reason for that to change.

"I really don't," Oz said. "More in the last few weeks than in the last few months. But she mentioned meeting Graham, and said she had three media passes for a competition exhibition that's coming up. Said we should all be there Thursday night."

Watching gaming, with these two, and just having fun? Epic. Doing it surrounded by more crowds where I needed to be the two-dimensional version of myself? Boo. But this was all part of the plan. This was what I needed to find an in. "I'm free."

"Same." Graham slid his hand under mine, palm up, and wove his fingers through mine. "Are you all right?"

I'd let my exhaustion bleed into my voice, and hadn't meant to. "Totally fine." I summoned the internal sunshine again, to match the warmth peeking over the tops of the mountains.

"Don't do that. Don't ever think you have hide how you feel." There was a light edge to Oz's voice.

I wasn't faking happy, I'd simply rather stay with joy than slide into unpleasant feelings. "I'm not."

Graham squeezed my hand. "If you're not up for Tuesday night, we don't have to do it."

"I'm not going to turn the opportunity down. I'm a little filtered is all. A day to recharge with my two favorite men, and I'll be fine."

Unless we worked all day, setting more appointments to fill my calendar with talking to people.

I swallowed the train of thought that would lead into blahness. Oz's and Graham's company was better than cupcakes and rainbows, and when they were like this, their energy was healing.

Oz's quiet sigh tickled my insecurity. Was he disappointed in me? I didn't want that.

"You ever play the original Hoarde games?" Graham's question was an obvious and welcome right turn in the conversation. "Before Digital Media ruined them?"

Cord's flagship title when they were a brand new company.

"I played them to death." Oz snorted. Of course he did. He helped write them.

I shook my head. "Not so much. The whole FPS, shoot-to-kill isn't my thing." I didn't have a problem with the video game violence when it was as pixelated as those games had been, but I hated the tension of sneaking around, waiting for something to jump out at me.

"I played those games so much." Graham sounded nostalgic. "They got me through pre-grad."

Oz laughed. An actual chuckle. "They got me out of having to do pre-grad." He'd learned most of his skills on the job, rather than going to college.

Every time I remembered that, I was impressed. "You know what? I've been talking about myself all week, and I already know about me. You guys should talk about you." I knew surprisingly little considering how much time I'd spent with each of them. They'd done an effective job of never letting the conversations delve too deeply into their personal lives.

"On one condition," Graham said.

What was I supposed to do with a reply like that?

I chose to be amused. "Talking about yourselves requires a negotiation?"

Oz nodded. "In this case it does. Terms are, you have to take a day off."

Wasn't this Graham's deal?

"I *have* to?"

"No work at all today," Graham said.

Oh gosh golly gee darn. "But why?" I let the mock despair bleed into my voice, trying to make it obvious I was joking.

Oz headed toward an exit. We were miles from his place. "Change of plans. We're doing something different today."

"It's going to be gorgeous and sunny," Graham said.

Oz glanced at him. "Picnic?"

"You don't strike me as a *picnic* kind of guy," Graham countered.

I had the distinct impression I was being set up. And I loved it.

Oz squeezed my knee. "I'm a make my baby girl happy kind of guy."

I wrinkled my nose at the nickname.

"No?" He glanced between me and the road.

I shook my head. "You're just not great with the names. You didn't come up with yours, did you?"

His clenched jaw was all the reply I needed. Where was he taking us? Along a series of hard packed dirt roads, up a back mountain path.

"What's the story there, with the name?" I'd asked before, and he'd always brushed off the question.

"You have to agree to the deal first." Graham was taking his side. How gloriously, wonderfully silly.

"It's not even your story. *Fine.*" I couldn't help my grin as I let out an exaggerated sigh. "We'll have a picnic. But only so I can learn things about you two."

We pulled around a tight curve and came to a stop at the edge of a huge clearing that was native grass and wildflowers. It wasn't really a park. It was like a tiny cove of amazing, tucked away in the mountains.

Graham grabbed a blanket out of the lockbox in the back of the truck, and Oz grabbed a cooler.

"So this was all spontaneous and you just came up with it on the drive?" I asked playfully as we laid out the blanket.

"No one ever said that." Oz pulled me to sit next to him.

"The two of you have been talking—plotting even—with each

other when I'm not around." It was perfect. "And getting along enough to make plans." I fit perfectly resting against Oz, especially with Graham on my other side.

"We have." Graham reached into the cooler. He handed each of us a can of iced coffee, and extracted a bowl of fruit.

I caught a glimpse of more food, sandwiches maybe. "How long do you plan for us to spend out here?"

"As long as you want." Graham popped the top on his drink and took a sip.

Oz set his can aside, and reached for the food. "This way, there are no excuses for checking in on anything."

"It's brilliant." Better than cake or ice cream or long drawn out conversations about the most efficient bash scripts ever written in Python.

Oz set the bowl of fruit on the blanket between us, plucked a slice of strawberry out, and trailed it along my bottom lip.

I gasped at the light touch, and drew my tongue along the same path, licking away the sweet-tart juice.

He pushed the fruit into my mouth, and I drew his finger in with my tongue. His groan was more delicious than the fruit.

"Now that's not fair." Graham's protest was playful. "We've been here less than ten minutes and you two are already at it."

The corner of Oz's mouth tugged up, and he faced Graham. "No one's leaving you out."

"No?" Graham challenged.

"Nope. I'm happy to feed you fruit, too."

Uh, first, what? And second, *hot*. "Yes, please." I didn't realize I'd said the last bit out loud until Graham raised his brows.

Oz plucked a piece of melon from the bowl next, and pressed it to Graham's lips.

It was alluring watching Graham react the same way I had. So that was what it looked like from the outside.

And Oz's moan when Graham sucked on his fingers…

Wowza.

Pink crept up Graham's neck, and he scooted back on the blanket. "You brought bowls or something, right?"

He may be pulling away, but the tension in the air didn't dissipate.

Could I push things further? I wanted to.

I'd been promised answers, and maybe I could use that to my advantage. "The nickname—Oz—did Judith come up with it?"

"Judith is capable of a large number of things. She's not a creative individual, though. Chloe came up with the name."

Someone else I had all the respect for. Chloe was one of those original Cord staffers who was still with Rinslet today. She'd been their head writer when the company started, and was responsible for the story line on most of the X games. She was their COO now.

I met her a few days ago, doing a podcast with her partner Jordan. She wasn't just brilliant, she was also kind and totally fun.

"You've got such a fascinating past, Cole." Graham's voice was a blend of awe and envy. But not in a mean way.

"It's not really. I simply avoid talking about the boring bits."

The heat between them had cooled, and I wanted it back. Maybe I wasn't so brilliant as I thought, if I couldn't fan this existing spark.

SEVENTEEN

"Be fair," Graham said. "You don't talk about most of the bits."

"You worked on the original team. You get to look back and say *I helped start that.*" I loved modern tech, but there was a teensy bit of me that was eternally sad that I'd never have a haven to be part of something as groundbreaking as Cord and their original games.

"Oh yeah, that too," Graham said.

I studied him, trying to puzzle out the words. "What bits were you talking about?"

Oz finished his can and crammed it into the small trash bag we had sitting next to us. "He meant the orgies."

Graham shrugged. "I led a sheltered life. My parents gave me a video to watch about sex, rather than having the talk with me themselves, and it was pretty much limited to *penis goes in vagina and babies happen.*"

"But you've expanded your horizons since." Did Oz sound... hopeful?

"I have. But when I was in my early twenties, a blow job was naughty. Group sex? That only happened in bad porn."

"To be fair, most porn was bad when we were in our early twenties."

At Oz's statement, Graham chuckled. "True. But I don't know if it's better now, or just more prolific."

This was better than Oz and Graham getting along. It was actually friendly.

"Three people aren't quite a *group*," Oz said, "but there are a lot fewer limbs to keep track of."

Inspiration struck. "Let's play a game."

"All right," Graham agreed easily.

"What are we playing?" Oz sounded more hesitant.

The kind of game that helped people open up, without feeling like twenty questions. "Firsts."

"Which is...?" Oz better not be a hard sell.

Graham leaned in, an easy smile on his face. "It's like *Truth or Dare* meets *Never Have I Ever*."

"Sounds complicated." Oz hadn't said *yes* yet, but he also hadn't said *no*. "And how do you know that?"

Probably the same way I did. "It was big on campus."

"All right," Oz's sigh was exaggerated. "How do we play *Firsts*?"

In my head, chibi Luna clapped and squealed in delight... and a smidge of anticipation. This game frequently ended with kissing or making out. I could get that here regardless, but this way was a different kind of fun.

"We each take a turn picking *first time you ever*... events, based on our own ages. First person who did it gets to dare the last person or the person who's never done it. For instance, first time I ever saw a movie in a theater, I was thirteen."

"Okay, I think I get it." Oz nodded. "My parents were huge sci-fi bugs, so the first time I ever saw a movie in theaters it was probably Return of the Jedi, and I was two. But the first time I remember, I was probably four or five."

"If I didn't know better, I'd say I was set up." Graham's grumble didn't hold any weight. "That sheltered childhood I mentioned? To my parents, the kind of movies they have in theaters were anti-intellectual shit. So first time was in college. I was eighteen."

"If it helps you feel any better, that's why it was so long for me, too." I'd snuck off to see something with my friends, when we were supposed to be back to school shopping at the mall.

"That means I win, right?" Oz looked smug. "What next?"

"Next you get to dare Graham," I said.

Oz smirked. "I like this game."

Graham rolled his eyes. "Because you're a fucking sadist."

"Not true. I don't want to see you in pain, just squirming in discomfort. Besides, I don't expect I'll win every round, and I'm not opening myself to retaliation on the first question."

"You've already formed a strategy?" I shouldn't be surprised, but I had hoped things would escalate quickly.

"I know I am," Graham said.

In that case, I needed one too. I set my brain working on the task of getting us toward fondling sooner rather than later. Within the confines of the game, of course. "Maybe I shouldn't have suggested this. I hope no one dares me to do anything too horrible."

"Fine." Graham slouched. "What do you want me to do? Streaking through the park doesn't matter, since there's no one else here."

"No streaking. I want to see that tattoo you're hiding," Oz said.

Graham had a tattoo? Wait. "How do you know that, Cole?"

"I caught a glimpse of it when he was buried to the hilt inside you."

I flushed at the memory summoned by the catch in Oz's voice.

"All right." Graham stood, unbuckled his belt, and undid his slacks. He tugged the waistband down his hip, exposing half a butt cheek in the process, and Celtic knot that looked like a circle woven around and through four pointed ellipses.

I brushed my fingers over the delicate ink, relishing Graham's soft skin and intoxicating groan. "What does it mean?"

"I was told it means the never-ending circle of internal strength," Graham said as he did his slacks up and sat.

"So cool." It didn't escape me that he left his belt undone. This was a good start. "Now Oz gets to go."

"First job—As in, first time someone paid you to do work for them. Fifteen. I had a paper route," Oz said.

Graham sighed heavily. "Twenty-one. TA."

I got to win a round early on. I needed a good dare, and I was pretty sure I had one. "Babysitting for the neighbors. I was twelve."

"Wait." Graham's voice brightened. "If babysitting counts, I was ten. My sister."

Oz knit his brows together. "Family doesn't count."

"Bullshit. My parents paid me, and expected me to do a good job."

As much as I wanted to hold onto my win, Graham had a point. "Oz didn't specify up front that family doesn't count. Graham wins."

Oz shook his head, but he was still smiling. "Fine. Do your worst, Graham But remember vengeance is delayed and antagonizing."

"Pretty sure that's not how the phrase goes," Graham said.

"It is now."

Graham urged his lips and furrowed his brow. His expression stayed frozen for a moment. "Why did you leave Rinslet?"

"Don't know if you've noticed"—a hint of sarcasm lined Oz's reply—"but they're a *very* public facing company. I was sitting through my millionth meeting about how to deal with both positive and negative press, and I realized it wasn't for me. I wanted to be working with computers, not playing Bad Boy Programmer for the gossip sites."

"The man behind the curtain." I understood his nickname better now than ever.

"Exactly. Scandalous enough for you?" He looked at Graham.

"Not looking for scandal. I was curious is all."

"Your turn, Graham," I said.

"First time I kissed someone the same gender as me, I was twenty." A whisper of melancholy ghosted over Graham's face. "Apparently college meant a lot of firsts."

"I think you're supposed to pick something you have a chance of winning at." A week ago, Oz probably would've said that with more disdain.

I liked that things weren't that way now.

"I think I'm supposed to pick something I want the answer to," Graham said. "Why? Are you going to come back with *ten*? Mister Bear was an early bloomer?"

"Nope." Oz *popped* on the *p*. "Same age as you. Twenty. I never let myself consider the possibility I might be attracted to men. Then one game release celebration, we were playing a game a little like this. You might be surprised to hear this, but I'm not one to back down from a dare."

Graham stared back with mock horror. "You? No."

I laughed, then shivered as a gust of chilly wind raced down my back. Clouds passed in front of the morning sun, shrouding us in shadows.

"How old, Luna?" Graham asked.

"Thirteen. Same first movie. D.E.B.S. And when I saw them falling in love on screen…" I sighed at the happy memories. "She tasted like Dr. Pepper lip gloss."

"The sexy lady is the winner." Oz boomed in an announcer voice.

"Which of us is the loser?" Graham asked.

Oz stared at him. "Don't. Make me answer that."

Graham raised an eyebrow.

I had my opening. "I get to dare you both. *Ha*. I want you to kiss."

Graham raised the second eyebrow.

Oz didn't hesitate. He captured Graham's neck, holding him captive as Oz claimed his mouth. I felt the kiss from beside them. The pressure. The intensity. The mingling of tongues and deep throaty groans.

Watching them together made my pulse race and sent need dancing over my skin. Two guys together had never been a thing for me, one way or the other, but I could masturbate to Oz and Graham doing all sorts of wicked things to each other.

Something wet struck my cheek and I swiped it away, too

enthralled in seeing this kiss to give it another thought. Then another raindrop landed on my cheek. And ten more.

The skies opened up and poured buckets on us.

Kisses in the rain were incredible. Water sliding down the sharp chisel of Oz's jaw. Glistening in Graham's short beard. I was surprised the water didn't sizzle and turn to steam the moment it struck them.

Graham finally broke away with a groaning sigh. "We're going to freeze out here."

But it would be a happy freezing.

"That's fair." Oz released his grip on Graham's neck.

We rushed to get the cooler and wet blanket secured in the back of the truck, before sliding into the cab. *Sliding* being the operative term, given our wet butts on vinyl seats.

I looked between them—Oz's drenched and brooding versus Graham's soaked and reserved—and joy bubbled up inside, turning to laughter. "Best. Day. Ever."

My breath stalled when I met Oz's gaze again and saw the heat in his eyes. He dragged a thumb across my cheek, brushing away the rain as he traveled a path down to my mouth. He tugged my bottom lip, and dipped in to nibble on the tender skin.

I sighed against his mouth. Was Graham watching us the way I'd watched them? Geez, I hoped so. The possibility lit my senses on fire.

Oz grabbed my wrist and moved my hand to his jeans, to cup his erection. "Graham got me started for you." His voice was a rough growl against my lips.

"And I'm already wet," I teased.

"I'd fuck you right now if I thought there was room for Graham to join us without someone's legs cramping."

Graham's laugh was light. "Appreciate the consideration."

"Anything for my girl's other favorite guy," Oz said.

My girl. Not the most unique nickname, but better than the alternatives.

Graham's phone rang and he sighed. "It's Adrienne. Give me a second." He swiped *Answer.* "What's up?"

Sister calling before sex? That was a bit of a mood killer.

A tinny, indistinguishable voice drifted from his phone, and deep creases etched themselves into his forehead. "They can't do that… I'm sorry… No. I'll make it right… It is on me, it's my fault… I'll call you back when I know."

Graham dropped his phone on dashboard with a sigh.

If I curled up next to him, would it comfort him the way it would me? "What's wrong?"

"Erol ran his complaint up to the Dean, about me being on campus and disrupting courses. She's been asked not to return."

"They can't do that." Oz stiffened behind me, and not in a sexy, *let's play* kind of way.

Graham shook his head. "No, they can't. I have to make this right for her." He raked his fingers through his hair. "I have to know someone there who still has clout who can speak up for her."

"I do," Oz said. "Let me make some calls."

"I don't need you to do this for me." Like that, our morning of fun evaporated in Graham's bitter retort.

Oz sighed. "This entire thing we're working on for Luna, it's your brainchild. These are things I could never do on my own. If it makes you feel better, think of it as returning the favor."

We wouldn't be here, none of this would be happening, if it weren't for me. I was costing Oz contacts. I was damaging Graham's chances of recovering career-wise, and now Adrienne was suffering the consequences too.

EIGHTEEN

My Thursday morning appointment was in Downtown Salt Lake, in an actual office building. The podcaster I was talking to ran several other shows as well, and was doing well enough to have an entire staff on hand.

Was I nervous?

Uh, *yeah.*

But she was friendly, greeting me shortly after I arrived and showing me around the studio. Making sure I knew where everything was, and what to expect from the show.

The *live* show.

Gulp.

But it was all right. Roxie was great about leading me through any stall-points. Filling in the dead air when I stumbled, so it wasn't obvious, and she was super friendly.

"I understand you ran into some trouble in college," she said.

No. This wasn't supposed to be part of any interview. What was she doing? My mouth was instantly dry. "I did."

"And that a member of the staff was involved."

Well, crap and double crap. I laughed nervously. "When you put it that way, it makes the entire thing sound illicit."

"Wasn't it?" Roxie's tone was kind rather than accusatory, but that didn't make me feel better about the question.

I shook my head. People wouldn't hear that. "No. Not like that."

"Like what?"

Shit. "Nothing. I don't know what I'm saying." I really didn't. How was I going to get out of this? Why wasn't I given a script? A heads-up?

"I hate that you're taking the heat for this." She still sounded nice. Concerned. "You were so young, and this older man—influential, respected—took advantage of you."

"Whoa. There was no *taking advantage*. This wasn't that kind of trouble." I could explain exactly what kind it was, but me saying *I was arrested for creating a piece of malware that threatened an entire industry. It wasn't like my teacher assaulted me* didn't seem like the right response.

Roxie's smile was sad and the way she studied me felt like pity. "I know it can be hard to admit, especially looking back on a younger you who wasn't as familiar with the world. It's easy for any of us to say now *I wouldn't let that happen to me*. But when you find yourself in that situation, at nineteen, and a person in a position of power forces their will on you—"

"I'm sorry, that's not at all what happened." I didn't want to delve into the details of my crime, but I wouldn't sit her and let her accuse Graham of things that would make him ill to even consider. "The trouble I got into was all my own doing. If you'd like, we can discuss the technical details of the code *I* created. I can decompile it for you right now." Offering to talk code should help her change the subject.

"Okay." Now she sounded condescending. How did she manage that in so few syllables? "But he got a heavier sentence than you, didn't he? What does that say about the situation?"

That my best friend's boyfriend knew people in politics and pulled some strings on my behalf. There was no way I could say that —Hunter got me this spot so Roxie knew exactly who Ramsey was. "It says I was more fortunate than he was."

Roxie finally changed the subject, but her implied accusations lingered with me through the whole hour. I gave her the most polite, sugary sweet goodbye when it was all over, and vowed to myself to never be on a show like that again.

I had to focus on keeping my hands from shaking as I waited for the bus. This was the worst kind of adrenaline rush ever, making my stomach churn and my knee bounce.

Violet called, and I almost dropped my phone trying to answer.

"I'm *so* sorry." Violet sounded as stressed as I was. "Ramsey's been on their show before, and they were always great. Hunter feels horrible. I'm so so sorry."

"It's okay." *I* wasn't okay, but this wasn't her or Hunter's fault. "They thought they were doing me a favor." But the things they implied about Graham. About my naiveté. I hated when people confused adoration with stupidity.

"I'll pick you up. We'll go for ice cream."

I smiled at her concern. "It's okay. I've got another thing tonight, and I'll use the bus ride to clear my head."

"Okay. But call me if you change your mind."

The ride home didn't do what I wanted. It wasn't the words that lingered with me so much as the implication. That I'd been too stupid to see Graham manipulating me. That this was anything other than my idea. That I was so naive I was willing to break the law for a grade. For sex? I wasn't even sure.

If I was going to be accused of doing reckless things, I wanted it to be for the right reason—because I wanted to prove I could—not because my vagina thought my teacher was pretty and I was too young and stupid to tell it *no*.

When I got home, I sifted through every piece of clothing I owned. Twice. I needed something that made me look less flighty. More mature. Smarter. Not a decade younger than the men I was dating.

The Captain Marvel dress wouldn't give me the look I wanted. Neither would the sweater with the Minnie Mouses on it.

What would Judith wear? She commanded respect just by standing in a room.

I finally landed on the same blouse I'd worn the day Oz told me he liked me. It was professional, it made my eyes bright, and it had that confidence of Oz's kisses attached to it.

I added my nicest jeans, went all out with my make-up, and pulled my hair up.

Oz and some of his people had been hired to do some higher end, last minute wiring for the exhibition we were going to. I should've taken him up on his offer to help, and skipped this morning's interview.

No going back now.

When I answered the door to Graham, he stared at me for a moment. "You look incredible."

"More than normal? Do you like this better?" I hated that my insecurities were showing through.

"There's no better or worse for you. Any way you look is another color on the rainbow of how gorgeous you are. If you answered the door in an Elmo costume, I'd be an instant furry."

His kiss was quick, but it warmed me from head to toe.

"Is this about the show earlier?" Graham asked.

And there was the memory I was trying to ignore. "Maybe."

"I'm not worried about it, and you shouldn't be either."

"But they implied—"

"And they were wrong. About you and me and every single one of their assumptions."

Hearing him back up my thoughts made me feel better. I grabbed my purse and we were on our way.

"Do you *want* me in an Elmo costume?" I asked as Graham drove. I needed to talk about anything but earlier, and that was the first ridiculous thought that flitted close.

"I want you. Full stop."

"But Elmo is super specific."

Graham moved his arm to drape over my shoulders. "Because I assume you giggle and squirm when you're tickled."

I was *super* ticklish. "Do not."

He brushed light fingers along my neck, his touch so barely there it was like a feather.

I sighed at the faint contact, until he hit a specific spot, and a squeal escaped my throat, turning to a laugh. I didn't want to break away, but the tickling became too much. "Okay. I yield. Elmo costume then?"

"No costume. But I am wishing now I'd tried that while we were back at your apartment."

I hadn't entertained that fantasy before. One where his fingers were gliding over my body until I was squirming and couldn't breathe and he was pinning me down with his full weight.

Graham was too sophisticated for something like tickling. But apparently not.

"Something to try next time," I said.

The corner of his mouth tugged up. "Definitely."

The expo was taking place in a different convention center than the auction had. Oz met us near a side entrance, away from everyone else. He gave us both a nod as we approached, and as I drew within his arm's reach, he pulled me close for a long kiss.

"Not sure which of you I'm more jealous of." Graham's teasing was gruff.

Was the other day in the park more than a one-time thing? I could handle that.

"Do you want a kiss too?" Oz asked.

Graham's cheeks darkened. "Maybe later."

Okay, that was super adorable that he was not only shy around Oz, but that they were actually being playful around each other.

I stepped between them, feeling ten million percent better with my hands occupied by theirs, and we headed inside. In the convention room, we were just another group of people that no one gave a second glance to.

Geez that felt good after more than a week of being everyone's focus. I was content to be at the center of my guys' world, and no one else's.

There was a stage at the far end of the room. Two long tables sat up there, holding four computers each. Giant screens hung behind them, presumably so everyone in the room could see what was being played.

There were maybe only a couple hundred people here. A huge crowd for a house party, but small for something like this.

"What is this for?" Maybe I should've asked sooner, but I hadn't been concerned with the details beyond spending the night with Oz and Graham.

"I'm sworn to secrecy," Oz said. "In fact, I didn't know until I got here this afternoon, and they only told me because I had to be on hand while they tested everything."

"Ooh." Graham dragged out the syllable. "Super Secret Secret Squirrel."

"Something like that." Oz chuckled.

"...be ashamed..."

The isolated snatch of conversation crawled up my neck.

"You guys made it." Judith joined us. She looked me over with a faint smile. "Hey. Twins."

Sure enough, our outfits could've been built from the same template. Except her trousers screamed *professional and tailored* while mine whimpered *off the rack at Walmart*, and her top was silk in a gorgeous wine color that complimented her perfectly.

Judith owned the room and I looked like a little girl playing pretend.

I pushed aside the doubt and smiled. "Apparently I've got good taste."

Graham raised my hand to lick the back. "Best taste ever."

Gross, but sweet.

"...no shame..."

"...years younger..."

I pushed out the background conversations. This morning's interview wasn't going to make me paranoid.

"We're going to start soon, but I wanted to talk to you first," Judith said. "Find me when the main event is over, because I want your opinions. Especially Luna's."

Now I was extra curious. "About what?"

"You'll see." Judith stepped away with a wave.

"...clueless..."

"...pedo..."

No. I heard that last one wrong.

"Grand denizens of industry." A booming voice flooded the room, drawing my attention to the stage. I'd met the man up there at the auction...

Dustin, that was right. He'd lost the costume and was dressed in a shirt with the same single spade on it that had been tattooed on his colleagues' arms.

"Thank you to everyone for coming out last minute." He spoke with the kind of confidence that kept everyone's attention on him. The Rinslet logo appeared on the screen behind him. "I'm sure you're all wondering what this is about. If you're not, I didn't do my job."

Light laughter rolled through the room.

"It's because tonight, we're excited to introduce AcesPlayed—because we're the first and we'll continue to be the best at what we do. Most of you know our team from our time at Rinslet—previously the most awesome gaming company in the world to work for."

The image on the large screens morphed from a Rinslet logo into the spade on his shirt, with AcesPlayed beneath it. "We're going to miss our colleagues. It's been an amicable parting of ways, but we have parted regardless."

Murmurs rolled through the crowd, and I felt the ambient curiosity and excitement in my bones.

"Tonight, we say goodbye to the people we came up in this industry with, in the most gaming way possible," Dustin said. "A little friendly competition, in the game we've built. This is where you want to be recording, if you're not, because this is where I get salesy and show you something you've never seen before."

Cell phones came up, raised above heads and all pointed at Dustin. He explained this was a new kind of multiplayer RPG. It wasn't an MMO, all the servers were private, because they offered two things no one else had in this configuration.

A strictly adult only game, complete with nudity. Sex. Any sorts of hookups a person wanted, as long as it didn't break any local or federal laws. And players could either be the adventurers or the monsters.

"Ballsy," Graham muttered.

"Because Judith has bigger balls than most of the people in this room." Oz's words were nothing but respect.

Wow. I was witnessing video game history. I was here for it. I channeled my excitement into my thoughts, where chibi Luna was clapping and bouncing and squealing with anticipation.

Dustin introduced developers from each team. Rinslet would play the adventurers, and AcesPlayed were the boss monster and his add-ons.

As the teams battled back and forth, the room erupted in a wave of cheers and friendly boos. It was a close game, with dead on both sides, and stat bars in the red for anyone left standing. In the end, giant red letters flashed on the screen announcing the adventurers' party had wiped, and evil maintained its control of the valley.

Applause and boos filled the room, all good-natured.

This was abso-freakin'-lutely incredible.

Judith rejoined us as Dustin stepped forward to take questions.

"Wow." It was the first thought that came to mind. I could be more articulate than that, but for three letters, *wow* encompassed a lot.

Judith opened her mouth and someone called her name. She scowled. "Hold that thought." And she was gone again.

"So that's what innovation in gaming looks like these days." Graham sounded as impressed as me.

Oz even managed to look stunned in a good way. "It's been a long time since I've seen something like that. Pretty cool."

"…guys like that do in a game like this…"

"…in the tavern with Loli's…"

I scowled at the nearby whispers. They weren't talking about us. They couldn't be. But the words tugged at doubts and insecurities that lingered near the surface.

"…who needs to fuck cartoon little girls when he's got a real one?"

I clenched my jaw.

"Luna." Oz worked my fingers loose from the fist I hadn't realized I'd clenched them into. "Do you want to step outside?"

I shook my head and pasted on a smile. "I'm fine."

We chatted with more people Oz knew, all of them kind. Complimentary. A few even asking for my information or offering to look at my resume.

But I couldn't ignore the murmurs that grew louder the longer we were here. People quoting the show from this morning. Calling me naive. Saying Graham was a pedo-wannabe, and that I was making the same mistake with Cole.

I'd been called young and immature all my life. Whatever. But implying I was stupid. Saying horrible things about the men I was with. These gossiping assholes having no idea who the three of us were.

But telling myself none of the anonymous words were true didn't erase them.

The podcasts were supposed to make me look better to the public. Make it possible for me to get a job in this industry. In any industry that dealt with programming.

As the night wore on, my heart crumpled more and more, until the best I could summon to any bit of conversation was a tight smile and a brief response.

I couldn't do this. Not if it came with this kind of backlash. Not if it dragged Oz and Graham down with me, or showed them I wasn't as great as they thought.

I stuck it out as long as I could before I asked Oz to take me home. Graham walked us out to the truck.

I hugged Graham tightly and pressed my lips softly to his. "'Night." I poured everything I could into the brief exchange, swallowing my *goodbye*. I didn't want to say it now, and have them try to talk me out of it. I knew this was the right thing to do and they'd figure it out too.

Oz tried to draw me out on the ride home, but I refused to let myself be sucked into a conversation. I had him park in front of the house, rather than in the driveway. I gave him a long kiss, memorizing the way his rough hands felt on my skin as he drew the moment out.

I pulled away before I could fall into more. "'Night." I hopped from the truck and tried to keep my gait casual as I headed inside.

I pressed my back to the door and listened for the sound of Oz's truck leaving, before I let the tears spill down my cheeks. I had to end things with them, before they suffered anymore backlash from my mistake. The thought clawed under my skin and ached in my throat and my heart and everywhere.

I didn't want to, but this was the only way to give them their lives back. To give them back the anonymity and respect they deserved.

NINETEEN

I wanted to sleep and let the world pass me by.

I wanted to call Oz or Graham and ask them to come get me. To keep me for the night.

I wanted to send them each a text saying things were over, so the temptation would be gone.

But if I did that now, at least one of them would show up on my doorstep. I couldn't have that while I was still here.

Instead, I spent the night staring blankly at anime I knew would make me cry. I could blame the ache in my chest on the cartoons instead of my me.

While I watched, a battle raged in my head, half of me arguing I was being stupid and the other half being logical and pointing out how Oz's and Graham's reputations had crumbled, and were continuing to deteriorate, because I was there.

As the sun came up, my eyes were raw and dry.

The cards would give me answers. They always helped me think my way through problems.

I started with my favorite deck, shuffling three times, cutting the cards, and muttering *what do I do?*

I pulled a card off the top and scowled at the reversed Two of

Cups. I didn't need the freaking cards to tell me I'd just walked away from love, and it hurt like hell. I wanted to know what to do next.

This was too complex an issue to rely on a single answer.

I laid out a spread instead. When the images taunted me with more suggestions I didn't like, I resisted the urge to fling the deck across the room, and shoved all the cards back together instead.

Fine. If that deck wouldn't behave, I'd try a different one.

But the next several results weren't any better. Every fucking card mocked me with the same things the people had said yesterday on the podcast. I was being naive. Immature. I didn't know what was right for myself.

I needed Violet's help for the next step in my plan, but if I called her this morning, she'd drop everything to get over here right away. I wasn't going to disrupt another life over this.

Instead, I sent cancellation messages to the two podcasts I was supposed to be on today, with a brief *I'm sorry. I'm not feeling well.*

I hopped on a bus downtown, having long ago memorized the schedule and route that took me to the library. I loved the downtown branch, with its five stories of glass and steel.

Inside was sunshine and warmth and a vast stretch of knowledge. It was also quiet, since this was a mid-week morning.

I made my way to their ever growing manga section, grabbed something high action that I'd been wanting to start, and settled into a bench seat by the windows.

I couldn't focus enough to read. Even my eyes hurt. How did this perfect scenario fall apart so quickly?

Because it had never been perfect. I'd ignored the consequences to live a fantasy.

As Violet's shift was coming to an end, I called her. "I'm so sorry. I need a favor." I tried to keep my voice clear, but my raw throat cracked on the words.

"Of course. What's wrong?"

I didn't want to ask this, but I was out of time and options. "I'm at the library. This is the weekend my lease is up. Can I stay in your guest bedroom for a little while? I'm looking for a place, I promise. I'll be out as soon as I can be."

"You can stay as long as you need. You know that. What's wrong?"

I couldn't tell her now. I'd break down crying if I did, and then I'd also have to explain to anyone who saw me, and deal with their sympathy, and that would bounce back on me and make me feel even worse. "I'll tell you when I see you."

"Okay. I'll be right there."

A short while later, we were in Ramsey's SUV—Violet managed to get a hold of it quickly—and headed back to my soon-to-be-former apartment.

"What happened?" Violet asked.

"I'm not seeing Cole or Graham anymore."

She frowned. "What happened?" She repeated.

I didn't want to worry her, and I wasn't ready to give details about the *why.* "It wasn't working out." *Please don't ask me for details.*

Violet clenched her jaw. "You can tell me."

"I know. Soon. Not yet."

"All right."

I couldn't ignore her tone. Now I'd hurt someone else I loved. This sucked so hard.

Hunter was already at my place with his truck. Usually his easy smile and warmth brightened my day.

Today, I didn't know if anything would ever again.

I didn't own much. My furniture all fit in Hunter's truck, and he promised to put it in storage for me. One more thing I owed someone for. My boxes went in the SUV.

When we got back to Violet, Hunter, and Ramsey's condo, it didn't take long to pack my boxes into a corner of the guest room.

Violet offered to order pizza, but I wasn't in the mood to socialize.

"We'll slide it under the door, if you prefer," Violet said. "You've gotta eat, L."

My stomach growled its agreement. "Okay. One more favor?" I had to force the words out.

"You know the answer is yes. Anything."

I did, and that made me feel even worse for asking. "If anyone

asks you where I am, unless it's like law enforcement or something"
—because that would be my luck—"don't tell them I'm here?"

"So *anyone* means Cole or Graham," Hunter said.

A fresh wave of doubt and pain shot through me at their names, and I nodded.

Violet scowled. She hated lying, which made this request even harder.

"Please." I spoke as plainly and emotionlessly as I could.

"All right," Violet said. She may not like it, but she'd do it. Her word meant everything.

TWENTY

G raham

WATCHING Luna's mood deteriorate over the course of the evening was hard.

The way she said goodnight was disconcerting.

Finding out she'd cancelled her appointments today was almost as troubling as realizing she'd had Cole drop her off and ending the night at her doorstep.

Now I was staring at a text from her that had to be the briefest thing she'd ever said.

I can't see you anymore.

I replied, asking for more, and got a system message that my note couldn't be delivered. It was the same thing as I retried every thirty seconds, for the next several minutes. I paced the short span of my apartment, alternating between trying to call her and resending my text.

No answer.

I went to her apartment and hammered on the door until the

upstairs neighbors told me she'd moved her things out a few hours ago, and said they'd call the cops if I didn't leave.

The threat didn't deter me. But if she was gone, there was no point in my being here.

Back home, I sank onto the couch and let disbelief wash over me.

What happened? I'd had Luna in my life again for such a short period of time, it couldn't be over already. She and I had what I'd never dared hope for.

Did I love her? Without a doubt. For years, but it felt more real after the last few weeks. I adored the person rather than the idea, because getting to know Luna proved daydreams couldn't hold a candle to reality.

I'd bet money she was with Violet, who I'd only met a few times when they were students. But Luna talked about her enough for me to know they were closer than sisters. Even if Luna wasn't there, Violet would know where she was.

It was inappropriate for me to either call Violet or show up on her doorstep, but it would only take me a few minutes to find her phone number or her address. It didn't matter that she was connected, I'd have the information quickly regardless.

God I was turning into a stalker.

Did that stop me from seriously considering reaching out to Violet? For about two point five seconds.

The only reason I let the possibility drift aside was because someone was ringing my doorbell. *Luna?* I couldn't help the hope that surged inside.

I peered through the peephole. *Cole.*

Not even in the same category as Luna, but not bad. I enjoyed his company far more than I expected when we met. I'd been grateful from that first day to see someone was looking out for Luna, and just as jealous of the way she looked at him.

I was happy to see him today, though.

"Where is she?" Cole asked before I finished opening the door. His demand was tinged with sadness.

I felt the sentiment on a spiritual level. I stepped away and he followed me inside, closing the door behind himself.

"You want something to drink?" I asked.

"No. I want to find Luna. You can't tell me you haven't looked yet."

How was I supposed to answer that without being insulting? Of course I'd fucking looked. But I hadn't exhausted all my options. "She's obviously hiding. Digging deeper runs a high risk of pissing her off." It was easier to tell him than to believe it myself.

Cole clenched his fist. "Seriously? This entire thing is bullshit. Don't get me wrong, I love her dearly—"

My heart caught. I knew he did, but hearing it was a different story. Cole was as much competition as he was a friend. Luna didn't see it that way, I believed her when she said that, but I hadn't moved past sentiment.

"*Fuck.*" Cole sank into the same spot on the couch, in the same way, that I had a short while ago, head in his hands. "I should've said that to her before you. But it's still bullshit. She's hiding for our own good, and she doesn't get to decide that any more than either of us."

"I don't have an argument."

"It took her months to find you," Cole said. "Tell me it won't take you that long to find her."

"She's with Violet." Though, now that I thought about it, Violet probably wouldn't say so, even if one of us did approach her. I know I'd lie for Luna if she asked. Without question.

TWENTY-ONE

C ole

I'D SPENT my life practicing control in all things.

Luna made me want to throw it all away, and until this afternoon, I thought that was a good thing.

Graham nodded at the hand I was favoring. "Your knuckles are scuffed. What happened?"

"I punched the dashboard when I got her text." I was lucky there hadn't been anything tougher nearby. What was I doing? I couldn't pinpoint a single moment in my life when I'd reacted with this level of frustration.

But Luna was different. She was delicate enough to need to be wrapped up and shielded, but strong enough to stand alone against the storm. She'd shown me the world through a new lens. Made me believe in magic again.

"What do we do?" I didn't know if I wasn't asking Graham or myself. The only thing I was certain of, besides wanting Luna back, was this was the only place I could think of going, after I got her message.

Graham shook his head. "Not a clue. Do you want something for your hand?"

I flexed my fingers. "I'm good." If I was here, I had a friend—how did Graham become that in such a short amount of time? But I also had someone to temper my bad ideas. If I walked out the door now, I'd drive straight to Violet's, throw Luna over my shoulder, and carry her out of there.

Luna would never forgive me for that. I'd never even consider it if she were anyone else.

"I'm calling Violet." I had to do something. My phone was already in my hand, and I was scrolling through to her phone number.

"Hey, Cole." Her friendly answer was flat.

Not the kind of reception I was used to from her. "Do you know where Luna is? Can I talk to her?"

"No."

Go figure. "I asked multiple questions."

"The answer is *no*."

It was tempting to push harder. In fact, all reason insisted I do so. It wouldn't get me anywhere. "Tell her I—we—miss her. That I just want to talk."

"*If* I talk to her, I'll tell her you called," Violet said.

I'd take it. "Thank you."

"Give her a little time."

Not helpful. "I'd give her all the time in the world if I knew she was coming back." I was intently aware of Graham watching me. I'd be doing the same if our roles were reversed.

"That's not all the time in the world. It's the opposite, because you're asking her to put a timer on it." The longer Violet talked, the tighter her voice grew.

"I could make the request in person." Stupid. I shouldn't have said that. I was about to go out of my head, but the words could come across as a threat.

"Do. Not."

I bit back a growl, despite her reacting exactly the way I thought she would.

"Tell me you won't."

I clenched my jaw, reason warring with something far more primal.

"*Cole.* If you show up on my doorstep, or if you go to where Luna is, looking for her… Don't make me turn this into a threat. Respect her wishes for distance."

"Fine." I wanted to add *for tonight.* Civility beat back my inner caveman. Barely. "Thank you for looking out for her." I disconnected before I could say something stupid.

Graham scrubbed his face. He must've heard enough of the conversation to understand. "Do you want a beer or something?"

"Yeah."

Graham stepped around the corner, and returned with two cans of Asahai.

He handed me one, and sank into a battered easy chair as he opened the other.

I pressed the chilled aluminum to my knuckles. I was an idiotic fucking brute. "Is the Japanese beer a fanboy thing, or do you really have a taste for it?" I kept my tone light. Easy conversation might take the edge off as much as the drink.

"Both. Started off as *look at me—I'm drinking Japanese beer.* Turned out I like it." Graham took a long swallow.

Watching him, it was easy to see why Luna was physically attracted to him. He was an elegant balance of formality and fun; a walking contradiction who was fascinating to observe and talk to. It was subtle and sexy.

"First time you knew you were sunk when it came to Luna." Graham met my gaze.

"If we're playing that game, I automatically lose, because you've known her longer." Though really, we'd both lost.

Graham shook his head. "We're not playing anything. I want to know when you first looked at her and realized you couldn't walk away."

"I don't think it was a single moment." Dozens flashed

through my mind as I traipsed through the last few years of knowing her. "I was doing wiring at the shelter Violet works at—upgrading the cable for internet—and this cute redhead was volunteering that day." My first thought when I'd met Luna was about how young she looked. My second, which seemed deeply irrational at the time, was *it doesn't matter as long as she's an adult.* "She was shy, but the instant we started talking tech, she opened up. By the time I realized I'd fallen for her, months later, well... I'd fallen for her."

I couldn't help my smile at the memories, despite the bitter ache in my chest. "This entire thing with Luna was one long, slow burn that flashed hot at the end, and now she's gone. It's not right."

"I know what you mean," Graham said.

"What's your moment?"

"It was my first time teaching sophomore programming, and this girl—woman? She was too young for me to be looking either way—walked in on Day One. She was wearing a green sweater as a dress, knee high socks, and Converse, and she owned it like no one's business. Even if she'd been older, while it hadn't been long since I was a student, I wasn't one anymore. It didn't matter. I couldn't take my eyes off her. She had this presence, and I had no idea how no one else noticed. And then she started challenging the lesson plan."

The easy conversation was a pleasant distraction. Focusing on how we fell for Luna? Not so much. I needed a different topic. "This idea you came up with, the planned viral concept, how did you get into teaching that?"

"I have an eye for seeing patterns in the data," Graham said. "If I pursue the research, I pick up even more, but just watching trends in different industries, I notice things. I had to know if I could reproduce what I saw, so I made it part of my thesis. When I moved into teaching, I had the support of my old teacher to try it first as a small class project, and then to put it on the curriculum."

He made it sound like a simple nothing, but he'd been teaching the kind of things most marketers would gnaw their right arm off know.

"You could've taken that anywhere," I said. "You could be

working for any of these tech giants and be at the top of the ladder."

"So could you."

"But I know why I chose not to. Why did you?" So many people didn't understand my decision. Judith was far from the only one who called me nuts for getting out of the industry.

"I already told you, I like the teaching. There's a unique level of satisfaction in showing someone how to do something, and seeing them make it their own. Watching as they grow a concept into more than it would've been if it had stayed mine alone. I like being part of that process."

Graham was so sincere with his reply. The longer he talked, the more I understood why Luna was drawn to him. My attraction ran along a different vein, but the two of them had that same thirst for discovery and sharing what they'd found.

"What did you do at Cord?" Graham asked.

I was surprised he didn't already know. "You've stalked me to the moon and back, you tell me."

"It's not stalking if I can type your name into a search engine and find it on the first page." He winced.

Because he knew he was wrong. "That's a technicality and you know it. Besides, my marriage to Judith isn't easy to find."

We didn't go out of our way to hide it, but the records weren't part of this *everything digitized* era. And Graham had known about her from the moment he showed up on Luna's doorstep, or he wouldn't have tried to use her name to trip me up.

Graham's wince became a cringe. "All right, so there was a little bit of… stalkerish behavior. I was worried about Luna." He worked his jaw. "And jealous," he said quietly. "But I found a lot of conflicting information about your job, and I never found a solid definition of what an *Entropy Engineer* is. Is that like a game physics thing?"

"Not quite. My job was to adapt. If they needed Quality Assurance, I did QA. Or coding. Or site design. Or networking. I never touched art or story"—those were Jordan and Chloe's babies from Day One—"but if it was tech related, I did it."

"So cool."

The conversation drifted from there.

I stayed later than I should, and was bleary-eyed on the drive home. Graham's company numbed my frustration while I was there, but the moment I left, I was intently aware of the Luna-shaped hole inside again.

The gaping need didn't vanish overnight, and as I trudged my way through business the next day, it only got worse.

I shouldn't have promised Violet I'd stay away, which was why I found myself at their condo that evening, regardless.

Ramsey answered. Even if we'd never met, I'd know who the guy was. He had that kind of public presence.

"Can I help you?" His voice was cool.

I didn't blame him, but it wouldn't stop me. "I'd like to see Luna."

"You've got the wrong place."

"Five minutes. I don't give a fuck if you all want to listen in. Let me talk to her."

"Can't help you."

Go get her now. The command roared in my head, and I was barely conscious of drawing myself to a straight-backed posture that emphasized my height. "Please." My voice was tight, and the word came out as an order rather than a request.

Ramsey clenched his jaw and his spine went rigid.

Hunter stepped up beside him, and rested a hand on Ramsey's arm, but his attention was on me. "Leave, or I'll call the police."

Barging my way into the place and forcing Luna to talk to me wouldn't help anything, and I'd feel like an ass. The desire was still there, though. I forced myself to relax as I exhaled. "All right. I'm gone."

I'd spent years living alone, and now I was reluctant to return to an empty house. I headed for Graham's instead. It would be easy to pretend the choice was strictly because of our shared interest in Luna, but I also wanted Graham's company.

He let me in and grabbed me a soda. I shrugged off the beer

this time, since I didn't need any help marring my judgment today. I settled on the couch. "I went to Violet's. It didn't go well."

Graham scoffed. "Me too. No one answered. Probably for the best."

"I held back for so long with Luna. Wanting her to have similar chances to what I had. I understand why you pushed her away *for her own good*. But telling her I was interested opened a floodgate. She pushed my inner hermit away. Somehow you do too." I didn't know where the confession came from, but it helped numb that emptiness again.

"So I'm your substitute Luna? Aren't I too old for you?" Graham teased.

I raised an eyebrow. "Touché."

Stopping by Graham's after work became an easy habit. Neither of us made the mistake of going to Violet's again, but I couldn't help leaving another message or two for Luna.

Four days in—was it wrong that I was keeping count—Violet called me.

"I get it, I do," she said. "It's not up to me to tell you if what you're doing is love or just obsession, but if Luna doesn't want it, it's stalking. Leave her alone."

Fuck.

TWENTY-TWO

G raham

THE LAST THING I wanted was to give up on Luna. I'd take another three years of probation, or even jail time, if it meant seeing her again.

I was that hooked on her.

But if she wasn't interested in hearing it, I didn't see a lot of options.

For the fourth night in a row, Cole and I were sitting in my living room, making idle chatter, and pretending there wasn't a Luna-sized crater in the room.

"I'm curious about something," Cole said.

I didn't know what to make of his tone. "What's that?"

He nodded to the shelves under my TV. "Is that an original PS2?"

"It is." All of my systems were originals, but that was the one I'd played most recently so the others were tucked away.

"Favorite game?"

That was like asking a parent who their favorite child was. "There are too many to list. Last thing I played was a cart racer, and I played the fuck out of it." Which was why it was the last thing I'd played.

"A racing guy, huh?" Competition sneaked into Cole's reply. "Wanna load up a game."

I'd love to. "We can't play anything on it."

Cole's expression barely shifted, but something told me that was disbelief staring at me. "You're not going to tell me it's because that's an antique and you don't touch it?" He asked.

"Saving that answer for next time." I laughed. "But now, it's the opposite. I killed the controllers. Turns out pressing the thumb stick to the wall only makes so much of a difference, but try telling me that when I'm pushing hard for that last hidden letter, and need the perfect angle to make a jump."

"So you broke your joystick playing with it too much."

Innuendo. Nice. "Pretty much."

"I can fix it."

I smirked. Something told me I'd very much enjoy Cole playing with my joystick. "You can fix my joystick? Are you going to show me how to wiggle it the right way?"

"If a man doesn't know that by the time he's your age, there's a problem. But I can finesse it from a different angle."

I'd seen his tender side, but I'd also seen hints of roughness in the bedroom. Not that I minded either, despite my protests. "You don't strike me as a joystick finessing kind of guy."

"No? How do I strike you?"

"Let's just say I suspect it would've broken a lot sooner if you were playing with it."

"I wouldn't snap it off or anything."

My hands flew to cover my crotch. "God, I hope not. Especially if you want me to believe you're not a sadist."

Cole's laugh was a deep, throaty sound that climbed up my spine and raced down again in a delicious shudder. "Being serious for a moment," he said. "If that's the only thing keeping you from using the system, I have the tools in my truck. I can fix it."

"You know how to fix a broken game controller."

"You and Luna aren't the only geniuses around here. I'll be right back."

Cole returned a moment later with a small toolbox. He set up on the kitchen table, where the lighting was best.

It was enthralling to watch him work—big hands doing such delicate things—and he had the devices repaired in no time.

We loaded up the game and settled next to each other on the couch. It was the best way to see the TV, but I couldn't ignore the heat of his arm and thigh brushing against mine.

I was great at most of the games I had, and this one lingered in my muscle memory, so I won the first few races. But Cole caught on fast. By the end of the night, we were evenly matched with him winning as many games as me.

We spent the next few nights playing PS2 games and taking turns kicking each other's asses. It was ridiculous, simple, and more fun than I'd had in a while, aside from those stolen moments I'd had with Luna.

"Have you ever modded this one to play anything else?" Cole asked shortly after he arrived one evening.

I shook my head. "Not the PS2. But I've got an extra Xbox I tweaked about a billion times. It's easier to play with the OS on that."

"Wanna put a copy of Hoarde on it?"

Seriously? Duh. "What kind of geek are you?"

"Same kind as you." Cole was unfazed by my teasing question. "Is that a *yes*?"

"It's a *hell yeah, I do*."

Cole pulled a USB stick from his pocket. "Original game and source code."

I grinned. "Fucking sexy." I grabbed the device, and we hooked it up to my laptop.

We spent the rest of the night tweaking the operating system on the Xbox to support the older game.

The next night, we dove into decompiling and modding the

code. But no matter what we tried, we couldn't get past the loading screen.

I was bummed when Cole had to head out at the end of the night and we didn't have the game up and running. The experience was fun, but success would've been better.

Day Three, we were spinning our wheels. Nothing we tried worked.

"We had some issues with this when we did our first builds." Cole sighed heavily. "Some of the anti-piracy security we had installed struggled on certain machines."

"If Luna were here…." I trailed off as her name tumbled past my lips. It hurt to think about her, but to bring her up made it worse. "Holy shit, I know what to do." Something she'd taught me. I made a few changes to trick the party check on load.

When we started up the game and made it to the character selection screens, I whooped loudly. Cole's *yes* was more reserved, but for him I assumed it was the equivalent of a cheer.

We fumbled our way through a level. It had been more than a decade for either of us, and games had changed a lot since this one was built, but it was a riot. We were laughing at how many times we each died, but better, it had been so much fun making this all work.

I looked up to see Cole watching me, heat in his gaze, and my laughter stuck in my throat.

Cole crushed his mouth to mine, and I grunted with surprise and desire. God, that felt even better than seeing it happen to someone else. He gripped the short hairs at the back of my neck, tugging and holding me captive at the same time, and deepened the kiss.

This was incredible. Not because it was physical contact and I needed to get laid, but because it was Cole. Fuck, the man could kiss.

I pressed a palm to his chest, hating that my brain had to put things on pause. "Is this… cheating?" I felt ridiculous asking, but the concern lingered.

"On whom?" Cole asked. "Our girlfriend dumped us."

"But neither of us is over her, and I know you haven't given up on getting her back any more than I have."

Oz relaxed his grip on my neck, but didn't let go. "She and I agreed to leave things open. That seeing other people was okay. In part so she could see you. I assumed the two of you talked about something similar."

"Not in so many words." Realization settled in. I'd let her assurances about the whole dating-two-guys thing make it okay, because part of me assumed I'd win her over in the end. I didn't want that now. Not in the way that would push Cole out of the picture. "We should have."

"I wouldn't do it if I thought it would hurt either of our chances of winning her back, and I won't keep it from her once she's here again, but this is about you and me."

I was good with that. Fantastic, even. I didn't want more because it had been too long since I got laid. Cole was tugging at parts of my heart and mind Luna didn't, and together the two pieces of desire built an incredible picture.

"Okay." I leaned in and kissed him lightly.

Cole shifted his angle and leaned into the kiss, crushing against me. He dragged rough fingers over my skin, amping my desire, and I pushed back.

I couldn't get close enough. I need more contact. More skin. We stripped each other's shirts off, and it still wasn't enough. Stroking him through his jeans, the way he gripped my cock hard though my slacks in return... none of it sated the raw need that roared inside.

I'd been fighting this for too long. Focusing on Luna. She forever had a part of my heart that no one else could touch, but Cole... things had been growing between us from the day we met. Yes, the day he pinned me to the doorframe and threatened me.

This desperate gropefest was an incredible next step between Cole and me.

"Do you have lube?" He asked.

"Don't you? You've got everything else in your toolbox," I teased.

His glare sent goosebumps dancing over my skin. "Yes. Bedroom."

We barely let up in the kissing and teasing long enough to stumble our way into my bedroom. I was reluctant to break away, even long enough to grab the lube out of a dresser drawer.

Cole pressed into my back, his erection digging into me, and nipped along my neck. He sank his teeth into my shoulder, and I groaned loudly. God, this felt good.

He took the bottle from me. "Pants off."

"Bossy much?"

"If you expected otherwise, you haven't been paying attention."

I had, and this entire series of events pushed me beyond turned on, and had me rock hard. My cock sprung free, eager for attention, as I shed the last of my clothes.

"Kneel on the bed," Cole ordered.

I'd never been with any sort of domineering boyfriend before. I liked that Cole was my first.

He spread my ass cheeks and glided a cold slippery finger along my crack. The sharp contrast in temperature warmed quickly as he liberally applied the liquid.

Then he was nudging my entrance with the head of his cock, and sliding in one agonizing inch at a time.

It had been a while, and I'd forgotten how much I loved this feeling of being entered. Being fucked.

Cole rested inside me, occasionally twitching, but not moving much otherwise.

He reached around and gripped my dick tightly, and stroked as he started to move in my ass. He thrust in time with slow even strokes of my shaft. In and out. Up and down.

The slow build was delicious and maddening. I pushed back into Cole to increase the pace, and covered his fist with my own.

"This ends quickly if you do that," Cole warned.

"I've used up a lot of my patience over the past few years."

Cole's throaty laugh rumbled through me, and he moved both hands to grip my hips as he picked up the pace to hammer inside me.

I managed to balance myself on one arm, and stroked my own cock as he hit just the right spot with each thrust. Intensity saturated the air and I wanted to breathe it all in.

I closed my eyes as I lost myself in the combination of my touch and Cole's, and climax inched closer. Without further warning, orgasm crashed around me, sending a shower of stars to dance behind my eyelids. I came hard, coating my hand, thrusting against my grip until my skin was too tender and slippery for any more.

Cole reached climax quickly after I did. Grunting. Pounding. Slowing to a stop. He kissed up my spine, pulling me upright as he moved higher and his dick slipped out of me. "Fuck." His simple statement rolled over me.

I didn't have a better word for it.

"Mess on the blanket," he said.

Great. I was the cause of the wet spot. "I have others."

We washed up, changed the comforter out, and collapsed naked together on the bed.

"I need to find a way to fall asleep with the two of you at my place," Cole said. "You've got some crummy mattresses."

I smiled and pressed closer into him. "Now you're a bed snob?"

"Yes."

"*And* you assume that *the two of us* are still an option."

"I need Luna back." Cole's conviction rumbled through me. "Tell me you don't."

"I do. Desperately." We had to figure out how to get her to hear us out.

TWENTY-THREE

L^{una}

I SPENT days walking up and down streets in different parts of different cities in the valley, applying for any job where there was a help wanted sign. I'd done this before, and it had never panned out, but I had to try again.

I missed Oz and Graham so much the ache overrode my sore feet and tired legs.

Violet had told me when Cole stopped by, and that he and Graham both called. They'd called me, too. The calls stopped when she threatened them. I was grateful I hadn't had to tell them myself to stop, because I would've cracked.

If that happened, if I went back to them, their lives would fall apart again. Their names and mine had vanished quickly from current media once I walked away.

Both men filled my nights in the form of dreams, but that was the case before, too. The longing was more potent than before I'd had a taste, but at least I had reality to flavor the fantasies now.

I wanted to lose track of the days to let time wash around me and make me forget what I'd had. I knew exactly how long it had been since I saw Oz and Graham, though. Thirteen days, twenty hours. If pressed, I could recite the minutes and seconds, too.

I was sitting on the bed, pretending I could focus on the book on my phone, when Violet knocked on the bedroom door.

She joined me without waiting for a reply, sitting next to me, back to the headboard, and knees propped up. "Why are you doing this?" She asked. "You're miserable."

"I have to. It's the only way." I thought Violet of all people would get it without me having to explain. "You almost left Ramsey because of the public attention."

"No. I almost left Ramsey because he was asking me to lie about who we were. You know the difference between that and bad press."

My insides twinged. I wanted comfort, not to be called out. "This isn't just bad press. It was ruining their lives. Oz's colleagues, the things they were saying about him. And Graham... he was already struggling to find work, and he loves teaching." I took that from him, and I didn't know how to give it back.

"So first of all, since when do you care what other people think, and just as important, they're adults. They can make their own decisions about what does and doesn't ruin their lives. They've survived this long."

I searched for words, but the only thing I found was *how dare you*, and I couldn't summon the indignation to go with the retort.

"Well?" Violet asked.

You're supposed to back me up. You're supposed to be my friend. "If you're worried about them calling or coming by again, I'll find somewhere else to go. I can get out of your hair."

Violet sighed and leaned her head against mine. "You know that's not what this is about. Why are you really here? Why are you really avoiding them?"

"I already told you." I pulled away in frustration and stood.

But her question reached inside and grabbed thoughts I'd been successfully shoving aside, and I pushed back on my own insecurities.

"L. I'm worried about you. I love you. I don't want to see you hurting, especially not yourself." Violet pushed to her feet as well. "I don't think I've ever seen you like this. Even after you were arrested. Even after you were sentenced. Something more is going on. Why did you walk away from Cole and Graham?"

"Because I'm a silly little girl who's really good at letting my curiosity fuck things up, and they deserve better." The confession tumbled out on a gasp of despair and I squeezed my eyes shut. I hadn't meant to say that out loud. I hadn't even let myself think that full thought.

"You're an adult ass woman, as much as they're adult men. You're not fucking up anyone's lives, and that's their decision, not yours. Did you even tell them *goodbye*?"

I ducked my head and hugged myself. If I stopped answering, would Violet leave me alone? Not that I wanted her gone. I couldn't lose her, too. What was I doing? The confusion hit me full force.

Violet wrapped me in a tight hug, squeezing before letting go. "You know my commute between the shelter and Loading Java takes me past Graham's."

No it didn't. "Not without doubling your travel time."

"Cole's truck has been out there the couple of times I've driven past."

"Your point is?" My chest was threatening to collapse in on itself.

"Why are you hiding from them?"

"I told you why."

Violet clucked. "That's not a good reason. If someone told you the same thing, you'd be furious."

I had been. When Graham said it, it was enough to push me away. I should've—

My mind refused to finishing putting words to the thought. "You know what makes me furious?" Speaking was better than falling into my head. "Doing podcast after podcast, for days on end. Applying for job after job, and not getting a call back, even though I'm the fucking best at what I do. Because why? Because I've got a record? Because I'm a girl? Because I'm a girl with a record?"

Now that the words were flowing, I couldn't stop them. "And Graham and Oz have expectations. Of me. They think I'm going somewhere. They've both told me this. They think that because I have this talent, that I'm going to do great things with it." I gasped at my own confession. "What if I'm not that person?" It hurt to say. I'd never vocalized that fear, even to myself, and it tied a knot in my heart to admit it. Despair bubbled up inside and a sob tried to work its way out. "There's nothing wrong with me waiting tables. Or working a cash register. Sweeping floors. I don't have to be great to make a difference."

"It's true." Violet's voice softened. "But those aren't the things you want to be doing."

"I wouldn't mind."

She tugged my arms apart and grasped my fingers. "Are you worried about letting the guys down, or are you worried about seeing your expectations for yourself reflected back at you, when you look at Cole and Graham?"

"That doesn't make any sense." But it did. If I pushed them away, I could say my success was their dream.

"Doesn't it? Come here." Violet led me into the guest bathroom and pointed me at the mirror. "What do you see?"

I didn't want to look at my reflection. Not figuratively or literally.

"Humor me." Violet gently forced my gaze up.

Sad green eyes stared back at me. Heavy shadows under pale skin were obvious underneath. I still wore the makeup I'd put on to fill out applications. Was still in the generic blouse and trousers, with my hair pulled back.

"What do you see?" Violet asked.

"I don't know. Me?"

"Are you sure?"

No. The person in the mirror was like pod person Luna. Made up to blend into the world, rather than explore her way through places most people never noticed. I turned away, stalked back to the bedroom and flopped on the bed.

Violet lingered in the bathroom doorway. "For as long as I've known you, you've had this drive to learn and to use that knowledge. To dissect the universe, figure out what makes it tick, and tweak until it ticks better. You've never been satisfied with the status quo. I know this has been hard on you. The arrest. The probation. The publicity."

"Are you going somewhere with this?"

"But you pulled through it all. You stayed true to you. Now that you've pushed Graham and Cole away, you've given yourself a reason to give up. To hate yourself, when you've never surrounded before."

"I don't—" My voice cracked.

"This is going to get better. The media. The trouble finding work. You will achieve great things, even though you're stumbling now. Not because someone else expects you to, but because that's who you are, L."

I rolled over on my side and pulled the blanket over me. "I'm going to sleep."

"It's five in the evening."

"It's a nap."

Violet yanked the covers off me. "Go take a shower. Put on some of *your* clothes. Not whatever you think will impress some small business, but something that you own that makes you smile. And then I'm taking you to Graham's."

I was tempted. Everything Violet said hurt. Pissed me off. Made me admit things to myself I didn't want to. She was also right.

"I'm scared." Another confession, but this one didn't hurt as much. "What if things stay hard?"

"They won't be forever. And they'll be a lot easier if you stop pushing people out of your life who you love. Who love you."

TWENTY-FOUR

In a way I was reluctant to admit Violet's kind version of tough love was working. But having my hair hanging loose and damp, knowing I didn't have to tame the messy waves that would dry, was oddly comforting. And this time I was wearing the Captain Marvel dress, with my old, battered pair of Vans.

This time the Luna who stared back at me in the mirror was almost smiling. Which made me smile more. Which made a big ball of warm sunshine spread through me.

Until I remembered how badly I'd screwed things up with Graham and Oz. And I still didn't know if Violet was right about going back to them.

Anxiety bubbled up inside as Violet drove me to Graham's. Sure enough, when we arrived, Oz's truck was parked out front.

Violet pulled me into a tight hug. "Call me if you need anything," she said. "You're brilliant, you're sexy, and you're going to be all right."

If I let the happy tears squeeze out, my eyeliner would smudge. It didn't matter how nervous I was, I still hoped the ruined makeup wouldn't happen until Oz was having his way with me.

"Thank you." I squeezed back, stepped from the car, and forced one foot in front of the other until I was in front of Graham's door.

As I knocked, I flashed back to just a few weeks ago, when I stood her for the first time with Cole, hoping above hope that Graham would want to see me.

Even the way he opened the door and stared at me was too much like last time. Except today, Oz was standing next to him, not me.

Silence stretched between us. It was only a second or two, but it felt like an eternity. My words stuck in my throat.

Graham placed a finger under my chin, tilted my head up, and kissed me hard. Hungrily. Devouring my gasp of surprise and my repeated *I'm sorry*.

"It's fine." He nipped at my lips. "As long as you're here now. As long as you're not leaving again." He pulled me into his apartment, still kissing me over and over, and the door closed behind us.

Hands rested on my hips and Oz spun me to face him. He lifted me as he crushed his mouth to mine, pressing my back to the door. I had to wrap my legs around his waist and my arms around his waist to hold on.

If he leaned into me any harder, we might melt together and become one. I was fine with that. I wanted to stay wrapped up here with him, with Graham, forever. All my reasons for leaving lay whimpering and useless by the side of my mind.

I could move into this feeling of warmth and belonging, start a little commune, and build a happy ranch of rainbows and sexy brilliant men. Two specifically.

Oz spun with me still wrapped around him, his hands on my ass holding me to him, and walked us into the bedroom to deposit me on the bed. He knelt at my feet, never breaking the kiss for more than a heartbeat.

Graham was behind me, lips gliding over my neck and fingers dancing up my sides.

"Should we talk?" I finally found enough of a pause to speak. Not that I didn't want this—I wanted it more than almost anything —but I couldn't ignore that the last few weeks happened.

"Does talking involve any form of you leaving?" Oz asked.

Now that I was here, I couldn't imagine being without either of them again. "I'm here to stay. I mean, not specifically. I'm not movi—"

Oz silenced me with another kiss.

"But yes, I suppose we should talk." Graham's words hummed against my shoulder.

Oz groaned into my mouth and broke away. "You know we're in this relationship with you because we want to be. Because we want you. Because we believe in you."

That last bit yanked on my insecurities again, because I did know that. "*We?* You speak for Graham now?"

"For this he does," Graham said.

"What if I can't live up to your expectations?" Or my own.

Graham wrapped his arms around my waist and pressed into my back. "This isn't about expectations. It's about hope and possibility and being happy. Don't let a couple of missed steps take your spark away"

The sentiment was sweet and painful and wonderful.

"You're like a unicorn." The adoration in Oz's voice made my heart catch. "You're magical, mystical, and the kind of elusive magic people spend their lives chasing, but never find."

I didn't know how to respond. "Are you going to name me *Horny?*"

Oz's smile was half amusement and half feral and completely delicious. "No. I'm going to call you Luna. *My* Luna. Every night that you've been gone I considered kicking down Violet's door to get you."

"She would've killed you." I was horrified by the idea, and that any part of me thought it was a sweet sentiment.

"You wouldn't have forgiven me, and that was what held me back. I've never been that guy before, but you make me surrender all reason. I love you, Luna."

My heart swelled in my chest. "I love you too. So much." The longer I sat here, pressed between them, the lighter I felt. It'd be neat if we just kind of floated away in a cloud of bliss.

"Feeling a little left out here," Graham said lightly.

I leaned more of my weight into him and pulled his arms tighter around me. "You're as much a part of this equation for me as Oz is. I'm sorry I ruined your life."

"Don't." Graham was stern. "It's like you keep saying, I made my own decisions. Some of them were for the challenge, a lot more of them of them were so I could spend time with you, but all of them brought us to this point. My life isn't ruined. There were downs, there were some amazing ups and there will be more. My world shines brighter with you in it. You're my heart. My mind. My sanity. And I was an idiot to push you away. I need you here with me. With us. I don't care what comes next as long as we're all facing it together."

My heart was soaring. Both Graham and Oz's repeated use of *we* and *us* to describe them both didn't escape me either. That must be quite a story. I felt their love and hope and both spoke to something I'd been missing since I cut myself off from them.

And then Oz was kissing me again. So was Graham. Mouths gliding along my neck, my lips, my jaw, my ears, my shoulders. Most if their attention stayed above my neck except for the occasional hand that glided up my side or over my stomach.

It was about as chaste as being pinned between two men could be.

"What do you want, right at this moment?" Oz asked. "Anything."

Double banana split with extra fudge probably wasn't the kind of mood-enhancing answer he was looking for. It wasn't what I wanted anyway. I wanted that first night with Oz, but times two. I bit my bottom lip.

Oz's wicked smile was back. "Tell me."

"Use me like a set of holes. Fuck me hard and fill me up until I'm sore and sticky."

Graham's groan rumbled against my back. "How is that a turn on when you say it?"

"Because you're as filthy and desperate as she is," Oz said. "And I'm gonna let you watch. If you're lucky, I'll let you have a taste."

He shifted me on the mattress enough to pull me from Graham and push me roughly onto my back, pinning me in place with his hand on my stomach.

Graham grabbed my wrists. He was more gentle than Oz had been doing the same thing, but I still couldn't break free. Not that I wanted to.

Oz forced his knee between my legs, pressing it against my pussy, prompting me to grind against him. He shoved my dress to my chest, and kneaded my breasts hard enough to draw a long groan from me.

Each new pinch, twist, and light slap from Oz had me whimpering louder. Squirming. Loving every minute of it as I fell into bliss.

Oz removed his knee to push the crotch of my panties aside and penetrate me with his fingers. Without the fabric, my thighs were coated in an instant as he fingerfucked me and abused my nipples.

I was lost enough in pleasure that I was barely aware of him removing one hand. I heard the sound of tearing foil. He slid his fingers from me, and my body groaned at the sudden absence of any sensation besides Graham pinning me in place.

I hoped he was fucking enjoying the show. I was certainly enjoying being part of it.

Oz thrust his cock inside me without warning, burying himself deep and stretching me out. I'd missed this far more than was reasonable considering it had only been a few weeks.

I rocked against him as he glided in and out, over and over, enough to work me to the brink of anticipation. I knew how this part of the game worked. If I wanted more, I'd have to beg, and I may or may not get it right away. The odds were part of the fun.

"Make me come, please?" I whimpered.

"No." Oz pulled out again. "In fact, if you touch yourself, no orgasms."

Geez, this was the most delicious torture.

Oz moved to kneel next to me instead, reached past me, and grabbed Graham by the back of the neck. Graham obeyed the silent prompting, crawling forward to draw Oz into his mouth, licking my juices away.

H. O. T.

Oz forced Graham's head up. "You can have Luna next," Oz said. "If you can make me come."

Wowza. I squeezed my thighs together to try to fight the throb. My fingers itched to slide between my legs. To stroke myself while I watched Graham on his knees in front of Oz.

I rolled up onto one elbow, partly to get a better view, but just as much to make it easier to resist the need pulsing under my skin.

The groans that filled the room drove me wild. The pleasure on both of their faces. The way Graham's cock hung hard and eager between his legs. The way Oz slammed against his face.

Oz's grunts said he was close. He let out a long sighing shudder, and stopped.

The way Graham looked up at him, eyes wide, chin wet, as if he needed permission, clenched around my chest and made me want to be a part of that sandwich.

Tilting Graham's head, Oz gave him a soft kiss. "She's all yours."

Graham rolled a condom on, scooted my butt toward him, and knelt between my legs. The heat and glazed look on his face probably reflected my own.

The way he slid inside me was both a relief, and not nearly enough to sate my roaring desperation.

Oz moved closer, dragging a thumb over my bottom lip. "My gorgeous little cock slut. Does he feel different than me?"

"Yes. Longer, but not thicker. He can still make me come hard, though."

Oz lowered himself to brush his lips over mine. "He'd better." He lowered his mouth to one nipple, and I arched into his mouth when he scraped his teeth over the tender skin before sucking hard.

Graham pounded inside me with reckless abandon, slamming harder and faster. From the sounds he was making, he wouldn't last long.

Oz dipped his fingers between my legs, stroking my clit, teasing me, easing off every time my breathing grew shorter.

When Graham reached that point where he was all fast grunts, Oz pushed me harder, drawing me into the longest, most delicious climax. I clenched around Graham, milking him as he came. Squeezing tight and savoring every inch of him deep inside me.

The rest of the world didn't exist as we slowed to a stop. The only thing here were my guys. Sweet. Protective. Utterly fuckable.

Oz cleaned me up, and Graham stayed curled around me while Oz changed out the comforter. Apparently that big wet spot was my fault. I didn't have the brainpower to ask when Oz had become so comfortable changing the bedding in Graham's apartment.

We all squeezed into the bed, and Oz pulled me into him.

Graham pressed into my back, trailing his fingers through my hair. "God, you're so stunning."

"Hmm." Oz's grunt rumbled through my cheek. "Indeed."

I ran my fingers through the fine hairs on Oz's chest, memorizing every sensation. His warmth. The tickles of his chest fuzz. The beat of his heart against my cheek and Graham's against my back. I could sink into this for a long, long time.

TWENTY-FIVE

I dozed, wrapped up my in my men and feeling safe. Each time I managed to register the clock, thirty minutes had passed, or sixty. The sun had set and the sky was growing dark. It was almost nine.

I forced myself to consciousness again when Oz extracted himself to answer a ringing phone. He came back into the room a moment later. "Call for..." He put the receiver back to his ear. "How did you phrase it?" He listened for a moment before holding the device toward me. "Call for the adorable little sprite who holds my leash."

"*Sprite* doesn't work for me," Graham said. "It's too much like Soda. *Imp?*"

I scrunched up my face. "No. Game of Thrones call backs."

Oz looked at us, brows raised. "Would you like to take this, or should I tell her to call back?"

"Her?" My curiosity swelled and I took the phone. "Hello?"

"You're a hard woman to get a hold of." It was Judith.

Calling for me? "I've been screening my calls."

"Never screen me again."

"Yes, ma'am." The agreement slipped out before I could consider the words.

"Damn straight." Her tone lightened. "I know it's late, but is now a good time?"

"For...?"

"A job interview."

What in the what? Did I even remember how to act in an interview? Was there a different protocol when it was with my boyfriend's ex-wife? Who also happened to own what was about to be the hottest game on the market. "Of course."

"What did you think of the game?" Judith asked.

In order to tell her, I'd have to separate the bad of that night from the good. Doing so would be a lot harder if I didn't have Graham next to me and Oz climbing into bed again. Was it weird to do a job interview naked? Was it irony, considering the kind of game Judith was making?

I pulled the sheet tighter around me, like it would make any difference in the grand scheme of things. "I love the idea. The gameplay looks incredible. The concept is top notch. It's been a long time since I saw something so innovative, and honestly I'm a little jealous of the people who get to work on it." But she'd said job interview. I didn't want to let my hope skip ahead several steps, but it was too late.

"A game like ours needs airtight security," Judith said. "Not just to keep the bots out, but to make sure minors can't get in. To ensure privacy. Protocols have to be top notch and impenetrable."

"No offense, but there's no such thing."

"If you were going to keep yourself out, how would you do it?"

The pieces slid into place in my mind in an instant. Age verification. Layers of checking. Firewalls. Encryption. Salt. Hashes.

I reeled off about three sentences before Judith said, "Hold up. Wow, you make me feel out of the loop, and I own the fucking company."

"Security development is a different mindset than game development." I had respect for both, and she could without a doubt teach me a few things about her side of the business.

"It is," Judith said. "I had to let one of our security developers go two weeks ago. A company like ours has to be twice as vigilant about things like harassment and privacy violations, and the lawyers won't let me say more beyond he wasn't working out."

"I'm sorry to hear it."

"I'm glad we caught it before it became more of an issue. Would you like to come work for me? On the hottest *coming soon* game in the industry?"

I hoped the offer was coming the moment she said *job interview*, but I still needed to process the word. "I'm sorry. What?"

"You heard me. You don't have to answer tonight, though. Text me your email, and I'll get you a contract so you can think things over."

"That won't be necessary." Crap. That might sound like I was turning her down. "I mean, yes. I want the job. *Yes.*" My excitement bubbled to overflowing. "I definitely want it. Yes over and over. When can I start?"

Judith laughed. "Are you sure?" She was lightly sarcastic. "How does Monday sound?"

"Brilliant. I love it. I'll be there. Thank you, thank you!" I disconnected and handed Oz his phone before I realized I hadn't gotten details. Office location. Dress code. Working hours. My mind was racing so fast it could barely keep up with itself, I was so excited.

Oz's phone buzzed, and he showed me the text from Judith with all the information and an *I'm looking forward to it.*

"*Yay.*" I clapped and bounced.

"I assume *congratulations* are in order?" Graham looked amused.

I should stop bouncing. I couldn't. I gave him a huge hug and kiss, and then one for Oz. "Do you know how amazing this is?" The question was rhetorical. Everyone must know.

"Should we be hurt that seeing us again didn't earn that kind of response?" Graham asked.

Seriously? There was no contest. "Do you want me to beg Judith to call me a filthy whore and plead for her to fuck me?"

"Definitely not," Oz said quickly. He pressed a long kiss to my lips, drawing out my breath and making my heart skip. "Congratulations."

This was so incredible. This was I couldn't have imagined a more perfect fantasy levels of wonderful. The job was the cherry on top of the banana split sundae. Being caught between Oz and Graham, feeling the warmth in the room, the love, was the best thing ever.

It set a high bar for what came next.

And I had no doubt we'd beat that benchmark over and over.

EPILOGUE 1

G raham

ONE MONTH Later

Luna spent weekdays at my place, with Cole stopping by after work more often than not, despite the cramped quarters with three of us here. It made getting Luna to work easier, but mostly it was because we all wanted to spend that time together.

Cole offered to buy Luna a car, and she made him promise not to. She was making more with this job than she knew want to do with, and a car was one of the first things on her to-buy list. She did agree to let Cole co-sign for her, though.

On weekends, all three of us spent our time at Cole's in Jeremy Ranch. We all had keys to both places. The entire thing became routine quickly, and I adored it.

I was still doing tutoring. That hadn't picked up, but I enjoyed the work, so I wasn't complaining. I was at the tail and of a video tutoring session when I heard my apartment door unlock.

The *Recording in Progress* sign on the front door would tell whoever it was that I was working, but the others were supposed to both be at their own jobs still.

Cole poked his head around the corner of the kitchen, where I sat at the table. I gave him a slight nod, but kept my attention on the lesson and my student's last minute questions. He settled on the couch, which I could see from my seat, and scrolled through his phone.

I wrapped up class about ten minutes later, and took the spot next to him. "You're here early."

"I wanted to watch you work." Cole rested a hand on my knee. He liked the contact with either Luna or I, and I certainly wasn't complaining.

I didn't know what to do with his statement, though. I still had a hard time telling when he was being serious and when he was joking. I got it right more often, but right now he sounded serious, and there was no way he could be. "Your own work was that dull?" I teased.

"It was that busy. I need to bring on a couple more externship supervisors."

"Very cool. Congrats." It made me happy to hear that things were going well for Cole, on several levels.

"So when can you start?" He asked.

"I—" I laughed. "What?"

"You heard me."

I had a brief flashback to the night Luna was offered a job. I flashed back a lot to that night, but usually the sex and *I love yous* that came before that moment. "You want me—"

"Frequently. But to finish the thought, yes, I want you to come work for me."

What was I missing? "I thought you didn't fuck people involved with the job." I'd heard the story about how Cole kept his distance from Luna for so long, and while I could image the kind of restraint that took, I also didn't understand why Cole made that choice. He was the boss. He didn't have to place those restrictions on himself.

"I said *with* me, not *for* me. Do you really think this is just fucking?"

"No." Not to me it wasn't.

Cole sighed. "When Luna was in my program, I told myself I wasn't making a move for her because she worked for me. It was an excuse. I wasn't doing it because… I didn't want to be the dirty old man corrupting her."

I knew this story all too well. "Everything you accused me of."

"We frequently accuse others of our own worst flaws."

"That's poetic."

He trailed his thumb along the seam of my jeans in a lazy path. "She's more to me than *a fuck*, obviously, and so are you. I want you in my life, in our lives. I need another person who can do both administration and training at the office, and I've never met anyone more qualified than you. I don't care if you keep doing the tutoring. You can set your own hours with me."

I was more of a nine-to-five kind of guy than a pick-my-own-schedule dude. Was it wrong that the idea of set hours was kind of a turn-on? And being a part of what Cole did… "Yes. I'd love to sign on."

"Welcome aboard, partner." The way he said *partner* heated my blood.

The way he pressed his lips to mine raised my temperature to scorching. God, I loved kissing this man.

The door clicked open again, interrupting the moment.

"You didn't wait for me?" Luna's voice was playful as she stepped into the apartment.

We had a *we don't all have to be there for sex* agreement that was working out great, so I wasn't worried about hurt feelings or jealousy. When we first discussed it, I thought it would be hard to adjust, but I couldn't imagine doing things any other way.

"I saved some things for you," Cole said.

"Oh my head." Luna pressed her palms to her cheeks in a perfect *Home Alone* impersonation. "There's more than watching the two of you kiss?" She crossed the room to join us.

We each grabbed a wrist and tugged her to sit across our laps. She winced and shifted her shoulder, but her smile returned so quickly I could've imagined it left at all.

"Not that I mind," I said. "But how did I get lucky enough to have both of you here at three on a weekday afternoon?" I was supposed to pick Luna up from work, so her arriving alone was a double surprise.

"Boss gave me the afternoon off to recover." Luna's tone was cheerful.

Cole frowned. "Recover from what?"

I shared his concern.

Luna pulled up her shirtsleeve to reveal a spade tattoo covered in plastic. A lot of the people at AcesPlayed had them.

My concern climbed higher at seeing the fresh ink. "You know that's—"

She silenced me with a look. "Permanent? Yes. I'm aware. You weren't going to question whether or not I thought about this, were you?"

I was, but not now.

"It's a good point." Cole didn't seem to have the same reservations.

Luna grinned. "Yeah, the job may not work out—not that I'm worried—but even if for some ungodly reason it doesn't, I still want a reminder that I was part of it. Of this new, incredible piece of technology."

"Did it hurt?" I asked. Mine hadn't been bad, but one never knew.

"Like you wouldn't believe. I want to get another one in a few months."

Cole nuzzled her neck. "My sexy little pain slut."

God, I loved everything about this. Cole. Luna. Our time together. The blend of brains, personalities, and fun…

I couldn't imagine a better future than one with the two of them in it. I never would've dreamed this up to begin with, it was so implausible and wonderful. I couldn't wait to see what came next, as long as it involved all of us.

EPILOGUE 2

C ole

"WHAT WAS this about saving something for me?" Luna asked.

Graham nodded toward the kitchen. "There's a piece of chocolate cake in the fridge. The kind with extra frosting that only you like."

Luna clapped with glee. *Fuck* that was adorable.

"But that's from you, not Oz," she said.

"True."

I was stalling. Which was stupid, since I hadn't hesitated about anything this way in a long time. Not since Judith. On second thought, I don't think even that meant this much to me.

"Are you nervous?" Graham asked in disbelief.

I stared back. "Fuck you." My tone was light.

He grinned. "Not until after you tell us. Distracting me with offers of sex doesn't get you off the hook."

"The commutes are getting to be a bit much." Best I get it over with, or he'd make a big deal out of things, and then Luna would join in… That would be fun, but it would delay what I really wanted.

"I get paid in a week, and it'll be enough for a down payment on a car." Luna's voice was meek.

I smiled. I was so excited to see her doing this. "Not what I meant. I don't mind chauffeuring you around. What I mind is leaving either of you at the end of the night. Also, sleeping in Graham's bed. I mind that lumpy piece of shit a lot."

"Fucking hell, really?" Graham's sigh was exaggerated.

Double adorable. "One of my rental homes just opened up. I'm doing a lot of work down here in the valley, you're both situated here, and I was wondering if I should take the rental off the market so we can make it our second home."

"I think I need a first home in order to have a second."

"The place up in Jeremy Ranch is the first," I said. "You know, that tiny little chateau where we spend our weekends?"

Graham scoffed. "Tiny. Pft."

"Wait…" The pieces clicking in Luna's head were almost audible.

"You're getting it."

She stuck her tongue out at me. "You're suggesting we all move in together."

"I'm *asking* that we make it official." I may control her in the bedroom, but I would never presume to order her around day to day.

Her grin brightened the room. "My cards said it was going to be an amazing day. I thought they meant the tattoos, but—"

"Is that a yes?" I didn't mean to cut her off. I was more anxious than I should be for an answer.

"Can I bring the bed?" Graham asked.

I fixed him with a glare. "No."

"I guess I'm in anyway." He sighed heavily.

Luna elbowed him lightly. "You can't see, but I'm cheering in my head. Full-blown chibi me, complete with pom poms. Yes. Yes, A million bazillion times, *yes*."

"Fuck, I love you." I brushed my lips over hers. I turned to

Graham, holding his gaze. "And you. I love you so very deeply." It was the first time I'd said that, and it felt incredible.

Graham's breath caught as he stared back. "I love you too. God, you irritate the hell out of me sometimes, but I love you immensely. I can't imagine a future that you're not a part of. Both of you."

As I kissed him, and Luna, and Graham again, I couldn't help but think this was perfect. Better than perfect. This was the ultimate in amazing, and it was ours.

THANK YOU FOR READING LUNA, Oz, and Graham's story, and I hope you've followed and loved the entire Three Player Co-op series.

THOUGH THIS SERIES IS OVER, I have so many more threesomes with geeky heroines and possessively sweet heroes, including Adrienne's book.

She's the new artist for the hottest, dirtiest game about to hit the market. But with her limited experience in the bedroom, she doesn't know if she can pull off realistic renderings. Her two sexy co-workers offer her a hands-on lesson in anatomy. Can they all get what they want and keep things professional, or will the lesson cost them their careers and hearts?

Check out RANDOM ENCOUNTER Today

ANTONIO WANTS his best friend and business partner, Justin. Justin wants the new contractor, Emily. Emily wouldn't mind all of the above. But giving in to desire will cost them everything.

Grab your copy of THEIR NERD now